BRITT-MARIE WAS HERE

ALSO BY FREDRIK BACKMAN

A Man Called Ove

My Grandmother Asked Me to Tell You She's Sorry

And Every Morning the Way Home Gets Longer and Longer

BRITT-MARIE WAS HERE

- A NOVEL -

FREDRIK BACKMAN

Translated by Henning Koch

WASHINGTON SQUARE PRESS

New York London Toronto Sydney New Delhi

WASHINGTON SQUARE PRESS
An Imprint of Simon & Schuster, Inc.
1230 Avenue of the Americas
New York, NY 10020

This book is a work of fiction. Any references to historical events, real people, or real places are used fictitiously. Other names, characters, places, and events are products of the author's imagination, and any resemblance to actual events or places or persons, living or dead, is entirely coincidental.

Copyright © 2014 by Fredrik Backman
Originally published in 2014 in Swedish as *Britt-Marie var här* by Partners in Stories, Stockholm, Sweden.
Published in the English language by arrangement with Hodder & Stoughton Ltd.
Translation © 2015 by Henning Koch

All rights reserved, including the right to reproduce this book or portions thereof in any form whatsoever. For information, address Atria Books Subsidiary Rights Department, 1230 Avenue of the Americas, New York, NY 10020.

First Washington Square Press trade paperback edition February 2017

WASHINGTON SQUARE PRESS and colophon are trademarks of Simon & Schuster, Inc.

For information about special discounts for bulk purchases, please contact Simon & Schuster Special Sales at 1-866-506-1949 or business@simonandschuster.com.

The Simon & Schuster Speakers Bureau can bring authors to your live event. For more information, or to book an event, contact the Simon & Schuster Speakers Bureau at 1-866-248-3049 or visit our website at www.simonspeakers.com.

Interior design by Paul Dippolito

Manufactured in the United States of America

10 9 8 7 6 5 4

The Library of Congress has cataloged the hardcover edition as follows:

Names: Backman, Fredrik, 1981– author.
Title: Britt-Marie was here : a novel / Fredrik Backman.
Other titles: Britt-Marie var här. English
Description: New York: Atria Books, 2016.
Identifiers: LCCN 2015047026 (print) | LCCN 2016004098 (ebook)
Classification: LCC PT9877.12.A32 B7613 2016 (print) | LCC PT9877.12.A32 (ebook) | DDC 839.73/8—dc23
LC record available at http://lccn.loc.gov/2015047026

ISBN 978-1-5011-4253-6
ISBN 978-1-5011-4254-3 (pbk)
ISBN 978-1-5011-4255-0 (ebook)

To my mother, who always made sure there was food in my stomach and books on my shelf.

Borg is an imaginary place, and any apparent resemblance to real places is coincidental.

BRITT-MARIE WAS HERE

1

Forks. Knives. Spoons.

In that order.

Britt-Marie is certainly not the kind of person who judges other people. Far from it.

But surely no civilized person would even think of arranging a cutlery drawer in a different way from how cutlery drawers are supposed to be arranged?

We're not animals, are we?

It's a Monday in January. She's sitting at a desk in the unemployment office. Admittedly there's no cutlery in sight, but it's on her mind because it sums up everything that's gone wrong recently. Cutlery should be arranged as it always has been, because life should go on unchanged. Normal life is presentable. In normal life you clean up the kitchen and keep your balcony tidy and take care of your children. It's hard work—harder than one might think. In normal life you certainly don't find yourself sitting in the unemployment office.

The girl who works here has staggeringly short hair, Britt-Marie thinks, like a man's. Not that there's anything wrong with that, of course—it's modern, no doubt. The girl points at a piece of paper and smiles, evidently in a hurry.

"Just fill in your name, social security number, and address here, please."

Britt-Marie has to be registered. As if she were a criminal. As if she has come to steal a job rather than find one.

"Milk and sugar?" the girl asks, pouring some coffee into a plastic mug.

Britt-Marie doesn't judge anyone. Far from it. But who would behave like that? A plastic mug! Are we at war? She'd like to say just that to the girl, but because Kent is always urging Britt-Marie to "be more socially aware" she just smiles as diplomatically as she can and waits to be offered a coaster.

Kent is Britt-Marie's husband. He's an entrepreneur. Incredibly, incredibly successful. Has business dealings with Germany and is extremely, extremely socially aware.

The girl offers her two tiny disposable cartons of the sort of milk that doesn't have to be kept in the fridge. Then she holds out a plastic mug with plastic teaspoons protruding from it. Britt-Marie could not have looked more startled if she'd been offered roadkill.

She shakes her head and brushes her hand over the table as if it was covered in invisible crumbs. There are papers everywhere, in any old order. The girl clearly doesn't have time to tidy them up, Britt-Marie realizes—she's probably far too busy with her career.

"Okay," says the girl pleasantly, turning back to the form, "just write your address here."

Britt-Marie fixes her gaze on her lap. She misses being at home with her cutlery drawer. She misses Kent, because Kent is the one who fills in all the forms.

When the girl looks like she's about to open her mouth again, Britt-Marie interrupts her.

"You forgot to give me a coaster," says Britt-Marie, smiling, with all the social awareness she can muster. "I don't want to make marks on your table. Could I trouble you to give me something to put my . . . coffee cup on?"

She uses that distinctive tone, which Britt-Marie relies on whenever she has to summon all her inner goodness, to refer to it as a "cup" even though it is a plastic mug.

"Oh, don't worry, just put it anywhere."

As if life was as simple as that. As if using a coaster or organizing the cutlery drawer in the right order didn't matter. The girl—who clearly doesn't appreciate the value of coasters, or proper cups, or even mirrors, judging by her hairstyle—taps her pen against the paper, by the "address" box.

"But surely we can't just put our cups on the table? That leaves marks on a table, surely you see that."

The girl glances at the surface of the desk, which looks as if toddlers have been trying to eat potatoes off it. With pitchforks. In the dark.

"It really doesn't matter; it's so old and scratched up already!" she says with a smile.

Britt-Marie is screaming inside.

"I don't suppose you've considered that it's because you don't use coasters," she mutters, not at all in a "passive-aggressive" way, which is how Kent's children once described her when they thought she wasn't listening. Britt-Marie is not actually passive-aggressive. She's considerate. After she heard Kent's children saying she was passive-aggressive she was extra considerate for several weeks.

The unemployment office girl looks a little strained. "Okay . . . what did you say your name was? Britt, right?"

"Britt-Marie. Only my sister calls me Britt."

"Okay, Britt-Marie, if you could just fill in the form. Please."

Britt-Marie peers at the paper, which requires her to give assurances about where she lives and who she is. An unreasonable amount of paperwork is required these days just to be a human being. A preposterous amount of administration for society to let one take part. In the end she reluctantly fills in her name, social security number, and her cell phone number. The address box is left empty.

"What's your educational background, Britt-Marie?"

Britt-Marie squeezes her handbag.

"I'll have you know that my education is excellent."

"But no formal education?"

"For your information, I solve an enormous number of crosswords. Which is not the sort of thing one can do without an education."

She takes a very small gulp of the coffee. It doesn't taste like Kent's coffee at all. Kent makes very good coffee. Everyone says so. Britt-Marie takes care of the coasters and Kent takes care of the coffee.

"Okay . . . what sort of life experience do you have?"

"My latest employment was as a waitress. I had outstanding references."

The girl looks hopeful. "And when was that?"

"Nineteen seventy-eight."

"Ah . . . and you haven't worked since then?"

"I have worked *every day* since then. I've helped my husband with his company."

Again the girl looks hopeful. "And what sorts of tasks did you perform in the company?"

"I took care of the children and saw to it that our home was presentable."

The girl smiles to hide her disappointment, as people do when they don't have the ability to distinguish between "a place to live" and "a home." It's actually thoughtfulness that makes the difference.

Because of thoughtfulness there are coasters and proper coffee cups and beds that are made so tightly in the mornings that Kent jokes with his acquaintances about how, if you stumble on the threshold on your way into the bedroom, there's "a smaller risk of breaking your leg if you land on the floor than the bedspread." Britt-Marie loathes it when he talks that way. Surely civilized people lift their feet when they walk across bedroom thresholds?

Whenever Britt-Marie and Kent go away, Britt-Marie sprinkles the mattress with baking soda for twenty minutes before she makes the bed. The baking soda absorbs dirt and humidity, leaving the mattress much fresher. Baking soda helps almost everything, in Britt-Marie's experience. Kent usually complains about being late; Britt-Marie clasps her hands together over her stomach and says: "I absolutely must be allowed to make the bed before we leave, Kent. Just imagine if we die!"

This is the actual reason why Britt-Marie hates traveling. Death. Not even baking soda has any effect on death. Kent says she exaggerates, but people do actually drop dead all the time when they're away, and what would the landlord think if they had to break down the door only to find an unclean mattress? Surely they'd conclude that Kent and Britt-Marie lived in their own dirt?

The girl checks her watch.

"*Okay*," she says.

Britt-Marie feels her tone has a note of criticism in it.

"The children are twins and we have a balcony. It's more work than you think, having a balcony."

The girl nods tentatively.

"How old are your children?"

"Kent's children. They're thirty."

"So they've left home?"

"Obviously."

"And you're sixty-three years old?"

"Yes," says Britt-Marie dismissively, as if this was highly irrelevant.

The girl clears her throat as if, actually, it's very relevant indeed.

"Well, Britt-Marie, quite honestly, because of the financial crisis and all that, I mean, there's a scarcity of jobs for people in your . . . situation."

The girl sounds a bit as if "situation" was not her first choice as a way of concluding the sentence. Britt-Marie smiles patiently.

"Kent says that the financial crisis is over. He's an entrepreneur, you must understand. So he understands these kind of things, which are possibly a little outside your field of competence."

The girl blinks for an unnecessary amount of time. Checks her watch. She seems uncomfortable, which vexes Britt-Marie. She quickly decides to give the girl a compliment, just to show her goodwill. She looks around the room for something to compliment her about, and finally manages to say, with as generous a smile as she can muster:

"You have a very modern hairstyle."

"What? Oh. Thanks," she replies, her fingertips moving self-consciously towards her scalp.

"It's very courageous of you to wear your hair so short when you have such a large forehead."

Why does the girl look offended? Britt-Marie wonders. Clearly that's what happens when you try to be sociable towards young people these days. The girl rises from her chair.

"Thanks for coming, Britt-Marie. You are registered in our database. We'll be in touch!"

She holds out her hand to say good-bye. Britt-Marie stands up and places the plastic mug of coffee in her hand.

"When?"

"Well, it's difficult to say."

"I suppose I'm supposed to just sit and wait," counters Britt-Marie with a diplomatic smile, "as if I didn't have anything better to do?"

The girl swallows.

"Well, my colleague will be in touch with you about a jobseekers' training course, an—"

"I don't want a course. I want a job."

"Absolutely, but it's difficult to say when something will turn up. . . ."

Britt-Marie takes a notebook from her pocket.

"Shall we say tomorrow, then?"

"What?"

"Could something turn up tomorrow?"

The girl clears her throat.

"Well, it could, or I'd rather . . ."

Britt-Marie gets a pencil from her bag, eyes the pencil with some disapproval, and then looks at the girl.

"Might I trouble you for a pencil sharpener?" she asks.

"A pencil sharpener?" asks the girl, as if she had been asked for a thousand-year-old magical artifact.

"I need to put our meeting on the list."

Some people don't understand the value of lists, but Britt-Marie is not one of those people. She has so many lists that she has to keep a separate list to list all the lists. Otherwise anything could happen. She could die. Or forget to buy baking soda.

The girl offers her a pen and says something to the effect of, "Actually I don't have time tomorrow," but Britt-Marie is too busy peering at the pen to hear what she's saying.

"Surely we can't write lists in *ink*?" she bursts out.

"That's all I've got." The girl says this with some finality. "Is there anything else I can help you with today, Britt-Marie?"

"Ha," Britt-Marie responds after a moment.

Britt-Marie often says that. "Ha." Not as in "ha-ha" but as in "aha," spoken in a particularly disappointed tone. Like when you find a wet towel thrown on the bathroom floor.

"Ha." Immediately after saying this, Britt-Marie always firmly closes her mouth, to emphasize this is the last thing she intends to say on the subject. Although it rarely is the last thing.

The girl hesitates. Britt-Marie grasps the pen as if it's sticky. Looks at the list marked "Tuesday" in her notebook, and, at the top, above "Cleaning" and "Shopping," she writes "Unemployment office to contact me."

She hands back the pen.

"It was very nice to meet you," says the girl robotically. "We'll be in touch!"

"Ha," says Britt-Marie with a nod.

Britt-Marie leaves the unemployment office. The girl is obviously under the impression that this is the last time they'll meet, because she's unaware of how scrupulously Britt-Marie sticks to her lists. Clearly the girl has never seen Britt-Marie's balcony.

It's an astonishingly, astonishingly presentable balcony.

It's January outside, a winter chill in the air but no snow on the ground—below freezing without any evidence of it being so. The very worst time of year for balcony plants.

After leaving the unemployment office, Britt-Marie goes to a supermarket that is not her usual supermarket, where she buys everything on her list. She doesn't like shopping on her own, because she doesn't like pushing the shopping cart. Kent always pushes the shopping cart while Britt-Marie walks at his side and holds on to a corner of it. Not because she's trying to steer, only that she likes holding on to things while he is also holding on to them. For the sake of that feeling they are going somewhere at the same time.

She eats her dinner cold at exactly six o'clock. She's used to sitting up all night waiting for Kent, so she tries to put his portion in the fridge. But the only fridge here is full of very small bottles of alcohol. She lowers herself onto a bed that isn't hers, while rubbing her ring finger, a habit she falls into when she's nervous.

A few days ago she was sitting on her own bed, spinning her wedding ring, after cleaning the mattress extra carefully with baking soda. Now she's rubbing the white mark on her skin where the ring used to be.

The building has an address, but it's certainly neither a place to live nor a home. On the floor are two rectangular plastic boxes for balcony flowers, but the hostel room doesn't have a balcony. Britt-Marie has no one to sit up all night waiting for.

But she sits up anyway.

2

The unemployment office opens at 9:00. Britt-Marie waits until 9:02 before going in, because she doesn't want to seem pigheaded.

"You were supposed to contact me today," she announces, not at all pigheadedly, when the girl opens her office door.

"What?" the girl exclaims, her face entirely liberated from any kind of positive emotion. She is surrounded by similarly dressed people clutching plastic mugs. "Erm, look, we're just about to begin a meeting. . . ."

"Oh, right. I suppose it's important?" says Britt-Marie, adjusting a crease in her skirt that only she can see.

"Well, yes . . ."

"And I'm not important, of course."

The girl contorts herself as if her clothes have suddenly changed size.

"You know, I told you yesterday I'd be in touch if something turned up. I never said it would be tod—"

"But I've put it on the list," says Britt-Marie, producing her notebook and pointing at it determinedly. "I wouldn't have put it on the list if you hadn't said it, you must understand that. And you made me write it in ink!"

The girl takes a deep breath. "Look, I'm very sorry if there's been a misunderstanding, but I have to go back to my meeting."

"Maybe you'd have more time to find people jobs if you didn't spend your days in meetings?" observes Britt-Marie as the girl shuts the door.

Britt-Marie is left on her own in the corridor. She notes there are two stickers on the girl's door, just under the handle. At a height where a child would put them. Both have soccer balls on them. This reminds her of Kent, because Kent loves soccer. He loves soccer in a way that nothing else in his life can live up to. He loves soccer even more than he loves telling everyone how much something costs after he's bought it.

During the big soccer championships, the crossword supplements are replaced by special soccer sections, and after that it's hardly possible to get a sensible word out of Kent. If Britt-Marie asks what he wants for dinner, he just mumbles that it doesn't matter, without even taking his eyes off the page.

Britt-Marie has never forgiven soccer for that. For taking Kent away from her, and for depriving her of her crossword supplement.

She rubs the white mark on her ring finger. She remembers the last time the morning newspaper replaced the crossword supplement with a soccer section, because she read the newspaper four times in the hope of finding a small, hidden crossword somewhere. She never found one, but she did find an article about a woman, the same age as Britt-Marie, who had died. Britt-Marie can't get it out of her head. The article described how the woman had lain dead for several weeks before she was found, after the neighbors made a complaint about a bad smell from her flat. Britt-Marie can't stop thinking about that article, can't stop thinking about how vexatious it would be if the neighbors started complaining about bad smells. It said in the article that the cause of death had been "natural." A neighbor said that "the woman's dinner was still on the table when the landlord walked into the flat."

Britt-Marie had asked Kent what he thought the woman had eaten. She thought it must be awful to die in the middle of your dinner, as if the food was terrible. Kent mumbled that it hardly made any difference, and turned up the volume on the TV.

Britt-Marie fetched his shirt from the bedroom floor and put it in the washing machine, as usual. Then she washed it and reorganized his electric shaver in the bathroom. Kent often maintained that she has "hidden" his shaver, when he stood there in the mornings yelling "Briiitt-Mariiie" because he couldn't find it, but she's not hiding it at all. She was reorganizing. There's a difference. Sometimes she reorganized because it was necessary, and sometimes she did it because she loved hearing him call out her name in the mornings.

After half an hour the door to the girl's office opens. People emerge; the girl says good-bye and smiles enthusiastically, until she notices Britt-Marie.

"Oh, you're still here. So, as I said, Britt-Marie, I'm really sorry but I don't have time for . . ."

Britt-Marie stands up and brushes some invisible crumbs from her skirt.

"You like soccer, I see," Britt-Marie offers, nodding at the stickers on the door. "That must be nice for you."

The girl brightens. "Yes. You too?"

"Certainly not."

"Right . . ." The girl peers at her watch and then at another clock on the wall. She's quite clearly bent on trying to get Britt-Marie out of there, so Britt-Marie smiles patiently and decides to say something sociable.

"Your hairstyle is different today."

"What?"

"Different from yesterday. It's modern, I suppose."

"What, the hairstyle?"

"Never having to make up your mind."

Then she adds at once: "Not that there's anything wrong with that, of course. In fact it looks very practical."

In actual fact it mainly looks short and spiky, like when someone has spilled orange juice on a shagpile rug. Kent always used to spill his drink when he was having vodka and orange juice during his soccer matches, until one day Britt-Marie had enough and moved the rug to the guest room. That was thirteen years ago, but she still often thinks about it. Britt-Marie's rugs and Britt-Marie's memories have a lot in common in that sense: they are both very difficult to wash.

The girl clears her throat. "Look, I'd love to talk further, but as I keep trying to tell you I just don't have time at the moment."

"When do you have time?" Britt-Marie asks, getting out her notebook and methodically going through a list. "Three o'clock?"

"I'm fully booked today—"

"I could also manage four or even five o'clock," Britt-Marie offers, conferring with herself.

"We close at five today," says the girl.

"Let's say five o'clock then."

"What? No, we close at five—"

"We certainly can't have a meeting later than five," Britt-Marie protests.

"What?" says the girl.

Britt-Marie smiles with enormous, enormous patience.

"I don't want to cause a scene here. Not at all. But my dear girl, civilized people have their dinner at six, so any later than five is surely a bit on the late side for a meeting, wouldn't you agree? Or are you saying we should have our meeting while we're eating?"

"No . . . I mean . . . What?"

"Ha. Well, in that case you have to make sure you're not late. So the potatoes don't get cold."

Then she writes "6:00. Dinner" on her list.

The girl calls out something behind Britt-Marie but Britt-Marie has already gone, because she actually doesn't have time to stand here going on about this all day.

3

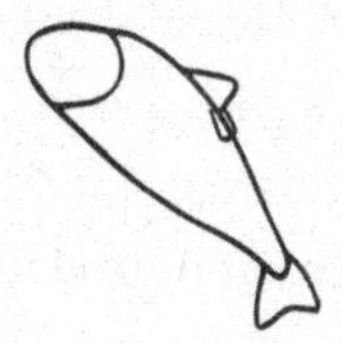

It's 4:55. Britt-Marie is waiting by herself in the street outside the unemployment office, because it would be impolite to go in too early for the meeting. The wind ruffles her hair gently. She misses her balcony so much, it pains her to even think about it—she has to squeeze her eyes shut so tightly that her temples start hurting. She often busies herself on the balcony at night while she's waiting for Kent. He always says she shouldn't wait up for him. She always does. She usually notices his car from the balcony, and by the time he steps inside, his food is already on the table. Once he's fallen asleep in their bed she picks up his shirt from the bedroom floor and puts it in the washing machine. If the collar is dirty she goes over it beforehand with vinegar and baking soda. Early in the morning she wakes and fixes her hair and tidies up the kitchen, sprinkles baking soda in the balcony flower boxes, and polishes all the windows with Faxin.

Faxin is Britt-Marie's brand of window-cleaner. It's even better than baking soda. She doesn't feel like a fully fledged human being unless she has a more-or-less full bottle at the ready. No Faxin? Anything could happen in such a situation. So she wrote "Buy Faxin" on her shopping list this afternoon (she considered adding exclamation marks at the end, to really highlight the seriousness of it, but managed to contain herself). Then she went to the supermarket that isn't her usual, where nothing is arranged as usual. She asked a young person working there for Faxin. He didn't even know what it was. When Britt-Marie explained that it's her brand of window-cleaner, he just shrugged and suggested a different brand. At which point Britt-Marie got so angry that she got out her list and added an exclamation mark.

The shopping cart was acting up and she even ran over her own foot with it. She closed her eyes and sucked in her cheeks and missed Kent. She found some salmon on sale and got some potatoes and vegetables. From a little shelf marked "Stationery" she took a pencil and two pencil sharpeners and put them in her cart.

"Are you a member?" asked the young man when she reached the cashier.

"Of what?" Britt-Marie asked suspiciously.

"The salmon is only on sale for members," he said.

Britt-Marie smiled patiently.

"This is not my usual supermarket, you see. In my usual supermarket my husband is a member."

The young man held out a brochure.

"You can apply here, it only takes a sec. All you do is fill in your name and address here an—"

"Certainly not," said Britt-Marie immediately. Because surely there's some kind of limit? Do you really have to register and leave your name and address like some suspected terrorist just because you want to buy a bit of salmon?

"Well, in that case you have to pay full price for the salmon."

"Ha."

The young man looked unsure of himself.

"Look, if you don't have enough money on you I ca—"

Britt-Marie gave him a wide-eyed stare. She wanted so badly to raise her voice, but her vocal cords wouldn't cooperate.

"My dear little man, I have plenty of money. Absolutely plenty." She tried to yell, and to slap down her wallet on the conveyor belt, but it was more like a whisper and a little pushing movement.

The young man shrugged and took her payment. Britt-Marie wanted to tell him that her husband was actually an entrepreneur, and that she was actually well able to pay the full price for some salmon. But the young man had already started serving the next customer. As if she didn't make any difference.

At exactly 5:00 Britt-Marie knocks on the door of the girl's office. When the girl opens the door, she's wearing her coat.

"Where are you going?" asks Britt-Marie. The girl seems to pick up an incriminating note in her voice.

"I . . . well, we're closing now . . . as I told you, I have t—"

"Are you coming back, then? What time should I expect you?"

"What?"

"I have to know when I'm supposed to put on the potatoes."

The girl rubs her eyelids with her knuckles.

"Yes, yes, okay. I'm sorry, Britt-Marie. But as I tried to tell you, I don't have the t—"

"These are for you," says Britt-Marie, offering her the pencil. When the girl takes it, in some confusion, Britt-Marie also holds out a pair of pencil sharpeners, one of them blue and the other pink. She nods at these, and then she nods in a wholly unprejudicial way at the girl's boyish hairstyle.

"You know, there's no knowing what sort you people like nowadays. So I got both colors."

The girl doesn't seem quite sure who Britt-Marie is referring to by "you people."

"Th . . . anks, I guess."

"Now, I'd like to be shown to the kitchen, if it's not too much bother to you, because otherwise I'll be late with the potatoes."

The girl very briefly looks as if she's going to exclaim, "Kitchen?" but at the last moment she holds back and, like small children next to bathtubs, seems to understand that protesting will only prolong the process and make it more tortuous. She simply gives up, points to the staff kitchen, and takes the food bag from Britt-Marie, who follows her down the corridor. Britt-Marie decides to acknowledge her civility with some sort of compliment of her own.

"That's a fine coat you have there," she says at long last.

The girl's hand slides in surprise over the fabric of her coat.

"Thanks!" She smiles sincerely, opening the door to the kitchen.

"It's courageous of you to wear red at this time of year. Where are the cooking implements?"

With diminishing patience, the girl opens a drawer. One half is a jumble of cooking implements. The other holds a plastic compartment for cutlery.

A single compartment.

Forks, knives, spoons.

Together.

The girl's irritation turns to genuine concern.

"Are . . . you . . . are you all right?" she asks Britt-Marie.

Britt-Marie has gone over to a chair to sit down, and looks on the verge of passing out.

"Barbarians," she whispers, sucking in her cheeks.

The girl drops onto a chair opposite. Seems at a loss. Her gaze settles on Britt-Marie's left hand. Britt-Marie's fingertips are uncomfortably rubbing the white mark on her skin, like the scar of an amputated limb. When she notices the girl looking, she hides her hand under her handbag, looking as though she's caught someone spying on her in the shower.

Gently, the girl raises her eyebrows.

"Can I just ask . . . sorry, but . . . I mean, what are you really doing here, Britt-Marie?"

"I want a job," Britt-Marie replies, digging in her bag for a handkerchief so she can wipe the table down.

The girl moves about in a confused attempt to find a relaxed position.

"With all due respect, Britt-Marie, you haven't had a job in forty years. Why is it so important now?"

"I have had a job for forty years. I've taken care of a home. That's why it's important now," says Britt-Marie, and brushes some imaginary crumbs off the table.

When the girl doesn't answer right away, she adds:

"I read in the newspaper about a woman who lay dead in her flat for several weeks, you see. They said the cause of death was 'natural.' Her dinner was still on the table. It's actually not very natural at all. No one knew she was dead until her neighbors reacted to the smell."

The girl fiddles with her hair.

"So . . . you . . . sort of want a job, so that . . ." she says, fumbling.

Britt-Marie exhales with great patience.

"She had no children and no husband and no job. No one knew she was there. If one has a job, people notice if one doesn't show up."

The girl, still at work long after her day should be over, sits looking for a long, long time at the woman who's kept her here. Britt-Marie sits with a straight back, like she sits on the chair on the balcony when she's waiting for Kent. She never wanted to go to bed when Kent wasn't home, because she didn't want to go to sleep unless someone knew she was there.

She sucks in her cheeks. Rubs the white mark.

"Ha. You believe it's preposterous, of course. I'm certainly aware that conversation isn't one of my strengths. My husband says I'm socially incompetent."

The last words come out more quietly than the rest. The girl swallows and nods at the ring that is no longer on Britt-Marie's finger.

"What happened to your husband?"

"He had a heart attack."

"I'm sorry. I didn't know he'd died."

"He didn't die," whispers Britt-Marie.

"Oh, I th—"

Britt-Marie interrupts her by getting up and starting to sort the cutlery as if it has committed some kind of crime.

"I don't use perfume, so I asked him to always put his shirt directly in the washing machine when he came home. He never did. Then he used to yell at me because the washing machine was so loud at night."

She stops abruptly, and gives the oven a quick lecture about its buttons being the wrong way around. It looks ashamed of itself. Britt-Marie nods again and says:

"The other woman called me after he'd had his heart attack."

The girl stands up to help, then sits down watchfully when Britt-Marie takes the filleting knife from the drawer.

"When Kent's children were small and stayed with us every other week, I made a habit of reading to them. My favorite was *The Master Tailor.* It's a fairy tale, you understand. The children wanted me to make up my own stories, but I can't see the point of it when there are perfectly good ones already written by professionals. Kent said it was because I don't have any imagination, but actually my imagination is excellent."

The girl doesn't answer. Britt-Marie sets the oven temperature. She puts the salmon in an oven dish. Then just stands there.

"It takes an excellent imagination to pretend one doesn't understand anything year in, year out, even though one washes all his shirts and one doesn't use perfume," she whispers.

The girl stands up again. Puts her hand fumblingly on Britt-Marie's shoulder.

"I . . . sorry, I . . ." she starts to say.

She stops although she hasn't been interrupted. Britt-Marie clasps her hands together over her stomach and looks into the oven.

"I want a job because I actually don't think it's very edifying to disturb the neighbors with bad smells. I want someone to know I'm here."

There's nothing to say to that.

When the salmon is ready they sit at the table and eat it without looking at each other.

"She's very beautiful. Young. I don't blame him, I actually don't," says Britt-Marie at long last.

"She's probably a slag," the girl offers.

"What does that mean?" asks Britt-Marie, uncomfortable.

"It's . . . I mean . . . it's something bad."

Britt-Marie looks down at her plate again.

"Ha. That was nice of you."

She feels as though she should say something nice back, so, with a certain amount of strain, she manages to say, "You . . . I mean . . . your hair looks nice today."

The girl smiles.

"Thanks!"

Britt-Marie nods.

"I'm not seeing as much of your forehead today, not like yesterday."

The girl scratches her forehead, just under her fringe. Britt-Marie looks down at her plate and tries to resist the instinct to serve up a portion for Kent. The girl says something. Britt-Marie looks up and mumbles: "Pardon me?"

"It was very nice, this," says the girl.

Without Britt-Marie even asking.

4

And then Britt-Marie got herself a job. Which happened to be in a place called Borg. Two days after inviting the girl from the unemployment office to have some salmon, that's where Britt-Marie heads off to in her car. So we should now say a few words about Borg.

Borg is a community built along a road. That's really the kindest possible thing one can say about it. It's not a place that could be described as one in a million, rather as one of millions of others. It has a closed-down soccer field and a closed-down school and a closed-down chemist's and a closed-down liquor store and a closed-down health care center and a closed-down supermarket and a closed-down shopping center and a road that bears away in two directions.

There is a recreation center that admittedly has not been closed down, but only because they haven't had time to do it yet. It takes time to close down an entire community, obviously, and the recreation center has had to wait its turn. Apart from that, the only two noticeable things in Borg are soccer and the pizzeria, because these tend to be the last things to abandon humanity.

Britt-Marie's first contact with the pizzeria and the recreation center are on that day in January when she stops her white car between them. Her first contact with soccer is when a soccer ball hits her, very hard, on the head.

This takes place just after her car has blown up.

You might sum it up by saying that Borg and Britt-Marie's first impressions of each other are not wholly positive.

If one wants to be pedantic about it, the actual explosion happens while Britt-Marie is turning into the parking area. On the passenger side. Britt-Marie is very clear about that, and if she had to describe the sound she'd say it was a bit like a "ka-boom." Understandably, she's in a panic, and she abandons both brake and clutch pedals, whereupon the car splutters pathetically. After a few unduly dramatic deviations across the frozen January puddles, it comes to an abrupt stop outside a building with a partially broken sign, the neon lights of which spell the name "PizzRai." Terrified, Britt-Marie jumps out of the car, expecting it (quite reasonably, under the circumstances) to be engulfed in flames at any moment. This does not happen. Instead, Britt-Marie is left standing on her own in the parking area, surrounded by the sort of silence that only exists in small, remote communities.

It's a touch on the annoying side. She adjusts her skirt and grips her handbag firmly.

A soccer ball rolls in a leisurely manner across the gravel, away from Britt-Marie's car and towards what Britt-Marie assumes must be the recreation center. After a moment there's a disconcerting thumping noise. Determined not to be distracted from the tasks at hand, she gets out a list from her handbag. At the top it says, "Drive to Borg." She ticks that point. The next item on the list is, "Pick up key from post office."

She gets out the cell phone that Kent gave her five years ago, and uses it for the first time. "Hello?" says the girl at the unemployment office.

"Is that how people answer the phone nowadays?" says Britt-Marie. Helpfully, not critically.

"What?" says the girl, for a few moments still blissfully unaware that Britt-Marie has not necessarily walked out of the girl's life just because she's walked out of the unemployment office.

"I'm here now, in this place, Borg. But something is making an awful racket and my car has blown up. How far is it to the post office?"

"Britt-Marie, is that you?"

"I can hardly hear you!"

"Did you say *blown up*? Are you okay?"

"Of course I am! But what about the car?"

"I don't know the first thing about cars," tries the girl.

Britt-Marie releases an extremely patient exhalation of air.

"You said I should call you if I had any questions," she reminds her. Britt-Marie feels it would be unreasonable for her to be expected to know everything about cars. She has only driven on very few occasions since she and Kent were married—she never goes anywhere in a car unless Kent is there, and Kent is an absolutely excellent driver.

"I meant questions about the *job*."

"Ha. That's the only important thing, of course. The career. If I'm killed in an explosion, that's not important of course," states Britt-Marie. "Maybe it's even good if I die. Then you'll have a job to spare."

"Please Britt-Mar—"

"I can hardly hear you!!" bellows Britt-Marie, in a very helpful way, and hangs up. Then she stands there, on her own, sucking in her cheeks.

Something is still thumping on the other side of the recreation center, which is still standing only because at the last councillors' meeting in December, there were so many other things already scheduled for closure. The local authority representatives were concerned it might cause a postponement of their annual Christmas dinner. In view of the importance of the Christmas dinner, the closure was pushed back to the end of January, after the holiday period of the local authority councillors. Obviously the communications officer of the local authority should have been responsible for communicating this to the personnel department, but unfortunately the communications officer went on holiday and forgot to communicate it. As a result, when the personnel department found that the local authority had a building without anyone to take care of it, a vacancy for a caretaker of the recreation center was advertised with the unemployment office in early January. That was the long and the short of it.

Anyway, the job is not only exceptionally badly paid, but also temporary and subject to the decision regarding the closure of the recreation center to be reached at the councillors' meeting in three weeks' time. And to top it all, the recreation center is in Borg. The number of applicants for the position were, for these reasons, fairly limited.

But it just so happened that the girl at the unemployment office, who very much against her will ate salmon with Britt-Marie the day before yesterday, promised Britt-Marie that she would really try to find her a job. The next morning at 9:02, when Britt-Marie knocked on the girl's door to learn how this was going, the girl tapped her computer for a while then eventually said: "There is one job. But it's in the middle of nowhere and so badly paid that if you're receiving unemployment benefits you'll probably lose money on it."

"I don't get any *benefits*," said Britt-Marie, as if they were a disease.

The girl sighed again and tried to say something about "retraining courses" and "measures" that Britt-Marie might be eligible for, but Britt-Marie made it clear that she certainly wouldn't welcome any of those measures.

"Please, Britt-Marie, this is just a job for three weeks, it's not really the kind of thing you want to be applying for at your . . . age . . . plus you'd have to move all the way to this place. . . ."

Now Britt-Marie is in Borg and her car has blown up. It's hardly the best possible first day in her new job, one might say. She calls the girl back.

"Where can I expect to find the cleaning equipment?" asks Britt-Marie.

"What?" asks the girl.

"You said I should call if I had any questions about the job."

The girl mutters something unintelligible, her voice sounding as if it's coming from inside a tin can.

"Now you have to listen to me, my dear. I fully intend to find the post office you have informed me about and pick up the keys to the recreation center, but I am not putting one foot inside the recreation center until you inform me of the whereabouts of the cleaning equip—!" Once again she is interrupted by the ball rolling across the parking area. Britt-Marie dislikes this. It's nothing personal, she hasn't decided to pick on this ball in particular. It's just that she just dislikes all soccer balls. Entirely without prejudice.

The ball is being pursued by two children. They are exceedingly dirty, all three of them if you include the ball.

The children's jeans are all torn down their thighs. They catch up with the ball, kick it back in the opposite direction, and once again disappear behind the recreation center. One of them loses his balance and steadies himself by putting his hand against the window, where he leaves a black handprint.

"What's happening?" asks the girl.

"Shouldn't those children be at school?" Britt-Marie exclaims, reminding herself to put an extra exclamation mark after "Buy Faxin!" on her list. If this place even has a supermarket.

"What?" says the girl.

"My dear girl, you have to stop saying 'what?' all the time, it makes you sound so untalented."

"What?"

"There are *children* here!"

"Okay, but please, Britt-Marie, I don't know anything about Borg! I've never been there! And I'm not hearing you—I think you . . . are you sure you're not holding the telephone upside down?"

Britt-Marie gives the telephone a scrutinizing look. Turns it around.

"Ha," she says into the microphone, as if the fault lay with the person at the other end of the line.

"Okay, I can hear you at last," says the girl encouragingly.

"I've never used this telephone. There are actually people who have other things to do than spending all day talking into their telephones, you understand."

"Oh, don't worry. I'm just the same when I have a new telephone!"

"I'm certainly not worrying! And this is absolutely not a new telephone, it's five years old," Britt-Marie corrects her. "I've never needed one before. I've had things to get on with, you see. I don't call anyone except Kent, and I call him on the home telephone, like a civilized person."

"But what if you're out?" asks the girl, instinctually unable to process what the world looked like before one could get hold of anyone, at any time of the day.

"My dear girl," she explains patiently, "if I'm out, I'm with Kent."

Britt-Marie was probably intending to say something else, but that's the point at which she sees the rat, more or less as big as a normal-sized flowerpot, scampering across patches of ice in the parking area. Looking back, Britt-Marie is of the firm opinion that she wanted to scream very loudly. But unfortunately she did not have time for that, because everything abruptly went black and Britt-Marie's body lay unconscious on the ground.

Britt-Marie's first contact with soccer in Borg is when the soccer ball hits her very hard on the head.

5

Britt-Marie wakes up on a floor. Somebody is leaning over her, saying something, but Britt-Marie's first thoughts are about the floor. She's worried that it may be dirty, and that people might think she's dead. These things happen all the time, people falling over and dying. It would be horrific, thinks Britt-Marie. To die on a dirty floor. What would people think?

"Hello, are you, what's-it-called? Deceased?" Somebody asks, but Britt-Marie keeps focusing on the floor.

"Hello, lady? Are you, you know, dead?" Somebody repeats and makes a little whistling sound.

Britt-Marie dislikes whistling, and she has a headache.

The floor smells of pizza. It would be awful to die with a headache while smelling of pizza.

She's not at all keen on pizza, because Kent smelled so much of pizza when he came home late from his meetings with Germany. Britt-Marie remembers all his smells. Most of all the smell of the hospital room. It was loaded with bouquets (it is common practice to receive flowers when you have a heart attack) but Britt-Marie can still remember that smell of perfume and pizza from the shirt by the side of his bed.

He was sleeping, snoring slightly. She held his hand a last time, without waking him. Then she folded up the shirt and put it in her handbag. When she came home she cleaned the collar with baking soda and vinegar and washed it twice before she hung it up. Then she polished the windows with Faxin and freshened up the mattress and brought in the balcony boxes and packed her bag and turned on her cell phone for the first time in her life. For the first time in their life together. She thought the children might call and ask how things were with Kent. They didn't. They both sent a single text message.

There was a time just after their teenage years when they still promised to come to visit at Christmas. Then they started pretending to have reasons for canceling. After a year or two they stopped pretending to have reasons for canceling. In the end they stopped pretending that they were coming at all. That's how life went.

Britt-Marie has always liked the theater, because she enjoys the way the actors get applauded at the end for their pretense. Kent's heart attack and the voice of the young, beautiful thing meant there'd be no applause for her. You can't keep pretending someone doesn't exist when she speaks to you on the telephone. So Britt-Marie left the hospital room with a shirt smelling of perfume and a broken heart.

You don't get any flowers for that.

"But, shit, are you . . . like . . . dead?" Somebody asks impatiently.

Britt-Marie finds it extremely impolite for Somebody to interrupt her in the midst of dying. Especially with such terrible language. There are certainly a good number of alternatives to "shit," if you have a particular need to express such a feeling. She looks up at this Somebody standing over her, looking down.

"May I ask where I am?" asks Britt-Marie, in confusion.

"Hi there! At the health center," says Somebody cheerfully.

"It smells of pizza," Britt-Marie manages to say.

"Yeah, you know, health center is also pizzeria," says Somebody, nodding.

"That hardly strikes me as hygienic," Britt-Marie manages to utter.

Somebody shrugs his shoulders. "First pizzeria. You know, they closed down that health center. Financial crisis. What a shit. So now, you know, we do what we can. But no worry. Have first aid!"

Somebody, who actually seems to be a woman, points jovially at an open plastic case marked with a red cross on the lid, and "First Aid" written on it. Then she waves a stinky bottle.

"And here, you know, second aid! You want?"

"Excuse me?" Britt-Marie squeaks, with her hand on a painful bump on her forehead.

Somebody, who on closer inspection is not standing over Britt-Marie but sitting over her, offers her a glass.

"They closed down the liquor store here, so now we do what we can. Here! Vodka from Estonia or some shit like that. Letters bloody weird, you know. Maybe not vodka, but same shit, burns your tongue but you get used to it. Good when you get those, what's-it-called? Flu blisters?"

Tormented, Britt-Marie shakes her head and catches sight of some red stains on her jacket.

"Am I bleeding?" she bursts out, sitting up in terror.

It would be terribly vexatious if she left bloodstains on Somebody's floor, whether it's been mopped or not.

"No! No! No shit like that. Maybe you get a bump on your head from the shot, huh, but that's just tomato sauce, you know!" yells Somebody and tries to mop Britt-Marie's jacket with a tissue.

Britt-Marie notices that Somebody is in a wheelchair. It's a difficult thing not to notice. Furthermore Somebody seems intoxicated. Britt-Marie bases this observation on the fact that Somebody smells of vodka and can't quite manage to dab the tissue in the right place. But Britt-Marie doesn't have any prejudices about it.

"I was waiting here for you to stop looking deceased. Got hungry, you know, so I had a bit of lunch," sniggers Somebody, pointing at a half-eaten pizza perched on a stool.

"Lunch? At this time of day?" mumbles Britt-Marie, because it isn't even eleven o'clock.

"If you hungry? Have pizza!" Somebody explains.

Only then does Britt-Marie register what was said.

"What do you mean, a bump from 'the shot'? Have I been shot?" she exclaims, fingering her scalp as if searching for a hole.

"Yeah, yeah, yeah. A soccer ball in the head, you know." Somebody nods and spills vodka on the pizza.

Britt-Marie looks as if she may even have preferred a pistol to a pizza. She imagines that pistols are less dirty.

Somebody, who seems to be in her forties, helps her up, assisted by a girl in her early teens who has turned up at their side. Somebody has one of the worst hairstyles Britt-Marie has ever laid eyes on, as if she's combed her hair with a terrified animal. The girl's hair is more respectable, but her jeans are torn to shreds across her thighs. Probably modern.

Somebody sniggers, without a care in the world.

"Bloody brats, you know. Bloody soccer. But don't get angry, they weren't aiming at you!"

Britt-Marie touches the bump on her forehead.

"Is my face dirty?" she asks, simultaneously reproachful and anxious.

Somebody shakes her head and rolls back towards her pizza.

Britt-Marie's gaze falls self-consciously on two men with beards and caps, sitting at a table in a corner, with cups of coffee and morning newspapers. It seems abominable to her, lying there passed out in front of people who are trying to have their coffee. Yet neither of the men even glances at her.

"You only passed out a little," says Somebody breezily, while shoveling the pizza into her mouth.

Britt-Marie gets out a small mirror from her handbag and starts rubbing her forehead. She found it very vexatious passing out, but nowhere near as vexatious as the thought of having passed out with a dirty face.

"How do you know if they were aiming at me?" she asks, with just a touch of criticism.

"They hit you!" laughs Somebody, throwing out her arms. "If they aim, they don't hit. These kids bloody terrible at soccer, huh?"

"Ha," says Britt-Marie.

"We're actually not that bad. . . ." mutters the teenage girl standing next to them, looking offended.

Britt-Marie notices that she's holding the soccer ball in her hands. The way you hold a ball when that's what you have to do to stop yourself from repeatedly kicking it.

Somebody gestures encouragingly at the girl.

"My name's Vega. I work here!" the girl says.

"Shouldn't you be at school?" asks Britt-Marie, without taking her eyes off the soccer ball.

"Shouldn't you be at work?" answers Vega, holding the ball as you do when you're holding on to someone you love.

Britt-Marie grips her handbag more firmly.

"Let me tell you something, I was on my way to work when I was hit on the head. I'm the caretaker of the recreation center, I'll have you know. This is my first day."

Vega's mouth opens in surprise. As if this, in some way, changes everything. But she remains silent.

"Caretaker?" asks Somebody. "Why didn't you say so, lady! I've got one of them, what's-it-called? Registered letters! With the key!"

"I've been informed I'm to pick up the keys at the post office."

"Are here! They closed down the post office, you see!" shouts Somebody, rolling round behind the counter, still with the bottle of vodka in her hand.

There's a short silence. There's a tinkle from the door and a pair of dirty boots cross the unmopped floor. Somebody yells out:

"All right, Karl! I have packaging for you, wait!"

Britt-Marie turns around and is almost knocked to the ground by someone crashing into her shoulder. She looks up and sees a thick beard just below an unreasonably dirty cap, the whole appendage looking back at her.

There's a growl from somewhere between the beard and the cap: "Look where you're going."

Britt-Marie, who wasn't even moving, is deeply puzzled. Then she grips her handbag even more firmly and says:

"Ha."

"*You* walked into *her*!" Vega hisses behind her.

Britt-Marie doesn't like it at all. She gets confused when anyone defends her—it doesn't happen very often.

Somebody comes back with Karl's packaging; Karl looks with irritation at Vega and hostility at Britt-Marie. Then he nods grumpily to the two men at the corner table. They nod back even more grumpily. The door tinkles merrily behind Karl as he lopes out.

Somebody pats Britt-Marie encouragingly on the shoulder.

"Never bloody mind about him. Karl has . . . like . . . what do you say? A lemon up his arse, you know what I mean? Pissed off at life and the universe and everything. People around here don't like visitors from the city," she says to Britt-Marie, and nods at the men by the table when she says "people." They keep reading their newspapers and drinking their coffee as if neither of the women are there.

"How did he know I was from the city?"

Somebody rolls her eyes. "Come on! I'll show you the recreation center, huh!" she shouts and rolls off towards the door.

Britt-Marie looks at a section that leads off the pizzeria, health care center, post office, or whatever it is. There are shelves of groceries in there. As if it were a mini market.

"Could I ask, is this a grocer's?"

"They closed down the supermarket, you know, we do what we can!"

Britt-Marie remembers the dirty windows in the recreation center.

"Might one ask if you have Faxin available here?" she asks.

Britt-Marie has never used any other brand than Faxin. She saw an advertisement for it in her father's morning newspaper when she was a child. A woman stood looking out of a clean window and underneath was written: FAXIN LETS YOU SEE THE WORLD. Britt-Marie loved that picture. As soon as she was old enough to have her own windows, she polished them with Faxin, continued doing so daily for the rest of her life, and never had any problems seeing the world.

It was just that the world did not see her.

"I know, you know, but there's no Faxin now . . . you know?" says Somebody.

"What's that supposed to mean?" asks Britt-Marie, only a touch reproachfully.

"Faxin is not anymore in manufacturer's . . . what's-it-called? Product range! Not profitable, you know."

Britt-Marie's eyes open wide and she makes a little gasp.

"Is . . . but how . . . is that even legal?"

"Not profitable," says Somebody with a shrug.

As if that's an answer.

"Surely people can't just behave like that?" Britt-Marie bursts out.

Somebody shrugs again. "Never mind though, eh? I have another brand! You want Russian brand, good shit, over there—" she starts to say, and gestures at Vega to run over and get it.

"Absolutely not!" Britt-Marie interrupts, walking towards the door as she hisses: "I'll use baking soda!"

Because you can't change Britt-Marie's way of seeing the world. Because once Britt-Marie has taken a position on the world there's no changing her.

6

Britt-Marie stumbles on the threshold. As if it's not just the people in Borg who are trying to push her away, but also the actual buildings. She stands on the wheelchair ramp leading up to the door of the pizzeria. Curls her toes, making her foot into a little fist in her shoe to dull the pain. A tractor goes past on the road in one direction, a truck in the other. And then the road lies desolate. Britt-Marie has never been in such a small community, only driven through places like this sitting next to Kent in the car. Kent was always very sneering about them.

Britt-Marie regains her composure and grips her handbag more firmly as she steps off the wheelchair ramp and crosses the large graveled parking area. She walks fast, as if she's being chased by someone. Somebody rolls behind her. Vega takes the soccer ball and runs towards a group of other children, who are all wearing jeans that are torn across their thighs. After a couple of steps, Vega stops, peers at Britt-Marie and mumbles:

"Sorry the ball hit your head. We weren't aiming at you."

Then she says quite curtly to Somebody:

"But we could have hit it if we'd been aiming!"

She turns around and shoots the ball past the boys into a wooden fence between the recreation center and the pizzeria. One of the boys is at the receiving end, and he fires it into the fence again. Only then does Britt-Marie realize where the thumping sounds in Borg come from. One of the boys takes aim at the fence but instead manages to shoot the ball right back to Britt-Marie, which, if you consider the angle, is quite an impressive feat as far as underachievements go.

The ball rolls back slowly to Britt-Marie. The children seem to be waiting for her to kick it back. Britt-Marie moves out of the way as if the ball was trying to spit at her. The ball rolls past. Vega comes running.

"Why didn't you kick it?" she asks, perplexed.

"Why on earth would I want to kick it?"

They glare at each other, filled with mutual conviction that the opposing party is utterly deranged. Vega kicks the ball back to the boys and runs off. Britt-Marie brushes some dust from her skirt. Somebody takes a gulp of vodka.

"Bloody brats, you know. Crap at soccer. They couldn't hit the water from, you know? A boat! But they don't have nowhere to play, right? Bloody crap. The council closed down the soccer pitch. Sold the land and now they're building flats there. Then the financial crisis and all that shit and now: no flats like they said, and no soccer pitch either."

"Kent says the financial crisis is over," Britt-Marie informs her amicably.

Somebody snorts.

"Maybe that Kent bloke has, what's-it-called? His head up his arse, huh?"

Britt-Marie doesn't know if she's more offended because she doesn't know what this means, or because she has an idea of what it means.

"Kent probably knows more about this than you do. He's an

entrepreneur, you have to understand. Incredibly successful. Does business with Germany," she says, putting Somebody to rights.

Somebody looks unimpressed. Points at the children with her vodka bottle and says:

"They closed down the soccer team when they closed down the pitch. Good players moved to crap team in town."

She nods down the road towards what Britt-Marie has to assume is "town," then back at the children.

"Town. Twelve miles that way, huh? These are, you know, the kids left behind. Like your what's-it-called? Faxin! Discontinued product line. You have to be profitable. So this Kent, huh, he may have his arse full of head, huh? Maybe financial crisis cleared out of the city, you know, but it likes Borg. It's living here now, the bastard!"

Britt-Marie notes the clear distinction between how she speaks of the "town" twelve miles away and the city Britt-Marie comes from. There are two different levels of contempt. Somebody takes such a big hit on her bottle that her eyes tear up as she goes on:

"In Borg, everyone drove trucks, you know. There was, what's-it-called, a trucking company here! Then you know, the bastard financial crisis. More people in Borg now than trucks, and more trucks than jobs."

Britt-Marie keeps a firm grasp on her handbag and feels a need, for reasons that are not entirely transparent, to defend herself.

"There are rats here," she informs Somebody, not at all unpleasantly.

"Rats have to live somewhere, don't they?"

"Rats are filthy. They live in their own dirt."

Somebody digs in her ear. Looks at her finger with interest. Drinks some more vodka. Britt-Marie nods and adds in a tone that, in every possible way, is extremely helpful:

"If you got involved in keeping things a bit cleaner here in Borg, then maybe you wouldn't have so much of a financial crisis."

Somebody doesn't give the impression that she's been listening very carefully.

"It's one of those, what's-it-called? Myths? Dirty rats. It's a myth, huh. They're, what's-it-called? Clean! Wash themselves like cats, you know, with tongue. Mice are crappy, crap everywhere, but rats have toilets. Always crap in same place, huh." She points at Britt-Marie's car with her bottle.

"You should move the car. They'll shoot the soccer ball at it, huh."

Britt-Marie shakes her head patiently.

"It certainly cannot be moved, it exploded as I was parking it."

Somebody laughs. She pushes her wheelchair around the car, and looks at the soccer ball–shaped dent in the passenger door.

"Ah. Flying stone." She chuckles.

"What's that?" asks Britt-Marie, reluctantly following behind and glaring at the soccer ball–shaped dent.

"Flying stone. When the car workshop call insurance company, huh. Then the workshop say, 'flying stone,'" chuckles Somebody.

Britt-Marie fumbles after her list in her handbag.

"Ha. Might I ask where I'll find the nearest mechanic?"

"Here," says Somebody.

Britt-Marie peers skeptically—at Somebody, obviously, not at the wheelchair. Britt-Marie is not one of those types who judges people.

"You repair cars, do you?"

Somebody shrugs.

"They shut down the car workshop, huh. We do what we can. But never bloody mind that now! I show you the recreation center, yeah?"

She holds up the envelope with the keys. Britt-Marie takes it, looks at Somebody's bottle of vodka, and keeps a firm grip on her handbag.

Then she shakes her head.

"That's perfectly all right, thank you. I don't want to create any bother."

"No bother for me," says Somebody and nonchalantly rolls her wheelchair back and forth.

Britt-Marie smiles superbly.

"I wasn't alluding to your bother."

Then she briskly turns around and marches off across the graveled courtyard, in case Somebody gets the idea of trying to follow her. She lifts out her bags and flowerboxes from the car and drags them over to the recreation center. Unlocks the door and steps inside, and locks it behind her. Not that she dislikes this Somebody person. Not at all.

It's just that the smell of vodka reminds her of Kent.

She looks around. The wall is thumping from the outside, and there are rat tracks in the dust on the floor. So Britt-Marie does what she always does when facing emergencies in life: she cleans. She polishes the windows with a rag dipped in baking soda and wipes them with newspaper dampened with vinegar. It's almost as effective as Faxin, but doesn't quite feel as good. She wipes the kitchen sink with baking soda and water and then mops all the floors, then mixes baking soda and lemon juice to clean the tiles and taps in the bathroom, and then mixes baking soda and toothpaste to polish the sink. Then she sprinkles baking soda over her balcony boxes, otherwise there'll be snails.

The balcony boxes may look as if they only contain soil, but underneath there are flowers waiting for spring. The winter requires whoever is doing the watering to have a bit of faith, in order to believe that what looks empty has every potential. Britt-Marie no longer knows whether she has faith or just hope. Maybe neither.

The wallpaper of the recreation center looks indifferently at her. It's covered in photos of people and soccer balls.

Everywhere, soccer balls. Every time Britt-Marie glimpses another one from the corner of her eye, she rubs things even more aggressively with her sponge. She keeps cleaning until the thumping against the wall stops and the children and the soccer ball have gone home. Only once the sun has gone down does Britt-Marie realize that the lights inside only work in the kitchen. So she stays in there, stranded on a little island of artificial, fluorescent light, in a soon-to-be-closed-down recreation center.

The kitchen is almost completely taken up by a dish rack, a refrigerator, and two wooden stools. She opens the refrigerator to find it empty apart from a packet of coffee. She curses herself for not bringing any vanilla extract. If you mix vanilla extract with baking soda, the refrigerator smells fresh.

She stands hesitantly in front of the coffee percolator. It looks modern. She hasn't made coffee in many years, because Kent makes very good coffee, and Britt-Marie always finds it's best to wait for him. But this percolator has an illuminated button, which strikes Britt-Marie as one of the most marvelous things she has seen in years, so she tries to open the lid where she assumes the coffee should be spooned in. It's stuck. The button starts blinking angrily.

Britt-Marie feels deeply mortified by this. She tugs at the lid in frustration. The blinking intensifies, upon which Britt-Marie tugs at it with such insistence that the whole machine is knocked over. The lid snaps open and a mess of coffee grounds and water sprays all over Britt-Marie's jacket.

They say people change when they go away, which is why Britt-Marie has always loathed traveling. She doesn't want change.

So it must be on account of the traveling, she decides afterwards, that she now loses her self-possession as never before. Unless you count the time Kent walked across the parquet floor in his golf shoes soon after they were married.

She picks up the mop and starts beating the coffee machine with the handle as hard as she can. It blinks. Something smashes. It stops blinking. Britt-Marie keeps hitting it until her arms are trembling and her eyes can no longer make out the contours of the dish rack. Finally, out of breath, she fetches a towel from her handbag. Turns off the ceiling light in the kitchen. Sits down on one of the wooden stools in the darkness, and weeps into the towel.

She doesn't want her tears to drip onto the floor. They could leave marks.

7

Britt-Marie stays awake all night. She's used to that, as people are when they have lived their entire lives for someone else.

She sits in the dark, of course, otherwise what would people think if they walked by and saw the light left on as if there was some criminal inside?

But she doesn't sleep, because she remembers the thick layer of dust on the floor of the recreation center before she started cleaning, and if she dies in her sleep she's certainly not going to risk lying here until she starts smelling and gets all covered in dust. Sleeping on one of the sofas in the corner of the recreation center is not even worth thinking about, because they were so filthy that Britt-Marie had to wear double latex gloves when she covered them with baking soda. Maybe she could have slept in the car? Maybe, if she were an animal.

The girl at the unemployment office kept insisting that there was a hotel in the town twelve miles away, but Britt-Marie can't even think of staying another night in a place where other people have made her bed. She knows that there are some people who do nothing else but dream of going away and experiencing something different, but Britt-Marie dreams of staying at home where everything is always the same. She wants to make her own bed.

Anytime she and Kent are staying at a hotel she always puts up the "Do Not Disturb" sign, and then makes the bed and cleans the room herself. It's not because she judges people, not at all; it's because she knows that the cleaning staff could very well be the sort of people who judge people, and Britt-Marie certainly doesn't want to run the risk of the cleaning staff sitting in a meeting in the evening discussing the horrible state of Room 423.

Once, Kent made a mistake about the check-in time for the flight when they were going home after a hotel visit, although Kent still maintains that "those sods can't even write the correct time on the sodding ticket," and they had to run off in the middle of the night without even having time to take a shower. So, just before Britt-Marie rushed out of the door, she ran into the bathroom to turn on the shower for a few seconds so there would be water on the floor when the cleaning staff came, and they would therefore not come to the conclusion that the guests in Room 423 had set off wearing their own dirt.

Kent snorted at her and said she was always too bloody concerned about what people thought of her. Britt-Marie was screaming inside all the way to the airport. She had actually mainly been concerned about what people would think of Kent.

She doesn't know when he stopped caring about what people thought of her.

She knows that once upon a time he did care. That was back in the days when he still looked at her as if he knew she was there. It's difficult to know when love blooms; suddenly one day you wake up and it's in full flower. It works the same way when it wilts—one day it is just too late. Love has a great deal in common with balcony plants in that way. Sometimes not even baking soda makes a difference.

Britt-Marie doesn't know when their marriage slipped out of her hands. When it became worn and scratched up no matter how many coasters she used. Once he used to hold her hand when they slept, and she dreamed his dreams. Not that Britt-Marie didn't have any dreams of her own; it was just that his were bigger, and the one with the biggest dreams always wins in this world. She had learned that. So she stayed home to take care of his children, without even dreaming of having any of her own. She stayed home another few years to make a presentable home and support him in his career, without dreaming of her own. She found she had neighbors who called her a "nag-bag" when she worried about what the Germans would think if there was rubbish in the foyer or the stairwell smelled of pizza. She made no friends of her own, just the odd acquaintance, usually the wife of one of Kent's business associates.

One of them once offered to help Britt-Marie with the washing-up after a dinner party, and then she set about sorting Britt-Marie's cutlery drawer with knives on the left, then spoons and forks. When Britt-Marie asked, in a state of shock, what she was doing, the acquaintance laughed as if it was a joke, and said, "Does it really matter?" They were no longer acquainted. Kent said that Britt-Marie was socially incompetent, so she stayed home for another few years so he could be social on behalf of the both of them. A few years turned into more years, and more years turned into all years. Years have a habit of behaving like that. It's not that Britt-Marie chose not to have any expectations, she just woke up one morning and realized they were past their sell-by date.

Kent's children liked her, she thinks, but children become adults and adults refer to women of Britt-Marie's type as nag-bags. From time to time there were other children living on their block; occasionally Britt-Marie got to cook them dinner if they were home alone. But the children always had mothers or grandmothers who came home at some point, and then they grew up and Britt-Marie became a nag-bag. Kent kept saying she was socially incompetent and she assumed this had to be right. In the end all she dreamed of was a balcony and a husband who did not walk on the parquet in his golf shoes, who occasionally put his shirt in the laundry basket without her having to ask him to do it, and who now and then said he liked the food without her having to ask. A home. Children who, although they weren't her own, came for Christmas in spite of everything. Or at least tried to pretend they had a decent reason not to. A correctly organized cutlery drawer. An evening at the theater every now and again. Windows you could see the world through. Someone who noticed that Britt-Marie had taken special care with her hair. Or at least pretended to notice. Or at least let Britt-Marie go on pretending.

Someone who came home to a newly mopped floor and a hot dinner on the table and, on the odd occasion, noticed that she had made an effort. It may be that a heart only finally breaks after leaving a hospital room in which a shirt smells of pizza and perfume, but it will break more readily if it has burst a few times before.

Britt-Marie turns on the light at six o'clock the following morning. Not because she's really missing the light, but because people may have noticed the light was on last night, and if they've realized Britt-Marie has spent the night at the recreation center she doesn't want them thinking she's still asleep at this time of the morning.

There's an old television by the sofas, which she could turn on to feel less lonely, but she avoids it because there will most likely be soccer on it. There's always soccer nowadays, and faced with that option Britt-Marie would actually prefer to be lonely. The recreation center encloses her in a guarded silence. The coffee percolator lies on its side and no longer blinks at her. She sits on the stool in front of it, remembering how Kent's children said Britt-Marie was "passive-aggressive." Kent laughed in the way that he did after drinking vodka and orange in front of a soccer match, his stomach bouncing up and down and the laughter gushing forth in little snorting bursts through his nostrils, and then he replied: "She ain't bloody passive-aggressive, she's aggressive-passive!" And then he laughed until he spilled vodka on the shagpile rug.

That was the night Britt-Marie decided she had had enough and moved the rug to the guest room without a word. Not because she's passive-aggressive, obviously. But because there are limits.

She wasn't upset about what Kent had said, because most likely he didn't even understand it himself. On the other hand she was offended that he hadn't even checked to see if she was standing close enough to hear.

She looks at the coffee percolator. For a fleeting, carefree moment the thought occurs to her that she might try to mend it, but she comes to her senses and moves away from it. She hasn't mended anything since she was married. It was always best to wait until Kent came home, she felt. Kent always said, "women can't even put together IKEA furniture," when they watched women in television programs about house building or renovation. "Quota-filling," he used to call it. Britt-Marie liked sitting next to him on the sofa solving the crossword. Always so close to the remote control that she could feel the tips of his fingers against her knee when he fumbled with it to flip the channel to a soccer match.

Then she fetches more baking soda and cleans the entire recreation center one more time. She has just sprinkled another batch of baking soda over the sofas when there's a knock at the door. It takes Britt-Marie a fair amount of time to open it, because running into the bathroom and doing her hair in front of the mirror without functioning lights is a somewhat complicated process.

Somebody is sitting outside the door with a box of wine in her hands.

"Ha," says Britt-Marie to the box.

"Good wine, you know. Cheap. Fell off the back of a truck, huh!" says Somebody quite smugly.

Britt-Marie doesn't know what that means.

"But, you know, I have to pour into bottle with label and all that crap, in case tax authority asks about it," says Somebody. "It's called 'house red' in my pizzeria, if tax authority asking, okay?" Somebody partly gives Britt-Marie the box and partly throws it at her before she forces her way inside, the wheelchair slamming across the threshold, to have a look around.

Britt-Marie looks at the goo of melted snow and gravel left behind by the wheels with only marginally less horror than if it had been excrement.

"Might I ask how the repair of my car is progressing?" asks Britt-Marie.

Somebody nods exultantly.

"Bloody good! Bloody good! Hey, let me ask you something, Britt-Marie: do you mind about color?"

"I beg your pardon?"

"You know, the door I got, huh. Bloody lovely door, huh. But maybe not same color as car. Maybe . . . more like yellow."

"What's happened to my door?" Britt-Marie asks, horrified.

"Nothing! Nothing! Just a question, huh! Yellow door? Not good? It's, what's-it-called? Oxidized! Old door. Almost not yellow anymore. Almost white now."

"I will certainly not tolerate a yellow door on my white car!"

Somebody waves the palms of her hands in circles.

"Okay, okay, okay, you know. Calm, calm, calm. Fix white door. No problem. Don't get lemon in arse now. But white door will have, what's-it-called? Delivery time!"

She nods at the wine in a carefree manner.

"You like wine, Britt?"

"No," answers Britt-Marie, not because she dislikes wine, but because if you say you like wine, people may come to the conclusion that you're an alcoholic.

"Everyone likes wine, Britt!"

"My name is Britt-Marie. Only my sister calls me Britt."

"Sister, huh? There's, what's-it-called? Another one of you? Nice for the world!"

Somebody grins as if this is a joke. At Britt-Marie's expense, Britt-Marie assumes.

"My sister died when we were small," she informs Somebody, without taking her eyes off the wine box.

"Ah . . . what the hell . . . I . . . what's-it-called? Condole," says Somebody sadly.

Britt-Marie curls up her toes tightly in her shoes.

"Ha. That's nice of you," she says quietly.

"The wine is good but a bit, what's-it-called? Muddy! You have to strain it a few times with a coffee filter, huh, everything okay then!" she explains expertly, before looking at Britt-Marie's bag and Britt-Marie's balcony boxes on the floor. Her smile grows.

"I wanted to give to you, you know, as your congratulations-for-new-job present. But now I can see it's more like a, what's-it-called? Moving-in present!"

Offended, Britt-Marie holds the box of wine in front of her as if it's making a ticking sound.

"I'd like to point out to you that I don't live here."

"Where did you sleep last night, then?"

"I didn't sleep," says Britt-Marie, looking as if she'd like to toss the wine box out of the door and cover her ears.

"There's one of them hotels, you know," says Somebody.

"Ha, I suppose you also have a hotel on your premises. I could imagine you do. Pizzeria and car workshop and post office and grocer's shop and a hotel? Must be nice for you, never having to make up your mind."

Somebody's face collapses with undisguised surprise.

"Hotel? Why would I have one of those? No, no, no, Britt-Marie. I keep to my, what's-it-called? Core activity!"

Britt-Marie shifts her weight from left foot to right, and finally goes to the refrigerator and puts the wine box inside.

"I don't like hotels," she announces and closes the door firmly.

"No, damn it! Don't put wine in fridge, you get lumps in it!" yells Somebody.

Britt-Marie glares at her.

"Is it really necessary to swear all the time, as if we were a horde of barbarians?"

Somebody propels her chair forward and tugs at the kitchen drawers until she finds the coffee filters.

"Shit, Britt-Marie! I show. You must filter. It's okay. Or, you know, mix with Fanta. I have cheap Fanta, if you want. From China!"

She stops herself when she notices the coffee percolator. The remains of it, at least. Britt-Marie, filled with discomfort, clasps her hands together over her stomach and looks as if she'd like to brush some invisible specks of dust from the opening of a black hole, and then sink into it herself.

"What . . . happened?" asks Somebody, eyeing first the mop and then the mop-sized dents in the coffee percolator. Britt-Marie stands in silence, with flaming cheeks. She may quite possibly be thinking about Kent. Finally she clears her throat, straightens her back and looks Somebody right in the eye as she answers:

"Hit by a flying stone."

Somebody looks at her. Looks at the coffee machine. Looks at the mop.

Then she starts laughing. Loudly. Then coughing. Then laughing even louder. Britt-Marie is deeply offended. It wasn't meant to be funny. At least Britt-Marie doesn't think it was; she hasn't said anything that was supposed to be funny in years, as far as she can remember. So she's offended by the laughter, because she assumes it's at her expense and not because of the actual joke. It's the sort of thing you assume if you've spent a sufficient amount of time with a husband who is constantly trying to be funny. There was not space in their relationship for more hilarity than his. Kent was funny and Britt-Marie went into the kitchen and took care of the washing-up. That was how they divided up their responsibilities.

But now Somebody sits here laughing so much that her wheelchair almost topples over. This makes Britt-Marie insecure, and her natural reaction to insecurity is irritation. She goes to the vacuum cleaner in a very demonstrative way—to attack the sofa covers, which are covered in baking soda.

Somebody's laughter slowly turns into a titter, and then into general mumbling about flying stones. "That's bloody funny, you know. Hey, you know there's a bloody big package in your car, huh?"

As if this would in any way be a surprise to Britt-Marie. Britt-Marie can still hear a trace of tittering in her voice.

"I'm well aware of that," she says tersely. She can hear Somebody rolling her wheelchair towards the front door.

"You want, you know, some help carrying it inside?"

Britt-Marie turns on the vacuum cleaner by way of an answer. Somebody yells to make herself heard:

"It's no trouble, Britt-Marie!"

Britt-Marie rubs the nozzle as hard as she can over the sofa cushions.

Repeatedly, until Somebody gives up and yells: "Well, you know, have Fanta like I said if you want some for wine! And pizza!" Then the door closes. Britt-Marie turns off the vacuum cleaner. She doesn't want to be unfriendly, but she really doesn't want any help with the package. Nothing is more important to Britt-Marie right now than her reluctance to be helped with the package.

Because there's a piece of furniture from IKEA inside.

And Britt-Marie is going to assemble it herself.

8

From time to time a truck drives through Borg, and whenever this happens, the recreation center shakes violently—as if, Britt-Marie thinks, it was built on the fault line between two continental shelves. Continental shelves are common in crossword puzzles, so it's the sort of thing she knows about. She also knows that Borg is the kind of place Britt-Marie's mother used to describe as "the back of beyond," because that was how Britt-Marie's mother used to describe the countryside.

Yet another truck thunders past. A green one. The walls shake.

Borg used to be the sort of community trucks came home to, but nowadays they only drive past. The truck makes her think of Ingrid. She remembers that she had time to see it through the back window when she was a child, on the very last day that she can recall thinking of herself as such. It was also green.

Britt-Marie has wondered the same thing an infinite number of times over the years: whether she had time to scream. And whether it would have made a difference. Their mother had told Ingrid to put on her belt, because Ingrid never put her belt on, and for that exact reason Ingrid had not put it on. They were arguing. That's why they didn't see it. Britt-Marie saw it because she always put her belt on, because she wanted her mother to notice. Which she obviously never did, because Britt-Marie never had to be noticed, for the simple reason that she always did everything without having to be told.

It came from the right-hand side. Green. That's one of the few things Britt-Marie remembers. It came from the right and there was glass and blood all over in the backseat of their parents' car. The last thing Britt-Marie remembered before she passed out was that she wanted to clean it up. Make it nice. And when she woke up at the hospital that is precisely what she did. Clean. Make things nice. When they buried her sister and there were strangers in black clothes drinking coffee in her parents' home, Britt-Marie put coasters under all the cups and washed all the dishes and cleaned all the windows. When her father began to stay at work for longer and longer and her mother stopped talking altogether, Britt-Marie cleaned. Cleaned, cleaned, and cleaned.

She hoped that sooner or later her mother would get out of bed and say, "How nice you've made everything," but it never happened. They never spoke about the accident, and, because they didn't, they also couldn't talk about anything else. Some people had pulled Britt-Marie out of the car; she doesn't know who, but she knows that her mother, silently furious, never forgave them for saving the wrong daughter. Maybe Britt-Marie didn't forgive them either. Because they saved the life of a person who from that day devoted herself to just walking around being afraid of dying and being left there to stink. One day she read her father's morning newspaper and saw an advertisement for a brand of window-cleaner. And in this way a life went by.

Now she's sixty-three and she's standing at the back of beyond, looking out at Borg through the kitchen window of the recreation center, missing Faxin and her view of the world.

Obviously, she stands far enough from the window for no one

outside to be able to see her looking out. What sort of impression would that make! As if she just stood there all day staring out, like some criminal. But her car is still parked in the graveled courtyard. She has accidentally left her keys inside and the IKEA package is still in the backseat. She doesn't know exactly how she's supposed to get it inside the recreation center, because it's so very heavy. She can't really say why it's so heavy because she doesn't know exactly what's inside. The idea was to buy a stool, not unlike the two stools in the kitchen at the recreation center, but after she had made her way to the IKEA self-service warehouse and found the appropriate shelf she found that all the stools had been sold.

Britt-Marie had taken all morning to make the decision that she was going to buy and assemble a stool, so this anticlimax left her standing there, frozen to the spot, for such a length of time that she began to worry that someone in the warehouse would see her there looking mysterious. What would people think? Most likely, that she was planning to steal something. Once this thought was firmly established, Britt-Marie panicked and with superhuman powers managed to drag over the next available package to her cart, in almost every conceivable way conveying the impression that this was the package she had been after all along. She hardly remembers how she got it into the car. She supposes that she was overcome with that syndrome they often talk about on the TV, when mothers pick up huge boulders under which their children are lying trapped. Britt-Marie is invested with that sort of power when she starts entertaining suspicions of strangers looking at her and wondering whether she's a criminal.

She moves farther away from the window, just to be on the safe side. At exactly twelve o'clock she prepares the table by the sofas for lunch. Not that there's much of either a table or a lunch, just a tin of peanuts and a glass of water, but the fact is that civilized people have lunch at twelve, and if Britt-Marie is anything in this world she's certainly civilized. She spreads a towel on the sofa before she sits down, then empties the tin of peanuts onto a plate. She has to force herself not to try to eat them with a knife and fork. Then she washes up and cleans the whole recreation center again so carefully that she almost uses up her whole supply of baking soda.

There's a little laundry room with a washing machine and a tumble dryer. Britt-Marie cleans the machines with her last bit of baking soda, like a starving person putting out her last bait on her fishing line.

Not that she was thinking of doing any washing, but she can't bear the thought of them all dirty. In a corner behind the tumble dryer she finds a whole sack of white shirts with numbers on them. Soccer jerseys, she understands. The entire recreation center is hung with pictures of various people wearing those shirts. Very likely they're covered in grass stains, of course. Britt-Marie can't for the life of her understand why anyone would choose to practice an outdoor sport while wearing white jerseys. It's barbaric. She wonders whether the corner shop/pizzeria/car workshop/post office would even be likely to sell baking soda.

She fetches her coat. Just inside the front door, next to several photos of soccer balls and people who don't know any better than to kick them, hangs a yellow jersey with the word "Bank" printed above the number "10." Just beneath is a photo of an old man holding up the same jersey with a proud smile.

Britt-Marie puts on her coat. Outside the front door is a person who was clearly just about to knock on it. The person has a face and the face is full of snuff. This, in every possible way, is an awful way of establishing the very short-lived acquaintance between Britt-Marie and the face, because Britt-Marie loathes snuff. The whole thing is over in twenty seconds, when the snuff-face moves off while mumbling something that sounds distinctly like "nag-bag."

At this point Britt-Marie picks up her telephone and dials the number of the only person her telephone has ever called. The girl at the unemployment office doesn't answer. Britt-Marie calls again, because actually a telephone is not a thing you decide whether or not to answer.

"Yes?" says the girl at long last, with food in her mouth. "Sorry. I'm having my lunch."

"Now?" Britt-Marie exclaims, as if the girl was joking. "My dear girl, we're not at war. Surely it's not necessary to be having your lunch at half past one?"

The girl chews her lunch quite hard. Bravely tries to change the topic of conversation:

"Did the pest control man come? I had to spend hours calling around but in the end I found someone who promised to make an emergency visit, and—"

"She was a pest control woman. Who took snuff," Britt-Marie goes on, as if this explains everything.

"Right," says the girl again. "So did she deal with the rat?"

"No, she most certainly did not," Britt-Marie affirms. "She came in here wearing dirty shoes and I'd just mopped the floor. Taking snuff as well, she was. Said she was putting out poison, that's how she put it, and you can't just do that. Do you really think one can just do that? Put out poison just like that?"

"*No . . .* ?" guesses the girl.

"No, you actually can't. Someone could die! And that's what I said. And then she stood there rolling her eyes with her dirty shoes and her snuff, and she said she'd put out a trap instead, and bait it with Snickers! Chocolate! On my newly mopped floor!" Britt-Marie says all this in the voice of someone screaming inside.

"Okay," says the girl, and immediately wishes she hadn't, because she realizes it is not okay at all.

“So I said it will have to be poison, then, and do you know what she told me? Listen to this! She said if the rat eats the poison you can’t know for certain where it will go to die. It could die in a cavity in the wall and lie there stinking! Have you ever heard of such a thing? Do you know that you called in a woman who takes snuff and thinks it’s absolutely in order to let dead animals die in the walls and stink the place out?”

“I was only trying to help,” says the girl.

“Ha. A fine lot of help that was. Some of us actually have other things to do than hanging about dealing with pest control women all day long,” says Britt-Marie well-meaningly.

“I couldn’t agree more,” says the girl.

There’s a queue in the corner shop. Or the pizzeria. Or the post office. Or the car workshop. Or whatever it is. Either way, there’s a queue. In the middle of the afternoon. As if people here don’t have anything better to do at this time.

The men with beards and caps are drinking coffee and reading the newspapers at one of the tables. Karl is standing at the front of the queue. He’s picking up a parcel. How very nice for him, thinks Britt-Marie, having all this leisure time on his hands. A cuboid woman in her thirties stands in front of Britt-Marie, wearing her sunglasses. Indoors. Very modern, muses Britt-Marie.

She has a white dog with her. Britt-Marie can’t think it’s very hygienic. The woman buys a pack of butter and six beers with foreign lettering on the cans, which Somebody produces from behind the counter. Also four packs of bacon and more chocolate cookies than Britt-Marie believes any civilized person could possibly need. Somebody asks if she’d like to have it on credit. The woman nods grumpily and throws it all in a bag. Britt-Marie would obviously never consider the woman to be "fat," because Britt-Marie is absolutely not the kind of person who pigeonholes people like that, but it does strike her how wonderful it must be for the woman to go through life so untroubled by her cholesterol levels.

"Are you blind, or what?" the woman roars as she turns around and charges directly into Britt-Marie.

Britt-Marie opens her eyes wide in surprise. Adjusts her hair.

"I most certainly am not. I have quite perfect vision. I've spoken to my optometrist about it. 'You have quite perfect vision,' he said!"

"In that case could you possibly get out of the way?" grunts the woman and waves a stick at her.

Britt-Marie looks at the stick. Looks at the dog and the sunglasses.

She mumbles, "Ha . . . ha . . . ha . . ." and nods apologetically before she realizes that nodding won't make any difference. The blind woman and the dog walk through her more than they walk past her. The door tinkles cheerfully behind them. It doesn't have the sense to do anything else.

Somebody rolls past Britt-Marie and waves encouragingly at her.

"Don't worry about her. She's like Karl. Lemon up her arse, you know."

She makes a gesture with her arm, which Britt-Marie feels is supposed to indicate how far up the latter the former is stuck, and then piles up a stack of empty pizza boxes on the counter.

Britt-Marie adjusts her hair and adjusts her skirt and instinctively adjusts the topmost pizza box, which isn't quite straight, and then tries to adjust her dignity as well and say in a tone that is absolutely considerate:

"I should like to know how the repair of my car is progressing."

Somebody scratches her hair.

"Sure, sure, sure, that car, yeah. You know, I have something to ask you, Britt-Marie: is a door important to Britt-Marie?"

"Door? Why . . . what in the world do you mean?"

"You know, only asking. Color: important for Britt-Marie, I understand. Yellow door: not okay. So I ask you, Britt-Marie: is a door important to Britt-Marie? If not important then Britt-Marie's car is, what's-it-called? Finish repaired! If a door is important . . . you know. Maybe, what's-it-called? Longer delivery time!"

She looks pleased. Britt-Marie does not look pleased.

"For goodness' sake, I must have a door on the car!" she fumes.

Somebody waves the palms of her hands defensively.

"Sure, sure, sure, no get angry. Just ask. Door: a little longer!" She measures out a few inches in the air between her thumb and index finger to illustrate how short a period of time "a little longer" really is.

Britt-Marie realizes that the woman has the upper hand in these negotiations.

Kent should have been here; he loves negotiating. He always says you have to compliment the person you're negotiating with. So Britt-Marie collects herself and says:

"Here in Borg people seem to have all the time in the world to go shopping in the afternoon. It must be nice for you to have so much leisure."

Somebody raises her eyebrows.

"And you? You're very busy?"

With a deep patience, Britt-Marie puts one hand in the other.

"I am *extremely* busy. Very, very busy indeed. But as it happens I am out of baking soda. Do you sell baking soda in this . . . shop?"

She says the word "shop" with divine indulgence.

"Vega!" Somebody roars at once so that Britt-Marie jumps into the air and almost knocks over the pile of pizza boxes.

The child from yesterday turns up behind the counter, still holding the soccer ball. Beside her stands a boy who looks almost exactly the same as her, but with longer hair.

"Baking soda for the lady!" says Somebody with an exaggerated theatrical bow at Britt-Marie, which is not at all appreciated.

"It's her," whispers Vega to the boy.

The boy immediately looks as if Britt-Marie is a lost key. He runs into the stockroom and stumbles back out with two bottles in his arms. Faxin. All the air goes out of Britt-Marie.

She assumes that she has what is sometimes in crossword clues known as an "out-of-body experience." For a few moments she forgets all about the grocery shop and the pizzeria and the men with beards and cups of coffee and newspapers. Her heart beats as if it's just been released from prison.

The boy places the bottles on the counter like a cat that's caught a squirrel. Britt-Marie's fingers brush over them before her sense of dignity orders them to leave off. It's like coming home.

"I . . . I was under the impression that they'd been discontinued," she whispers.

The boy points eagerly at himself: "Chill! Omar fixes everything!"

He points even more eagerly at the bottles of Faxin.

"All the foreign trucks stop at the petrol station in town! I know them all there! I fix whatever you like!"

Somebody nods wisely.

"They shut down petrol station in Borg. Not, you know, profitable."

"But I fix petrol in can, if you like, free home delivery! And I can get you more Faxin if you want!" the boy hollers.

Vega rolls her eyes.

"I'm the one who told you she needed Faxin," she hisses at the boy and puts the jar of baking soda on the counter.

"I'm the one who fixed it!" the boy maintains, without taking his eyes off Britt-Marie.

"This is my younger brother, Omar," sighs Vega to Britt-Marie.

"We're born the same year!" protests Omar.

"In January and December, yeah," snorts Vega. If anything, Britt-Marie notices, the brother looks slightly older than her. Still a child, but approaching that age when they can become quite pungent.

"I'm the best fixer in Borg. The king of the castle, you know. Whatever you need, come to me!" says Omar to Britt-Marie, winking confidently without paying any attention to his sister, who's kicking him on the shin.

"Twit," says Vega with a sigh.

"Cow!" answers Omar.

Britt-Marie doesn't know if she should be concerned or proud that she actually knows that this means something bad, but she doesn't have much time to reflect on this before Omar is lying on the floor, holding his lip. Vega goes out of the door with the soccer ball in one hand and the other still formed into a fist.

Somebody titters at Omar.

"You have, what's-it-called? Marshmallows for brains! Never learn, do you?"

Omar wipes his lip and then looks as if he's letting go of the whole business. Like a small child forgetting to cry over a dropped ice cream when he catches sight of a glittering power ball.

"If you want new hubcaps for your car I can fix it. Or anything. Shampoo or handbags or anything. I'll fix it!"

"Maybe some Band-Aids?" hollers Somebody mischievously and points at his lip.

Britt-Marie keeps a firm grip on her handbag and adjusts her hair, as if the boy has offended the both of them.

"I certainly don't need either shampoo or a handbag."

Omar points at the bottles of Faxin.

"Those are thirty kronor each but you can have them on credit."

"On *credit*?"

"Everyone shops on credit in Borg."

"I certainly don't shop on credit! I can see maybe you don't understand such a thing in Borg, but there are some of us that can pay our way!" hisses Britt-Marie.

That last bit just slips out of her. It wasn't quite how she meant to put it.

Somebody is not grinning anymore. Both the boy and Britt-Marie have red faces, caused by different kinds of shame. Britt-Marie briskly lays down the money on the counter and the boy picks it up and runs out of the door. Soon the thumping can be heard again. Britt-Marie stays where she is and tries to avoid Somebody's eyes.

"I didn't get a receipt," Britt-Marie states in a low voice, which is not at all incriminating.

Somebody shakes her head and smacks her tongue.

"What does he look like, IKEA or something? He doesn't have, what's-it-called? Limited company, you know. Just a kid with a bicycle."

"Ha," says Britt-Marie.

"What else do you want?" asks Somebody, her tone noticeably less hospitable as she puts the jar of baking soda and the bottles of Faxin in a bag.

Britt-Marie smiles as helpfully as she can.

"You have to understand that one has to get a receipt. Otherwise one actually can't prove that one isn't a criminal," she explains.

Somebody rolls her eyes, which Britt-Marie feels is unnecessary.

Somebody presses a few keys on her register. The money tray opens, revealing not very much money at all inside, and then the register spits out a pale yellow receipt.

"That'll be six hundred and seventy-three kronor and fifty öre," says Somebody.

Britt-Marie stares back as if she's got something stuck in her throat.

"For baking soda?"

Somebody points out of the door.

"For dent in car. I have done one of those, what's-it-called? Bodywork inspection! I don't want to, what's-it-called? Insult you, Britt-Marie! So you can't have credit. Six hundred and seventy-three kronor and fifty öre."

Britt-Marie almost drops her handbag. That's how grave the situation is.

"I have . . . who . . . for goodness' sake. No civilized person walks around with that much cash in her handbag."

She says that in an extra-loud voice. So that everyone in there can hear, in case one of them is a criminal. On the other hand, only the bearded coffee-drinking men are there, and neither of them even look up, but still. Criminal types do sometimes have beards. Britt-Marie actually has no prejudices about that.

"Do you take cards?" she says, registering a certain amount of rising heat along her cheekbones.

Somebody shakes her head hard.

"Poker players do cards, huh, Britt-Marie. Here we do cash."

"Ha. In that case I'll have to ask for directions to the nearest cash machine," says Britt-Marie.

"In town," says Somebody coldly, crossing her arms.

"Ha," says Britt-Marie.

"They closed down the cash machine in Borg. Not profitable," says Somebody with raised eyebrows, nodding at the receipt.

Britt-Marie's gaze flickers desperately across the walls, in an attempt to deflect attention from her bloodred cheeks. There's a yellow jersey hanging on the wall, identical to the one in the recreation center, with the word "Bank" written above the number 10 on its back.

Somebody notices her looking at it, so she closes the register, knots the bag of baking soda and Faxin, and pushes it across the counter.

"You know, no shame here with credit, huh, Britt-Marie. Maybe shame where you come from, but no shame in Borg."

Britt-Marie takes the bag without knowing what to do with her eyes.

Somebody takes a slug of vodka and nods at the yellow jersey on the wall.

"Best player in Borg. Called 'Bank,' you know, because when Bank play for Borg it was like, what's-it-called? Like money in the bank! Long time ago. Before financial crisis. Then, you know: Bank got ill, huh. Like another sort of crisis. Bank moved away. Gone now, huh."

She nods out of the door. A ball thumps against the fence.

"Bank's old man trained all the brats, huh. Kept them going. Kept all of Borg going, huh? Everyone's friend! But God, you know, God got a shit head for numbers, huh. The sod gives both profitable and unprofitable person heart attack. Bank's dad died a month ago."

The wooden walls creak and groan around them, as old houses do, and old people. One of the men with papers and cups of coffee fetches more coffee from the counter. Britt-Marie notes that you get a free top-up here.

"They found him on the, what's-it-called? Kitchen floor!"

"Pardon me?"

Somebody points at the yellow jersey. Shrugs.

"Bank's old man. On the kitchen floor. One morning. Just dead."

She snaps her fingers. Britt-Marie jumps. She thinks of Kent's heart attack. He had always been very profitable. She takes an even firmer grip on her bag of Faxin and baking soda. Stands in silence for so long that Somebody starts to look concerned.

"Hey, you need something else? I have that, what's-it-called? Baileys! Chocolate spirit! You know, it's a copy, but you can put O'boy and vodka in it, and then, it's okay to drink, if you drink it, you know . . . fast!"

Britt-Marie shakes her head briskly. She walks towards the door, but something about that kitchen floor may possibly cause her some hesitation. So she cautiously turns around, before she changes her mind, and then turns around again.

Britt-Marie is not a very spontaneous person, one certainly needs to be clear about that. "Spontaneous" is a synonym for "irrational"—that's Britt-Marie's firm view, and if there's one thing Britt-Marie isn't, it's irrational. This is not so very easy for her, in other words. But at last she turns around, then changes her mind and turns around another time, so that by the end she's facing the door when she lowers her voice and asks, with all the spontaneity that she can muster:

"Do you possibly stock Snickers chocolate bars?"

Darkness falls early in Borg in January. Britt-Marie goes back to the recreation center and sits by herself on one of the kitchen stools, with the front door open. The chill doesn't concern her. Not the waiting either. She is used to it. You do get used to it. She has plenty of time to think about whether what she is going through now is a sort of life crisis. She has read about them. People have life crises all the time.

The rat comes in through the open door at twenty past six. It settles on the threshold and focuses a very watchful gaze on the

Snickers bar, which is on a plate on top of a little towel. Britt-Marie gives the rat a stern look and cups one hand firmly in the other.

"From now on we have dinner at six o'clock. Like civilized people."

After thinking this over for a certain amount of time, she adds:

"Or rats."

The rat looks at the Snickers. Britt-Marie has removed the wrapper and placed the chocolate in the middle of the plate, with a neatly folded napkin next to it. She looks at the rat. Clears her throat.

"Ha. I'm not especially good at starting these types of conversations. I'm socially incompetent, you see, that's what my husband says. He's very socially gifted, everyone says that. An entrepreneur, you see."

When the rat doesn't answer, she adds:

"Very successful. Very, very successful."

She briefly considers telling the rat about her life crisis. She imagines she'd like to explain that it's difficult to know who you are once you are alone, when you have always been there for the sake of someone else. But she doesn't want to trouble the rat with it. So she adjusts a crease in her skirt and says, very formally:

"I would like to propose a working arrangement. For your part, it would mean that a dinner would be arranged for you every evening at six o'clock."

She makes an explanatory gesture at the chocolate.

"The arrangement, if we find it mutually beneficial, would mean that, if you die, I won't let you lie and smell bad in the wall. And you will do the same for me. In case people don't know we are here."

The rat takes a tentative step towards the chocolate. Stretches its neck and sniffs it. Britt-Marie brushes invisible crumbs from her knee.

"It's the sodium bicarbonate that disappears when one dies, you have to understand. That's why people smell. I read that after Ingrid had died."

The rat's whiskers vibrate with skepticism. Britt-Marie clears her throat apologetically.

"Ingrid was my sister, you have to understand. She died. I was worried she'd smell bad. That's how I found out about sodium bicarbonate. The body produces sodium bicarbonate to neutralize the acidic substances in the stomach. When one dies, the body stops producing the sodium bicarbonate, so the acidic substances eat their way through the skin and end up on the floor. That's when it smells, you have to understand."

She thinks about adding that she has always found it reasonable to assume that the human soul is found in the sodium bicarbonate. When it leaves the body, there's nothing left. Only complaining neighbors. But she doesn't say anything. Doesn't want to cause bother.

The rat eats its dinner but doesn't comment on whether or not it enjoyed it.

Britt-Marie doesn't ask.

Everything begins in earnest this evening. The weather is mild, the snow turns to rain as it falls from sky to earth. The children play soccer in the dark, but neither the dark nor the rain seems to concern them in the least. The parking area is only blessed with light here and there, where it's cast by the neon sign of the pizzeria, or from the kitchen window where Britt-Marie stands hidden behind the curtain watching them, but, to be quite honest, most of them are so bad at soccer that more light would only have a marginal effect on their ability to hit the ball.

The rat has gone home. Britt-Marie has locked the door and washed up and cleaned the whole recreation center one more time. She is standing by the window looking out at the world. From time to time, the ball bounces through the puddles onto the road, and then the children play Rock, Paper, Scissors to decide who has to go and fetch it.

Kent used to tell David and Pernilla when they were small that Britt-Marie couldn't play with them because she "didn't know how," but that isn't true. Britt-Marie knows perfectly well how to play Rock, Paper, Scissors. She just doesn't think it sounds very hygienic to keep stones in paper bags. As for the scissors, it's not even worth thinking about. Who knows where they've been?

Of course Kent is always saying Britt-Marie is "so darned negative." It's a part of her social incompetence. "Darn it! Just be happy instead!" Kent fetches the cigars and takes care of the guests and Britt-Marie does the washing-up and takes care of the home, and that's how they have divided up their lives. Kent is a bit happy, darn it, and Britt-Marie is darned negative. Maybe that's how it goes. It's easier to stay optimistic if you never have to clear up the mess afterwards.

The two siblings, Vega and Omar, play on opposing sides. She is calm and calculating, gently moving the ball with the insides of her feet, as you might twiddle your toes against someone you love while sleeping. Her brother, on the other hand, is angry and frustrated, hunting the ball down as if it owes him money. Britt-Marie doesn't know the first thing about soccer, but anyone can see that Vega is the best player in the parking area. Or at least the least bad one.

Omar is constantly in his sister's shadow. They are all in her shadow. She reminds Britt-Marie of Ingrid.

Ingrid was never negative. As always with people like this, it's difficult to know whether everyone loved Ingrid because she was so positive, or if she was so positive because everyone loved her. She was one year older than Britt-Marie and five inches taller—it doesn't take much to put someone in your shadow. It never mattered to Britt-Marie that she was the one who receded into the background. She never wanted much.

Sometimes she actually yearned to want something, so much that she could hardly bear it. It seemed so vital, wanting things. But usually the feeling passed.

Ingrid, of course, was always falling to bits with wanting things—her singing career, for instance, and the celebrity status she was predestined to achieve, and the boys out there in the world who were so much more than the usual ones on offer in their apartment block. The usual boys who, Britt-Marie realized, were infinitely too unusual to even look at Britt-Marie and yet far too usual in every way to deserve her sister.

They were brothers, the boys on their floor. Alf and Kent. They fought about everything. Britt-Marie couldn't understand it. She followed her sister everywhere. It never bothered Ingrid. Quite the opposite. "It's you and me, Britt," she used to whisper at nights when she told her the stories of how they were going to live in Paris in a palace filled with servants. That was why she called her little sister "Britt"—because it sounded American.

Admittedly it seemed a bit odd to have an American name in Paris, but Britt-Marie had certainly never been the sort of person who opposed things needlessly.

Vega is grim, but when her team scores in the dark yard, in the rain, in a goal made of two soft-drink cans, her laugh sounds just like Ingrid's. Ingrid also loved to play. As with all people like that, it's difficult to know if she was the best because she loved the games, or if she loved them because she was the best.

A little boy with ginger hair gets hit hard in the face with the ball. He falls headlong into a muddy puddle. Britt-Marie shudders. It's the same soccer ball they shot at Britt-Marie's head, and when she sees the mud on it she wants to give herself a tetanus shot. Yet she has difficulties taking her eyes off the game, because Ingrid would have liked it.

Of course, if Kent had been here he would have said the children were playing like big girls' blouses. Kent is able to describe almost anything bad by adding, before or after, that it's a bit of a "big girl's blouse." Britt-Marie is actually not especially fond of irony, but she notes a certain amount of that very thing in the fact that the only player out there not playing like a girl's blouse is the girl.

Britt-Marie finally comes to her senses and leaves the window before anyone out there starts getting any ideas. It's past eight, so the recreation center is steeped in darkness. Britt-Marie waters her balcony boxes in the dark. Sprinkles baking soda over the soil. She misses her balcony more than anything. You're never quite alone when you can stand on a balcony—you have all the cars and houses and the people in the streets. You're among them, but also not. That's the best thing about balconies. The second best is standing out there early in the morning before Kent has woken up, closing your eyes and feeling the wind in your hair. Britt-Marie used to do that, and it felt like Paris. Of course she has never been to Paris, because Kent doesn't do any business there, but she has solved an awful lot of crossword clues about Paris. It's the world's most crossword-referenced city, full of rich and famous celebrities with their very own cleaners. Ingrid used to go on about how they'd have their own servants, which was the only bit of the dream Britt-Marie wasn't sure about—she didn't want them to think that Britt-Marie's sister was so bad at cleaning that she had to employ someone to do it. Britt-Marie had heard their mother talking about those sorts of mothers with contempt, and Britt-Marie didn't want anyone talking about Ingrid like that.

So while Ingrid would excel at everything out there in the world, Britt-Marie imagined herself being really good at things inside of it. Cleaning. Making things nice. Her sister noticed this. Noticed her. Britt-Marie did her hair every morning, and her sister never forgot to say, "Thanks, you did that really well, Britt!" while she turned her head in front of the mirror to a tune from one of her vinyl records. Britt-Marie never had records. You don't need any when you have an older sister who truly sees you.

When there's a bang on the door Britt-Marie jumps as if someone just drove an ax through it. Vega is standing outside, but without an ax. Worse still, she's dripping mud and rain on the floor. Britt-Marie screams on the inside.

"Why don't you turn on the lights?" asks Vega, squinting into the darkness.

"They don't work, dear."

"Have you tried changing the bulbs?" asks Vega with a frown, as if she has to totally control herself not to add "dear" at the end of her question.

Omar pops up next to her. He has mud in his nostrils. Inside his nostrils. Britt-Marie cannot get her head around how something like that could happen. Surely there's such a thing as gravity.

"You need to buy lightbulbs. I have the baddest low-energy bulbs! Special price!" he says eagerly, producing a rucksack from somewhere.

Vega kicks him on the shin and looks at Britt-Marie with the strained diplomacy of the teenager.

"Can we watch the match here?" she asks.

"What . . . match?" asks Britt-Marie.

"*The* match!" Vega replies, not entirely unlike how you'd say "*the* Pope" if someone asked, "what Pope?"

Britt-Marie switches her hands around on her stomach, and then reclasps them together.

"The match in what?"

"Soccer!" Vega and Omar burst out.

"Ha," mutters Britt-Marie and looks with revulsion at their muddy clothes. Not at the children, obviously. At their clothes. Britt-Marie is obviously not revolted by children.

"He always let us watch it here," says Vega and points at the photo on the wall inside the door of the elderly man with the "Bank" jersey in his hands.

In another photo just next to it stands the same man in front of a truck, and he's wearing a white jacket on which Borg SC is written on one of his breast pockets and Coach on the other. It could have done with a wash, Britt-Marie notes.

"I have not been informed about this. You'll have to contact the man, in that case."

The silence depletes the air between them of oxygen.

"He's dead," says Vega at long last, looking down at her shoes.

Britt-Marie looks at the man in the photo. Then at her hands.

"That's . . . ha. Very sad to hear it. But I actually can't be held responsible for it," she says.

Vega peers at her with hate. Then shoves Omar in the side and hisses:

"Come on, Omar, let's get out of here. Never bloody mind about her."

She has already turned around and started walking away when Britt-Marie notices the other children, three of them, waiting a few feet away. All in their early teens. One with ginger hair, one with black, and another with high cholesterol. She senses the accusation in their eyes.

"Can I ask why you don't watch the soccer in the pizzeria or the car workshop or whatever it is, if it's so important?" asks Britt-Marie in a polite and not at all confrontational manner.

Omar kicks his ball across the parking area and says in a quiet voice:

"They drink in there. If they lose."

"Ha. And if they win?"

"Then they drink even more. So he always let us watch in here."

"And I suppose in these parts you wouldn't have homes of your own to go to, with televisions in them? Would you?"

"There isn't space for the whole team at anyone's house," snaps

Vega suddenly, "and besides, we watch the matches together. Like a team."

Britt-Marie brushes some dust off her skirt.

"I was under the impression that you didn't have a team anymore."

"We have a team!" roars Vega and stamps back towards Britt-Marie.

"We're here, aren't we? We're here! So we are a team! Even if they take our bloody pitch and our bloody club and our trainer has a bloody heart attack and goes and bloody dies on us we're a team!"

Britt-Marie is practically shaking as the child's furious eyes focus on her. This is certainly no suitable way for a human being to express herself. But tears are now running down Vega's cheeks, and Britt-Marie can't properly determine whether the child is going to give her a hug or a wallop.

Britt-Marie looks as if she would find either alternative similarly threatening.

"I have to ask you to wait here," she says in a panic, and closes the door.

That's how it all happens before everything begins in earnest.

Britt-Marie stands inside the door, breathing in the smell of wet potting soil and baking soda. She remembers the smell of alcohol and the sound of Kent's soccer matches. He never went onto the balcony, so the balcony belonged to Britt-Marie and no one else, which was something quite unique. She always lied and said she had bought the plants, because she knew he'd say something horrible if she told him she'd found them in the garbage room and sometimes in the street, left behind by some neighbors when they moved away. Plants reminded her of Ingrid, because Ingrid loved things that were alive. And for this reason Britt-Marie repeatedly saved homeless plants, to give her the strength to remember a sister whose life she was not even able to save once. You couldn't explain things like this to Kent.

Kent doesn't believe in death, he believes in evolution. "That's evolution," he said, nodding approvingly, on one occasion when he was watching a nature program in which a lion killed an injured zebra: "It's sorting out the one that's weak, right? It's about the survival of the species, you have to get that. If you're not the best from the start, you have to accept the consequences and leave space for someone stronger, right?"

You can't discuss balcony plants with a person like that.

Or the feeling of missing someone.

Britt-Marie's fingertips are trembling slightly when she picks up the cell phone.

The girl from the unemployment office answers on the third attempt.

"Hello?" says the girl in a panting voice.

"Is that how you answer the phone? Out of breath?"

"Britt-Marie? I'm at the gym!"

"That must be very nice for you."

"Has something happened?"

"There are some children here. They say they want to see some sort of match here."

"Oh yeah, the match! I'm going to watch it as well!"

"I wasn't notified that my range of duties included taking care of children. . . ."

The girl at the other end of the line groans in what is, to be honest, quite an uncalled-for way.

"Britt-Marie, sorry, but I'm not supposed to talk on the phone in the gym."

Then she exclaims, without a thought:

"But . . . you know . . . it's a good thing, isn't it? If the children are there watching the soccer and you drop dead, they'll know all about it!"

Britt-Marie laughs curtly. Then there's a silence for a very, very long time.

The girl inhales grimly, and there's a sound of a jogging machine stopping.

"Okay, sorry Britt-Marie, I was joking. It was a silly thing for me to say. I didn't mean it that way . . . hello?"

Britt-Marie has already hung up. She opens the door half a minute later with the newly washed soccer jerseys neatly folded into a pile in her arms.

"But you're not coming in with those muddy clothes, I have just mopped the floors!" she says to the children before she stops herself.

There's a policeman standing among them. He's small and chubby and has a head of hair like a lawn the day after an impromptu barbecue.

"What have you done now?" Britt-Marie hisses at Vega.

The policeman looks ambivalent. The woman who stands in front of him is very different to the one the children described. Fussy, yes, and bossy, clearly, but something else as well. Determined, immaculately neat, and somehow . . . unique. He stares dumbly for a moment while he tries to think of something to say to her, but in the end decides the most civic thing he can do is to hold out a big glass jar towards Britt-Marie.

"My name is Sven. I just wanted to welcome you to Borg. This is jam."

Britt-Marie looks at the jam jar. Vega looks at Sven. At a loss, Sven scratches himself on various parts of his police uniform.

"Blueberry jam. I made it myself. I did a course. In town."

Britt-Marie gives him a careful once-over from top to bottom and back again. She stops in both directions when she comes to the uniform shirt, which is tight over his stomach.

"I don't have a jersey in your size," she informs him.

Sven blushes.

"No, no, no, of course, that's not what I meant. I want . . . just welcome to Borg, just that. That's all I wanted to say."

He presses the jam jar into Vega's hands and totters away from the threshold into the parking area, heading towards the pizzeria. Vega looks at the jam jar. Omar looks at Britt-Marie's bare ring finger and grins.

"Are you married?" he asks.

Britt-Marie is shocked at herself when she notices how quickly she blurts out:

"I'm divorced."

It's the first time she's said it out loud. Omar's grin widens as he nods at Sven.

"Sven is free, just so you know!"

Britt-Marie hears the other children tittering. She presses the jerseys into Omar's arms, snatches the jam jar from Vega, and disappears into the gloom of the recreation center. About half a dozen children remain on the threshold, rolling their eyes.

That's how it all begins.

10

Soccer is a curious game, because it doesn't ask to be loved. It demands it.

Britt-Marie wanders about inside the recreation center like a confounded spirit whose grave someone has opened in order to start a discotheque.

The children sit on the sofa, wearing the white jerseys and drinking soft drinks. Britt-Marie has obviously ensured that they are sitting on towels, because she doesn't have enough baking soda to clean all the children. It goes without saying that they have coasters under their soft drinks. Admittedly there weren't any proper coasters, so Britt-Marie has used two pieces of toilet paper folded over. Necessity has no rule, but even necessity has to understand that you can't just put a soft-drink can on the table.

She also puts glasses in front of the children. One of them, the one that Britt-Marie would obviously never refer to as "overweight" but who looks as if he's had quite a few soft drinks belonging to other children, tells her cheerfully that he'd "rather just drink straight from the can."

"You certainly won't, here we drink from glasses," Britt-Marie interjects with uncompromising articulation.

"Why?"

"Because we're not animals."

The boy looks at his lemonade can, thinks about it, and then asks:

"What animal apart from human beings can drink from a can?"

Britt-Marie doesn't answer. Instead she picks up the remote controls from the floor and puts them on the table. As soon as she's done it she bounces back in terror when the until-now timid boys on the sofa all roar "Nooo!" as if she's flung the remote controls in their faces.

"No remotes on the table!" hisses the lemonade boy fearfully.

"That's the worst jinx! We'll lose if you do that!" yells Omar and runs up to throw them back on the floor.

"What do you mean, 'we'll lose'?" asks Britt-Marie, as if he's taken leave of his senses.

Omar points at the grown men on the TV, who quite clearly do not even know he exists.

"We will!" he repeats with conviction, as if this somehow explains anything.

Britt-Marie notes that he's wearing his soccer jersey back to front.

"I don't appreciate yelling indoors. I also don't appreciate the wearing of clothes back to front like gangsters," she points out, picking up the remotes from the floor.

"We'll lose if we wear our shirts the right way around!"

Britt-Marie doesn't even know how to respond to such nonsense, so she takes the remote controls and the children's muddy clothes into the laundry. When she turns around after starting the washing machine, the ginger-haired boy is standing in front of her. He looks embarrassed. Britt-Marie cups one hand into the other and doesn't look ready for more conversation.

"They're superstitious, everything has to be the same as the last time we won," says the boy, at the same time explanatory and defensive. He suddenly looks slightly nervous.

"I'm the one who shot the soccer ball at your head yesterday. I didn't do it on purpose. I'm pants at aiming. I hope it didn't ruin your hair," he says. "Your hair is . . . nice," he adds with a smile, then turns to go back to the sofa.

Britt-Marie keeps her eyes on him and by and large doesn't entirely dislike him. He sits on the far side against the wall behind the boy with black hair and the boy who's had the most soft drinks, so that he's out of sight.

"We call him Pirate," says Vega.

She has popped up next to Britt-Marie. Apparently it's what she does: pops up, all the time. Her jersey is slightly too big. Or her body too small, possibly.

"Pirate," echoes Britt-Marie, in the way that Britt-Marie echoes when she has to drum up all the well-meaning feelings she's capable of in order not to have to explain that Pirate is not much of a name for anyone except an actual pirate.

Vega points to the other two children on the sofa.

"And that's Toad. And that's Dino."

And there goes the limit of Britt-Marie's well-meaningness.

"For goodness' sake, those aren't even proper names!"

Vega doesn't look as if she understands what this is supposed to mean.

"It's because he's a Somalian," she says, pointing at one of the boys, as if this explains everything.

When Britt-Marie doesn't look as if it does explain everything, Vega sighs in a very bored sort of way and explains:

"When Dino moved to Borg and Omar heard that he was a Somalian he thought it sounded like a 'sommelier,' you know one of those people who drink wine on the TV. So we called him 'Wino.' And it rhymes with 'Dino.' So now we just call him 'Dino.' "

Britt-Marie stares at Vega as if Vega had just fallen asleep drunk in Britt-Marie's bed.

"So your real names weren't good enough, I suppose, were they?"

Vega doesn't seem to comprehend the difference.

"He can't have the same name as us, can he? Or we wouldn't know who to pass to when we're playing."

Britt-Marie snorts hard through her nose, because that's how Britt-Marie's irritation comes steaming out when it grows too large inside her head.

"Surely the boy has a proper name," she fumes.

Vega shrugs.

"He didn't do much talking when he moved here, so we didn't know what his name was, but he laughed when we called him Dino and we liked it when he laughed. So he kept the name.

"Toad we called Toad because he can burp so loud that it's just sick. And Pirate we call Pirate because we . . . I don't know, we just do."

She nods towards the ginger-haired boy, who still can't be seen. Britt-Marie smiles graciously and says:

"And I don't suppose there are any girls' teams for you to play on? No, of course not."

Vega shakes her head.

"All the girls play for the team in town."

Britt-Marie nods with absolute, absolute helpfulness.

"I suppose that team wasn't good enough for you, was it?"

Vega looks annoyed.

"This is my team!" she says.

A player on the TV is rolling about on the pitch. Omar uses the stoppage time to climb up on one of the kitchen stools and start changing the lightbulbs on credit. Britt-Marie circles nervously.

Vega starts looking around as if there's a person missing.

"Where's the ball?" she calls out into the room.

"Shit! Outside!" Omar cries, looking out at the rain outside the window.

"You can't possibly be thinking about bringing that ball in here!" gasps Britt-Marie in terror.

"It can't just stay out there in the rain!" says Vega, with a similar level of terror in her voice, as if this was a question of a human life.

Before Britt-Marie has time to realize what's going on, a chain of Stones and Scissors being put in Paper Bags is initiated across the room, until ginger-haired Pirate in some way loses and is on his way up from the sofa towards the door in a fluid movement.

"Mother of God! Not in your newly washed jersey! No!" She catches hold of his collar but he's already wearing his shoes and has already gone over the threshold. Britt-Marie, in absolute agitation, gets into her own shoes and runs after him.

The boy is standing six feet away, with the muddy soccer ball in his arms.

"Sorry," he mumbles, staring down at the leather.

Britt-Marie doesn't know if he is apologizing to her or to the soccer ball. She holds her hands over her hair so the rain doesn't ruin her coiffure. The boy peers at her, smiling sincerely, and then, embarrassed, looks down at the ground.

"Can I ask you something?" he says.

"Excuse me?" says Britt-Marie, the rain running down her face.

"Would you help me fix my hair?" he mumbles, avoiding eye contact.

"I'm sorry, what was that?" asks Britt-Marie while she keeps her gaze focused on a patch of mud left by the soccer ball on the boy's newly washed jersey.

"I have a date tomorrow. I was going to . . . I was thinking . . . I wanted to ask if you could help me fix my hair," he manages to say.

Britt-Marie nods as if this was quite typical.

"I don't suppose you have any hairdressers in Borg, oh no. I suppose that will also be my responsibility now, is that what you mean? Is it?"

The boy shakes his head at the ball.

"Your hair's really nice. I was thinking you're good at doing hair, because your hair is nice. There isn't a hairdresser in Borg because it closed down."

The rain tails off somewhat. Britt-Marie is still holding the palms of her hands like a pitched roof over the top of her head, and the rain is running down into her sleeves.

"Is that what it's known as these days? A 'date'?" she says, a touch thoughtfully.

"What did you call it before?" asks the boy, peering up from the ball.

"In my days it was known as a 'meeting,'" says Britt-Marie firmly.

Possibly she's not an expert at this, she'd be willing to admit. She has only ever been on two meetings with boys. One of them she ended up marrying. The rain stops completely while they are standing there, she and the boy with the ginger hair and the muddy soccer ball.

"We say date, or at least I do," mumbles the boy.

Britt-Marie takes a deep breath and avoids his avoidance of eye contact.

"You really must understand that I can't give you an answer now, because I have my list in my handbag," she says in a low voice.

The boy immediately starts nodding with altogether worrying enthusiasm.

"It doesn't matter! I can make it anytime tomorrow!"

"Ha. I imagine school isn't of much concern here in Borg."

"It's still Christmas holiday."

And then their silence is so abruptly broken by the children's howls of euphoria from within that Britt-Marie is startled and makes a grab for the boy's jersey, and the boy in turn is so surprised that he tosses the ball into her arms. She gets mud on her jacket. Half a second later the men in the pizzeria burst into fits of braying until the neon sign above the door rattles.

"What's going on?" Britt-Marie wants to know, with panic in her eyes, as she throws the ball on the ground.

"We scored a goal!" howls the Pirate boy ecstatically.

"What do you mean, 'we'?" asks Britt-Marie.

"Our team!"

"I thought you didn't have a team!"

"But I mean: our team, the one we're supporting! On the TV!" the boy tries to explain.

"But how is it your team if you don't *play* in it?"

The boy thinks this over for a moment. Then he seems to take a firm grip on the ball.

"We've supported this team for longer than most of the players in it. So it's more our team than theirs."

"Preposterous," snorts Britt-Marie.

In the next second the sound of a front door being slammed cuts through the January night. Britt-Marie spins around in pure dismay and starts running towards it. The boy runs after. The door is locked from the inside.

"Like, they've locked it so we can't come in! Because we were out here when we scored!" puffs Pirate, jubilant and out of breath.

"What on earth are you trying to say?" Britt-Marie demands and tugs frantically at the door handle.

"I mean it's important that we stay out here, because while we were out here we scored! We're bringing good luck out here!" hollers the boy as if that's reasonable. Britt-Marie stares at him as if it certainly isn't. But then they stand in the parking area, despite the rain that's falling again, and Britt-Marie doesn't say anything else.

Because it's the first time in an absolute age that anyone has told Britt-Marie it's important for her to be somewhere.

Soccer is a curious game in that way. Because it doesn't ask to be loved.

11

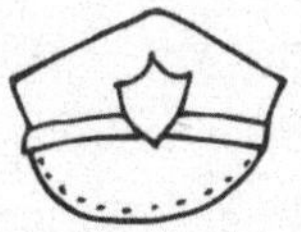

The children open the door at half-time to let Britt-Marie and Pirate back in. Britt-Marie spends the second half in front of the mirror in the bathroom. Firstly because she doesn't want to come out and risk having to talk to any of the children, and secondly because their team scores again so they forbid her from coming out until the match is over. So Britt-Marie stays in there and dries her hair and brings them luck and has a life crisis. It's possible to do all of these things at the same time. Her mirror image belongs to someone else, someone whose face has been touched by many winters. The winters have always been the worst, both for the balcony plants and for Britt-Marie. It's the silence that Britt-Marie struggles most of all to live with, because while immersed in silence you don't know if anyone knows you are there, and winter is also the quiet season because the cold insulates people. Makes the world soundless.

It was the silence that paralyzed Britt-Marie when Ingrid died.

Her father started coming home later and later from his work, and at a certain point he started to come home so late that Britt-Marie would already be asleep by the time he walked in. Then she woke up one morning and he was only just coming home. And in the end she woke up one morning and he hadn't come home at all. Her mother said less and less about it. Stayed in bed for longer and longer in the mornings. Britt-Marie meandered around the flat as children do when they have to live in silent worlds. Once she knocked over a vase just so her mother would yell at her from the bedroom. Her mother didn't yell. Britt-Marie swept up the glass herself. And never knocked over a vase again. The next day her mother stayed in bed until Britt-Marie had made dinner. The day after that she got up even later. And in the end she didn't get up at all. Of course several of her mother's girlfriends sent beautiful flowers and condolences, but they were too busy with their lives to pay their respects to someone who was already dead anyway. Britt-Marie cut little notches in the flower stalks and put them in newly washed vases. She cleaned the flat and polished all the windows and the day after, when she took out the rubbish, she met Kent on the stairs. They stared at each other as children who have turned into adults tend to do. He had been married with two children, but he had recently been divorced and had now come back to the house to visit his mother. He smiled when he saw Britt-Marie. Because in those days he used to see her.

Britt-Marie rubs her ring finger in front of the mirror. The white line there is like a tattoo. Taunting her. There's a knock on the bathroom door.

Pirate is standing outside.

"Ha . . . Did you win?"

"Two to zero!" Pirate nods blissfully.

"Because actually I have only stayed in here all this time because you told me so. I have no intestinal problems," says Britt-Marie very seriously.

Pirate nods, in some confusion, mumbles, "*Okay*," and points at the front door, which is open.

"Sven is here again."

The policeman stands on the threshold and lifts his hand in a fumbling wave. Britt-Marie draws back, deeply affronted but not sure why, and closes the bathroom door behind her. Once she has fixed her hair properly she takes a deep breath and reemerges.

"Yes?" she says to the policeman.

The policeman smiles and holds out a piece of paper, which he drops just as he's giving it to Britt-Marie.

"Whoops, whoops, sorry, sorry, I just thought I'd give you this. Well, I thought, or we, we thought . . ."

He makes a gesture towards the pizzeria. Britt-Marie assumes he means he has spoken to Somebody. He smiles again. Clasps his hands together on top of his stomach, then changes his mind and crosses his arms just below his chin.

"We were thinking you need somewhere to live, of course, of course, and I understood you didn't want to stay at the hotel in town . . . Not that you can't live anywhere you want to. Of course! We just thought this might be a good alternative for you. Perhaps?"

Britt-Marie looks at the paper. It's a handwritten, misspelled advertisement for a room that's available for rent. At the bottom is an image of a little man wearing a hat, who appears to be dancing. The relationship between the man and the advertisement is extremely unclear.

"I'm the one who helped her make the ad," says the policeman enthusiastically. "I did a course in it, in town. She's a very nice lady, the one who's letting the room, I mean, she's just moved back to Borg. Or, I mean, it's just temporary, of course, she's selling the house. But it's here in Borg, not far at all . . . it's walkable but I can give you a lift, if you like?"

Britt-Marie's eyebrows inch closer together. There's a police car parked outside.

"In that?"

"Yes, I heard your car's at the workshop. But I can drive you, it's no trouble at all!"

"It's obviously not a problem for you. Whereas I'm supposed to be driven around this community in a police car, am I, so everyone thinks I'm a criminal, is that what you are telling me?"

The policeman looks ashamed of himself.

"No, no, no. Of course, you wouldn't want that."

"I certainly would not," says Britt-Marie. "Was there anything else?"

He shakes his head despondently and turns to leave. Britt-Marie closes the door.

The children stay in the recreation center until she has tumble-dried their clothes.

Clothes that cannot be tumble-dried she hangs up to dry, so the children can pick them up the next day. Most of them go home in their soccer jerseys. In a certain sense this is how Britt-Marie turns into their team coach. It's just that no one has told her about it yet.

None of the children thank her for doing their laundry. The door closes behind them and the recreation center is steeped in the sort of silence that only children and soccer balls can fill. Britt-Marie puts away plates and soft-drink cans from the sofa table. Omar and Vega have left their plates on the dish rack. They haven't washed them up or put them in the dishwasher, haven't even rinsed them off. All they've done is put them there.

Kent also used to do that sometimes as if expecting to be thanked for it. As if he wanted Britt-Marie to know that when the plate was back in its place, washed and dried, in the cupboard tomorrow, he had certainly done his allotted share of the task.

There's a knock at the front door of the recreation center. It's not a civilized hour, so Britt-Marie assumes that it's one of the children who's forgotten something. She opens with a:

"Ha?"

Then she sees that it's the policeman standing outside again. He smiles awkwardly. Britt-Marie immediately changes the tone to a:

"Ha!"

Which is something quite different. At least the way Britt-Marie says it. The policeman swallows and seems to be drumming up some courage. A little too abruptly he whips out a bamboo curtain, almost smacking it into Britt-Marie's forehead.

"Sorry, yes, well, I just wanted to . . . this is a bamboo screen!" he says and almost drops it into the mud.

"Ha . . ." says Britt-Marie, more guarded now.

He nods enthusiastically.

"I made it! I did a course in town. 'Far Eastern Home Design.' "

He nods again. As if Britt-Marie is supposed to say something. She doesn't. He holds the bamboo screen in front of his face.

"You can hold it against the window. So no one sees it's you."

He points cheerfully at the police car. Then at the bamboo screen.

Then at the rain that has started falling again. As rain does in Borg. Which must obviously be quite pleasant for the rain, not having anything better to do with its time.

"And you can keep it over your head when we go out to the car, like an umbrella, so you don't ruin your hair." He swallows again and fingers the bamboo.

"You don't have to, of course, of course. I was just thinking that you have to live somewhere while you're in Borg. I was thinking, so to speak, well, hmm, you understand. That it's hardly suitable for a lady to live in a recreation center, so to speak."

They stand in silence for a long time after that. Britt-Marie switches her hands the other way, and then at long last exhales deeply with immeasurable patience. Not at all a sigh. Then she says:

"I need to get my things."

He nods eagerly. She closes the door and leaves him out there in the rain.

That is how it goes on—the thing that has started.

12

Britt-Marie opens the door. He gives her the bamboo screen and she gives him the balcony boxes.

"I was told there was a large flat-pack from IKEA in the backseat of your car, should I load it into my car?" he asks helpfully.

"You certainly shall not!" answers Britt-Marie, as if he had suggested setting fire to it.

"Of course not, of course not," he says apologetically.

Britt-Marie sees the men with the beards and caps leave the pizzeria. They nod at the policeman, he waves back. They seem not to see Britt-Marie at all.

The policeman hurries off towards his patrol car with the balcony boxes, then he hurries back to walk alongside Britt-Marie. He doesn't hold her arm, but he does position his arm a few inches under hers without actually touching her. So he can catch her in case she slips.

She holds the bamboo screen like an umbrella over her hair (because in fact bamboo screens work quite brilliantly as umbrellas), and keeps it in a firm grip over her head throughout the journey, so the policeman doesn't notice that her hairstyle has been ruined.

"I should like to stop by a cash machine on the way, so I can pay for the room," she says. "If it's no bother to you. I obviously don't want to cause you any bother," she adds in a bothered tone of voice.

"It's no bother at all!" says the policeman, who seems free of any kind of bothered tendencies. He doesn't mention the fact that the nearest cash machine is actually a twelve-mile detour.

He talks all the way, just as Kent used to do when they were in the car. But it was different, because Kent always told her things, whereas the policeman asks her questions. It irritates Britt-Marie. You do get irritated by someone taking an interest in you, when you're not used to it.

"What did you think of the match, then?" he asks.

"I was in the toilet," says Britt-Marie.

She gets incredibly irritated when she hears herself saying this. Because anyone making hasty conclusions might believe she has serious intestinal problems. The policeman doesn't answer straight away, so she comes to the conclusion that he is indeed sitting there making hasty conclusions, and she doesn't at all appreciate that he is doing so. So she adds sharply:

"I actually don't have serious intestinal problems, but it was important for me to be in the toilet, otherwise apparently something would have gone wrong in the match."

He laughs. She doesn't know if it's at her expense. He stops when he notices that she doesn't much appreciate it.

"How did you end up here in Borg?"

"I was offered employment here."

She has her feet semi-buried among empty pizza boxes and paper bags from the hamburger place. In the backseat is a painter's easel and a jumble of brushes and canvases.

"Do you like paintings?" the policeman asks her, in an upbeat mood, when he sees her looking at them.

"No."

He fidgets with embarrassment at the steering wheel.

"I mean, I don't mean my own paintings, of course. I'm just a bit of a happy amateur. I'm doing a course in watercolor painting in town. No, I mean paintings in general. Real paintings. Beautiful paintings."

There's something inside Britt-Marie that wants to say, "Your paintings are also beautiful," but another more down-to-earth part of her answers in its place:

"We don't have any paintings at home. Kent doesn't like art."

The policeman gives her a silent nod. They drive into town, which is actually also more like a large village than a proper town. Similar to Borg, just a bit more of it. Heading in the same direction, but not as quickly. Britt-Marie stops at a cash machine next to a tanning salon, which Britt-Marie doesn't find so very hygienic because she's read that solariums cause cancer, and you can hardly say cancer is hygienic.

It takes a bit of time to get her money out, because she's so careful about hiding her code that she ends up pressing the wrong buttons. She is also hardly helped along by the fact that she still has a bamboo screen on top of her head.

But the policeman doesn't tell her to hurry up. She realizes to her own surprise that she likes this. Kent always told her to hurry up, however quickly she was doing something. She gets back into the police car, and starts feeling she ought to say something sociable. So she takes a deep breath and points at the empty takeaway boxes and bags on the floor, and says:

"I don't suppose they were offering a cooking course in town, oh no."

The policeman lights up.

"Yes, as a matter of fact, I did a sushi-making course. Have you ever made sushi?"

"Certainly not. Kent doesn't like foreign food."

"True, true, well, there isn't much cooking when you make sushi. Mainly just . . . cutting. And I haven't done it so many times, actually, to be honest with you. I mean since I did the course. It's not much fun cooking for yourself, if you understand what I mean?"

He smiles with embarrassment. She doesn't smile at all.

"No," she says.

They drive back into Borg. Finally the policeman seems to build up enough courage to bring up another subject:

"Well, anyway, it's nice of you to take on the youngsters like you have. Borg is not an easy place to grow up in these days. The young people need someone, as you know, to see them."

"I have not taken anyone on. They are certainly not my responsibility!" protests Britt-Marie.

"I don't mean it like that, of course, I just mean they *like* you. The young people. I haven't seen them liking anyone since their last coach died."

"What do you mean, their 'last coach'?"

"I, well, yes, I suppose I just mean they are very glad you moved here," says the policeman, opting for "they" when really he would have preferred to say "we," and then he asks:

"What did you do before you came here?"

Britt-Marie doesn't answer. Instead she glares out of the window at the houses they are passing. Outside almost every one of them, a "For Sale" sign has been hammered into the lawn, so she states drily:

"There don't seem to be many people living in Borg who want to stay in Borg."

The corners of the policeman's mouth do what the corners of mouths do when trying to overcome wistfulness.

"The financial crisis hit hard here, after the trucking company laid off all the drivers. Those who have signs up are the ones who still have hopes of selling. The others have given up. Young people escape to the cities, and only the oldies like us stay on, because we're the only ones who still have jobs."

"The financial crisis is over. My husband told me that, and he's an entrepreneur," Britt-Marie informs him, keeping both her hair and the white mark on her ring finger well hidden under the bamboo screen. He looks away, awkwardly, while she firmly stares out of her window at a community in which even those who live there would rather not.

"And you're also keen on soccer, I understand," she says at last.

"I was once told that 'You love soccer because it's instinctive. If a ball comes rolling down the street you give it a punt. You love it for the same reason that you fall in love. Because you don't know how to avoid it.' " The policeman smiles, slightly embarrassed.

"Who made this suggestion?"

"The children's old coach said it once. Lovely, isn't it?"

"Ludicrous," says Britt-Marie, although part of her wants to say "poetic."

He grips the steering wheel even harder.

"Probably so, probably so, I just mean that . . . I mean everyone loves soccer, don't they? So to speak?"

She doesn't say a word.

They pass the corner shop, carry on for a few moments, then stop outside a small, gray, squat house built on two floors. In a garden on the other side of the road stand two women who are so old that they look as if they lived in this community before it became a community. Leaning on their walkers, they cast suspicious glances at the police car. Sven waves at them as he and Britt-Marie get out of the car; they do not wave back. It has stopped raining, but Britt-Marie is still holding the bamboo screen over her hair. Sven rings the doorbell of the house. The blind woman, no less cube-shaped than the house itself—although Britt-Marie would never dream of referring to her as fat—opens the door.

"Hi, Bank," says Sven cheerfully.

"Hello, Sven. So you've brought her along?" says Bank indifferently, waving her stick towards Britt-Marie. "The rent for the room is two hundred and fifty kronor a week, no credit. You can only rent it until I get the house sold," Bank goes on, grunting, and stomps back into the house without inviting them in.

Britt-Marie enters behind her, slightly on her tiptoes because the floor is so dirty that she doesn't even want to walk on it in her shoes. The white dog lies in the hall, surrounded by carelessly packed moving boxes in an utter disarray. Britt-Marie assumes this is all because of carelessness, not the fact that this "Bank" person is blind. Although Britt-Marie doesn't have preconceived opinions, she's quite convinced that even blind people can be careless.

All over the house are photos of a girl in a yellow soccer jersey, and in a few of them she is standing next to the old man who is also in the photos at the recreation center. In these pictures he is younger. He must have been about Britt-Marie's age when they found him on the kitchen floor in that house, Britt-Marie realizes. She doesn't know if that makes her old. She hasn't had so many people to compare herself to in recent years.

Sven stands by the door with the balcony boxes and her bag in his arms.

He's about the same age as her, and this feels rather old when she looks at him.

"We miss your dad very much, Bank. All of Borg misses him," he says wistfully into the hall.

Bank doesn't answer. Britt-Marie doesn't know what to do, so she snatches the balcony boxes from Sven. He takes off his police cap, but remains on the threshold as men of that kind always do because as far as they are concerned it is not appropriate to go inside a lady's home without an invitation.

Britt-Marie doesn't invite him in, although it irks her to see him standing there on her threshold in uniform. She sees the ancient women on the other side of the road, still standing in the garden glaring at them.

What will the neighbors think?

"Was there anything else?" she says, although what she really means is, "Thanks."

"No, no, nothing at all . . ."

"Thank you," says Britt-Marie so that it sounds more like "Good-bye" than "Thanks."

He nods awkwardly and turns round. When he has got halfway to the car, Britt-Marie takes a deep breath and clears her throat and only raises her voice a little:

"For the lift. I should like to . . . well, what I'm saying is: I should like to thank you for the lift."

He turns around and his whole face lights up. She quickly shuts the door before he gets any ideas.

Bank goes up the stairs. Seems to use the stick more as a sort of walking cane than for orienting herself. Britt-Marie comes stumbling after with the balcony boxes and the bag in her arms.

"Toilet. Sink. You'll have to eat somewhere else, because I don't want the smell of frying in the house. Make yourself scarce in the daytime, because that's when the estate agent brings buyers over," she snorts and starts moving off towards the staircase.

Britt-Marie goes after her and says diplomatically:

"Ha. I should like to apologize for my behavior earlier. I was unaware of your being blind."

Bank grunts something and tries to go downstairs, but Britt-Marie hasn't finished.

"But I'd like to point out that you actually can't expect people to know you're blind when they have only seen you from behind," she says helpfully.

"Goddamn it, woman, I'm not blind!" roars Bank.

"Ha?"

"I have impaired vision. Close up I can see just fine."

"How close?"

"I can see where the dog is. The dog sees the rest," says Bank, pointing at the dog, about three feet away on the stairs.

"Well, then you're practically blind."

"That's what I said. Good night."

"I'm certainly not the sort of person who gets hung up on semantics, I really am not, but I did certainly hear you say 'blind' . . ."

Bank looks like someone weighing up the possibility of causing damage to the wall with the front of her head.

"If I say I'm blind, people are too ashamed to ask any more questions, and they leave me in peace. If I say I have impaired vision they want to prattle on endlessly about the difference between that and being properly blind. Good night now!" she concludes, and moves on down the stairs.

"Might I ask why you have a stick and a dog and sunglasses if you're not even blind?"

"My eyes are sensitive to light, and I had the dog before my eyes started acting up. It's a normal bloody dog. Good night!"

The dog looks as if it has taken offense at this.

"And the stick?" Britt-Marie asks.

"It's not a blind stick, it's a walking cane. I have a bad knee. And it's also quite convenient when people don't get out of the way."

"Ha," says Britt-Marie. Bank shoves the dog out of the way with the cane.

"Payment in advance. No credit. And I don't want to see you here in the daytime. Good night!"

"Could I ask when you expect to sell this house?"

"As soon as I find anyone balmy enough to want to live in Borg."

Britt-Marie stands at the top of the stairs, which seem desolate and very steep as soon as Bank and the dog are out of sight. A moment later the front door slams and the house drowns in the silence that follows.

Britt-Marie looks around. It's raining again. The police car has gone. A lone truck goes by. Then more silence. Britt-Marie feels cold on the inside.

She takes the bedclothes off the bed and covers the mattress in baking soda.

She gets her list out of her bag. There's nothing on it. No items to tick. Darkness comes sweeping in through the window, enveloping Britt-Marie. She doesn't turn on any lights. She finds a towel in her bag and weeps into it, while standing up. She doesn't want to sit on the mattress until it has been properly cleaned.

It's past midnight by the time she notices the door. It's next to one of the windows, facing out onto nothing. Britt-Marie has difficulties at first believing what she is seeing. She has to go and fetch a bottle of Faxin, then clean all the window glass in the door, before she can even bring herself to touch the door handle. It's stuck. She pulls at it for all she's worth, wedges herself against the doorframe and uses her body weight, which admittedly isn't much. For a fleeting moment she sees the world through the glass and thinks about Kent and all the things he always said she couldn't do and, in that moment, something makes her gather all her strength in a furious show of defiance that finally overpowers the door. She flies backwards through the room when the door opens wide. Rain falls in over the floor.

Britt-Marie sits leaning against the bed, breathing heavily and staring out.

It's a balcony.

13

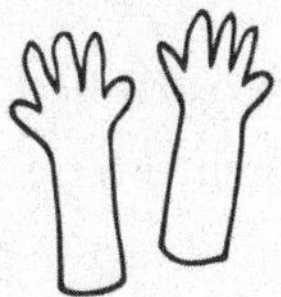

A balcony can change everything.

It's six in the morning and Britt-Marie is enthusiastic. It's a new experience for her. Somebody's state of mind would rather have to be described as the hungover, irascible kind. Britt-Marie has woken her by knocking on the door of the pizzeria at six o'clock to ask her, excitedly, for a drill.

Somebody grudgingly opens up and informs Britt-Marie that the pizzeria and all its other financial activities are closed at this time of day. Britt-Marie then questions why Somebody is there at all, because, as far as Britt-Marie can see, it can't possibly be hygienic to live in a pizzeria. Somebody explains as well as she can in her condition—eyes half-closed, with various scraps of food on her jersey that never quite made it to her mouth or for one reason or another came back out again—that she was "too much drunk" after the soccer match last night to make it home. Britt-Marie nods appreciatively at this, and says she thought this was a wise decision, because one really shouldn't drink and drive. She doesn't look at the wheelchair at all when she says it.

Somebody mutters and tries to close the door. But, as we already said, Britt-Marie is enthusiastic and will not be deterred. For Britt-Marie now has somewhere to put her balcony boxes.

Everything changes when you have somewhere to put your balcony boxes. Britt-Marie feels ready to take on the world. Or, at least, Borg.

Somebody doesn't seem to respond so very well to enthusiasm at six in the morning, so Britt-Marie asks if Somebody happens to own an electric drill. And in fact Somebody does own one. She fetches it. Britt-Marie takes it with both hands and accidentally turns it on and, as a result of this, happens to drill Somebody's hand just a little. Somebody then takes back the drill and demands to know what Britt-Marie was intending to do with the drill. Britt-Marie announces that she plans to put up a picture.

So now Somebody is in the recreation center, hungover and a little irascible, with a drill in her hand. Britt-Marie stands in the middle of the room, looking enthusiastically at the picture. She found it in the recreation center storage room early this morning, because Bank, as we know, had ordered her to make herself scarce in the house in the daytime, and in any case Britt-Marie was having trouble sleeping, what with all the emotions surfacing after the discovery of the balcony. The picture had been leaning up against the wall behind an unmentionable pile of rubbish, covered in a layer of dust so thick that it looked like volcanic ash. Britt-Marie took it inside the recreation center and cleaned it with a damp rag and baking soda. It looks very stylish now.

"I've never put up a picture before, you have to understand," explains Britt-Marie, very considerately, when she notices that Somebody is looking exhausted.

Somebody finishes her drilling and then hangs up the picture. It's not actually a painting, just a very, very old information chart with a black-and-white map of Borg. "Welcome to Borg" it says at the top. For someone who loathes traveling, Britt-Marie has always had a great love of maps. There's something reassuring about them, she's always found, ever since Ingrid used to speak to her at night about Paris when they were children. You can look at a map and point at Paris. Things are understandable when you can point at them. She nods soberly at Somebody.

"We don't have any pictures at home, me and Kent, you have to understand. Kent doesn't like art."

Somebody raises her eyebrows at the information chart when Britt-Marie mentions "art."

"Could we possibly hang it a little higher?"

"Higher?"

"It's very low," Britt-Marie observes, obviously not in a critical way.

Somebody looks at Britt-Marie. Looks at her wheelchair. Britt-Marie looks at the wheelchair too. "But obviously it's fine where it is, also. Obviously."

Somebody mutters something best not heard by anyone and rolls off towards the door, back to the pizzeria across the parking area. Britt-Marie follows her because she needs Snickers and baking soda.

Inside there's an overwhelming smell of cigarette smoke and beer. The tables are covered in dirty glasses and crockery. Somebody roots around behind the counter, grunting something to the effect of, "Headache tablets . . . where does Vega keep that shit?" She disappears into the kitchen.

Britt-Marie is tentatively reaching for two dirty plates when Somebody, as if she can sense what she is up to, yells:

"Don't touch washing-up!"

Britt-Marie opens the cutlery drawer and starts arranging the cutlery in the right order. Somebody rolls forward and closes the cutlery drawer. Britt-Marie inhales patiently.

"I'm just trying to make things look nice around here."

"Stop changing! I won't find a crap!" Somebody exclaims when

Britt-Marie turns her attention to the cupboard where drinking glasses are kept, not as if she's choosing to do it but rather as if she has no choice.

"It's quite extraordinary how you manage to find anything here at all," Britt-Marie informs her.

"You're putting in wrong place!" Somebody objects.

"Ha, ha, whatever I do is wrong, of course, isn't that always the case?"

Somebody mumbles something incoherent, throws her arms up at the ceiling as if it's the fault of the ceiling, and rolls out of the kitchen. Britt-Marie stays where she is and tries to stop herself from opening the cutlery drawer again. It works fairly well for about fifteen seconds. When she goes out of the kitchen, she finds Somebody sitting in the shop eating fist-sized piles of cornflakes straight from the pack.

"You could at least use a plate," says Britt-Marie and fetches a plate.

Somebody, extremely displeased, eats fist-sized piles of cornflakes straight from the plate.

"I don't suppose you're having any natural yogurt with that, are you?"

"I am, what's-it-called? Lactose intolerant."

"Ha," says Britt-Marie tolerantly, and rearranges a few cans on a shelf.

"Please Britt-Marie, don't move shit," whispers Somebody, like you do when you have a severe headache.

"You mean my cleaning is wrong as well, is that what you mean?" asks Britt-Marie and goes over to the cash register, where she starts sorting cartons of cigarettes into color-coded piles.

"Stop!" Somebody yells and tries to snatch them out of Britt-Marie's hands.

"I'm only trying to make it a bit nice in here!"

"Not together!" whines Somebody and points at one brand of cigarettes with foreign letters on the cartons, and another that doesn't have foreign letters. "Because of tax authority!" says Somebody, looking very serious as she points at the cartons with the foreign letters: "Flying stones!"

Britt-Marie looks like she needs something to grab hold of so she doesn't lose her balance.

"You mean they're contraband?"

"Nah, you know, Britt-Marie. These, huh, they fall off a truck," says Somebody apologetically.

"That's *illegal*!"

Somebody rolls back into the kitchen. She opens the cutlery drawer and swears very loudly, then a long harangue follows in which Britt-Marie can only make out, "Comes here for to borrow drill and hang picture, I want to sleep but oh no, I'm criminal, Mary Poppins out there is starting recreation center and moving crap around."

Britt-Marie stays in the demarcation area between the groceries and the pizzeria, rearranging cans and cigarette cartons. In actual fact she only meant to buy some baking soda and Snickers and then leave, but as it doesn't seem responsible to purchase baking soda from someone who is clearly drunk, she has decided to wait until Somebody sobers up.

Somebody seems to have decamped to the kitchen, so in the meantime Britt-Marie does what she always does in these types of situations: she cleans. It looks quite decent when she's finished, it really does. Unfortunately there are no flowers, but there is a vase on the counter next to the register with a white piece of tape stuck to it, where someone has written, "Tips." It's empty. Britt-Marie washes it out and puts it back next to the register. Then she gets all the coins out of her handbag and drops them in. She tries to make them look fluffy, as if they were potting soil. By the time she has finished, the vase looks a good deal more decorative.

"Maybe you wouldn't develop so many allergies if you kept things a little more hygienic in here," she explains considerately to Somebody when Somebody comes out of the kitchen.

Somebody massages her temples, spins the wheelchair around, and disappears back into the kitchen. Britt-Marie keeps working on the coins in the vase to make them look even more decorative.

The front door tinkles and the two men with beards and caps step inside. They also look hungover.

"I have to ask you to wipe your feet outside," Britt-Marie informs them at once. "I've just mopped the floor, you see." They look bemused, but comply.

"Ha. How can we help you?" asks Britt-Marie when they come back in.

"Coffee?" the men manage to say and look around as if they have stepped into a parallel dimension where there's a pizzeria just the same as the one where they usually drink their coffee, except this one is clean.

Britt-Marie nods and goes into the kitchen. Somebody is sleeping with a can of beer in her hand and her head resting in the cutlery drawer. Britt-Marie cannot find any tea towels, so she takes two paper towel rolls, carefully lifts Somebody's head, and pushes the paper towel rolls into the cutlery drawer as cushions, onto which she gently lowers Somebody's head. She makes coffee in an entirely normal coffee percolator unaffected by flying stones, and serves this to the men with caps and beards. Stands there by their table for a while, in the vague hope that one of them might say that the coffee's decent. Neither of them do.

"Ha. Are you intending to solve the crossword?"

The men stare at her as if she has just addressed them without using vowels, then go back to their newspapers. Britt-Marie nods helpfully.

"If you don't have the intention of solving it, may I?"

The men look a little as if she has asked whether they're planning on using their kidneys in the foreseeable future or if she can take them.

"Who are you, anyway?" asks one of the men.

"I'm Britt-Marie."

"Are you from the city?"

"Yes." She smiles.

The men nod, as if this explains everything.

"Buy your own bloody newspaper, then," says one of them. The other grunts in agreement.

"Ha," says Britt-Marie and decides not to offer them a top-up.

Somebody keeps sleeping in the kitchen; possibly it is Britt-Marie's fault because she's made her too comfortable, but nonetheless Britt-Marie feels obliged to take care of the customers until Vega comes in. Not that there's a particularly large number of customers. Or any at all, you might say, if you were being pedantic about it. The only one who comes in is the ginger-haired boy whose name is Pirate, even though that's not a name. He diffidently asks if Britt-Marie has time to do his hair. She informs him that she is terribly busy right now. He nods, excited, and waits in a corner.

"If you're just going to stand there you may as well help out," says Britt-Marie eventually.

He nods so eagerly it's a wonder he doesn't bite his tongue.

Vega shows up. She stops in the doorway and looks as if she's come to the wrong place.

"What's . . . happened here?" she pants, as if the pizzeria has been burgled in the night by a group of pedants who have cleaned it up as a way of making a political statement.

"What are you trying to say?" says Britt-Marie, a bit offended.

"It's so . . . clean!" She heads for the kitchen, but Britt-Marie stops her.

"She's sleeping in there."

Vega shrugs.

"She's hungover. She always is when soccer's been on."

Karl, who always seems to have some parcel to pick up, walks in.

"Can we be of assistance?" asks Britt-Marie, in every way mindful of providing good service, without any hint of incrimination.

"I'm picking up a parcel," says Karl, not at all mindful of anyone's good service.

His sideburns reach all the way to his chin, Britt-Marie notes. They look like snowdrops—one of Britt-Marie's favorite flowers—except in his case the snowdrops are upside down.

"We haven't had any parcels today," says Vega.

"I'll wait, then," says Karl, and goes over to the cap-wearing men.

"And obviously you are not ordering yourself anything. You're just going to sit here," says Britt-Marie in a thoroughly, thoroughly friendly way.

Karl stops. The men at the table look at him as if to clarify that, as far as they are concerned, he should not be negotiating with terrorists.

"Coffee," Karl rumbles at last.

Pirate is already on his way with the jug.

The next person who steps inside is Sven. A smile lights up his round little face when he catches sight of Britt-Marie.

"Hello, Britt-Marie!"

"Wipe your shoes."

He nods eagerly. Goes outside and then comes back inside again.

"Nice to see you here," he says.

"Ha. Are you working today?" asks Britt-Marie.

"Yes, yes, of course, of course." He nods.

"It's not so easy knowing, you seem to keep your uniform on whether you're working or not," says Britt-Marie, not at all critically.

Sven doesn't entirely look as if he's sure what she's talking about. Instead, his gaze alights on what is clearly a foreign carton of cigarettes, left on the counter next to the register after Somebody and Britt-Marie's argument about smuggling.

"Interesting letters, those . . ." he says inquiringly.

Britt-Marie and Vega's eyes meet, and the girl's sense of panic transmits back.

"Those are mine!" Britt-Marie exclaims and snatches up the cigarettes.

"Oh," says Sven, surprised.

"It's certainly no crime to smoke!" says Britt-Marie, although she certainly thinks it ought to be.

Then she makes herself exceedingly, exceedingly busy with rearranging a shelf in the grocery section.

"Has everything worked out with the room at Bank's?" asks Sven behind her, but to Britt-Marie's relief he's interrupted by Vega groaning:

"Nooo, not him . . ."

Britt-Marie looks out of the window. A BMW has stopped in the parking area. Britt-Marie knows that because Kent has a BMW. The door makes a tinkling sound and a man more or less the same age as Somebody and a boy more or less the same age as Vega come walking in.

It is unclear which one of them Vega doesn't want to see. The man is wearing a very expensive jacket. Britt-Marie knows this because Kent has one just the same. The boy is wearing a beaten-up tracksuit top, on which the name of the town twelve miles away is written followed by the word HOCKEY. He looks at Vega with interest and she looks at him with contempt. The man smiles jeeringly at the men in the corner, and they look back at him as if hoping that by doing so they'll eventually set him on fire. He looks away and starts jeering at Vega instead.

"Frantic business activity here, as usual?"

"Why? Are you here to give someone the sack?" Vega answers acidly, then, pretending to have suddenly realized something, slaps her forehead dramatically: "Oh no! That's right, you can't because you don't work here! And where you work there's no one left to sack, because you already sacked them all!"

The man's eyes go black. The boy looks spectacularly uncomfortable.

The man thumps two soft-drink cans on the counter.

"Twenty-four kronor," says Vega indifferently.

"We're having pizzas as well," says the man, trying to regain the upper hand.

"The pizzeria is closed," says Vega.

"What do you mean?"

"The pizza baker is temporarily out of order."

The man snivels disdainfully and slaps a five-hundred krona note on the counter.

"A pizzeria without pizzas, seems a pretty effective business venture you have here."

"A bit like a trucking company with one manager and no drivers," Vega responds sarcastically.

The man clenches his fist on the counter, but from the corner of his eye he sees Karl getting out of his chair, though the other two men are doing their best to make him sit back down.

"I'm six kronor short here," he says grimly at Vega, after examining the change she's flung back.

"We don't have any coins left," Vega says through her teeth.

Sven is standing beside them now. He looks unsure of himself.

"It might be best if you leave now, Fredrik," he says.

The man's gaze moves from Vega to the policeman. It stops on the vase, where the tips are kept.

"No problem," he says, his face cracking open in a scornful smile as he stuffs his hand into the vase and fishes out six kronor.

He grins at Sven, then at the boy with the ice hockey tracksuit top. The boy looks down at the floor and walks back to the door. Sven stays where he is, beaten. The man with the expensive jacket makes eye contact with Britt-Marie.

"Who are you?" asks the man.

"I work at the recreation center," says Britt-Marie, glaring at the fingerprints on the newly polished vase for the tips.

"I thought the council had closed it down? Bloody waste of taxpayers' money if you ask me. Invest it in juvenile detention centers, that's where the kids end up anyway!"

Britt-Marie looks helpful.

"My husband has a jacket like that," she says.

"Your husband has good taste," says the man with a grin.

"Except his is the right size," says Britt-Marie. There's a long, long silence. Then Vega first, and Sven after, burst into peals of laughter. Britt-Marie can't think what they're laughing about. The boy runs out, the man marches behind him and slams the door so hard that the fluorescent tube on the ceiling flickers. The BMW does a wheelspin as it leaves the parking area.

Britt-Marie doesn't know where to look. Sven and Vega are still laughing loudly, which makes her uncomfortable. She assumes it must be at her expense. So she also hurries towards the door.

"I have time for your hair now," she whispers to Pirate and then flees across the parking area.

The door closes with a merry tinkling.

14

All marriages have their bad sides, because all people have weaknesses. If you live with another human being you learn to handle these weaknesses in a variety of ways. For instance, you might take the view that weaknesses are a bit like heavy pieces of furniture, and based on this you must learn to clean around them. To maintain the illusion.

Of course the dust is building up unseen, but you learn to repress this for as long as it goes unnoticed by guests. And then one day someone moves a piece of furniture without your say-so, and everything comes into plain view. Dirt and scratch marks. Permanent damage to the parquet floor. By then it's too late.

Britt-Marie stands in the bathroom at the recreation center, looking at all of her worst sides in the mirror. She's afraid—she's fairly certain this is her worst side. More than anything she'd like to go home. Iron Kent's shirts and sit on her own balcony. More than anything she'd like everything to go back to normal.

"Do you want me to leave?" asks Pirate anxiously from the doorway.

"I'm not going to tolerate your laughing at me," says Britt-Marie with all the strictness she can summon.

"Why would I laugh at you?" asks Pirate.

She sucks in her cheeks without answering. Hesitant, he holds out a carton of cigarettes with foreign lettering.

"Sven said you forgot this."

Britt-Marie takes it, dismayed. Contraband. Which she has now either stolen or bought on credit, depending on how positively you want to look at it. This is all highly vexatious, because Britt-Marie is not even sure now what sort of criminal she is. But there's no doubt that she's a criminal. Although Kent would certainly agree with Somebody that there's nothing criminal about withholding cigarettes from the tax authorities and the police. "Get over it, darling! It's not cheating if you don't get caught!" he always used to say when she was signing off her tax return and she asked what all those other pieces of paper were that Kent's accountant had slipped into the envelope. "Don't worry, they're completely legal tax deductions! Get on with it!" he'd say reassuringly. Kent loved deductions and loathed tax bills. Britt-Marie never dared admit to him that she did not understand the rights and wrongs of it.

Pirate gently touches her shoulder.

"They weren't laughing at you. In the pizzeria, I mean. They were laughing at Fredrik. He was the boss at the trucking company when they all got fired, so they don't like him."

Britt-Marie nods and tries to look as if, in fact, she hadn't been especially worried about it in the first place. Pirate seems encouraged by this response, because he goes on:

"Fredrik trains the hockey team in town, they're wicked! The tall one who was with him in the pizzeria is his son, he's as old as me but he's almost got a beard already! You get that? Sick, isn't it? He's wicked at soccer as well but Fredrik wants him to play hockey because he thinks hockey's better!"

“Why on earth does he think that?” asks Britt-Marie, because on the basis of her slight knowledge of hockey it seems to her one of the few things in the universe that is more ludicrous than soccer.

“Probably because it’s expensive. Fredrik likes things that most people can’t afford,” says Pirate.

“Why are you so dreadfully amused by soccer, then?” asks Britt-Marie.

Pirate seems to find the question mystifying.

“What do you mean? People like soccer just because they like soccer, that’s all.”

Ludicrous, thinks Britt-Marie, but she doesn’t say it. Instead, she points to a bag in the boy’s hand.

“What’s that?”

“Scissors and a comb and products and stuff!” says the boy blissfully.

Britt-Marie doesn’t ask what he means by “products” but she notes that he has a heck of a lot of jars, anyway. She fetches a stool from the kitchen, puts down towels on the floor, and gestures for him to take a seat. Then she washes his hair and cuts the uneven bits. She used to do that for Ingrid.

Suddenly words come tumbling out of her; she can’t understand why on earth she had to open her mouth, but:

“From time to time I feel unsure whether people are laughing at me or something else, you must understand. My husband says I don’t have a sense of humor.”

She is quickly silenced by her common sense. Embarrassed, she clamps her lips together.

The boy stares at her in the mirror with consternation.

“That’s a horrific thing to say to someone!”

Britt-Marie doesn’t answer. But she agrees. It is a horrific thing to say to someone.

"Do you love him? Your husband?" asks the boy so suddenly that Britt-Marie almost snips him in the ear.

She brushes down his shoulder with the back of her hand. Buries her gaze in his scalp.

"Yes."

"Why isn't he here, then?"

"Because sometimes love isn't enough."

Then they remain silent until Britt-Marie has finished cutting, and Pirate's unruly mop has been tenderly coaxed into a hairstyle as neat as biological circumstances will allow. He stays where he is, admiring himself in the mirror. Britt-Marie cleans up and looks out into the parking area. Two young men are standing there, neither of them even twenty years old, smoking and leaning against a big black car. They're wearing the same kind of jeans, ripped across the thighs, as the children in the soccer team. But these two are no children. They look like the sort of young men who would make Britt-Marie take a firmer grip on her handbag while passing. Not that she judges people, not at all, but one of these men actually has tattoos on his hands.

"That's Sami and Psycho," says Pirate behind her.

He sounds scared.

"Those are not names," Britt-Marie informs him.

"Sami is a name, I think. But Psycho is called Psycho because he's a psycho," says Pirate quietly, as if he doesn't dare utter their names too loudly.

"I don't suppose they have jobs to go to?"

Pirate shrugs.

"No one here has a job. Apart from some really old people."

Britt-Marie puts one hand in the other. Then the other in the one. While trying not to be offended.

"The one on the right has tattoos on his hands," she notes.

"That's Psycho. He's mad. Sami's quite all right, but Psycho's . . . you know, he's dangerous. You have to avoid any trouble with him. My mother says I'm not allowed in Vega and Omar's house when Psycho's there."

"Why on earth would he be in Vega and Omar's home?"

"Sami is their older brother."

The door of the pizzeria opens. Vega emerges with two pizzas and hands them to Sami. He kisses her on the cheek. Psycho grins insolently at her. She looks at him as if she just bought a new bag and he vomited in it. Then he slams the door. The black car pulls out of the parking area.

"They don't eat in the pizzeria when Sven's there. Vega said they're not allowed to," explains Pirate.

"Ha. Quite understandable. Because she knows they're worried about the police, of course."

"No, because she knows the police are afraid of them."

Societies are like people in that way. If you don't ask too many questions and don't shift any heavy furniture around, there's no need to notice their worst sides. Britt-Marie brushes down her skirt. Then she brushes Pirate's sleeve. She'd like to change the subject, and without further ado he helps her out:

"Has Vega asked you yet?"

"About what?" asks Britt-Marie.

"If you want to be our coach?"

"Absolutely not!"

Extremely offended, she cups one hand into the other and asks:

"Anyway, what does that mean?"

"I mean a trainer. We have to have one. There's a challenge cup in town; you can only enter if you have a team with a coach."

"A cup? Like a competition?"

"Like a cup."

"In this weather? Outdoors? That's ludicrous!"

"No, I mean it's an indoor competition. In a sports center, in town," says Pirate. Britt-Marie is about to say a few choice words about the sort of people who like to kick balls around indoors when there's a knock on the door. A boy about the same age as Pirate is standing outside. Long-haired, one might also add.

"Ha?" says Britt-Marie.

"Is Ben, like, here?" asks the boy.

It seems fairly unclear what the meaning of "like" is in the construction of the sentence. As if the boy just asked, "Is Ben almost here?"

"Who?" says Britt-Marie.

"Ben? Or, like, what they call him in his team. Pirate?"

"Ha. Ha. Ha. He is here, but he's occupied," says Britt-Marie firmly and is about to close the door.

"With what, sort of thing?" asks the boy.

"He's meeting someone. Or he has a date. Or whatever it's called."

"I know. With me!" says the boy with a frustrated groan.

Britt-Marie, who is not encumbered with any prejudice, puts one hand in the other and says:

"Ha."

The boy is chewing gum. She dislikes that. It's actually quite all right to dislike chewing gum, even if you are a person without any prejudices.

"It's, like, epically lame saying 'date,'" says the boy.

"It was Pir . . . it was Ben who said it. In my time we said 'meeting,'" says Britt-Marie, defending herself.

"Also epically lame," snorts the boy.

"What do you say, then?" asks Britt-Marie, just a touch critically.

"Nothing. Just 'out,' sort of thing," says the boy.

"I have to ask you to wait here," says Britt-Marie and firmly closes the door.

Pirate stands in the bathroom, fixing his hair. He starts jumping up and down on the spot when he sees her in the mirror.

"Is he here? Isn't he fantastic?"

"He's strikingly rude," says Britt-Marie, but Pirate obviously can't hear anything, because the sound of his jumping echoes quite a lot in the bathroom.

Britt-Marie takes a piece of toilet paper, carefully picks a hair off Pirate's jumper and folds it into the toilet paper, then flushes it down the toilet.

"I was under the impression that you went on dates with girls."

"I do go on dates with girls sometimes," says Pirate.

"But this is a boy," says Britt-Marie.

"This is a boy," confirms Pirate with a nod, as if they are playing some sort of parlor game, the rules of which have not been explained to him.

"Ha," says Britt-Marie.

"Do you have to decide on one or the other?"

"I know nothing about that. I don't have any prejudices about it," Britt-Marie assures him.

Pirate adjusts his hair, smiles, and asks:

"Do you think he'll like my hair?"

Britt-Marie doesn't seem to have heard his question, and instead she says:

"Your friends in the soccer team obviously don't know that you go on dates with boys. Obviously I won't mention it."

Pirate looks surprised.

"Why wouldn't they know?"

"Have you told them?"

"Why wouldn't I have told them?"

"What did they say?"

"They said 'okay.'" Then he looks unsure. "What else should they have said?"

"Ha, ha, obviously nothing, obviously," says Britt-Marie in a way you could describe as not at all defensive, and then adds: "I have no prejudices about this!"

"I know," says Pirate.

Then he smiles nervously.

"Is my hair looking nice?"

Britt-Marie can't quite bring herself to answer, so she just nods. She picks off one last hair from his jumper, and awkwardly holds it in her hand. He hugs her. She can't think why on earth he would get it into his head to do such a thing.

"You shouldn't be alone. It's a waste when someone whose hair looks as nice as yours is alone," he whispers.

He's almost at the door when Britt-Marie, still holding his hair in her hand, collects herself, clears her throat, and whispers back:

"If he doesn't say your hair is looking lovely, then he doesn't deserve you!"

Pirate turns around, runs back through the room, and hugs her again. She pushes him away, friendly but firm, because one mustn't forget one's boundaries. He asks her if he can borrow her cell phone. She looks doubtful, and warns him not to run up a large bill. He dials his own number, lets it ring once, then hangs up. Then he tries to embrace her again, laughs when she squirms, and runs off. The door closes.

Fifteen minutes later Britt-Marie gets a text message: "He said it! :)"

The recreation center goes quiet around her. She vacuums up all the hair from the floor just to make some noise. Washes and tumble-dries the towels.

Then she dusts all the pictures, taking extra care with the information chart and map, which Somebody hung three feet lower than all the other frames.

She removes the wrapper from a Snickers bar, puts it on a plate, puts the plate on a towel, and leaves it all on the threshold. Opens the front door. Sits for a long time on her stool trying to feel the wind in her hair. At long last she picks up the telephone.

"Hello?" says the girl at the unemployment office.

Britt-Marie inhales deeply.

"It was impolite of me to say that you had a boy's hairstyle."

"Britt-Marie?"

Britt-Marie swallows with concentration.

"Obviously I shouldn't have got involved in that, I mean the sort of hairstyle you have. Or if you go out on dates with boys or girls. Not at all."

"You didn't mention anything about . . . that."

"Ha. Ha. Ha. It's not beyond the realm of possibility that I just thought it, maybe so. In either case it was impolite of me," says Britt-Marie irritably.

"What . . . but I mean, what do you mean by . . . what's wrong with my hairstyle?"

"Nothing at all. That's what I'm saying," insists Britt-Marie.

"I'm not . . . I mean, I'm . . . I don't like . . ." says the girl defensively in a slightly overbearing voice.

"That's not for me to stick my nose into."

"I mean, not that . . . you know . . . there's anything wrong with being that way! Or not," the girl persists.

"I certainly haven't said anything of the kind!"

"Nor me!" protests the girl.

"Well, then," says Britt-Marie.

"Absolutely!" says the girl.

There's such a long silence between them that at long last the girl says, "Hello?" because she thinks Britt-Marie has hung up. And that's when Britt-Marie hangs up.

The rat is one hour and six minutes late for dinner. It rushes in and lunges at the biggest possible piece of Snickers that it could carry, stops for a second and stares at Britt-Marie, then runs back outside into the darkness. Britt-Marie wraps the rest of the chocolate in plastic wrap and puts it in the fridge. Washes up the plate. Washes and tumble-dries the towel and hangs it in its place. Through the window she sees Sven emerging from the pizzeria. He stops by the police car and looks over at the recreation center. Britt-Marie hides behind the curtain. He gets in the car and drives off. For a short moment she was afraid he was going to come over and knock on the door. Then she got disappointed when he didn't.

She turns off all the lights except in the bathroom. The sheen of the lone lightbulb finds its way out from under the door and lights up the exact area of the wall where Somebody hung up the information chart, slightly too low but obviously not too low. "Welcome to Borg," Britt-Marie reads, while she sits on a stool in the darkness and looks at the red dot that first made her fall in love with the picture. The reason for her love of maps. It's half worn away, the dot, and the red color is bleached. Yet it's there, flung down there on the map halfway between the lower left corner and its center, and next to it is written, "You are here."

Sometimes it's easier to go on living, not even knowing who you are, when at least you know precisely where you are while you go on not knowing.

15

People sometimes refer to darkness as something that falls, but in places like Borg it doesn't just fall, it collapses. It engulfs the streets in an instant. In cities there are so many people who don't want to sit at home all night that you can open dedicated premises and run entertainment industries that are open only at these times. But in Borg, life is encapsulated once darkness falls.

Britt-Marie locks the door of the recreation center and stands on her own in the parking area.

Her pockets are full of neatly folded toilet paper, because she did not find an envelope. The sign above the pizzeria is turned off, but she can make out the shadow of Somebody moving around inside. Something in Britt-Marie wants to go and talk to her, possibly to buy something. Another considerably more rational something orders her to do no such thing. It's dark outside. It's not civilized to walk into shops when it's dark outside.

She stands by the door listening to the radio inside, which is playing some sort of pop music. Britt-Marie knows this because she's not at all unfamiliar with pop music. There are many crossword questions about it, and Britt-Marie likes to keep herself informed. But this particular song is new to her; a young man is singing in a cracked voice about how you can either be "someone" or "no one at all."

Britt-Marie is still holding on to the carton of cigarettes covered in foreign letters. She doesn't know how much foreign cigarettes cost, but she gets out a considerably larger than reasonable amount of money from her handbag and folds it in the toilet paper until it looks like a small envelope with a phenomenal capacity for water absorption. Then she carefully tucks it under the door.

The young man keeps singing on the radio. As hard as he can. About nothing much.

"Love has no mercy," he sings. Again and again. Love has no mercy. Kent wells up in Britt-Marie's chest until she can't breathe.

Then she walks by herself along a road that heads out of the community in two directions. As darkness collapses. Towards a bed and a balcony that are not her own.

The truck comes up on her right, from behind. Too close. Too fast.

That's why she throws herself across to the other side of the road. The human brain has a monstrous ability to re-create memories of such clarity that the rest of the body loses all sense of time. An approaching truck can make the ears believe they are hearing a mother screaming, can make the hands believe they are cutting themselves on glass, can make the lips taste blood. Deep inside, Britt-Marie has time to yell Ingrid's name a thousand times.

The truck thunders by, so close that her heart can't tell whether it's been run over or not, in a rain of hard lumps of mud gouged out of the road surface. Britt-Marie takes a few tottering steps; her coat is wet and dirty, and there's a howling in her ears. Maybe a single second passes and maybe a hundred. She blinks at the headlights with a growing awareness that the howling is not coming from inside. There's actually a car sounding its horn. She hears someone yelling. She holds up her hand to shield her eyes from the headlights of the BMW. Fredrik, the man who came to the café earlier, is standing in front of her, shouting furiously.

"Are you bloody senile or what, you old bat?! What are you doing walking in the middle of the fucking road! I almost killed you!"

The way he puts it, it's as if her death would have been an inconvenience to him more than anyone else. She doesn't know what to say. Her heart is racing so frantically that it's giving her a stitch. Fredrik throws out his arms.

"Can you hear what I'm saying or are you a spastic?"

He takes two steps towards her. She doesn't know why. Looking back on it, she's unsure whether he was intending to hit her, but neither of them ever find out because he's interrupted by another voice. A different kind of voice. Cold.

"Problem?"

Fredrik turns around first, so that Britt-Marie has time to see his eyes register the danger before she has time to see what he's worried about. He swallows.

"No . . . she was wal—"

Sami is standing a few feet away, with his hands in his pockets. He is twenty years old at most, but judging by the suffocating grip of his presence in the darkness, you might describe him as a "spirit of violence." Britt-Marie wonders whether in a crossword this might be rendered as "God of aggression." Vertical, fifteen letters. People have time to think of all sorts of things while they face up to what they imagine is their imminent violent death, and this happens to be the first thing that comes to Britt-Marie's mind. Fredrik stutters indecipherably. Sami says nothing. Another young man is moving up behind him. He's taller. It's not at all difficult to guess why he's known as Psycho. His mouth is grinning, but it's not so much a grin as a display of teeth.

Britt-Marie has heard tell of this sort of thing on the natural history programs Kent used to watch when there was no soccer on the TV. Human beings are the only animals that smile as a gesture of peace, whereas other animals show their teeth as a threat. This is perfectly understandable now; she can see the animal inside the human being.

Psycho's smile grows wider. Sami doesn't take his hands out of his pockets. Doesn't even raise his voice.

"Don't you touch her," he says, nodding towards Britt-Marie while keeping his gaze fixed on Fredrik.

Fredrik totters back to his BMW. His self-confidence seems to grow with every step he takes towards it, as if the car is giving him superpowers. But he waits until he's standing right by the door before he hisses:

"Spastic! This whole bloody place is completely spastic!"

Psycho takes half a step forward. The BMW does a wheelspin in the mud and gravel and makes its escape in the rain. Britt-Marie has time to see the boy in the passenger seat, the one who's the same age as Ben and Vega and Omar, but taller and more grown up. Wearing the tracksuit top on which it says HOCKEY. He looks scared.

Psycho looks at Britt-Marie. Displays his teeth. Britt-Marie turns around and does her absolute best to walk briskly without breaking into a run, because in the natural history programs they always say you shouldn't try to run away from wild animals. She hears Sami calling out behind her, without anger or menace, in fact almost softly:

"See you around, Coach!"

She's three hundred feet away when she finally has the courage to stop and catch her breath. When she turns around the two men have gone back to a group of other young men on a patch of asphalt between some apartment blocks and a cluster of trees. The black car is there, with its engine running and the headlights on. The young men are moving about in the beams of light. Sami yells something and surges forward, kicking his right leg into the air. Then he punches his fists up and cheers loudly at the sky.

It takes Britt-Marie a minute to understand what they are doing.

They're playing soccer.

Playing.

The temperature drops below freezing in the night. Rain turns to snow.

Britt-Marie stands on the balcony watching all this happening. She finds herself spending an inordinate amount of time thinking about sushi and how you make it.

She cleans the mattress. Hangs up her coat. When she hears Bank coming back and closing the door downstairs, she paces around the room three times and thumps her feet as hard against the floor as she can. Just to clarify that she's there. Then she sleeps the dreamless sleep of exhaustion, because she couldn't even begin to say whose dreams she might have.

The sun is already up when she wakes. She almost falls out of bed when she realizes. Waking up long after the late-rising January sun! What will people think? Still half asleep, she's making her way to her clothes when she realizes why she's woken up. Someone is knocking on the door. The whole thing is terribly vexatious, actually, waking up at an hour when people are actually quite entitled to knock on your door.

She fixes her hair as quickly as she can, then stumbles down almost the entire length of the stairs, very nearly breaking her neck. It's the sort of thing that happens every few minutes—people falling down stairs and killing themselves. She just about manages to land on her two feet at the bottom, in the hall, and then sets about gathering her wits. After a certain amount of hesitation she rushes into the kitchen, which is obviously as dirty as you can possibly imagine, and then looks in all the drawers until she finds an apron.

She puts this on.

"Ha?" she says with raised eyebrows when she opens the door.

She adjusts her apron, as you do when you are interrupted by someone knocking at your door while you are busy with the washing-up. Vega and Omar are standing there.

"What are you doing?" asks Vega.

"I'm busy," Britt-Marie answers.

"Were you asleep?" asks Omar.

"Certainly not!" Britt-Marie protests, while adjusting both her hair and her apron.

"We heard you coming down the stairs," says Vega.

"That's not a crime, is it?"

"Cool it, will you? We only asked if you were asleep!"

Britt-Marie clasps her hands together.

"It's possible that I may have overslept. It's not something that happens often."

"Did you have something you had to get up for?" asks Omar.

Britt-Marie doesn't have a convincing answer to that one. There's a silence for a few moments, until Vega's patience runs out and she gets to the point with a frustrated groan:

"We were wondering if you wanted to eat with us tonight."

Omar nods energetically.

"And then we're wondering if you want to be our new coach, for our team!"

Then Omar shrieks, "Ouch!" and Vega hisses, "Idiot!" and tries to kick him again on the shin, but this time he gets out of the way.

"We wanted to invite you for dinner so we could ask you to be our coach. Sort of like when they offer a contract in *proper* soccer teams," says Vega sourly.

"I'm not particularly taken with soccer," says Britt-Marie as politely as she can, which quite possibly is not very politely at all.

"You don't need to do anything, all you have to do is sign a bloody form and come to our bloody training sessions!" protests Vega.

"There's this wicked knockout competition in town. The council is organizing it, and any team can take part, but you have to have a coach."

"There has to be someone else in Borg you could give this assignment to," says Britt-Marie and starts backing away into the hall.

"No one else has time," says Vega.

"But we were thinking you don't have anything to do, sort of thing!" says Omar with a cheerful nod.

Britt-Marie pauses and looks thoroughly offended.

Adjusts her apron.

"I'll have you know I have a great deal to do."

"Like what?"

"I have a list!"

"But I mean, God, this will hardly take anytime at all. You only have to be there when we're training in case one of the competition organizers comes by! So they can see we have a sodding coach!" Vega groans.

"We're training at six this evening in the parking area by the recreation center," says Omar with a nod.

"But I don't know anything about soccer!"

"Nor does Omar, but we still let him play with us," says Vega.

"You bloody what?!" Omar exclaims.

Vega, apparently losing her patience, shakes her head at Britt-Marie.

"Never bloody mind, then! We thought you had it in you to be decent about it. This is Borg, so it's not like there are so many other bloody adults to choose from. You're the only one."

Britt-Marie has nothing to say to that. Vega starts going down the steps and makes an irritated gesture at Omar to come with her. Britt-Marie stays in the doorway, keeping her hands clasped together while opening and closing her mouth repeatedly, until at long last she calls out:

"I can't at six o'clock!"

Vega turns around. Britt-Marie stares at her apron.

"Civilized people have their dinner at six. You actually can't play soccer in the middle of your dinner."

Vega shrugs. As if it doesn't make any difference.

"Okay. Come over to ours and have dinner at six, then, and we'll train afterwards."

"We're having tacos!" says Omar, nodding with great satisfaction.

"What's tacos?"

The children stare at her.

"Tacos," says Omar, as if the problem could only have been that she didn't hear him properly.

"I don't eat foreign food," says Britt-Marie, even though what she really means is, "Kent doesn't eat foreign food."

Vega shrugs her shoulders again.

"If you don't eat the tortillas it's like having salad."

"We live in one of the high-rises, block two, second floor," says Omar and points down the road.

Of course it's not there and then that Britt-Marie becomes the coach of a soccer team. It's just the point at which someone tells her that's what she's become.

She closes the door. Removes her apron. Puts it back in the drawer. Then cleans the kitchen, because she doesn't know how not to. Then she goes upstairs and fetches her cell phone. The girl at the unemployment office picks up after a single ring.

"Do you know anything about soccer?"

"Is that Britt-Marie?" asks the girl, although she should have learned by now.

"I need to know how one trains a soccer team," Britt-Marie informs her. "Do you need a permit from the local authority for that type of thing?"

"No . . . or what I mean is . . . what do you mean?" says the girl.

Britt-Marie exhales. But does not sigh.

"My dear, if for example you want to have your balcony glazed, you need a permit. I'm assuming the same thing applies to soccer teams. Surely they're not beyond the rule of law just because the players run about kicking things all over the place?"

"No . . . I've . . . or, I mean I assume their parents have to sign some letter to say they're allowed to play in the team," says the girl dubiously.

Britt-Marie makes a note of that on her list. Nods soberly to herself and asks:

"Ha. So can I ask, what's the first thing you have to do at soccer practice?"

"I'd say . . . but I don't know . . . the first thing you do at training . . . I mean, is to take the register?"

"I beg your pardon?"

"You have a register. You tick off the people who are there," says the girl.

"A list?"

"Yes . . . ?"

Britt-Marie has already hung up.

She may not know a lot about soccer, but even the gods know that no one is more skilled at lists than Britt-Marie.

16

Dino opens the door. He laughs when he sees Britt-Marie, who assumes she has pressed the wrong doorbell, but in fact it turns out Dino always has his dinner with Vega and Omar, and Dino isn't necessarily laughing at her. Apparently, in spite of her first impressions, that is how things are done in Borg. People seem to have their dinners at other people's homes just like that, and then go around laughing as if they hadn't a care in the world. Omar comes running into the hall and points at Britt-Marie.

"Take off your shoes. Sami gets really pissed off otherwise because he just mopped the floor!"

"I do not get pissed off!" comes a voice from the kitchen, sounding fairly pissed off.

"He's always in a foul one when it's our cleaning day," explains Omar to Britt-Marie.

"Maybe I wouldn't be in a foul one if *we* had a fucking cleaning day, but it's always *me* who has a fucking cleaning day in this place. *Every day!*" yells Sami from the kitchen.

Omar nods meaningfully at Britt-Marie.

"You see. Pissed off."

Vega turns up in the doorway with a slumped upper-body posture, waving an invisible bottle of spirits, in imitation of Somebody.

"You know, Britt-Marie, Sami he has, what's-it-called? Citrus fruit up the anus, huh?"

Dino and Omar laugh until they are hyperventilating. Britt-Marie responds with a brisk series of polite nods, because this is as close as she gets to laughing out loud. She removes her shoes, goes into the kitchen, and nods cautiously at Sami. He points at a chair.

"The food is ready," he says and removes his apron, before immediately roaring towards the hall:

"Grub's up!"

Britt-Marie checks her watch. It's exactly six o'clock.

"Are we waiting for your parents?" she asks considerately.

"They're not here," says Sami and starts putting coasters on the table.

"I suppose they're delayed coming home from work," Britt-Marie says pleasantly.

"Mum drives a truck. Abroad. She's not home much," says Sami curtly, putting glasses and bowls on the coasters.

"And your father?"

"He cleared off."

"Cleared off?"

"That's right. When I was small. Omar and Vega were just born. I guess he couldn't take it. So we don't talk about him in this home. Mum took care of us. *The food's ready now so come here before I fucking beat the hell out of you!*"

Vega, Omar, and Dino saunter into the kitchen and start devouring their food, hardly stopping to chew it; it might as well have been liquidized and served up with straws.

"But who takes care of you now, then, when your mother's not here?" asks Britt-Marie.

"We take care of us," says Sami, offended.

She doesn't know exactly what common conversational practice is after that, so she gets out the carton of cigarettes with the foreign letters on it.

"Of course I usually bring flowers when I'm invited for dinner, but there's no florist in Borg. I've noticed you like cigarettes. I suppose cigarettes must be like flowers for someone who likes cigarettes," she explains, as if to defend herself.

Sami takes the carton of cigarettes. He looks almost emotional. Britt-Marie sits in a spare seat and clears her throat.

"You're not afraid of cancer, I suppose?"

"There are worse things to be afraid of," says Sami with a smile.

"Ha," says Britt-Marie, and picks up something from her plate that she has to assume is a taco.

Omar and Vega start talking at the same time. Mostly about soccer, as far as Britt-Marie can make out. Dino says almost nothing, but he laughs the whole time. Britt-Marie doesn't understand what he's laughing at. He and Omar don't even need to say anything before they burst out laughing, all they have to do is look at each other. Children are unfathomable that way.

Sami points at Omar with his fork.

"How many times do I have to tell you, Omar? Take your fucking elbows off the fucking table!"

Omar rolls his eyes. Removes his elbows.

"I don't get why you can't have your elbows on the table. What difference does it make?"

Britt-Marie observes him intensely.

"It makes a difference, Omar, because we're not animals," she explains.

Sami looks at Britt-Marie appreciatively. Omar looks at them both with puzzlement.

"Animals don't have elbows," he objects.

"Eat your fucking food," says Sami.

When Omar and Dino are done, they stand up and run into another room, still laughing. Vega puts her plate on the dish rack and looks as if she's expecting a diploma for effort. After that she also runs off.

"You could say thanks for the food," Sami calls out after them, pissed off.

"*Thanks for the food!*" the children roar from an indefinable part of the flat.

Sami stands up and clatters demonstratively with the plates in the sink. Then he looks at Britt-Marie.

"Right. So you didn't like the food, then?"

"Excuse me?" says Britt-Marie.

Sami shakes his head, says something to himself punctuated by several "fucking" references, then snatches up the carton of cigarettes and disappears onto the balcony.

Britt-Marie stays in the kitchen on her own. Eats what she is almost sure must be tacos. They taste less odd than she expected. She stands up, puts what's left of the food into the fridge, washes up and dries the plates and cutlery, and opens the cutlery drawer. Leans over it, catches her breath. Forks-knives-spoons. In the right order.

Sami is standing on the balcony, smoking, when she comes out.

"Very nice dinner, Sami. Thanks for that," she says, one hand firmly clasped in the other.

He nods.

"Sometimes it's nice if someone says it tastes good without your having to ask every time, you get what I mean?"

"Yes," she says. Because she does get it.

Then she feels that it would be in order to say something polite, so she says:

"You have a very nice cutlery drawer."

He looks at her for a long time, and then grins.

"You're okay, Coach."

"Ha. Ha. You're also . . . okay. Sami."

He drives them all to their practice session in his black car. Vega argues loudly with him all the way—which, in Borg, is not very far. Britt-Marie doesn't understand what the argument is about, but it seems to have something to do with that Psycho fellow. Something about money. When they stop, Britt-Marie has a sense that something ought to be done to change the subject, because this Psycho makes her nervous in much the same way as too much talk about poisonous spiders. So she says:

"Do you also have a team, Sami? You and those boys you were playing with the other night?"

"No, we don't have a . . . team," says Sami, and looks as if it was a bit of a strange question.

"So why do you play soccer, then?" asks Britt-Marie, puzzled.

"What do you mean, 'why'?" asks Sami, just as puzzled.

Neither of them are able to come up with a good answer.

The car stops. Vega, Omar, and Dino jump out. Britt-Marie checks the contents of her bag to make sure she hasn't forgotten anything.

"Are you ready, Britt-Marie?" asks Vega, as if she's already bored.

Britt-Marie nods with a good deal of concentration and points at her bag.

"Yes, yes, obviously I'm ready. I should like to tell you that I have made a list!"

Sami parks the car with the engine running, so that the headlights illuminate the parking area. The children put out four fizzy-drink cans as goalposts. Fizzy-drink cans are magical in this way—they can transform parking areas into soccer pitches by their mere existence.

Britt-Marie holds up her list.

"Vega?" she asks, loud and clear, while the children run about kicking the ball with varying degrees of success.

"What?" says Vega, who's standing right in front of her.

"Is that a 'yes'?"

"What are you talking about?"

Britt-Marie taps her pen against the list with extreme patience.

"My dear, I am reading the register. What one does is, one reads out the names and then each respective person says 'yes.' It's common practice."

Vega squints disapprovingly.

"You can see I'm standing here!"

Britt-Marie nods considerately.

"My dear, if we could just tick people off in any old way there wouldn't be any point doing the register, you have to understand."

"Never mind about your bloody register! Let's just play!" Vega says and kicks the ball.

"Vega?"

"*Yes?!* Jesus . . ."

Britt-Marie nods intently and ticks Vega's name off on the list. Once she's done the same with the other children, she distributes handwritten notes to them with a short, very formal message followed by two neat lines at the bottom, where it is written "Parental signature." Britt-Marie is very proud of the notes. She has written them in ink. Anyone who knows Britt-Marie understands what an outstanding achievement it is for Britt-Marie to control her compulsion never to write anything in ink. People really do change when they travel.

"Do both parents have to sign?" asks Pirate, who has arranged his hair so neatly that it really pains Britt-Marie when, in the next second, a ball strikes his head.

"Sorry! I was aiming at Vega!" yells Omar.

Vega and Omar end up having a fight. The other children fling themselves into the chaos. Britt-Marie walks around in circles, trying to figure out how to give Vega and Omar their notes among all the flying fists, but in the end she gives up and walks determinedly across the parking area and hands their slips to Sami instead. He's sitting on the hood of the black car, drinking one of the goalposts.

Britt-Marie brushes dust off every part of herself. Soccer is certainly not very hygienic.

"You need help?" asks Sami.

"I'm not familiar with what a soccer coach is supposed to do when the players fight like wild dogs," Britt-Marie admits.

"You let them run—you know, idiot!" Sami grins.

"I'm certainly not an idiot!" protests Britt-Marie.

"No, it's an exercise. It's called 'Idiot.' I'll show you."

He slides off the hood and walks around the car. Britt-Marie follows him. Clasps one hand in the other and asks, not at all accusingly:

"Might I trouble you for an answer as to why you don't train these children yourself, if you know so much about this soccer thing?"

Sami gets half a dozen soft-drink cans out of the trunk. Hands one of them to Britt-Marie.

"I don't have time," he says.

"Maybe you would if you didn't spend such an inordinate amount of time buying soft drinks," Britt-Marie notes.

Sami laughs again.

"Come on, Coach, you do get that the council wouldn't let someone with my criminal record coach a youth team," he says. As if it's hardly worth mentioning. Britt-Marie keeps an extra-firm grip on her handbag after that. Not because she judges people, obviously, but because there's a pretty strong wind in Borg tonight. No other reason.

Idiot, the way it's done in Borg, is an exercise based on half a dozen soft-drink cans being positioned at intervals of a couple of yards. The children stand by the fence between the recreation center and the pizzeria, then they run as fast as they can to the first soft-drink can, and as fast as they can back to the fence, then as fast as they can to the second soft-drink can a little farther away, and then back as fast as they can. And then to the third soft-drink can, and so on.

"For how long are they supposed to do that?" asks Britt-Marie.

"As long as you like," says Sami.

"For goodness' sake, I can't make them do that!" Britt-Marie objects.

"You're the coach now. If they don't do what you tell them, they can't play in the competition."

It sounds quite deranged, in Britt-Marie's opinion, but Sami doesn't go into more detailed explanations because his telephone starts ringing.

"What did you say the exercise was called?" asks Britt-Marie.

"Idiot!" says Sami and then answers "Yeah" into his telephone, as people do who have no use for either exclamation marks or question marks.

Britt-Marie mulls this over at length until at long last she manages to say:

"That's a good name for both the exercise and the person who came up with it."

By now, Sami has started walking back to his car with the telephone pressed to his ear, so he can't hear her. No one can. But this doesn't actually concern Britt-Marie so much. The children run between the soft-drink cans and Britt-Marie stands there beside them with a sort of happy fizziness in her whole body, repeating, “A good name for the exercise and the person who came up with it,” very, very quietly to herself. Over and over again.

It’s the first time for as long as she can remember that she has intentionally made a joke.

17

In the children's defense, they didn't do it on purpose. Or rather, it was obviously done on purpose but none of them believed Toad would actually hit the mark, so to speak. They never hit anything they aim at. Especially not Toad, who's the youngest and worst player in an already dismal team.

It so happens that Bank, in an even blacker mood than usual, comes walking across the parking area with her white dog in the middle of a training session.

Omar sees her go into the pizzeria or the corner shop or car workshop or whatever it is, and after a while come out again with one bag that seems to contain chocolate and another that seems to contain beer. Omar elbows Toad in the side and says:

"You think she has superpowers?"

Toad answers with a sound made by children whose mouths are full of goalpost. Omar gestures in an explanatory way to Britt-Marie, as if Britt-Marie might be more receptive to his line of reasoning, which must be reckoned as fairly exaggerated optimism.

"You know, what the hell, in films blind types get superpowers! Like Daredevil!"

"I'm not familiar with Daredevil," explains Britt-Marie with as much amicability as she can drum up, considering how enormously stupid this conversation is.

Bank moves across the parking area with her stick in her hand, next to and slightly behind the white dog. Omar points at her exultantly:

"Daredevil! Is a superhero! Except blind! So he has super-senses instead. You think she does? Could she sort of sense it if you shot a soccer ball at her head even though she couldn't see it?"

"She is not blind. She merely has impaired vision," says Britt-Marie. Omar, who has long since stopped listening to Britt-Marie, turns around and says:

"Do it, Toad!"

Toad, who happens to have the ball at that moment, doesn't seem to think it's a very good idea. But then Omar utters those golden words that have the magical power to obliterate every child's self-restraint anywhere in the world:

"You don't have the guts to do it!"

In fairness to Toad, he obviously never thought he'd hit her. They're all quite surprised that he does.

Most surprised of all, obviously, is Bank.

"*Whatthebloody* . . . !" she roars.

The children stand still at first, their mouths agape. Like you do. Then Omar starts tittering. Then Vega follows suit. Bank storms towards them, incandescent, her stick cleaving the air.

"Was that funny? Brats!"

Britt-Marie clears her throat and almost holds out her arms.

"Please . . . Bank, he didn't mean to, he obviously wasn't aiming at you, he obviously wasn't. It was obviously an accident."

"*Accident! Accident, yeah!*" howls Bank, and it's a little unclear what she means by this.

"What do you mean not on purpose? He was aiming, wasn't he?" yells Omar confidently, while at the same time moving out of cleaving range behind Britt-Marie.

"Did you really?" Britt-Marie asks Toad in astonishment.

"*Who did this?!*" yells Bank, her entire face throbbing like a single thick vein emerging from her throat.

Toad, paralyzed, nods and backs away. Britt-Marie enthusiastically clasps one hand in the other, and doesn't quite know what to do with herself.

"But . . . it's absolutely marvelous!" she manages to blurt out.

"*What* are *you saying, you old bat?*" howls Bank.

At this stage, everything that's reasonable inside Britt-Marie insistently tries to curb her enthusiasm, but clearly it doesn't have much success, because Britt-Marie leans in and whispers chirpily:

"They never hit anything they aim at, you see. This is really an excellent sign of progress!"

Bank stares at Britt-Marie. At least she seems to be staring. It's difficult to know for sure, with those sunglasses. Britt-Marie gulps hesitantly.

"It's obviously not marvelous that he hit . . . you. That is obviously not what I mean. But it is excellent that he hit . . . anything at all."

Bank leaves the parking area in a hailstorm of the ugliest and most colorful words Britt-Marie has ever heard. Britt-Marie actually didn't even know it was possible to combine words for genitalia with words describing other parts of the body in that way. You don't even come across that level of verbal innovation in crosswords.

A thoughtful silence envelops the parking area. Obviously, it's the voice of Somebody that breaks it.

"Like I said about that one. Lemon. Up the. Arse."

She's sitting in the pizzeria doorway, grinning in the direction of Bank.

Britt-Marie brushes her skirt down.

"I wouldn't want to suggest that you're wrong, I certainly wouldn't. But I do really think that on this occasion Bank's problem was not a lemon in the arse, but a soccer ball in the head."

They all laugh. Britt-Marie doesn't get angry about it. It's a new feeling for her.

The boy with the tracksuit jacket with HOCKEY written on it walks out of the pizzeria with a pizza box in his hands. He fails to hide his interest in the soccer training, realizes his mistake, and tries to quickly get moving, but Vega has already seen him.

"What are you doing here?" she calls out.

"Buying pizza," says the boy in the tracksuit repentantly.

"Don't you have pizza in town, or what?"

The boy looks down at his pizza box.

"I like the pizza here."

Vega clenches her fists but doesn't say anything else. The boy squeezes past Somebody in the doorway and runs out towards the road. The BMW is parked three hundred feet down the road, with its engine running.

Somebody turns to Vega with a grimace.

"He's not his dad. Dad can be pig, kid could be good. You should know if anyone."

Vega looks as if the words have wounded her. She turns around and kicks the ball so hard that it flies over the fence into the darkness.

Somebody rolls a few feet towards Britt-Marie, nods at the pizzeria.

"Come! Have something for you!"

By this stage, Toad has drunk all the goalposts and Vega kicks off a noisy dispute with Sami, of which Britt-Marie can only distinguish something about "Psycho" and "owes money," by which she comes to the conclusion that the training session is over. She's unsure whether she should be doing anything in particular, such as blowing a whistle or something similar, but she chooses not to. Mainly because she doesn't have a whistle.

Inside the pizzeria, Somebody slides a fistful of money and a piece of paper across the counter.

"Here. This change, and this receipt, huh."

She gestures towards the bottom of the door, where Britt-Marie pushed the money through last night.

"Next time, you can, what's-it-called? Come in!" She grins.

When Britt-Marie doesn't seem to know what to say, she adds:

"You left too much money for cigarettes, Britt-Marie. You are, what's-it-called? Either your maths is crap or you're very generous, huh? I think: Britt-Marie is generous, huh? Not like that Fredrik, for example, he's so mean he yells every time he takes a shit!"

She nods cheerfully. Britt-Marie mumbles "Ha" repeatedly. Neatly folds the receipt and puts it in her handbag. Takes the change and puts it in the vase for tips. Somebody rolls half a turn forward, then half a turn back.

"It looked nice, you know. Looked nice when you . . . cleaned, huh. Thanks!" she says.

"It was not my intention to hide your belongings so you could not find them," says Britt-Marie, directing her voice into her handbag.

Somebody scratches her chin.

"The cutlery, huh. Fork, knife, spoon. That order. I can, what's-it-called? Get used to it!"

Britt-Marie sucks in her cheeks. Goes to the door. She has reached the threshold when she stops and summons her strength and says:

"I should just like to inform you that there's no urgency, at the moment, to have my car repaired."

Somebody looks out of the door at the children and their soccer pitch. She nods. Britt-Marie also nods. It's the first time for as long as Britt-Marie can remember that she has had a friend. The children take off their dirty jerseys and drop them off in the recreation center, without Britt-Marie even having offered to wash them. There's no one left in the parking area by the time she's washed and tumble-dried the jerseys and put them in a neat pile, ready for tomorrow's training. Borg is empty except for a lone silhouette by the bus stop on the road. Britt-Marie didn't even know there was a bus stop there until she saw someone waiting by the streetlight.

She doesn't recognize Pirate until she's just a few feet away. His red hair is tangled and muddy and he stands motionless as if trying to ignore that she's there. Her common sense tries to make her walk away. But instead she says:

"I was under the impression that you lived in Borg."

He keeps a firm grip on the note that Britt-Marie handed out at the start of the training session.

"It says here you have to have both your parents' signatures. So I have to go and ask my father to sign it."

Britt-Marie nods.

"Ha. Have a good evening, then," she says and starts walking towards the darkness.

"You want to come with me?" he calls out after her.

She turns around as if he's out of his mind. The paper in his hands is stained with sweat.

"I . . . it . . . I think it would feel better for me if you were there," he manages to say.

It's obviously wholly ludicrous. Britt-Marie is scrupulous about telling him that throughout the whole bus journey.

Which takes almost an hour. And ends abruptly in front of an enormous white building. Britt-Marie is holding on to her handbag so tightly that she gets a cramp in her fingers. She is, in spite of everything, a civilized person with a normal life to get on with.

Civilized people with normal lives are actually not in the habit of visiting prisons.

18

"Bloody gangsters," Kent always used to call them, the people who were responsible for things such as street violence, extortionate taxes, pickpocketing, graffiti in public toilets, and hotels where all the deck chairs were occupied when Kent came down to the pool. All things of this kind were caused by "gangsters." It was an effective system, always having people there to blame for everything without ever having to define who they really were.

Britt-Marie never found out what he really wanted. What would have satisfied him? Would a lot of money have been enough, or was every last penny required? One time when David and Pernilla were teenagers, they gave him a coffee mug with a message on it: "He Who Dies with the Most Toys Wins." They said it was "ironic" but Kent seemed to take it as a challenge. He always had a plan, there was always a "bloody big deal" just round the corner. His company was just about to strike bigger and bigger deals in Germany; the flat they inherited from Britt-Marie's parents could finally be converted to a freehold so they could sell it for more money. Just a few more months. Just a few years. They got married because Kent's accountant said it made sense from a "tax-planning perspective." Britt-Marie never had a plan, she hoped it would be enough if you were faithful and in love. Until the day came when it wasn't enough.

"Bloody gangsters," Kent would have said if he'd been sitting with Britt-Marie this evening, in the little waiting room in the prison. "Put the criminals on a deserted island with a pistol each, and they'll clean up the sorry mess themselves." Britt-Marie never liked him talking like that, but she never said anything. Now when she thinks about it she has difficulties remembering the last time she said anything at all, until one day she left him without a word. Because of this, it always feels as if the whole thing was her fault.

She wonders what he's doing now. If he feels well and wears clean shirts. If he takes his medicine. If he looks for things in kitchen drawers and yells out her name before he remembers that she's no longer there. She wonders if he is with her, the young and beautiful woman, and if she likes pizza. Britt-Marie wonders what he would say if he knew she was sitting in a waiting room in a prison full of gangsters. If he'd be worried. If he'd tell a joke at her expense. If he'd touch her and whisper that everything would be all right, like he used to do in the days after she had buried her mother.

They were very different people in those days. Britt-Marie doesn't know if it was Kent or herself who changed first. Or how much of it was her fault. She was ready to say "everything" if she could only have her life back.

Pirate sits next to her, holding her hand, and Britt-Marie clutches his very hard in return.

"You mustn't tell my mum we were here," he whispers.

"Where is she?"

"At the hospital."

"Was she in an accident?"

"No, no, she works there," says Pirate, before adding as if explaining a law of nature: "All the mums in Borg work at the hospital."

Britt-Marie doesn't know what to say to that.

"Why do they call you Pirate?" she asks instead.

"Because my father hid the treasure."

As soon as she hears this, she decides she'll never call him Pirate again.

A thick metal door opens and Sven stands in the doorway, sweaty and red-nosed, with his police cap in his hands.

"Is Mum livid again?" says Ben at once, with a sigh.

Sven slowly shakes his head. Puts his hand on the boy's shoulder.

Meets Britt-Marie's eyes.

"Ben's mother is on the night shift. She called me as soon as they called from here. I came as quick as I could."

Britt-Marie would like to hug him, but she's a sensible person. The guards won't let Ben see his father because it isn't visiting hours, but after much persuasion Sven manages to get them to agree to take the paper into the prison. They come back with a signature. Next to the signature his father has written: "LOVE YOU!"

Ben holds the paper so hard on their way back that it's illegible by the time they get to Borg. Neither he, Britt-Marie, nor Sven utter a single word. There's not much you can say to a teenager who has to ask strangers in uniforms for permission to see his father. But when they drop Ben off outside his house and his mother comes out, Britt-Marie feels it's appropriate to say something encouraging, so she makes an attempt with:

"It was very clean, Ben, I have to say. I have always imagined prisons to be dirty places, but this one certainly seemed very hygienic. That is something to be pleased about at least."

Ben folds the paper with his father's signature without meeting her eyes, and then hands it to her. Sven quickly says:

"You should keep that, Ben."

Ben nods and smiles and holds the paper even more tightly.

"Is there training tomorrow?" he murmurs.

Britt-Marie fumbles for her list in her bag, but Sven calmly assures him:

"Of course there's training tomorrow, Ben. Usual time."

Ben peers at Britt-Marie. She tries to nod affirmatively. Ben starts up the path, then turns, smiles faintly and waves. They wait until he's buried his face in his mother's arms. Sven waves, but she doesn't see, just presses her face into her boy's hair and whispers something.

Sven drives slowly through Borg. Clears his throat uncomfortably as you do when you have a bad conscience.

"They haven't had such an easy time, Ben and her. She's working triple shifts so they can keep the house. He's a good boy, and his dad wasn't a bad man. Well, sure, I know what he did was wrong, tax evasion is a crime. But he was desperate. Financial crises can make people desperate, and desperation makes people foolish. . . ."

He goes silent. Britt-Marie doesn't say anything about the financial crisis being over. For various reasons it doesn't strike her as appropriate on this particular occasion.

Sven has cleaned up the police car. All the pizza boxes have been removed from the floor, she notes. They drive past the patch of asphalt where Sami and Psycho are playing soccer again this evening with their friends.

"Ben's father is not like them. I just want you to understand that he isn't a criminal. Not in the same way as those boys," explains Sven.

"Sami is not like those boys either!" protests Britt-Marie, and the words slip out of her quickly: "He's no gangster, he has a spectacularly well-organized cutlery drawer!"

Sven's laughter comes abruptly, deep and rolling, like a lit fire to warm your hands.

"No, no, there's nothing wrong with Sami. He just keeps bad company. . . ."

"Vega seems to be of the opinion that he owes people money."

"Not Sami, but Psycho does. Psycho always owes people money," says Sven, and his laughter fades, spills onto the floor, and disappears.

The police car slows down. The boys playing soccer see it, but they hardly react. There's a certain swagger about their disregard for the police. Sven narrows his eyes by half.

"Sami didn't have an easy time growing up either. More disasters have hit that family than you'd consider fair by anyone's reckoning, if you ask me. He's both mother and father as well as older brother to Vega and Omar, and that's not a responsibility anyone should put on the shoulders of a kid who hasn't even turned twenty."

Possibly Britt-Marie wants to ask what this means, the bit about "both mother and father," but she manages not to, so he continues:

"Psycho is his best friend, and has been since they were big enough to kick that ball around. Sami could have been a really good player; everyone saw his talent, but he was too busy surviving, perhaps."

"What does that mean?" asks Britt-Marie, slightly wounded by the way Sven says it, as if she should understand without an explanation.

Sven holds up his palm apologetically.

"Sorry, I . . . was thinking out loud. He, they, how should I explain it? Sami, Vega, and Omar's mother did all she could but their father, he . . . he was not a good man, Britt-Marie. When he came home and had his anger attacks, people heard him all over Borg. And Sami was hardly old enough to go to school back then, but he took his younger siblings' hands and ran for it. Psycho met them outside their door, every time. Psycho carried Omar on his back and Sami carried Vega, and then they ran into the forest. Until their dad fell into a drunken stupor. Night after night, until their dad just cleared out one day. And then that thing happened with their mother . . . it . . ."

He falls silent, as you do when you realize once again that you're thinking out loud. He doesn't try to hide that he's hiding something, but Britt-Marie doesn't stick her nose in. Sven smooths the back of his hand over his eyebrows.

"Psycho grew into a properly dangerous lunatic, Sami knows that, but Sami's not the sort of person to turn his back on someone who once carried his younger siblings on his back. Maybe in a place like Borg you don't have the luxury of being able to choose your best friend."

The police car once again starts rolling slowly down the road. The boys' soccer match continues. Psycho scores, roars something into the night, and runs around the pitch with his arms extended as if he were an aircraft. Sami laughs so much that he keels over, hands on his knees. They look happy.

Britt-Marie doesn't know what to say, or what to believe.

She has never met a gangster with a correctly organized cutlery drawer.

Sven's gaze loses itself in some place where the headlights end and darkness begins.

"We do what we can in Borg. We always have done. But there's a fire burning in those boys, and sooner or later it will consume everyone around them, or themselves."

"That was nicely put," says Britt-Marie.

He smiles bashfully.

She looks down into her handbag. Then she dismays herself by going further:

"Do you have any children yourself?"

He shakes his head. Looks out of the window as you do if you don't have any children, yet in spite of all have a whole village full of children.

"I was married, but . . . ah. She never liked Borg. She said it was a place where you came to die, not live."

He tries to smile. Britt-Marie wishes she had brought the bamboo screen along.

He bites his lip. When they should turn off by Bank's house, he seems to hesitate, then summons his courage and says:

"If it isn't, I mean, if it's not inconvenient to you I'd like to show you something."

She doesn't protest. He smiles in a way you'd hardly notice. She smiles in a way no one could ever notice.

He drives the police car through Borg and out the other side. Turns off down a gravel track. It apparently goes on forever, but when they finally stop it suddenly seems inconceivable that they were just in a built-up area. The car is surrounded by trees, and the silence is of a sort that only exists where there are no people.

"It's . . . well . . . ah. It's probably ridiculous, of course, but this is my . . . well, my favorite place on earth. . . ." mumbles Sven.

He blushes. Looks like he wants to turn the car around and drive away fast and never mention it again. But Britt-Marie opens her door and gets out.

They are standing on a rock over a lake held tight by trees on all sides.

Britt-Marie peers down over the edge until she feels a queasiness in her stomach. The sky is clear and bright with stars. Sven opens his door and comes up behind her and clears his throat.

"I . . . ah. It's silly, but I wanted you to see that Borg can be beautiful as well," he whispers.

Britt-Marie closes her eyes. She feels the wind in her hair.

"Thank you," she whispers back.

They don't speak on the way back. He gets out of the car outside Bank's house, runs around, and opens Britt-Marie's door. Then he opens the door of the backseat and fumbles with something, coming back with a well-thumbed plastic folder.

"It's . . . ah, it's just . . . something," he manages to say.

It's a drawing. Of the recreation center and the pizzeria, and in between the children playing soccer. Britt-Marie in the middle of the picture. Everything done in pencil. Britt-Marie holds on to it a little too hard, and Sven removes his police cap a little too suddenly.

"Well, it's probably silly, of course, of course it is, but I was thinking . . . there's a restaurant in town . . ."

When Britt-Marie doesn't answer at once he adds briskly:

"A proper restaurant, I mean! Not like the pizzeria here in Borg, but a nice one. With white tablecloths. And cutlery."

It will be quite a long time before Britt-Marie realizes that he tries to hide his insecurity with jokes, rather than the other way around. But when she does not immediately seem to understand, he holds up his palm and apologizes:

"Not that there's anything wrong with the pizzeria, of course not, of course not, but . . ."

He's holding his police cap in both hands now, and looking like considerably younger men do when they want to ask considerably younger women something specific. There is so much inside Britt-Marie that yearns to know what it is. But the sensible part inside her has already gone into the hall and closed the door.

19

"The other woman" is what it's called, but Britt-Marie always had difficulties viewing Kent's other woman as that. Maybe because she herself knew how it felt to be that woman. Admittedly Kent had already divorced when he came back to the house that day, a lifetime earlier, after Britt-Marie had buried her mother, but his children never saw it that way. Children never see it that way. As far as David and Pernilla were concerned, Britt-Marie was the other woman regardless of how many fairy tales she read them and how many dinners she cooked—and maybe Kent also regarded her as such. And despite the number of shirts she had washed, maybe Britt-Marie never quite felt like the primary woman herself.

She sits on the balcony watching the morning dawdling over Borg, as mornings in Borg have a habit of doing in January. Daylight comes apparently without any need for the sun to rise. She is still holding Sven's drawing.

He is not an especially good drawer, far from it, and if she'd been more critical by nature she might have had reservations about what the blurred contours and irregular silhouettes were saying about the way he saw her. But at least he saw her. It's difficult to steel oneself against that.

She fetches her cell phone and calls the girl at the unemployment office.

The girl's voice answers very gaily, so Britt-Marie understands it has to be the telephone answering machine. Obviously she intends to hang up, because she doesn't find it appropriate to be leaving messages on answering machines unless you're calling from a hospital or selling narcotics. But for some reason or other she doesn't hang up; instead she sits in silence after the beep and declares at last:

"This is Britt-Marie. One of the children in the soccer team hit something he was aiming for today. I felt you might be interested to hear that."

She feels silly when she hangs up. Obviously the girl won't be interested in that. Kent would have laughed at her if he was here.

Bank is sitting in the kitchen having soup when Britt-Marie comes down the stairs. The dog is sitting next to the table, waiting. Britt-Marie stops in the hall and looks at the soup plate. She wonders how the soup was cooked, because she sees no saucepan and the kitchen doesn't have a microwave. Bank is slurping.

"Did you have something to say, or is it just that you never saw a blind person having soup before?" she asks without lifting her head.

"I was under the impression you had *impaired vision*."

Bank slurps loudly by way of an answer. Britt-Marie presses the palms of her hands against her skirt.

"You like soccer, I understand," she says, nodding at the photographs on the walls.

"No," says Bank.

Britt-Marie clasps her hands together over her stomach and looks at the rows of photographs on the wall, each one of them of Bank and her father and at least one soccer ball.

"I've become a sort of coach for a team."

"I heard." She starts slurping again. Doesn't raise her head. Britt-Marie brushes some specks of dust from various objects in the hall.

"Ha. At any rate I noticed all the photographs, so I felt it was appropriate under the circumstances, bearing in mind your obvious experience of soccer, that I asked you for a piece of advice."

"A piece of advice about what?"

"About soccer." She doesn't know if Bank rolls her eyes, but it certainly feels as if she does. The dog goes into the living room. Bank walks behind, running her stick along the walls.

"Where are these photos you're talking about?" she asks.

"Higher up."

Bank's stick taps the glass of one of the framed photos, in which a younger version of her is standing, wearing a jersey so badly stained that not even baking soda would have helped. Bank leans towards the photo until her nose is almost touching the glass. Then she moves around the room and taps systematically at all the photos, as if memorizing where they are.

Britt-Marie stands in the hall and waits for what she considers to be an appropriate length of time, until the whole thing stops being merely uncomfortable and starts getting downright odd. Then she puts on her coat and opens the door. Just before it closes, Bank grunts behind her:

"You want some good advice? That team can't play. Nothing you do will make any difference."

Britt-Marie whispers, "Ha," and walks out.

She locks herself into the laundry at the recreation center. Sits on one of the stools while her skirt, still muddy from the truck incident, spins around in the washing machine. Once she has gotten dressed and fixed her hair, she stands for a long time in the kitchen observing the coffee percolator that was destroyed by flying stones.

Britt-Marie decides to assemble an entire piece of IKEA furniture that day and for some reason ends up doing so at the pizzeria. Almost completely on her own. No screwdriver is required, but it takes the best part of ten hours, because there are actually three items of furniture—one table and two chairs. Intended for balconies. Britt-Marie pushes them as far as they'll go into a corner, puts out kitchen roll as a tablecloth, and then sits there on her own eating pizza that Somebody has baked for her. It is a remarkable day in Britt-Marie's life, unique even among the consistently remarkable days she's had since arriving in Borg.

Sven has his dinner at another table in the pizzeria, but they have their coffee together. Without saying anything to each other. Just trying to get used to the presence of the other person. As you do when it's been a long time since anyone's presence had a physical effect on you. A long time since a person could be sensed without physically touching at all.

Karl comes in to pick up a parcel. Sits down at a table in the corner and has a cup of coffee beside the men with caps and beards. They continue to intentionally ignore Britt-Marie, as if this might make her disappear. Vega comes in with the soccer ball under her arm, as dirty as only a child can get in the short distance between her older brother's car and a pizzeria. Omar comes in behind her and, when he sees Britt-Marie's newly assembled balcony furniture, immediately tries to sell her some furniture polish.

When Britt-Marie walks out to go to the training session, Sven stands up with his police cap in his hands, but he doesn't say anything and she speeds up to make sure he doesn't have the opportunity.

Ben's mother is standing outside the door. She is wearing her hospital clothes and holding something in her hands.

"Hello, Britt-Marie. We haven't met, but I'm Ben's mo—"

"I'm aware of who you are," says Britt-Marie guardedly, as if preparing to be spattered with mud again by a passing truck.

"I just wanted to say thank you for, well . . . for seeing Ben. Not many grown-ups do," says Ben's mother, and holds out what she has in her hands.

It's a bottle of Faxin. Britt-Marie is dumbstruck. Ben's mother clears her throat awkwardly.

"I hope it doesn't seem silly. Ben asked Omar what you liked and Omar said you liked this. He gave us a special deal, so we . . . well, Ben and I, we wanted to say thanks. For everything."

Britt-Marie holds the bottle as if she's afraid of dropping it. Ben's mother takes a step back, then stops and adds:

"We want you to know there's another Borg than the one with a couple of old blokes sitting in a pizzeria boozing all day. There are the rest of us as well. Those of us who haven't given up."

With that she turns around before Britt-Marie has a chance to respond, gets into a little car and drives off. The training begins and Britt-Marie calls the register and makes a note on her list, and the children do the Idiot, because that's the next item on Britt-Marie's list after "Take register."

The children hardly complain at all, the one exception being when Vega asks if they've practiced enough, and Britt-Marie says they have, and Vega immediately gets stirred up and yells something about how this team will never improve if their coach goes easy on them!

Children are beyond understanding, this much is abundantly clear. So Britt-Marie writes in her list how they have to "do the Idiot" more and that's precisely what they do. After that they gather in a ring around Britt-Marie and look like they expect her to say something, and Britt-Marie goes to Sami, who's sitting on the hood of his black car, and asks him what sort of thing this might be.

"Ah, you know. They've been running and now they want to play. Give them a pep talk and just toss the ball to them."

"A pep talk?"

"Something encouraging," he clarifies.

Britt-Marie thinks about it for a while, then turns to the children and says with all the encouragement she can muster:

"Try not to get too dirty."

Sami laughs. The children look utterly perplexed, and start a practice match. Toad, who's the goalkeeper at one end, lets in more goals than anyone else. Seven or eight, one after the other. Every time it happens his face turns completely scarlet and he roars: "Come on now! Let's *turn this thing around*!"

Sami laughs about that every time. This makes Britt-Marie nervous, so she asks:

"Why is he behaving like that?"

"He has a dad who supports Liverpool," Sami answers, without elaboration.

He grabs two cans from the back of the car, and gives one of them to Britt-Marie. "If you have a dad who supports Liverpool you always fucking think you can turn anything around. You know! Ever since that Champions League final."

Britt-Marie sips her soft drink from the can and thinks that, by doing this, she is finally beyond all limits of honor and decency. So she decides she might as well say what she feels:

"I don't want to be unpleasant in any way, Sami, because you have a quite impeccable cutlery drawer. But by and large I find everything you say utterly mystifying!"

Sami guffaws.

"You too, Britt-Marie. You too."

Then he tells her about a soccer game, almost a decade ago, at a time when Vega and Omar were hardly out of their diapers, yet nonetheless sat there with him and Psycho in the pizzeria. Liverpool were up against Milan in the Champions League final. Britt-Marie asks whether this is a competition, and Sami answers that it's a cup, and Britt-Marie asks what a cup is, and Sami says it's a sort of competition, whereupon Britt-Marie points out that he could just have said that from the start instead of giving himself airs and graces.

Sami gives a deep breath, which is not at all a sigh.

Then he explains that Milan were in the lead by 3–0 at half-time, and no team in any final of any soccer competition for as long as Sami can remember had ever been so exposed and outplayed as Liverpool in this match. But in the changing rooms, one of the players from the Liverpool team stood yelling like a madman at the others, because he would not go along with a world where there were certain things that could not be turned around. In the second half he headed in a goal to make it 3–1, then waved his arms like crazy and ran back down the pitch. When his team scored again to make it 3–2 he was on his way to heaven, because he and all the others saw it now, saw that there was an avalanche in motion and no one could stop them from turning it around. Not with walls, moats, and ten thousand wild horses would it be possible to hold them back.

They tied to make it 3–3, survived extra time, then won on penalties.

You can't tell someone with a father who supports Liverpool that everything can't be turned around after that.

He looks at Vega and Omar and smiles.

"Or an older brother, I suppose. It could be an older brother too."

Britt-Marie sips her goalpost. "It sounds almost poetic, the way you describe it."

Sami grins.

"Soccer is poetry for me, you know. I was born in the summer of 1994, right in the middle of the World Cup."

Britt-Marie doesn't have a clue what that's supposed to mean, but she doesn't ask because she thinks there has to be some limit to the anecdotes, even if they happen to be poetic.

"Does Toad's dad come here to watch him play?" she asks.

"He's standing right there," says Sami, pointing at the pizzeria.

Karl stands in the doorway drinking coffee. He has a red cap on his head. Looks almost happy. It's a very remarkable day for Britt-Marie. A remarkable game.

Sven is waiting for her in the pizzeria at the end of the session. He offers her a lift home, but she insists that there's no need. Then he asks her if he can drive her balcony furniture back instead, and at long last she agrees to that. He's carried it out and loaded it and almost got into the driver's seat when she closes her eyes and summons all the energy she has in order to blurt out:

"I have dinner at six."

"Sorry?" says Sven after his head has popped up on the other side of the police car.

She digs her heels into the mud.

"It's not as if I have to have a white tablecloth on the table. But I want cutlery and I want us to eat at six."

"Tomorrow?" he says effervescently.

She nods grimly and gets her list out.

When the police car has disappeared down the road, Vega, Omar, and Sami call out to her from the other side of the parking area. Sami is grinning. Vega shoots the ball all the way across the gravel and mud, and it comes to a stop a few feet away from her. Britt-Marie puts her list in her handbag and holds on to the latter so hard that her knuckles turn white, as you do when you have waited a whole life for something to begin.

Then she takes a few very small steps forward and kicks the soccer ball as hard as she can.

Because she no longer knows how not to.

20

Today is the day after, and it's one of the absolute worst days of Britt-Marie's life. She has a bump on her head and apparently she has broken two fingers. At least that is what Ben's mother tells her, and Ben's mother is a nurse, after all, so Britt-Marie has to assume she is qualified to comment on such matters. They are sitting on a little bench behind a curtain at a hospital in town. Britt-Marie has a Band-Aid on her forehead and her hand in a bandage, and she's doing her absolute utmost not to cry. Ben's mother keeps her hand on her sore wrist, but she doesn't ask how all this happened. Britt-Marie is grateful for that, because she'd rather no one ever found out.

Having said that, this is how it all did happen:

To begin with, Britt-Marie slept all night through for the first time since she had come to Borg. She slept the unreflective sleep of a child, and she woke up in great spirits. Another day. This alone should immediately have made her suspicious, because little good can come of waking up all enthusiastic like that. She leapt out of bed and immediately started cleaning Bank's kitchen. Not because she needed to but rather because Bank wasn't at home and the kitchen was just there when Britt-Marie came down the stairs. Simply put, she had never met a kitchen she did not want to clean. After this was done, she took a walk through Borg to the recreation center. Then cleaned it from top to bottom. Made sure all the pictures were hanging straight, even the ones with soccer balls in them. She stood absolutely still in front of them and looked at her reflection in the glass of the frames.

Then she rubbed the white mark on her ring finger. People who have not worn a wedding ring for almost their entire lives are unaware of how a mark like that looks. Some people take theirs off from time to time—while doing the washing-up, for instance—but Britt-Marie had never once taken off her ring until the day she took it off once and for all. So the white mark is permanent, as if her skin had another color when she was married. As if this is what is left of her, underneath, if you scrape off everything she turned into.

With this thought in mind Britt-Marie set off for the pizzeria, to wake up Somebody. They drank coffee and Britt-Marie inquired in a friendly way about postcards and whether Somebody happened to stock them. Somebody did indeed. They were extremely old and had the caption "Welcome to Borg" written across them. That was how you knew they were old, said Somebody; it was a long time since anyone uttered those words.

Britt-Marie wrote a postcard to Kent. Her message was very short. "Hello. This is from Britt-Marie. Sorry for all the pain I have caused you. I hope you are feeling well. I hope you have clean shirts. Your electric shaver is in the third drawer in the bathroom. If you need to get onto the balcony to polish the windows you have to wiggle the door handle a bit, pull it towards you, and give the door a little shove. There is Faxin in the broom cupboard." She wanted to describe how much she missed him. But didn't. Didn't want to cause any bother.

"Might I ask for directions to the nearest postbox?" she asked Somebody.

"Here," Somebody replied and pointed to the palm of her hand.

Britt-Marie immediately looked skeptical, but Somebody promised that her postal service was "the fastest in town!"

Then the two women had a short discussion about the yellow jersey hanging on the wall in the pizzeria, with the word BANK emblazoned on its back, because Britt-Marie couldn't quite manage to stop looking at it.

As if it was a clue to some mystery. Somebody explained helpfully that Bank did not know it had been hung up there, and if she found out she would probably be so angry that Somebody thought she might behave like a person "with something shoved up her arse, like a whole bloody what's-it-called? Lemon tree orchard!"

"Why?"

"You know, Bank hate soccer, huh! What's-it-called? No one like memories of good time when times are bad, huh?"

"I was under the impression that you and Bank were good friends."

"We are! We were! Best mates before, you know. The whole thing with eyes. Before Bank moved, huh."

"But you never talk about soccer?"

Somebody laughed drily.

"In the old days—Bank loved soccer, huh. Loved more than life. Then this thing with eyes, huh. Eyes took soccer from her, so now she hates soccer. You understand? That's how life is, huh? Love, hate, one or the other. So she went away. Long, long time, huh. Bank's old man not like Bank at all, huh, without soccer they had nothing to, what's-it-called? Converse about! Then the old man died. Bank came here to bury and sell the house, huh. She and me now, we are more like, what's-it-called? Drinking buddies! You could say, we talk less now. Drink more."

"Ha. Might one ask where she went when she left Borg?"

"You know, here and there, when you have lemon in your arse you don't want to sit still, do you?" laughed Somebody.

Britt-Marie didn't laugh. Somebody cleared her throat.

"She was in London, Lisbon, Paris, I got one of them postcards! Have it somewhere, huh. Bank and dog, around the world. You know, sometimes I think she left because she was angry. But sometimes I think she went because this thing with eyes gets worse and worse, you know? Maybe Bank want to see the world before completely blind, you see?"

She found the postcard from Paris. Britt-Marie wanted so badly to hold it in her hand, but she stopped herself. Instead, she tried to distract both Somebody and herself by pointing at the wall and asking:

"Why is the jersey yellow? I was under the impression that soccer jerseys in Borg are white."

"National team."

"Ha. Is that something special?"

"It's . . . national team," said Somebody, as if she found the question odd.

"Is it hard to get into that?"

"It's . . . national team," answered Somebody, looking bemused.

Britt-Marie was annoyed by this, so she didn't ask anything else. Instead she suddenly blurted out, to her own consternation:

"How did it happen? How did Bank lose her sight?"

Not that Britt-Marie is the sort who sticks her nose into other people's business, obviously, but still. She did wake up feeling enthusiastic today, and obviously anything can happen when you do. Her common sense was yelling at her inside, but by then it was already too late.

"Disease. Bloody crap. Came, what's-it-called? Sneaking along! Many years. Like financial crisis . . ."

Somebody's eyebrows sank towards her sweater. "You know, Britt-Marie, people say Bank good *in spite* this thing with the eyes, huh. I say Bank good *because* this thing with her eyes. You understand? Had to fight harder than everyone else. Therefore—she became the best. What's-it-called? Incentive! You understand?"

Britt-Marie wasn't entirely sure that she did. She wanted to take the chance of asking Somebody how it had come to pass that she was in a wheelchair, but at this point the sensible part of Britt-Marie put a stop to things, and in this she was backed up by common practice, because it certainly wasn't seemly to ask questions of this nature. So the conversation tailed off. Whereupon Somebody rolled back one full turn of the wheels, and then forward one turn.

"I fell off one of them boats. When I was small, huh. If you wondering."

"I certainly wasn't wondering!" insisted Britt-Marie.

"I know, Britt, I know," said Somebody, grinning. "You don't have prejudice. You get that I am human, huh. Happen to have the wheelchair. I not wheelchair that happens to have human in it, huh." She patted Britt-Marie on the arm and added: "That is why I like you, Britt. You are also human."

Britt-Marie wanted to say she also liked Somebody, but she was sensible about it.

So they didn't say anything else. Britt-Marie bought a Snickers for the rat and asked if Somebody happened to know of anywhere that sold flowers.

"Flower? For who?"

"For Bank. It strikes me as impolite when I am renting a room from her for all this time that I have never offered her so much as a flower, it's common practice to give flowers."

"But Bank likes beer! Take her beer instead, huh?"

Britt-Marie didn't find this very civilized, but she accepted that beer might be a little like flowers to someone who liked beer. She insisted on Somebody finding a bit of cellophane, which Somebody failed to do, but after a few minutes Omar showed up in the doorway and cried: "You need cellophane? I have some! Special price for a friend!"

Because that is clearly how things happen in Borg.

With this cellophane, which came at a price that Britt-Marie was certainly not prepared to categorize as very friendly at all, Britt-Marie wrapped up a can of beer to make it look decorative, with a little bow at the top and everything. Then she went to the recreation center, left the front door ajar, and put a plate with the Snickers on the threshold. Next to the plate she put a note, written neatly in ink: "Out on a date. Or a meeting. Or whatever it's called nowadays. No need to put away your plate when you have finished, it's no trouble at all for me." She wanted to write something about how she hoped the rat would find someone else to share its dinner with, because she did not feel the rat deserved to eat alone. Loneliness is a waste of both rats and people. But her common sense ordered her not to get involved in the rat's personal choices about social relationships, so she left it at that.

She turned off the lights and waited for dusk, because, conveniently enough, at this time of year the sun set well in advance of dinnertime. Once she had made sure that no one could see her, she briskly set off for the bus stop on the road leading out of Borg in two directions and left in one of those two available directions on a bus. It felt like an adventure. Like freedom. Not to the extent that she was unconcerned about the state of the seat, obviously, so she tidily spread four white napkins over it before sitting down. You had to have some limits, after all, even when you were out adventuring.

But in spite of all: it felt like something new, traveling on a bus on her own.

All the way, she rubbed the white mark on her ring finger.

The tanning salon next to the cash machine in the town was deserted. Britt-Marie followed the instructions on a machine that told her to put coins in it. Its display started flashing, and then half a dozen large fluorescent tubes in the hard plastic bed turned themselves on.

Britt-Marie is no connoisseur when it comes to solariums, and as a result she was possibly not very familiar with the basic functions of the machine. Her idea had been to sit on a stool next to the lit-up bed, sticking her hand into the light, and gently closing the lid on top of it. How long she would have to sit there bronzing her hand into one without a white mark on it she did not know, but she imagined that the process could not be more elaborate than cooking salmon in the oven. Her plan was to simply remove her hand now and then and see how it was all going.

It must have been something to do with the soporific humming of the machine, perhaps, as well as the heat of it, especially as she had gone around all day being enthusiastic—that was how it happened. Her head slumped, as one's head has a way of doing when one goes to sleep on a stool, and then her forehead struck the lid of the tanning machine very hard, and her hand got horribly twisted under the lid. She rolled onto the floor and passed out, and now she's in the hospital. With a bump on her head and broken fingers.

Ben's mother is sitting next to her, patting her on the arm.

The cleaning staff found her, and this makes Britt-Marie even more indignant, because everyone knows how cleaning staff gossip at their meetings.

"Don't be upset, things like this happen to the best of us," whispers Ben's mother encouragingly.

"No, they don't," says Britt-Marie, so that her voice cracks. She slips off the bench. Ben's mother holds out her hand but Britt-Marie glides away. "Enough people in Borg are giving up, Britt-Marie. Don't become one of them, please."

Britt-Marie may want to retort something, but humiliation and common sense compel her to leave the room. The children from the soccer team are sitting in the waiting room. Quite decimated, Britt-Marie avoids their eyes. This is something new to her—the feeling of having yearned for something, only to collapse on the ground. Britt-Marie is not used to hoping.

So she walks past the children and wishes with all her heart that they were not here.

Sven is waiting with his cap in his hands. He has brought a little basket with baguettes in it.

"Well, ah, I thought that . . . well, I thought you wouldn't want to go to the restaurant now . . . after all this, so I made a picnic. I thought . . . but, yeah, maybe you'd rather just go home. Of course." Britt-Marie shuts her eyes hard and holds her bandaged hand behind her back. He looks down into his basket.

"I bought the baguettes but I wove the basket myself."

Britt-Marie sucks her cheeks in and bites them. There's no way Sven and the children knew what she was doing in the salon, but this makes her feel all the more ridiculous. So she whispers:

"Please, Sven, I just want to go home."

So Sven drives her to Bank's house, even though she wishes he wouldn't. And wishes he'd never seen her like this. She hides her hand under the bamboo screen and more than anything she'd like to be taken back to her proper home. Her real life. And be dropped off there. She's not ready for enthusiasm.

He tries to say something when they stop, but she gets out before he has time. He's still standing outside his police car with his cap in his hands when she closes the front door. She stands motionless on the other side, holding her breath until he leaves.

She cleans Bank's house from top to bottom. Has soup for dinner, alone. Then slowly walks up the stairs, fetches a towel, and sits on the side of the bed.

Bank comes home spectacularly drunk somewhere between midnight and dawn. She is carrying a pizza box from Somebody's pizzeria, and is singing songs so uncivilized that they'd make a sailor blush. Britt-Marie sits on the balcony and the dog seems to look up at her, establishing eye contact as Bank stands there swearing and fidgeting with the key in the lock. The dog almost appears to shrug its shoulders in weary resignation. Britt-Marie can empathize.

The first thump from downstairs is the sound of a picture frame being knocked off the wall by Bank's stick. The second thump is followed by a splintering sound, when the frame hits the floor and the sheet of glass on a photograph of a soccer-playing girl and her father is broken and scatters all over the floor. This continues methodically for almost an hour. Bank wanders about on the ground floor, here and there, then here again, smashing all her memories, not furiously and violently but with the simple, systematic approach of grief. One by one the pictures are broken, until only empty walls and abandoned nails remain. Britt-Marie sits motionless on the balcony and wishes she could call the police. But she doesn't have Sven's telephone number.

And then finally the noise stops. Britt-Marie stays on the balcony until she realizes Bank must have given up and gone to sleep. Shortly afterwards she hears soft steps on the stairs, a creak of her door, and then feels something touching the tips of her fingers. The dog's nose. It lies beside her, sufficiently far away not to be intrusive, but close enough for each to sense the other's presence in case of movement. After that everything is quiet until morning comes to Borg, to the extent that morning comes at all to Borg.

When Britt-Marie and the dog finally dare to come downstairs, Bank is sitting on the floor in the hall, leaning against the wall. She smells of alcohol. Britt-Marie doesn't know if she's sleeping, but she's certainly not about to lift her sunglasses to check, so instead she just fetches a broom and starts sweeping up the glass. Collects all the photographs and puts them in a neat pile. Stacks the frames one against the other in a corner. Gives the dog breakfast.

Bank is still not moving by the time Britt-Marie puts on her coat and makes sure she has her list in her handbag, but Britt-Marie nonetheless collects herself and puts the beer next to her and says:

"This is a present. I should like to insist that you don't drink it today, because it seems to me that you had quite enough yesterday, and if you're ever to smell like a civilized person again you'll need a bath in baking soda and vanilla extract, but don't think I'm trying to stick my nose into your business."

Bank is sitting so still that Britt-Marie has to lean forward to assure herself that she is breathing. The fact that Bank's breath seems to be burning off the surface of Britt-Marie's retinas indicates that she's doing exactly that. Britt-Marie blinks and straightens up and suddenly hears herself saying the following:

"I suppose I have to assume you're not the sort of person whose father was a supporter of Liverpool. You see, I've been informed that anyone whose father supported Liverpool never gives up. . . .

Or an older brother. As I understand it, in some cases the same thing also goes for an older brother who supports Liverpool."

She stands on the front porch and has all but closed the front door behind her when she hears Bank mumbling from inside the gloom:

"Dad was a Tottenham supporter."

Somebody is sitting in the kitchen of the pizzeria and smelling just like Bank, though her mood is a good deal better. If she notices Britt-Marie's bandaged hand she certainly says nothing about it. She hands Britt-Marie a letter that "some bloke from town" apparently brought in.

"Something about that soccer coach. 'For the attention of the coach.' "

"Ha," says Britt-Marie. She reads the paper without properly understanding what it means—something about "the need for registration" and "a license."

She is far too busy to concern herself with some silly letter, so she stuffs it in her bag and sets about serving coffee to the men with caps and beards, who have their heads buried in their newspapers. She doesn't ask for the crossword supplements and they don't offer her any either. Karl picks up a parcel and has some coffee. When he's done, he takes his cup to the counter, nods at Britt-Marie without looking at her and mumbles, "Thanks, that was nice."

Britt-Marie's common sense prevents her from asking what he could possibly be getting in the post all the time, which is probably just as well. Those parcels could have anything in them. Maybe he's building a bomb. That's the sort of thing you read about. Admittedly Karl seems a taciturn sort of man who mostly keeps himself to himself and doesn't bother other people, but in fact this is precisely the sort of person neighbors describe whenever a bit of bomb-making has been going on.

Crossword puzzle writers like bombs, so Britt-Marie knows all about it.

Sami and Psycho come in after lunch. Psycho lingers by the door, with something doleful in his eyes as he scans the premises, apparently looking for something he's lost. Britt-Marie must be visibly unsettled by this, because Sami gives her a calming look and then turns to Psycho and says:

"Can you go and check if I left my phone in the car?"

"Why?" asks Psycho.

"Because I'm fucking asking you to!"

Psycho does something with his lips as if he's spitting without any saliva in his mouth. The door tinkles cheerfully behind him. Sami turns to Britt-Marie.

"Did you win?"

Britt-Marie stares at him, nonplussed. His face cracks open in a purposeful grin as he points at her bandaged fingers:

"Looks like you've been in a fight. What kind of state did you leave the other lady in?"

"I'll have you know it was an accident," protests Britt-Marie, praying she'll be able to avoid going into the details.

"Okay, Coach, okay," laughs Sami, with a flurry of play punches in the air. He produces a bag, gets out three soccer jerseys from it, and puts them on the counter. "This is Vega, Omar, and Dino's kit. I've washed them over and over, but some of the stains won't bloody go away whatever I do."

"Have you tried baking soda?"

"Would that help?"

Britt-Marie has to grab hold of the register to contain her enthusiasm.

"I . . . it's . . . I can try to get rid of the stains for you. It's no trouble at all!"

Sami nods gratefully.

"Thanks, Coach. I could do with a few pointers. I mean the stains on these kids' clothes, anyone would think they live in the fucking trees."

Britt-Marie waits until he has left with Psycho before she goes to the recreation center. The stains do go away with baking soda. She also washes towels and aprons for Somebody, even though Somebody insists there's no need. Not that Somebody has a problem with Britt-Marie doing the washing for her; it's more because she really doesn't think the laundry needs doing. They have a brief dispute about this. Somebody calls Britt-Marie "Mary Poppins" again and Britt-Marie retorts that she's a "filthy little piglet." Somebody bursts out laughing about this, at which point the argument runs out of steam.

Britt-Marie puts out some Snickers for the rat. She doesn't wait until it appears, because she doesn't want to explain how things went with her date. Not that she's sure the rat will be keen to know about it, but either way she's not ready to talk about it yet. Afterwards, she goes back to the pizzeria to have her dinner with Somebody, because Somebody seems to care either too little or too much about Britt-Marie to ask.

Sven doesn't pass by the pizzeria that evening, but Britt-Marie catches herself leaping out of her chair, and also her heart racing, every time there's a tinkle from the door. It wouldn't have annoyed her even if he showed up in the middle of their meal. But it's never Sven. Just one or other of the children, until they're all assembled, with crisp, clean soccer jerseys, because the children seem to have someone at home taking care of that.

This fills Britt-Marie with a sort of hope for Borg. That there are still people here who understand the value of a freshly washed soccer jersey.

The children are on their way out to start their training when the boy turns up in the doorway. He is wearing his tracksuit top with HOCKEY written on it, but there's no sign of his dad.

"What the hell are you doing here?" Vega wants to know.

The boy pushes his hands deep into his pockets and nods at the soccer ball in her hands.

"I was hoping to play with you—can I?"

"You can clear off to town and play there!" hisses Vega.

The boy's chin is resting against his collarbone, but he doesn't back off.

"The soccer team in town trains at six o'clock. That's when I have my hockey training. But I noticed that you train later. . . ."

Britt-Marie has a clear perception of needing to defend that decision, so she says:

"You actually can't train in the middle of dinner!"

"Not in the middle of hockey either," says the boy.

"You don't belong here, bloody rich kid," sneers Vega as she elbows past him. "We're not as good as the team in town, anyway, so why don't you clear off and play with them if you want to play soccer!"

Still he doesn't back off. She stops. He raises his chin.

"I couldn't give a shit if you're good. I just want to play. That's how a team is made."

Vega pushes her way outside with a choice of words that, as far as Britt-Marie is concerned, is far from civilized, but Omar gives the boy a soft shove in the back and says:

"If you can get the ball off her you're in. I don't think you've got the guts to do it, though."

The boy has rushed across the parking area before the sentence comes to an end. Vega elbows him in the face. He stumbles onto his knees with blood in his nostrils, but at the same time he sticks out his foot and scoops out the ball, in a long hook. Vega falls and scrapes her entire body through the gravel, a warlike expression in her eyes. Omar nudges Britt-Marie, standing in the pizzeria doorway, and points at them with excitement: "Check it out now, when Vega gives him, like, the worst sliding tackle!"

"What does that mean?" asks Britt-Marie, but she soon finds out when Vega darts across the pitch and, a few feet behind the boy, catapults herself through the air with both legs stretched out, sliding across the gravel until she collides with the boy's feet, and sends his body into a wild half somersault through the gloom.

That is how Britt-Marie comes to realize why all the children in Borg have jeans that are ripped across their thighs. Vega stands up and puts her foot on the ball in a gesture not so much of ownership but of domination. The boy brushes himself off a bit, displaying an alarming need for baking soda, and digs sharp pebbles out of the skin of his face. Vega looks at Britt-Marie, shrugs her shoulders, and snorts:

"He's okay."

Britt-Marie gets out the list from her handbag.

"Would you be good enough to state your name?" she asks.

"Max," says the boy.

Omar, with great seriousness, points first at Vega and then at Max.

"You *cannot* play in the same team when we're playing two-goals!"

Then they do the Idiot. Play two-goals. And they are a team. Sami couldn't come tonight to light up the field with his headlights, but there's another vehicle in the same place with its headlights turned on. It's Karl's truck, with such an impressive amount of rust down its sides it seems unlikely that such a length of time could have passed since the invention of trucks.

22

When the woman and the man in the red car stop at the far end of the parking area, neither Britt-Marie nor the children react at first, because they're starting to get used to new players and spectators turning up at Borg soccer team's training sessions as if it was the most natural thing in the world. Only when Max points at them and says, "They're from town, aren't they? She's the head of the district soccer association. My dad knows her," does play stop and the players and coach wait suspiciously for the strangers to present themselves.

"Are you Britt-Marie?" asks the woman as she comes closer.

She is neatly dressed, as is the man. The red car is extremely clean, notes Britt-Marie with an initial sense of approval from her old life, which is quickly replaced by an instinctual skepticism that she has picked up in Borg for all things that seem neat and clean. "I am," answers Britt-Marie.

"I dropped off a document for you earlier today, have you had time to look through it?" asks the woman, with a gesture at the pizzeria.

"Ha. Ha. No, no, I haven't. I have been otherwise engaged."

The woman looks at the children. Then at Britt-Marie.

"It's about the rules of the competition, the January Cup, for which this . . . *team* . . . has been entered."

She says the word "team" in much the same way as Britt-Marie says "cup" when she's got a plastic mug in her hand.

"Ha," says Britt-Marie, picking up her notebook and pen, as if arming herself.

"You are named as the soccer coach in the application. Do you have a license for that?"

"I beg your pardon?" says Britt-Marie, while at the same time writing "license" in her notebook.

"*License*," the woman repeats, pointing at the man beside her as if he was someone Britt-Marie ought to recognize: "The District Soccer Association and the County Council only allow teams to participate in the January Cup if they have a coach with a local authority coaching license."

Britt-Marie writes, "Acquire local authority coaching license" in her notebook.

"Ha. Might I trouble you to tell me how I can get my hands on such a license? I will immediately see to it that my contact at the unemployment office ensures th—"

"But good Lord, it's not something you just *pick up*! You have to do an entire *course* in it!" the man next to the woman in front of the red car bursts out a touch hysterically.

Angrily he waves his hand over the parking area. "You're not a proper team! You don't even have a pitch to train on!"

At this stage Vega gets fed up, because Vega's patience is quite clearly of the very shortest kind, and she hisses back at him:

"Hey, you miserable old sod, are we playing soccer here or not?"

"What?" says the old sod.

"Are you deaf? I said: are we playing bloody soccer here or are we bloody not?" roars Vega.

"Well?" says the old sod with a mocking smile, throwing out his arms.

"If we're playing soccer here then it *is* a bloody soccer pitch," Vega establishes.

The old sod looks at Britt-Marie in shock, as if he feels she ought to say something. Britt-Marie actually feels this would not be so appropriate, because just for once, apart from her use of language, she feels that Vega is absolutely right. So she stays silent. The woman next to the old sod clears her throat.

"There's an absolutely excellent soccer club in town, I'm quite sure that—"

"We have an absolutely excellent soccer club here!" Vega interrupts.

The woman is breathing spasmodically through her nostrils.

"We have to have rules and regulations for the January Cup. Otherwise more or less anyone could turn up and play. That would be chaotic, you have to understand that. If you don't have an accredited trainer we can't let you participate, unfortunately; in that case you'll have to reapply next year and then we'll process the—"

The voice that interrupts her, somewhere in the dark between the red car and Karl's truck, is hungover and in no mood to be talked back to, this much is amply clear.

"I have a license. Write my name on the paper if it's so damned important."

The woman stares at Bank. All the others do the same. Where Bank is staring, without being at all prejudicial about it, is unclear. But the dog is at least looking at Britt-Marie. Britt-Marie peers back at it shiftily, as a conspiring criminal type might do.

"Good God, is *she* back in Borg?" hisses the old codger to the woman as soon as he catches sight of Bank.

"Shush!" shushes the woman.

Bank steps out of the shadows and waves her stick in the direction of the woman and the old codger, so that she accidentally strikes the old codger quite hard on his thigh. Twice.

"Oh, dear," Bank says apologetically, then points the stick at the woman.

"Put my name down. I suppose you haven't forgotten it," she says, and happens to strike the old codger fairly hard across one of his arms three or possibly four times.

"I didn't even know you were back in Borg," the woman says with a cold smile.

"Now you do."

"We . . . I mean . . . the regulations of the competition stipulate that . . ." the woman tries to say.

Bank groans, loud and hungover.

"Shut your mouth will you, Annika, just shut your mouth. The kids just want to play. There used to be a time when we also just wanted to play, and old blokes like this one tried to stop us."

Bank thrusts her stick in the direction of the old sod when she says that last bit, but this time he manages to jump out of the way. The woman stands there for a good while, and seems to be pondering a variety of answers. She looks younger and younger for every moment that passes. She opens her mouth, then closes it again. Finally, in a resigned sort of way, she writes down Bank's name in her papers. The old sod is still spitting and hissing when they get into the red car and leave Borg behind as they head back to town.

Bank doesn't waste any time on superficialities. In her hungover condition, her patience seems comparable to Vega's. She waves her stick menacingly at the children and mutters:

"If you're not blind you must have noticed by now that I am, pretty well. But I have no need to watch you play to get the fact that you're useless. We have a few days until their idiotic cup, so we have to use that time as well as we can to make you as un-useless as possible."

She thinks about this for a moment and then adds:

"You should probably keep your expectations low."

It's not an excellent pep talk, far from it. Possibly, Britt-Marie has a sense that she liked Bank better when she hardly did any talking. But of course Omar is the first of them to drum up enough courage to disagree with her, partly because he dares say what the whole team is thinking, and partly because he's dumb enough to do it.

"Shit! Fat chance we've got with a blind coach!"

Britt-Marie clasps her hands together.

"You're not supposed to say things like that, Omar. It's incredibly uncivilized."

"She's blind! What can she know about soccer?"

"It's actually more a case of impaired vision," Britt-Marie points out, adding with a slight note of outrage: "It has nothing to do with corpulence."

Omar swears. Bank just nods calmly. She points her stick at the soccer ball with a precision that makes even Omar feel slightly caught out.

"Give the ball here," she says, and at the same time whistles to her dog. The dog shuffles off at once and positions itself immediately behind Omar.

Omar's eyes flick nervously between the dog behind him and Bank in front of him.

"Right . . . what I . . . hold on, I didn't mean . . ."

Bank runs forward with a surprising turn of speed to claim the ball. At the same time the dog, behind Omar, places itself with its legs wide apart and starts peeing. The dog pee forms itself into a neat, round puddle in the gravel. Bank's foot caresses the leather soccer ball and makes a sudden movement as if about to kick it hard at Omar's head. He ducks and throws himself back, startled, stumbling over the dog and stepping neatly into the puddle.

Bank stops abruptly with her foot on the ball. Points with her stick at Omar and mutters:

"At least I know what a dummy shot is. And even if I'm almost blind I'd bet quite a lot of money you're standing in dog pee right now. So maybe we could agree that at least I know more about soccer than you do?"

Vega stands at the edge of the wee pool, fascinated by all this.

"How did you teach the dog to do that?"

Bank whistles for the dog. Scratches its nose. Opens her jacket pocket and lets it have what's inside.

"The dog knows lots of tricks. I had it before I went blind. I know how to train things."

Britt-Marie is already on her way to the recreation center to fetch baking soda.

When she comes back to the parking area, the children are playing soccer so you can hear it. It has to be experienced before you can understand it, the difference between silent and nonsilent soccer. Britt-Marie stops in the darkness and listens. Every time one of the children gets the ball, their teammates are shouting: "Here! I'm here!"

"If you can be heard then you exist," mutters hungover Bank, massaging her temples.

The children play. Call out. Explain where they are. Britt-Marie squeezes her container of baking soda until it has dents in it.

"I'm here," she whispers, wishing that Sven was here so she could tell him.

It's a remarkable club. A remarkable game.

They part ways at the end of the training session. Toad goes back with his dad in the truck, Sami picks up Vega, Omar, and Dino. Max wanders home on his own, along the road. Ben is met by his mother. She waves at Britt-Marie and Britt-Marie waves back. Bank doesn't say a word on the way home and Britt-Marie feels it's inappropriate to challenge destiny. Above all she does not believe it is appropriate to challenge a stick that has been both in the mud and inside at least one person's mouth this evening. So she makes do with silence.

Back at the house, Bank opens the cellophane around the beer and drinks it straight from the bottle. Britt-Marie goes and fetches a glass and a coaster.

"Enough's enough, actually," she says firmly to Bank.

"You're a bloody nag-bag, did anyone ever tell you that?"

"Many times," says Britt-Marie and, depending on what sort of system you are using, you could say that Britt-Marie finds her second real girlfriend tonight.

On her way to the stairs, she changes her mind, turns around, and asks:

"You said your father supports Tottenham. If it's not too much trouble, what does that mean?"

Bank drinks her beer from the glass. Slumps in her chair. The dog lays its head in her lap.

"If you support Tottenham you always give more love than you get back," she says.

Britt-Marie cups her uninjured hand over the bandage on the other. There's certainly an awful lot of unnecessary complication about liking soccer.

"I assume what you mean by that is that it's a bad team."

The corners of Bank's mouth bounce up.

"Tottenham is the worst kind of bad team, because they're almost good. They always promise that they're going to be fantastic. They make you hope. So you go on loving them and they carry on finding more and more innovative ways of disappointing you."

Britt-Marie nods as if this sounded reasonable. Bank stands up and states:

"In that sense his daughter was always like his favorite team."

She puts the empty bottle on the kitchen counter and, without relying on the stick, walks past Britt-Marie into the living room.

"The beer was nice. Thanks."

Britt-Marie sits on the edge of her bed for hours that evening. She stands on the balcony, waiting for a police car. Then back to the bed. She doesn't cry, isn't despondent; in fact it's almost the other way around. She's almost eager. Just doesn't know what to do with herself. Like a sort of restlessness. The windows are polished, the floors have been scoured, and the balcony furniture wiped down. She's poured baking soda into the flowerpots and onto the mattress. She rubs the fingers of her uninjured hand across the bandages that cover the white mark that used to be covered by the wedding ring. So in a way she did achieve the desired result of her visit to the tanning salon, even if not in the exact way she had thought. Nothing has gone as she thought it would since she came to Borg.

For the first time since she got here, she accepts it may not be something altogether bad.

When she hears the knock at the front door she has been hoping for it for so long that at first she thinks it must be a figment of her imagination. But then there's another knock, and Britt-Marie jumps out of bed and stumbles down the stairs like a complete lunatic. It's obviously not at all like her, highly uncivilized in every possible way. She has not run down the stairs like this since she was a teenager, when your heart reaches the front door before your feet. For a moment she stops and summons all the common sense at her disposal, in order to fix her hair and adjust all the invisible creases in her skirt.

"Sven! I . . ." she has time to say, holding on to the door handle.

Then she just stands there. Trying, but failing, to breathe. She feels her legs giving way beneath her.

"Hello, my darling," says Kent.

23

Sweet boys don't get to kiss pretty girls," Britt-Marie's mother sometimes used to say. Even though what she really meant was that pretty girls should not kiss sweet boys, because when dealing with sweet boys there's absolutely no certainty of being able to look forward to a reliable income.

"We have to pray that Britt-Marie finds a man who can support her, otherwise she'll have to live in the gutter, because she has absolutely no talents of her own," Britt-Marie used to hear her mother say into the telephone. "I got her for my sins," she also used to say, into the telephone if she was drunk, or pointedly at Britt-Marie after tippling sherry.

It's impossible to be good enough for a parent after losing a sister who, in all important respects, was a better version of yourself. Britt-Marie did try, nonetheless. But with a father who came home later and later and, in the end, not at all, she did not have very many options. Instead, Britt-Marie learned not to have any expectations of her own, and to put up with her mother's skepticism about her prospects.

Alf and Kent lived on the same floor, and they fought, as brothers tend to do. Sooner or later they both wanted the same girl. Whether they wanted Britt-Marie because they really did want her, or because brothers always want what their brother wants, she was never quite sure. If Ingrid had been there they would have courted her instead, Britt-Marie had no illusions about that. You tend not to if you're used to living in someone's shadow. But the boys were persistent, competed, fought for her attention in very different ways.

One of the brothers was too insensitive to her, always going on about how much money he was going to make; the other was too kind. Britt-Marie didn't want to disappoint her mother, so she chose Alf and ruled out Kent.

Kent stood in the stairwell with flowers in his hands and his eyes closed when she walked off with his brother. By the time she came back, he had gone.

She was only with Alf for a short length of time. He was weary, she remembers. Already bored. Like a victor after the adrenaline has worn off. One morning he left her to go and do his military service and was gone for months.

The morning that he was due back, Britt-Marie spent hours in front of the mirror for the first time in her life and tried on a new dress. Her mother gave her a look, and said:

"I see you're trying to make yourself look cheap. Well, mission accomplished." Britt-Marie tried to explain that this was modern. Her mother told her not to raise her voice, it made her sound very ordinary. Britt-Marie tried to gently explain that she wanted to surprise Alf at the train station, and her mother snorted: "Oh, he'll be surprised all right." She was right.

Britt-Marie turned up in an old dress and with sweaty hands and her heart clattering like horse's hooves on cobblestones. Obviously she had heard the stories of how soldiers have a girl in every town, she had just never thought this would be true of Alf. At least she'd never thought he'd have two girls in the same town.

She'd been sitting all night in the kitchen weeping into a towel when her mother finally got out of bed and scolded her for making too much noise. Britt-Marie told her about the other girl she'd seen Alf with. "Ha, what did you expect when you picked a man like that?" hissed her mother before going back to bed. She got up later than usual the following day. In the end she didn't get up at all. Britt-Marie found a job as a waitress instead of getting herself an education, so she could take care of things at home. Brought dinner into the bedroom for her mother, who had stopped talking, yet was capable now and then of sitting up in the bed and saying, "Ha, working as a waitress—it must be nice for you not to feel you owe more to your parents after all the advantages we've given you. I don't suppose any education was good enough for you, you obviously prefer to stay here at home and live off my savings instead."

The flat grew increasingly quiet. And finally absolutely silent. Britt-Marie polished the windows and waited for something new to begin.

One day, Kent was just standing there on the landing. The day after her mother's funeral. He spoke of his divorce and his children.

Britt-Marie had been hoping for so long that she thought this must be a figment of her imagination, and when he smiled at her it felt like sunlight on her skin. She made his dreams her own. His life became her life. She was good at this, and people want to do the things they're good at. People want someone to know they are there.

Now Kent stands in her doorway in Borg, holding flowers. He smiles. Sunlight on her skin. It's hard not to want to go back to your normal life once you know how difficult it is to start again.

"Were you waiting for someone?" asks Kent insecurely, and once again he is like that boy on the landing.

Britt-Marie shakes her head in shock. He smiles.

"I got your postcard. And I . . . well . . . the accountant checked your cash withdrawals," he says almost with embarrassment and gestures at the road towards town.

When Britt-Marie doesn't know what to say he goes on:

"I asked for you in the pizzeria. That woman in the wheelchair didn't want to say where you were, but a couple of old blokes drinking coffee there were pretty keen to tell me. Do you know them?"

"No," whispers Britt-Marie, unsure whether he's making that up.

Kent holds out the flowers.

"Darling . . . I . . . damn it, I'm sorry! Me, her, that woman, it never meant a thing. It's over. You're the one I love. Damn it. Darling!"

Britt-Marie looks with concern at the stick he's using to prop himself up.

"What on earth's happened to you?"

He waves dismissively at her.

"Ah, don't make a fuss about that, the doctors just wanted me to have it for a while after the heart attack, that's all. The chassis has rusted up a bit, after it's been parked up in the garage for half the winter!" He grins, with a nod at his legs.

She wants to hold his hand.

It doesn't feel natural to have to invite him in. It never did, not even when they were teenagers. At her mother's she wasn't allowed to bring boys into the bedroom, so the first time Britt-Marie brought a boy in there, it was Kent. After her mother's death. That boy stayed. Made her home his own and his life hers. So now it seems very natural to them both to be driving around Borg in their BMW, because in many ways they were always at their best when they were in the car. He in the driver's seat, she the passenger. At this moment they can pretend they have only been passing through, and leave Borg, as you do with places you send postcards from.

They drive into town and back. Kent keeps his hand on the gear-stick, so that Britt-Marie can carefully reach out with the tips of her fingers of the hand that is not injured, and put them on top of his. Just to feel that they are both heading in the same direction. His shirt is creased and has coffee stains over his stomach. Britt-Marie remembers Sami talking about how some children look as if they live in the trees, and Kent does look as if he fell out of a tree in his sleep, hitting every branch on his way down. He smiles apologetically.

"I couldn't find that blasted iron, darling. There's no order to anything when you're not at home. You know that."

Britt-Marie doesn't answer. She's worrying about what people will think. Will they say he had a wife who left him while he was walking about with a stick and everything? Her ring finger feels cold, and she's infinitely grateful for the bandage, which stops Kent seeing it. She knows he let her down, but she can't get away from the feeling that she also let him down. What is love worth if you leave someone when he needs you the most?

Kent coughs and takes his foot off the accelerator, although the road lies empty ahead of them.

Britt-Marie has never seen him slow down for no particular reason.

"The doctors say I haven't been so well. For a long time, I mean. I haven't been myself. I've been given some darned tablets, antidepressants or whatever they're called."

The way he says it is the same as when he's talking about his plans, as if they are all a foregone conclusion.

As if what made him come home late smelling of pizza was nothing but a production fault, perfectly easy to mend. Now everything is fine.

She wants to ask why he never called her, after all she had a cell phone with her. But she realizes he would have assumed she couldn't switch it on. So she stays quiet about it. He peers out of the window as they drive back into Borg.

"Darned strange place for you to end up in, isn't it? What was it your mum used to call the countryside? 'Sheer mediocrity'? She was darned funny, your mum. And it is a bit ironic that you should end up in the sticks out here, isn't it? You, who hardly put your foot outside our flat in forty years!"

He says it as a joke. She can't quite accept it in that spirit. But when they stop outside Bank's house he's breathing so heavily that she can hear the pain he's in. His tears are the first she's ever seen in his eyes. There were no tears there even when he buried his own mother, while clutching Britt-Marie's hand.

"It's over. With her. That woman. She never meant a thing. Not like you, Britt-Marie."

He holds the fingers of her unscathed hand, caresses them gently, and says in a low voice:

"I need you at home, darling. I need you there. Don't throw away a whole life we've lived together just because I made one stupid mistake!"

Britt-Marie brushes invisible crumbs from his shirt. Breathes in the fragrance of the flowers in her arms.

"Boys are not allowed in my bedroom. Not then and not now either," she whispers.

He laughs out loud. Her skin is burning.

"Tomorrow?" he calls out behind her as she's getting out of the car.

She nods.

Because life is more than the shoes your feet are in. More than the person you are. It's the togetherness. The parts of yourself in another. Memories and walls and cupboards and drawers with compartments for cutlery, so you know where everything is.

A life of adaptation towards a perfect organization, a streamlined existence based on two personalities. A shared life of everything that's normal. Cement and stone, remote controls and crosswords, shirts and baking soda, bathroom cabinets and electric shavers in the third drawer. He needs her for all that. If she's not there, nothing is as it should be.

She goes up to her room. Opens drawers. Folds towels.

The cell phone rings, the display showing the number of the girl from the unemployment office, but Britt-Marie declines the call. Sits on her own on the balcony all night. With her packed bags next to her.

24

"You look at me as if you're judging me. I should like to inform you that I don't appreciate it at all," Britt-Marie affirms. When she doesn't get an answer, she continues more diplomatically:

"It may not be your intention to look at me as if you're judging me, but that is how it feels."

When she still gets no answer, she sits down on a stool with her hands clasped together in her lap, and points out:

"I should like to point out that the towel has been left where it is so you can wipe your paws on it. Not as a decoration."

The rat eats some Snickers. Doesn't say anything. But Britt-Marie senses she is being judged. She snorts defensively.

"Love doesn't necessarily have to be fireworks and symphony orchestras for every human being, I do believe you can look at it like that. For some of us, love can be other things. Sensible things!"

The rat eats Snickers. Makes a foray over the towel. Goes back to the Snickers.

"Kent is my husband. I am his wife. I'm certainly not going to sit here and be lectured by a rat," Britt-Marie clarifies. Then she collects her thoughts a bit, switches her hands around, and adds:

"Not that there's anything wrong with that, of course. Being a rat. I'm sure it's quite excellent."

The rat makes no attempt to be anything but a rat. Britt-Marie's next words come out in a long exhalation.

"It's just that I've been a melancholic for a long time, you have to understand."

The rat eats Snickers. The children play soccer in the parking area outside the recreation center. Britt-Marie sees Kent's BMW through the doorway. He's playing with the children. They like him; everyone likes Kent when they first meet him. It takes years to see his bad side. With Britt-Marie it's the other way around.

In fact she doesn't know if "melancholic" is the right word. She looks for a better expression, as in a crossword. Vertical: "Dejected individual." "As felt by a non-happy person." Or possibly: "Greek for black, followed by stomachache."

"Maybe 'heavyhearted' would be a better word," she tells the rat.

She has been feeling heavyhearted for a long time now.

"It may seem ludicrous to you, but in some ways I've had less time to be heavyhearted in Borg than I did at home. . . . It's not as if I've been forced into the life I've lived. I could have made changes. I could have found myself some employment," says Britt-Marie, and she can hear that she's actually defending Kent rather than herself.

But on the other hand it's quite true. She could have found herself a job. It was just that Kent thought it would be good if she waited awhile. Just a year or so. Who else would take care of everything at home, he asked, and by his way of asking it was clear to her that he wasn't volunteering to do it himself.

So after waiting at home with her mother for a few years, Britt-Marie waited at home with Kent's children for a few years, and then Kent's mother became ill and Britt-Marie waited at home with her quite a bit for another few years. Kent felt it was best that way, obviously just during a transitional period until all of Kent's plans had fallen into place, and, of course, it was best for the whole family if Britt-Marie was at home in the afternoons in case the Germans wanted to have dinner. When he said "the whole family" he was obviously referring to everyone in the family except Britt-Marie. "Corporate entertainment is tax-deductible," Kent always explained, but he never explained who would benefit by it.

A year turned into several years, and several years turned into all the years. One morning you wake up with more life behind you than in front of you, not being able to understand how it's happened.

"I could have found myself employment. It was my choice to stay at home. I'm not a victim," Britt-Marie points out.

She doesn't say anything about how close she got. She went to job interviews. Several of them. She didn't tell Kent about them, obviously, because he would only have asked what salary she'd get, and if she had told him he would have laughed and said: "Isn't it bloody better, then, if I pay you to stay at home?" He would have meant that as a joke, but she would not have been able to take it in that spirit, and so, as a result, she never said anything. She was always there in good time for the interviews, and there was always someone else waiting there in the visitors' room. Almost exclusively young women. One of them started talking to Britt-Marie, because she couldn't imagine that someone so old was there for the same job as herself. She had three children and had been left by her husband. One of the children had an illness. When she was called in for her interview, Britt-Marie stood up and went home. You could say a lot of things about Britt-Marie, but she was certainly not someone who'd steal a job from someone more in need of it.

Obviously she doesn't tell the rat about this; she doesn't want to make herself out to be some sort of martyr. And then, of course, you never know what sort of life experiences the rat has had.

Maybe it lost its whole family in a terrorist attack, for instance; it's the sort of thing you read about.

"There's a lot of pressure on Kent, you have to understand," she explains.

Because there is. Providing for a whole family takes time and has to be respected.

"It takes a long time to get to know a person," says Britt-Marie to the rat, her voice growing progressively quieter with every word.

Kent digs his heels in when he walks. Not everyone notices these kinds of things, but that's how it is. He curls up when sleeping, as if he's cold, irrespective of how many blankets she gently spreads over him. He's afraid of heights.

"And his general knowledge is outstanding, especially when it comes to geography!" she points out.

Geography is a very good skill to share the sofa with when solving crossword puzzles. Not so very easy to acquire, actually. Love doesn't have to be fireworks for everyone. It could be a question of capital cities with five letters or knowing exactly when it's time to reheel your shoes.

"He could change." Britt-Marie wants to say it in a loud, clear voice, but instead it comes out in a whisper.

But he might, certainly. He doesn't even need to become an entirely new person. It's enough if he can become who he used to be before he was unfaithful.

He is taking medicine, after all, and they can do really amazing things with medicine nowadays.

"A few years ago they cloned a sheep, can you imagine?" says Britt-Marie to the rat.

At this point the rat decides to leave.

She puts away the plate. Washes up. Cleans. Polishes the window and looks out at Kent playing soccer with Omar and Dino. She can also change, she's sure about that. She doesn't have to be so boring. Life may not turn out differently if she goes home with Kent, but at least it will go back to normal.

"I'm not ready for an unusual life," says Britt-Marie to the rat, before she remembers that it has gone.

It takes time to get to know a person. She is not ready to get to know a new one. She has decided she has to learn to live with herself as she is.

She stands in the doorway watching Kent score a goal. He props himself up against the stick and leaps into the air, making a pirouette. It could not possibly be the sort of behavior the doctors would recommend after a heart attack, but Britt-Marie stops herself from criticizing him, because he looks so happy. She assumes there could also be advantages, health-wise, in being happy after a heart attack.

Omar nags about having a ride in the BMW, justifying this by the argument that it's "wicked as hell," and Britt-Marie realizes this must be something good, so she manages to stop herself from criticizing this as well. Kent manages to tell the boys how much it cost, which seems to impress them terrifically. The third time around he lets Omar drive, and Omar looks as if he's just been given permission to ride a dragon.

Sven isn't wearing his uniform when he steps out of the pizzeria, so she hardly notices him until they're just a few feet apart. He looks at the BMW, looks at Britt-Marie, and clears his throat.

"Hello, Britt-Marie," he says.

"Hello," she says, surprised.

She holds on to her handbag very hard. He digs his hands deep into his pockets like a teenager. He's wearing a shirt and his hair is water-combed. He doesn't say it was for her sake, and before she has time to say anything irrational her common sense blurts out:

"That's my husband!"

She points at the BMW. Sven's hands sink even deeper into his jacket pockets.

Kent stops the car when he sees them, gets out with his stick swinging self-confidently in one hand. He reaches out to Sven and his handshake is a little longer and harder than it needs to be.

"Kent!" Kent crows.

"Sven," Sven mumbles.

"My husband," Britt-Marie reminds him.

Sven's hand goes back to his jacket pocket. His clothes seem to be rubbing uncomfortably.

Britt-Marie's grip on her handbag gets harder and harder, until her fingers hurt, and maybe also some other parts of her. Kent grins jauntily.

"Nice kids! That curly-haired one wants to be an entrepreneur, did he tell you?"

He laughs in the direction of Omar. Britt-Marie looks down at the ground. Sven is grim when he looks up at Kent.

"You can't park there," he notes, moving his elbow towards the BMW without taking his hand out of his pocket.

"Oh, right," Kent says dismissively, tiredly waving his hand at him.

"I'm telling you you can't park there and we don't let teenagers drive cars around here. It's irresponsible!" Sven says insistently, with a ferocity Britt-Marie has never seen in him before.

"Relax, will you?" Kent grins, with a superior air.

Sven is vibrating. He points through the lining of his jacket with both index fingers.

"Either bloody way you can't park there, and it's illegal to let minors drive your car. You just have to accept that, wherever you come from. . . ."

The last words are spoken at a much lower volume. As if they have already started regretting themselves. Kent supports himself against his stick and coughs, slightly at a loss.

He looks at Britt-Marie, but she doesn't look back at him, so he peers at Sven instead.

"What's the matter with you—what are you, a cop?"

"Yes!" says Sven.

"Well, I'll be damned," laughs Kent, immediately sobering up his face and straightening his back and making a scornful salute.

Sven blushes and fixes his gaze on the zipper of his jacket. Britt-Marie's breathing speeds up and she steps forward as if she's about to move between them physically. In the end she just puts her feet down hard in the gravel and says:

"Please Kent, why don't you just move the car. It is actually in the middle of the soccer pitch."

Kent sighs, then nods mischievously at her, and holds up both hands as if someone is threatening him.

"Sure, sure, sure, if the sheriff insists. No problem. Just don't shoot!"

He takes a few demonstrative steps forward and leans over Britt-Marie. She can't remember the last time he kissed her on the cheek.

"I checked into the hotel in town. Bloody rathole, you know how it is in places like this, but I noticed there was a restaurant opposite. It looked okay, under the circumstances," he says so Sven will hear. When he says "circumstances" he makes a superior sort of gesture at the pizzeria and the recreation center and the road. He revs the engine more than he needs to when he moves the car. When he's done, he gives his business card to Omar, because Kent likes giving people his business card almost as much as he likes telling people what his belongings cost. The boy is deeply impressed. Britt-Marie realizes that she doesn't know at what exact point Sven turned around and left, only that he's gone now.

She stands alone outside the pizzeria. If something within her has been knocked down and shattered, she tries to tell herself, it is all her own fault, because these feelings she has inside should never have been set free in the first place. It is far too late to start a new life.

She has dinner with Kent at the restaurant in town. It has white tablecloths and a menu without photographs and seems to have a serious attitude about the cutlery. Or at least it does not treat it like a joke. Kent says he feels alone without her. "Lost" is the word he uses. He seems to be taking her seriously, or at least he isn't treating her as a joke. He's wearing his old, broken belt, she notices, and she realizes this is because he did not find his usual one that she mended just before she left. She wants to tell him it's lying neatly rolled up in the second drawer of the wardrobe in the bedroom. Their bedroom. She wants him to shout out her name.

But all he does is scratch his beard stubble and try to sound unconcerned when he asks:

"But this copper, then . . . is he . . . how did you become . . . friends?"

Britt-Marie does her utmost to sound similarly unconcerned when she answers:

"He's just a policeman, Kent."

Kent nods and blinks with emphasis.

"You have to trust me when I say I know I made a mistake, darling. It's over now. I'll never ever have contact with her again. You can't punish me for the rest of my life because of just one false move, right?" he says, and softly grabs her bandaged hand across the table.

He's wearing his wedding ring. She can feel the white mark on her finger. It's burning and denouncing her. He pats the bandage, as if not even reflecting on why it's there.

"Come on now, darling, you've made your point. Loud and clear! I understand!"

She nods. Because it's true. Because she never wanted him to suffer, only that he should know that he was wrong.

"You obviously think this thing with the soccer team is ludicrous," she whispers.

"Are you joking? I think it's absolutely fantastic!"

He lets go of her hand as soon as the food comes, and she immediately misses it. Feels like you do when you come out of the hairdresser after having more hair taken off than you wanted.

She places her napkin neatly in her lap, pats it tenderly as if it were sleeping, and whispers:

"Me too. I also think it's fantastic."

Kent lights up. Leans forward. Looks deep into her eyes.

"Hey, darling, let's put it like this: you stay here until the kids have played in this cup that the curly-haired one was going on about today. And then we go home. To our life. Okay?"

Britt-Marie inhales so deeply that her breath starts faltering halfway through.

"I would appreciate that," she whispers.

"Anything for you, darling," says Kent with a nod, and then stops the waitress to ask for the pepper mill even though he hasn't tried the food yet.

It's normal food, of course, but before common sense puts the brakes on, Britt-Marie briefly considers telling Kent about how she has tried tacos. She wants him to know that there have been a lot of things going on in her life lately. But she stops herself, because it probably doesn't really matter now, and anyway Kent wants to tell her things about his business affairs with the Germans.

Britt-Marie orders French fries with her food. She doesn't eat French fries because she doesn't like them, but she always orders them anyway whenever she goes with Kent to restaurants; she always worries that he won't have enough food to satisfy him.

While he's reaching across the table for her fries, Britt-Marie peers out of the window and for a moment she has a feeling that there was a police car in the street. But this could merely have been a figment of her imagination. Ashamed of herself, she looks down at her napkin. Here she is, a grown woman, with fantasies of emergency vehicles. What would people think?

Kent drives her to soccer practice and waits in his BMW until it's over. Bank is also there, so Britt-Marie lets her take care of the training while Britt-Marie mainly just stands there holding on to the list. When it's over, Britt-Marie can hardly remember what they did, or if she even spoke to the children, or said good-bye to them.

Kent drives her and Bank and the dog back to Bank's house. Bank and the dog hop out without asking how much the car cost, which seems to upset Kent terribly. Bank accidentally taps her stick against the paintwork and it's almost certainly not deliberate the first two times. Kent fiddles with his telephone and Britt-Marie sits waiting next to him, because she's very good at doing that. Finally he says:

"I have to go and see the accountant tomorrow. There are big things in motion with the Germans, you know, big plans!"

He nods persistently, to show just how big the plans are.

Britt-Marie smiles encouragingly. She opens the door at the same time as the thought strikes her, and as a result she asks without really thinking it through:

"What soccer team do you support?"

"Manchester United," he answers, surprised, looking up from his telephone.

She nods and gets out.

"That was a very nice dinner, Kent. Thank you."

He leans across the seat and looks up at her.

"When we're home we'll go to the theater, just the two of us. Okay, darling? I promise!"

She stays in the hall with the door open until he's driven off. Then she sees the ancient women in the garden opposite staring at her while leaning against their walkers. She hurries inside.

Bank is in the kitchen having some bacon.

"My husband supports Manchester United," Britt-Marie informs her.

"Might have bloody known," says Bank.

Britt-Marie doesn't have a clue what that's supposed to mean.

25

Britt-Marie devotes the next morning to cleaning the balcony furniture. She'll miss it. The women with the walkers on the other side of the road emerge to pick up their newspapers from the postbox. In a sudden fit of wanting to seem sociable, Britt-Marie waves at them, but they only glare back at her and slam the door.

Bank is frying bacon when she comes downstairs, but obviously she hasn't turned on the extractor fan. It must be nice for Bank, thinks Britt-Marie, not to be bothered about the smell of burnt pork or concerned about what the neighbors might think.

Hesitantly she places herself in the doorway between the hall and the kitchen. As Bank seems unaware of her presence, she clears her throat twice, because she has a feeling that she may, after all, owe her landlady an explanation.

"I suppose you feel you're owed an explanation about this whole business of my husband," she says.

"No," says Bank firmly.

"Oh," says Britt-Marie, disappointed.

"Bacon?" grunts Bank, and pours a lick of beer into the pot.

"No thanks," says Britt-Marie, not at all disgusted by this, and goes on:

"He is my husband. We never actually divorced. I just haven't been at home for a while. Almost like a holiday. But now I'm going home, you have to understand. I understand very well that perhaps you don't understand this sort of thing, but he is my husband. It's certainly not an appropriate thing, to leave one's husband at my age."

Bank looks as one does when one doesn't want to discuss Britt-Marie and Kent's relationship.

"Sure you don't want any bacon?" she mutters.

Britt-Marie shakes her head.

"No, thank you. But I want you to understand that he's not a bad man. He made a mistake, but anyone can make a mistake. I'm sure he had masses of opportunities to make a mistake before, without ever doing it. You can't write off a human being forever, just for the sake of a single mistake."

"It's good bacon," says Bank.

"There are obligations. Marital obligations. One doesn't just give up," Britt-Marie explains.

"I would have offered you eggs if there were any eggs. But the dog had them. So you'll have to make do with bacon."

"You can't just leave each other after a whole life."

"So you'll have some bacon, then?" Bank establishes, and turns on the extractor fan.

You might infer from this that she's more bothered about the sound of Britt-Marie's voice than the smell of fried bacon. So Britt-Marie stamps her foot on the floor.

"I don't eat bacon! It's not good for the cholesterol. Kent has also cut down, I can tell you. He was at the doctor in the autumn. We have an exceedingly capable doctor. He's an immigrant, you know. From Germany!"

Bank turns up the extractor fan to its maximum level, so that Britt-Marie has to raise her voice to make herself heard over all the noise, and as a result she's almost shouting when she points out:

"It's actually not very edifying leaving your husband when he's just had a heart attack! I'm not that sort of a woman!"

The plate is slammed down on the table in front of her, so the fat splashes over the rim.

"Eat your bacon," says Bank.

Britt-Marie gives it to the dog. But she doesn't say anything else about Kent. Or at least she tries not to. Instead she asks:

"What does it mean when someone supports Manchester United or whatever it's called?"

Bank answers with her mouth full of bacon.

"They always win. So they've started believing they deserve to."

"Ha."

Bank doesn't say anything else. Britt-Marie stands up and washes her plate. Dries it. Stands there in case Bank has something else to add, but when Bank starts behaving as if she's forgotten that Britt-Marie is even there, Britt-Marie clears her throat and says with irrepressible emphasis:

"Kent is not a bad man. He has not always won."

The dog looks at Bank as if it feels Bank ought to have a bad conscience. Bank seems to pick up on this, because she continues eating, in an even surlier silence than usual. Britt-Marie has already left the kitchen and put on her coat and neatly stashed her list away in her handbag when the dog growls from the kitchen and Bank groans loudly by way of an answer, and then at long last calls out into the hall:

"You want a lift?"

"Excuse me?" says Britt-Marie.

"Shall I drive you to the recreation center?" asks Bank.

Britt-Marie goes to the kitchen doorway and stares at her and almost drops her handbag.

"Drive? How . . . I . . . no, that's fine . . . thank you. I don't want to . . . I don't know . . . I'm certainly not judging, but how . . ."

She stops when she sees the satisfied grin on Bank's face.

"I'm almost blind. I don't drive. I was joking, Britt-Marie."

The dog signals its encouragement. Britt-Marie adjusts her hair.

"Ha. That was . . . nice of you."

"Don't worry so much, Britt-Marie!" Bank calls out after her, and Britt-Marie has absolutely no idea what to say to that sort of absurd notion.

She walks to the recreation center. Cleans. Polishes the windows and looks out of them. She sees other things now than when she first came to Borg. Faxin can do that for a person.

She serves up the Snickers by the door. Walks across the soccer pitch that she used to think was just a parking area. Sven's car is parked outside the pizzeria. Britt-Marie takes a deep breath before she walks inside.

"Hello," she says.

"Britt! All right there!" yells Somebody and rolls out of the kitchen gripping a pot of coffee.

Sven is standing by the register, wearing his uniform. Quickly he removes his police cap and holds it in his hands.

"Hello, Britt-Marie," he says. He smiles, and seems to grow a few inches taller.

Then comes another voice from the window:

"Good morning, darling!"

Kent is sitting at a table, drinking coffee. He has taken off his shoes and has one of his feet propped up on a chair. It's one of his main talents. He can sit anywhere drinking coffee and looking as comfortable as if he was in his own living room. No one is quite his equal when it comes to making himself at home anywhere, without being invited to do so.

Sven shrinks again. As if he's leaking air. Britt-Marie tries not to look as if her heart has jumped twice inside of her.

"I thought you were going to your accountant," she manages to say.

"I'm going in a minute, that kid Omar just wanted to show me a couple of things first," says Kent, smiling as if he has all the time in the world, and then he winks playfully at Sven and points out loudly:

"Don't worry, Sheriff, I haven't parked illegally today. I'm on the other side of the road."

Sven wipes the palms of his hands on his trouser legs and looks down at the floor as he answers:

"You can't park there either."

Kent nods with feigned seriousness.

"Does the sheriff want to issue a fine? Will the sheriff accept cash?"

He takes out his wallet, which is so thick that he has to have a rubber band around it to get it into his trouser back pocket, and puts it on the table. Then he laughs as if all this is just a joke. He's good at that, Kent—good at looking as if everything is just a joke. Because if it is, then no one can take offense, and then Kent can always say: "Ah, come on, don't you have a sense of humor?" The person with less of a sense of humor always loses in this world.

Sven looks down at the floor.

"I don't issue parking fines. I'm not a traffic warden."

"Okay, Sheriff! Okay! But the sheriff himself obviously parks wherever the sheriff feels like parking." Kent grins and nods at the police car, which can be seen through the window.

Before Sven has time to answer, Kent hollers at Somebody:

"Don't worry about the sheriff's coffee, I'll pay for it! I mean it's us taxpayers who pay the sheriff's salary anyway, so just put it on our bill!"

Sven doesn't answer. He just puts some cash on the counter and says in a low voice to Somebody:

"I can pay for my own coffee."

Then he glances at Britt-Marie and mumbles:

"I'll have it to take away, if that's all right."

She wants to say something. Doesn't have time.

"Check this out, darling! I had these printed for Omar!" yells Kent and waves a fistful of business cards.

When every available person in the pizzeria does not immediately run to his table, Kent stands up very elaborately and sighs as if none of them have a sense of humor. Then he walks up to the counter in his socks, which makes Britt-Marie scream inside, and hands Sven a business card.

"Here, Sheriff! Take a business card!"

Then he grins at Britt-Marie and shows her one of them, on which it is written: OMAR—ENTREPRENEUR.

"There's a printing place in that town place. They printed these on the bloody double this morning, over the moon they were, poor things don't get any customers!" Kent tells them jovially and makes emphatic quotation marks in the air when he says "town."

Sven stands there swallowing hard. As soon as Somebody has poured his coffee into a paper mug, Sven takes it and walks directly towards the door.

When he passes Britt-Marie he slows down and meets her eyes very briefly.

"Have a . . . have a good day, won't you," he mumbles.

"You . . . well, I mean . . . you too," says Britt-Marie, sucking in her cheeks.

"Be careful out there, Sheriff!" Kent yells in an American accent.

Sven stands still, with his gaze focused on the floor. Britt-Marie has time to see his fist, clenched until his knuckles turn white, before he forces it into his trouser pocket like an animal into a sack. The door tinkles cheerfully behind him.

Britt-Marie stands in front of the register, feeling at a loss. One curious thing Kent can do is that he can feel so at ease in a place that Britt-Marie immediately feels like a stranger. He thumps her back and waves the business cards around.

"Please, Kent. Could you not at least put on your shoes?" she whispers.

Kent looks at his socks in surprise. Waves his big toe through a hole in one of them.

"Sure, sure, darling. Of course. I have to get going now anyway. Give these to the kid when he comes in!"

He shakes his wrist in a dramatic way, so that his watch makes a rattling sound. It's a very expensive one, Britt-Marie knows that, and everyone who's ever run into Kent while queuing up to pay at the petrol station knows it. Then he presses the business cards into her hand and kisses her cheek.

"I'll be back this evening!" he cries on his way out of the door, and the next second he's gone.

Britt-Marie stands there, more at a loss than ever. When she doesn't know what to do with herself, she deals with it in her usual way. She cleans.

Somebody lets her get on with it. Either because she doesn't care or precisely because she does care.

Omar turns up at lunchtime. He immediately starts chasing Britt-Marie around the pizzeria as if they were the last two people on the planet and she was holding the last bag of crisps.

"Is Kent here? Is he coming? Is he here?" he hollers, tugging at her arm.

"Kent is with his accountant. He'll be back this evening."

"I've fixed him the coolest rims for his BMW! Wicked! You want to check them? He's getting a special price for them . . . you know!"

Britt-Marie doesn't ask what this means, because she assumes that some truck or other, despite never being scheduled to stop in Borg, has left the community slightly lighter than when it pulled in.

When Britt-Marie gives the boy the business cards he goes abruptly silent. Holds them as if they were made of priceless silk. The door tinkles and Vega comes in. She doesn't even look at Britt-Marie.

"Hello, Vega," says Britt-Marie.

Vega ignores her.

"Hello, Vega!" Britt-Marie repeats.

"Check these *ultimate* business cards, they're wicked. I got them off Kent!" Omar yells, his eyes glittering.

Vega takes in this information with indifference and storms into the kitchen. Soon you can hear that she's washing up. It sounds like something is crawling about in the sink while she attempts to beat it to death. Somebody rolls out of the kitchen and shrugs apologetically at Britt-Marie.

"Vega very angry, you know."

"How do you know?" asks Britt-Marie.

"Teenager. Washing up without being told. Bloody angry when that happening, huh?"

Britt-Marie has to admit there's a good logic to that.

"Why is she so angry?"

Omar answers eagerly:

"Because she knows Kent's been here, so she's twigged you'll be clearing out!"

He doesn't sound too upset about it himself, because the opportunity of exchanging a soccer coach for an investor in tire rims seems like an acceptable deal to him.

"I'm staying in Borg until after the competition," says Britt-Marie, directing this as much to herself as to anyone else.

The boy doesn't look as if he's been listening. He doesn't even bother correcting her by saying it's called a "cup." Britt-Marie almost wishes he would. The men with beards and caps come in, drink coffee, and read newspapers without any acknowledgment of Britt-Marie, but there's a certain ease about them today, as if they know that soon they won't have to pretend not to notice her.

Evidently Vega has run out of things to slam about, so she comes storming out of the kitchen towards the front door.

"Ha. I suppose you're leaving?" says Britt-Marie in a well-meaning way.

"As if you're bothered," hisses Vega.

"Will you be back in time for training?"

"Bloody difference does it make?"

"At least put a jacket on? It's cold out ther—"

"Go to hell, you old bat! Go back to your crappy life with your shitty bloke!"

The girl slams the door, which tinkles cheerfully. Omar gathers up his business cards and runs after her. Britt-Marie calls out to him but he either doesn't hear, or doesn't care.

After that, Britt-Marie cleans the entire pizzeria in grim silence. No one tries to stop her.

When she's done she sinks onto a stool in the kitchen. Somebody sits next to her, drinking a beer and watching her thoughtfully.

"Beer, Britt-Marie. You want?"

Britt-Marie blinks at her.

"Yes, you know what? Absolutely. I think I'd absolutely like to have a beer."

So they drink beer without saying anything else. Britt-Marie must have had two or three sips of hers when the door tinkles again.

She just about has time to see the young man coming inside, and she's certainly not used to having alcohol levels of this magnitude in her blood at this time of the afternoon, which may be the reason why she does not immediately notice that the man is wearing a black hood over his head.

But Somebody does notice. She puts down her beer. Rolls up behind Britt-Marie and tugs at the arm of her jacket.

"Britt-Marie. Down on the floor. Now!"

And that's when Britt-Marie sees the pistol.

26

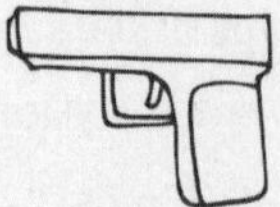

It's a very strange thing staring into the barrel of a gun. It embraces you. You fall into it.

A few hours later some police from town come to the pizzeria to ask Britt-Marie if she can describe the young man, what he was wearing and whether he was short or tall and spoke with a dialect or accent. The only description she's able to give them is, "He was holding a pistol." One of the police explains she "mustn't take it personally" because a robbery is only about the money.

This may be easy for the police to say, but it is actually extremely difficult to have a pistol pointed at one and *not* take it personally—at least that is Britt-Marie's considered opinion.

"Open the fucking register then, for Christ's sake!" hisses the robber at her.

She will come to remember this afterwards, being addressed as if she's an instrument, not a person. Somebody tries to roll up to the register but Britt-Marie is in the way and seems frozen to the spot.

"*Open it!*" bellows the robber so that both Somebody and the men with caps instinctively cover their faces with their hands, as if this might help.

But Britt-Marie does not move. Her terror paralyzes her so she's not even capable of feeling afraid. Why she reacts the way she does is something she's incapable of understanding, but there are an awful lot of things you are not equipped to know about yourself until you have a pistol pointing at your face. And so, to Britt-Marie's own surprise and the consternation of Somebody and the men with caps, she hears some words coming out of her mouth:

"First you have to buy something."

"*Ooopen it!*" howls the robber.

But Britt-Marie doesn't move. She puts her bandaged hand into the other. Both hands are trembling, and Britt-Marie thinks briefly that surely there are limits, but in the final analysis it's been the sort of day that Britt-Marie feels has gone beyond the limit. So she replies in a wholly considerate way:

"You have to put in an amount before you can open the register, you see. Otherwise the receipt is wrong."

The pistol judders up and down in the robber's hand. Equal amounts of fury and surprise.

"Just bloody put in anything then!"

Britt-Marie changes her hands around. Her fingers are slippery with sweat. But something within her decides, against her most reasonably protesting common sense, that this is a good point in Britt-Marie's life to stand her ground a bit.

"You have to understand you can't just put anything in. Then the receipts aren't right."

"I couldn't give a fuck about your fucking receipts, you old bag . . . !" screams the robber.

"There's no need to raise your voice," Britt-Marie interrupts firmly, and then goes on to patiently tell him:

"And there's certainly no cause to use that sort of language!"

Somebody's wheelchair comes careering across the floor and

tackles Britt-Marie at thigh-height, sending Somebody, the wheelchair, and Britt-Marie to the floor. The sound of the gunshot into the ceiling leaves a piercing ringing sound in Britt-Marie's ears that makes her lose all sense of direction. Fragments of glass from the fluorescent tube come snowing down and she doesn't know if she is lying on her back or her stomach, where the walls are, or where the floors are. She can feel Somebody's heavy breathing in her ear and far away something seems to be making a tinkling sound.

Then she hears Vega and Omar's voices.

"What the he—" Vega manages to say, and Britt-Marie instinctively gets to her feet at that point, even though her ears are still ringing and her common sense is telling her to sharpen up and stay there on the floor like a civilized person.

There's a lot you can't know about a person until you become one with her. What her capabilities are. The courage she has. The robber turns to Vega and Omar with his sense of shock radiating heatedly through the holes in his balaclava.

"What are you doing here?"

"Psycho?" whispers Omar.

"The hell you doing here? I waited until you'd gone! What you bloody doing here, fucking kids?"

"I forgot my jacket," Vega manages to say.

Psycho furiously waves his pistol at her, but Britt-Marie is already standing between the pistol barrel and the children. She stretches her arms out behind her to make sure she's covering the girl and the boy with her body, but she doesn't move an inch. She's frozen to the spot, held in place by a whole lifetime of thwarted ambitions.

"That's just about enough now!" she hisses menacingly.

She actually can't remember ever having done anything menacing in her entire life.

There's a slightly ambivalent atmosphere in the pizzeria after that; that is probably how you'd have to describe it. Psycho clearly doesn't quite know what to do with his pistol and, until he makes his decision, no one else in the pizzeria knows what to do about it either. Britt-Marie looks at his shoes with annoyance.

"I just mopped the floor."

"Shut your fucking mouth, motherfucker!"

"I certainly will not!"

Psycho has broken into a sweat, which drips from the holes in his balaclava. He spins his pistol two turns around the pizzeria at eye level, sending the men with caps down on the floor again. Then he stares hatefully at Britt-Marie one last time, and runs.

The bell on the door tinkles obediently and Britt-Marie's body starts melting onto the floor, although Vega and Omar are doing their best to hold her up with their trembling arms. Her coat is wet with tears, but she can't tell if they are hers or the children's, or exactly at what point she stops being in their arms and instead they are in hers. When she realizes that they are about to fall, she summons the strength to stand on her own two feet. Because that is what women like Britt-Marie do. They find the strength when they have to do something for others.

"Sorry, sorry, sorry, sorry, sorry," pants Vega.

"Shhhh," whispers Britt-Marie and rocks both her and Omar in her arms.

"Sorry for calling you an old bat," sobs Vega.

"It's certainly nothing I haven't heard before," Britt-Marie says to calm her.

Gently she sits the children down on two chairs. Wraps them in blankets and makes hot chocolate with real cocoa, because that was what Kent's children used to want when they woke in the night after having horrible nightmares. Admittedly the quality of the cocoa is a little dubious, because Somebody boasts that it's "almost cocoa, huh! From Asia!"—but in any case the children are too shaken up to be concerned about it.

Omar keeps stammering about how they have to find Sami, and Vega repeatedly calls her older brother's cell phone. Britt-Marie tries to calm them by saying that she's quite certain Sami had nothing to do with the robbery, upon which the two children stare openmouthed at her and Omar whispers:

"You don't get it. When Sami finds out that Psycho pointed a gun at us, he'll find him and kill him. We have to get hold of Sami!"

But Sami isn't picking up. The children get more and more frightened. Britt-Marie wraps them up even tighter in blankets and makes more hot chocolate. Then she does what she can. What she knows. She fetches a broom and a mop and baking soda and sweeps up the glass and swabs the floor.

When she's done with that she stands behind the register, holding on for all she's worth so that she doesn't pass out. Somebody gets her a headache tablet and another beer. The men with caps and beards get up from their table, bring their coffee cups to the counter, and silently put them down in front of Britt-Marie. Then they take off their caps, look down at their newspapers, and start rifling through them until they find what they are looking for and duly hand these over to Britt-Marie.

Crossword supplements.

27

Britt-Marie doesn't know if it's Kent or Sven's voice she hears first.

Sven comes because Vega has called him; Kent comes because Omar has called him.

The police car and the BMW both come plowing into the parking area. The two men come stumbling in, white-faced, standing crestfallen inside the door and looking at the shot-to-pieces fluorescent tube on the ceiling. Then they stare at Britt-Marie. She sees their fear. Sees how they are plagued by bad conscience because they weren't here to protect her. She sees how much this pains them, this missed opportunity to be her hero. They gulp. They don't seem to know which foot to stand on. Then they instinctively do what almost all men in that situation would do.

They start arguing with each other about whose fault this is.

"Is everyone okay?" Sven asks first of all, but he's interrupted by Kent, who points across the premises with his whole arm and orders everyone:

"Now let's take it easy until the police get here!"

Sven spins around like an offended mannequin.

"What do you think I'm wearing, you damned yuppie! A carnival outfit?"

"I mean the real police, the kind that can *stop* robberies!" splutters Kent.

Sven takes two small, angry steps forward and lifts his chin:

"Of course, of course, you would have stopped it with your *wallet* if you'd been here!"

Their white faces turn red in an instant. Britt-Marie has never seen Sven angry in this way before, and judging by the facial expressions of Vega, Omar, and Somebody, none of them have either. Kent, who immediately senses his leadership position in the room is under threat, tries to raise his voice even more to take command of the situation.

"Are you okay, kids?" he asks Omar and Vega.

"Don't you ask them if they're okay! You don't even *know* these children!" Sven says, cutting him off and furiously pushing Kent's pointing hand away, then turns to the children and points with his own whole arm. "Are you okay, kids?"

Vega and Omar nod, confused. Somebody tries to say something but she doesn't have a chance. Kent pushes in front of Sven and waves the palms of his hands about.

"Everyone calm down now so we can call the police."

"I'm *standing right here*!"

Britt-Marie's ears are still ringing. She clears her throat and says:

"Please, Kent. Please, Sven. Can I just ask you to calm yourselves dow—"

But the men are not listening to her. They continue rowing and gesticulating as if she were something you could just switch off with a remote control.

Kent snorts something about how Sven couldn't "protect a hand with a glove" and Sven snorts back that he's sure Kent is "very brave inside his BMW with the doors locked." Kent yells that Sven shouldn't get ideas about himself because he's nothing but "a copper in a little crappy village," and Sven yells back that Kent shouldn't think he can just come here and "buy people's admiration with business cards and shit like that!" Upon which Kent yells that "the kid wants to be a bloody entrepreneur, doesn't he!" Upon which Sven yells that "being an entrepreneur is not a job!" Upon which Kent rails at him, "What, so you want him to be a cop instead, do you? Huh? What sort of pay does a policeman take home?" Upon which Sven flies into a rage: "We get a two-and-a-half-percent raise every year and I have very good yields on my pension funds! I've done a course in it!"

Britt-Marie tries to step between them, but they don't notice her.

"I've done a *cooouuurse*," Kent imitates disdainfully.

"Hey! It's an offense to pull at a policeman's uniform, damn it!" roars Sven and grabs hold of Kent's shirt.

"Watch the shirt! Do you have any idea how much this cost?!"

"You vain ponce, no wonder Britt-Marie left you!"

"Left me?! You think she'll be staying here with *you*, you glorified security guard?!"

Britt-Marie waves her arms as hard as she can in front of them, trying to make them see her.

"Please, Kent! Please, Sven! Stop at once! I just mopped this floor!"

But it's useless, as each of the men has just employed their respective right arms to put the other in a headlock, and they have started tottering about doubled over in a swearing, panting dance, and seconds later, with a mighty crash, the front door of the pizzeria shatters into splintered wood when the two men tumble through it like drunken bears. They land in an indecorous pile in the gravel and, in so doing, seem to draw even more attention to their physical imperfections.

Britt-Marie runs forward and stares at them. They stare up at her, suddenly silent and well aware of the trouble they have caused.

Kent tries to get on his feet first.

"Darling, you can see for yourself, can't you? The bloke is a complete idiot!"

"He started it!" Sven protests at once, crawling to his feet next to Kent.

And that's the point when Britt-Marie has had enough. Enough of the whole thing. She's been shouted at and pushed and threatened with pistols and now she has to mop the floor one more time because of splinters of wood all over the pizzeria. Enough is enough.

They don't hear her the first, second, or third time. But then she fills her lungs with air and says as emphatically as she can:

"I should like to ask you to leave."

When they still don't listen to her she does something she hasn't done in twenty years, not since one of her flowers was blown off the balcony. She yells.

"Get out of here! The pair of you!"

The pizzeria grows more silent than it could possibly have been even if a new pistol-wielding robber had stepped inside. Kent and Sven are left standing with their mouths wide open, making noises that would probably have been words if they had closed their mouths between the syllables. Britt-Marie digs her heels even deeper into the floor and points at the broken door.

"Get out. At once."

"But for God's sake, darl—" Kent begins to say, but Britt-Marie chops her bandaged hand through the air in what could probably have qualified as a new form of martial arts and abruptly silences him.

"You might have asked how I hurt my hand, Kent. You might have asked, because then I might have believed that you actually cared."

"I thought, oh, come on now, darling, I thought you'd got your hand caught in the dishwasher or some shit like that . . . you know how it is. I didn't think it was anything seri—"

"Because you didn't ask!"

"But . . . darling . . . don't get all piss—" stammers Kent.

Sven sticks out his chest towards him.

"Exactly! Exactly! Get out of here, you bloody yuppie, Britt-Marie doesn't want you here! Don't you underst—" he starts saying, brimming with self-confidence.

But Britt-Marie's hand cleaves the air in front of him so that he staggers back at the draft.

"And you, Sven! Don't tell me what I feel! You don't know me! Not even I know myself, quite clearly, because this is certainly not normal behavior for me!"

Somewhere on the premises Somebody is trying not to laugh. Vega and Omar look as if they'd like to keep notes so they never forget any of the details. Britt-Marie collects herself and adjusts her hair and brushes some wooden splinters from her skirt and then places her bandaged hand neatly in the other, and clarifies in an altogether well-meaning, considerate way:

"Now I'm going to clean in here. Good afternoon to you both."

The bell above the door tinkles dolefully and halfheartedly behind Kent and Sven. They stay outside for a good while yelling, "See what you've done?" at each other. Then everything goes silent.

Britt-Marie starts cleaning.

Somebody and the children hide in the kitchen until she has finished. They daren't even laugh.

28

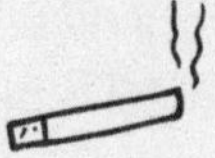

Admittedly it is not the two policemen's fault, it really isn't. They've come to Borg from town and are just trying to do their jobs as best they can.

But Britt-Marie is possibly just slightly irascible. That is how you get when people shoot at you.

"We can appreciate that you're in shock, but we need our questions answered," one of the policemen tries to explain.

"I see you're not at all concerned about stomping in with muddy shoes on a newly mopped floor, I see that. It must be very nice for you."

"We've already said we're sorry about that. Really sorry. But as we've already explained now several times we have to question all the witnesses on the scene," the other policeman tries to say.

"My list has been destroyed."

"What do you mean?"

"You asked for my testimony. My list is destroyed. None of this was on my list when I left home this morning, so now my entire list is in disarray."

"That's not quite what we meant," says the first policeman.

"Aha. So now my testimony is wrong as well, is it?"

"We need to know if you got a good look at the perpetrator," the other policeman attempts to say.

"I should like to inform you that I have perfectly good vision. I've spoken to my optometrist about it. He's an excellent optician, you should understand. Very well brought up. He doesn't walk around indoors with muddy shoes."

The police emit synchronized sighs. Britt-Marie exhales very pointedly back.

"It would be a great help to us if you could describe the perpetrator," one of the policemen asks.

"Of course I can do that," hisses Britt-Marie.

"And how would you describe him?"

"He had a pistol!"

"But you really don't remember anything else? Any distinguishing characteristics?"

"Isn't a pistol a distinguishing characteristic?" wonders Britt-Marie.

This is the moment when the police decide to go back into town.

Britt-Marie mops the floor again. So hard that in the end Somebody has to stop her.

"Careful with mop, Britt-Marie, expensive mop for God's sake!" She grins.

Britt-Marie does not think this is the best of days to roll about in your wheelchair, grinning at people, she certainly doesn't. But Somebody makes sure she drinks her beer and eats a bit of pizza, and then she hands over her car keys.

"I was under the distinct impression that the car had not been repaired yet!" Britt-Marie bursts out.

Somebody shrugs, ashamed of herself.

"Ah, you know. Been ready many days, huh, but . . . you know."

"No. I absolutely don't know at all."

Somebody guiltily rubs her hands in her lap.

"The car is ready many days. But if Britt has no car: can't drive off and leave Borg, huh?"

"So you pulled the wool over my eyes? You lied to my face?" Britt-Marie says in an injured tone of voice.

"Yes," Somebody admits.

"Might I ask why you did that?"

Somebody shrugs. "I like you. You're, what's-it-called? A breath of fresh air! Borg is boring without Britt, huh?"

Britt-Marie doesn't have a particularly good answer on hand for this, it has to be said. So Somebody fetches another beer and calls out, as if in passing:

"But Britt, you know, let me put question to you: how do you feel about blue car?"

"What do you mean by that?" pants Britt-Marie.

Then they spend a fairly lengthy amount of time on the soccer pitch, arguing about this, because Somebody is quite persistent about explaining that she could without any trouble respray Britt-Marie's car the same color as the new blue door. It wouldn't be any trouble at all. In fact, Somebody is almost a hundred percent sure that at some point she registered a paint-shop business with the local authority.

In the end Britt-Marie gets so worked up about this that she takes her notebook and tears out her list for the whole day, and starts one completely fresh. She has never done this in her whole life, but desperate times call for desperate measures.

She walks back through Borg with Vega and Omar, because Britt-Marie has by this point consumed half a can of beer, meaning it's quite out of the question for her to get behind the wheel. Especially not in a car with a blue door. What would people think? Omar stays absolutely silent until they get home, which is more minutes of silence than Britt-Marie has ever heard from him since they first got to know each other.

Vega keeps calling Sami without getting an answer. Britt-Marie tries to convince her that Sami may not have heard news of the robbery, but Vega tells her that this is Borg. Everyone knows everything about everyone in Borg. So Sami knows and Sami isn't answering because he's busy tracking Psycho down and killing him.

Under these circumstances, Britt-Marie can't bring herself to leave the children on their own, so she goes up to the flat with them and starts making dinner. They have it at exactly six o'clock. The children eat staring down at their plates, as children do who have learned to expect the worst. When Britt-Marie's telephone rings the first time they bounce up, but it's only Kent so Britt-Marie doesn't answer. When Sven calls a minute later she doesn't answer either, and when the girl from the unemployment office calls three times in a row she switches off the telephone.

Vega calls Sami again. Gets no answer. That's when she starts washing up, without anyone having asked her, and then Britt-Marie realizes the situation is really serious.

"I'm sure nothing serious has happened," says Britt-Marie.

"The hell you know about it?" Vega says.

Omar mumbles from the table:

"Sami is never late for dinner. He's a dinner-Nazi."

Then he puts his plate in the dishwasher. Voluntarily. Which is the point at which Britt-Marie understands something extremely drastic has to be done, so she concentrates on breathing in and out half a dozen times, and then she hugs the children hard. When they burst into tears she does the same.

When the doorbell finally rings they're stumbling over one another to get there. None of them gives a second thought to the fact that if this was Sami coming back he would just have opened the door with his key, so when they tug at the door handle only to find the white dog sitting outside, Omar feels disappointed, Vega is angry, and Britt-Marie anxious. Because these seem to be their most basic emotions in life.

"You can't come in with dirty paws," Britt-Marie informs the dog.

The dog glances at its paws, and seems overwhelmed by a lack of self-confidence.

Next to it stands Bank, and next to her stand Max, Ben, Dino, and Toad.

Bank points her stick, gently poking Britt-Marie in the stomach.

"Hi there, Rambo!"

"How dare you!" protests Britt-Marie instinctively.

"You scared off the robber," explains Toad. "Like Rambo. That means you're an ice-cool motherfucker!"

Britt-Marie patiently puts her bandaged hand in the other and turns her eyes to Ben. He smiles and nods encouragingly.

"And that's, like, good."

Britt-Marie absorbs this information and then her eyes wander all the way back to Bank.

"Ha. Very nice of you to say so."

"Don't mention it," mutters Bank impatiently and makes a gesture at her wrist, as if she was wearing a watch: "What about training?"

"What training?" asks Britt-Marie.

"The training!" answers Max, who's wearing his national hockey team jersey and dancing up and down as if he needs the bathroom.

Britt-Marie uncomfortably rocks back and forth from her heels to her toes.

"I assumed it was self-evident that it had been canceled. In view of the circumstances."

"What circumstances?"

"The robbery, my dear."

Max looks as if he's working his brain hard to bring clarity to what these two separate things could feasibly have to do with each other. Then he comes to the only possible logical conclusion: "Did the robber nick the ball?"

"I'm sorry?"

"If he didn't nick the ball we can still play, can't we?"

The group gathered on the landing takes this conclusion into consideration, and when none of them seems able to come up with any rational line of argument to oppose it, there's not much else to do.

So they play. In the yard outside the apartment block, between the refuse room and the bicycle stand, using three gloves and a dog as the goalposts.

Max tackles Vega just as she's about to score, and she takes two swings at him with both fists. He backs off. She roars: "Don't touch me, rich kid!" They all shuffle away. Omar avoids the ball as if it's frightening to him.

The black car stops on the road just as Toad has hit one of the goalposts on the nose for the third time, and it's refusing to take part anymore. Omar rushes into Sami's arms, and Vega turns around and marches into the house without a word.

The goalpost is having some sweets from Bank's pocket and getting scratched behind its ears as Sami draws closer.

"Hey there, Bank," he says.

"Did you find him?" asks Bank.

"No," says Sami.

"Lucky for Psycho!" yells Toad excitedly, waving his thumb and index finger like a pistol, then cutting this activity short when Britt-Marie gives him a look as if he just refused to use a coaster.

Bank pokes Sami's stomach with her stick.

"Lucky for Psycho. But mainly lucky for you, Sami."

She heads for home with Max, Dino, Toad, and Ben in tow. Before they go around the corner Ben stops and calls out to Britt-Marie:

"You're still coming tomorrow, aren't you?"

"Coming to what?" Britt-Marie wants to know, and is met by a collective stare from the group as if she's lost her reason.

"To the cup! Tomorrow's the cup!" thunders Max.

Britt-Marie brushes her skirt so they don't see she's got her eyes closed and is sucking her cheeks in.

"Ha. Ha. Obviously I will. Obviously."

She doesn't say anything about how it will be her last day in Borg. They don't say anything either.

She sits in the kitchen until Sami comes out of Vega and Omar's bedroom.

"They're sleeping," he says with a somewhat forced smile.

Britt-Marie stands up, collects herself, and informs him coolly:

"I don't want to stick my nose in, because I'm certainly not the sort of person who does that, but if it's true that you were intending to do away with this Psycho tonight for the sake of Vega and Omar, I should like to clarify to you that it's not suitable for a gentleman to run around doing away with people."

He raises his eyebrows. She closes her fingers around her handbag.

"I'm not a gentleman," he says with a smile.

"No, but you could become one!"

He laughs. She doesn't laugh. So he stops laughing.

"Ah, drop it, I wouldn't have killed him. He's my best friend. He's just so fucking sick in the head, you get what I mean? He owes people money. The wrong kind of people. So he's desperate. He didn't think Vega and Omar would be there."

"Right," says Britt-Marie.

"That's not to say you're not important as well!" Sami corrects himself.

"Sorry. I need a cig," says Sami with a sigh, and only then does Britt-Marie realize his hands are trembling.

She goes with him onto the balcony, coughing dubiously and not at all demonstratively. He blows the smoke away from her and apologizes.

"Sorry, is this bothering you?"

"I should like to ask if you have any more cigarettes," says Britt-Marie without blinking an eye.

He starts laughing.

"I didn't think you were a smoker."

"I'm certainly not," she says defensively. "I've just had a long day."

"Okay, okay," he smirks, handing her one and lighting it for her.

She takes slight, shallow puffs. Closes her eyes.

"I'd like you to know that you're certainly not the only one with tendencies to live a wild, irresponsible existence. I smoked any number of cigarettes in my youth."

He laughs out loud, and she feels it's more at her than with her, so she goes on to clarify her statement:

"For a period in my youth I was actually employed as a waitress!"

She nods with emphasis, just to underline that she's by no means just making this up off the top of her head. Sami looks impressed and gestures at her to take a seat on an upside-down drinks crate.

"You want a whiskey, Britt-Marie?"

Britt-Marie's common sense has obviously locked itself in its room, because suddenly Britt-Marie hears herself saying:

"Yes, absolutely, you know what, Sami? I would like one very much!"

And so they drink whiskey and smoke. Britt-Marie tries to blow some smoke rings, because she knows she wished she could do this at the time when she was working as a waitress. The chefs knew how to do it. It looked so very relaxing.

"Dad didn't leave, we chased him away, me and Magnus," Sami tells her without any preamble.

"Who's Magnus?"

"He likes 'Psycho' better, people don't get as scared of a 'Magnus,'" says Sami with a grin.

"Ha," says Britt-Marie, but it's actually more of a "huh?" than a "ha."

"Dad hit Mum whenever he'd been drinking. No one knew about it, you know, but once Magnus was picking me up to go to soccer training when we were small, and he'd never seen anything like it. He comes from a right nuclear family, his dad worked for an insurance company and drove an Opel, sort of thing. But he . . . I don't bloody know. He saw me step in between Mum and Dad, and I got a hiding from Dad as usual, and then out of fucking nowhere Magnus was standing there yelling, with a knife at Dad's throat. And I don't think I got it until then, that not all kids lived like we did. Not all kids were afraid every time they came home. Omar cried. Vega cried. So, you know . . . it felt like that was enough right there. See what I mean?"

Britt-Marie coughs smoke through her nose. Sami pats her helpfully on the back and fetches water for her. Then stands by the balcony railing, peering over the edge as if he's measuring the distance to the ground.

"Magnus helped chase Dad away. You don't find friends like that just anywhere."

"Where's your mother, Sami?"

"Just away for a while, she'll be coming back soon," Sami attempts.

Britt-Marie collects herself and points her cigarette at him menacingly.

"I may be many things, Sami, but I'm no idiot."

Sami empties his glass. Scratches his head.

"She's dead," he admits at last.

Exactly how long it takes Britt-Marie to get absolutely clear about the whole story, she can't say. Night has fallen over Borg, and she thinks it may be snowing. When Sami, Vega, and Omar's father left, their mother took on more driving work with the trucking company. Year after year. When the trucking company fired all its drivers, she started working for foreign companies, whenever she could find them, to the best of her ability. Year after year, as mothers do. One evening she got caught up in a traffic jam, got delayed, and her bonus hung in the balance. So she drove through the night in bad weather, in a truck that was too old. At dawn she met an oncoming car, the driver of which was reaching for his cell phone, so that he'd veered onto the wrong side of the road. She swerved, the tires of the truck lost their purchase on the road in the rain, and the whole thing overturned. There was a deluge of blood and glass, and three children sat waiting two thousand miles away for the sound of a key in the front door.

"She was a bloody good mum. She was a warrior," whispers Sami.

Britt-Marie has to refill her glass before she manages to say:

"I am so very, very sorry, Sami."

It may sound paltry and less than you might expect. But it's all she's got.

Sami pats her on the arm understandingly, as if he's the one to console her and not the other way around.

"Vega's afraid, even though she mainly seems angry. Omar is angry, though you'd probably think he was afraid."

"And you?"

"I don't have time to feel things, I have to take care of them."

"But . . . how . . . I mean . . . the authorities," Britt-Marie starts, in a welter of disconnected thoughts.

Sami lights her another cigarette, then one for himself.

"We never informed anyone that Dad cleared off. He must be abroad somewhere, but he's still registered at this address. We had his old driving license, so Omar bribed a truck driver at the petrol station to go to the police in town pretending to be him and signing some papers. We got a couple of thousand on Mum's insurance. No one else ever asked anything about it."

"But you can't just . . . Good God, Sami, this is not *Pippi Longstocking*, is it! Who will take care of the children—"

"I will. I will take care of them," he says simply, cutting her short.

"For . . . how long?"

"As long as I can. I get the fact they'll catch us out pretty soon, I'm not an idiot. But I only need a bit of time, Britt-Marie. Just a bit. I have plans. I just have to show that I can support them financially, you understand? Otherwise they'll take Vega and Omar and put them in some fucking children's home. I can't let them do that. I'm not the type that just walks out."

"They might let you take care of the children. If you explain it exactly as it is, they might—"

"Look at me, Britt-Marie. Criminal record, unemployed, and mates with people like Psycho. Would you let me take care of two children?"

"We can show them your cutlery drawer! We can explain that you have the potential to become a gentleman!"

"Thanks," he says and puts his hand on her shoulder.

She leans against him.

"And Sven knows everything?"

Sami runs his hands over her hair to calm her.

"He's the one who took the international call from the police who found the truck. He came here to give us the news. Cried as much as we did. It's like having a parent in the army, you know, when your mum drives a truck. If someone in uniform comes to your door you know what it's about."

"So . . . Sven . . ."

"He knows everything."

Britt-Marie's eyes blink very hard as they stare at his shirt. It's a curious thing to do. A grown woman on a young man's balcony in the middle of the night, just like that. What on earth would people think about that?

"I was under the impression that one became a policeman because one believed in rules and regulations."

"I think Sven became a policeman because he believes in justice."

Britt-Marie straightens up. Wipes her face down.

"We're going to need more whiskey. And if it's not too troublesome, I should like to ask for a bottle of window-cleaner as well."

After a considerable amount of reflection she adds:

"Under present circumstances I could see myself making do with any old brand."

29

Britt-Marie wakes up with a headache of the most spectacular kind. She's lying in her bed in Bank's house. A neighbor seems to be drilling the wall. The whole room sways when she gets up. She's sweating, her body aching and her mouth laced with a sort of sharp bitterness. Britt-Marie is obviously a woman with a certain amount of life experience, so she understands her condition immediately. The day after she has drunk more alcohol in Sami's home than her total intake in the last forty years there can only be one reasonable conclusion:

"I've got flu!" she explains to Bank in a knowing sort of way, when she comes down to the kitchen.

Bank is making bacon and eggs. The dog sniffs the air and moves a little farther away from Britt-Marie.

"You smell of spirits," Bank states, without quite managing to stop herself looking amused.

"That's right. Which is obviously why I feel the way I do today," says Britt-Marie with a nod.

"I thought you said you'd come down with flu," says Bank.

Britt-Marie nods helpfully.

"But my dear, that's precisely what I'm saying! It's the only reasonable explanation. When you drink alcohol your immune system is knocked out, you have to understand. And that's why I've got the flu."

"Flu, right then," mumbles Bank and puts the eggs on the table for Britt-Marie.

Britt-Marie closes her eyes, holding back her nausea, and gives the eggs to the dog. Bank puts a glass of cold water in front of her instead. Britt-Marie drinks. Flu makes people dehydrated. She's read all about it.

"Mine and Kent's children were ill all the time; if it wasn't one thing it was another—but as for myself I am never ill. 'Britt-Marie, you're as healthy as a nut kernel!' That's what my doctor always says, he really does!"

When neither Bank nor the dog answer, Britt-Marie breathes deeply and her eyes blink forlornly. Her words seem drained of oxygen when she corrects herself:

"I mean Kent's children."

She drinks her water in silence. The dog and Bank have their eggs. They go with her to meet the soccer team, because Britt-Marie is not the sort of woman who bunks off work just because she has flu. The dog makes a demonstrative loop around the flower bed outside the house because it stinks as if someone has vomited there in the course of the night.

Somebody is sitting inside the broken front door of the pizzeria, drinking coffee, when they get there. She grimaces when Britt-Marie comes too close, and Britt-Marie pulls an even uglier face back.

"It stinks in here. Have you been smoking inside?" she asks, almost with a note of accusation.

Somebody wrinkles her nose.

"And you, Britt? Have you been, what's-it-called? On fire and trying to put it out with whiskey?"

"I'll have you know that I've got the flu," snorts Britt-Marie.

Bank pokes Somebody's wheelchair with her stick.

"Stop going on now and give her a Bloody Mary."

"What's that?" asks Britt-Marie as brightly as she's able.

"It helps against . . . flu," mutters Bank.

Somebody disappears into the kitchen and comes back with a glass filled with what looks like tomato juice. Britt-Marie sips it skeptically, before spitting it out at the dog. It does not look at all pleased about it.

"This tastes of *pepper*!" splutters Britt-Marie.

The dog goes to sit in the gravel, carefully placing itself upwind. Bank holds out her stick with her arm straightened to make sure she's out of spitting range. Somebody frowns and fetches a cloth to wipe down the table between them, while muttering:

"Don't know what flu you have, Britt, but do me a favor, huh, what's-it-called? Don't light a match near your breath before you brush your teeth, huh? Pizzeria has no fire insurance, you know."

Britt-Marie certainly has no idea what that's supposed to mean. But she makes her polite apologies to Somebody and Bank and explains she has a few things to do in the recreation center and actually can't stay here all morning making a fuss about things. Then she briskly walks across the parking area, continues in a controlled manner into the recreation center toilet, and locks the door behind her.

When she comes out Sven is squatting by the pizzeria door, putting the hinges back in. He stumbles to his feet and removes his police cap when he catches sight of her. There's a toolbox at his feet. He tries to smile.

"I just thought that I, well, that I would mend the door. I thought . . ."

"Ha," says Britt-Marie and looks at the wood splinters around his feet.

"Yes, I mean, I'll sweep up here. It was . . . I'm, I mean, I'm sorry!"

He looks as if that last bit is about more important things than wood splinters. He moves out of the way, and she slinks past. Holding her breath even though she has brushed her teeth.

"I'm, I mean, I'm very sorry about yesterday," he says wretchedly to her back.

She stops without turning around. He clears his throat.

"I mean, I never meant to make you feel . . . the way you felt. I would never want to be the one to make you feel . . . like that."

She closes her eyes and nods. Waits until her common sense has silenced the part of her that wishes he'd touch her.

"I'll get the vacuum cleaner," she whispers after that. She knows he's looking at her as she walks away. Her steps become awkward, as if she's forgotten how to walk without putting one foot on top of the other. All her words to him are like staying in a hotel, new and curious and tentatively fumbling for switches on the wall, repeatedly turning on different lights than those she wanted to turn on.

Somebody comes rolling after her into the kitchen, where she's opening the broom cupboard to get out the pizzeria's vacuum cleaner.

"Here. Came for you."

Britt-Marie stares at the bouquet in her hands. Tulips. Purple. Britt-Marie loves purple tulips, to the extent that Britt-Marie can love anything without viewing it as an unseemly burst of emotion. Tenderly she holds it in her hands and does her utmost not to get the shivers. "I love you," it says on the card. From Kent.

It takes years to get to know a human being. An entire life. It's what makes a home a home.

At a hotel you're only a visitor. Hotels don't know your favorite flowers.

She fills her lungs with tulips; during one long inhalation she is there again, at her own dish rack and in her own broom cupboard and on rugs that she knows the whereabouts of because she put them there herself. White shirts and black shoes and a damp towel on the bathroom floor. All Kent's things. All Kent-things. You just can't rebuild things like that. You wake up one morning and realize that you're too old to check in to a hotel.

She doesn't meet Sven's eyes when she comes back out of the kitchen. Is grateful that the noise of the vacuum cleaner is drowning out with its noise all the things that should not be said.

Then come Vega, Omar, Ben, Toad, and Dino, exactly on time, and Britt-Marie busies herself with fitting them out in their newly washed soccer kits. Vega looks searchingly at Britt-Marie and asks if she's hungover, because actually she looks hungover, says the girl. Britt-Marie makes it clear in every possible way that she's certainly no such thing, that she's merely come down with the flu.

"Ah. That sort of flu. Sami had that this morning as well," laughs Omar.

The first little tinkle from the friendly bell above the door, after Sven has mended it, rings out when the men with beards and caps come in to drink their coffee and read their newspapers. But one of them asks when the first match is starting and when Omar tells them, the men check their wristwatches. As if for the first time in ages they have a schedule to keep to.

The second tinkle from the bell above the door comes when the two ancient women with walkers come dragging themselves over the threshold.

One of them rivets her eyes into Britt-Marie and points at her.

"Err yow thoon she oa treena de boos?"

Britt-Marie can't tell if these are words or sounds. Vega leans forward and whispers:

"She's asking if you're our coach."

Britt-Marie nods without taking her eyes off the tip of the ancient woman's finger, as if it's about to open fire. At this confirmation, the ancient woman produces a bag from a little shelf under the handle of the walker, and presses it into Britt-Marie's arms.

"Frout aia de boos!"

"She says it's fruit for the boys on the team," Vega interprets helpfully.

"Ha. I should like to inform you there's also a girl in the team," informs Britt-Marie.

The ancient woman glares at her. Then she glares at Vega and the soccer jersey she's wearing. The other ancient woman pushes her way forward and grunts something to the first ancient woman, whereupon the first ancient woman points at Vega and glares at Britt-Marie:

"Shera havan esstrofrout!"

"They're saying I should have extra fruit," says Vega, pleased to hear this and taking the bag from Britt-Marie to peer inside.

"Ha," says Britt-Marie, frenetically adjusting her skirt in every possible way she can think of.

When she looks up again the two ancient women are standing so close to her that you couldn't get an A4 sheet of paper between them. The women point at her and Bank.

"Yer yunguns shall teek th' chouldrin un goo ter de blousted folk in toon un tall erm Borg ainnit derd! We ainitt derd hire! Tell doose bastourds dait, hire wha' I see?"

"She's saying you and Bank have to take us to town and tell those bastards Borg isn't dead," says Vega, with her mouth full of apple.

Bank stands on the other side of Britt-Marie with a grin on her face.

"And she called you a 'young one,' Britt-Marie."

Britt-Marie, who wasn't even referred to as a "young one" when she was young, can't quite think what to say to that. So she just pats one of the women's walkers, slightly at a loss, and says:

"Ha. Thank you, then. Thank you kindly."

The women grunt and drag themselves out again. Somebody fetches the keys to the white car with the blue door and, in between chewing, Vega informs Britt-Marie that they have to pick up Max on the way.

"Ha. I was under the impression that you didn't like him," says Britt-Marie with surprise.

"*Are you going to start now as well?!*" roars Vega at once, so that the apple sprays out of her mouth and ricochets between them.

Omar laughs loudly and mockingly. Vega chases him out into the parking area with apples and mangos whizzing past the back of his head.

Britt-Marie closes her eyes and squeezes her eyelids tightly until her headache retreats. Then she nervously fidgets with the car keys, coughs quietly, and holds them out to Sven without making eye contact.

"It's not appropriate driving a car when you have . . . the flu."

Sven removes his cap when they get into the car. He doesn't even need to say he's doing it out of empathy. He doesn't want Britt-Marie to start worrying about what people might think if she's driven to the soccer competition by a policeman. Especially not in a white car with a blue door.

Nor does he say anything about how there are considerably more passengers and dogs in the car than what is suitable from both a legal and a hygienic point of view, especially as the dog and Toad have to sit in the trunk because there isn't any other space available. In the end, he does timidly point out that the car needs filling up. And asks her if she'd like him to do it. She answers that there's certainly no need for that, because she can absolutely manage that bit herself. It's her car, after all, whether it has a blue door or not.

After she's stood with one hand clasped in the other in front of the petrol pump for ten minutes, the back door opens and Vega crawls out of a tangle of arms, legs, soccer boots, and dog heads, and comes to stand next to her, carefully positioning herself so that she blocks Sven's point of view.

"It's the one in the middle," she says in a low voice to Britt-Marie without herself reaching for the petrol pump.

Britt-Marie looks at her in a panic.

"I didn't think about it until I got out of the car, you have to understand. That I don't know how you . . ."

Her voice cracks. Vega tries to make herself as broad-chested as she can so Sven can't see anything from the window. She reaches out and touches Britt-Marie's hand.

"It doesn't matter, Coach."

Britt-Marie smiles faintly and tenderly removes a loose hair from the shoulder of Vega's jersey.

"Kent always filled up the car. He was always the one who . . . it's always been him."

Vega points at the pump in the middle. Britt-Marie grabs hold of it as if worried that it might be alive. Vega leans forward and unscrews the petrol cap.

"Who taught you all this?" asks Britt-Marie.

"My mother," says Vega.

Then she grins so you can see more clearly than ever that she's Sami's sister.

"You don't have to support Liverpool from the day you're born, Coach. You can learn to do it when you're grown up."

It's a day for the soccer cup, and for farewells, and it's the day Britt-Marie puts fuel in her own car. She would have been capable of climbing mountains or crossing oceans, if someone had asked her to.

30

Britt-Marie is not sure exactly at what point the sun broke through the eternal gray haze of the January sky, but it seems to be looking ahead into the new season. Borg somehow looks different today. They drive past Toad's house, the one with the greenhouse outside. A pregnant woman is moving about inside. They pass more gardens, with more people in them, which is deeply strange now that Britt-Marie has got used to Borg's only road always being deserted. A few of them are young, a few have children, a few of them wave at the car. A man with a cap is standing there with a sign in his hand.

"Is he putting out a 'For Sale' sign?" asks Britt-Marie.

Sven slows down and waves at the man.

"He's taking it down."

"Why?"

"Things have changed. They're going to the soccer cup. They no longer want to go, they want to see what happens next. It's been awhile since anyone in Borg wanted to know what happens next."

The white car with the blue door travels through Borg, and only when they go past the sign announcing that they are now leaving Borg does Britt-Marie realize that they are being followed by other vehicles. History will remember this as the first time there's ever been a traffic jam in Borg.

Max lives in one of the big houses beyond the boundaries of the village, on its own secluded street and with windows so big that they could only have been put there by someone who thought it more important for people to be able to look in than out. Sven explains to Britt-Marie that the residents here have fought with the local council for years, with mounting hostility, to put them under the jurisdiction of the town rather than remaining a part of Borg. In the next moment he slams on his brakes as a BMW backs out, without looking, from a garage at the far end of the street. Fredrik is wearing sunglasses, spinning the wheel as if it's fighting his efforts to do so. Sven waves, but the BMW roars past; it might as well have driven straight through them.

"Bloody lemon arse," mutters Vega and gets out of the backseat.

Britt-Marie follows on behind. Max opens the door before they have even pressed the doorbell, barges his way out and, looking stressed out, closes the door behind him. He's still wearing the tracksuit top with HOCKEY printed across the chest, but he has a soccer ball under his arm.

"No need to bring a ball, Vega has already put one in the car," Britt-Marie informs him.

Max blinks uncomprehendingly.

"Surely you don't need more than one ball?" Britt-Marie goes on.

Max looks at the ball. Looks at Britt-Marie.

"Need?"

As if that's a word that bears any relation to soccer balls.

"Well *I* need to use your bathroom," moans Vega, moving impatiently towards the door. Max's hand catches her shoulder; she instantly slaps it away.

"You can't!" he says, looking worried. "Sorry!"

Vega peers suspiciously at him.

"Are you worried I'll see how bloody over-the-top your house is? You think I care if you're millionaires?"

Max tries to push her away from the door, but she's too quick; she slips under his arm and goes in. He bundles in after her, then they stand there, both rooted to the spot. She with her mouth wide open, he with his eyes closed.

"I . . . what the hell . . . where's your furniture?"

"We had to sell it," mumbles Max after a moment, closing the door without looking at the room.

Vega peers at him.

"Don't you have any money?"

"No one has any money in Borg," says Max, opening the door and stepping out, heading towards the car.

"So why doesn't your dad just sell his bloody BMW, then?" Vega calls out after him.

"Because then everyone will know he's given up," says Max with a sigh, and climbs into the backseat.

"But . . . what the . . ." Vega starts saying as she climbs in after him, until she's stopped by a hard shove from Omar.

"Drop it, sis, what are you? A cop or something? Leave him alone."

"I only want to kn—" she protests, but Omar gives her another shove.

"Leave it! He talks like one of them but he plays soccer like one of us. You got it? Leave him alone."

Max doesn't say a word on the way into town. When they stop outside the leisure center, he gets out of the backseat with his soccer ball tucked under his arm, drops it onto the asphalt, and drills a shot into the wall that is just about the hardest Britt-Marie has ever seen a ball being struck. Britt-Marie lets out the dog and Toad from the trunk. Bank follows them inside. Dino, Omar, and Vega come behind. Sven is at the back. Britt-Marie counts them several times and tries to work out who's missing, then hears Ben's voice, sounding rather pathetic, from somewhere around the far corner of the backseat.

"Sorry, Britt-Marie. I didn't mean to."

When she can't immediately locate the voice he manages to say:

"I've never played in a cup before. I got so . . . nervous. I didn't want to say anything when we were at the petrol station."

Britt-Marie still isn't quite sure she can hear what he's saying, so she sticks her head into the car. Sees the dark patch on his trousers and the seat where he's sitting.

"Sorry," he says, squeezing his eyes shut.

"Oh . . . I . . . sorry. Don't worry about it! It'll come off with baking soda!" Britt-Marie stutters, and goes to dig out some spare clothes from the trunk.

Because that's the sort of person she's become in Borg, she realizes. Someone who goes to soccer competitions with spare clothes in the trunk.

She holds the bamboo screen over the window while Ben gets changed inside. Then she covers the seat with baking soda. Brings his trousers into the sports hall and rinses them in a sink in a dressing room.

He stands beside her with an embarrassed pout around his mouth, but his eyes are sparkling, and when she's done he blurts out:

"Mum's coming here to watch today. She's taken the day off work!"

The way he says it, it's as if the building they're in is made of chocolate.

The other children are kicking two soccer balls around the corridor outside, and Britt-Marie has to exert considerable self-control not to rush out and give them a stern talking to about the unsuitability of kicking balls around indoors. She actually feels it's inappropriate even having sports arenas indoors, but she has no intention of being looked at as if *she's* the one with crazy opinions on the matter, so she keeps silent about it.

The sports hall consists of a tall spectators' stand and a flight of stairs of equal height, leading down to a rectangular surface full of colorful lines running to and fro, which Britt-Marie assumes is where the soccer matches will be played. Indoors.

Bank gathers the children in a circle at the top of the stairs and tells them things that Britt-Marie does not understand, but she comes to the conclusion this is another one of those pep talks they're all so taken with.

After Bank has finished she waves her stick in the air towards where she's figured out Britt-Marie is standing, and then says:

"Do you have anything you want to say before the match, Britt-Marie?"

Britt-Marie has not prepared for this sort of eventuality, it's not on her list, so she grips her handbag firmly and thinks it over for a moment before saying:

"I think it's important that we try to make a good first impression."

She doesn't know what exactly she's driving at with this; it's just something Britt-Marie finds a good general rule in life. The children watch her, with their eyebrows at varying heights. Vega keeps eating fruit from the bag and nodding sourly at the spectators in the stands.

"A good impression on who? That lot? They hate us, don't you get it?"

Britt-Marie has to admit that most of the people in the stands, many of them wearing jerseys and scarfs emblazoned with the name of their own team from their own town, are looking at them as you might look at a stranger on the underground who just sneezed in your face.

Halfway down the stairs stands the old codger from the council and the woman from the soccer association, the same ones that paid a visit to the training session in Borg a couple of days ago. The woman looks concerned, the old codger has his arms full of papers, and next to them stands a very serious man wearing a jersey on which it says "Official," and another person with long hair and a tracksuit top with the name of the team from town printed on one side and the word "Coach" on the other. He's pointing at Team Borg and bellowing something about how this is "a serious competition, not a nursery!"

Britt-Marie doesn't know what that's supposed to mean, but when Toad hauls out a soft-drink can from his pocket she decides that this is certainly not a way of making a good first impression, so she cautions him not to open it. Toad immediately insists that his blood sugar is a bit on the low side, whereupon Vega gets involved and shoves his shoulder, while hissing:

"Are you deaf or what? Don't open that can!" Unfortunately she catches Toad off balance and he falls backwards helplessly. He tumbles halfway down the stairs, shrieking with every step, until his body thumps into the legs of the woman from the soccer association, the old codger from the local council, the official, and the coach person.

"*Don't open that can!*" roars Vega.

Upon which he decides to open the can.

It's not what you'd in any way describe as a top-notch first impression, it really isn't.

By the time Britt-Marie and Bank have reached the section of the stairs where Toad came to a stop, the coach person is yelling with even greater indignation, for reasons already described. The old codger and the woman and the papers are whirling about in a persistent rain of lemonade. The coach person has such an amount of lemonade in his hair, on his face, and over his clothes that the amount of lemonade in the can must in some way have bypassed the natural laws of physics. The coach person points at Bank and Britt-Marie, so angry by this stage that the pointing action is executed by both hands, which, at this kind of distance, makes it difficult to determine whether he's actually pointing at all, or just demonstrating the approximate size of a badger.

"Are you the *coach* of this so-called *team*?"

He makes deranged quotation marks in the air when he says "coach" and "team." Bank's stick pokes at the coach person by accident the first time, and possibly a little less by accident the following five times. The woman looks concerned. The old codger with the papers moves behind her and, chastened by experience, keeps his hand over his mouth.

"We're the coaches," Bank confirms.

The coach person grins and looks angry at the same time.

"An old biddy and a blind person, *seeeriously*? Is this a *seeerious* competition? Huh?"

The official shakes his head gravely. The woman, more concerned than ever, peers at Bank.

"One of the players in your team, this Patrik Ivars . . ."

"What about me?" Toad bursts out anxiously from the floor.

"What about him?" growls Bank.

"Yeah, what about Patrik?" asks a third voice.

Toad's father is standing behind Britt-Marie now. He has combed his hair neatly, and dressed up. There's a red tulip tucked into the lapel of his jacket. Kent stands next to him in a wrinkled shirt. He smiles at Britt-Marie, and she immediately wants to take him by the hand.

"Patrik is two years younger than the others. He's too young to play in this competition without exemption being granted," says the woman, coughing down at the floor.

"So organize the exemption then!" snorts Bank.

"Rules are rules!"

"Really? *Really! Come here you little . . .*" yells Bank, striking furiously at the coach person with her stick, whereupon the coach person tries to grab her stick in order to avoid falling, and at the same time manages to pull her with him down the stairs, whereupon they both lose their footing and drop over the ledge, before a big hand in a single, forcible movement closes like a handcuff around the tracksuited arm and stops their fall.

The coach person hovers, leaning backwards over the stairs, with eyes wide open as he looks at Kent, who keeps his implacable grip on his arm and leans forward and declares in that clear and straightforward way of his, which he makes use of when explaining to people that he's actually going to do business with Germany:

"If you try to push a blind woman down a staircase I'll sue you in the courts until your family is buried in debt for the next ten generations."

The coach person stares at him. Bank regains her balance by happening to put her stick in the coach person's stomach two or maybe three times. The concerned woman, trying a different tack, holds out a piece of paper.

"There has also been a protest from your opponents concerning this 'Viga' in your team. We can see by her social security number that . . ."

"My name is *Vega*!" snarls Vega from farther up the stairs.

The woman scratches her earlobe self-consciously. Then smiles, as if after a local anaesthetic. And turns to Britt-Marie, who by now seems to be the only reasonable person in the assembled company.

"You have to have an exemption before girls and younger players can take part."

"So you're going to ban Patrik and Vega, purely because this town team is too scared to play against a girl and a kid who's two years younger!!" says Kent.

"*You're scared!*" yells Bank and accidentally pokes her stick into the tracksuit top and a bit into the old codger with papers.

"We're not bloody sc—" mumbles the coach person.

And that is how Vega and Patrik get their exemptions so they can play. Patrik goes down the stairs to the pitch with his dad's arms around his shoulders, looking so happy you'd think he'd sprouted wings.

The other children run onto the pitch and start taking some warm-up shots at the goal, which admittedly looks as if they're taking general warm-up shots at everything except the goal.

Britt-Marie and Kent stay there on the stairs, just the two of them. She picks up a hair from the shoulder of his shirt, and adjusts a crease on his arm so softly that it's as if she never even touched him.

"How did you know to say that thing about them being scared?" she asks.

Kent laughs in a way that makes Britt-Marie also start laughing inside.

"I have an older brother. It always worked for me. You remember when I jumped off the balcony and broke my leg? All the dumbest things I ever did started with Alf telling me he didn't think I had the guts to do them!"

"It was nice of you. And you were sweet to leave the tulips," whispers Britt-Marie, without asking if she was also one of those dumb things he did.

Kent laughs again.

"I bought them off that Toad boy's dad. He's growing them in a greenhouse in the garden. What a lunatic, eh? He nagged the heck out of me about how I had to get the red ones instead because they're 'better,' but I told him you like the purple ones."

She brushes some invisible dust from his chest. Controls herself.

In a commonsense approach, she clasps one hand in the other and says:

"I have to go. They'll be on soon."

"Good luck!" says Kent, leaning forward and kissing her on the cheek so warmly she has to grasp the metal banister to avoid falling down the stairs.

When he goes to sit in the last empty seat in the away section, she realizes that this is the first time Kent is somewhere for her sake. The first time in their lives that he has to present himself as being in her company, rather than the other way around.

In the seat next to him sits Sven. With his eyes fixed on the floor.

Britt-Marie breathes in deeply with each step. Bank and the dog are waiting for her on a bench next to the pitch. Somebody as well, with a particularly satisfied expression on her face.

"How did you get here?" asks Britt-Marie.

"Drove, you know," Somebody answers casually.

"What about the pizzeria and the grocery store and the post office, then? What about the opening hours?"

Somebody shrugs.

"Who will come to shop, Britt? Everyone in Borg—here!"

Britt-Marie adjusts invisible creases in her skirt at such a speed that it looks as if she's trying to start a fire. Somebody pats her calmingly.

"Nervous, huh? No problem, Britt, I said to that official, huh: 'I will sit on the sideline with Britt. Because I have one of those, what's-it-called . . . calming effect on Britt, huh.' The official just said 'Forget it,' so I said 'Can't see one of those disability areas here, illegal, huh.' I said: 'Could sue you, you know.' So now: I sit here. Best seat, isn't it?"

Britt-Marie excuses herself, leaves the sideline, walks down a corridor and into a toilet, where she vomits. When she comes back to the bench, Somebody is still talking, her fingers nervously drumming against anything within reach. The dog sniffs in Britt-Marie's direction. Bank offers her a pack of chewing gum.

"It's normal. You often get food poisoning just before important games."

Britt-Marie chews the gum with her hand covering her mouth, because people might come to the conclusion that she has tattoos (or something similar). Then the spectators burst into applause, the referee walks onto the pitch, and a team from Borg that does not even have its own pitch starts playing.

With vocal support from an entire community where just about everything has been closed down. But only just about.

The first thing that happens is that Dino gets tackled—or elbowed, to be more precise—by a large boy with a complicated haircut. The next time Dino gets the ball, exactly the same thing happens, only even harder. A few feet away from Britt-Marie the coach person bounces up and down in a soaking wet tracksuit jacket while yelling his encouragement:

"*Exaaactly* like that! Make them *respeeect* you!"

Britt-Marie is convinced she's about to have a heart attack, but when she explains this to Bank, Bank says, "That's how it's meant to be when you're watching soccer." Who on earth would want to watch soccer, then, Britt-Marie thinks to herself. The third time Dino gets the ball the big boy accelerates from the other side of the pitch and runs at full speed with his elbow raised. The next moment he's lying on his back. Max stands over him with his chest out and his arms straightened. He's already walking back towards the bench before the referee has sent him off.

"Max! Huh! You're such a, what's-it-called?" Somebody says, overwhelmed with joy.

Bank taps her stick against Max's shoes.

"He talks like one of them. But he plays like one of us."

Max smiles and says something, but Britt-Marie can't hear what.

The match resumes, and Britt-Marie finds, to her surprise, that she's standing up. Her mouth is hanging open and she doesn't even know how. On the pitch, three players have collided and the ball has bounced haphazardly towards the touchline, and suddenly it's just lying there right at Ben's feet with a clear shot at the goal. He stares at it. The entire crowd in the sports hall stares at him.

"Shoot," whispers Britt-Marie.

"Shoot!" yells a voice from the stand.

It's Sami. Next to him stands a red-faced woman. It's the first time Britt-Marie has ever seen her wearing anything but a nurse's uniform.

"*Shooooooooooooooot!!!*" cries Bank, waving her stick to and fro in the air.

So Ben shoots. Britt-Marie hides her face in the palms of her hands; Bank almost overturns Somebody's wheelchair while she yells:

"What's happening? Tell me what's happening!"

The stands are silent as if no one can quite believe how this has happened. At first, Ben looks as if he's going to burst into tears, then as if he's looking for a hiding place. And he doesn't have time to do much more than that before he finds himself at the bottom of a screaming pile of arms and legs and white shirts. Borg is in the lead by 1–0. Sami charges around in the stand with his arms held out, like an aircraft. Kent and Sven bounce up from their seats so abruptly that they accidentally start hugging each other.

A red-faced woman makes her way out of the chaos and runs down the stairs. A couple of officials try to get in her way when they see she's going to run onto the pitch, but they can't stop her. They couldn't have stopped her even if they were carrying guns. Ben dances with his mum as if no one can take this away from him.

Borg lose the match 14–1. It makes no difference. They play as if it makes all the difference in the universe.

It does make a difference.

31

At a certain age almost all the questions a person asks him or herself are really just about one thing: how should you live your life?

If a human being closes her eyes hard enough and for long enough, she can remember pretty well everything that has made her happy. The fragrance of her mother's skin at the age of five and how they fled giggling into a porch to get out of a sudden downpour. The cold tip of her father's nose against her cheek. The consolation of the rough paw of a soft toy that she has refused to let them wash. The sound of waves stealing in over rocks during their last seaside holiday. Applause in a theater. Her sister's hair, afterwards, carelessly waving in the breeze as they're walking down the street.

And apart from that? When has she been happy? A few moments. The jangling of keys in the door. The beating of Kent's heart against the palms of her hands while he lay sleeping. Children's laughter. The feel of the wind on her balcony. Fragrant tulips. True love.

The first kiss.

A few moments. A human being, any human being at all, has so perishingly few chances to stay right there, to let go of time and fall into the moment. And to love someone without measure. Explode with passion.

A few times when we are children, maybe, for those of us who are allowed to be. But after that, how many breaths are we allowed to take beyond the confines of ourselves? How many pure emotions make us cheer out loud, without a sense of shame? How many chances do we get to be blessed by amnesia?

All passion is childish. It's banal and naive. It's nothing we learn; it's instinctive, and so it overwhelms us. Overturns us. It bears us away in a flood. All other emotions belong to the earth, but passion inhabits the universe.

That is the reason why passion is worth something, not for what it gives us but for what it demands that we risk. Our dignity. The puzzlement of others and their condescending, shaking heads.

Britt-Marie yells out loud when Ben scores that goal. The soles of her feet are catapulted off the floor of the sports hall. Most people are not blessed with that sort of thing in the month of January. The universe.

You have to love soccer for that.

It's late at night, the cup was over several hours ago, and Britt-Marie is at the hospital. She's rinsing the blood out of a white soccer jersey in the sink while Vega sits on the toilet next to her, her voice still euphorically effervescent. As if she can't sit still. As if she could have run vertically.

Britt-Marie's heart is still beating so wildly that she still can't understand how anyone could have the energy to live like this—that is, if it's true what the children are saying, that it's possible to have a soccer team that plays a match every week. Who would be willing to do this to themselves on a weekly basis?

"I absolutely can't understand how you could get it into your head to behave in this sort of way," Britt-Marie manages to whisper, because her voice no longer carries, having been yelled to shreds.

"They would have scored otherwise!" explains Vega for the thousandth time.

"You threw yourself right in front of the ball," hisses Britt-Marie, with a reproachful gesture from the sink and the bloodstains on the jersey.

Vega blinks. It hurts when she does that, because half her face is dark purple and swollen from her lacerated eyebrow down across her bloodshot eye, her nose with coagulated blood in her nostrils, and her split lip at the bottom so big that it looks as if she's tried to eat a wasp.

"I covered the shot," she asserts.

"With your face, yes. For goodness' sake, one doesn't cover shots with one's face," but it's unclear if she's mainly angry because Vega got blood on her face or blood on her jersey.

"They would have scored." Vega shrugs.

"I can't for the life of me understand why you love soccer so much that you're prepared to risk your life in that way," hisses Britt-Marie as she furiously rubs baking soda on the jersey.

Vega looks thoughtful. Then hesitant.

"Have you never loved anything like that?"

"Ha. No. I . . . ha. I don't know. I actually don't know."

"I don't feel pain anymore when I'm playing soccer," says Vega, her eyes fixed on the number on the back of the jersey soaking in the sink.

"What pain do you mean?"

"Any pain."

Britt-Marie goes silent, ashamed of herself. Turns on the hot water. Closes her eyes. Vega leans her head back and peruses the ceiling of the bathroom.

"I dream about soccer when I'm sleeping," she says, as if this is quite reasonable, and then she asks, with sincere curiosity, as if she cannot understand what else you could dream about:

"What do you dream about?"

It just slips out of Britt-Marie; she whispers instinctively:

"Sometimes I dream about Paris."

Vega nods understandingly.

"In that case soccer for me is like Paris for you. Have you been there a lot?"

"Never."

"Why not?"

"It's one of those things that just . . . never happened. Come here now and wash your face—"

"Why not?"

Britt-Marie adjusts the tap so the water is not too hot.

Her heart is still thumping so hard that she can count the beats. She looks at Vega, tries to smooth away a few hairs from her forehead and gently probes the swelling at the edge of her eye, as if it is hurting Britt-Marie more than Vega. Then she whispers:

"You have to understand that when I was small my family and I went to the seaside. My sister always found the highest rocks to jump off into the water, and when she dived and came up to the surface, I was always still there at the top of the rock, and she would call out to me, 'Jump, Britt! Just jump!' You have to understand that when one is just standing there looking, then just for a second one is ready to jump. If one does it, one dares to do it. But if one waits, it'll never happen."

"Did you jump?"

"I'm not the sort who jumps."

"But your sister was?"

"She was like you. Fearless."

Then she folds a paper tissue and whispers:

"But not even she would have got it into her head to throw herself face-first in front of a soccer ball like an utter madwoman!"

Vega stands up and lets Britt-Marie dab her cuts.

"So that's why you don't go to Paris now? Because you're the type that doesn't jump?" asks the girl.

"I'm too old for Paris."

"How old is Paris?"

To which Britt-Marie has no decent answer. Even though it sounds like an absolutely excellent crossword clue. She glimpses herself in the mirror. It's all quite ludicrous, of course. She's a grown woman, she is, and here she stands in a hospital for the second time in just a few days. A child sits here on a toilet seat, her face covered in blood, while, in another room at the end of the corridor, another child lies with a broken leg.

Because they were covering shots. Who would want to live like that?

Vega meets her eyes in the mirror, then laughs so the blood runs from her lip across her teeth. Which makes her laugh even more, the lunatic.

"If you're not the type that jumps, Britt-Marie, how did you bloody well end up in Borg, then?"

Britt-Marie presses the paper tissue against her lip and hisses something at her about not using inappropriate language. Vega mumbles something angrily through the tissue, so Britt-Marie presses it down even harder. Then she pulls the girl outside into the waiting room before she says anything else.

Which is obviously not a very well-thought-through idea, because that's where Fredrik is. He's pacing back and forth outside the toilet door. Toad, Dino, Ben, and Omar are sleeping on the benches in a corner. Fredrik immediately points at Britt-Marie in a hostile manner.

"If Max has broken his leg and misses elite training camp, I'll make sure you never get anywhere near h . . ."

His voice fades as he closes his eyes and tries to calm himself down. Vega pushes in front of Britt-Marie and slaps at his finger.

"Shut up, will you! The leg will heal! Max was covering a shot!"

Fredrik clenches his fists and backs away from her, as if, in his despair, he's afraid of what might otherwise happen.

"I banned him from playing soccer before the elite training camp. I told him that if he injures himself now it could damage his whole career. I told hi—"

"What bloody career is that? He's at bloody secondary school!" Vega cuts in.

Fredrik points at Britt-Marie again. Sinks down on a bench as if someone just dropped him.

"Do you know what it means to go to elite training camp when you play ice hockey? Do you understand what we have sacrificed to give him this opportunity?"

"Did you ask Max if he wants to, or not?"

"Are you spastic or something? It's the elite camp! Of course he wants to!" bellows Fredrik.

"No one needs to shout at him for playing soccer!" Vega bellows back.

"Maybe you could do with someone shouting at you!"

"And maybe you could do with some furniture!"

They stand with their foreheads locked together, breathing heavily, and both utterly exhausted. Both have tears in their eyes. Neither of them will ever forget the cup matches Borg played today. No one in Borg will.

Admittedly they lost their second game 5–0. The match had to be stopped for several minutes halfway through because Toad saved a penalty and everyone had to wait until he had stopped running around the pitch like an aircraft. The crowd sounded as if Borg had won the World Cup, which, after repeated explanations, Britt-Marie understood was another soccer competition of particular importance if you were that way inclined.

In the third and last game the noise in the sports hall was so loud that all Britt-Marie could hear was a sort of sustained roar, and her heart thumped so hard that she lost her sense of touch, while her arms waved around her body as if they were no longer hers. Their opponents were in the lead by 2–0, but with another few minutes to go, Vega thumped in a goal for Borg with her whole body. Immediately afterwards, Max dribbled his way through the entire opposing team and scored, watched every step of the way by his begrudging father. When his head popped out of the pile of arms and legs of his teammates, Fredrik turned around in disappointment and walked out of the door. Max stood motionless by the sideline, staring at him as the referee blew the whistle to restart the game. By the time the roaring spectators had woken the boy up, their opponents had hit the post once and the crossbar once, and the whole team except for Vega was lying scattered on the floor. Then one of the opposing players gathered himself to take a shot at the open goal, and that was when Vega threw herself in front of the ball and covered the shot. With her face. There was blood on the ball when it bounced back to the player.

He could have killed the match by tapping the ball in with the side of his foot, but despite this, the player stretched his foot for a hard shot. Max ran straight into the pile of bodies and threw himself forward with his leg stretched out. He made contact with the ball but the opponent hit his leg. Max yelled so loudly that Britt-Marie felt as if she was the one with the broken leg.

The match finished 2–2. It was the first time in a very, very long time that Borg had not lost a soccer match. Vega sat next to Max on their way to the hospital, singing extremely unsuitable songs all the way.

Ben's mother is standing in the doorway. She looks at Vega, then at Britt-Marie, then she nods as you do at the end of a long shift.

"Max wants to see you two. Just you two."

Fredrik swears loudly, but Ben's mother is implacable.

"Just these two."

"I thought you were having the evening off," says Vega.

"I was. But when Borg plays soccer the hospital has to call in extra staff," she says severely, even though she's quite clearly trying not to laugh.

She throws a blanket over Ben on one of the benches, and kisses him on the cheek. Then she does the same with Dino, Toad, and Omar, all still sleeping on the other benches.

Britt-Marie feels Fredrik's hateful stare at her back as she and Vega follow her down the corridor, so she slows and walks behind Vega, to stop his stares hitting the girl. Max lies in a bed with his leg hoisted up towards the ceiling. He grins when he sees Vega's swollen face as she comes walking in.

"Nice face! Totally an improvement on how you looked before!"

Vega snorts and nods at his leg.

"You think the doctors can screw on your leg straight this time, so you can learn to shoot properly, or what?"

He sniggers. So does she.

"Is my dad pissed off?" asks Max.

"Do bears shit in the woods?" Vega answers.

"Really, Vega! Is that the sort of language you use when you're in a hospital? Well, is it?"

Vega laughs. Max too. Britt-Marie inhales, deeply self-controlled, turns, and leaves them and their language to it.

Fredrik is still standing in the waiting room where they left him. Britt-Marie stops, at a loss. Resists the impulse to pick one of Vega's hairs from his arm, where it landed while they were locking heads and yelling at each other.

"Ha," whispers Britt-Marie.

He doesn't answer. Just glares down at the floor. So she summons what voice she has left in her throat and asks:

"Have you ever loved anything as much as these children do, Fredrik?"

He raises his head and drills his eyes into her.

"Do you have any children of your own, Britt-Marie?"

She swallows heavily and shakes her head. He looks down at the floor again.

"Don't ask me about what I love, then."

They sit on their chairs without saying anything else until Ben's mother reemerges. Britt-Marie stands up, but Max's dad stays seated as if he can't summon any more energy. Ben's mother puts her hand consolingly on his shoulder and says:

"Max wanted me to tell you that he'll most likely be able to start playing ice hockey within six months. His leg will be completely back to normal. His career shouldn't be in any danger at all."

Max's father doesn't move. Presses his chin hard against his throat. Ben's mother nods at Britt-Marie. Britt-Marie sucks in her cheeks. Ben's mother is heading for the door when Max's father finally lifts his hands to his eyes in two quick movements, tears dripping between his fingers, down into his beard. He doesn't have a towel. The tears stain the floor.

"Soccer, then? When can he start playing soccer again?"

At a certain age almost all the questions a person asks himself are about one thing: how should you live your life?

32

Britt-Marie sits alone on a bench on the pavement outside the accident and emergency wing. She has a bouquet of tulips in her arms, can feel the wind in her hair, and is thinking about Paris. It's strange, the power a place can have over you, even if you've never been there. If she closes her eyes she can nonetheless feel its cobblestones under her feet. Maybe more clearly now than ever. As if when she jumped into the air when Ben scored, she came back down to earth as a different person. The sort of person who jumps.

"Mind if I sit with you?" asks the voice.

She can hear the voice is smiling. She also smiles, even before she has opened her eyes.

"Please do," she whispers.

"Your voice is hoarse," says Sven with a smile.

She nods.

"It's the flu."

He laughs out loud. She laughs inside. He sits down and holds out a ceramic vase for her.

"Well, yeah, I made it for you. I'm doing a course. You know, I thought you could put your tulips in it."

She grips it and holds it tightly in her arms. The surface is slightly rough against her skin, like a soft toy you wouldn't let your parents wash.

"It was quite fantastic today. I have to admit it. Absolutely wonderful," she manages to say.

"It's a wonderful sport," says Sven.

As if life was so simple.

"It's been heavenly to feel enthusiastic again," she whispers.

He smiles and turns to her, looking as if he's about to tell her something, so she stops him by gathering up all her common sense in a single, suffocating breath and saying:

"If it's not too much trouble I'd be very grateful if you had time to run the children home."

She sees him sitting there growing smaller in the seconds that follow. Her heart twists inside her. Also inside him.

"I have to assume that this, that this means that, well . . . I have to assume that it'll be Kent who's driving you home then," he manages to say.

"Yes," she whispers.

He sits in silence with his hands gripping the edge of the bench. She does the same, because she likes holding it while he's also holding it. She peers at him and wants to say that it's not his fault. That she's just too old to fall in love. She wants to tell him that he can find himself someone better. That he deserves something perfect. But she doesn't say anything, because she's afraid he'll say she is perfect.

She's still clutching the vase as she sits in the car, the town and the road swishing by. Her chest is aching with held-back longings. Kent talks all the way, of course. Initially about the soccer and the children, but before long his focus switches to business and Germans and plans. He wants to go on holiday, he says, just the two of them. They can go to the theater. Go to the sea. Very soon; a few plans just have to fall into place first. When they drive into Borg he makes a joke about how this place is so small that two people could stand on top of the welcome signs at either end, having a conversation without even having to raise their voices.

"If you lie down here you'll find your feet are already in the next village!" he guffaws, and when she doesn't immediately laugh he says it again.

"Okay, pop in and get your stuff now, and then we'll be off!" he says as the BMW stops outside Bank's house.

"Right away?"

"Yes, I have a meeting tomorrow. Let's get going now so we're ahead of the traffic." He drums his fingers against the dashboard impatiently.

"We actually can't just leave in the middle of the night," protests Britt-Marie, her voice scarcely audible.

"Why not?"

"Well, only criminals drive around in the middle of the night."

"Oh, good God, darling, you have to pull yourself together now," he groans.

Her nails dig into the vase.

"I haven't even handed in notice to my employers yet. I can't just disappear without handing in my notice. The keys have to be returned, you have to understand."

"Please, darling, it's not exactly much of a 'job,' is it?"

Britt-Marie sucks her cheeks in.

"It's a job as far as I'm concerned."

"Yes, yes, yes, that's not how I mean it, darling. Don't get irate now. Can't you just call them while we're on the road? It's not that important, is it? Come on, I have a meeting tomorrow!" He says this as if he's the one who's being flexible here. She doesn't answer.

"Do you even get a salary for this 'job'?"

Britt-Marie's nails hurt as they bend against the ceramic vase in her lap.

"I'm not some criminal. I'm not traveling around in the car at night. I just won't do it, Kent," she whispers.

"No, no, no, okay then," sighs Kent. "Tomorrow morning if it's so important. I can't believe how this village has got under your skin, my darling. You don't even like soccer!"

Britt-Marie's nails start slowly retracting from the ceramic vase. Her thumb dives over the rim and adjusts the tulips inside.

"I was given a crossword the other day, Kent. There was a question about Maslow's Hierarchy of Needs in it."

Kent has started fidgeting with his cell phone, so she raises her voice:

"It's popular in crosswords, it really is. The Hierarchy of Needs. So I read about it in a newspaper. The first stage is about people's most basic needs. Food and water."

"Mmm," says Kent, tapping away.

"Air as well, I have to assume," adds Britt-Marie so quietly that she's almost not sure herself whether she says anything.

The second stage of the Hierarchy of Needs is "safety," the third is "love and belonging," the fourth is "self-esteem." She remembers it quite clearly, because this Maslow fellow is remarkably popular in crosswords. "The highest step of the ladder is self-actualization. That was how all this felt to me, Kent. It was a way of actualizing myself."

She bites her lip.

"You just think it's silly, I suppose."

He looks up from his telephone. Looks at her, breathing deeply and loudly, like he does just before he falls asleep and starts snoring.

"Yes, yes! Of course I can understand the whole darned thing, darling. I get it. It's superb, really superb! Self-actualizing. Bloody superb. So now you've got it out of your system. And tomorrow we can go home!"

She bites her lip and lets go of his hand. Takes a firm grip on the vase and clambers out of the car.

"Damn it, darling! Don't get annoyed again! I mean how long does this job last? How long will you be employed?"

"Three weeks," she forces herself to say.

"And then? When those three weeks are over and you don't have a job anymore? Will you be staying on in Borg as an unemployed person, then?"

When she doesn't answer he sighs and gets out of the car.

"You do understand this is not your home, don't you, darling?"

She is walking away, but she knows he's right.

He breaks into a run and catches up with her. Takes the ceramic pot with the tulips from her, and carries them into the house. She walks slowly behind him.

"I'm sorry, my darling," he says, with his hands cupped softly around her face, as they stand there in the hall.

She closes her eyes. He kisses her on the eyelids. He always used to do that, in the beginning, just after her mother had died. When she was at her loneliest in the world, until one day when he stood there on the landing in their apartment building, and then she was no longer at her loneliest. Because he needed her, and you are not alone when someone needs you. So she loves it when he kisses her eyelids.

"I'm just a bit stressed. Because of the meeting tomorrow. But everything is going to be all right. I promise."

She wants to believe him. He grins and kisses her cheek and tells her not to worry. And that he will be picking her up tomorrow morning at six o'clock, so they don't end up in the morning rush hour traffic.

Then he scoffs: "But you never know, if all three cars in Borg are out at the same time it could get a bit crowded!" She smiles, as if that's funny. Stands in the hall with the door closed until he drives away.

Then she goes up the stairs and makes the bed. Puts her bags in order. Folds all the towels. Goes down the stairs again, out of the door, and walks through Borg. It's dark and silent as if no one lives here, as if the soccer cup never even took place.

But the lights are on in the pizzeria; she can hear Bank and Somebody laughing in there.

There are other voices too. Clinking glasses. Songs about soccer, and other songs sung by Bank, the lyrics of which, certainly as far as Britt-Marie is concerned, do not bear repeating.

She unlocks the recreation center and turns on the kitchen light. Sits on a stool and hopes the rat will turn up. It fails to do so. Then she sits with her cell phone held in her cupped hands, as if it was liquid and might otherwise be spilled. She waits for a long time before she can bring herself to make the call.

The girl from the unemployment office answers on her third attempt.

"Britt-Marie?" she manages to say, sounding drowsy.

"I should like to hand in my notice," Britt-Marie whispers.

It sounds as if the girl is stumbling about and knocking something over at the other end of the line. A lamp, perhaps.

"No, no, Mummy is just talking on the telephone, darling, go back to sleep, sweetie. . . ."

"I beg your pardon?"

"Sorry. I was talking to my daughter. We fell asleep on the sofa."

"I wasn't aware you had a daughter."

"I have two," the girl replies, and it sounds as if she walks into a kitchen and turns on a lamp and starts making coffee. "What time is it?"

"Hardly a good time to be drinking coffee," answers Britt-Marie.

"What can I do for you, Britt-Marie?"

"I should like to hand in my notice. I need to . . . come home," whispers Britt-Marie.

"How did the soccer cup go?" the girl asks after a long silence.

Something about that question impacts Britt-Marie. It may be the case that after Ben's goal she really did come back to earth as a different human being. She doesn't know. But she takes a deep breath and tells the girl everything.

About communities situated by main roads and rats and people who wear their caps indoors. About boys' first dates and jerseys hung up on pizzeria walls. It all pours out of her. About Faxin and bamboo screens, beer bottles presented in cellophane, and IKEA furniture. Pistols and crossword supplements. Policemen and entrepreneurs. Doing the Idiot in the beam of a truck's headlights. Blue doors and old soccer matches. Purple tulips and whiskey and cigarettes and dead mothers. Flu. Soft-drink cans. 1–0 against the team from the town. A girl who covers a shot with her face. The universe.

"I suppose this must all sound very . . . silly," she concludes.

The girl at the other end of the line can't quite keep her voice steady as she replies:

"Have I told you why I work here, Britt-Marie? I don't know if you know this, but you're at the receiving end of an unbelievable amount of crap when you work at the unemployment office. People can be incredibly mean. And when I say 'crap,' Britt-Marie, you should know that I really do mean that quite literally. One time, someone sent me some shit in an envelope. As if it's my fault that there's a financial crisis, sort of thing?"

Britt-Marie coughs.

"Might one ask how on earth they got it into the envelope?"

"The shit?"

"It must have been quite hard to . . . aim."

The girl laughs loudly for several minutes. Britt-Marie is pleased about losing her voice, because it means the girl can't hear that she's also laughing. It may not be the universe, maybe not so, but the emotion levitates her slightly off the stool.

"Do you know why I work when there's all this crap, Britt-Marie?"

"Why?"

"My mother worked for the social services all her life. She always said that in the middle of all the crap, in the thick of it all, you always had a sunny story turning up. Which makes it all worthwhile." The next words that come are smiling:

"You're my sunny story, Britt-Marie."

Britt-Marie swallows.

"It's inappropriate to talk on the telephone in the middle of the night. I should like to contact you again tomorrow."

"Sleep well, Britt-Marie," says the girl softly.

"You too."

Britt-Marie sits on the stool with the palms of her hands cupped around the telephone.

She catches herself wishing so fervently for the rat to turn up that when there's a knock on the door, she thinks it finally has. Then she comes to her senses and realizes that rats can't knock on doors, because they don't have knuckles. At least she thinks they don't.

"Anyone home?" Sami calls out from the door.

Britt-Marie flies off her stool.

"Did something happen? Has there been an accident?"

He stands calmly leaning against the doorpost.

"No. Why?"

"It's the middle of the night, Sami. Surely one doesn't just show up unannounced at people's homes like some vacuum cleaner salesman unless something has happened!"

"Do you live here?" asks Sami, with a grin.

"You must surely understand what I mean—"

"Chill, Britt-Marie. I was driving past and I saw your lights were on. Wanted to see if you fancied a cigarette. Or a drink." He laughs at her expense.

She doesn't appreciate that at all.

"Certainly not," she hisses.

"Okay, cool," he laughs.

She adjusts her skirt.

"But if you'll make do with a Snickers instead you can come in."

They each take a stool by the kitchen window. Look at the stars through the cleanest windows in Borg.

"It was nice today," says Sami.

"Yes. It was . . . nice." She smiles.

She wants to tell him she has to leave Borg first thing tomorrow and go home, but before she has time to open her mouth he says:

"Right, I have to go into town. I have to help a friend."

"What sort of friend is that? It's the middle of the night."

"Magnus. He's having problems with a few guys there. Owes them money, you know."

Britt-Marie stares at him. He nods. Smiles ironically at himself.

"I know what you're thinking. But this is Borg. We forgive each other in Borg. We don't have a choice. If we didn't there wouldn't be any friends left to get pissed off at."

She stands up. Gently takes his plate. Hesitates for a long time, then at long last tenderly lays her bandaged hand against his cheek.

"You don't always have to be the one who steps in, Sami."

"Yes, I do."

She washes up. He stands next to her, drying the plates.

"If something happens to me can you promise you'll look out for Omar and Vega and make sure they're all right? Can you promise me you'll find good people to look after them?"

"Why would something happen to you?" she asks, the color draining from her face.

"Ah, nothing is going to happen to me, I'm fucking Superman. But you know. If something does happen. Will you make sure they can live with some good people?"

She elaborately dries her hands on the towel, so he won't notice that they are shaking.

"Why are you asking me? Why don't you ask Sven or Bank or . . ."

"Because you're not the type to walk out, Britt-Marie."

"Neither are you!"

He places himself on the threshold and lights a cigarette. She stands to one side behind him, breathing in the smoke.

The sun hasn't come up yet. She picks a hair off the arm of his jacket. Puts it in a handkerchief and folds it up.

"What soccer team did your mother support?" she asks quietly.

He grins, as if it's quite obvious, and answers the question as all sons with mothers do:

"Our team."

He drives her to Bank's house. Kisses her hair. She sits on the balcony with her packed bags and watches him driving off towards town. He has made her promise that she won't sit up all night waiting for his car to come back.

But she does it anyway.

33

I should like you to know that I've handed in my notice. I have to go home, you understand."

Britt-Marie fiddles with the bandage around her ring finger.

"Admittedly I can perfectly understand that you don't understand. But I belong with Kent. A person has to have a home. Obviously I don't mean to say that you also have to have a home. I'm not sticking my nose into that. I'm quite sure you have a perfectly adequate home."

The rat sits on the floor, looking at the plate in front of it as if the plate had stepped on its tail and called it a blithering idiot.

"I ran out of Snickers," Britt-Marie says apologetically.

The rat looks at the jars on the plate.

"That one is peanut butter. And this is something known as Nutella," she says proudly. "They'd run out of Snickers in the grocery, but I've been informed that in all important respects this is the same thing."

It's still the middle of the night. Somebody was not at all pleased about being woken up, but Britt-Marie couldn't bring herself to sit on her own with her bags on Bank's balcony. Couldn't bear it. So she came back here, to say good-bye. To both the rat and the village.

Britt-Marie stands by the window. It'll soon be dawn. Somebody has turned out the lights in the pizzeria and gone to bed again, in the hope that Britt-Marie won't be banging on her door because she needs peanut butter and chocolate. The party is long since over. The road lies deserted. Britt-Marie rubs her wedding ring with a potato smeared with baking soda, because that is the best way to clean wedding rings. She often does that with Kent's wedding ring; he often leaves it on his bedside table. He's often so distracted, Kent is, whenever he's about to meet with the Germans.

Britt-Marie usually cleans the ring until it gleams, so he won't be able to avoid noticing it when he gets out of bed the next morning.

This is the first time she has cleaned her own ring. The first time she has not worn it on her finger. She whispers, without looking at the rat:

"Kent needs me. A person needs to be needed, you have to understand."

She doesn't know if rats sit awake in their kitchens at night, thinking about how they are going about their lives. Or who they are going about their lives with.

"Sami told me I'm not the type to clear off, but you have to understand that that is most certainly exactly what I am. Whichever way I turn, I'm leaving someone behind. So the only thing that's right must be to blasted well stay where you belong. In your normal life."

Britt-Marie tries to sound sure of herself. The rat licks its feet. Makes a little semi-loop on the napkin. Then dashes out of the door.

Britt-Marie doesn't know if it thinks she talks too much. Doesn't know why it keeps coming here. The supply of Snickers, obviously, but she hopes there's something more to it. She takes the plate and puts plastic wrap over the remains of the peanut butter and Nutella, then puts everything in the fridge out of an old habit, because she's not one to throw away food. She wipes her wedding ring carefully and folds it in a piece of paper towel before tucking it into her jacket pocket. It'll be nice to take off the bandage and put the ring back on her finger. Like getting into her own bed after a long journey.

A normal life—she has never wanted anything but a normal life. She could have made other choices, she tells herself, but she chose Kent. A human being may not choose her circumstances, but she does choose her actions, she insists quietly to herself. Sami was right. She's not the kind that clears off. So she must go home, where she is needed.

She sits on the stool in the kitchen, staring at the wall and waiting for a black car. It does not come. She wonders if Sami thinks about how one should live one's life, if he has ever had that luxury. A human being can't choose his circumstances, admittedly, but in Sami's life there have been more circumstances than events. She asks herself if choices or circumstances make us the sort of people we become—or what it was that made Sami the sort of person who steps in. She wonders what takes the most out of a person: to be the kind that jumps, or the kind that doesn't?

She wonders how much space a person has left in her soul to change herself, once she gets older. What people does she still have to meet, what will they see in her, and what will they make her see in herself?

Sami went to town to protect someone who doesn't deserve it, and Britt-Marie is getting ready to go home for the same reason. Because if we don't forgive those we love, then what is left? What is love if it's not loving our lovers even when they don't deserve it?

The headlights from the road give off a sudden gleam, slowly reach out of the darkness like arms in the water, passing the "Welcome to Borg" sign.

They slow down by the bus stop. Turn off into the graveled parking area. Britt-Marie is already standing in the doorway.

—

Later, when people speak of it, it will be said that a few young men found Magnus in the early hours of morning, standing outside a bar. One of them was holding a knife. Another man stepped in between them. He was the kind that always steps in.

The car stops gently on the gravel. Makes a little warm sigh as the engine is turned off. The headlights are switched off at the same time as the pizzeria lights are turned on. In certain types of communities people always know what it means when cars stop outside their windows before dawn. People know it is never because something good has happened. Somebody comes rolling onto the porch; her wheelchair stops at once when she sees the police uniform.

Sven stands with his cap in both hands and his bottom lip full of teeth marks, caused by his attempt to hold it all in. Despair, which has run down his cheeks and caused red lines, speaks volumes about just how futile his attempt has been.

Britt-Marie yells out. Falls to the ground. And lies there under the weight of another human being, who no longer exists.

34

This is no slow grief. It does not emerge at the tail end of denial, anger, negotiation, depression, or acceptance. It flares up at once, like an all-consuming fire within her, a fire that takes all the oxygen from the air until she's lying on the ground, lashing at the gravel and panting for air. Her body tries to twist into itself, as if there's no spine, as if it is desperately trying to quench the flames inside.

Death is the ultimate state of powerlessness. Powerlessness is the ultimate despair.

Britt-Marie doesn't know how she gets back on her feet. How Sven gets her into the car. He must have carried her. They find Vega halfway between the flat and the recreation center, and she's lying in the gravel. Her hair is plastered to her skin, her words come out in stuttered gurgles, as if tears have filled her lungs. As if the girl is drowning from the inside.

"Omar. We have to find Omar. He'll kill them."

Britt-Marie doesn't know if, sitting there in the backseat, she's holding Vega so tightly herself, or if, in fact, it's the other way around.

Around them, the dawn gently wakes Borg like someone breathing into the ear of someone they love. With sun and promises. Tickling light falls over warm duvets, like the smell of freshly brewed coffee and toasted bread. It shouldn't be doing this. It's the wrong day to be beautiful, but the dawn doesn't care.

The police car hurtles along in these first few moments of morning, the only thing moving on the road. Sven's fingers are curled so hard around the steering wheel it must surely be hurting him. As if he has to keep the pain in some place. He speeds up when he sees the other car. The only car that has any reason to leave Borg at this time of morning. The only brother left for Vega to save.

Every death is unjust. Everyone who mourns seeks someone to blame. Our fury is almost always met by the merciless insight that no one bears responsibility for death. But what if someone was responsible? And what if you knew who had snatched away the person you love? What would you do? Which car would you be sitting in, and what would you be holding in your hands?

The police car roars past and cuts off the other car. Sven's feet hit the asphalt before any of them have even come to a stop. For an eternity he stands there in the road, alone, his face streaked with red lines and his lip buckled with bite marks. Finally a car door opens and Omar steps out. A man's eyes in the body of a boy. Is this the end of a childhood?

It's the sort of night that can't be undone in a person.

"What, Sven? What are you going to tell me? That I have too much to lose? What the fuck do I have to lose?"

Sven holds out his palms. His eyes flicker towards what Omar is holding in his hands. His voice hardly makes itself heard.

"Tell me where it ends, Omar. When you've killed them, and they've killed you. Tell me where it ends after that."

Omar just stands there dumbly, as if he also has to focus his pain somewhere. Two young men in the back of the car open the doors, but they don't get out, merely sit there waiting for Omar to make a choice. Britt-Marie recognizes them. They play soccer with Sami and Magnus in the glare of headlights from Sami's black car . . . how long ago did they last play? Days? Weeks? A whole lifetime ago. They are almost boys.

Death is powerlessness. Powerlessness is desperation. Desperate people choose desperate measures. Britt-Marie's hair moves in the draft when the door of the police car opens and Vega steps out. She looks at her brother. He's on his knees now. She keeps his head pressed against her throat and whispers:

"Where would Sami have stood?"

When he doesn't immediately answer she repeats:

"Where. Would. Sami. Have stood?"

"Between us," he pants.

The two young men give Sven one last look. At another time, perhaps, they could have been stopped. One day it may be possible to stop them again. But not tonight.

The car leaves Britt-Marie, Sven, and two children in the road.

Dawn rises over them.

The police car slowly drives back through Borg, exits on the other side, continues down a gravel track. Keeps driving forever, until Britt-Marie no longer knows if she has fallen asleep or just gone numb. They stop by a lake.

Britt-Marie wraps the pistol in every handkerchief she's got in her bag, she doesn't know why, perhaps mainly because she doesn't want the girl to get dirty. Vega insists she's got to be the one that does it. She gets out and throws it as hard as she can into the lake.

Britt-Marie doesn't know how the hours turn into days, or how many of them pass by. By night, she sleeps between the children in

Sami's bed. The beating of their hearts in her hands. She stays there for several nights. It is not something she plans, no decision has been made, she just stays there. One dawn after another seems to merge with dusk. Looking back, she has a vague memory of having spoken to Kent on the telephone, but she can't remember what was said. She thinks she may have asked him to arrange some practical things, possibly she asks him to make some telephone calls, he's good at those things. Everyone says Kent is good at those things.

One afternoon, she's unsure when it is, Sven comes to the apartment. He has brought a young woman with him from the social services. She is warm and pleasant. Sven's neck doesn't seem capable of holding up all his thoughts any longer. The woman sits with them all at the kitchen table, speaking slowly and softly, but no one is able to concentrate. Britt-Marie's eyes keep straying out of the window, one of the children is looking up at the ceiling, and the other is looking down at the floor.

The following night, Britt-Marie is woken by a sound of slamming in the flat. She gets up and fumbles for the light switch. The wind is blowing in through the balcony door. Vega moves maniacally back and forth in the kitchen. Tidying up. Cleaning everything she finds. Her hands scrub frenetically at the dish rack and frying pans.

Again and again. As if they were magic lamps that could give her everything back. Britt-Marie's hands hesitate in the air behind her shaking shoulders.

Her fingers grip without touching.

"I'm so sorry, I know you must feel—"

"I don't have time to feel things. I have to take care of Omar," the girl interrupts vacantly.

Britt-Marie wants to touch her, but the girl moves away, so Britt-Marie fetches her bag. Gets out some baking soda. The girl meets her eyes, and her sorrow has nothing else to say. Words cannot achieve anything.

So they keep cleaning until morning comes again. Although not even baking soda can help against this.

It's a Sunday in January. While Liverpool are playing Stoke six hundred miles away, Sami is buried next to his mother, sleeping softly under a carpet of red flowers. Mourned by two siblings, missed by a whole community. Omar leaves a scarf in the churchyard.

Britt-Marie serves coffee in the pizzeria and makes sure each of the mourners has a coaster. Everyone in Borg is there. The graveled parking area has lit candles around its boundary. White jerseys have been neatly hung up on the wooden plank fence next to it. Some of them are new, and some so old and faded that they've turned gray. But they all remember.

Vega stands in the doorway, in a freshly ironed dress and with her hair combed. She receives people's condolences as if they have a greater right to mourn than she does. Mechanically shakes their hands. Her eyes are empty, as if someone has turned off a switch inside her. Something is making a thumping noise outside in the parking area but no one listens to it. Britt-Marie tries to get Vega to eat, but Vega doesn't even answer when spoken to. She allows herself to be led to the table and lowered into a chair, but her body reacts as if it's sleeping. It turns so that she faces the wall, as though she wants to avoid any possible physical contact. The thumping gets louder.

Britt-Marie's despair intensifies. People have different ways of experiencing powerlessness and grief, but for Britt-Marie it's never so strong as when she's unable to get someone to eat.

The mumbling voices from the crowded pizzeria grow into a hurricane in her ears, her resigned hand fumbles for Vega's shoulder as if it were reaching over the edge of a precipice. But the shoulder moves away. Glides towards the wall. And the eyes flee inwards. The plate remains untouched.

When the thumping from the parking area gets even louder, as if trying to prove something, Britt-Marie turns angrily towards the door with her hands clenched so tightly that the bandage comes loose from her fingers. She's just about to scream when she feels the girl's body pushing past her, through the throng of people.

Max is standing outside, leaning on his crutches. He suspends himself from his armpits, his whole weight swinging through the air, and then swings his uninjured leg at the soccer ball, firing it at a tight angle so it flies first against the wall of the recreation center, then at the wooden fence where the white jerseys are hanging, then back at him. *Du-dunk-dunk*, it sounds like. *Du-dunk-dunk. Du-dunk-dunk.*

Du-dunk-dunk.

Like a heartbeat.

When Vega gets close enough he lets the ball roll past him without turning around. It rolls up to her, and stops against her feet. Her toes touch it through her shoes. She leans over it and runs her fingertips over the stitched leather.

Then she cries without measure.

Six hundred miles away, Liverpool win 5–3.

35

Omar and Dino are the first to throw themselves into the game with Vega. At first they are guarded, as if every movement is made in sorrow, but before long they are playing as if it's just another evening. They play without memory, because they don't know any other way of doing it. More children turn up, first Toad and Ben but soon others too. Britt-Marie doesn't recognize every one of them, but they all have jeans that are ripped over their thighs. They play as if they live in Borg.

"Britt-Marie?" says Sven in a formal tone that she's not used to.

He's standing beside her with a very tall man. Really astonishingly tall. Britt-Marie doesn't even know how one could manage to have fully functional lighting at home with him around.

"Ha?" she says.

Sven presents Dino's uncle in English marred by a heavy accent, but Britt-Marie doesn't criticize; she's not the sort of person that criticizes.

"Hello," says Britt-Marie, this being about the long and short of the conversation for her part.

It's not that Britt-Marie can't speak English. It's just that she doesn't know how to speak it without feeling like an utter idiot. She wouldn't even know how to say "utter idiot" in English. As far as she's concerned this illustrates her point very well.

The very tall man, who really is quite unreasonably tall, points at Dino and explains that they lived in three countries and seven cities before they came to Borg. Sven helpfully translates. Britt-Marie understands English perfectly well, but she lets him go on, fearing that she might otherwise be expected to say something. The tall man's mouth judders up and down in a melancholy way when he says that small children don't remember things, which is a blessing. But Dino was old enough to see and hear and remember. He remembers everything they had to flee from.

"He's saying he still hardly says anything. Only with them . . ." Sven explains, pointing out of the window.

Britt-Marie clasps one hand in the other. The tall man does the same.

"Sami," he says with a sort of music in the way he pronounces the name, as if he's nursing every nuance of sound. Her eyelashes grow heavy.

"He says that Sami saw a boy walking on his own in the road. Vega and the others called out and asked him if he wanted to play, but he didn't understand. So Sami rolled a ball over to him, and then he kicked it," says Sven.

Britt-Marie looks at the tall man and her common sense prevents her from saying that once when she and Kent were staying at a hotel and someone had left a foreign newspaper behind, she almost solved a crossword in English entirely on her own.

"Thank you," says the tall man.

"He wants to thank you for coaching the team. It meant a lo—"

Britt-Marie interrupts him, because she understands:

"I'm the one who should say thank you."

Sven starts translating to the tall man, but he stops him because he also understands. He presses Britt-Marie's hand.

She goes back into the pizzeria, with Sven following, and helps Somebody clear glasses and plates from the tables.

"It was a beautiful funeral," says Sven, because that's what you say.

"Very beautiful," says Britt-Marie, because you have to say that as well.

He gets something out of his pocket and hands it to her. The keys to her car. His eyes flicker. Through the window they see Kent's BMW pulling into the parking area.

"I assume you'll be going home now, you and Kent," says Sven, his eyes remote.

"It's best that way," says Britt-Marie, sucking in her cheeks, but then a few more words slip out of her in spite of it all: "Unless I'm needed here with . . . Vega and Omar . . ."

Sven looks up and crumples in the brief instant between the first question and the realization that what she's asking is whether the children need her. Not whether he does.

"I . . . I, of course, of course, I have contacted the social services. They have sent a girl to Borg," he says with a grim expression, as if he's already forgotten that it was actually several nights earlier that he first brought the girl to the children.

"Of course," she says.

"She's . . . you'll like her. I've worked with her many times before. She's a good person. She wants what's best for them, she's not like . . . like you imagine the social services could be."

Britt-Marie mops the sweat from her brow with a handkerchief, so he doesn't notice that she's also mopping her eyes.

"I promised Sami they'd be all right. I promised . . . I want . . .

they have to have an opportunity to . . . there must be a sunny story in their lives, Sven. At some point," she manages to say at long last.

"We're going to do our best. We'll all do everything we possibly can."

"Of course, of course," she replies, directing her words at her shoes.

Sven fingers the police cap in his hands.

"The girl from the council, yes, she'll be staying with the children for a few days. Until they've sorted it all out. She's very considerate. You don't have to worry about that, I, well, I've been asked to drive the children home tonight."

It takes a few seconds before the significance of what he has said sinks in for Britt-Marie. Before she's hit with the insight that she's no longer needed.

"Obviously, obviously. It's best that way, obviously," she whispers.

Outside on the soccer pitch, Kent has gotten out of his BMW. He sees Britt-Marie and Sven through the window and puts his hands in his pockets, slightly nonplussed, looking as if he's standing on a street corner and not quite willing to admit that he's lost. He's never been good at talking about death, Britt-Marie knows that. He's the kind of person who can sort out all the practicalities; he can make calls; he'll kiss your eyelids. But he's never been good at feeling things.

His eyes seem to be considering walking into the pizzeria, but his feet steer off in the opposite direction. He makes a few movements with which he seems to be heading back into the BMW, but then the soccer ball comes rolling up and stops by his feet. Omar is standing a few feet away. Kent puts the sole of his shoe on the ball and looks at the boy. Kicks the ball to him. Omar stops it with the side of his foot, so it bounces back to Kent.

Thirty seconds later Kent is in the middle of the pile of children, his shirt creased and hanging down outside his belt, his hair untidy. Instantly, he's happy. When the ball comes flying to him at knee-height, he gathers himself and kicks as hard as he can, misses the ball, and watches one of his shoes flying off and clearing the top of the fence along the side of the recreation center.

"Mother of God," mumbles Britt-Marie from the window. The children watch the shoe flying off. Turn to Kent. He looks back at them and starts laughing. They also laugh. He plays the rest of the match with one shoe, and when he scores he runs around the pitch with Omar perched on his back.

Omar hugs him a little too hard. A little too long. As teenagers get few chances to do outside of a soccer pitch. Kent hugs him back. Because soccer allows him to do it.

Sven has turned away from the window when he mumbles:

"Don't dislike me, Britt-Marie, for not calling the social services earlier. I just wanted to give Sami the chance to get things organized. I thought . . . I . . . I . . . I just wanted to give him the chance. Don't dislike me for it."

Her fingers skim through the air between them as close as they can without actually touching him.

"Quite the opposite, Sven. Quite the opposite."

He looks about to say something, so she quickly interjects:

"There are more kids here now than earlier. Where are they all from?"

Sven puts his police cap back on his head. It ends up slightly wonky.

"They've been coming here every evening since the cup. More and more of them every evening. If it carries on like this, soon Borg won't be a team, it'll be a club."

Britt-Marie doesn't know what that means, but it sounds beautiful. She thinks Sami would have liked it.

"They look so happy. Even in the midst of all this they can look so happy when they're playing," she says, almost enviously.

Sven rubs the back of his hand against his beard stubble. He looks tired. She has never seen him tired. But at long last the corners of his mouth twitch slightly, his eyes glitter at her, and he says:

"Soccer forces life to move on. There's always a new match. A new season. There's always a dream that everything can get better. It's a game of wonders."

Britt-Marie straightens out a crease in his shirt, her hand landing as lightly as a butterfly, without actually touching his body under the fabric.

"If it's not too inappropriate, I should like to ask you a very personal question, Sven."

"Of course."

"What soccer team do you support?"

Surprised, his face releases and changes.

"I've never supported a team. I think I love soccer too much. Sometimes your passion for a team can get in the way of your love for the game."

It seems quite fitting for a man like Sven that he should believe more in love than in passion. He's a policeman who believes more in justice than in the law. It suits him, she thinks to herself. But she doesn't tell him as much.

"Poetic," she says.

"Course." He smiles back.

She wants to say so much more. Maybe he does too. But in the end all he can manage to utter is: "I want you to know, Britt-Marie, that every time there's a knock on my front door, I hope it's you."

Maybe he is also intending to say something bigger, but he holds off and walks away. She wants to call out to him, but it's too late.

The door tinkles cheerfully behind him, because doors really don't seem to get when the moment is or isn't right.

Britt-Marie dabs her cheeks with her handkerchief so no one can see she's wiping her eyes. Then she walks purposefully through the pizzeria to Somebody. There are still people everywhere. Ben's mother and Dino's uncle and Toad's parents, but also a lot of other people whose faces Britt-Marie can only dimly recall from the soccer cup. They are cleaning up and putting the chairs in order, and she only just manages to resist the urge to straighten them again.

"It was, what's-it-called? Beautiful funeral, huh?" says Somebody, her voice a little gravelly.

"Yes," agrees Britt-Marie, before getting out her wallet and immediately continuing: "I should like to ask what I owe you for the car door."

Somebody drums the edge of her wheelchair.

"Well. I been, you know, thinking about that car, huh, Britt-Marie. I don't have good car mechanic, huh? Maybe did it wrong, you know? So first you check the work, huh? Then you come back. Pay."

"I don't understand."

Somebody scratches her cheek so no one can see she's wiping her eyes as well.

"Britt-Marie very honest person, huh. Britt-Marie does not steal. So then I know Britt-Marie comes back to Borg, huh. To pay."

"Of course," she replies, turning away. "Of course."

She wants to get busy cleaning up, but then has a merciless realization that the people she does not know, inside the pizzeria, have already done it. Somebody has already told them all what to do. And now there is nothing left to finish.

Britt-Marie is not needed here anymore.

She stands on her own in the doorway until the children stop playing. They go home, one after the other. At a distance, Sven waits patiently for Vega and Omar. He lets the children take the time they need. Vega goes directly to the backseat and closes the door behind her, but Omar wanders on his own along the plank and runs his fingers across the white jerseys. He leans over the candles on the ground, carefully picks one up that has gone out, and relights it by holding it over the flame of another, then puts it back. When he straightens up he sees Britt-Marie in the doorway. His hand moves almost unnoticeably away from his hip, in a little wave. A wave from a young man is much more than a wave from a child. She waves back as much as she can without showing him that she is crying.

She goes down to the parking area just as the police car pulls into the road and heads off towards the children's house. Kent is waiting for her, sweaty, his shirt creased and hanging loose, his hair on end to one side of his large head—and he still only has one shoe. He looks quite, quite mad. It reminds her of how he used to look when they were children. Back then it never bothered him that other people would shake their heads at him; he was never afraid of making a fool of himself. He never needed anyone's affirmation except hers.

He takes her hand and she presses her eyelids against his lips. Says, almost panting:

"Vega is afraid even if she mainly seems angry. Omar is angry, even if he mostly seems afraid."

"Everything is going to be all right," says Kent into her hair.

"I promised Sami their lives would work out," sobs Britt-Marie.

"They're going to be fine, you have to let the authorities take care of this," he says calmly.

"I know. Of course I do know that."

"They're not your children, darling."

She doesn't answer. Because she knows. Obviously she knows that. Instead, she straightens her back and wipes her eyes with a tissue, adjusts a crease in her skirt and several in Kent's shirt. Collects herself and clasps her hands over her stomach and asks him:

"I should like to take care of a last errand. Tomorrow. In town. If it's not too much trouble."

"I'll go with you."

"You don't always have to stand next to me, Kent."

"Yes, I do."

Then he smiles. And she tries to.

But when he starts walking back to the BMW she stays where she is with her heels dug into the gravel, as you do when enough is finally enough:

"No, Kent, certainly not! I am certainly not going into town with you if you don't first put on both your shoes!"

36

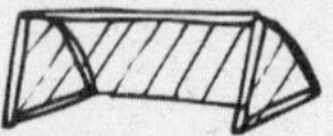

One remarkable thing about communities built along roads is that you can find just as many reasons for leaving them as excuses to stay. Some people never quite stop devoting themselves to one or the other.

In the end it's almost a whole week after the funeral before Britt-Marie gets into her white car with its blue door and drives off along the road that leaves Borg. Admittedly it's not entirely the fault of the council employees in the town hall. Possibly, they are only trying to do their jobs. It is not their fault that they are not wholly aware of Britt-Marie's precision when ticking off her lists.

So on the first day, a Monday, the young man who's working temporarily on reception at the town hall looks as if he thinks Britt-Marie is trying to be amusing. The reception opens at 8:00, so Britt-Marie and Kent have turned up at 8:02 because Britt-Marie doesn't want to come across as pigheaded.

"Borg?" says the temporary receptionist in the sort of tone you might use when pronouncing the names of beasts in fairy tales.

"My dear boy, surely you can't be working for the council without knowing that Borg is a part of the local council!" Britt-Marie says.

"I'm not from here. I'm a temp."

"Ha. And I suppose that's meant to be an excuse for not having to know anything at all."

But Kent nudges her encouragingly in the side, and whispers to her that she should try to be a little more diplomatic, so she grimly collects herself, smiles considerately at the young man, and says:

"It was very brave of you, putting that tie on. Because it looks absolutely preposterous."

Following this, there is a series of opinions exchanged that could not exactly be described as "diplomatic." But in the end Kent manages to calm down both combatants to the extent that the young man promises not to call the security guards, and Britt-Marie promises not to try to strike him with her handbag again.

One curious thing about communities built along roads is that you don't need to spend very long in them before you're deeply and personally offended when young men don't even know these places are there—that they even exist.

"I've come here to demand that a soccer pitch should be built in Borg, for your information," Britt-Marie explains with her most goddess-like patience.

She points at her list. The young man looks through a file. He turns demonstratively to Kent and says something about a "committee," which is currently held up in a meeting.

"For how long?"

The young man continues going through the file.

"It's a breakfast meeting. So, more or less, until about ten o'clock."

Whereupon both she and Kent have to leave the town hall, because a newly aggressive Britt-Marie has taken umbrage at the idea of a breakfast that lasts until ten o'clock, causing the young man to break his promise about not calling the security guards. They come back at ten o'clock, only to learn that the committee is in a meeting until after lunch. They come back after lunch, when they find out that the committee is in a meeting for the rest of the day. Britt-Marie clarifies her errand to the young man, because she does not believe it should have to take a whole day to get it done. The security guard who the young man has called takes the view that her clarity is somewhat overstated. He tells Kent that if Britt-Marie does this one more time he'll have no option but to take her handbag away from her. Kent sniggers and says in that case the security guard is a braver man than Kent. Britt-Marie doesn't know whether to feel insulted or proud about it.

"We'll come back tomorrow, darling, don't worry about it," Kent says soothingly as they are walking out.

"You have your meetings, Kent. We have to go home, I understand that, of course I do understand that. I just hope that we manage to . . ."

She takes a breath so deep that it seems to be extracted from the bottom of her handbag.

"When Vega plays soccer she doesn't feel any pain anymore."

"Pain about what?"

"Everything."

Kent lowers his head for a moment in thought.

"It doesn't matter, darling. We'll come back tomorrow."

Britt-Marie adjusts the bandage on her hand.

"I'm aware of the fact that the children don't need me. Obviously I am aware of that, Kent. I just wish I could give them something. At least if I could give them a soccer pitch."

"We'll come back tomorrow," Kent repeats, as he opens the car door for her.

"Yes, yes, you have your meetings, I understand that you have your meetings, we have to go home," she says with a sigh.

Kent scratches his head distractedly. Coughs gently. Fixes his gaze on the rubber seal between the glass and the metal of the door, and answers:

"The fact is, darling, I only have one meeting. With the car dealer."

"Ha. I didn't realize you were planning to buy a new car."

"I'm not buying. I'm selling this one," says Kent, with a nod at the BMW that she has just got into.

His face is dejected, as if it knows this is what is expected of it. But when he shrugs he does it as a young boy might, and his shoulders are light and relaxed as if they have just been liberated from a heavy burden.

"The company has gone bankrupt, darling. I tried to save it for as long as I could, but . . . well. It's the financial crisis."

Britt-Marie gawps at him.

"But I thought . . . I thought you said the crisis was over?"

He considers this for a moment, then simply says, "I was wrong, darling. Totally, totally wrong."

"What are you going to do?"

He smiles, unconcerned and youthful.

"Start again. That's what you do, isn't it? Once upon a time I had nothing, remember?"

She does remember. Her fingers seek out his. They may be old, but he's laughing:

"I built a whole life. A whole life! I can do it again."

He holds her hands in his and looks into her eyes when he promises:

"I can become that man again, my darling."

They're halfway between town and Borg when Britt-Marie turns to him and asks how things have gone for Manchester United. He laughs out loud. It's heavenly.

"Ah, it's gone to pot. They've had their worst season in more than twenty years. The manager is going to get kicked out any moment."

"How come?"

"They forgot what made them successful."

"What do you do when that happens?"

"You start again."

He rents a room from Toad's parents for the night. Britt-Marie doesn't ask if he'd prefer to stay in Bank's house, because Kent admits "that blind old bat scares me a bit."

The next day they go back to the town hall. And the next. Probably some of the people who work at the town hall believe that sooner or later Britt-Marie and Kent will give up, but these people are simply not aware of the profound implications of writing your lists in ink. On the fourth day they are allowed to see a man in a suit who's a member of a committee. By lunchtime he has called in a woman and a man, both wearing suits. Whether this is because of their expertise in the relevant area, or simply because the first suited man wants to improve his odds of not being hit in the event Britt-Marie starts lashing out with her handbag, is never clarified.

"I've heard a lot of good things about Borg. It seems so charming there," says the woman encouragingly, as if the village some twelve miles from her office is an exotic island only accessible through reliance on magic spells.

"I am here about a soccer pitch," Britt-Marie begins.

"There's no budget for that," the second suited man informs them.

"As I already said," the first suited man points out.

"In that case I have to demand that you change the budget."

"That's absolutely out of the question! How would that look? Then we'd have to start making changes in all the budgets!" says the second suited man, terrified.

The suited woman smiles and asks if Britt-Marie wants some coffee. Britt-Marie doesn't. The suited woman's smile intensifies.

"The way we understood it, Borg already has a soccer pitch."

The second man in a suit makes a dissatisfied humming sound from between his teeth, and almost yells:

"No! The soccer pitch was sold off for the eventual building of apartments. It's in the budget!"

"Well, in that case I have to ask you to buy back the land."

The humming from between the suited man's teeth is now also accompanied by a fountain of saliva. "How would that look? If that happened *everyone* would want to sell their land back! We actually can't just go around building soccer pitches everywhere! We'd be swimming in soccer pitches!"

"Well," says the first man in a suit and looks at his watch with a very bored expression.

Kent has to grip Britt-Marie's handbag quite firmly at that point. The suited woman leans forward disarmingly and pours coffee for everyone, although no one actually wants any.

"We understand that you were employed at the recreation center in Borg," she says with a mild smile.

"Yes. Yes, that's right, but I have . . . I have handed in my notice," says Britt-Marie, sucking in her cheeks.

The woman smiles even more mildly and pushes the coffee cup closer to Britt-Marie.

"There was never meant to be a position there, dear Britt-Marie. The intention was to close down the recreation center before Christmas. The vacancy was a mistake."

The second suited man is droning like an outboard engine.

"A position not in the budget. How would that look?"

The first suited man stands up.

"You'll have to excuse us. We actually have an important meeting."

And on this note, Britt-Marie leaves the town hall. Having come to realize that her arrival in Borg was all a mistake. They are right. Obviously they are right.

"Tomorrow, darling. We'll come back here tomorrow," Kent tries to tell her again as they sit in the BMW. Silent and dejected, she leans her head against the window and keeps a tissue under her chin. A sort of determination appears in Kent's eyes when he sees this, almost like something vengeful, but she doesn't notice it at that point.

The fifth day at the town hall is a Friday. It's raining again.

Kent has to force Britt-Marie to go. When she insists that it's all useless anyway, he has no choice in the end but to threaten to write a lot of mischievous, quite irrelevant things in ink on her list. At this point she snatches back the list as if it were a flowerpot he had threatened to throw off a balcony, and then she reluctantly gets into the BMW, all the while muttering that Kent is a "hooligan."

A woman is waiting for them when they arrive at the town hall. Britt-Marie recognizes her as the woman from the soccer association.

"Ha. I suppose you're here to stop us?" notes Britt-Marie.

The woman looks at Kent, surprised. Nervously starts wringing her hands.

"No. Kent here called me. I am here to help you."

Kent pats Britt-Marie on the shoulder.

"I made a couple of calls. I took the liberty of doing what I'm good at."

When Britt-Marie steps into the suited people's office, there are even more suits in there. Under existing circumstances, it seems, the soccer pitch in Borg has become a matter of interest for more committees than just the one.

"It has come to our attention that strong interests are backing the initiative for more soccer pitches within our council boundaries," says a new suit, with a nod at the woman from the soccer association.

"It has also come to our attention that local business interests are ready to exert a certain amount of . . . pressure," says another suit.

"Fairly unpleasant pressure, actually!" a third suit interjects, producing a plastic folder with various papers inside, and putting this on the table in front of Britt-Marie.

"We have also been reminded both by mail and various telephone calls that this is an election year," says the aforementioned suit.

"We have been reminded in a fairly abrasive and persistent way, in fact!" the latter suit adds.

Britt-Marie leans forward. The papers are headed as "Working Group of Borg's Official Partnership of Independent Business Interests." In these papers it can be clearly seen that the owners of Borg's pizzeria, Borg's corner shop, Borg's post office, and Borg's car repairs workshop have sat down together over the course of the night and signed a collective demand for a soccer pitch. For safety's sake, the owners of the very recent start-ups, "Law Firm Son & Son," "Hairdressing and That," and "Borg Good Wine Importers Ltd." have also signed this demand. As it happens, all in the same handwriting. The only document that stands out as different is one from a man named Karl, who according to the document has just opened a florist's.

Everything else is in Kent's handwriting. He stands behind Britt-Marie with his hands in his pockets, slouching slightly as if he does not wish to make too much of his presence. The woman with a suit serves coffee and nods excitedly:

"Actually, I had no idea there was such a flourishing business community in Borg! How charming!"

Britt-Marie's common sense has to work hard to stop her running around the room with her arms stretched out like an aircraft, because she's almost certain this would not be very appropriate.

The first man with a suit clears his throat and wishes to say another few words. He says:

"The thing is, we have now also been contacted by the unemployment office in your hometown."

"Twenty-one times. *Twenty-one* times, we've been contacted," another suit points out.

Britt-Marie turns and looks at Kent for guidance, but he's now standing with his mouth agape, looking just as shocked as she is. An apparently randomly picked suit points at another paper.

"It has come to our attention that you have been employed at the recreation center in Borg."

"Mistakenly so!" the woman in a suit says with a mild smile.

The random suit continues without missing a beat:

"The unemployment office in your town has made us aware of certain political responsibilities arising out of this. We have also been made aware of a certain amount of flexibility in the local council budget concerning further recruitment, which could be acted on now that . . . well . . . now that we are in an election year."

"Twenty-one times. Twenty-one times we have been made aware of this!" another suit interjects angrily.

Words fail Britt-Marie. She stutters and clears her throat and then at long last manages to burst out:

"Might I just ask what on earth all this is supposed to mean?"

All of the suits in the room make restrained groans about how this must surely be quite plain and obvious. The suit sleeves slide back collectively to check if it isn't time to have lunch. It is. A great impatience arises. One of the suits finally takes it upon himself to clarify the whole thing, and then looks wearily at Britt-Marie:

"It means that the local council will either budget for a new soccer pitch, or budget for you to keep your job. We can't afford to do both."

It's not a reasonable choice to give a human being.

One remarkable thing about communities built along roads is that you can find just as many reasons for leaving them as excuses to make you stay.

37

"I must ask you to try to understand that it isn't a reasonable choice to give a human being," says Britt-Marie.

When she doesn't get an answer, she explains:

"It's just intractable, you have to understand. I want to ask you to try not to hold it against me."

She still doesn't get an answer, so she sucks in her cheeks and adjusts her skirt.

"It's very neat and tidy here. Of course I don't know if this makes any difference to you now, but I hope it does. It's a very neat and tidy churchyard, this."

Sami doesn't answer, but she hopes he's listening when she says:

"I want you to know, darling boy, I'll never regret coming to Borg."

It's Saturday afternoon. The day after the local council gave her an unreasonable choice and the very same day that Liverpool are playing Aston Villa six hundred miles from Borg. Early this morning Britt-Marie went to the recreation center.

On Monday there'll be bulldozers on the gravel outside, the council has promised. Kent forced them to promise, because he said otherwise he would not let them go to have their lunch. And so they promised and crossed their hearts that turf would be laid down and there would be proper goals with nets. Proper chalked sidelines. It was not a reasonable choice to give a human being, but Britt-Marie remembered what it was like losing a sibling, she remembered just how much one could lose oneself. With this in mind, she felt this was the best possible thing she could give someone who was every bit as lost. A soccer pitch.

She could hear voices through the open door of the pizzeria, but she didn't go in. It was best that way, she felt. The recreation center was empty, but the door of the refrigerator was ajar. The rat teeth marks on the rubber seal of the door made it clear enough what had happened. The cellophane over the plate had been chewed away and every last crumb of peanut butter and Nutella on it had been licked clean. On its way out the rat had stumbled on Britt-Marie's tin of baking soda, overturning it on the dish rack. There were tracks in the white dust. Two pairs, in fact. The rat had been there on a date, or a meeting, or whatever they called it these days.

Britt-Marie sat on one of the stools for a long time, with a towel in her lap. Then she mopped her face and cleaned the kitchen. Washed up and disinfected and made sure everything was spotless. Patted the coffee machine, which had once been damaged by flying stones; ran her hand over a picture with a red dot hanging at precisely the right height on the wall, telling her exactly where she was.

The knocking on the door didn't surprise her, oddly enough. The young woman from social services standing in the doorway gave her the impression of being exactly in the right place. As if she belonged here.

"Hello, Britt-Marie," said the girl, "I hope I'm not disturbing you. I saw that the lights were on."

"Certainly not. I only came to leave the keys," Britt-Marie informed her in a low voice, feeling like a guest in someone else's house.

She held out the keys to the recreation center, but the girl did not take them. Just smiled warmly as she looked at the premises.

"It's very nice here. I've understood that this place means so much to Vega and Omar, and I wanted to have a look at it so I could understand them better."

Britt-Marie fumbled with the keys. Stifled everything welling up inside her. Checked several times that she had put all of her things in her handbag, and that she had really turned off the lights in the bathroom and kitchen. Galvanized herself several times to say what she wanted to say, even though her common sense was fighting tooth and nail to stop her.

"Would it make any difference if someone offered to take care of the children?" she wanted to ask. Obviously she knew it was preposterous. Obviously she did. Yet she had time to open her mouth, and then to say:

"Would it . . . I should just like your leave to ask whether . . . obviously it's quite preposterous, certainly it is, but I should like to inquire about the whither and whether of whether it might happen to make any difference if someone . . ."

Before she got to the end of the sentence she noticed Toad's parents standing in the doorway. The mother had her hands on her pregnant stomach, and the father held his cap in his hands.

"Are you the one who's picking up the children?" Karl demanded to know.

The mother elbowed him softly in his side, and then turned in a very forthright manner to the girl from the social services.

"My name is Sonja. This is Karl. We're Patrik's parents; he plays in the same soccer team as Vega and Omar."

Of course it is quite possible that the girl from the social services was intending to answer, but Karl did not give her the chance:

"We want to take care of the children. We want them to come and live with us. You can't take them away from Borg!"

Sonja looked at Britt-Marie. Saw her hands, perhaps, so she crossed the room and, without any sort of prior warning, gave her a hug. Britt-Marie mumbled something about having washing-up liquid on her fingers but despite that Sonja kept hugging her. Something was rattling in the doorway. The girl from the social services began to laugh a little, as if this was her natural impulse every time she opened her mouth.

"The fact is I've had the same suggestion from both Ben's mother and the uncle of . . . Dino . . . is that his name?"

The rattling sounds from the doorway intensified and were complemented by a person demonstratively clearing her throat.

"Those kids! Can live with me, huh? They're like, what's-it-called? Children for me, huh?" Somebody looked ready to fight about it with everyone in the room. She waved at the soccer pitch; there were still white jerseys hanging along the fence and the candles had been thoughtfully lit again earlier that morning.

"It takes, what's-it-called? Takes a village to bring up a child, huh? We have a village!"

Sonja reluctantly let go of Britt-Marie, like you do with a balloon that you know will fly off as soon as you loosen your grip.

Karl wrung his cap and pointed both exactingly and fearfully at the girl from the social services. "You can't take the children away from Borg, they could end up living with anyone! They could end up with a Chelsea supporter!"

By that stage, Britt-Marie had already put the keys to the recreation center on the dish rack and sneaked out behind them. If they did notice, and maybe they did, they let her go without a word, because they liked her enough to do that.

Afternoon turns to evening in Borg, quick and merciless, as if dusk is pulling a Band-Aid off the daylight. Britt-Marie kneels with her forehead against Sami's headstone.

"My darling boy, I'll never regret that I was here."

On Monday the bulldozers are coming to Borg. Britt-Marie doesn't know if she is religious, but she imagines that it's good enough, the knowledge that God has plans for Borg.

She has grass stains on her tights when she walks on her own down the road through the village. The white jerseys are still there on the fence. New candles have been lit underneath. The recreation center is lit up by the glow of a television and she can see the shadows of the children's heads inside. More children now than ever. A club more than a team. She wants to go in, but she understands this would not be appropriate. Understands that it's best this way.

In the graveled parking area between the recreation center and the pizzeria are two quite gigantic old trucks with their headlights turned on. A group of grown men with beards and caps are moving about in the beams of light, huffing and puffing, groaning and shoving each other. It takes a good while before Britt-Marie understands they are playing soccer.

They are playing.

She continues down the road. Stands for a few heartbeats outside a modest little house with a modest little garden. If you didn't know it was there you could easily walk past without paying any attention to it and, in this sense, the house has a great deal in common with its owner. The police car is not parked outside, the windows are not lit up. Once she's absolutely certain that Sven is not at home, Britt-Marie sneaks up to the door and knocks on it. Because she wanted to do that once in her life.

Then she quickly moves off, keeping herself to the shadows, and walks the remaining distance to Bank's house. The flower bed outside no longer stinks. The "For Sale" sign on the lawn has been removed. There's a smell of fried eggs when Britt-Marie steps into the hall; the dog is sleeping on the floor, Bank is sitting in her armchair in the living room with her face pressed up so close to the TV that Britt-Marie actually wants to warn her that it might be harmful to her eyes, but on second thought realizes it would be better not to.

"Might one ask who's playing?" she says instead.

"Aston Villa and Liverpool! Aston Villa are leading two to none!" says Bank, very agitated.

"Ha. So should I presume, then, that you also support Liverpool, like all the children seem to?"

"Are you mad? I support Aston Villa!" hisses Bank.

"Might I ask why?" asks Britt-Marie, because when she thinks about it more closely, it occurs to her that this is the first time she has ever seen Bank pay any attention to a televised soccer match.

Bank looks as if this is a preposterous question. Thinks for a moment. Then answers, grumpily:

"Because no one else supports Aston Villa . . . and because they have nice jerseys."

Britt-Marie finds the second argument a touch more rational than the first. Bank lifts her head, turns down the volume on the TV. Takes a pull at her beer and clears her throat.

"There's food in the kitchen. If you're hungry."

Britt-Marie shakes her head, clutches her handbag hard.

"Kent is coming soon. We're going home. He's driving his car, and I am driving mine, but he'll drive in front of me of course. I don't like driving in the dark. It's best if he's at the front."

Bank gets to her feet with a lot of laborious cursing at the armchair, as if it's the chair's fault that people get older.

"Not that I want to get involved, but I think you should learn to drive in the dark."

"That's very sweet of you," answers Britt-Marie into her handbag.

Bank and the dog give her a hand with the bags and the balcony box from upstairs. Britt-Marie washes up and cleans the kitchen. Sorts cutlery. Pats the dog behind its ears. A person on the TV starts yelling loudly. Bank disappears into the living room and comes back looking irascible.

"Liverpool just scored. Now it's two to one," she mutters.

Britt-Marie walks around the house one last time. Straightens rugs and curtains.

When she comes down into the kitchen she says:

"I'm not the kind to stick my nose in, but I could hardly avoid noticing that the 'For Sale' sign on the lawn has been taken down. I'd just like to congratulate you on getting your house sold."

Bank laughs bitterly.

"Are you joking? Who would buy a house in Borg?"

Britt-Marie adjusts her skirt.

"It wasn't an unreasonable assumption to make given that you'd just removed the sign . . ."

"Ah, I thought I'd stay on in Borg for a while, that's all. I was thinking I'd go and have a word with my old man. I thought it might be easier now he's dead, because he can't interrupt me all the time."

Britt-Marie wants to pat her on the shoulder, but she realizes it's best to leave it. Not least because Bank has her stick within reach.

There's a knock. Bank goes into the hall but then continues on into the living room without opening the door, because she knows who it is.

Britt-Marie looks around the kitchen one last time. Runs her fingers close enough to the walls to feel them, but not close enough to touch them. They are very dirty, after all. She hasn't had time to sort them out. She would have needed more time in Borg for that.

Kent smiles with relief when she opens the door.

"Are you ready to go?" he says anxiously, as if he still fears she may change her mind.

She nods and grasps her bag. Then the commentator on the TV suddenly starts roaring like mad. It sounds as if someone has walloped him.

"What on earth is going on?" Britt-Marie exclaims.

"Let's go now! Or we could get stuck in the traffic!" Kent tries, but it's too late. Britt-Marie goes into the living room. Bank is swearing and hissing at a young man in a red shirt who's charging about yelling until his face turns purple.

"Two to two, Liverpool has tied, it's two to two," she mutters, kicking the armchair as if it's responsible for the situation.

Britt-Marie is already halfway out the door.

Kent's BMW is parked in the street. He comes running and reaches out to her, but she pulls away. Of course, it's not appropriate at all, a grown woman running as if she were a criminal fleeing justice. She stops herself by the edge of the pavement, her breath hot in her throat, and she turns around and looks at Kent with tears streaming down her face.

"What are you doing, darling? We have to go now," he says, but his voice breaks because he can probably recognize very clearly what she's doing.

Her skirt is creased, but she doesn't adjust it. Her hair is almost untidy, as untidy as it is possible for Britt-Marie's hair to be. Her common sense throws in the towel in the end, and allows her to raise her voice:

"Liverpool have tied! I think they're going to win!"

Kent allows his chin to sink towards his chest. He shrinks.

"You can't be their mother, darling. And even if you can, what'll happen after that? When they don't need you anymore? What happens then?"

She shakes her head. But defiantly, rebelliously, not with sadness and dejection. As if she's fully intending to jump off an edge, even if only the edge of the pavement.

"I don't know, Kent. I don't know what happens after that."

He closes his eyes, looking once again like a young boy on a landing, and then says in a quiet voice:

"I can only wait till tomorrow morning, Britt-Marie. I'll stay with Toad's parents. If you don't come knocking on the door in the morning I'm going home on my own."

He tries to say it in a confident way, even though he knows he has already lost her.

She is already halfway to the recreation center.

Omar and Vega see her before she sees them. She has already run past them when she hears them calling out irritably to her.

"Goodness grac . . . Liverpool have . . . well I certainly don't know exactly what they've done, but I am under the impression that they're going to win against these . . . whatever their name was. Villa something!" pants Britt-Marie, so out of breath that she sees stars and has to steady herself, in the middle of the road, by resting her hands on her knees. The neighbors must surely be wondering whether she's started using narcotics.

"We know!" Omar joins in eagerly. "We're going to win! You could see it in Gerrard's eyes when he scored that we're going to win!"

Britt-Marie looks up, breathing so heavily that she feels a migraine coming on.

"May I ask what on earth you are doing here in the middle of the road, then?"

Vega faces her with her hands in her pockets, shaking her head as if she has come to the conclusion that Britt-Marie is even slower than she'd thought.

"When we turn it around we want to see it with you."

Liverpool never turn that match around. The final score is 2–2. It makes no difference and it makes all the difference in the world.

They have eggs and bacon in Bank's kitchen that night. Vega and Omar and Britt-Marie and Bank and the dog. When Omar puts his elbows on the table, it's Vega who tells him to take them off.

Their eyes meet for a moment, and then he does as she says without protest.

Britt-Marie stands in the hall as they put on their jackets. She curls up her toes in her shoes and brushes their arms until they have to hold her hands to make her stop.

The young woman from the social services is standing on the lawn, waiting for them.

"She's okay, she doesn't like soccer but she's okay," says Vega to Britt-Marie.

"We'll teach her," Omar assures her.

Britt-Marie sucks in her cheeks and nods.

"I . . . the thing is that I . . . I just want to say that I . . . that you . . . that I never," she begins.

"We know," mumbles Vega deep into the fabric of Britt-Marie's jacket.

"It's cool," Omar promises.

The children have reached the road when the boy turns around. Britt-Marie hasn't moved at all, as if she wants to preserve the image of them on her retinas until the very last. So he asks:

"What are you doing tomorrow?"

Britt-Marie clasps her hands together on her stomach. Inhales for as long as she can.

"Kent will be waiting for me to knock on his door."

Vega shoves her hands in her pockets. Raises her eyebrows.

"And Sven?"

Britt-Marie inhales. Exhales. Lets Borg bounce around inside her lungs.

"He told me he hopes it's me every time there's a knock on his door."

The children look so small, illuminated by the streetlights. But Vega stretches, straightens her back, and says:

"Do me a favor, Britt-Marie."

"Anything," she whispers.

"Don't knock on any door tomorrow. Just get in the car and drive!"

Britt-Marie stands on her own in the dark long after they have gone. She never said anything, has not promised anything. She knows it would have been a promise she could not keep.

She stands on the balcony of Bank's house, feeling Borg blowing tenderly through her hair. Not so hard that it ruins her hairstyle, just enough to feel the breeze. The newspaper delivery drives past while it's still dark. The women with the walkers slowly make their way out of the house opposite, towards their postbox. One of them waves at Britt-Marie and she waves back. Not with her whole arm, obviously, but with a controlled movement, a discreet movement of one hand at the level of her hips. The way a person with common sense waves. She waits until the women have gone back into the house. Then she sneaks down the stairs and carries her bags out to the white car with the blue door.

Before dawn she's standing outside a door, and knocking.

38

If a human being closes her eyes hard and long enough, she can remember all the times she has made a choice in her life just for her own sake. And realize, perhaps, that it has never happened. If she drives a white car with a blue door slowly down a road through a village, while it's still dark, and if she winds down the window and takes deep breaths, then she can remember all the men she has fallen in love with.

Alf. Kent. Sven. One who deceived her and left her. Another who deceived her and was left by her. A third who is many things she has never had, but possibly none of the ones she has been longing for. And she can slowly, slowly, slowly unwrap the bandage from her hand and look at the white mark on her ring finger. While dreaming of first love and other chances, and weighing up forgiveness against love. Counting the beats of her heart.

If a human being closes her eyes she can remember all the choices in her life. And realize they have all been for the sake of someone else.

It's early morning in Borg, but the dawn seems to be holding off. As if it wants to give her time to raise her hand. Make up her mind.

And jump.

She knocks on the door. It opens. She wants to say everything she feels inside, everything she has been carrying, but she never gets the chance. She wants to explain exactly why she's here and nowhere else, but she is interrupted. It makes her disappointed to realize she was expected—and that she's so predictable.

She wants to say something about how it feels, to open her chest and let everything flow for the first time, but she is not given the opportunity. Instead she is led with a firm hand back to the road. The pavement is dotted with plastic petrol cans. As if they've fallen off the back of a truck.

"Everyone in the team collected money. We've worked out the exact distance," says the boy.

"Those of us who can count have worked it out, yes," the girl interjects.

"I can count!" the boy cries angrily.

"Just about as much as you can kick a ball, so, yeah, like, you can count to three!" The girl grins.

Britt-Marie leans forward and feels the plastic jerrycans. They stink.

Something brushes against her arms and it takes a good while before she realizes the children are holding both of her hands.

"It's petrol. We've worked it out. There's enough here to get all the way to Paris," whispers Omar.

"And all the way back," adds Vega.

They stand there waving while Britt-Marie gets into the driver's seat. They wave with their entire bodies, the way grown-ups never do. Morning comes to Borg with a sun that controls itself and waits respectfully on the horizon, as if wanting to give her enough time to make a last choice, and then to choose for herself for the first time. When daylight finally streams in over the rooftops, a white car with a blue door starts pulling away.

Maybe she stops. Maybe she knocks on just one more door.

Maybe she just drives.

God knows Britt-Marie certainly has enough fuel.

It's January in a place that is one of millions rather than one in a million. A place like all the others, and a place like no other.

In a few months, six hundred miles away, Liverpool will almost win the English Premier League. In one of the last matches they will be leading 3–0 against Crystal Palace, but in eight surreal minutes they will let in three goals and lose the League title. No one in Liverpool will ever know anything about Borg, they won't even know the place exists, but no one who drives down this road with their windows rolled down will be able to avoid hearing the whole thing as it happens.

Manchester United fire their manager and start again. Tottenham promise that next season will be better. Somewhere out there, people can still be found who support Aston Villa.

It's January now, but spring will come to Borg. A young man will rest beside his mother in a churchyard under a blanket of scarves; two children will fall over themselves to deplore useless referees and pathetic sliding tackles. A ball will come rolling and a foot will kick it, because this is a community where no one knows how not to. A summer will come when Liverpool loses everything, and then autumn will arrive and along with it a new season, when they have another chance to win everything. Soccer is a mighty game in that way, because it forces life to go on.

Borg is exactly where it is. Where it has always been. Borg is a place by a road that exits in two directions. One direction home and one to Paris.

If you merely drive through Borg it's easy to notice only the places that have been closed down. You have to slow down to see what's still there. There are people in Borg. There are rats and walkers and greenhouses. Wooden fences and white jerseys and lit candles. Newly laid turf and sunny stories. There's a florist where you can only buy red flowers. There's a corner shop and a car mechanic and a postal service and a pizzeria where the TV is always on whenever there's a match, and where it's no shame to buy on credit. There isn't a recreation center anymore, but there are children who eat bacon and eggs with their new coach and her dog in a house with a balcony, in a living room where there are new photos on the wall. There are marginally fewer "For Sale" signs along the road today than there were yesterday. There are grown men with beards and caps who play soccer in the beams of headlights from old trucks.

There's a soccer pitch. There's a soccer club.

And whatever happens.

Wherever she is.

Everyone will know Britt-Marie was here.

Acknowledgments

Neda. The greatest blessing in life is to be able to share it with someone who's much smarter than oneself. I'm sorry you'll never get to experience that, it really is unbeatable. *Asheghetam.* Sightseeing.

Jonas Axelsson. My publisher and agent, who never loses sight of the fact that I am still a beginner, and that his foremost task is to help me get better at writing. Niklas Natt och Dag, who, in his texts and his respectful artistry, reminds me every day that this is a privilege. Céline Hamilton and Agnes Cavallin at Partners in Stories, where a large houseful of competence is slotted into the walls of a fairly small house; using equal parts of brain and heart they have kept this project on course. It wouldn't have worked without you. Karin Wahlén at Kult PR, who got it from day one. Vanja Vinter, grammatical elite soldier and uncompromising, outstanding proofreader, editor, and critic, although her cutlery drawer is one prolonged disappointment. Nils Olsson, who patiently, sensitively, and with great love, has designed three fantastic book covers. Andrea Fehlauer, who stepped in as the editor of key sections of the book, bringing both his experience and his precision to the task, and without a doubt improving the book as a result.

The readers of my blog, who were there from the very start. All this is actually mostly your fault.

Torsten Wahlund, Anna Maria Käll, and Martin Wallström, who recorded my stories as audiobooks and gave voices to my characters in ways I did not think possible. They are more yours than mine now. Julie Lærke Løvgren, who has overseen the publication of my books internationally. Judith Toth, who got me there. Siri Lindgren at Partners in Stories, who makes sure the boat does not capsize when Jonas refuses to sit still in it. Johan Zillén. First in, last out.

Everyone who was and still is involved in my books at Forum, Månpocket, Bonnier Audio, and Bonnier Rights. Especially John Häggblom, without whose help I would not be here today. Liselott Wennborg, the editor of *Saker min son behöver veta om världen* [*Things My Son Needs to Know about the World*]. Adam Dahlin, who saw the potential. Sara Lindegren and Stephanie Tärnqvist, who have always been far more patient with me than I deserve.

Natur och Kultur, who have given us their support, especially Hannah Nilsson and John Augustsson.

Pocketförlaget and A Nice Noise, who believed in all this.

All who have reviewed, written about, blogged, tweeted, Facebooked, Instagrammed, and spoken about my books. Especially those of you who really did not like them, and took your time to rationally and instructively explain why. I can't promise that I became a better writer as a result, but at least you forced me to think. I don't think that can be a bad thing.

Lennart Nilsson in Gantofta. The best football trainer I ever had.

Most of all, thanks to all of you who read my books. Thanks for your time.

Praise for

MY GRANDMOTHER ASKED ME TO TELL YOU SHE'S SORRY

"Believable and fanciful. Backman's smooth storytelling infuses his characters with charm and wit. . . . Engaging . . . A delightful story."

—*St. Louis Post-Dispatch*

"In his second offering, Backman continues to write with the same whimsical charm and warm heart as in his debut."

—*Publishers Weekly*

"An eclectic cast of characters, fairy-tale wisdom, and a little mystery . . . one of our favorite novels of the year so far."

—SFGate.com

Praise for

A MAN CALLED OVE

"A charming debut . . . You'll laugh, you'll cry, you'll feel new sympathy for the curmudgeons in your life."

—*People*

"Even the most serious reader of fiction needs light relief, and for that afternoon when all you want is charm, this is the perfect book."

—*San Francisco Chronicle*

"A lighthearted, deeply moving novel . . . This quirky debut is a thoughtful and charming exploration of the impact one life has on countless others—and an absolute delight."

—*CBS Local*

"Exquisite. The lyrical language is the confetti thrown liberally throughout this celebration-of-life story, adding sparkle and color to an already spectacular party."

—Shelf Awareness (starred review)

"Readers seeking feel-good tales with a message will rave about the rantings of this solitary old man with a singular outlook. If there was an award for 'Most Charming Book of the Year,' this first novel by a Swedish blogger-turned-overnight-sensation would win, hands down."

—*Booklist* (starred review)

"A funny crowd-pleaser that serves up laughs to accompany a thoughtful reflection on loss and love . . . The author writes with winning charm."

—*Publishers Weekly* (starred review)

"Poignant and unpredictable, Backman's book is filled with many twists and turns, as well as enjoyable characters and humorous situations."

—*Columbia Daily Tribune* (Missouri)

ALSO BY FREDRIK BACKMAN

A Man Called Ove

Britt-Marie Was Here

And Every Morning the Way Home Gets Longer and Longer

MY GRANDMOTHER ASKED ME TO TELL YOU SHE'S SORRY

- A NOVEL -

FREDRIK BACKMAN

WASHINGTON SQUARE PRESS

New York London Toronto Sydney New Delhi

WASHINGTON SQUARE PRESS
An Imprint of Simon & Schuster, Inc.
1230 Avenue of the Americas
New York, NY 10020

This book is a work of fiction. Any references to historical events, real people, or real places are used fictitiously. Other names, characters, places, and events are products of the author's imagination, and any resemblance to actual events or places or persons, living or dead, is entirely coincidental.

Copyright © 2013 by Fredrik Backman
Translation © 2015 by Henning Koch

All rights reserved, including the right to reproduce this book or portions thereof in any form whatsoever. For information, address Atria Books Subsidiary Rights Department, 1230 Avenue of the Americas, New York, NY 10020.

This Washington Square Press trade paperback edition April 2016
Originally published in Swedish in 2015 as *Min mormor hälsar och saäger förlåt*
Published by arrangement with Hodder & Stoughton

WASHINGTON SQUARE PRESS and colophon are trademarks of Simon & Schuster, Inc.

For information about special discounts for bulk purchases, please contact Simon & Schuster Special Sales at 1-866-506-1949 or business@simonandschuster.com.

The Simon & Schuster Speakers Bureau can bring authors to your live event. For more information or to book an event, contact the Simon & Schuster Speakers Bureau at 1-866-248-3049 or visit our website at www.simonspeakers.com.

Interior design by Paul Dippolito

Manufactured in the United States of America

20 19 18

The Library of Congress has cataloged the hardcover edition as follows:

Backman, Fredrik, 1981–
[Min mormor hälsar och saäger förlåt. English]
My grandmother asked me to tell you she's sorry : a novel / by Fredrik Backman ; translated from the Swedish by Henning Koch.
pages cm
1. Originally published as: Min mormor hälsar och saäger förlåt. Stockholm : Mån-pocket, 2013. 2. Grandparent and child—Fiction. 3. Grandmothers—Death—Fiction. 4. Girls—Fiction. 5. Individuality—Fiction. 6. Fairy tales—Fiction. 7. Life change events—Fiction. I. Koch, Henning, 1962– translator. II. Title.
PT9877.12.A32M5613 2015
839.73'8—dc23

2015000829

ISBN 978-1-5011-1506-6
ISBN 978-1-5011-1507-3 (pbk)
ISBN 978-1-5011-1508-0 (ebook)

To the monkey and the frog.

For an eternity of ten thousand tales.

MY GRANDMOTHER ASKED ME TO TELL YOU SHE'S SORRY

1

TOBACCO

Every seven-year-old deserves a superhero. That's just how it is. Anyone who doesn't agree needs their head examined.

That's what Elsa's granny says, at least.

Elsa is seven, going on eight. She knows she isn't especially good at being seven. She knows she's different. Her headmaster says she needs to "fall into line" in order to achieve "a better fit with her peers." Other adults describe her as "very grown-up for her age." Elsa knows this is just another way of saying "massively annoying for her age," because they only tend to say this when she corrects them for mispronouncing "déjà vu" or not being able to tell the difference between "me" and "I" at the end of a sentence. Smart-asses usually can't, hence the "grown-up for her age" comment, generally said with a strained smile at her parents. As if she has a mental impairment, as if Elsa has shown them up by not being totally thick just because she's seven. And that's why she doesn't have any friends except Granny. Because all the other seven-year-olds in her school are as idiotic as seven-year-olds tend to be, but Elsa is different.

She shouldn't take any notice of what those muppets think, says Granny. Because all the best people are different—look at superheroes. After all, if superpowers were normal, everyone would have them.

Granny is seventy-seven years old, going on seventy-eight. She's not very good at it either. You can tell she's old because her face looks like newspaper stuffed into wet shoes, but no one ever accuses Granny of being grown-up for her age. "Perky," people sometimes say to Elsa's mum, looking either fairly worried or fairly angry as Mum sighs and asks how much she owes for the damages. Or when Granny's smoking at the hospital sets the fire alarm off and she starts ranting and raving about how "everything *has to be* so bloody politically correct these days!" when the security guards make her extinguish her cigarette. Or that time she made a snowman in Britt-Marie and Kent's garden right under their balcony and dressed it up in grown-up clothes so it looked as if a person had fallen from the roof. Or that time those prim men wearing spectacles started ringing all the doorbells and wanted to talk about God and Jesus and heaven, and Granny stood on her balcony with her dressing gown flapping open, shooting at them with her paintball gun, and Britt-Marie couldn't quite decide if she was most annoyed about the paintball-gun thing or the not-wearing-anything-under-the-dressing-gown thing, but she reported both to the police just to be on the safe side.

Those are the times, Elsa supposes, that people find Granny perky for her age.

They also say that Granny is mad, but in actual fact she's a genius. It's just that she's a bit of a crackpot at the same time. She used to be a doctor, and she won prizes and journalists wrote articles about her and she went to all the most terrible places in the world when everyone else was getting out. She saved lives and fought evil everywhere on earth. As superheroes do.

But one day someone decided she was too old to save lives, even if Elsa quite strongly suspects what they really meant by "too old" was "too crazy." Granny refers to this person as "Society" and says it's only because everything has to be so bloody politically correct nowadays that she's no longer allowed to make incisions in people. And that it was really mainly about Society getting so bleeding fussy about the smoking ban in the operating theaters, and who could work under those sorts of conditions?

So now she's mainly at home driving Britt-Marie and Mum around the bend. Britt-Marie is Granny's neighbor, Mum is Elsa's mum. And really Britt-Marie is also Elsa's mum's neighbor because Elsa's mum lives next door to Elsa's granny. And Elsa obviously also lives next door to Granny, because Elsa lives with her mum. Except every other weekend, when she lives with Dad and Lisette. And of course George is also Granny's neighbor, because he lives with Mum. It's a bit all over the place.

But anyway, to get back to the point: lifesaving and driving people nuts are Granny's superpowers. Which perhaps makes her a bit of a *dysfunctional* superhero. Elsa knows this because she looked up "dysfunctional" on Wikipedia. People of Granny's age describe Wikipedia as "an encyclopedia, but on the net!" Encyclopedias are what Elsa describes as "Wikipedia, but analog." Elsa has checked "dysfunctional" in both places and it means that something is not quite functioning as it's supposed to. Which is one of Elsa's favorite things about her granny.

But maybe not today. Because it's half past one in the morning and Elsa is fairly tired and would really like to go back to bed. Except that's not going to happen, because Granny's been throwing turds at a policeman.

It's a little complicated.

Elsa looks around the little rectangular room and yawns listlessly and so widely that she looks like she's trying to swallow her own head.

"I *did* tell you not to climb the fence," she mutters, checking her watch.

Granny doesn't answer. Elsa takes off her Gryffindor scarf and puts it in her lap. She was born on Boxing Day seven years ago (almost eight). The same day some German scientists recorded the strongest-ever emission of gamma radiation from a magnetar over the earth. Admittedly Elsa doesn't know what a magnetar is, but it's some kind of neutron star. And it sounds a little like "Megatron," which is the name of the evil one in *Transformers*, which is what simpletons who don't read enough quality literature call "a children's program." In actual fact the Transformers are robots, but if you look at it academically they could also be counted as superheroes. Elsa is very keen on both *Transformers* and neutron stars, and she imagines that an "emission of gamma radiation" would look a bit like that time Granny spilled Fanta on Elsa's iPhone and tried to dry it out in the toaster. And Granny says it makes Elsa special to have been born on a day like that. And being special is the best way of being different.

Granny is busy distributing small heaps of tobacco all over the wooden table in front of her and rolling them into rustling cigarette papers.

"I said I told you not to climb the fence!"

Granny makes a snorting sound and searches the pockets of her much-too-large overcoat for a lighter. She doesn't seem to be taking any of this very seriously, mainly because she never seems to take anything seriously. Except when she wants to smoke and can't find a lighter.

"It was a tiny little fence, for God's sake!" she says breezily. "It's nothing to get worked up about."

"Don't you 'for God's sake' me! You're the one who threw shit at the police."

"Stop fussing. You sound like your mother. Do you have a lighter?"

"I'm seven!"

"How long are you going to use that as an excuse?"

"Until I'm not seven anymore?"

Granny mumbles something that sounds like "Not a crime to ask, is it?" and continues rifling through her pockets.

"I don't think you can smoke in here, actually," Elsa informs her, sounding calmer now and fingering the long rip in the Gryffindor scarf.

"Course you can smoke. We'll just open a window."

Elsa looks skeptically at the windows.

"I don't think they're the sort of windows that open."

"Why not?"

"They've got bars on them."

Granny glares with dissatisfaction at the windows. And then at Elsa.

"So now you can't even smoke at the police station. Jesus. It's like being in *1984*."

Elsa yawns again. "Can I borrow your phone?"

"What for?"

"To check something."

"Where?"

"Online."

"You invest too much time on that Internet stuff."

"You mean, 'spend.'"

"I beg your pardon?"

"What I mean is, you don't use 'invest' in that way. You wouldn't go round saying, 'I invested two hours in reading *Harry Potter and the Sorcerer's Stone*,' would you?"

Granny just rolls her eyes and hands her the phone. "Did you ever hear about the girl who blew up because she did too much thinking?"

The policeman who shuffles into the room looks very, very tired.

"I want to call my lawyer," Granny demands at once.

"I want to call my mum!" Elsa demands at once.

"In that case I want to call my lawyer first!" Granny insists.

The policeman sits down opposite them and fidgets with a little pile of papers.

"Your mother is on her way," he says to Elsa with a sigh.

Granny makes the sort of dramatic gasp that only Granny knows how to do.

"Why did you call *her*? Are you mad?" she protests, as if the policeman just told her he was going to leave Elsa in the forest to be raised by a pack of wolves. "She'll be bloody livid!"

"We have to call the child's legal guardian," the policeman explains calmly.

"*I* am also the child's legal guardian! I am the child's *grandmother*!" Granny fumes, rising slightly out of her chair and shaking her unlit cigarette menacingly.

"It's half past one in the morning. Someone has to take care of the child."

"Yes, me! *I'm* taking care of the child!" she splutters.

The policeman makes a fairly strained attempt to gesture amicably across the interrogation room.

"And how do you feel it's going so far?"

Granny looks slightly offended.

"Well . . . everything was going just fine until you started chasing me."

"You broke into a zoo."

"It was a *tiny little* fence—"

"There's no such thing as a 'tiny' burglary."

Granny shrugs and makes a brushing movement over the table, as if she thinks they've stretched this out long enough. The policeman notices the cigarette and eyes it dubiously.

"Oh, come on! I can smoke in here, can't I?"

He shakes his head sternly. Granny leans forward, looks him deep in the eyes, and smiles.

"Can't you make an exception? Not even for little old me?"

Elsa gives Granny a little shove in the side and switches to their secret language. Because Granny and Elsa have a secret language, as all grannies must have with their grandchildren, because by law that's a requirement, says Granny. Or at least it should be.

"Drop it, Granny. It's, like, illegal to flirt with policemen."

"Says who?"

"Well, the police for starters!" Elsa replies.

"The police are supposed to be there for the sake of the *citizens*," Granny hisses. "I pay my taxes, you know."

The policeman looks at them as you do when a seven-year-old and a seventy-seven-year-old start arguing in a secret language in a police station in the middle of the night. Then Granny's eyelashes tremble alluringly at him as she once again points pleadingly at her cigarette, but when he shakes his head, Granny leans back in the chair and exclaims in normal language:

"I mean, this political correctness! It's worse than apartheid for smokers in this bloody country nowadays!"

"How do you spell that?" asks Elsa.

"What?" Granny sighs as you do when precisely the whole world is against you, even though you pay taxes.

"That *apartight* thing," says Elsa.

"A-p-p-a-r-t-e-i-d," Granny spells.

Elsa immediately Googles it on Granny's phone. It takes her a few attempts—Granny's always been a terrible speller. Meanwhile the policeman explains that they've decided to let them go, but Granny will be called in at a later date to explain the burglary and "other aggravations."

"What aggravations?"

"Driving illegally, to begin with."

"What do you mean, illegally? That's my car! I don't need permission to drive my own car, do I?"

"No," replies the policeman patiently, "but you need a driver's license."

Granny throws out her arms in exasperation. She's just launched into another rant about this being a Big Brother society when Elsa whacks the phone sharply against the table.

"It's got NOTHING to do with that apartheid thing!!! You compared not being able to smoke with apartheid and it's not the same thing at all. It's not even CLOSE!"

Granny waves her hand resignedly.

"I meant it was . . . you know, more or less like that—"

"It isn't at all!"

"It was a metaphor, for God's sake—"

"A bloody crap metaphor!"

"How would you know?"

"WIKIPEDIA!"

Granny turns in defeat to the policeman. "Do your children carry on like this?" The policeman looks uncomfortable.

"We . . . don't let the children surf the Net unsupervised. . . ."

Granny stretches out her arms towards Elsa, a gesture that seems to say "You see!" Elsa just shakes her head and crosses her arms very hard.

"Granny, just say sorry for throwing turds at the police, and we can go home," she snorts in the secret language, though still very expressly upset about that whole apartheid thing.

"Sorry," says Granny in the secret language.

"To the police, not me, you muppet."

"There'll be no apologizing to fascists here. I pay my taxes. And *you're* the muppet." Granny sulks.

"Takes one to know one."

Then they both sit with their arms crossed, demonstratively looking away from each other, until Granny nods at the policeman and says in normal language:

"Would you be kind enough to let my spoilt granddaughter know that if she takes this attitude, she's quite welcome to walk home?"

"Tell *her* I'm going home with Mum and *she's* the one who can walk!" Elsa replies at once.

"Tell HER she can—"

The policeman stands up without a word, walks out of the room, and closes the door behind him, as if intending to go into another room and bury his head in a large, soft cushion and yell as loud as he can.

"Now look what you did," says Granny.

"Look what YOU did!"

Eventually a heavyset policewoman with piercing green eyes comes in instead. It doesn't seem to be the first time she's run into Granny, because she smiles in that tired way so typical of people who know Granny, and says: "You have to stop doing this, we also have real criminals to worry about."

Granny just mumbles, "Why don't you stop, yourselves?" And then they're allowed to go home.

Standing on the pavement waiting for her mother, Elsa fingers the rip in her scarf. It goes right through the Gryffindor emblem.

She tries as hard as she can not to cry but doesn't make much of a success of it.

"Ah, come on, your mum can mend that," says Granny, trying to be cheerful, giving her a little punch on the shoulder.

Elsa looks up anxiously.

"And, you know . . . we can tell your mum the scarf got torn when you were trying to stop me climbing the fence to get to the monkeys."

Elsa nods and runs her fingers over the scarf again. It didn't get torn when Granny was climbing the fence. It got torn at school when three older girls who hate Elsa without Elsa really understanding why got hold of her outside the cafeteria and hit her and tore her scarf and threw it down the toilet. Their jeers are still echoing in Elsa's head. Granny notices the look in her eyes and leans forward before whispering in their secret language:

"One day we'll take those losers at your school to Miamas and throw them to the lions!"

Elsa dries her eyes with the back of her hand and smiles faintly.

"I'm not stupid, Granny," she whispers. "I know you did all that stuff tonight to make me forget about what happened at school."

Granny kicks at some gravel and clears her throat.

"I didn't want you to remember this day because of the scarf. So I thought instead you could remember it as the day your Granny broke into a zoo—"

"And escaped from a hospital," Elsa says with a grin.

"And escaped from a hospital," says Granny with a grin.

"And threw turds at the police."

"Actually, it was soil! Or mainly soil, anyway."

"Changing memories is a good superpower, I suppose."

Granny shrugs.

"If you can't get rid of the bad, you have to top it up with more goody stuff."

"That's not a word."

"I know."

"Thanks, Granny," says Elsa and leans her head against her arm.

And then Granny just nods and whispers: "We're knights of the kingdom of Miamas, we have to do our duty."

Because all seven-year-olds deserve superheroes.

And anyone who doesn't agree needs their head examined.

2

MONKEY

Mum picked them up at the police station. You could tell that she was very angry, but she was controlled and full of composure and never even raised her voice, because Mum is everything Elsa's granny is not. Elsa fell asleep almost before she'd fastened her seat belt. By the time they were on the highway, she was already in Miamas.

Miamas is Elsa and Granny's secret kingdom. It is one of six kingdoms in the Land-of-Almost-Awake. Granny came up with it when Elsa was small and Mum and Dad had just got divorced and Elsa was afraid of sleeping because she'd read on the Internet about children who died in their sleep. Granny is good at coming up with things. So when Dad moved out of the flat and everyone was upset and tired, Elsa sneaked out the front door every night and scampered across the landing in her bare feet into Granny's flat, and then she and Granny crawled into the big wardrobe that never stopped growing, and then they half-closed their eyes and set off.

Because you don't need to close your eyes to get to the Land-of-Almost-Awake. That's the whole point of it, sort of thing. You only need to be *almost* asleep. And in those last few seconds when your eyes are closing, when the mists come rolling in across the boundary between what you think and what you just know, that's when you set off. You ride into the Land-of-Almost-Awake on the backs of cloud animals, because that's the only way of getting there. The cloud animals come in through Granny's balcony door and pick her and Elsa up, and then they fly higher and higher and higher until Elsa sees all the magical creatures that live in the Land-of-Almost-Awake: the enphants and regretters and the Noween and wurses and snow-angels and princes and princesses and knights. The cloud animals soar over the endless dark forests, where Wolfheart and all the other monsters live, then they sweep down through the blindingly bright colors and soft winds to the city gates of the kingdom of Miamas.

It's difficult to say for sure whether Granny is a bit odd because she's spent too much time in Miamas, or Miamas is a bit odd because Granny's spent too much time there. But this is the source of all of Granny's amazing, monstrous, magical fairy tales.

Granny says that the kingdom has been called Miamas for an eternity of at least ten thousand fairy tales, but Elsa knows that Granny only made this up because Elsa couldn't say "pajamas" when she was small and used to say "mjamas" instead. Except of course Granny insists that she never made up a bloody thing and Miamas and the other five kingdoms in the Land-of-Almost-Awake are not only real, but actually far *more* real than the world we're in now, where "everyone is an economist and drinks lactose-free milk and makes a right fuss." Granny isn't particularly good at living in the real world. There are too many rules. She cheats when she plays Monopoly and drives Renault in the bus lane and steals those yellow carrier bags from IKEA and won't stand behind the line when she's at the conveyor belt at the airport. And when she goes to the bathroom she leaves the door open.

But she does tell the very best fairy tales ever, and for that Elsa can forgive quite a few character defects.

All fairy tales that are worth something come from Miamas, says Granny. The other five kingdoms in the Land-of-Almost-Awake are busy doing other things: Mirevas is the kingdom where they stand guard over dreams, Miploris is the kingdom where they store all sorrow, Mimovas is where music comes from, Miaudacas is where courage comes from, and Mibatalos is the kingdom where the bravest warriors, who fought against the fearsome shadows in the War-Without-End, were raised.

But Miamas is Granny and Elsa's favorite kingdom, because there storytelling is considered the noblest profession of all. The currency there is imagination; instead of buying something with coins, you buy it with a good story. Libraries aren't known as libraries but as "banks," and every fairy tale is worth a fortune. Granny spends millions every night: tales full of dragons and trolls and kings and queens and witches. And shadows. Because all imaginary worlds have to have terrible enemies, and in the Land-of-Almost-Awake the enemies are the shadows, because the shadows want to kill the imagination. And if we're going to talk about shadows, we must mention Wolfheart. He was the one who defeated the shadows in the War-Without-End. He was the first and greatest superhero Elsa ever heard about.

Elsa was knighted in Miamas; she gets to ride cloud animals and have her own sword. She hasn't once been afraid to fall asleep since Granny started taking her there each night. Because in Miamas no one says girls can't be knights, and the mountains reach up to the sky, and the campfires never go out, and no one tries to shred your Gryffindor scarf.

Of course, Granny also says that no one in Miamas closes the door when they go to the bathroom. An open-door policy is more or less legally enforceable in every situation across the Land-of-Almost-Awake. But Elsa is pretty sure she is describing another version of the truth there. That's what Granny calls lies: "other versions of the truth." So when Elsa wakes up in a chair in Granny's room at the hospital the next morning, Granny is on the toilet with the door open, while Elsa's mum is in the hall, and Granny is in the midst of telling another version of the truth. It's not going all that well. The real truth, after all, is that Granny escaped from the hospital last night and Elsa sneaked out of the flat while Mum and George were sleeping, and they went to the zoo together in Renault, and Granny climbed the fence. Elsa quietly admits to herself that it now seems a little irresponsible to have done all this with a seven-year-old in the middle of the night.

Granny, whose clothes are lying in a pile on the floor and still very literally smelling a bit monkey-ish, is claiming that when she was climbing the fence by the monkey cage and the guard shouted at her, she thought he could have been a "lethal rapist," and *this* was why she started throwing muck at him and the police. Mum shakes her head in a very controlled way and says Granny is making all this up. Granny doesn't like it when people say that things are made-up, and reminds Mum she prefers the less derogatory term "reality-challenged." Mum clearly disagrees but controls herself. Because she is everything that Granny isn't.

"This is one of the worst things you've done," Mum calls out grimly towards the bathroom.

"I find that very, very unlikely, my dear daughter," Granny answers from within, unconcerned.

Mum responds by methodically running through all the trouble Granny has caused. Granny says the only reason she's getting so worked up is that she doesn't have a sense of humor. And then Mum says Granny should stop behaving like an irresponsible child. And then Granny says: "Do you know where pirates park their cars?" And when Mum doesn't answer, Granny yells from the toilet, "In a gAAARRRage!" Mum just sighs, massages her temples, and closes the bathroom door. This makes Granny really, really, really angry because she doesn't like feeling enclosed when she's on the toilet.

She's been in the hospital for two weeks now, but absconds almost every day and picks up Elsa, and they have ice cream or go to the flat when Mum isn't home and make a soapsud slide on the landing. Or break into zoos. Basically whatever appeals to her, whenever. But Granny doesn't consider this an "escape" in the proper sense of the word, because she believes there has to be some basic aspect of challenge to the whole thing if it's to count as an escape—a dragon or a series of traps or at least a wall and a respectably sized moat, and so on. Mum and the hospital staff don't quite agree with her on this point.

A nurse comes into the room and quietly asks for a moment of Mum's time. She gives Mum a piece of paper and Mum writes something on it and returns it, and then the nurse leaves. Granny has had nine different nurses since she was admitted. Seven of these she refused to cooperate with, and two refused to cooperate with her, one of them because Granny said he had a "nice ass." Granny insists it was a compliment to his ass, not to him, and he shouldn't make such a fuss about it. Then Mum told Elsa to put on her headphones, but Elsa still heard their argument about the difference between "sexual harassment" and "basic appreciation of a perfectly splendid ass."

They argue a lot, Mum and Granny. They've been arguing for as long as Elsa can remember. About everything. If Granny is a dysfunctional superhero, then Mum is very much a fully operational one. Their interaction is a bit like Cyclops and Wolverine in *X-Men*, Elsa often thinks, and whenever she has those types of thoughts she wishes she had someone around who could understand what she means. People around Elsa don't read enough quality literature and certainly don't understand that *X-Men* comics count as precisely that. To such philistines Elsa would explain, very slowly, that X-Men are indeed superheroes, but first and foremost they are mutants, and there is a certain academic difference. Anyway, without putting too fine a point on it, she would sum it up by saying that Granny's and Mum's superhero powers are in direct opposition. As if Spider-Man, one of Elsa's favorite superheroes, had an antagonist called Slip-Up Man whose superpower was that he couldn't even climb onto a bench. But in a good way.

Basically, Mum is orderly and Granny is chaotic. Elsa once read that "Chaos is God's neighbor," but Mum said if Chaos had moved onto God's landing, it was only because Chaos couldn't put up with living next door to Granny anymore.

Mum has files and calendars for everything and her telephone plays a little jingle fifteen minutes before she has a meeting. Granny writes down things she needs to remember directly on the wall. And not only when she's at home, but on any wall, wherever she is. It's not a perfect system, because in order to remember a particular task she needs to be in exactly the same place where she wrote it down. When Elsa pointed out this flaw, Granny replied indignantly, "There's still a smaller risk of me losing a kitchen wall than your mother losing that poxy telephone!" But then Elsa pointed out that Mum never lost anything. And then Granny rolled her eyes and sighed: "No, no, but your mother is the exception, of course. It only applies to . . . you know . . . people who aren't perfect."

Perfection is Mum's superpower. She's not as much fun as Granny, but on the other hand she always knows where Elsa's Gryffindor scarf is. "Nothing is ever really gone until your mum can't find it," Mum often whispers into Elsa's ear when she's wrapping it around her neck.

Elsa's mum is the boss. "Not just a job, but a lifestyle," Granny often snorts. Mum is not someone you go with, she's someone you follow. Whereas Elsa's granny is more the type you're dodging rather than following, and she never found a scarf in her life.

Granny doesn't like bosses, which is a particular problem at this hospital, because Mum is even more of a boss here. Because she *is* the boss here.

"You're overreacting, Ulrika, good God!" Granny calls out through the bathroom door just as another nurse comes in, and Mum again writes on a bit of paper and mentions some numbers. Mum gives her a controlled smile; the nurse smiles back nervously. And then things go silent inside the bathroom for a long while and Mum suddenly looks anxious, as one does when things go quiet around Granny for too long. And then she sniffs the air and pulls the door open. Granny is sitting naked on the toilet seat with her legs comfortably crossed. She waves her smoldering cigarette at Mum.

"Hello? A little privacy, perhaps?"

Mum massages her temples again, takes a deep breath, and rests her hand on her belly. Granny nods intently at her, waving her cigarette at the bump.

"You know stress isn't good for my new grandchild. Remember you're worrying for two now!"

"I'm not the one who seems to have forgotten," replies Mum curtly.

"Touché," Granny mumbles and inhales deeply.

(That's one of those words Elsa understands without even having to know what it means.)

"Does it not occur to you how dangerous that is for the baby, not to mention Elsa?" Mum says, pointing at the cigarette.

"Don't make such a fuss! People have been smoking since the dawn of time and there have been perfectly healthy babies born the whole way through. Your generation forgets that humanity has lived for thousands of years without allergy tests and crap like that before you showed up and started thinking you were so important. When we were living in caves, do you think they used to put mammoth skins through a scalding-hot machine-wash program?"

"Did they have cigarettes back then?" asks Elsa.

Granny says, "Don't you start." Mum puts her hand on her belly. Elsa is unsure if she's doing it because Halfie is kicking in there or because she wants to cover her/his ears. Mum is Halfie's mum but George is Halfie's dad, so Halfie is Elsa's half sibling. Or she/he will be, anyway. She/he will be a proper full-size human; a half sibling, but not in any way half a person, Elsa has been promised. She had a couple of confused days until she understood the difference. "Considering how smart you are, you can certainly be a bit of a thickie sometimes," Granny burst out when Elsa asked her about it. And then they bickered for nearly three hours, which was almost a new bickering record for them.

"I only wanted to show her the monkeys, Ulrika," mumbles Granny as she extinguishes the cigarette in the sink.

"I don't have the energy for this. . . ." Mum answers with resignation, although she's absolutely controlled about it, and then goes into the corridor to sign a piece of paper covered in numbers.

Granny really did want to show Elsa the monkeys. They'd been arguing on the phone last night about whether there was a certain type of monkey that slept standing up. Granny was wrong, of course, because it said on Wikipedia and everything. And then Elsa had mentioned the scarf and what had happened at school, which was when Granny decided that they were going to the zoo, and Elsa sneaked out while Mum and George were sleeping.

Mum disappears down the corridor, her head buried in her phone, while Elsa climbs into Granny's bed so they can play Monopoly. Granny steals money from the bank and, when Elsa catches her out, also steals the car so she can skip town. After a while Mum comes back looking tired and tells Elsa they have to go home now, because Granny has to rest. And Elsa hugs Granny for a long, long, long time.

"When are you coming home?" asks Elsa.

"Probably tomorrow!" Granny promises chirpily.

Because that is what she always says. And then she pushes the hair out of Elsa's eyes, and when Mum disappears into the corridor again, Granny suddenly looks very serious and says in their secret language: "I have an important assignment for you."

Elsa nods, because Granny always gives her assignments in the secret language, only spoken by initiates of the Land-of-Almost-Awake. Elsa always gets them done. Because that is what a knight of Miamas has to do. Anything except buying cigarettes or frying meat, which is where Elsa draws the line. Because they make her feel sick. Even knights have to have certain principles.

Granny reaches down next to the bed and picks up a big plastic bag from the floor. There are no cigarettes or meat in it. Just sweets.

"You have to give the chocolate to Our Friend."

It takes a few seconds before Elsa understands exactly what friend she is referring to. And she stares at Granny with alarm.

"Have you gone MAD? You want me to DIE?"

Granny rolls her eyes.

"Don't faff about. Are you telling me a knight of Miamas is too scared to complete a quest?"

Elsa gives her an offended glare.

"That's very mature of you to threaten me with that."

"Very mature of you to say 'mature.'"

Elsa snatches up the plastic bag. It's full of small, crinkly packets of Daim chocolate. Granny says, "It's important that you remove the wrapper from each piece. Otherwise he gets cross."

Elsa peers sulkily into the bag.

"He doesn't know me, though. . . ."

Granny snorts so loudly that it sounds as if she's blowing her nose.

"Course he knows! Good God. Just tell him your granny sent you to tell him she's sorry."

Elsa raises her eyebrows.

"Sorry for what?"

"For not bringing him any sweets for days and days," Granny replies, as if this was the most natural thing in the world.

Elsa looks into the bag again.

"It's irresponsible to send out your only grandchild on a mission like this, Granny. It's insane. He could actually kill me."

"Stop faffing about."

"Stop faffing about yourself!"

Granny grins; Elsa can't help but grin back. Granny lowers her voice.

"You have to give Our Friend the chocolate secretly. Britt-Marie mustn't see. Wait till they have that residents' meeting tomorrow evening and then sneak over to him."

Elsa nods, though she's terrified of Our Friend and still thinks it's pretty irresponsible to send a seven-year-old on such a perilous mission. But Granny grabs her fingers and squeezes them in her hands like she always does, and it's difficult to be afraid when someone does that. They hug again.

"See you, oh proud knight of Miamas," Granny whispers in her ear.

Granny never says "good-bye," only "see you."

While Elsa is putting on her jacket in the hall she hears Mum and Granny talking about "the treatment." And then Mum tells Elsa to listen to her headphones. And that's what Elsa does. She put the headphones on her wish list last Christmas and was very particular about Mum and Granny splitting the cost, because it was only fair.

Whenever Mum and Granny start arguing, Elsa turns up the volume and pretends they're both actresses in a silent movie. Elsa is the sort of child who learned early in life that it's easier to make your way if you get to choose your own soundtrack.

The last thing she hears is Granny asking when she can pick up Renault at the police station. Renault is Granny's car. Granny says she won it in a game of poker. It obviously should be "a" Renault, but Elsa learned that the car was a Renault when she was small, before she understood that there were other cars with the same name. So she still says "Renault" as if it's a name.

And it's a very suitable name, because Granny's Renault is old and rusty and French and when you change gears it makes an ungodly racket, like an old Frenchman with a cough. Elsa knows that because sometimes when Granny is driving Renault while smoking and eating a kebab, she only has her knees to steer with, and then she stamps on the clutch and shouts "NOW!" and then Elsa has to change gear.

Elsa misses doing that.

Mum tells Granny that she won't be able to go and pick up Renault. Granny protests that it's actually her car; Mum just reminds her that it's illegal to drive without a license. And then Granny calls Mum "young lady" and tells her she's got drivers' licenses in six countries. Mum asks in a restrained voice if one of these countries happens to be the one they live in, after which Granny goes into a sulk while a nurse takes some blood from her.

Elsa waits by the lift. She doesn't like needles, irrespective of whether they're being stuck into her own arm or Granny's. She sits reading *Harry Potter and the Order of the Phoenix* on the iPad for about the twelfth time. It's the Harry Potter book she likes the least; that's why she's read it so few times.

Only when Mum comes to get her and they're about to go down to the car does Elsa remember that she's left her Gryffindor scarf in the hall outside Granny's room. So she runs back.

Granny is sitting on the edge of the bed with her back to the door, talking on the phone. She doesn't see her, and Elsa realizes Granny is talking to her lawyer, because she's instructing him about what sort of beer she wants the next time he comes to the hospital. Elsa knows that the lawyer smuggles in the beer in large encyclopedias. Granny says she needs them for her "research," but in fact they are hollowed out inside with beer-bottle-shaped slots. Elsa takes her scarf from the hook and is just about to call out to Granny when she hears Granny's voice fill with emotion as she says, into the telephone:

"She's my grandchild, Marcel. May the heavens bless her little head. I've never met such a good and clever girl. The responsibility must be left to her. She's the only one who can make the right decision."

There's silence for a moment. And then Granny goes on determinedly:

"I KNOW she's only a child, Marcel! But she's a damn sight smarter than all the other fools put together! And this is my will and you're my lawyer. Just do what I say."

Elsa stands in the hall holding her breath. And only when Granny says, "Because I don't WANT TO tell her yet! Because all seven-year-olds deserve superheroes!"—only then does Elsa turn to quietly slip away, her Gryffindor scarf damp with tears.

And the last thing she hears Granny say on the telephone is:

"I don't want Elsa to know that I am going to die because all seven-year-olds deserve superheroes, Marcel. And one of their superpowers ought to be that they can't get cancer."

3

COFFEE

There's something special about a grandmother's house. You never forget how it smells.

It's a normal building, by and large. It has four floors and nine flats and the whole block smells of Granny (and coffee, thanks to Lennart). It also has a clear set of regulations pinned up in the laundry, with the heading FOR EVERYONE'S WELL-BEING in which WELL-BEING has been underlined twice. And a lift that's always broken and rubbish separated for recycling in the yard, and a drunk, a very large animal of some sort, and, of course, a granny.

Granny lives at the top, opposite Mum and Elsa and George. Granny's flat is exactly like Mum's except much messier, because Granny's flat is like Granny and Mum's flat is like Mum.

George lives with Mum and that's not always the easiest of things, because it means he also lives next door to Granny. He has a beard and a very small hat and is obsessed with jogging, during which he insists on wearing his shorts over the top of his tracksuit. He cooks in English, and so when he's reading the recipes he says "pork" instead of "flask." Granny never calls him "George," just "Loser," which infuriates Mum, but Elsa knows why Granny's doing it. She just wants Elsa to know she's on Elsa's side, no matter what. Because that's what you do when you're a granny and your grandchild's parents get divorced and find themselves new partners and suddenly tell your grandchild there's a half sibling on its way. That it irritates the hell out of Mum is something Granny views purely as a bonus.

Mum and George don't want to know if Halfie is a boy-half or a girl-half, even though it's easy to find out. It's especially important for George not to know. He always calls Halfie she/he, so he doesn't "trap the child in a gender role." The first time he said it, Elsa thought he said "gender troll." It ended up being a very confusing afternoon for all involved.

Halfie is either going to be called Elvir or Elvira, Mum and George have decided. When Elsa told Granny this, she just stared at her.

"*ELV-ir*?!"

"It's the boy version of Elvira."

"*Elvir,* though? Are they planning to send him to Mordor to destroy the ring, or what?" (This was soon after Granny had watched all of the *Lord of the Rings* films with Elsa, because Elsa's mum had expressly told Elsa she wasn't allowed to watch them.)

Obviously Elsa knows that Granny doesn't dislike Halfie. Or even George, really. She just talks that way because she's Granny. One time Elsa told Granny she really did hate George, and that sometimes she even hated Halfie too. It's very difficult not to love someone who can hear you say something as horrible as that and still be on your side.

In the flat under Granny's live Britt-Marie and Kent. They like owning things, and Kent especially likes telling you how much everything costs. He's hardly ever at home because he's an entrepreneur, or a "Kentrepreneur" as he likes to joke loudly to people he doesn't know. And if people don't laugh right away, he repeats it even louder. As if their hearing is the problem.

Britt-Marie is almost always at home, so Elsa assumes she is not an entrepreneur. Granny calls her "a full-time nag-bag who will forever be the bane of my life." She always looks a little like she just popped the wrong chocolate into her mouth. She's the one who put up the sign in the laundry with that FOR EVERYONE'S WELL-BEING bit on it. Everyone's well-being is very important to Britt-Marie, even though she and Kent are the only people in the house with a washing machine and tumble-dryer in their flat. One time after George had done some laundry, Britt-Marie came upstairs and asked to have a word with Elsa's mum. She'd brought a little ball of blue fluff from the tumble-dryer filter, which she held out towards Mum as if it were a newly hatched chick, and said: "I think you forgot this when you were doing the laundry, Ulrika!" And then when George explained that actually he was in charge of their laundry, Britt-Marie looked at him and smiled, though she didn't seem very genuine about it. And then she said, "How very modern," and smiled well-meaningly at Mum and handed her the fluff and said: "For *everyone's* well-being, in *this* leaseholders' association we clear the dryer filter when we've finished, Ulrika!"

It actually isn't a leaseholders' association yet. But it's going to become one, Britt-Marie is at pains to point out. She and Kent will see it done. And in Britt-Marie's leaseholders' association it's going to be very important to keep to the rules. That is why she is Granny's antagonist. Elsa knows what "antagonist" means, because you do if you read quality literature.

In the flat opposite Britt-Marie and Kent lives the woman with the black skirt. You hardly ever see her except when she scurries between the front entrance and her door early in the morning and late at night. She always wears high heels and a perfectly ironed black skirt and talks extremely loudly into a white cord trailing from her ear. She never says hello and she never smiles. Granny says that her skirt is too well ironed and "if you were the cloth hanging off that woman, you'd be terrified of getting yourself creased."

Under Britt-Marie and Kent's flat live Lennart and Maud. Lennart drinks at least twenty cups of coffee per day and always looks triumphantly proud every time his percolator is turned on. He is the second-nicest person in the world, and he's married to Maud. Maud is the nicest person in the world and she has always just baked some cookies. They live with Samantha, who's almost always asleep. Samantha is a bichon frisé but Lennart and Maud talk to her as if she wasn't. When Lennart and Maud drink coffee in front of Samantha they don't say they're having "coffee," they call it "a drink for grown-ups." Granny says they're soft in the head, but Elsa just thinks they're nice. And they always have dreams and hugs—dreams are a kind of cookie; hugs are just normal hugs.

Opposite Lennart and Maud lives Alf. He drives a taxi and always wears a leather jacket under a layer of irascibility. His shoes have soles as thin as greaseproof paper because he doesn't lift his feet when he walks. Granny says he has the lowest center of gravity in the entire bloody universe.

In the flat under Lennart and Maud live the boy with a syndrome and his mum. The boy with a syndrome is a year and a few weeks younger than Elsa, and never speaks. His mother loses things all the time. Objects seem to rain from her pockets, like in a cartoon when the crook gets frisked by the police and the pile of stuff from his pockets ends up bigger than they are. Both the boy and his mother have very kind eyes, and not even Granny seems to dislike them. And the boy's always dancing. He dances his way through his existence.

In the flat next to theirs, on the other side of the lift that never works, lives The Monster. Elsa doesn't know what his real name is, but she calls him The Monster because everyone is afraid of him.

Even Elsa's mum, who isn't scared of anything in the entire world, gives Elsa's back a little shove when they're about to walk past his flat. No one ever sees The Monster because he never goes out in the daytime, but Kent always says "People like that shouldn't be let loose! But that's what happens when the authorities go for the soft option. People in this bloody country get psychiatric care instead of prison!" Britt-Marie has written letters to the landlord, demanding that The Monster be evicted in view of her firm conviction that he "attracts other substance abusers into the building." Elsa is not sure what that means, and she's not even sure Britt-Marie knows. She asked Granny one day, but she just went a bit quiet and said, "Certain things should be left well alone." And this is a granny who fought in the War-Without-End, the war against the shadows in the Land-of-Almost-Awake, and who has met the most terrifying creatures that have been dreamed up in an eternity of ten thousand fairy tales.

That's how you measure time in the Land-of-Almost-Awake: in *eternities*. There are no watches in the Land-of-Almost-Awake, so time is measured according to how you feel. If it feels like an eternity, you say, "This is a lesser eternity." And if it feels sort of like two dozen eternities, you say, "An utter eternity." And the only thing that feels longer than an utter eternity is the eternity of a fairy tale, because a fairy tale is an eternity of utter eternities. And the very longest kind of eternity in existence is the eternity of ten thousand fairy tales. That's the biggest number in the Land-of-Almost-Awake.

Anyway, to get back to the point: at the bottom of the house where all these people live, there's a meeting room, where residents' meetings are held once every month. This is a bit more than in most buildings, but the flats are rented, and Britt-Marie and Kent really want everyone living there, by "a democratic process," to make a request to the landlord to sell them the building so they can become flat owners. And to do that, you must have residents' meetings. Because no one else in the house actually wants to be a flat-owner. The democratic bit of the democratic process is the one Kent and Britt-Marie like the least, you might say.

And the meetings are obviously terrifically boring. First everyone argues about what they were arguing about in the last meeting, and then they all look at their agendas and argue about when to have the next meeting, and then the meeting is over. But Elsa still goes there today because she needs to know when the arguing starts, so no one notices when she sneaks off.

Elsa arrives early. Kent hasn't got there yet, because Kent is always late. Alf hasn't arrived either, because Alf is always exactly on time. But Maud and Lennart are sitting at the big table and Britt-Marie and Mum are in the pantry discussing the coffee. Samantha is sleeping on the floor. Maud pushes a big tin of dreams towards Elsa. Lennart sits next to her, waiting for the coffee. Meanwhile he sips from a thermos he has brought with him. It's important to Lennart to have standby coffee available while he's waiting for the new coffee.

Britt-Marie is by the kitchen counter in the pantry with her hands clasped together in frustration over her stomach, while she looks nervously at Mum. Mum is making coffee. This is making Britt-Marie nervous because she thinks it would be best if they waited for Kent. Britt-Marie always thinks it would be best to wait for Kent, but Mum is not so big on waiting. She is more about taking control. Britt-Marie smiles well-meaningly at Mum.

"Everything all right with the coffee, Ulrika?"

"Yes, thanks," says Mum curtly.

"Maybe we should wait for Kent after all?"

"Oh, I think we can manage to make some coffee without Kent," Mum answers pleasantly.

Again, Britt-Marie clasps her hands together over her stomach. Smiles.

"Well, of course, please yourself, Ulrika. You always do."

Mum looks as if she's counting to some three-digit number and continues measuring the scoops of coffee.

"It's only coffee, Britt-Marie."

Britt-Marie nods her understanding of the situation and brushes some invisible dust off her skirt. There is always a bit of invisible dust on Britt-Marie's skirt, which only Britt-Marie can see, and which she absolutely must brush off.

"Kent always makes very nice coffee. Everyone always thinks Kent makes very nice coffee."

Maud sits at the table looking worried. Because Maud doesn't like conflict. That's why she bakes so many cookies, because it's much more difficult to have conflict when there are cookies around.

"Well, it's lovely that you and your little Elsa are here today. We all think it's . . . lovely," says Britt-Marie.

There's a patient "mmm" from Mum. A bit more coffee is measured out. A bit more dust is brushed off.

"I mean, it must be hard for you to find time for little Elsa, we can appreciate that, what with you being so ambitious about your career."

And then Mum spoons the coffee a little as if she's having fantasies of flinging it in Britt-Marie's face. But in a controlled way.

Britt-Marie goes to the window and moves a plant and says, as if thinking out aloud: "And your partner's so good, isn't he, staying at home to take care of the household. That's what you call it, isn't it? *Partner*? It's very modern, I understand." And then she smiles again. Well-meaning. Brushes a little more and adds, "Not that there's anything wrong with that, of course. Nothing at all."

Alf comes in, in a very bad mood, wearing his creaking leather jacket with a taxi logo on its chest. He has an evening newspaper in his hand. Checks his watch. It's seven o'clock sharp.

"Bloody says seven on the note," he grunts across the room at no one in particular.

"Kent is a little late," says Britt-Marie, and smiles and clasps her hands together over her stomach again. "He has an important group meeting with Germany," she goes on, as if Kent is meeting the entire population of Germany.

Fifteen minutes later Kent comes storming into the room, his jacket flapping like a mantle around him, and yelling, "Ja, Klaus! Ja! We will dizcuzz it at ze meeting in Frankfurt!" into his telephone. Alf looks up from his evening newspaper and taps his wristwatch and mutters, "Hope we didn't cause you any inconvenience by being here on time." Kent ignores him and instead claps his hands excitedly towards Lennart and Maud and says, with a grin, "Shall we kick things off, then? Eh? It's not like we're getting any babies made here, are we?" And then he turns quickly to Mum and points at her belly and laughs: "At least no more than we've already got!" And when Mum doesn't immediately laugh, Kent points at her belly again and repeats, "At least no more than we've already got!" in a louder voice, as if his levels weren't quite right the first time.

Maud brings in cookies. Mum serves coffee. Kent takes a gulp, pauses, and announces that it's rather strong. Alf sweeps down the whole cup in one go and mutters, "Just right!" Britt-Marie takes a tiny, tiny mouthful and rests the cup in the palm of her hand before offering her verdict: "I do think it's a little strong, personally." Then she throws a furtive glance at Mum and adds, "And you're drinking coffee, Ulrika, even though you're pregnant." And before Mum has time to answer, Britt-Marie immediately excuses herself: "Not that there's anything wrong with that, obviously. Obviously not!"

And then Kent declares the meeting open and then everyone argues for two hours about what they argued about at the last meeting. Which is when Elsa sneaks out without anyone noticing.

She tiptoes up the stairs to the mezzanine floor. She peers at the door to The Monster's flat, but calms herself with the thought that there is still daylight outside. The Monster never goes outside while it's still light.

Then she looks at the door of the flat next to The Monster's, the one without a name on the mail slot. That is where Our Friend lives. Elsa stands a few feet from it, holding her breath because she's afraid it will smash the door and come charging out of the splintered remains and try to close its jaws around her throat if it hears her coming too close. Only Granny calls it Our Friend; everyone else says "the hound." Especially Britt-Marie. Elsa doesn't know how much fight there is in it, but either way she's never seen such a big dog in her life. When you hear it barking from behind the door it's like being whacked in the stomach by a medicine ball.

But she has only seen it once, in Granny's flat, a few days before Granny got taken ill. She couldn't have imagined feeling more afraid, even if facing a shadow eye-to-eye in the Land-of-Almost-Awake.

It was a Saturday and Granny and Elsa were going to an exhibition about dinosaurs. That was the morning Mum put the Gryffindor scarf in the wash without asking and made Elsa take another scarf—a vomit-green one. Mum knows Elsa hates green. She really lacks empathy sometimes, that woman.

Our Friend had been lying on Granny's bed, like a sphinx outside a pyramid. Elsa stood transfixed in the hall, staring at that gigantic black head and the terrifying, depthless eyes. Granny had come out of the kitchen and was putting on her coat as if it were the most natural thing in the whole universe to have the biggest thing ever lying on her bed.

"What is . . . that thing?" Elsa had whispered. Granny carried on rolling her cigarette and replied indifferently: "That's Our Friend. It won't hurt you if you don't hurt it."

Easy for her to say, Elsa thought—how was she supposed to know what would provoke one of those? Once, one of the girls at school had hit her because she had "an ugly scarf." That was apparently all Elsa had done to her, and she got hit for it.

And so Elsa stood there, her usual scarf in the wash and in its place an ugly scarf chosen by her mother, worrying that vomit-green might provoke the beast. In the end Elsa had explained that it was her mum's scarf, not hers, and her mum had terrible taste, before backing away towards the door. Our Friend just stared at her. Or at least that was what Elsa thought, if she was right in thinking those were its eyes. And then it also bared its teeth, Elsa was almost sure of it. But Granny just muttered something about "kids, you know" and rolled her eyes at Our Friend. Then she went to find the keys to Renault and then she and Elsa went to the dinosaur exhibition. Granny left the front door wide open, Elsa remembers, and when they sat in Renault and Elsa asked what Our Friend was doing in Granny's flat, Granny just answered: "Visiting." When Elsa asked why it was always barking behind its door, Granny answered cheerily, "Barking? Ah, it only does that when Britt-Marie goes past." And when Elsa asked why, Granny grinned from ear to ear and answered: "Because that's what he likes doing."

And then Elsa had asked who Our Friend lived with, and then Granny said: "Not everyone needs to live with someone, good God. For instance, I don't live with anybody." And even though Elsa insisted that this might have some connection with the fact that Granny was not a *dog*, Granny never explained anything else about it.

And now here Elsa stands, on the landing, peeling off wrappers from the Daim chocolate. She throws in the first one so quickly that the flap slams when she lets go of it. She holds her breath and feels her heart thumping in her whole head. But then she remembers Granny saying that this needs to be done quickly, so Britt-Marie doesn't get suspicious during the residents' meeting downstairs.

Britt-Marie really hates Our Friend. Elsa tries to remind herself that, in spite of it all, she is a knight of Miamas, and after that she opens the mail slot with more courage.

She hears its breath. It sounds like there's an avalanche going on in its lungs. Elsa's heart thumps until she's sure Our Friend will feel the vibrations through the door.

"My granny says to tell you she's sorry for not bringing you any sweets for such a long time!" she says diligently through the mail slot, removing fistfuls of wrappers and dropping them on the floor.

Then she hears it moving and snatches back her hand, startled. There's silence for a few seconds. She hears the abrupt crunch of Our Friend taking the chocolate in its jaws.

"Granny's ill," Elsa explains while it's eating.

She isn't prepared for the way the words tremble as they come out of her. She convinces herself that Our Friend is breathing more slowly. She empties in more chocolate.

"She has cancer," whispers Elsa.

Elsa has no friends, so she isn't quite sure of the normal procedure for these types of errands. But she imagines that if she did have friends, she'd want them to know if she had cancer. Even if they happened to be the biggest things of anything. "She sends her best and says sorry," she whispers into the darkness and drops in the rest of the chocolate and gently closes the flap.

She stays there for a moment, looking at Our Friend's door.

And then at The Monster's. If this wild animal can be hiding behind one of the doors, she doesn't even want to know what might be behind the other.

Then she jogs down the stairs to the front entrance.

George is still in the laundry. In the meeting room, they are all drinking coffee and arguing.

Because it's a normal house.

By and large.

4

BEER

The room in the hospital smells as bad and feels as cold as hospital rooms tend to when it is barely above freezing outside and someone has hid beer bottles under her pillow and opened a window to try to get rid of the smell of cigarette smoke. It hasn't worked.

Granny and Elsa are playing Monopoly. Granny doesn't say anything about cancer, for Elsa's sake. And Elsa doesn't say anything about death, for Granny's sake. Because Granny doesn't like talking about death, especially not her own. So when Elsa's mum and the doctors leave the room to talk in low, serious voices in the corridor, Elsa tries not to look worried. That doesn't really work either.

Granny grins secretively.

"Did I ever tell you about the time I fixed a job for the dragons in Miamas?" she asks in their secret language.

It's good to have a secret language in the hospital, because hospitals have ears in their walls, says Granny. Especially when the walls have Elsa's mum as their boss.

"Duh—obviously!"

Granny nods as a courtesy and tells the whole story anyway. Because no one ever taught Granny how not to tell a story. And Elsa listens, because no one ever taught her how not to.

That's why she knows that one of the things people say about Granny most often when she's not around is, "This time she's really crossed the line." Britt-Marie is *always* saying it. Elsa assumes this is why Granny likes the kingdom of Miamas so much: you can't cross the line in Miamas, because the kingdom is endless. And not like on television when people toss their hair about and say that they "have no boundaries," but properly, without any limits, because no one knows for certain where Miamas begins and ends. This is partly because unlike the other five kingdoms in the Land-of-Almost-Awake, which are mainly built of stone and mortar, Miamas is wholly made of imagination. It could also be slightly because the Miamas city wall has an insanely moody temperament and may suddenly one morning have the idea of moving itself a mile or two into the forest because it needs a bit of "me time." Only to move twice as far back in the opposite direction the next morning, because it has decided to wall in some dragon or troll that for one reason or another it has decided to be grumpy with. (Usually because the dragon or the troll has been up all night drinking schnapps and weeing on the wall while sleeping, Granny suggests.)

There are more trolls and dragons in Miamas than in any other of the five kingdoms in the Land-of-Almost-Awake, you see, because the main export industry in Miamas is fairy tales. Trolls and dragons have excellent employment prospects in Miamas because stories need villains. "Of course, it hasn't always been like this," Granny sometimes muses. "There was a time when the dragons had been almost forgotten by Miamas's storytellers, particularly the ones who'd grown a little long in the tooth." Then she recounts the whole story about how the dragons were causing too much trouble in Miamas, drifting about without jobs, drinking schnapps and smoking cigars and getting involved in violent confrontations with the city wall. So in the end the people of Miamas begged Granny to help them come up with some kind of practical job-creation scheme. And that's when Granny had the idea that dragons should guard treasures at the ends of the tales.

Up until that point, it had actually been a massive narrative problem, the fact that heroes in fairy tales looked for a treasure and, once they had located it in some deep cave, only had to nip inside to pick it up. Just like that. No epic closing battles or dramatic apexes or anything. "All you could do was play worthless video games afterwards," Granny said, nodding somberly. Granny knows all about it, because last summer Elsa taught her how to play a game called World of Warcraft and Granny played it around the clock for several weeks until Mum said she was beginning to "exhibit disturbing tendencies" and banned her from sleeping in Elsa's room from then on.

But anyway, when the storytellers heard Granny's idea the whole problem was solved in an afternoon. "And that's why all fairy tales nowadays have dragons at the end! It's my doing!" Granny chortles. Like she always does.

Granny has a story from Miamas for every situation. One of them is about Miploris, the kingdom where all sorrow is kept in storage, and its princess who was robbed of a magical treasure by an ugly witch whom she's been hunting ever since. Another story is about two princeling brothers, both in love with the princess of Miploris, and practically breaking the Land-of-Almost-Awake into pieces in their furious battle for her love.

One story was about the sea-angel, burdened by a curse that forced her to drift up and down the coast of the Land-of-Almost-Awake after losing her beloved. And another story was about the Chosen One, the most universally loved dancer in Mimovas, which is the kingdom all music comes from. In the fairy tale the shadows tried to abduct the Chosen One in order to destroy Mimovas, but the cloud animals saved him and flew him all the way back to Miamas.

And when the shadows came after them, all the inhabitants of the six kingdoms of the Land-of-Almost-Awake—the princes, princesses, knights, soldiers, trolls, angels, and the witch—agreed to protect the Chosen One. And that was when the War-Without-End started. It raged for an eternity of ten thousand fairy tales, until the wurses and Wolfheart came out of the forest and led the good army into the last battle and forced the shadows back across the sea.

Of course, Wolfheart is a whole fairy tale in his own right, because he was born in Miamas but just like all other soldiers he grew up in Mibatalos. He has a warrior's heart but the soul of a storyteller, and he's the most invincible fighter ever seen in any of the six kingdoms. He had been living deep in the dark forests for many eternities of fairy tales, but he came back when the Land-of-Almost-Awake needed him most.

Granny has been telling these fairy tales for as long as Elsa can remember. In the beginning they were only to make Elsa go to sleep, and to get her to practice Granny's secret language, and a little because Granny is just about as nutty as a granny should be. But lately the stories have another dimension as well. Something Elsa can't quite put her finger on.

"Put 'Pennsylvania Railroad' back," says Elsa tersely.

"I bought it . . . ?" Granny tries.

"Mmm, sure you did. Put it back."

"This is how it must have been playing bloody Monopoly with Hitler!"

"Hitler would only have wanted to play Risk," mutters Elsa, because she's checked out Hitler on Wikipedia, after there were some rows between her and Granny about her use of Hitler as a metaphor.

"Touché," mutters Granny.

And then they play in silence for about a minute. Because that is about the usual length of time they can be bothered to keep feuding.

"Did you give the chocolate to Our Friend?" asks Granny.

Elsa nods. But she doesn't mention how she told it about Granny's cancer. A little bit because she thinks Granny would be annoyed, and quite a bit because she doesn't want to talk about cancer. She checked it on Wikipedia yesterday. And then she checked what a will is and then she was so angry that she couldn't sleep all night.

"How did you and Our Friend become friends?" she asks instead.

Granny shrugs. "The usual way."

Elsa doesn't know what the usual way is, because she has no friends other than Granny. But she doesn't say anything, because she knows Granny would be upset if she heard that.

"Anyway, the mission is done," she says in a low voice.

Granny nods keenly and throws a searching look at the door, as if concerned someone could be watching them. Then she reaches under her pillow. The bottles clink against each other and she swears when she spills some beer on the pillowcase, but then she hauls out an envelope and presses it into Elsa's hand.

"This is your next mission, my knight Elsa. But you mustn't open it until tomorrow."

Elsa looks at the envelope skeptically.

"Haven't you heard of e-mail?"

"You can't e-mail something this important."

Elsa weighs the envelope in her hand, presses the lumpy bit at the bottom of it.

"What is it?"

"A letter and a key," says Granny. And then she looks both serious and frightened, both of which are very rare emotions in Granny. She reaches out and grabs hold of Elsa's index fingers. "Tomorrow I'm going to send you out on the biggest treasure hunt you've ever seen, my brave little knight. Are you ready for that?"

Granny has always loved treasure hunts. In Miamas, treasure

hunting is considered a sport. You can compete in it, because it's an approved Olympic field event. But in Miamas it's not called the Olympic Games, it's actually known as the Invisible Games, because all the participants are invisible. Not exactly a spectator sport, as Elsa pointed out when Granny told her about it.

Elsa also loves treasure hunts, but not as much as Granny. No one in any kingdom in the eternity of ten thousand fairy tales could love them like she does. She can make anything into a treasure hunt: if they've been out shopping and Granny can't remember where she parked Renault; or when she wants Elsa to go through her mail and pay her bills because Granny finds this insanely boring; or when there's a sports day at school and Elsa knows the older children are going to lash her in the shower with rolled-up towels. Granny can make a parking area into magic mountains, and rolled-up towels into dragons that must be outsmarted. And Elsa is always the heroine.

This sounds like a different kind of treasure hunt altogether, though.

"The one who's supposed to have the key will know what to do with it. You have to protect the castle, Elsa."

Granny has always called their house "the castle." Elsa always just thought it was because she's a bit nutty. But now she's not so sure.

"Protect the castle, Elsa. Protect your family. Protect your friends!" Granny repeats determinedly.

"What friends?"

Granny puts her hands against Elsa's cheeks and smiles.

"They'll come. Tomorrow I am sending you out on a treasure hunt, and it's going to be a fairy tale of marvels and a grand adventure. And you have to promise not to hate me for it."

Elsa blinks, and there's a burning sensation.

"Why would I hate you?"

Granny caresses her eyelids.

"It's a grandmother's prerogative never to have to show her worst sides to her grandchild, Elsa. Never to have to talk about what she was like before she became a grandmother."

"I know loads of your worst sides!"

She's hoping to make Granny laugh with that one. But it doesn't work. Granny just whispers in a sad voice: "It's going to be a grand adventure and a fairy tale of marvels. But it's my fault that you'll find a dragon at the end, my darling knight."

Elsa squints at her. Because she has never heard Granny talking like this. She always claims credit for the dragons at the end. It's never her "fault." Granny sits before her, tinier and more fragile than Elsa can remember ever having seen her. Not at all like a superhero.

Granny kisses her forehead.

"Promise you won't hate me when you find out who I've been. And promise me you'll protect the castle. Protect your friends."

Elsa doesn't know what any of this means, but she promises. And then Granny embraces her for longer than ever before.

"Give the letter to him who's waiting. He won't want to accept it, but tell him it's from me. Tell him your granny asked you to tell him she's sorry."

And then she wipes the tears from Elsa's cheeks. And Elsa points out that you're supposed to say "to he who's waiting," not "him." And they argue a bit about that, as usual. And then they play Monopoly and eat cinnamon buns and talk about who'd win a fight between Harry Potter and Spider-Man. Bloody pathetic discussion, of course, thinks Elsa. But Granny likes nattering on about these types of things because she's too immature to understand that Harry Potter would have crushed Spider-Man.

Granny gets out some more cinnamon buns from large paper

bags under another pillow. Not that she has to hide the cinnamon buns from Elsa's mum the way she has to hide the beer from Elsa's mum, but she likes keeping them together because she likes eating them together. Beer and cinnamon buns is Granny's favorite snack. Elsa recognizes the name of the bakery on the bags; Granny only eats cinnamon buns from that one bakery, because she says no one else knows how to make real Mirevas cinnamon buns. In fact, it's the national dish of the Land-of-Almost-Awake. One very bad thing about it is that one can only have the national dish on the national day. But a very good thing about it is that in the Land-of-Almost-Awake, every day is the national day. As Granny likes to put it, "In the end the problem disappears, said the old lady who crapped in the sink." Elsa hopes with all her might that this doesn't mean Granny is going to start using the kitchen sink with the door left open.

"Are you really going to get well?" Elsa asks with the reluctance of an almost-eight-year-old asking a question to which she already knows she doesn't want to know the answer.

"Course I will!" Granny says with complete confidence, although she can see well enough that Elsa knows she's lying.

"Promise," Elsa insists.

And then Granny leans forward and whispers into her ear, in their secret language:

"I promise, my beloved, beloved knight. I promise that it will get better. I promise that everything will be fine."

Because that is what Granny always says. That it will get better. That everything will be fine.

"But I still think that Spider-Man fellow would have wiped the floor with this Harry," Granny adds with a grin. And, in the end, Elsa grins back at her.

They eat more cinnamon buns and play more Monopoly. And this makes it much more difficult to stay grumpy.

The sun goes down. Everything goes silent. Elsa lies very close to Granny in the narrow hospital bed. And they mainly just close their eyes, and the cloud animals come to fetch them, and they go to Miamas together.

And in an apartment block on the other side of town, everyone wakes up with a start when the hound in the first-floor flat, without any warning, starts howling. Louder and more heartrendingly than anything they have ever heard coming out of the primal depths of any animal. As if it is singing with the sorrow and yearning of an eternity of ten thousand fairy tales. It howls for hours, all through the night, until dawn.

And when the morning light seeps into the hospital room, Elsa wakes up in Granny's arms. But Granny is still in Miamas.

5

LILIES

Having a grandmother is like having an army. This is a grandchild's ultimate privilege: knowing that someone is on your side, always, whatever the details. Even when you are wrong. Especially then, in fact.

A grandmother is both a sword and a shield. When they say at school that Elsa is "different," as if this is something bad; or when she comes home with bruises and the headmaster says she "has to learn to fit in," this is when Granny backs her up. Won't let her apologize. Refuses to let her take the blame. Granny never says to Elsa that she shouldn't let it get to her because "then they won't enjoy teasing you as much." Or that she should "just walk away." Granny knows better than that.

And the lonelier Elsa gets in the real world, the larger her army in the Land-of-Almost-Awake. The harder the lashes of rolled-up towels in the day, the more astounding the adventures she gets to ride into in the night. In Miamas, no one says she has to learn to fit in. That's why Elsa wasn't especially impressed when Dad took her to that hotel in Spain and explained that it was "all-inclusive" there. Because if you have a granny, your whole life is all-inclusive.

Her teachers at school say that Elsa is having "concentration issues." But it isn't true. She can recite more or less all of Harry Potter by memory. She can outline the exact superpowers of all the X-Men and knows exactly which of them Spider-Man could and could not take out in a fight. And she can draw a fairly okay version of the map at the start of *The Lord of the Rings* with her eyes closed. Unless Granny is standing next to her, tugging at the paper and moaning about how this is insanely boring and how she'd rather take Renault out and "do something." She's a bit restless, Granny. But she has shown Elsa every corner of Miamas and all the corners of the other five kingdoms in the Land-of-Almost-Awake. Even the ruins of Mibatalos, which was sacked by the shadows at the end of the War-Without-End. Elsa has stood with Granny on the rocks by the coast, where the ninety-nine snow-angels sacrificed themselves; she has looked out over the sea, where one day the shadows will come back. And she knows all about the shadows, because Granny always says one should know one's enemies better than oneself.

The shadows were dragons in the beginning, but they had an evil and a darkness of such strength within themselves that it made them into something else. Something much more dangerous. They hate people and their stories; they have hated for so long and with such intensity that in the end the darkness enveloped their whole bodies until their shapes were no longer discernible. That is also why they are so difficult to defeat, because they can disappear into walls or into the ground or float up. They're ferocious and bloodthirsty, and if you're bitten by one you don't just die; a far more serious and terrible fate lies in store: you lose your imagination. It just runs out of your wound and leaves you gray and empty. You wither away year by year until your body is just a shell. Until no one remembers any fairy tales anymore.

And without fairy tales, Miamas and the whole Land-of-Almost-

Awake die a death without imagination. The most repellent kind of death.

But Wolfheart defeated the shadows in the War-Without-End. He came out of the forests when the fairy tales needed him most and drove the shadows into the sea. And one day the shadows will come back, and maybe that is why Granny tells her all the stories now, thinks Elsa. To prepare her.

So the teachers are wrong. Elsa has no problems concentrating. She just concentrates on the right things.

Granny says people who think slowly always accuse quick thinkers of concentration problems. "Idiots can't understand that non-idiots are done with a thought and already moving on to the next before they themselves have. That's why idiots are always so scared and aggressive. Because nothing scares idiots more than a smart girl."

That is what she often says to Elsa when Elsa has had a particularly concentration-challenged day at school, and they lie on Granny's gigantic bed under all the black-and-white photographs on Granny's ceiling, and close their eyes until the people in the photographs start dancing. Elsa doesn't know who they are, Granny just calls them her "stars," because when the streetlight comes through the blinds they glitter like the sky at night. Men in uniforms stand there and other men in doctors' coats and a few men with hardly any clothes on at all. Tall men and smiling men and men with moustaches and heavyset men wearing hats, and they all stand next to Granny and they look as if she just told them a cheeky joke. None of them are looking into the camera, because none of them can tear their eyes away from her.

Granny is young. She is beautiful. And immortal. She stands by road signs whose letters Elsa can't read; she stands outside tents in deserts between men with rifles in their hands. And everywhere in the photos are children. Some of them have bandages around their heads and some lie in hospital beds with tubes inserted into their bodies, and one of them only has one arm and a stump where the other arm should have been. But one of the boys hardly looks hurt at all. He looks like he could run fifty miles in his bare feet. He's about the same age as Elsa, and his hair is so thick and tangled that you could lose your keys in it, and there's something in his eyes as if he'd just found a secret stash of fireworks and ice cream. His eyes are big and perfectly round and so black that the surrounding white is like chalk on a blackboard. Elsa doesn't know who he is, but she calls him the Werewolf Boy, because that is what he looks like to her.

She always thinks about asking Granny more about the Werewolf Boy. But the minute the thought occurs to Elsa, her eyelids start drooping and in the next moment she is sitting on a cloud animal and Granny is next to her on her own and they're gliding over the Land-of-Almost-Awake and landing by the city gates of Miamas. And then Elsa thinks that she'll ask Granny in the morning.

And then one morning there is no morning anymore.

Elsa is sitting on the bench outside the big window. She's so cold that her teeth are chattering. Her mum is inside talking to the woman who sounds like a whale, or, at least, the way Elsa imagines a whale would sound. Which is difficult to know, admittedly, when you have never happened to run into a whale, but she sounds like Granny's record player after Granny tried to build a robot out of it. It was slightly unclear what sort of robot she was intending to build, but whatever the case it wasn't a very good one. And then it sounded like a whale after that whenever you tried to play a record on it. Elsa learned all about LPs and CDs that afternoon. That was when she worked out why old people seem to have so much free time, because in the olden days until Spotify came along they must have used up almost all their time just changing the track.

She tightens her coat collar and her Gryffindor scarf around her chin. The first snow came in the night. Gradually, almost reluctantly. Now it's so deep you can make snow-angels. Elsa loves doing that.

In Miamas there are snow-angels all year round. But as Granny constantly reminds Elsa, they are not especially polite. They're quite arrogant and self-important, in fact, and always complain about the service when they're eating out at one of the inns. "There's a right fuss, smelling the wine and all that crap," snorts Granny.

Elsa holds out her foot and catches the snowflakes on her shoe. She hates sitting on benches outside, waiting for Mum, but she still does it, because the only thing Elsa hates more is sitting *inside* waiting for Mum.

She wants to go home. With Granny. It's as if the whole house is missing Granny now. Not the people living in it, but the actual building. The walls are creaking and whining. And Our Friend has been howling without pause in its flat for two whole nights.

Britt-Marie forced Kent to ring the doorbell of Our Friend's flat, but no one answered. It just barked so loudly that Kent stumbled into a wall. So Britt-Marie called the police. She has hated Our Friend for a long time. A couple of months ago she went round the house with a petition, to get everyone to sign it so she could send it to the landlord and demand "the eviction of that horrendous hound."

"We can't have dogs in the leaseholders' association. It's a question of safety! It's dangerous for the children, and one *must* think of the children!" Britt-Marie explained this to everyone in the manner of someone who is concerned about children, although the only children in the house are Elsa and the boy with a syndrome, and Elsa is pretty sure that Britt-Marie is not massively worried about Elsa's safety.

The boy with a syndrome lives opposite the terrifying dog, but his mother lightheartedly told Britt-Marie she believed the hound was more bothered by her son than the other way around. Granny couldn't stop herself laughing when she heard this, but it made Elsa worry about Britt-Marie trying to prohibit children as well.

Elsa jumps off the bench and starts traipsing around in the snow, to warm up her feet. Next to the big window where the whale-woman is working there's a supermarket with a sign outside: MINCEBEEF 49.90. Elsa tries to control herself because her mum is always telling her to control herself. But in the end she takes her red felt-tip pen from her jacket pocket and adds a neat "D" and a slash, to show that it should be two words.

She looks at the result and nods slightly. Then puts the pen back in her pocket and sits down again on the bench. Leans her head back and closes her eyes and feels the cold little feet of the snowflakes landing on her face. When the smell of smoke reaches her nostrils she thinks she's imagining it. At first it's even wonderful to feel that acrid smell at the back of her throat and, though Elsa can't think why, it makes her feel warm and secure. But then she feels something else. Something thumping behind her ribs. Like a warning signal.

The man is standing a distance away. In the shadow of one of the high-rise apartment buildings. She can't see him clearly, only pick out the red glow of his cigarette between his fingers and the fact that he's very thin. As if he's lacking in contours. He stands partially turned away from her, as if he hasn't even seen her.

And Elsa doesn't know why she gets so scared, but she finds herself fumbling around the bench for a weapon. It's very odd; she never does that in the real world. In the real world, her first instinct is always to run. Only in Miamas would she reach for her sword, as a knight does when sensing danger. But there are no swords here.

When she looks up again the man is still turned away from her, but she could swear that he's moved closer. And he's still in the shade, although he's moved away from the high-rise. As if the shadow isn't cast by the house, but by the man himself. Elsa blinks, and when she opens her eyes she no longer thinks the man has moved closer.

She knows he has.

She slips off the bench and reverses towards the big window, fumbling for the door handle. Stumbles inside. Stands there panting, gasping, trying to calm down. Only when the door closes behind her with a little friendly *pling* does she understand what she found reassuring about the cigarette smoke.

The man smokes the same tobacco as Granny. Elsa would recognize it anywhere, because Granny used to let her help out with the cigarette rolling, because Granny says that Elsa has "such small fingers, and they're perfect for these little sods."

When she looks out the window she no longer knows where the shadows begin and end. One moment she imagines the man is still standing there on the other side of the street, but then she starts wondering if she actually saw him at all.

She jumps like a startled animal when Mum's hands alight on her shoulders. She spins round with wide-open eyes, before her legs give way. Tiredness disarms all her senses once she is in her mother's arms. She has not slept for two days. Mum's distended belly is big enough to rest a teacup on. George says it is nature's way of giving a pregnant woman a break.

"Let's go home," Mum whispers softly in her ear.

Elsa stares, forcing her tiredness away and sliding out of her mother's grip.

"First I want to talk to Granny!"

Mum looks devastated. Elsa knows that because "devastated" is a word for the word jar.

(We'll get to the word jar later in this story.)

"It's . . . darling . . . I don't know if it's a good idea," whispers Mum.

But Elsa has already run past the reception desk and into the next room. She can hear the whale-woman yelling behind her, but then she hears her mother's composed voice asking her to let Elsa go inside.

Granny is waiting for her in the middle of the room. There's a fragrance of lilies, Mum's favorite flower. Granny doesn't have any favorite flowers because no plant lives for longer than twenty-four hours in Granny's flat, and in a fairly rare instance of compliance, possibly also because of the enthusiastic encouragement of her favorite grandchild, Granny has decided it would be bloody unfair to nature for her to have any favorite flowers.

Elsa stands to one side with her hands pushed moodily into her jacket pockets. Defiantly she stamps snow from her shoes onto the floor.

"I don't want to be a part of this treasure hunt, it's idiotic."

Granny doesn't answer. She never answers when she knows that Elsa is right. Elsa stamps more snow off her shoes.

"YOU are idiotic," she says cuttingly.

Granny doesn't rise to that one either. Elsa sits on the chair next to her and holds out the letter.

"You can take care of this idiotic letter yourself," she whispers.

Two days have gone by since Our Friend started howling. Two days since Elsa was last in the Land-of-Almost-Awake and the kingdom of Miamas. No one is being straight with her. All the grown-ups try to wrap it in cotton wool, so it doesn't sound dangerous or frightening or unpleasant. As if Granny hasn't been ill. As if the whole thing was an accident. But Elsa knows they're lying, because Elsa's granny hasn't ever been laid low by an accident. Usually it's the accident that gets laid low by Granny.

And Elsa knows what cancer is. It says all about it on Wikipedia.

She gives the edge of the coffin a shove, to get a reaction. Because deep down she's still hoping this could be one of those occasions when Granny is just pulling her leg. Like that time Granny dressed the snowman so he looked like a real person who'd fallen from the balcony, and Britt-Marie got so furious when she realized it was a joke that she called the police. And the next morning when Britt-Marie looked out the window, she discovered that Granny had made another identical snowman, and then Britt-Marie "went loopy," as Granny put it, and came charging out with a snow shovel. And then the snowman jumped up and roared, "WAAAAAAAAH!!!" Granny told her afterwards that she'd lain in the snow for hours waiting for Britt-Marie and at least two cats had weed on her in the meantime, "but it was well worth it!" Britt-Marie called the police again, of course, but they said it wasn't a crime to scare someone.

This time, though, Granny doesn't get up. Elsa bangs her fists against the coffin, but Granny doesn't answer, and Elsa bangs harder and harder as if it's possible to put right all the things that are wrong by banging. In the end she slips off the chair and sinks onto her knees on the floor and whispers:

"Do you know that they're lying, they say you've 'passed away,' or, that we've 'lost you?' No one says 'dead.'"

Elsa digs her nails into her palms and her whole body trembles.

"I don't know how to get to Miamas if you're dead. . . ."

Granny doesn't answer. Elsa puts her forehead against the lower edge of the coffin. She feels the cold wood against her skin and warm tears on her lips. Then she feels Mum's soft fingers against her neck, and she turns around and throws her arms around her, and Mum carries her out of there. When she opens her eyes again she's sitting in Kia, Mum's car.

Mum is standing outside in the snow talking to George on the telephone. Elsa knows she doesn't want her to hear them talking about the funeral. She's not an idiot. She's still got Granny's letter in her hand. She knows you're not supposed to read other people's letters, but she must have read this one a hundred times these last two days. Granny must have known she'd do this, because she's written the entire letter in symbols that Elsa can't understand. Using the strange alphabet she saw on the road signs in Granny's photographs.

Elsa glares at it. Granny always said she and Elsa shouldn't have any secrets from each other, only secrets together. She's furious with Granny for the lie, because now Elsa sits here with the greatest secret of them all and she can't understand a crapping thing. And she knows that if she falls out with Granny at this point, it will set a personal record that they can never beat.

The ink smudges over the paper when she blinks down at it. Although there are letters that Elsa doesn't know, Granny has probably misspelled things. When Granny writes, it's as if she is just scattering words over the page while she's already mentally on her way somewhere else. It's not that Granny can't spell, it's just that she thinks so fast that the letters and words can't keep up. And unlike Elsa, Granny can't see the point of spelling things correctly; anyway she was always better at science and numbers. "You bloody understand what I mean!" she hisses when she passes Elsa secret notes while they're eating with Mum and George and Elsa adds the dashes and spaces in the right places with her red felt-tip pen.

It's one of the few things they really row about, Granny and Elsa, because Elsa thinks letters are something more than just a way of sending messages. Something more important.

Or used to. They used to row about it.

There's only one word in the whole letter that Elsa can read. Just one, which has been written in normal letters, tossed down almost haphazardly in the middle of the text. It's so anonymous that Elsa didn't notice it the first time she read it. She reads it again and again until she can't see it through all her blinking. She feels let down and angry for tens of thousands of reasons and probably another ten thousand she hasn't even thought of yet. Because she knows it's not a coincidence. Granny put that word right there so Elsa would see it.

The name on the envelope is the same name as the one on The Monster's mailbox. And the only word Elsa can read in the letter is "Miamas."

Granny has always loved treasure hunts.

6

CLEANING AGENTS

She has three scratch marks on her cheek. As if from claws. She knows they'll want to know how it all began. Elsa ran, is the short answer. She's good at running. That's what happens when you get chased all the time.

This morning she lied to Mum about starting school an hour earlier than usual. And when Mum pulled her up on it, Elsa played the bad mother card. The bad mother card is like Renault: hardly a beauty but surprisingly effective. "I've told you like a hundred times I start earlier on Mondays! I even gave you a slip but you never listen to me anymore!"

Mum mumbled something about "pregnant airhead" and looked guilty. The easiest way of getting her off balance is if you can manage to persuade her she's lost control. There used to be just two people in the world who knew how to make Mum lose control. And now there's only one. That's a lot of power to put into the hands of someone who's not even eight yet.

At lunchtime, Elsa took the bus home, because she figured she had a better chance of dodging Britt-Marie during the day. She stopped and bought four bags of Daim in the supermarket. The house was as dark and silent as only Granny's house could be without the presence of Granny, and it felt as if even the house were missing her. Elsa hid carefully from Britt-Marie, who was on her way to the space where the trash bins are kept, although she didn't even have any bags of separated rubbish. After Britt-Marie had checked the contents of all the bins and pursed her mouth the way she does when she decides to raise some issue at the next residents' meeting, she set off down the street to the supermarket so she could walk about and purse her mouth in there for a while. Elsa sneaked in and went up the stairs to the mezzanine floor. There she stood, shaking with fear and anger outside the flat, still with the letter in her hand. Her anger was reserved for Granny. Her fear was of The Monster.

Not long after, she was running through the playground so fast she thought her feet were on fire. And now she sits in a small room with luminous red marks on her cheek as if from claws, waiting for Mum and fully aware that she'll demand to know what's happened.

She spins the globe at one end of the desk. The headmaster looks particularly vexed when she does it. So she keeps doing it.

"Well?" the headmaster asks, pointing at her cheek, "Are you ready to tell me what happened?"

She doesn't even grace him with an answer.

It was smart of Granny, Elsa has to admit it. She's still insanely irritated about this stupid treasure hunt, but it was smart of Granny to write "Miamas" in normal characters in the letter. Because Elsa had stood there earlier on the landing, summoning her courage for at least a hundred eternities before she rang the doorbell. And if Granny hadn't known that Elsa would read the letter even though one mustn't read other people's letters, and if she hadn't written "Miamas" in normal characters, Elsa would just have thrown the envelope in The Monster's mail slot and run away. Instead, she stood there ringing the doorbell, because she had to press The Monster for some answers.

Because Miamas belongs to Granny and Elsa. It's only theirs. Elsa's fury at the thought of Granny bringing along some random muppet was bigger than any fear she might have of monsters.

Okay, not *much* bigger than her monster fear, but big enough.

Our Friend was still howling in the flat next door, but nothing happened when she rang at The Monster's door. She rang again and banged on the door until the wood was creaking and then peered inside through the mail slot, but it was too dark to see anything. Not a movement. Not a breath. All she could feel was an acrid smell of cleaning agents, the sort of smell that rushes up your nasal membranes and starts kicking the back of your eyeballs when you breathe it in.

But no sign of a monster. Not even a little one.

Elsa took off her backpack and got out the four bags of Daim and emptied them through Our Friend's mail slot. For a few brief, brief moments the creature stopped howling in there. Elsa has decided to call it "the creature" until she has figured out what it really is, because, irrespective of what Britt-Marie says, Elsa is pretty damn sure that this is no mere dog.

"You have to stop howling; Britt-Marie will call the police and they'll come here and kill you," she whispered through the slot.

She didn't know if the creature understood. But at least it was being quiet and eating its Daim. As any rational creature does, when offered Daim.

"If you see The Monster, tell him I have mail for him," said Elsa.

The creature didn't answer, but Elsa felt its warm breath when it sniffed at the door.

"Tell him my granny sends her regards and says she is sorry," she whispered.

And then she put the letter in her backpack and took the bus back to school. And when she looked out of the bus window she thought she saw him again. The thin man who'd been standing outside the undertaker's yesterday while Mum was talking to the whale-woman. Now he was in the shadows on the other side of the street. She couldn't see his face behind the cigarette smoke, but a cold, instinctual terror wrapped itself around her ribs.

And then he was gone.

Elsa reckons this may have been why she couldn't make herself invisible when she got to school. Invisibility is the sort of superpower you can train yourself to have, and Elsa practices it all the time, but it doesn't work if you are angry or frightened. When she got to school Elsa was both. Afraid of men turning up in the shadows without her knowing why, and angry at Granny for sending a letter to a monster, and both angry at and afraid of monsters. Normal monsters have the decency to live deep inside black caves or at the bottoms of ice-cold lakes. Normal, terrifying monsters don't actually live in flats and get their mail delivered.

And anyway Elsa hates Monday. School is always at its worst on Monday mornings, because people who like chasing you have had to hang about all weekend with no one to chase. The notes in her locker are always the worst on Mondays. Which could also be why the invisibility thing is not working.

Elsa starts fidgeting with the headmaster's globe again. Then she hears the door opening behind her and the headmaster stands up, looking relieved.

"Hello! Sorry I'm so late! It's the traffic!" Elsa's mum pants, out of breath, and Elsa feels her fingers brushing her neck.

Elsa doesn't turn around. She also feels Mum's telephone brushing against her neck, because Mum always carries it. As if she were a cyborg and it was a part of her organic tissue.

Elsa fingers the globe a little more demonstratively. The headmaster sits down in his chair, then leans forward and discreetly tries to move the globe out of her reach. He turns hopefully to Mum.

"Shall we wait for Elsa's father, perhaps?"

The headmaster prefers Dad to be present at these types of meetings, because he seems to find dads easier to reason with when it comes to this sort of thing. Mum doesn't look especially pleased.

"Elsa's father is away and unfortunately he won't be back until tomorrow." The headmaster looks disappointed.

"Of course, there's no intention on our part to create a sense of panic here. Especially not in your condition. . . ."

He nods at Mum's belly. Mum looks like she needs to control herself quite a lot not to ask exactly what he's driving at. The headmaster clears his throat and pulls the globe even farther from Elsa's reaching fingers. He looks as if he's going to impress on Mum that she should think of the child, which is what people try to impress on Mum when they're nervous that she may get angry.

"Think about the child." They used to mean Elsa when they said that. But now they mean Halfie.

Elsa straightens her leg and kicks the wastepaper basket. She can hear the headmaster and Mum talking, but she doesn't listen. Deep inside, she's hoping Granny will come storming in at any moment with her fists raised, like in a boxing match in an old film. The last time Elsa was called in to see the headmaster, he only called Mum and Dad, but Granny came along all the same. Granny was not the sort of person you had to call.

Elsa had sat there spinning the headmaster's globe on that occasion too. The boy who'd given her a black eye had been there with his parents. The headmaster had turned to Elsa's father and said: "There's an element of a typical boyish prank about this. . . ." And then he had to devote quite a long time to explaining to Granny what a typical girlish prank might be, because Granny really wanted to know.

The headmaster had tried to calm Granny by telling the boy who'd given Elsa the black eye that "only cowards hit girls," but Granny was not the least bit calmed by that.

"It's not bloody cowardly to hit girls!" she had roared at the headmaster. "This kid isn't a little asswipe for hitting a girl, he's an asswipe for hitting anyone!" And then the boy's father got upset and started being rude to Granny for calling his son an asswipe, and then Granny had replied that she was going to teach Elsa how to "kick boys in the fuse box" and then they'd see "how much bloody fun it is fighting with girls!" And then the headmaster had asked everyone to compose themselves a little. And then they all tried that for a bit. But then the headmaster wanted the boy and Elsa to shake hands and apologize to each other, and then Granny sprang out of her chair asking, "Why the hell should Elsa apologize?" The headmaster said that Elsa must take her share of the guilt because she had "provoked" the boy and one had to understand that the boy had experienced difficulties in "controlling himself." And that was when Granny had tried to throw the globe at the headmaster, but Mum managed to catch hold of Granny's arm at the very last moment, so that the globe ended up hitting the headmaster's computer instead and smashing the screen. "I WAS PROVOKED!" Granny had roared at the headmaster while Mum tried to drag her into the corridor, "I COULDN'T CONTROL MYSELF!"

That's why Elsa always tears up the notes she gets in her locker. The notes about how she is ugly. That she's disgusting. That they're going to kill her. Elsa rips them into such tiny pieces that they can hardly be seen and then throws them into different wastepaper bins all over the school. It's an act of mercy to those who wrote the notes, because Granny would have beaten them to death if she'd found out.

Elsa rises slightly from the chair and quickly reaches across the desk to give the globe another spin. The headmaster looks close to despair. Elsa sinks back into her chair, satisfied.

"My God, Elsa! What happened to your cheek!" Mum bursts out with exclamation marks at the end, when she sees the three red lacerations.

Elsa shrugs without answering. Mum turns to the headmaster. Her eyes are burning.

"What happened to her cheek?!"

The headmaster twists in his seat.

"Now, then. Let's calm ourselves down, now. Think about . . . I mean, think about your child."

He isn't pointing at Elsa when he says that last bit, he's pointing at Mum. Elsa stretches her leg and kicks the wastepaper bin again. Mum takes a deep breath and closes her eyes, then determinedly moves the wastebasket farther under the desk. Elsa looks at her, offended, sinks so deep into the chair that she has to hold on to the armrests to stop herself sliding out, and reaches out with her leg until her toe almost, almost, touches the rim of the wastebasket. Mum sighs. Elsa sighs even louder. The headmaster looks at them and then at the globe on his desk. He pulls it closer to him.

"So . . ." he begins at last, smiling halfheartedly at Mum.

"It's been a difficult week for the whole family," Mum interrupts him at once and sounds as if she's trying to apologize.

Elsa hates it.

"We can all empathize with that," says the headmaster in the manner of someone who doesn't know the meaning of the word. He looks nervously at the globe. "Unfortunately it's not the first time Elsa has found herself in conflict at this school."

"Not the last either," Elsa mutters.

"Elsa!" snaps Mum.

"Mum!!!" Elsa roars with three exclamation marks.

Mum sighs. Elsa sighs even louder. The headmaster clears his throat and holds the globe with both hands as he says:

"We, and by that I mean the staff at this school, obviously in collaboration with the guidance counselor, feel that Elsa could be helped by a psychologist to channel her aggressions."

"A psychologist?" says Mum hesitantly, "Surely that's a bit dramatic?"

The headmaster raises his hands defensively as if apologizing, or possibly as if he's about to start playing an air tambourine.

"It's not that we think anything is *wrong*! Absolutely not! Lots of special-needs children benefit from therapy. It's nothing to be ashamed of!"

Elsa reaches out with the tips of her toes and pushes over the wastepaper basket. "Why don't you go to a psychologist yourself?"

The headmaster decides to make the globe safe by putting it on the floor next to his chair. Mum leans towards Elsa and exerts herself incredibly not to raise her voice.

"If you tell me and the headmaster which of the children are causing you trouble, we can help you solve the conflicts instead of things always ending up like this, darling."

Elsa looks up, her lips pressed into a straight line.

The scratch marks on her cheek have stopped bleeding but they are still as bright as neon lights.

"Snitches get stitches," she says succinctly.

"Elsa, please try to cooperate," the headmaster says, attempting a grimace that Elsa assumes to be his way of smiling a little.

"You be cooperative," Elsa replies without an attempt to smile even a little.

The headmaster looks at Mum.

"We, well, I mean the school staff and I, believe that if Elsa could just try to walk away sometimes when she feels there's a conflict about to happ—"

Elsa doesn't wait for Mum's answer, because she knows Mum won't defend her. So she snatches up her backpack from the floor and stands up.

"Can we go now, or what?"

And then the headmaster says she can go into the corridor. He sounds relieved. Elsa marches out, while Mum stays in there, apologizing. Elsa hates it. She just wants to go home so it won't be Monday anymore.

During the last lesson before lunch, one of their smarmy teachers told them their assignment over the Christmas holiday would be to prepare a talk on the theme of A Literary Hero I Look Up To. And they were to dress up as their hero and talk about the hero in the first person singular. Everyone had to put up their hands and choose a hero. Elsa was going to go for Harry Potter, but someone else got him first. So when her turn came she said Spider-Man. And then one of the boys behind her got annoyed because he was going for that. And then there was an argument. "You can't take Spider-Man!" shouted the boy. And Elsa said, "Pity, because I just did!" And then the boy said, "It's a pity for YOU, yeah!" And then Elsa snorted in English. "Sure!" Because that is Elsa's favorite word in English. And then the boy shouted that Elsa couldn't be Spider-Man because "only boys can be Spider-Man!" And then Elsa told him he could be Spider-Man's girlfriend. And then he pushed Elsa into a radiator. And then Elsa hit him with a book.

Elsa still thinks he should thank her for it, because that's probably the nearest that boy ever got to a book. But then the teacher came running and put a stop to it all and said that no one could be Spider-Man because Spider-Man only existed in films and so he wasn't a "literary character." And then Elsa got possibly a bit disproportionally worked up and asked the teacher if he'd heard of something called Marvel Comics, but the teacher hadn't. "AND THEY LET YOU TEACH CHILDREN?!" Then Elsa had to sit for ages after the class "having a chat" with the teacher, which was just a lot of teacher-babbling.

The boy and a few others were waiting for her when she came out. So she tightened the straps of her backpack until they hugged her tight like a little koala hanging on to her back, and then she ran.

Like many children who are different, she's good at running. She heard one of the boys roar, "Get her!" and the clattering of footsteps behind her across the icy asphalt. She heard their excited panting. She ran so fast that her knees were hitting her rib cage, and if it hadn't been for her backpack she would have made it over the fence and into the street, and then they would never have caught up with her. But one of the boys got a grip on her backpack. And of course she could have wriggled out of it and got away.

But Granny's letter to The Monster was inside. So she turned around and fought.

As usual she tried to shield her face so Mum wouldn't get upset when she saw the damage. But it wasn't possible to shield both her face and the backpack. So things took their course. "You should choose your battles if you can, but if the battle chooses you, then kick the sod in his fuse box!" Granny used to tell Elsa, and that is what Elsa did. Even though she hates violence, she's good at fighting because she's had a lot of practice. That's why there are so many of them now when they chase her.

Mum comes out of the headmaster's office after at least ten eternities of fairy tales, and then they cross the deserted playground without saying anything. Elsa gets into the backseat of Kia with her arms around her backpack. Mum looks unhappy.

"Please, Elsa—"

"It wasn't me that started it! He said girls can't be Spider-Man!"

"Yes, but why do you fight?"

"Just because!"

"You're not a little kid, Elsa. You always say I should treat you like a grown-up. So stop answering me like a little kid. Why do you fight?"

Elsa pokes at the rubber seal in the door.

"Because I'm tired of running."

And then Mum tries to reach into the back and caress her gently across her scratch marks, but Elsa snatches her head away.

"I don't know what to do." Mum sighs, holding back her tears.

"You don't have to do anything," Elsa mumbles.

Mum backs Kia out of the parking area and drives off. They sit there in the sort of silent eternity that only mothers and daughters can build up between themselves.

"Maybe we should go to a psychologist after all," she says at last.

Elsa shrugs.

"Whatever." That's her second-favorite word in English.

"I . . . Elsa . . . darling, I know what's happened with Granny has hit you terribly hard. Death is hard for everyone—"

"You don't know anything!" Elsa interrupts and pulls so hard at the rubber seal that, when she lets go, it snaps back against the window with a loud noise.

"I'm sad as well, Elsa," says Mum, swallowing. "She was my mother, not just your grandmother."

"You hated her. So don't talk rubbish."

"I did not hate her. She was my mother."

"You were always fighting! You're probably just GLAD she's dead!!!"

Elsa wishes she'd never said that last bit. But it's too late. There's a silence lasting for all imaginable eternities, and she pokes at the rubber seal until its edge comes away from the door. Mum notices, but she doesn't say anything. When they stop at a red light she puts her hands over her eyes and says resignedly, "I'm really trying here, Elsa. Really trying. I know I'm a bad mother and I'm not at home enough, but I'm really trying. . . ."

Elsa doesn't answer. Mum massages her temples.

"Maybe we should talk to a psychologist anyway."

"You talk to a psychologist," says Elsa.

"Yeah. Maybe I should."

"Yeah. Maybe you should!"

"Why are you so horrible?"

"Why are YOU so horrible?"

"Darling. I'm really sad about Granny dying but we have t—"

"No you're not!" And then something happens that hardly ever, ever happens. Mum loses her composure and yells:

"YES I BLOODY AM! TRY TO UNDERSTAND THAT YOU'RE NOT THE ONLY ONE WHO'S CAPABLE OF BEING UPSET AND STOP BEING SUCH A LITTLE BRAT!"

Mum and Elsa stare at each other. Mum covers her mouth with her hand.

"Elsa . . . I . . . darl—"

Elsa shakes her head and pulls off the entire rubber seal from the door in a single tug. She knows she's won. When Mum loses control, Elsa wins every time.

"Cut it out. It's not good shouting like that," she mumbles. And then she adds without so much as glancing at her mother: "Think about the baby."

7

LEATHER

It's possible to love your grandmother for years and years without really knowing anything about her.

It's Tuesday when Elsa meets The Monster for the first time. School is better on Tuesdays. Elsa only has one bruise today, and bruises can be explained away by saying she's been playing soccer.

She sits in Audi. Audi is Dad's car. It's the exact opposite of Renault. Normally Dad picks her up from school every other Friday, because that's when she stays with Dad and Lisette and Lisette's children. Granny used to pick her up on all the other days and now Mum will have to do it. But today Mum and George have gone to a doctor to look at Halfie, so today Dad is picking her up even though it's a Tuesday.

Granny always came on time and stood at the gate. Dad is late and stays in Audi in the parking area.

"What did you do to your eye?" Dad asks nervously.

He came back from Spain this morning, because he went there with Lisette and Lisette's children, but he hasn't caught any sun because he doesn't know how to.

"We played soccer," says Elsa.

Granny would never have let her get away with the soccer story.

But Dad isn't Granny, so he just nods tentatively and asks her to be good enough to put on her seat belt. He does that very often. Nods tentatively. Dad is a tentative person. Mum is a perfectionist and Dad is a pedant and that was partly why their marriage didn't work so well, Elsa figures. Because a perfectionist and a pedant are two very different things. When Mum and Dad did the cleaning, Mum wrote a minute-by-minute breakdown of the cleaning schedule, but then Dad would sort of get caught up with descaling the coffee percolator for two and a half hours, and you really can't plan a life with a person like that around you, said Mum. The teachers at school always tell Elsa that her problem is her inability to concentrate, which is very odd, Elsa thinks, because Dad's big problem is that he can't stop concentrating.

"So, what do you want to do?" asks Dad, indecisively putting his hands on the wheel.

He often does that. Asks what Elsa would like to do. Because he very rarely wants to do anything himself. And this Tuesday was very unexpected for him: Dad is not very good at dealing with unexpected Tuesdays. That's why Elsa only stays every other weekend with him, because after he met Lisette and she and her children moved in, Dad said it was too "messy" for Elsa there. When Granny found out, she phoned him and called him a Nazi at least ten times in a minute. That was a Nazi record, even for Granny. And when she'd hung up she turned to Elsa and spluttered, "Lisette? What sort of name is that?" And Elsa knew she didn't really mean it, of course, because everyone likes Lisette—she has the same superpower as George. But Granny was the sort of person you brought with you when you went to war, and that was what Elsa loved about her.

Dad's always late picking Elsa up from school. Granny was never late. Elsa has tried to understand exactly what "irony" means and she's fairly sure it's that Dad is never late for anything other than picking up Elsa from school, and Granny was always late for everything except for that one thing.

Dad fiddles with the wheel again.

"So . . . where would you like to go today?"

Elsa looks surprised, because it sounds as if he really means they're going somewhere. He twists in his seat.

"I was thinking maybe you'd like to do . . . something."

Elsa knows he's only saying it to be nice. Because Dad doesn't like doing things, Dad is not a doing type of person. Elsa looks at him. He looks at the steering wheel.

"I think I'd just like to go home," she says.

Dad nods and looks disappointed and relieved at the same time, which is a facial expression that only he in the whole world has mastered. Because Dad never says no to Elsa, even though she sometimes wishes he would.

"Audi is really nice," she says when they're halfway home and neither of them has said a word.

She pats the glove compartment of Audi, as if it were a cat. New cars smell of soft leather, the polar opposite of the smell of old split leather in Granny's flat. Elsa likes both smells, though she prefers living animals to dead ones that have been made into car seats. "You know what you're getting with an Audi," Dad says, nodding. His last car was also called Audi.

Dad likes to know what he's getting. One time last year they rearranged the shelves in the supermarket near where Dad and Lisette live, and Elsa had to run those tests she had seen advertised on the television, to make sure he hadn't had a stroke.

Once they get home, Dad gets out of Audi and goes with her to the entrance. Britt-Marie is on the other side of the door, hunched up like a livid little house pixie on guard. It occurs to Elsa that you always know no good can come from catching sight of Britt-Marie. "She's like a letter from the tax authorities, that old biddy," Granny used to say. Dad seems to agree—Britt-Marie is one of the few subjects on which he and Granny were in agreement. She's holding a crossword magazine in her hand. Britt-Marie likes crosswords very much because there are very clear rules about how to do them. She only ever does them in pencil, though—Granny always said Britt-Marie was the sort of woman who would have to drink two glasses of wine and feel really wild and crazy to be able to fantasize about solving a crossword in ink.

Dad offers a tentative hello, but Britt-Marie interrupts him.

"Do you know whose this is?" she says, pointing at a stroller padlocked to the stair railing under the noticeboard.

Only now does Elsa notice it. It's odd that it should be there at all, because there are no babies in the house except Halfie, and she/he still gets a lift everywhere with Mum. But Britt-Marie seems unable to attach any value to this deeper philosophical question.

"Strollers are not allowed in the entrance vestibule! They're a fire risk!" she declares, firmly clasping her hands together so that the crossword magazine sticks out like a rather feeble sword.

"Yes. It says on the notice here," says Elsa, nodding helpfully and pointing at a neatly written sign right above the stroller, on which it is written: DO NOT LEAVE STROLLERS HERE: THEY ARE A FIRE RISK.

"That's what I mean!" Britt-Marie replies, with a slightly raised—but still well-meaning—voice.

"I don't understand," says Dad, as if he doesn't understand.

"I am obviously wondering if you put this sign up! That's what I'm wondering!" says Britt-Marie, taking a small step forward and then a very small step back as if to emphasize the gravity of this.

"Is there something wrong with the notice?" asks Elsa.

"Of course not, of course not. But it's not *common practice* in this leaseholders' association to simply put up signs in any old way without first clearing it with the other residents in the house!"

"But there is no leaseholders' association, is there?" asks Elsa.

"No, but there's going to be! And until there is, I'm in charge of information in the association committee. It's not common practice to put up signs without notifying the head of information in the association committee!"

She is interrupted by the bark of a dog, so loud that it rattles a pane of glass in the door.

They all jump. Yesterday Elsa heard Mum telling George that Britt-Marie had called the police to say that Our Friend should be put down. It seems to have heard Britt-Marie's voice now, and just like Granny, Our Friend can't shut up for a second when that happens. Britt-Marie starts ranting about how that dog needs to be dealt with. Dad just looks uncomfortable. "Maybe someone tried to tell you but you weren't home?" Elsa suggests to Britt-Marie, pointing at the sign on the wall. It works, at least temporarily. Britt-Marie forgets to be upset about Our Friend when she gets re-upset by the sign. Because the most important thing for her is not to run out of things to be upset about. Elsa briefly considers telling Britt-Marie to put up a sign letting the neighbors know that if they want to put up a notice they have to inform their neighbors first. For instance, by putting up a notice.

The dog barks again from the flat a half-flight up. Britt-Marie purses her mouth.

"I've called the police. I have! But of course they won't do anything! They say we have to wait until tomorrow to see if the owner turns up!"

Dad doesn't answer, and Britt-Marie immediately interprets his silence as a sign that he'd love to hear more about Britt-Marie's feelings on the topic.

"Kent has rung the bell of that flat lots of times, but no one even lives there! As if that wild animal lives there on its own! Would you believe it?"

Elsa holds her breath, but no more barking can be heard—as if Our Friend has summoned some common sense at last.

The entrance door behind Dad opens and the woman in the black skirt comes in. Her heels click against the floor and she's talking loudly into the white cord attached to her ear.

"Hello!" says Elsa, to deflect Britt-Marie's attention from any further barking.

"Hello," says Dad, to be polite.

"Well, well. Hello there," says Britt-Marie, as if the woman is potentially a criminal notice-poster. The woman doesn't answer. She just talks even louder into the white cable, gives all three of them an irritated look, and disappears up the stairs.

There's a long, strained silence in the stairwell after she has gone. Elsa's dad is not so good at dealing with strained silences.

"Helvetica," he manages to say, in the middle of a nervous bout of throat-clearing.

"Pardon me?" says Britt-Marie and purses her mouth even harder.

"Helvetica. The font, I mean," says Dad skittishly, nodding at the sign on the wall. "It's a good . . . font."

Fonts are the sort of thing Dad finds important. One time when Mum was at a parents' evening at Elsa's school and Dad had called at the very last possible moment to say he couldn't make it because of something that had come up at work, Mum, as a punishment, signed him up as a volunteer to do the posters for the school's tag sale. Dad looked very doubtful about it when he found out. It took him three weeks to decide what sort of font the posters should have. When he brought them in to school, Elsa's teacher didn't want to put them up because they'd already had the sale—but Elsa's father had apparently not understood what this had to do with it.

It's a little like Britt-Marie not really comprehending what the Helvetica font has to do with anything at all right now.

Dad looks down at the floor and clears his throat again.

"Do you have . . . keys?" he asks Elsa.

She nods. They hug briefly. Relieved, Dad disappears out the door, and Elsa darts up the stairs before Britt-Marie has time to start talking to her again. Outside Our Friend's flat she stops briefly, peers back over her shoulder to make sure Britt-Marie is not watching, then opens the mail slot to whisper, "Please, be quiet!" She knows that it understands. She hopes that it cares.

She runs up the last flight of stairs with the keys to the flat in her hand, but she doesn't go into Mum and George's flat. Instead she opens Granny's door. There are storage boxes and a scouring bucket in the kitchen; she tries not to pay any attention to those, but fails. She hops into the big wardrobe. The darkness inside the wardrobe settles around her, and no one knows she is crying.

It used to be magic, this wardrobe. Elsa used to be able to lie full-length in it and only just reach the walls with her toes and fingertips. However much she grew, the wardrobe was exactly the right size. Granny maintained, of course, that it was all "faffing about because this wardrobe has always been exactly the same size," but Elsa has measured it. So she knows.

She lies down, stretching herself as far as she can. Touching both walls. In a few months she won't have to reach. In a year she won't be able to lie here at all. Because nothing will be magic anymore.

She can hear Maud's and Lennart's muted voices in the flat, can smell their coffee. Elsa knows Samantha is also there long before she hears the sound of the bichon frisé's paws in the living room and, shortly after, its snoring under Granny's sofa table. Maud and

Lennart are tidying up Granny's flat and starting to pack up her things. Mum has asked them to help, and Elsa hates Mum for that. Hates everyone for it.

Soon she hears Britt-Marie's voice as well. As if she's pursuing Maud and Lennart. She's very angry. Only wants to talk about who's had the cheek to put up that sign in the vestibule, and who's been impudent enough to lock up that stroller directly under the sign. It seems very unclear, also to Britt-Marie herself, which of these two occurrences is the most upsetting to her. But at least she doesn't mention Our Friend again.

Elsa has been in the wardrobe for an hour when the boy with a syndrome comes crawling in. Through the half-open door Elsa sees his mother walking about, tidying, and how Maud carefully walks behind her, picking up the things that are falling all around her.

Lennart puts a big platter of dreams outside the wardrobe. Elsa pulls them inside and closes the door, and then she and the boy with a syndrome eat them in silence. The boy doesn't say anything, because he never does. That is one of Elsa's favorite things about him.

She hears George's voice in the kitchen. It's warm and reassuring; it asks if anyone wants eggs, because in that case he'll cook eggs. Everyone likes George, it's his superpower. Elsa hates him for that. Then Elsa hears her mum's voice, and for a moment she wants to run out and throw herself into her arms. But she doesn't, because she wants her mother to be upset. Elsa knows she has already won, but she wants Mum to know it too. Just to make sure she's hurting as much as Elsa is about Granny dying.

The boy falls asleep at the bottom of the wardrobe. His mother gently opens the door soon after, and crawls inside and lifts him out. It's as if she knew he had fallen asleep the minute he did. Maybe that is her superpower.

Moments later Maud crawls inside and carefully picks up all the things the boy's mother dropped when she was picking him up.

"Thanks for the cookies," whispers Elsa.

Maud pats her on the cheek and looks so upset on Elsa's behalf that Elsa gets upset on Maud's behalf.

She stays in the wardrobe until everyone has stopped tidying and stopped packing and gone back to their own flats. She knows that Mum is sitting in the front hall of their flat, waiting for her, so she sits in the big deep window on the stairs for a long time. To ensure that Mum has to keep waiting. She sits there until the lights in the stairwell automatically switch off.

After a while the drunk comes stumbling out of a flat farther down in the house, and starts hitting the banister with her shoehorn and mumbling something about how people aren't allowed to take baths at night. The drunk does this a few times every week. There's nothing abnormal about it.

"Turn off the water!" mutters the drunk, but Elsa doesn't answer.

Nor does anyone else. Because people in houses like this seem to believe that drunks are like monsters, and if one pretends they are not there they actually disappear.

Elsa hears how the drunk, in a passionate exhortation for water rationing, slips and falls and ends up on her ass with the shoehorn falling on her head. The drunk and the shoehorn have a fairly long-drawn-out dispute after that, like two old friends at loggerheads about money. And then at last there's silence. And then Elsa hears the song. The song the drunk always sings. Elsa sits in the darkness on the stairs and hugs herself, as if it is a lullaby just for her. And then even that falls silent. She hears the drunk trying to calm down the shoehorn, before disappearing into her flat again. Elsa half-closes her eyes. Tries to see the cloud animals and the first outlying fields of the Land-of-Almost-Awake, but it doesn't work.

She can't get there anymore. Not without Granny. She opens her eyes, absolutely inconsolable. The snowflakes fall like wet mittens against the window.

And that's when she sees The Monster for the first time.

It's one of those winter nights when the darkness is so thick it's as if the whole area has been dipped headfirst in a bucket of blackness, and The Monster steals out the front door and crosses the half circle of light around the last light in the street so quickly that if Elsa had blinked a little too hard, she would have thought she was imagining it. But as it is she knows what she saw, and she hits the floor and makes her way down the stairs in one fluid movement.

She's never seen him before, but she knows from his sheer size that it must be him. He glides across the snow like an animal, a beast from one of Granny's fairy tales. Elsa knows very well that what she's about to do is both dangerous and idiotic, but she runs down the stairs three steps at a time. Her socks slip on the last step and she careers across the ground-floor vestibule, smacking her chin into the door handle.

Her face throbbing with pain, she throws the door open and breathlessly churns through the snow, still only in her socks.

"I have mail for you!" she cries into the night. Only then does she realize that her tears have lodged in her throat. She's so desperate to know who this person is that Granny secretly talked to about Miamas.

There's no answer. She hears his light footfalls in the snow, surprisingly agile considering his enormity. He's moving away from her. Elsa ought to be afraid, she should be terrified of what The Monster could do to her. He's big enough to tear her apart with a single tug, she knows that. But she's too angry to be afraid.

"My granny says to tell you she's sorry!" she roars.

She can't see him. But she no longer hears the creaking of his steps in the snow. He's stopped.

Elsa isn't thinking. She rushes into the darkness, relying on pure instinct, towards the spot where she last heard him put down his foot. She feels the movement of air from his jacket. He starts running; she stumbles through the snow and catapults herself forward, catching hold of his trouser leg. When she lands on her back in the snow, she sees him staring down at her, by the light of the last streetlight. Elsa has time to feel her tears freezing on her cheeks.

He must be a good deal more than six feet tall. As big as a tree. There's a thick hood covering his head and his black hair spills out over his shoulders. Almost his entire face is buried under a beard as thick as an animal pelt, and, emerging from the shadows of the hood, a scar zigzags down over one eye, so pronounced that it looks as if the skin has melted. Elsa feels his gaze creeping through her circulating blood.

"Let go!"

The dark mass of his torso sinks over Elsa as he hisses these words at her.

"My granny says to tell you she's sorry!" Elsa pants, holding up the envelope.

The Monster doesn't take it. She lets go of his trouser-leg because she thinks he'll kick her, but he only takes a half-step back. And what comes out of him next is more of a growl than a word. As if he's talking to himself, not to her.

"Get lost, stupid girl. . . ."

The words pulsate against Elsa's eardrums. They sound wrong, somehow. Elsa understands them, but they chafe at the passages of her inner ear. As if they didn't belong there.

The Monster turns with a quick, hostile movement. In the next moment he's gone. As if he's stepped right through a doorway in the darkness.

Elsa lies in the snow, trying to catch her breath while the cold stamps on her chest. Then she stands up and gathers her strength, crumpling the envelope into a ball and flinging it into the darkness after him.

She doesn't know how many eternities pass before she hears the entrance porch opening behind her. Then she hears Mum's footsteps, hears her calling Elsa's name. Elsa rushes blindly into her arms.

"What are you doing out here?" asks Mum, scared.

Elsa doesn't answer. Tenderly, Mum takes her face in her hands.

"How did you get that black eye?"

"Soccer," whispers Elsa.

"You're lying," whispers Mum.

Elsa nods. Mum holds her hard. Elsa sobs against her stomach.

"I miss her. . . ."

Mum leans down and puts her forehead against hers.

"Me too."

They don't hear The Monster moving out there. They don't see him picking up the envelope. But then, at last, burrowing into her mum's arms, Elsa realizes why his words sounded wrong.

The Monster was talking in Granny and Elsa's secret language.

It's possible to love your grandmother for years and years without really knowing anything about her.

8

RUBBER

It's Wednesday. She's running again.

She doesn't know the exact reason this time. Maybe it's because it's one of the last days before the Christmas holidays, and they know they won't be able to chase anyone for several weeks now, so they have to get it out of their systems. Or maybe it's something else altogether—it doesn't matter. People who have never been hunted always seem to think there's a reason for it. "They wouldn't do it without a cause, would they? You must have done something to provoke them." As if that's how oppression works.

But it's pointless trying to explain to these people, as fruitless as clarifying to a guy carrying around a rabbit's foot—because of its supposed good luck—that if rabbits' feet really *were* lucky, they'd still be attached to the rabbits.

And this is really no one's fault. It's not that Dad was a bit late picking her up, it's just that the school day finished slightly too early. And it's difficult making oneself invisible when the hunt starts inside the school building.

So Elsa runs.

"Catch her!" yells the girl somewhere behind her.

Today it all started with Elsa's scarf. Or at least Elsa thinks it did. She has started learning who the chasers are at school, and how they operate. Some only chase children if they prove to be weak. And some chase just for the thrill of it; they don't even hit their victims when they catch them, just want to see the terror in their eyes. And then there are some like the boy Elsa fought about the right to be Spider-Man. He fights and chases people as a point of principle because he can't stand anyone disagreeing with him. Especially not someone who's different.

With this girl it's something else. She wants a reason for giving chase. A way of justifying the chase. She wants to feel like a hero while she's chasing me, thinks Elsa with unfeasibly cool clarity as she charges towards the fence, her heart thumping like a jackhammer and her throat burning like that time Granny made jalapeño smoothies.

Elsa throws herself at the fence, and her backpack lands so hard on her head when she jumps down on the pavement on the other side that for a few seconds her eyes start to black out. She pulls hard on the straps with both hands to tighten it against her back. Hazily she blinks and looks left towards the parking area where Audi should show up at any moment. She hears the girl behind her screaming like an insulted, ravenous orc. She knows that by the time Audi arrives it'll be too late, so she looks right instead, down the hill towards the big road. The trucks are thundering by like an invading army on its way towards a castle still held by the enemy, but in the gaps between the traffic Elsa sees the entrance to the park on the other side.

"Shoot-up Park," that's what people call it at school, because there are drug addicts there who chase children with heroin syringes. At least that's what Elsa's heard, and it terrifies her. It's the sort of park that never seems to catch any daylight, and this is the kind of winter's day when the sun never seems to rise.

Elsa had managed just fine until lunchtime, but not even someone who's very good at being invisible can quite manage it in a cafeteria. The girl had materialized before her so suddenly that Elsa was startled and spilled salad dressing on her Gryffindor scarf. The girl had pointed at it and roared: "Didn't I tell you to stop going around with that ugly bloody scarf?" Elsa had looked back at the girl in the only way one can look back at someone who has just pointed at a Gryffindor scarf and said, "Ugly bloody scarf." Not totally dissimilar to how one would look at someone who had just seen a horse and gaily burst out, "Crocodile!" The first time the scarf caught the girl's attention, Elsa had simply assumed that the girl was a Slytherin. Only after she'd smacked Elsa in the face, ripped her scarf, and thrown it in a toilet had Elsa grown conscious of the fact that the girl hadn't read Harry Potter at all. She knew who he was, of course, everyone knows who Harry Potter is, but she hadn't read the books. She didn't even understand the most basic symbolism of a Gryffindor scarf. And while Elsa didn't want to be elitist or anything, how could one be expected to reason with a person like that?

Muggles.

So today when the girl in the cafeteria had reached out to snatch away Elsa's scarf, Elsa decided to continue the discussion on the girl's own intellectual level. She simply threw her glass of milk at her and ran for it. Through the corridors, up to the second floor of the school, then the third, where there was a space under the stairs that the cleaners used as a storage cupboard. Elsa had curled up in there with her arms around her knees, making herself as invisible as possible while she listened to the girl and her followers run up to the fourth floor. And then she hid in the classroom for the rest of the day.

It's the distance between the classroom and the school gates that's impossible; even a seasoned expert can't be invisible there. So Elsa had to be strategic.

First she stayed close to the teacher while her classmates were crowding to get out of the classroom. Then she slipped out the door in the general tumult and darted down the other flight of stairs, the one that does not lead to the main gates. Of course her pursuers knew she'd do that, they may even have wanted her to do it, because she'd be easier to catch on those stairs. But the lesson had finished early, and Elsa took a chance that lessons on the floor below were still in progress, so she had perhaps half a minute to run down the stairs and through the empty corridor and establish a small head start while her pursuers got entangled with the pupils welling out of the classrooms below.

She was right. She saw the girl and her friends no more than ten yards behind her, but they couldn't reach her.

Granny has told her thousands of stories from Miamas about pursuit and war. About evading shadows when they're on your tail, how to lay traps for them and how to beat them with distraction. Like all hunters, shadows have one really significant weakness: they focus all their attention on the one they're pursuing, rather than seeing their entire surroundings. The one being chased, on the other hand, devotes every scrap of attention to finding an escape route. It may not be a gigantic advantage, but it is an advantage. Elsa knows this, because she's checked what "distraction" means.

So she shoved her hand into her jeans pocket and got out a handful of coins she kept there for emergencies. Just as the throng of children was starting to disperse and she was getting close to the second stair towards the main entrance, she dropped the coins on the floor and ran.

Elsa has noticed one odd thing about people. Almost none of us can hear the tinkling sound of coins against a stone floor without instinctively stopping and looking down. The sudden crush and eager arms blocked her pursuers and gave her another few seconds to get clear of them. She made full use of the moment and bolted.

But she hears them throwing themselves at the fence now. Trendy winter boots scraping against the buckled steel wire. Just a few more moments until they catch her. Elsa looks left, towards the parking area. No Audi. Looks right, down at the chaos of the road and the black silence of the park. She looks left again, thinks to herself that this would be the safe option if Dad turned up on time for once. Then she looks right, feels an abrasive fear in her gut when she glimpses the park between the roaring trucks.

And then she thinks about Granny's stories from Miamas, about how one of the princes once evaded a whole flock of pursuing shadows by riding into the darkest forest in the Land-of-Almost-Awake. Shadows are the foulest foulnesses ever to live in any fantasy, but even shadows feel fear, said Granny. Even those bastards are afraid of something. Because even shadows have a sense of imagination.

"Sometimes the safest place is when you flee to what seems the most dangerous," said Granny, and then she described how the prince rode right into the darkest forest and the shadows stopped, hissing, at the edge. For not even they were sure what might be lurking inside, on the other side of the trees, and nothing scares anyone more than the unknown, which can only be known by reliance on the imagination. "When it comes to terror, reality's got nothing on the power of the imagination," Granny said.

So Elsa runs to the right. She can smell the burning rubber when the cars brake on the ice. That's how Renault smells almost all the time. She darts between the trucks and hears their blaring horns and her pursuers screaming at her. She's reached the pavement when she feels the first of them grab her backpack. She is so near the park that she could reach into the darkness with her hand, but it's too late. By the time she's being pulled down into the snow, Elsa knows that the blows and kicks will rain down on her quicker than her hands can shield her, but she pulls up her knees and closes her eyes and tries to cover her face so Mum won't be upset again.

She waits for the dull thuds against the back of her head. Often it doesn't hurt when they hit her; usually it doesn't hurt until the day after. The pain she feels during the actual beating is a different kind of pain.

But nothing happens.

Elsa holds her breath.

Nothing.

She opens her eyes and there's deafening noise all around her. She can hear them yelling. Can hear that they're running. And then she hears The Monster's voice. Something is booming out of him, like a primeval power.

"NEVER! TOUCH! HER!"

Everything echoes.

Elsa's eardrums are rattling. The Monster is not roaring in Granny and Elsa's secret language, but in normal language. The words sound strange in his mouth, as if the intonation of every syllable slips and ends up wrong. As if he hasn't spoken such words for a very long time.

Elsa looks up. The Monster stares down at her through the shadow of the upturned hood and that beard, which never seems to end. His chest heaves a few times. Elsa hunches up instinctively, terrified that his huge hands are going to grab her and toss her into the traffic like a giant flicking a mouse with a single finger. But he just stands there breathing heavily and looking angry and confused. At last he raises his hand, as if it's a heavy mallet, and points back at the school.

When Elsa turns around she sees the girl who doesn't read Harry

Potter and her friends scattering like bits of paper thrown into the wind.

In the distance she sees Audi turning into the parking area. Elsa takes a deep breath and feels air entering her lungs for what seems like the first time in several minutes.

When she turns around again, The Monster has gone.

9

SOAP

There are thousands of stories in the real world, but every single one of them is from the Land-of-Almost-Awake. And the very best are from Miamas.

The other five kingdoms have produced the odd fairy tale now and then of course, but none of them are anywhere near as good. In Miamas, fairy tales are still produced around the clock, lovingly handmade one by one, and only the very, very finest of them are exported. Most are only told once and then they fall flat on the ground, but the best and most beautiful of them rise from the lips of their tellers after the last words have been spoken, and then slowly hover off over the heads of the listeners, like small, shimmering paper lanterns. When night comes they are fetched by the enphants. The enphants are very small creatures with decorous hats who ride on cloud animals (the enphants, not the hats). The lanterns are gathered up by the enphants with the help of large golden nets, and then the cloud animals turn and rise up towards the sky so swiftly that even the wind has to get out of the way. And if the wind doesn't move out of the way quickly enough, the clouds transform themselves into an animal that has fingers, so the cloud animals can give the finger to the wind. (Granny always bellowed with laughter at this; it was a while before Elsa worked out why.)

And at the peak of the highest mountain in the Land-of-Almost-Awake, known as the Telling Mountain, the enphants open their nets and let the stories fly free. And that is how the stories find their way into the real world.

At first when Elsa's granny started telling her stories from Miamas, they only seemed like disconnected fairy tales without a context, told by someone who needed her head examined. It took years before Elsa understood that they belonged together. All really good stories work like this.

Granny told her about the lamentable curse of the sea-angel, and about the two princelings who waged war on each other because they were both in love with the princess of Miploris. She also talked about the princess engaged in a fight with a witch who had stolen the most valuable treasure in the Land-of-Almost-Awake from her, and she described the warriors of Mibatalos and the dancers of Mimovas and the dream hunters of Mirevas. How they all constantly bickered and nagged at each other about this or that, until the day the Chosen One from Mimovas fled the shadows that had tried to kidnap him. And how the cloud animals carried the Chosen One to Miamas and how the inhabitants of the Land-of-Almost-Awake eventually realized that there was something more important to fight for. When the shadows amassed their army and came to take the Chosen One by force, they stood united against them. Not even when the War-Without-End seemed unlikely to end in any other way than crushing defeat, not even when the kingdom of Mibatalos fell and was leveled to the ground, did the other kingdoms capitulate. Because they knew that if the shadows were allowed to take the Chosen One, it would kill all music and then the power of the imagination in the Land-of-Almost-Awake. After that there would no longer be anything left that was different. All fairy stories take their life from the fact of being different. "Only different people change the world," Granny used to say. "No one normal has ever changed a crapping thing."

And then she used to talk about the wurses. And Elsa should have understood this from the beginning. She really should have understood everything from the beginning.

Dad turns off the stereo just before she jumps into Audi. Elsa is glad that he does, because Dad always looks very downhearted when she points out to him that he listens to the worst music in the world, and it's very difficult not pointing it out to him when you have to sit in Audi and listen to the worst music in the world.

"The belt?" Dad asks as she takes a seat.

Elsa's heart is still thumping in her chest.

"Well, hi there, you old hyena!" she yells at Dad. Because that's what she would have yelled if Granny had picked her up. And Granny would have bellowed back, "Hello, hello, my beauty!" And then everything would have felt better. Because you can still feel scared while you're yelling "Well, hi there, you old hyena!" to someone, but it's almost insane how much more difficult it is.

Dad looks unsure about it. Elsa sighs and straps herself in and tries to slow her pulse by thinking about things she isn't afraid of. Dad looks even more hesitant.

"Your mum and George are at the hospital again. . . ."

"I know," says Elsa, as you do when something has not succeeded in allaying your fears.

Dad nods. Elsa throws her backpack between the seats and it lands lying across the backseat. Dad turns around and straightens it up very neatly.

"You want to do something?" he says, sounding slightly anxious when he says "something."

Elsa shrugs.

"We can do something . . . fun?"

Elsa knows he's only offering to be nice. Because he has a bad conscience about seeing her so seldom and because he pities Elsa because her granny has died and because this Wednesday thing was rather sudden for him. Elsa knows this because Dad would never usually suggest doing something "fun," because Dad doesn't like having fun. Fun things make Dad nervous. One time when they were on holiday when Elsa was small, he went with Elsa and Mum to the beach, and then they had so much fun that Dad had to take two ibuprofen and lie down all afternoon for a rest at the hotel. He had too much fun once, said Mum.

"A fun overdose," said Elsa, and then Mum laughed for a really long time.

The strange thing about Dad is that no one brings out the fun in Mum as much as he does. It's as if Mum is always the opposite pole of a battery. No one brings out order and neatness in Mum like Granny, and no one makes her as untidy and whimsical as Dad. Once when Elsa was small and Mum was talking on the phone with Dad, and Elsa kept asking, "Is it Dad? Is it Dad? Can I talk to Dad? Where is he?" Mum finally turned around and sighed dramatically: "No, you can't talk to Dad because Dad is in heaven now, Elsa!" And when Elsa went absolutely silent and just stared at her mum, Mum grinned. "Good God, I'm only joking, Elsa. He's at the supermarket."

She grinned just like Granny used to do.

The morning after, Elsa came into the kitchen with shiny eyes when Mum was drinking coffee with loads of lactose-free milk, and when Mum, looking worried, asked why Elsa was looking so upset,

Elsa replied that she had dreamed that Dad was in heaven. And then Mum went out of her mind with guilt and hugged Elsa hard, hard, hard and said sorry over and over and over, and then Elsa waited almost ten minutes before she grinned and said: "Good God, I was only joking. I dreamed he was at the supermarket."

After that, Mum and Elsa often used to joke with Dad and ask him what it was like in heaven. "Is it cold in heaven? Can one fly in heaven? Is one allowed to meet God in heaven?" asked Mum. "Do you have cheese-graters in heaven?" asked Elsa. And then they laughed until they couldn't sit straight. Dad used to look really quite hesitant when they did that. Elsa misses it. Misses when Dad was in heaven.

"Is Granny in heaven now?" she says to him and grins, because she means it as a joke, and she imagines he'll start laughing.

But he doesn't laugh. He just looks *that way*, and Elsa feels ashamed of saying something that makes him look *that way*.

"Oh, never mind," she mumbles and pats the glove compartment. "We can go home, it's cool," she adds quickly.

Dad nods and looks relieved and disappointed.

They see the police car from a distance, in the street outside the house. And Elsa can already hear the barking as they are getting out of Audi. The stairs are full of people. Our Friend's furious howling from inside its flat is making the whole building shake.

"Do you have . . . a key?" asks Dad.

Elsa nods and gives him a quick hug. Stairwells filled with people make Dad very tentative. He gets back into Audi and Elsa goes inside by herself. And somewhere beyond that ear-splitting noise from Our Friend she hears other things too. Voices.

Dark, composed, and threatening. They have uniforms and they move about outside the flat where the boy with a syndrome and his mother live.

Eyeing Our Friend's door intently but clearly afraid of getting too close, they press themselves to the wall on the other side. One of the policewomen turns around. Her green eyes meet Elsa's—it's the same policewoman she and Granny met at the station that night Granny threw the turds. She nods morosely at Elsa, as if trying to apologize.

Elsa doesn't nod back, she just pushes past and runs.

She hears one of the police talking into a telephone, mentioning the words "Animal Control" and "to be destroyed." Britt-Marie is standing halfway up the stairs, close enough to be able to give the police suggestions about what they should do, but at a safe distance in case the beast manages to get out the door. She smiles in a well-meaning way at Elsa. Elsa hates her. When she reaches the top floor, Our Friend starts baying louder than ever, like a hurricane of ten thousand fairy tales. Looking down the shaft between the flights of stairs, Elsa can see that the police are backing away.

And Elsa should have understood it all from the beginning. She really should have.

There is an absolutely unimaginable number of very special monsters in the forests and mountains of Miamas. But none were more legendary or more deserving of the respect of every creature in Miamas (even Granny) than the wurses.

They were as big as polar bears, moved as fluidly as desert foxes, and were as quick on the attack as cobras. They were stronger than oxen, with the stamina of wild stallions and jaws more ferocious than tigers'. They had lustrous black pelts as soft as a summer wind, but underneath, their hides were thick as armor. In the really old fairy tales they were said to be immortal. These were the tales from the elder eternities, when the wurses lived in Miploris and served the royal family as castle guards.

It was the Princess of Miploris who banished them from the

Land-of-Almost-Awake, Granny used to explain, a sense of guilt lingering in the silences between her words. When the princess was still a child she'd wanted to play with one of the puppies while it was sleeping. She tugged its tail and it woke in a panic and bit her hand. Of course, everyone knew that the real blame lay with her parents, who had not taught her never ever to wake the wurse that's sleeping. But the princess was so afraid and her parents so angry that they had to put the blame on someone else, so they could live with themselves. For this reason the court decided to banish the wurses from the kingdom forever. They gave a particularly merciless group of bounty-hunting trolls permission to hunt them with poison arrows and fire.

Obviously the wurses could have hit back; not even the assembled armies of the Land-of-Almost-Awake would have dared face them in battle, that was how feared the animals were as warriors. But instead of fighting, the wurses turned and ran. They ran so far and so high into the mountains that no one believed they would ever be found again. They ran until the children in the six kingdoms had grown up without seeing a single wurse in their entire lives. Ran for so long that they became legendary.

It was only with the coming of the War-Without-End that the Princess of Miploris realized her terrible mistake. The shadows had killed all the soldiers in the warrior kingdom of Mibatalos and leveled it to the ground, and now they pressed in with terrific power against the rest of the Land-of-Almost-Awake. When all hope seemed lost, the princess herself rode away from the city walls on her white horse. She rode like a storm into the mountains and there, after an almost endless search that made her horse succumb to exhaustion and almost crushed her too, the wurses found her.

By the time the shadows heard the thunder and felt the ground shaking, it was already too late for them. The princess rode at the front on the greatest of all wurse warriors. And that was the moment of Wolfheart's return from the forests. Maybe because Miamas was teetering on the edge of extinction and needed him more than ever. "But maybe . . ." Granny used to whisper into Elsa's ear when they sat on the cloud animals at night, "maybe most of all because the princess, by realizing how unjust she had been to the wurses, proved that all the kingdoms deserved to be saved."

The War-Without-End ended that day. The shadows were driven across the sea. And Wolfheart disappeared back into the forests. But the wurses remained, and to this day they are still serving as the princess's personal guard in Miploris. On guard outside her castle gate.

Elsa hears Our Friend barking quite madly down there now. She remembers what Granny said about how "making a racket amuses it." Elsa feels a bit unsure about Our Friend's sense of humor, but then remembers what Granny said about Our Friend not needing to live with anyone. Granny didn't live with anyone herself, of course, and when Elsa pointed out that perhaps she shouldn't compare herself to a dog, Granny rolled her eyes. Now Elsa understands why.

She should have got all this from the start. She really should have.

Because this is no dog.

One of the police fumbles with a big bunch of keys. Elsa hears the main door opening downstairs and between Our Friend's barks she hears the boy with a syndrome dancing up the stairs.

The police gently shove him and his mother into their flat. Britt-Marie minces back and forth with tiny steps on her floor. Elsa hates her through the banisters.

Our Friend is completely quiet for a moment, as if it has made a strategic retreat for a moment to gather its strength for the real battle. The police jingle the bunch of keys and talk about being "ready in case it attacks." They all sound fuller of themselves now, because Our Friend is no longer barking.

Elsa hears another door opening, and then she hears Lennart's voice. He asks timidly what's happening. The police explain that they have come to "take charge of a dangerous dog." Lennart sounds a bit worried. Then he sounds a little like he doesn't know what to say. Then he says what he always says: "Does anyone want a cup of coffee? Maud just made some fresh."

Britt-Marie interrupts, hissing at him that surely Lennart can understand that the police have more important things to get on with than drinking coffee. The police sound a little disappointed about this. Elsa sees Lennart going back up the stairs. At first he seems to consider staying on the landing, but then seems to realize this might lead to a situation of his own coffee getting cold and conclude that whatever is going on here, it could not possibly be worth a risk like that. He disappears into the flat.

The first bark after that is short and defined. As if Our Friend is merely testing its vocal cords. The second is so loud that all Elsa can hear for several eternities is a ringing sound in her ears. When it finally ebbs away, she hears a terrific thud. Then another. And one more. Only then does she understand what the noise means. Our Friend is launching itself with all its strength at the inside of the door.

Elsa hears one of the police talking on the telephone again. She can't hear most of what's being said, but she hears the words "extremely large and aggressive." She peers down through the railings and sees the police standing a few yards from the door of Our Friend's flat, their self-confidence dwindling as Our Friend throws itself at the door with increasing force. Two more police have turned up, Elsa notices. One of them has brought a German Shepherd on a leash. The German Shepherd doesn't seem to think it's a terrific idea to go wherever that thing, whatever it is, is trying to get out. It watches its handler a little like Elsa looked at Granny that time she tried to rewire Mum's microwave.

"Call in Animal Control, then," Elsa hears the policewoman with green eyes saying, at last, with a disconsolate sigh.

"That's what I said! Exactly what I said!" Britt-Marie calls out eagerly.

The green eyes throw a glance at Britt-Marie that causes her to shut up abruptly.

Our Friend barks one last time, horrifyingly loud. Then grows silent again. There's a lot of noise on the stairs for a moment, and then Elsa hears the main entrance door closing. The police have clearly decided to wait farther away from whatever is living in that flat, until Animal Control gets there. Elsa watches through the window as they make off, something in their body language suggesting coffee. Whereas the German Shepherd has something in its body language that suggests it is considering early retirement.

Everything is suddenly so quiet on the stairs that Britt-Marie's lone tripping steps farther down are giving off an echo.

Elsa stands there of two minds. (She knows that "of two minds" is a phrase for the word jar.) She can see the police through the window, and in retrospect Elsa will not be able to explain exactly why she does it. But no true knight of Miamas could stand and watch a friend of Granny's being killed without trying to do something about it. So she quickly sneaks down the stairs, taking extra care as she passes Britt-Marie and Kent's flat, and taking the precaution of stopping on every half-landing to listen and make sure the police are not coming back in.

Finally she stops outside Our Friend's flat and carefully opens the mail slot. Everything is black in there, but she hears Our Friend's rumbling breath.

"It's . . . me," Elsa stammers.

She doesn't know exactly how to start this type of conversation. And Our Friend doesn't answer. On the other hand, it doesn't throw itself against the door either. Elsa sees this as a clear sign of progress in their communication.

"It's me. The one with the Daim bars."

Our Friend doesn't answer. But she can hear its breathing slowing down. Elsa's words tumble out of her as if someone had toppled them over.

"Hey . . . I mean this might sound mega-weird . . . but I sort of think my granny would have wanted you to get out of here somehow. You know? If you have a back door or something. Because otherwise they'll shoot you! Maybe that sounds mega-weird, but it's pretty weird that you've got your own flat as well . . . if you get what I mean. . . ."

Only once all the words have fallen out of her does she realize that she's spoken them in the secret language. Like a test. Because if there's just a dog on the other side of the door, it won't understand. But if it does understand, she thinks, then it's something quite different. She hears a sound made by a paw the size of a car tire, quickly scraping the inside of the door.

"Hope you understand," Elsa whispers in the secret language.

She never hears the door opening behind her. The only thing she has time to register is Our Friend backing away from the door. As if preparing itself.

Elsa grows aware of someone standing behind her, as if a ghost has appeared behind her. Or a . . .

"Look out!" growls the voice.

Elsa throws herself against the wall as The Monster silently sweeps past with a key in his hand. In the next moment, she is caught halfway between The Monster and Our Friend. And these really are the biggest damned wurse and the biggest damned monster Elsa has ever seen. It feels as if someone is standing on her lungs. She wants to scream, but nothing comes out.

Everything goes terribly fast after that. They hear the door opening at the bottom of the stairs. The voices of the police. And someone else who, Elsa realizes, must be Animal Control. Looking back, Elsa is not completely convinced that she's in control of her own movements. If she's been placed under a spell or something it wouldn't be so unlikely, considering that even if it was unlikely, it would be far less unlikely than running into a flipping wurse. But when the door closes behind her, she's standing in the front hall in The Monster's flat.

It smells of soap.

10

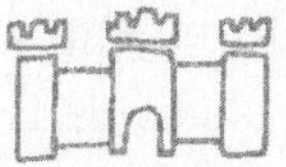

ALCOHOL

The sound of splintering wood fills the stairwell as the police drive the crowbar into the doorframe.

Elsa stands in the hall in The Monster's flat and watches them through the spyhole. Technically, her feet aren't touching the floor, though, because the wurse has sat down on the hall mat so that she's wedged between the rear end of the enormous animal and the inside of the door. The wurse looks extremely irritated. Not threatening, just irritated. As if there's a wasp in its bottle of lemonade.

It occurs to Elsa that she's more panicked by the police on the other side of the door than by the two creatures in the hall with her. Maybe it doesn't seem so very rational, but she's decided to trust more in Granny's friends than Britt-Marie's. She rotates carefully by the door until she's facing the wurse, then whispers in the secret language:

"You mustn't bark now, please be good. Or they'll kill you!"

The wurse doesn't look entirely convinced that it would come off worse if she opened the door and let it out among the police, and turns away dismissively. It stays silent, though seemingly more for Elsa's sake than its own.

Outside on the landing, the police have almost forced the door open. Elsa hears them yelling command words at each other, about being "ready."

She looks around the hall and into the living room. It's a very small flat but the tidiest one of any description she has ever set foot in. There is hardly any furniture, and the few items that there are have been arranged face-to-face, looking as if they'll commit furniture hara-kiri if a single speck of dust lands on them. (Elsa knows that because she had a samurai phase about a year ago.)

The Monster disappears into the bathroom. The tap runs in there for a long time before he comes out again. He dries his hands elaborately on a small white towel, which he then folds neatly and goes to put in a laundry basket. He has to stoop to fit through the doorway. Elsa feels as Odysseus must have felt when he was with that giant, Polyphemus, because Elsa recently read about Odysseus. Apart from the fact that Polyphemus probably didn't wash his hands as carefully as The Monster. And apart from Elsa thinking she's not as high-and-mighty and self-righteous as Odysseus seems to be in the book. Obviously. But apart from that, sort of like Odysseus.

The Monster looks at her. He doesn't look angry. More confused, actually. Almost startled. Maybe that's what gives Elsa the courage to blurt right out:

"Why did my granny send you a letter?"

She says it in normal language. Because, for reasons not yet entirely clear to her, she doesn't want to talk to him in the secret language. The Monster's eyebrows sink under his black hair so that it's difficult to make out any facial expressions at all behind it, and the beard and the scar. He's barefoot, but wears those blue plastic shoe covers you get at a hospital. His boots are neatly placed just inside the door, very precisely in line with the edge of the doormat.

He hands Elsa another two blue plastic bags, but jerks back his hand once she touches them, as if worried that Elsa might also touch him. Elsa bends down and puts the plastic bags over her muddy shoes. She notices that she has slightly stepped off the mat and left two halves of her footprints in melted snow on the parquet floor.

The Monster bends down with impressive fluidity and starts wiping the floor with a fresh white towel. When he has finished, he sprays the area with a small bottle of a cleaning agent that makes Elsa's eyes smart, and wipes it with another small white towel. Then he stands up and neatly puts the towels in the laundry basket, and places the spray bottle very exactly on a shelf.

Then he stands for a very long time and stares uncomfortably at the wurse. It lies splayed across the hall, covering the floor almost in its entirety. The Monster looks like he's about to hyperventilate. He disappears into the bathroom and comes back and starts carefully arranging towels in a tight ring around the wurse while taking extreme care not to touch any part of it. Then he goes back to the bathroom and scrubs his hands so hard under the tap that the basin vibrates.

When he comes back he's got a little bottle of antibacterial alcogel. Elsa recognizes it, because she had to rub that sort of stuff into her hands every time she was visiting Granny at the hospital. She peers into the bathroom through the gap under The Monster's armpit when he reaches out. There are more bottles of alcogel in there than she could imagine there would be in Mum's entire hospital.

The Monster looks infinitely vexed. He puts down the bottle and smears his fingers with alcogel, as if they were covered in a layer of extra skin that he had to try to rub off. Then he demonstratively holds up his two palms, each the size of a flatbed dolly, and nods firmly at Elsa.

Elsa holds up her own palms, which are more tennis ball–size. He pours alcogel on them and does his best not to look too disgusted. She quickly rubs the alcogel into her skin and wipes off the excess on her trouser legs. The Monster looks a little as if he's about to roll himself up in a blanket and start yelling and crying. To compensate, he pours more alcogel on his own hands and rubs, rubs, rubs. Then he notices that Elsa has knocked one of his boots out of position in relation to the other. He bends down and adjusts the boot. Then more alcogel.

Elsa tilts her head and looks at him.

"Do you have compulsive thoughts?" says Elsa.

The Monster doesn't answer. Only rubs his hands together, as if trying to get a fire started.

"I've read about it on Wikipedia."

The Monster's chest heaves up and down, taking frustrated breaths. He disappears into the bathroom and she hears the sound of gushing water again.

"My dad is sort of slightly compulsive as well!" Elsa calls out behind him, adding quickly, "But, God, not like you. You're properly barmy!"

Only afterwards does she realize it sounded like an insult. That was not at all how she meant it. She just didn't mean to compare Dad's amateurish compulsive behavior with The Monster's obviously professional obsessions.

The Monster returns to see the wurse nibbling at her backpack, where it clearly believes there are some Daim bars. The Monster looks as if he's trying to go to a happier place inside his head. And there they stand, all three of them: a wurse, a child, and a monster with a need for cleanliness and order that clearly is not at all well suited to the company of wurses and children.

On the other side of the door, the police and Animal Control have just broken into a flat where there's a lethal hound, only to discover the telling absence of said hound.

Elsa looks at the wurse. Looks at The Monster.

"Why do you have the key to . . . that . . . flat?" she asks The Monster.

The Monster seems to start breathing more heavily.

"You left letter. From Granny. In envelope," he replies at long last, deep-throated.

Elsa tilts her head the other way.

"Did Granny write that you should take care of it?"

The Monster nods reluctantly.

"Wrote 'protect the castle.'"

Elsa nods. Their eyes meet fleetingly. The Monster looks a great deal as one does when wishing that people would just go home and filthify their own halls. Elsa looks at the wurse.

"Why does it howl so much at night?"

The wurse doesn't look as if it greatly appreciates being spoken of in the third-person singular. That is, if it counts as a third person; the wurse seems unsure about the grammatical rules of the case. The Monster is getting tired of all the questions.

"Has grief," he says in a low voice towards the wurse, rubbing his hands together although there is nothing left to rub in.

"Grief about what?" asks Elsa.

The Monster's gaze is fixed on his palms.

"Grief about your grandmother."

Elsa looks at the wurse. The wurse looks at her with black, sad eyes. Later, when she thinks about it, Elsa assumes this is when she really, really starts liking it a lot. She looks at The Monster again.

"Why did my granny send you a letter?"

He rubs his hand harder.

"Old friend," he mutters from behind his mountain of black hair.

"What did it say?"

"Just said sorry. Just sorry . . ." he says, disappearing even deeper into his hair and beard.

"Why is my granny saying sorry to you?"

She is starting to feel very much excluded from this story, and Elsa hates feeling excluded from stories.

"Not matter for you," says The Monster quietly.

"She was MY granny!" Elsa insists.

"Was my 'sorry.'"

Elsa clenches her fists.

"Touché," she admits at last.

The Monster doesn't look up. Just turns around and goes back into the bathroom. More running of water. More alcogel. More rubbing. The wurse has picked up Elsa's backpack now with its teeth and has its whole snout inserted into it. It growls with great disappointment when it finds there is a palpable absence of chocolate-related materials in it.

Elsa squints at The Monster, her tone stricter and more interrogative:

"When I gave you the letter you spoke our secret language! You said 'stupid girl!' Was it Granny who taught you our secret language?"

And then The Monster looks up properly for the first time. His eyes open wide, in surprise. And Elsa stares at him, her mouth agape.

"Not she who taught me. I . . . taught her," says The Monster in a low voice, in the secret language.

Now Elsa sounds out of breath.

"You are . . . you are . . ."

And just at that moment as she hears the police closing up the remains of the door to the wurse's flat and walking out, while Britt-Marie protests wildly, Elsa looks directly into The Monster's eyes.

"You are . . . the Werewolf Boy."

And, a breath later, she whispers in the secret language:

"You're Wolfheart."

And The Monster nods sadly.

11

PROTEIN BARS

Granny's fairy tales from Miamas were fairly dramatic, as a rule. Wars and storms and pursuits and intrigues and stuff, because these were the sorts of action stories that Granny liked. They were hardly ever about everyday life in the Land-of-Almost-Awake. So Elsa knows very little about how monsters and wurses get along, when they don't have armies to lead and shadows to fight.

It turns out they don't really get along.

It starts with the wurse totally losing its patience with The Monster when The Monster tries to wash the floor under the wurse while the wurse is still lying on it, and then, because The Monster is extremely reluctant to touch the wurse, he accidentally spatters some alcogel in its eye. Elsa has to intervene to stop a full-blown fight, and later when The Monster with extreme frustration insists that Elsa must put one of those blue plastic bags on each of the wurse's paws, the wurse thinks it's gone far enough. In the end, once twilight is falling outside and she's certain that the police are not still hanging about on the stairs, Elsa forces them both outside into the snow, to give herself a bit of peace and quiet to think over the situation and decide what to do next.

She would have worried about being seen by Britt-Marie from

the balcony, except that it's six o'clock sharp and Britt-Marie and Kent have their dinner at exactly six o'clock because "only barbarians" eat their dinner at any other time. Elsa nestles her chin into her Gryffindor scarf and tries to think clearly. The wurse, still looking quite offended by the blue plastic bags, backs into a bush until only its nose is sticking out of the branches. It stays there, its eyes focused on Elsa with a very dissatisfied expression. It takes almost a minute before The Monster sighs and makes a pointed gesture.

"Crapping," mumbles The Monster, and looks the other way.

"Sorry," says Elsa guiltily to the wurse and turns away. They are using normal language again, because something in Elsa's stomach turns into a dark lump when she talks in the secret language to anyone but Granny. Either way, The Monster doesn't seem too keen on any language. Meanwhile, the wurse looks like you or I might if someone came barging in while you were attending to nature's needs, and it took a while before they understood how inappropriate it was to stand there gawking. Only then does Elsa realize that it actually couldn't have had a chance to relieve itself for several days, unless it did so inside its flat. Which she rules out because she can't see how it could have maneuvered itself into using a toilet, and it certainly wouldn't have crapped on the floor, because this is not the sort of thing a wurse would demean itself by doing. So she assumes that one of the wurse's superpowers is clenching.

She turns to The Monster. He rubs his hands together and looks down at the tracks in the snow as if he'd like to smooth out the snow with an iron.

"Are you a soldier?" asks Elsa, pointing at his trousers.

He shakes his head. Elsa continues pointing at his trousers, because she has seen this type of trousers on the news.

"Those are soldier trousers."

The Monster nods.

"Why are you wearing soldier's trousers if you're not a soldier, then?" she interrogates.

"Old trousers," The Monster replies tersely.

"How did you get that scar?" asks Elsa, pointing at his face.

"Accident," The Monster replies even more tersely.

"No shit, Sherlock—I wasn't implying you did it on purpose."

("No shit, Sherlock" is one of her favorite expressions in English. Her father always says one should not use English expressions if there are perfectly good substitutes in one's own language, but Elsa actually doesn't think there is a substitute in this case.)

"Sorry, I didn't mean to sound rude. I just wanted to know what sort of accident."

"Normal accident," he growls, as if that settles matters. The Monster disappears under the huge hood of his jacket. "Late now. Should sleep."

She understands that he is alluding to her, not to himself. She points at the wurse.

"That one has to sleep with you tonight."

The Monster looks at her as if she just asked him to get naked, roll in saliva, and then run through a postage stamp factory with the lights off. Or maybe not exactly like that. But more or less. He shakes his head, so that his hood sways like a sail.

"Not sleep there. Can't. Not sleep there. Can't. Can't. Can't."

Elsa puts her hands on her stomach and glares at him.

"Where's it going to sleep, then?"

The Monster retracts deeper into his hood. Points at Elsa.

Elsa snorts.

"Mum didn't even let me get myself an owl! Do you get how she'd react if I came home with that thhhiiinng?"

The wurse comes out of the bushes, making a lot of noise and looking offended. Elsa clears her throat and apologizes.

"Sorry. I didn't mean 'that thing' in a bad sense."

The wurse looks a bit as if it's close to muttering, "Sure you didn't." The Monster rubs his hands in circles faster and faster, and starts to look as if he's panicking, and hisses down at the ground:

"Shit on fur. Has shit on fur. Shit on fur."

Elsa rolls her eyes, realizing that if she presses the point he'll probably have a heart attack. The Monster turns away and looks as if he is trying to insert an invisible eraser into his brain to banish that image from his memory.

"What did Granny write in the letter?" she asks him.

The Monster breathes grimly under his hood.

"Wrote 'sorry,'" he says without turning around.

"But what else? It was a really long letter!"

The Monster sighs and shakes his head and nods towards the entrance of the house.

"Late now. Sleep," he growls.

"Not until you tell me about the letter!"

The Monster looks like a very tired person being kept awake by someone thumping him at regular intervals, as hard as he can, with a pillowcase filled with yogurt. Or more or less, anyway. He looks up and frowns and evaluates Elsa, as if trying to work out how far he could fling her.

"Wrote 'protect castle,'" he repeats.

Elsa steps closer to show him that she's not afraid of him. Or to show herself.

"And what *else*?"

He hunches up inside his hood and starts walking off through the snow.

"Protect you. Protect Elsa."

Then he disappears in the darkness and is gone. He disappears a lot, Elsa will learn in due course. He's surprisingly good at it for someone so large.

Elsa hears muted panting from the other side of the yard and turns around. George comes jogging towards the house. She knows it's George because he's wearing shorts over his leggings and the greenest jacket in the world. He doesn't see her and the wurse, because he's too busy bouncing up and down from a bench. George trains a lot at running and jumping up and down from things. Elsa sometimes thinks he's in a permanent audition to be in the next Super Mario game.

"Come!" whispers Elsa quickly to the wurse to get it inside before George catches sight of it. And to her surprise, the mighty animal obeys her.

The wurse brushes past her legs so its coat tickles her all the way up to her forehead, and she's almost knocked down by the force of it.

She laughs. It looks at her and seems to be laughing as well.

Apart from Granny, the wurse is the first friend Elsa has ever had.

She makes sure Britt-Marie is not prowling about on the stairs and that George still hasn't seen them, and then she leads the wurse down into the cellar. The storage units are each assigned to a flat, and Granny's unit is unlocked and empty.

"You have to stay here tonight," she whispers. "Tomorrow we'll find you a better hiding place."

The wurse doesn't look hugely impressed, but it lies down and rolls onto its side and peers nonchalantly into the parts of the cellar that still lie steeped in darkness. Elsa checks where it's looking, then focuses on the wurse.

"Granny always said there were ghosts down here," she says firmly. "You mustn't scare them, d'you hear?"

The wurse lies unconcerned on its side on the floor, its hatchet-sized incisors glinting through the darkness.

"I'll bring more chocolate tomorrow if you're nice," she promises.

The wurse looks as if it is taking this concession into consideration. Elsa leans forward and kisses it on the nose. Then she darts up the stairs and closes the cellar door carefully behind her. She sneaks up without turning on the lights, to minimize the risk of anyone seeing her, but when she comes to Britt-Marie and Kent's flat she crouches and goes up the last flight in big leaps. She's almost sure that Britt-Marie is standing inside, peering out of the spyhole.

The next morning both The Monster's flat and the cellar storage unit are dark and empty. George drives Elsa to school. Mum has already gone to the hospital because, as usual, there's some emergency going on there and it's Mum's job to sort out emergencies.

George talks about his protein bars the whole way. He bought a whole box of them, he says, and now he can't find them anywhere. George likes talking about protein bars. And various functional items. Functional clothes and functional jogging shoes, for example. George loves functions. Elsa hopes no one ever invents protein bars with functions, because then George's head will probably explode. Not that Elsa would find that such a bad thing, but she imagines Mum would be upset about it, and there'd be an awful lot of cleaning. George drops her off in the parking area after asking her one more time if she's seen his missing protein bars. She groans with boredom and jumps out.

The other children keep their distance, watching her guardedly. Rumors of The Monster's intervention outside the park have spread, but Elsa knows it will only last a short while. It happened too far from school. Things that happen outside school may as well be happening in outer space, because she is protected in here anyway. She may have a respite of a couple of hours, but those who are chasing her will keep testing the boundaries, and once they drum up the courage to have another pop at her they'll hit her harder than ever.

And she knows that The Monster will never get anywhere near the fence even for her sake, because schools are full of children and children are full of bacteria, and there's not enough alcogel in the whole world for The Monster after that.

But she enjoys her freedom that morning in spite of all. It's the second-to-last day before the Christmas holidays and after tomorrow she can have a couple of weeks of rest from running. A couple of weeks without notes in her locker about how ugly she is and how they're going to kill her.

In the first break she allows herself a walk along the fence. She tightens her backpack straps from time to time, to make sure it isn't hanging too loose. She knows they won't be chasing her now, but it's a difficult habit to break. You run slower if your backpack's loose.

Eventually she lets herself drift off in her own thoughts. That is probably why she doesn't see it. She's thinking about Granny and Miamas, wondering what plan Granny had in mind when she sent her out on this treasure hunt; that is, if she had any plan at all. Granny always sort of made her plans as she went along, and now that she's no longer there Elsa is having problems recognizing what the next step of the treasure hunt is supposed to be. Above all she wonders what Granny meant when she said she was worried that Elsa would hate her when she found out more about her. Up until now Elsa has only found out that Granny had some pretty dodgy friends, which was hardly a shock, you might say.

And Elsa obviously understands that Granny's statement about who she was before she became a granny must have something to do with Elsa's mum, but she'd rather not ask Mum unless she has to. Everything Elsa says to Mum these days seems to end in an argument. And Elsa hates it. She hates that one can't be allowed to know things unless one starts arguing.

And she hates being as alone as one can only be without Granny.

So it must be for that reason that she doesn't notice it. Because she's probably no more than two or three yards away when she finally sees it, which is an insane distance not to see a wurse from. It's sitting by the gate, just outside the fence. She laughs, surprised. The wurse seems to be laughing as well, but internally.

"I looked for you this morning," she says, and goes into the street, even though this is not allowed during breaks. "Were you nice to the ghosts?"

The wurse doesn't look as if it was, but she throws her arms around its neck all the same, buries her hands deep in its thick black fur, and exclaims: "Wait, I've got something for you!" The wurse greedily sticks its nose into her backpack, but looks remarkably disappointed when it pulls it back out again.

"They're protein bars," says Elsa apologetically. "We don't have any sweets at home because Mum doesn't want me to eat them, but George says these are mega-tasty!"

The wurse doesn't like them at all. It only has about nine of them. When the bell goes, Elsa hugs it hard, hard, hard one more time and whispers, "Thanks for coming!"

She knows that the other children in the playground see her do it. The teachers may be able to avoid noticing the biggest, blackest wurse appearing out of nowhere in the morning break, but no child in the entire universe could.

No one leaves any notes in Elsa's locker that day.

12

MINT

Elsa stands alone on the balcony of Granny's flat. They used to stand here often. It was here that Granny first pointed at the cloud animals and talked about the Land-of-Almost-Awake, just after Mum and Dad had got divorced. That night Elsa got to see Miamas for the first time. She stares out blindly into the darkness and misses her more than ever. She has been lying on Granny's bed, looking up at the photos on the ceiling and trying to figure out what Granny was talking about at the hospital when she said Elsa mustn't hate her. And also, "it's a grandmother's privilege never to have to show her grandchild who she was before she became a grandmother." Elsa has spent hours trying to work out what this treasure hunt is for, or where the next clue can be found. If there even is one.

The wurse sleeps in the storage unit in the cellar. In the midst of all this it's good to know that the wurse is close at hand. It makes Elsa feel a little bit less lonely.

She peers over the balcony railing. Has a sense of something moving down there on the ground, in the darkness. She can't see anything, obviously, but she knows The Monster is there. Granny has planned the fairy tale in this way. The Monster is guarding the castle. Guarding Elsa.

She's just angry with Granny for never explaining what he's guarding it from.

A voice farther off saws through the silence.

" . . . Yeah, yeah, I've got all the booze for the party, I'm only just getting back home now!" the voice declares irritably as it draws closer.

It's the woman in the black skirt, talking into the white cord. She's heaving four heavy plastic bags along, and they knock into each other and then against her shins at every step. The woman swears and fumbles with her keys by the door.

"Oh there'll be at least twenty of us—and you know how well the guys in the office hold their drink. Not that they had any time to help, mind. . . . Yeah, isn't it? I know! As if I didn't have a full-time job as well?" is the last thing Elsa hears before the woman marches into the house.

Elsa doesn't know much at all about the woman in the black skirt, except that everything smells of mint and she always has very well-ironed clothes and always seems to be stressed-out. Granny used to say it was "because of her boys." Elsa doesn't know what that's supposed to mean.

Inside, Mum is sitting on a high stool in the kitchen, talking on the telephone and fiddling restlessly with one of Granny's tea towels. She never seems to have to listen very much to what the person at the other end of the line is saying. No one ever disagrees with Mum. Not that she raises her voice or interrupts; she's just not the sort of person anyone wants to get on the wrong side of. Mum likes to keep it like this, because conflict is bad for efficiency and efficiency is very important to her. George sometimes jokes that Mum will give birth to Halfie during her lunch break, to avoid any negative effect on the hospital's general efficiency. Elsa hates George for making all those stupid jokes. Hates him because he thinks he knows Mum well enough to make jokes about her.

Of course, Granny thought efficiency was rubbish, and she couldn't give a crap about the negative effect of conflict. Elsa heard one of the doctors at Mum's hospital saying that Granny "could start a fight in an empty room," but when Elsa told Granny she just looked miffed and said, "What if it was the room that started it?" And then she told the fairy tale about the girl who said no. Even though Elsa had already heard it at least an eternity of times.

"The Girl Who Said No" was one of the first stories Elsa ever heard from the Land-of-Almost-Awake. It was about the Queen of Miaudacas, one of the six kingdoms. In the beginning the queen had been a courageous and fair-minded princess very much liked by all, but unfortunately she grew up and became a frightened adult, as adults tend to be. She started loving efficiency and avoiding conflict. As adults do.

And then the queen simply forbade all conflict in Miaudacas. Everyone had to get along all the time. And because nearly all conflicts start with someone saying "no," the queen also made this word illegal. Anyone breaking this law was immediately cast into a huge Naysayers' Prison, and hundreds of soldiers in black armor who were known as Yea-Sayers patrolled the streets to make sure there were no disagreements anywhere. Dissatisfied with this, the queen had soon outlawed not only the word "no" but also other words including "not" and "maybe" and "well." Any of these were enough to get you sent straight to prison, where you'd never again see the light of day.

After a couple of years, words like "possibly" and "if" and "wait and see" had also been made illegal. In the end no one dared say anything at all. And then the queen felt that she might as well make all talking illegal, because almost every conflict tended to start with someone saying something. And after that there was silence in the kingdom for several years.

Until one day a little girl came riding in, singing as she went. And everyone stared at her, because singing was an extremely serious crime in Miaudacas, because there was a risk of one person liking the song and another disliking it. The Yea-Sayers sprang into action to stop the girl, but they couldn't catch her because she was very good at running. So the Yea-Sayers rang all the bells and called for reinforcements. Upon which the queen's very own elite force, known as the Paragraph Riders—because they rode a very special kind of animal that was a cross between a giraffe and a rule book—came out to stop the girl. But not even the Paragraph Riders could lay their hands on her, and in the end the queen in person came rushing out of her castle and roared at the girl to stop singing.

But then the girl turned to the queen, stared her right in the eye, and said "No." And as soon as she had said it, a piece of masonry fell off the wall around the prison. And when the girl said "No" one more time, another piece of masonry fell. And before long, not only the girl but all the other people in the kingdom, even the Yea-Sayers and the Paragraph Riders, were shouting "No! No! No!" and then the prison crumbled. And that was how the people of Miaudacas learned that a queen only stays in power for as long as her subjects are afraid of conflict.

Or at least Elsa thinks that was the moral of the story. She knows this partly because she checked out "moral" on Wikipedia and partly because the very first word Elsa learned to say was "no." Which led to a *lot* of arguing between Mum and Granny.

They fought about a lot of other things as well, of course. Once Granny said to Elsa's mum that she only became a manager as a way of expressing teenage rebellion—because the very worst rebellion Elsa's mum could dream up was to "become an economist." Elsa never really understood what was meant by that. But later that night, when they thought Elsa was sleeping, Elsa heard Mum rebuff

Granny by saying, "What do you know about my teenage years? You were never here!" That was the only time Elsa ever heard Mum saying anything to Granny while holding back tears. And then Granny went very quiet and never repeated the comment about teenage rebellion to Elsa.

Mum finishes her call and stands in the middle of the kitchen floor with the tea towel in her hand, looking as if she's forgotten something. She looks at Elsa. Elsa looks back dubiously. Mum smiles sadly.

"Do you want to help me pack some of your granny's things into boxes?"

Elsa nods. Even though she doesn't want to. Mum insists on packing boxes every night despite being told by both the doctor and George that she should be taking it easy. Mum isn't very good at either—taking it easy or being told.

"Your dad is coming to pick you up from school tomorrow afternoon," says Mum in passing as she ticks things off on her Excel packing spreadsheet.

"Because you're working late?" asks Elsa, as if she means nothing in particular by the question.

"I'll be . . . staying on for a while at the hospital," says Mum, because she doesn't like lying to Elsa.

"Can't George pick me up, then?"

"George is coming with me to the hospital."

Elsa packs things haphazardly into the box, deliberately ignoring the spreadsheet.

"Is Halfie sick?"

Mum tries to smile again. It doesn't go so very well.

"Don't worry, darling."

"That's the quickest way for me to know that I should be mega-worrying," answers Elsa.

"It's complicated." Mum sighs.

"Everything is complicated if no one explains it to you."

"It's just a routine checkup."

"No it isn't, no one has so many routine checkups in a pregnancy. I'm not that stupid."

Mum massages her temples and looks away.

"Please, Elsa, don't you start making trouble about this as well."

"What do you mean, 'as well?' What ELSE have I been making trouble with you about?" Elsa hisses, as one does when one is almost eight and feels slightly put upon.

"Don't shout," says Mum in a composed voice.

"I'M NOT SHOUTING!" shouts Elsa.

And then they both look down at the floor for a long time. Looking for their own ways of saying sorry. Neither of them knows where to begin. Elsa thumps down the lid of the packing crate, stomps off into Granny's bedroom, and slams the door.

You could hear a pin drop in the flat for about thirty minutes after that. Because that is how angry Elsa is, so angry that she has to start measuring time in minutes rather than eternities. She lies on Granny's bed and stares at the black-and-white photos on the ceiling. The Werewolf Boy seems to be waving at her and laughing. Deep inside, she wonders how anyone who laughs like that can grow up into something as incredibly doleful as The Monster.

She hears the doorbell go and then a second ring following incredibly fast, much faster than would be feasible for a normal person when ringing a doorbell. So it can only be Britt-Marie.

"I'm coming," Mum answers politely. Elsa can tell by her voice that she's been crying.

The words come flowing out of Britt-Marie, as if she's fitted with a windup mechanism and someone has cranked it up using a key on her back.

"I rang your bell! No one opened!"

Mum sighs.

"No. We're not home. We're here."

"Your mother's car is parked in the garage! And that hound is still loose on the property!" She's talking so quickly it's clear she can't prioritize her various upsets.

Elsa sits up in Granny's bed, but it takes almost a minute before she manages to take in what Britt-Marie just said. Then she bounces out of bed and opens the door, and has to muster all her self-control to stop herself dashing off down the hall, because she doesn't want to make the old busybody suspicious.

Britt-Marie stands on the landing with one hand very firmly inserted into the other, smiling at Mum in a well-meaning way, nattering on about how in this leaseholders' association they can't have rabid dogs running around.

"A sanitary nuisance, a sanitary nuisance is what it is!"

"The dog is probably far away by now, Britt-Marie. I wouldn't worry about it—"

Britt-Marie turns to Mum and smiles well-meaningly.

"No, no, of course you wouldn't, Ulrika. Of course you wouldn't. You're not the type to worry yourself about other people's safety, even your own child's, are you? It's something you've inherited, I see. Putting the career before the children. That is how it's always been in your family."

Mum's face is utterly relaxed. Her arms hang down, apparently relaxed. The only thing that gives her away is that she's slowly, slowly clenching her fists. Elsa has never seen her do that before.

Britt-Marie also notices. Again she switches the position of her hands on her stomach. Looks as if she's sweating. Her smile stiffens.

"Not that there's anything wrong with that, Ulrika, obviously. Obviously not. You make your own choices and prioritizations, obviously!"

"Was there anything else on your mind?" says Mum slowly, but something in her eyes has changed hue, which makes Britt-Marie take a small, small step back.

"No, no, nothing else. Nothing else at all!"

Elsa sticks out her head before Britt-Marie has time to turn around and leave.

"What was that you said about Granny's car?"

"It's in the garage," she says curtly, avoiding Mum's eye. "It's parked in *my* space. And if it isn't moved *at once,* I'll call the police!"

"How did it get there?"

"How am I supposed to know?!" Then she turns to Elsa's mum again, with renewed courage. "The car has to be moved at once, otherwise I'm calling the *police*, Ulrika!"

"I don't know where the car keys are, Britt-Marie. And if you don't mind, I need to sit down—I seem to be getting a headache."

"Maybe if you didn't drink so much coffee you wouldn't get headaches so often, Ulrika!" She turns and stomps down the stairs so quickly no one has time to answer her.

Mum closes the door in a slightly less self-controlled and composed way than usual, and heads into the kitchen.

"What did she mean by that?" asks Elsa.

"She doesn't think I should drink coffee when I'm pregnant," Mum replies. Her phone starts ringing.

"That's not what I meant," says Elsa. She hates it when Mum pretends to be stupid.

Mum picks up her telephone from the kitchen counter.

"I have to answer this, sweetheart."

"What did Britt-Marie mean when she said in our family we 'put the career before the children'? She meant Granny, didn't she?"

The telephone continues ringing.

"It's from the hospital, I have to answer."

"No you don't!"

They stand in silence looking at each other while the telephone rings two more times. Now it's Elsa's turn to clench her fists.

Mum's fingers steal across the display.

"I have to take this, Elsa."

"No you *don't*!"

Mum closes her eyes and answers the telephone. By the time she starts talking into it, Elsa has already slammed the door to Granny's bedroom behind her.

When Mum gently opens the door half an hour later, Elsa pretends to be asleep. Mum sneaks up and tucks her in. Kisses her cheek. Turns off the lamp.

By the time Elsa gets up an hour after that, Mum is sleeping on the sofa in the living room. Elsa sneaks up and tucks her and Halfie in. Kisses Mum on the cheek. Turns out the lamp. Mum is still holding Granny's tea towel in her hand.

Elsa fetches a flashlight from one of the boxes in the hall and puts on her shoes.

Because now she knows where to find the next clue in Granny's treasure hunt.

13

WINE

It's a bit tricky to explain, but some things in Granny's fairy tales are like that. You have to understand, first of all, that no creature in the Land-of-Almost-Awake is sadder than the sea-angel, and it's actually only once Elsa remembers this whole story that Granny's treasure hunt begins to make sense.

Elsa's birthday was always extremely important to Granny. Maybe because Elsa's birthday is two days after Christmas Eve and Christmas Eve, when most people celebrate the holiday, is very important to everyone else, and as a result no child with a birthday two days after Christmas Eve ever gets quite the same amount of attention as a child born in August or April. So Granny had a tendency to overcompensate. Mum had banned her from planning surprise parties, after that time Granny let off fireworks inside a hamburger restaurant and accidentally set fire to a seventeen-year-old girl who was dressed up as a clown and apparently supposed to be providing "entertainment for the children." She really was entertaining, Elsa should say in her defense. That day, Elsa learned some of her very best swearwords.

The thing is, in Miamas you don't get presents on your birthday. You *give* presents. Preferably something you have at home and are very fond of, which you then give to someone you like even more. That's why everyone in Miamas looks forward to other people's birthdays, and that's the origin of the expression "What do you get from someone who has everything?" When the enphants took this fairy tale into the real world, someone here managed to get the wrong end of the stick, of course, making it "What do you GIVE to someone who has everything?" But what else would you expect? These are the same muppets who managed to misinterpret the word "interpret," which means something completely different in Miamas. In Miamas an interpreter is a creature most easily described as a combination between a goat and a chocolate cookie. Interpreters are extremely gifted linguistically, as well as excellent to grill on the barbecue. At least they were until Elsa became a vegetarian, after which Granny was not allowed to mention them anymore.

Anyway: so Elsa was born two days after Christmas Eve almost eight years ago, the same day that the scientists registered the gamma radiation from that magnetar. The other thing that happened that day was a tsunami in the Indian Ocean. Elsa knows that this is a sickeningly big wave caused by an earthquake. Except sort of at sea. So more like an ocean-quake, really, if you want to be persnickety about it. And Elsa is quite persnickety.

Two hundred thousand people died at the same time that Elsa started to live. Sometimes when Elsa's mum thinks Elsa can't hear, she tells George she still feels guilty—it cuts her to the quick to think that this was the happiest day of her life.

Elsa was five and about to turn six when she read about it online for the first time. On her sixth birthday, Granny told her the story of the sea-angel. To teach her that not all monsters are monsters in the beginning, and not all monsters look like monsters. Some carry their monstrosity inside.

The very last thing the shadows did before the ending of the

War-Without-End was to destroy all of Mibatalos, the kingdom where all the warriors had been brought up. But then came Wolfheart and the wurses, and everything turned, and when the shadows fled the Land-of-Almost-Awake they charged out over the sea with terrible force from all the coastlines of the six kingdoms. And their imprint on the surface of the water stirred up hideous waves, which, one by one, smashed into each other until they had formed a single wave as high as the eternity of ten thousand fairy tales. And to stop anyone pursuing the shadows, the wave turned and threw itself back in towards land.

It could have crushed the whole Land-of-Almost-Awake. It could have broken over the land and decimated the castles and the houses and all those who lived in them far more terribly than all the armies of the shadows could have managed through all eternity.

That was when a hundred snow-angels saved the remaining five kingdoms. Because, while everyone else was running from the wave, the snow-angels rushed right into it. With their wings open and the power of all their epic stories in their hearts, they formed a magical wall against the water and stopped it coming in. Not even a wave created by shadows could get past a hundred snow-angels prepared to die so that a whole world of fairy tales could live.

Only one of them turned back from the massive body of water.

And even if Granny always said that those snow-angels were arrogant sods who sniffed at wine and made a right fuss, she never tried to take away from them the heroism they showed on that day. For the day when the War-Without-End came to an end was the happiest day ever for everyone in the Land-of-Almost-Awake, apart from the hundredth snow-angel.

Since then, the angel had drifted up and down the coast, burdened by a curse that prevented it from leaving the place that had taken away all those it loved. It did this for so long that the people in the villages along the coast forgot who it used to be and started calling it "the sea-angel" instead. And as the years went by, the angel was buried deeper and deeper in an avalanche of sorrow, until its heart split in two and then its whole body split, like a shattered mirror. When the children from the villages sneaked down to the coast to catch a glimpse of it, one moment they might see a face of such beauty it took their breath away; but in the next, they would see something so terrible and deformed and wild looking back at them that they would run screaming all the way home.

Because not all monsters were monsters in the beginning. Some are monsters born of sorrow.

According to one of the most-often-told stories in the Land-of-Almost-Awake, it was a small child from Miamas who managed to break the curse on the sea-angel, releasing it from the demons of memory that held it captive.

When Granny told Elsa that story for the first time on her sixth birthday, Elsa realized she was no longer a child. So she gave Granny her cuddly toy lion as a present. Because Elsa didn't need it anymore, she realized, and wanted it to protect her granny instead. And that night Granny whispered into Elsa's ear that if they were ever parted, if Granny ever got lost, she would send the lion to go and tell Elsa where she was.

It has taken Elsa a few days to work it out. Only tonight, when Britt-Marie mentioned that Renault had suddenly been parked in the garage without anyone knowing how it got there, did Elsa remember where Granny had put the lion on guard.

The glove compartment in Renault. That was where Granny kept her cigarettes. And nothing in Granny's life needed a lion guarding it more than that.

So Elsa sits in the passenger seat in Renault and inhales deeply. As usual, Renault's doors weren't locked, because Granny never locked anything, and he still smells of smoke. Elsa knows it's bad, but because it's Granny's smoke she takes deep breaths of it anyway.

"I miss you," she whispers into the upholstery of the backrest.

Then she opens the glove compartment. Moves the lion aside and takes out the letter. On it is written: "For Miamas's Bravest Knight, to be delivered to:" And then—scrawled in Granny's awful, awful handwriting—a name and an address.

Later that night Elsa sits on the top step outside Granny's flat until the ceiling lights switch themselves off. Runs her finger over Granny's writing on the envelope again and again, but doesn't open it. Just puts it in her backpack and stretches out on the cold floor and mostly keeps her eyes closed. Tries one more time to get off to Miamas. She lies there for hours without succeeding. Stays there until she hears the main door at the bottom of the house opening and closing again. She lies on the floor and mostly keeps her eyes closed until she feels the night embracing the windows of the house and hears the drunk start rattling around with something a couple floors farther down.

Elsa's mum doesn't like it when she calls the drunk "the drunk." "What do I call her then?" Elsa used to ask, and then Mum used to look very unsure and sound a bit smarmy, while managing to suggest something like: "It's . . . I mean, it's someone who's . . . tired." And then Granny used to chime in, "Tired? Hell yeah, of course you get tired when you're up boozing all night!" And then Mum used to yell, "Mum!" and then Granny used to throw out her hands and ask, "Oh, good God, what did I say wrong *now*?" and then it was time for Elsa to put on her headphones.

"Turn off the water, I said! No bathing at night!!!" the drunk stammers from below at no one in particular, whacking her shoehorn against the banister.

That's what the drunk always does. Roars and screams and

bashes things with that shoehorn. Then sings that same old song of hers. Of course, no one ever comes out and quiets her down, not even Britt-Marie, for in this house drunks are like monsters. People think if they ignore them they'll cease to exist.

Elsa sits up into a squatting position and peers down through the gap between the stairs. She can only make out a glimpse of the drunk's socks as she shambles past, swinging the shoehorn as if scything tall grass. Elsa can't quite explain to herself why she does it, but she heaves herself up on her tiptoes and sneaks down the first flight of stairs. Out of pure curiosity, perhaps. Or more likely because she is bored and frustrated about no longer being able to get to Miamas.

The door of the drunk's flat is open. There's a faint light cast by an overturned floor lamp. Photos on all the walls. Elsa has never seen so many photos—she thought Granny had a lot of them on her ceiling, but these must be in the thousands. Each of them is framed in a small white wooden frame and all are of two teenage boys and a man who must be their father. In one of the photos, the man and the boys are standing on a beach with a sparkling green sea behind them. The boys are both wearing wetsuits. They smile. They are bronzed. They look happy.

Under the frame is one of those cheap congratulatory cards, the kind you buy in a gas station when you've forgotten to get a proper card. "To Mum, from your boys," it says on the front.

Beside the card hangs a mirror. Shattered.

The words reverberating over the landing are so sudden and so filled with fury that Elsa loses her balance and slips down the bottom four or five steps, right into the wall. The echo throws itself at her, as if determined to claw her ears.

"WHATAREYOUDOINGHERE?"

Elsa peers up through the railings at the deranged person wielding the shoehorn at her, looking simultaneously incandescent and terrified. Her eyes flicker. That black skirt is full of creases now. She smells of wine, Elsa can feel it all the way from the floor below. Her hair looks like a bundle of string in which two birds have got themselves tangled up during a fight. She has purple bags under her eyes.

The woman sways. She probably means to yell, but it comes out as a wheeze:

"You're not allowed to bathe at night. The water . . . turn off the water. Everyone will drown. . . ."

The white cable she always talks into sits in her ear, but the other end just dangles against her hip, disconnected. Elsa realizes there has probably never been anyone there, and that's not an easy thing for an almost-eight-year-old to understand. Granny told many fairy tales about many things, but never about women in black skirts pretending to have telephone conversations while they went up the stairs, so their neighbors wouldn't think they'd bought all that wine for themselves.

The woman looks confused. As if she has suddenly forgotten where she is. She disappears and, in the next moment, Elsa feels her mum gently plucking her from the stairs. Feels her warm breath against her neck and her "ssshhh" in her ear, as if they were standing in front of a deer and had got a bit too close.

Elsa opens her mouth, but Mum puts her finger over her lips.

"Shush," whispers Mum again, and keeps her arms tight around her.

Elsa curls up in her arms in the dark, and they see the woman in the black skirt drifting back and forth down there like a flag that's torn itself free in the wind. Plastic bags lie scattered on the floor of her flat. One of the wine boxes has toppled over. A few last drops of red are dripping onto the parquet floor. Mum makes a gentle movement against Elsa's hand. They stand up quietly and go back up the stairs.

And that night Elsa's mum tells Elsa what everyone except Elsa's parents was talking about on the day Elsa was born. About a wave that broke over a beach five thousand miles away and crushed everything in its path. About two boys who swam out after their father and never came back.

Elsa hears how the drunk starts singing her song. Because not all monsters look like monsters. There are some that carry their monstrosity inside.

14

TIRES

So many hearts broke the day Elsa was born. Shattered with such force by the wave that the shards of glass were dispersed all around the world. Improbable catastrophes produce improbable things in people, improbable sorrow and improbable heroism. More death than human senses can comprehend. Two boys carrying their mother to safety and then turning back for their father. Because a family does not leave anyone behind. And yet, in the end, that is precisely what they did, her boys. Left her alone.

Elsa's granny lived in another rhythm from other people. She operated in a different way. In the real world, in relation to everything that functioned, she was chaotic. But when the real world crumbles, when everything turns into chaos, then people like Elsa's granny can sometimes be the only ones who stay functional. That was another of her superpowers. When Granny was headed for some far-off place, you could only be sure of one thing: that it was a place everyone else was trying to get away from. And if anyone asked her why she was doing it, she'd answer, "I'm a doctor, for God's sake, and ever since I became one I've not allowed myself the luxury of choosing whose life I should be saving."

She wasn't big on efficiency and economics, Granny, but everyone listened to her when there was chaos. The other doctors wouldn't be seen dead with her on a good day, but when the world collapsed into pieces they followed her like an army. Because improbable tragedies create improbable superheroes.

Once, late one night when they were on their way to Miamas, Elsa had asked Granny about it, about how it felt to be somewhere when the world crumbles. And how it was being in the Land-of-Almost-Awake during the War-Without-End and what it was like when they saw that wave breaking over the ninety-nine snow-angels. And Granny had answered: "It's like the very worst thing you could dream up, worked out by the most evil thing you could imagine and multiplied by a figure you can't even imagine." Elsa had been very afraid that night, and she had asked Granny what they would do if one day their world crumbled around them.

And then Granny had squeezed her forefingers hard and replied, "Then we do what everyone does, we do everything we can." Elsa had crept up into her lap and asked: "But what can we do?" And then Granny had kissed her hair and held her hard, hard, hard and whispered: "We pick up as many children as we can carry, and we run as fast as we can."

"I'm good at running," Elsa had whispered.

"Me too," Granny had whispered back.

The day Elsa was born, Granny was far away. In a war. She had been there for months, but was on her way to an aircraft. On her way home. That was when she heard about the wave in another place even farther away, from which everyone was in desperate flight. So she went, because they needed her. She had time to help many children escape death, but not the boys of the woman with the black skirt. So she brought home the woman with the black skirt instead.

"That was your grandmother's last journey," says Mum. "She came home after that."

Elsa and Mum sit in Kia. It's morning and there's a traffic jam. Snowflakes as big as pillowcases are falling on the windshield.

Elsa can't remember the last time she heard Mum tell such a long story. Mum hardly ever tells stories, but this one was so long that Mum fell asleep in the middle of it last night and had to pick it up in the car on the way to school.

"Why was it her last journey?" asks Elsa.

Mum smiles with an emotional combination of melancholy and joy that only she in the entire world has fully mastered.

"She got a new job."

And then she looks as if she is remembering something unexpected. As if the memory just fell out of a cracked vase.

"You were born prematurely. They were concerned about your heart so we had to stay at the hospital for several weeks with you. Granny came back with her on the same day we came home. . . ."

Elsa realizes that she means the woman in the black skirt. Mum clutches Kia's steering wheel hard.

"I've never spoken much to her. I don't think anyone in the house wanted to ask too many questions. We let your grandmother handle it. And then . . ."

She sighs, and regret floods her gaze.

". . . then the years just went by. And we were busy. And now she's just someone who lives in our house. To be quite honest with you, I'd forgotten that was how she first moved in. You two moved in on the same day. . . ."

Mum turns to Elsa. Tries unsuccessfully to smile.

"Does it make me a terrible person that I've forgotten?"

Elsa shakes her head. She was going to say something about The Monster and the wurse, but she doesn't because she's worried Mum won't let her see them anymore if she knows. Mums can have a lot of strange principles when it comes to social interaction between their children and monsters and wurses. Elsa understands that everyone is scared of them, and that it will take a long time to make them all understand that The Monster and the wurse—like the drunk—are not what they seem.

"How often did Granny go away?" she asks instead.

A silver-colored car behind them sounds its horn when she allows a space to develop between her and the car in front. Mum releases the brake and Kia slowly rolls forward.

"It varied. It depended on where she was needed, and for how long."

"Was that what you meant that time Granny said you became an economist just to spite her?"

The car behind them sounds its horn again.

"What?"

Elsa fiddles with the rubber seal in the door.

"I heard you. Like a mega-long time ago. When Granny said you became an economist because you were in teenage rebellion. And you said, 'How do you know? You were never here!' That was what you meant, wasn't it?"

"I was angry, Elsa. Sometimes it's hard to control what you say, when you're angry."

"Not you. You never lose control."

Mum tries to smile again.

"With your grandmother it was . . . more difficult."

"How old were you when Grandfather died?"

"Twelve."

"And Granny left you?"

"Your grandmother went where she was needed, darling."

"Didn't you need her, though?"

"Others needed her more."

"Is that why you were always arguing?"

Mum sighs deeply as only a parent who has just realized that she has strayed considerably further into a story than she was intending is capable of sighing.

"Yes. Yes, sometimes it was probably for that reason we were arguing. But sometimes it was about other things. Your grandmother and I were very . . . different."

"No. You were just different in different ways."

"Maybe."

"What else did you argue about?"

The car behind Kia beeps its horn again. Mum closes her eyes and holds her breath. And only when she finally releases the hand brake and lets Kia roll forward does she release the word from her lips, as if it had to force its way through.

"You. We always argued about you, darling."

"Why?"

"Because when you love someone very much, it's difficult to learn to share her with someone else."

"Like Jean Grey," Elsa observes, as if it were absolutely obvious.

"Who?"

"A superhero. From *X-Men*. Wolverine and Cyclops both loved her. So they argued so much about her, it was totally insane."

"I thought those X-Men were mutants, not superheroes. Isn't that what you said last time we spoke about them?"

"It's complicated," says Elsa, even though it isn't really, if one has read enough quality literature.

"So what kind of superpower does this Jean Grey have, then?"

"Telepathy."

"Good superpower."

"Insane." Elsa nods in agreement.

She decides not to point out that Jean Grey can also do telekinesis, because she doesn't want to make things more complicated than necessary for Mum right now. She is pregnant, after all.

So instead, Elsa pulls the rubber seal on the door. Peers down into the gap. She is incredibly tired, as tired as an almost-eight-year-old gets after staying up all night feeling angry. Elsa's mum never had a mum of her own, because Granny was always somewhere else, to help someone else. Elsa has never thought of Granny in that way.

"Are you angry with me because Granny was so much with me and never with you?" she asks carefully.

Mum shakes her head so quickly and vehemently that Elsa immediately understands whatever she's about to say will be a lie.

"No, my darling, darling girl. Never. Never!"

Elsa nods and looks down again into the gap in the door.

"I'm angry with her. For not telling the truth."

"Everyone has secrets, darling."

"Are you angry with me because Granny and I had secrets?" She thinks about the secret language, which they always spoke so Mum wouldn't understand. She thinks about the Land-of-Almost-Awake, and wonders if Granny ever took Mum there.

"Never angry. . ." whispers Mum, and reaches across the seat before she adds, in a whisper: "Jealous."

The feeling of guilt hits Elsa like cold water when you're least expecting it.

"So that's what Granny meant," she states.

"What did she say?" Mum asks.

Elsa snorts.

"She said I'd hate her if I found out who she was before I was born. That's what she meant. That I'd find out that she was a crappy mum who left her own child—"

Mum turns to her with eyes so shiny that Elsa can see her own reflection in them.

"She didn't leave me. You mustn't hate your granny, darling."

And when Elsa doesn't answer, Mum puts her hand against Elsa's cheek and whispers, "All daughters are angry with their mothers about something. But she was a good grandmother, Elsa. She was the most fantastic grandmother anyone could imagine."

Elsa defiantly pulls at the rubber seal.

"But she left you by yourself. All those times she went off, she left you on your own, didn't she?"

"I had your grandfather when I was small."

"Yeah, until he died!"

"When he died I had the neighbors."

"What neighbors?" Elsa wants to know.

The car behind beeps its horn. Mum makes an apologetic gesture at the back window and Kia rolls forward.

"Britt-Marie," says Mum at last.

Elsa stops fiddling with the rubber seal in the door.

"What do you mean, Britt-Marie?"

"She took care of me."

Elsa's eyebrows sink into a scowling V-shape.

"So why is she such a nightmare to you now, then?"

"Don't say that, Elsa."

"But she is!"

Mum sighs through her nose.

"Britt-Marie wasn't always like that. She's just . . . lonely."

"She's got Kent!"

Mum blinks so slowly that her eyes are closed.

"There are many ways of being alone, darling."

Elsa goes back to fiddling with the rubber seal on the door.

"She's still an idiot."

"People can turn into idiots if they're alone for long enough," agrees Mum.

The car behind them beeps its horn again.

"Is that why Granny isn't in any of the old photos at home?" asks Elsa.

"What?"

"Granny isn't in any of the photos from before I was born. When I was small I thought it was because she was a vampire, because they can't be seen in photos, and they can smoke as much as they want without getting a sore throat. But she wasn't a vampire, was she? She was just never at home."

"It's complicated."

"Yes, until someone explains it to you! But when I asked Granny about it, she always changed the subject. And when I ask Dad, he says, 'Eh . . . eh . . . what do you want? You want an ice cream? You can have an ice cream!'"

Mum suddenly laughs explosively. Elsa does a mean impersonation of her dad.

"Your dad doesn't exactly like conflict." Mum giggles.

"Was Granny a vampire or not?"

"Your granny traveled around the world saving children's lives, darling. She was a . . ."

Mum looks as if she's looking for the right word. And once she finds it, she brightens and smiles radiantly.

"A superhero! Your granny was a superhero!"

Elsa stares down into the cavity in the door.

"Superheroes don't leave their own children."

Mum is silent.

"All superheroes have to make sacrifices, darling," she tries at last.

But both she and Elsa know she doesn't mean it.

The car behind them beeps its horn again. Mum's hand shoots up apologetically towards the back window, and Kia rolls forward a few yards. Elsa realizes that she's sitting there hoping Mum will start yelling. Or crying. Or anything. She just wants to see her feel something.

Elsa can't understand how anyone can be in such a hurry to move five yards in a traffic jam. She looks in the rearview mirror at the man in the car behind them. He seems to think the traffic jam is being caused by Elsa's mum. Elsa wishes with every fiber of her being that Mum would do what she did when she was pregnant with Elsa, and get out of the car and roar at the guy and tell him enough's bloody enough.

Elsa's father told that story. He almost never tells stories, but one Midsummer Eve—at the time when Mum was looking sadder and sadder and going to bed earlier and earlier and Dad sat on his own in the kitchen at night and reorganized the icons on Mum's computer screen and cried—they were at a party together, all three of them. And then Dad drank three beers and told a story about how Mum, while heavily pregnant with Elsa, got out of the car and went up to a man in a silver car and threatened to "give birth here and now on his sodding hood if he honked at her again!" Everyone laughed a lot at that story. Not Dad, of course, because he's not a big fan of laughing. But Elsa saw that even he found it funny. He danced with Mum that Midsummer. That was the last time Elsa saw them dancing together. Dad is spectacularly bad at dancing; he looks like a very large bear that has just got up and realizes its foot has gone to sleep. Elsa misses it.

And she misses someone who gets out and shouts at men in silver-colored cars.

The man in the silver-colored car behind them beeps again. Elsa picks up her backpack from the floor, gets out the heaviest book she can find, throws the door open, and jumps out onto the highway. She hears Mum shouting for her to come back, but without turning around she runs towards the silver car and slams the book as hard as she can into its hood. It leaves a big dent. Elsa's hands are shaking.

The man in the silver car stares at her as if he can't quite believe what just happened.

"ENOUGH, you muppet!"

When he doesn't answer right away, she slams the book down again three more times, and points at him menacingly.

"Do you get that my mum is PREGNANT?"

At first, the man looks as if he's going to open the door. But then he seems to change his mind, and watches in amazement as she pummels the hood with her book.

Elsa hears the click of the doors locking.

"One more peep and my mum comes out and gives birth to Halfie on YOUR BLOODY HOOD!" roars Elsa.

She stays where she is on the highway between the silver car and Kia, hyperventilating, until she gets a headache. She hears Mum yelling, and Elsa is actually on her way back into Kia, she really is. It's not as if she planned all this. But then she feels a hand on her shoulder and hears a voice, asking:

"Do you need help?"

And when she turns around there's a policeman standing over her.

"Can we help you?" he says again in a friendly tone of voice.

He looks very young. As if he's only working as a policeman as a summer job. Even though it's winter.

"He keeps beeping his horn at us!" Elsa says defensively.

The summer-intern policeman looks at the man in the silver car. The man inside the car is now terrifically busy not looking back.

Elsa turns towards Kia, and she really doesn't mean to say it, it's almost as if the words accidentally fall out of her mouth.

"My mum's about to give birth and we're sort of having a hard day here—"

"Your mother's in labor?" he asks, visibly tightening.

"I mean, it's not . . ." Elsa begins.

But of course it's too late.

The policeman runs up to Kia. Mum has managed to get out with great effort, and is on her way towards them with her hand against Halfie.

"Are you able to drive? Or . . . ?" shouts the policeman so loudly that Elsa irately shoves her fingers in her ears and moves demonstratively to the other side of Kia.

Mum looks slightly as if she's been caught off balance.

"What? Or what? Of course I can drive. Or what? Is there something wro—"

"I'll go on ahead!" yells the policeman without listening to the end of the sentence, shoving Mum back into Kia and running back to his patrol car.

Mum thumps back into the seat. Looks at Elsa. Elsa searches the glove compartment for a reason not to have to look back at her.

The patrol car thunders past with its sirens turned on. The summer-intern policeman waves frantically at them to follow behind.

"I think he wants you to follow him," mumbles Elsa without looking up.

"What's going on?" whispers Mum while Kia carefully potters along behind the patrol car.

"I guess he's escorting us to the hospital, because he thinks you're about to, y'know, give birth," mumbles Elsa into the glove compartment.

"Why did you tell him I was about to give birth?"

"I didn't! But no one ever listens to me!"

"Right! And what should I do now, do you think?" hisses Mum back, sounding possibly a bit less self-controlled now.

"Well, we've been driving behind him for ages now, so he'll probably get quite pissed if he finds out you're not actually going to give birth for real," Elsa states pedagogically.

"OH, REALLY, YOU THINK SO?!" Mum roars in a way that is neither pedagogical nor especially self-controlled.

Elsa chooses not to enter into a discussion of whether Mum is being sarcastic or ironic there.

They stop outside the hospital's emergency entrance and Mum attempts to get out of the car and confess everything to the summer-intern policeman. But he pushes her back into the car and yells that he's going to fetch help. Mum looks mortified. This is her hospital. She's the boss here.

"This is going to be a nightmare to explain to the staff," she mumbles and rests her forehead in despair against the steering wheel.

"Maybe you could say it was some sort of exercise?" Elsa suggests.

Mum doesn't answer. Elsa clears her throat again.

"Granny would have thought this was fun."

Mum smiles faintly and turns her head so her ear is on the steering wheel. They look at each other for a long time.

"She would have found it bloody funny," agrees Mum.

"Don't swear," says Elsa.

"You're always swearing!"

"I'm not a mum!"

Mum smiles again.

"Touché."

Elsa opens and closes the glove compartment a few times. Looks up at the hospital façade. Behind one of those windows, she slept in the same bed as Granny the night Granny went off to Miamas for the last time. It feels like forever ago. Feels like forever since Elsa managed to get to Miamas on her own.

"What job was it?" she asks, mainly so she doesn't have to think about it.

"What?" Mum exclaims.

"You said that thing with the tsunami was Granny's last journey because she had found a new job. What job was it?"

Mum's fingertips brush against Elsa's when she whispers the answer.

"As a grandmother. She got a job as a grandmother. She never went away again."

Elsa nods slowly. Mum caresses her arm. Elsa opens and closes the glove compartment. Then she looks up as if she's just thought of something, but mostly because she'd like to change the subject, because she doesn't want to think about how angry she is with Granny right now.

"Did you and Dad get divorced because you ran out of love?" she asks so quickly that the question actually surprises her.

Mum leans back. Pulls her fingers through her hair and shakes her head.

"Why are you asking?"

Elsa shrugs.

"We have to talk about something while we're waiting for the policeman to come back with the people you're the boss of and everything gets mega-embarrassing for you. . . ."

Mum looks unhappy again. Elsa fiddles with the rubber seal. Realizes that it was obviously too early to start making jokes about it.

"Don't people get married because they're full of love and then divorced when they run out of it?" she says in a low voice.

"Did you learn that one in school?"

"It's my own theory."

Mum laughs very loudly, without any warning. Elsa grins.

"Did Granddad and Granny run low on love as well?" she asks, when Mum has finished laughing.

Mum dabs her eyes.

"They were never married, darling."

"Why not?"

"Your granny was special, Elsa. She was difficult to live with."

"How do you mean?"

Mum massages her eyelids.

"It's difficult to explain. But in those days it can't have been so common for women to be like her. I mean . . . it can't have been so common for *anyone* to be like her. It wasn't common for women to become doctors in those days, for example. As for surgeons, forget it. The academic world would have been quite different . . . so . . ."

Mum goes quiet. Elsa raises her eyebrows as a way of telling her to get to the point.

"I think if your granny had been a man of her generation rather than a woman, she would have been called a 'playboy.'"

Elsa is silent for a long while. Then she nods soberly.

"Did she have many boyfriends?"

"Yes," says Mum cautiously.

"There's someone in my school who has many boyfriends," states Elsa.

"Oh, well I wouldn't want to suggest that the girl in your school is a—" says Mum, feverishly backtracking.

"He's a boy," Elsa corrects.

Mum looks confused.

Elsa shrugs. "It's complicated," she says.

Even though it really isn't. But Mum doesn't look massively less confused.

"Your granddad loved your granny very much. But they were never a . . . couple. Do you understand?"

"I get it," says Elsa, because she has the Internet.

Then she reaches out and takes Mum's index fingers and squeezes them in her hands.

"I'm sorry that Granny was a crappy mum, Mum!"

"She was a fantastic grandmother, Elsa. You were all her second chances," says Mum and caresses Elsa's hair as she goes on: "I think your grandmother functioned so well in chaotic places because she was herself chaotic. She was always amazing in the midst of a catastrophe. It was just all this, everyday life and normality, that she didn't quite know how to handle.

"And it was just . . . I mean . . . the reason there aren't any old photos of Granny is partly because she wasn't home very often. And slightly because I tore up all the ones there were."

"Why?"

"I was a teenager. And angry. The two belong together. There was always chaos at home. Bills that didn't get paid and food that went off in the fridge when we actually had food, and sometimes no food at all, and . . . God. It's hard to explain, darling. I was just angry."

Elsa crosses her arms and leans back in her seat and glares out of the window.

"People shouldn't have children if they don't want to take care of them."

Mum reaches out, touches her shoulder with her fingertips.

"Your granny was old when she had me. Or, what I mean is, she was as old as I was when I had you. But that was old in Granny's times. And she didn't think she could have children. She'd had herself tested."

Elsa presses her chin down over her wishbone.

"So you were a mistake?"

"An accident."

"In that case, I'm an accident as well."

Mum's lips fold in on themselves.

"No one has ever wanted something as much as your father and I wanted you, darling. You're about as far from an accident as anyone can get."

Elsa looks up at Kia's ceiling and blinks the haziness out of her eyes.

"Is that why order is your superpower? Because you don't want to be like Granny?"

Mum shrugs. "I taught myself to fix things on my own, that's all. Because I didn't trust your grandmother. In the end, things were even worse when she was actually here. I was angry at her when she was away, and even angrier when she was home."

"I'm angry too. . . . I'm angry because she lied about being sick and no one told me and now I know and I still miss her and THAT makes me angry!!!"

Mum shuts her eyelids tight and puts her forehead against Elsa's forehead.

Elsa's jaw is trembling.

"I'm angry with her for dying. I'm angry with her for dying and disappearing from me," she whispers.

"Me too," whispers Mum.

And that is when the summer-intern policeman comes charging out of the emergency doors. He has two nurses with a stretcher running behind him.

Elsa turns a couple of inches towards Mum. Mum turns a couple of inches towards Elsa.

"What do you think your granny would have done now?" asks Mum calmly.

"She would have cleared out," says Elsa, still with her forehead against Mum's forehead.

The summer-intern policeman and the nurses with the stretcher are only a few yards from the car when Mum slowly nods. Then she puts Kia into gear and, with the tires spinning in the snow, skids out into the road and drives off. It's the most irresponsible thing Elsa has ever seen her mother do.

She'll always love her for it.

15 WOOD SHAVINGS

Perhaps the most curious of all the curious creatures in the Land-of-Almost-Awake, even by Granny's yardstick, are the regretters. They are wild animals living in herds, whose grazing areas are just outside Miamas, where they forage widely, and really nobody knows how they survive, considering the circumstances. At first sight, regretters look more or less like white horses, although they are far more ambivalent and suffer from the biological defect of never being able to make up their minds. This obviously causes certain practical problems, because regretters are flock animals, and one regretter therefore almost always crashes into another when heading off in one direction and then changing its mind. For this reason regretters always have enormous, oblong swellings on their foreheads, which, in various fairy tales from Miamas that have ended up in the real world, has made people consistently get them confused with unicorns. But in Miamas the storytellers learned the hard way not to cut costs by hiring a regretter to do the job of a unicorn, because, whenever they did, the fairy tales had a tendency never to get to the point. And also no one, really no one at all, feels good after standing behind a regretter in the line for the lunch buffet.

"So there's no point changing your mind, all you get is a headache!" Granny used to say, smacking herself on her forehead. Elsa thinks about that now, sitting in Kia outside school and looking at Mum.

She wonders if Granny ever regretted all the times she left Mum. She wonders if Granny's head was full of bumps. She hopes so.

Mum is massaging her temples and swearing repeatedly through gritted teeth. She is obviously regretting speeding away from the hospital like that, since the first thing she has to do after dropping Elsa off at school is drive straight back to the hospital so she can go to work. Elsa pats her on the shoulder.

"Maybe you can blame it on your baby brain?"

Mum shuts her eyes in resignation. She's had rather too much baby brain lately. So much so that she could not even find Elsa's Gryffindor scarf when they looked for it this morning, and so much so that she keeps putting her telephone in strange places. In the refrigerator and in the trash bin and the laundry basket and on one occasion in George's jogging shoes. This morning Elsa had to call Mum's telephone three times, which is not entirely uncomplicated as the display on Elsa's telephone is quite fuzzy after its encounter with the toaster. But in the end they found Mum's telephone ringing inside Elsa's backpack. The Gryffindor scarf was also there.

"You see!" Mum tried to say. "Nothing is really gone until your mum can't find it!" But Elsa rolled her eyes and then Mum looked ashamed of herself and mumbled, "It's my baby brain, I'm afraid."

She looks ashamed of herself now as well. And full of regret.

"Darling, I don't think they'll let me be the head of a hospital if I tell them I had a police escort to the emergency entrance"

Elsa reaches out and pats Mum on the cheek.

"It'll get better, Mum. It'll be fine."

Granny used to say that, Elsa realizes as soon as she says it. Mum puts her hand on Halfie and nods with fake self-assurance in order to change the subject.

"Your dad will pick you up this afternoon, don't forget. And George will take you to school on Monday. I have a conference then and—"

Elsa patiently gives Mum's head a scratch.

"I'm not going to school on Monday, Mum. It's the Christmas holidays."

Mum puts her hand on Elsa's hand and inhales deeply from the point where they are touching, as if trying to fill her lungs with Elsa. As mums do with daughters who grow up too fast.

"Sorry, darling. I . . . forget."

"It doesn't matter," says Elsa.

Even though it does a little.

They hug each other hard before Elsa hops out of the car. She waits until Kia has disappeared before she opens her backpack and gets out Mum's cell phone, then scrolls to Dad's name in the address book and sends him a text: ACTUALLY: THERE IS NO NEED FOR YOU TO PICK UP ELSA THIS AFTERNOON. I CAN MANAGE IT! Elsa knows this is how they talk about her. She is something that needs to be "picked up" or "sorted." Like doing the laundry. She knows they mean no harm by it, but come on! No seven-year-old who has seen films about the Italian Mafia wants to be "sorted" by her family.

Mum's phone vibrates in Elsa's hand. She sees Dad's name on the display. And underneath, I UNDERSTAND. Elsa deletes it. And deletes the text she sent to Dad from the outgoing messages. Then stands on the pavement, counting down from twenty. When she's got to seven, Kia screeches back into the parking area and Mum, slightly out of breath, winds down the window. Elsa gives her the phone. Mum mumbles, "It's my baby brain." Elsa kisses her on the cheek.

Mum touches her throat and asks if Elsa has seen her scarf.

"In your right-hand coat pocket," says Elsa.

Mum pulls the scarf out. Takes Elsa's head in her hands and pulls her closer and kisses her forehead very hard. Elsa closes her eyes.

"Nothing is really gone until your daughter can't find it," she whispers into Mum's ear.

"You're going to be a fantastic big sister," Mum whispers back.

Elsa doesn't answer. She just stands there waving as Kia drives off. She couldn't answer because she doesn't want Mum to know that she doesn't want to be a big sister. Doesn't want anyone to know that she is this horrible person who hates her own half sibling, just because Halfie is going to be more loved by them than Elsa. Doesn't want anyone to know she's afraid they'll abandon her.

She turns around and looks into the playground. No one has seen her yet. She reaches into her backpack and gets out the letter she found in Renault. She doesn't recognize the address, and Granny was always terrible at giving directions. Elsa isn't even sure this address exists in real life, because quite often when Granny was explaining where things were, she used landmarks that were no longer there. "It's right by where those morons with the budgerigars lived, past the old tennis club down where the old rubber factory or whatever it was used to be," she'd ramble on, and when people didn't get exactly what she was talking about, Granny got so frustrated that she had to smoke two cigarettes one after the other, lighting the second by the embers of the first. And then when someone said she couldn't do that indoors, she got so angry that it was utterly impossible after that to get any decent directions out of her, impossible in fact to get anything except her expletive middle finger.

Really what Elsa wanted to do was rip the letter into ten thousand pieces and let the wind blow it all away. That was what she had decided last night. Because she was angry at Granny. But now, after

Mum has told her the whole story and Elsa has seen all that brokenness in Mum's eyes, she's made the decision not to do that. Elsa is going to deliver the letter, this and all the other letters Granny has left for her. This is going to be a grand adventure and a monstrous fairy tale, just as Granny planned it. But Elsa isn't doing it for Granny's sake.

First of all she's going to need a computer.

She looks at the playground again. And at the precise moment when the bell goes and everyone turns away from the street, she runs past the fence towards the bus stop. Gets off a few stops later, runs into the shop, and goes straight to the ice cream counter, then back to the house, where she sneaks into the cellar storage unit and buries her face in the wurse's fur. It's her new favorite place on earth.

"I've got ice cream in the bag," she says at last when she lifts her head.

The wurse points its nose with interest.

"It's Ben and Jerry's New York Super Fudge Chunk—my favorite," Elsa elaborates.

The wurse has eaten more than half the ice cream before she reaches the end of that sentence. She caresses its ears.

"I just have to get hold of a computer. Stay here and . . . you know . . . try to stay out of sight!"

The wurse looks at her like a very big wurse that has just been told to behave like a considerably smaller wurse.

Elsa promises to find it a much better hiding place. Soon.

She runs up the stairs. Checks carefully that Britt-Marie is not lurking anywhere, and once she's sure she's not, rings The Monster's doorbell. He doesn't open. She rings the bell again. Everything is silent. She groans and opens his mail slot and peers inside. All of the lights are out, but that doesn't dissuade her.

"I know you're there!" she calls out.

No one answers. Elsa takes a deep breath.

"If you don't open, I'll sneeze right inside! And I've got a mega-col—" she starts to say threateningly, before from behind her interrupts a hiss, like someone trying to make a cat jump down from a table.

She spins around. The Monster steps out of the shadows on the stairs. She can't understand how such a huge person can make himself invisible all the time. He's rubbing his hands together, turning the skin around his knuckles red.

"Don't sneeze, don't sneeze," he implores anxiously.

"I need to borrow your computer, because I think George could be at home and I can't surf on my cell phone because the display is screwed because Granny had a Fanta-and-toaster-related incident with it. . . ."

The hood over The Monster's head moves slowly from side to side.

"No computer."

"Just let me borrow it so I can check the address!" Elsa whines, waving Granny's letter in the air.

The Monster shakes his head again.

"Fine, just give me your Wi-Fi password, then, so I can connect my iPad!" she manages to say, rolling her eyes until it feels as if her pupils are out of position when she stops. "I don't have 3G on the iPad, because Dad bought the iPad and Mum got pissed because she didn't want me to have such expensive stuff, and she doesn't like Apple, so it was a compromise! It's complicated, okay? I only need to borrow your Wi-Fi, that's all! Good God!"

"No computer," repeats The Monster.

"No . . . computer?" Elsa repeats with extreme disbelief.

The Monster shakes his head.

"You don't have a computer?"

The hood moves from side to side. Elsa peers at him as if he's having her on, is clinically insane, or both.

"How can you not have a COMPUTER?"

The Monster produces a small sealed plastic bag from one of his jacket pockets, and inside it is a small bottle of alcogel. Carefully he squeezes out some of its contents and starts rubbing it into his palms and skin.

"Don't need computer," he growls.

Elsa takes a deep, irritated breath and takes a look around the stairs. George may still be at home so she can't go inside, because then he'll ask why she's not at school. And she can't go to Maud and Lennart, because they're too kind to lie, so if Mum asks if they've seen Elsa they'll tell her the truth. The boy with a syndrome and his mum aren't here in the daytime. And forget Britt-Marie.

Which doesn't exactly leave a wealth of possibilities. Elsa collects herself and tries to think about how a knight of Miamas is never afraid of a treasure hunt, even if it's difficult. And then she goes up the stairs.

Alf opens the door after the seventh ring. His flat smells of wood shavings. He's wearing a sorry excuse for a dressing gown, and the remaining hairs on his head look like the last tottering bits of buildings after a hurricane. He's holding a large white cup on which it says "Juventus" and there's a smell of coffee, strong like Granny always drank it. "After Alf has made coffee, you have to drive standing up all morning," she used to say, and Elsa didn't quite know what she meant, although she understood what she was saying.

"Yes?" he grunts.

"You know where this is?" says Elsa, and holds out the envelope with Granny's handwriting on it.

"Are you waking me up to ask about a bloody address?" answers Alf in every way inhospitably before taking a big gulp of coffee.

"Were you still sleeping?"

Alf takes another mouthful and nods at his wristwatch.

"I drive the late shift. This is nighttime for me. Do I come to your flat in the middle of the night to ask you random questions?"

Elsa looks at the cup. Looks at Alf.

"If you're asleep, why are you drinking coffee?"

Alf looks at the cup. Looks at Elsa. Looks totally puzzled. Elsa shrugs.

"Do you know where this is or not?" she asks and points at the envelope.

Alf looks a little as if he's repeating her question to himself inside his head, in a very exaggerated and contemptuous tone. Has another sip of coffee.

"I've been a taxi driver for more than thirty years."

"And?" wonders Elsa.

"And so of course I bloody know where that is. It's by the old waterworks," he says, then drains his cup.

"What?"

Alf looks resigned.

"Young people and their lack of history, I tell you. Where the rubber factory was until they moved it again. And the brickyard."

Elsa's expression gives away the possibility that she doesn't have a clue what he's talking about.

Alf claws at the remains of his hair and disappears into the flat. Comes back with a topped-up cup of coffee and a map. Puts down the coffee cup with a slam on a shelf in the hall and marks the map with a thick ring using a ballpoint pen.

"Oh, theeere! That's where the shopping center is. Why didn't you just say?"

Alf says something that Elsa can't quite make out and closes the door in her face.

"I'll keep the map!" Elsa hollers cheerfully into his mail slot.

He doesn't answer.

"It's the Christmas holidays, if you're wondering! That's why I'm not at school!" she calls out.

He doesn't answer that either.

The wurse is lying on its side with two legs comfortably stretched up into the air when Elsa walks into the storage unit, as if it has very gravely misunderstood a Pilates exercise. The Monster is standing in the passage outside, rubbing his hands. He looks very uncomfortable.

Elsa holds up the envelope to him.

"Are you coming?"

The Monster nods. The hood glides away a few inches from his face, and the big scar gleams momentarily in the fluorescent light. He doesn't even ask where they're going. It's difficult not to feel a pang of affection for him.

Elsa looks first at him and then at the wurse. She knows that Mum is going to be angry with her for playing hooky and going off without permission, but when Elsa asks her why she's always so worried about her, Mum always says, "Because I'm so bloody afraid something may happen to you." But Elsa is having a pretty hard time thinking that anything can happen to you when you have a monster and a wurse tagging along. So she feels it should be okay, given the circumstances.

The wurse tries to lick The Monster when it walks out of the storage unit. The Monster jumps in terror and snatches back his hand and grabs a broom leaning up against another storage unit. The wurse, as if it's teasing and having a bit of a laugh, sweeps its tongue back and forth in long, provocative movements.

"Stop it!" Elsa tells it.

The Monster holds out the broom like a lance and tries to force the wurse back by pushing the bristles into its nose.

"I said stop it!" Elsa snaps at both of them.

The wurse closes its jaws around the broom and crunches it to smithereens.

"Stop i—" Elsa begins but doesn't have time to finish the last "it" before The Monster has thrown both broom and wurse across the cellar with all his might, sending the heavy animal crashing hard into the wall several yards away.

The wurse rolls up and flexes its body in one movement, and is in the middle of a terrifying spring before it has even landed. Its jaws are open, and rows of kitchen knife–size teeth exposed. The Monster faces it with a broad chest and the blood pumping in his fists.

"CUT IT OUT, I SAID!" Elsa roars, throwing her little body right between the two furious creatures, unprotected between claws as sharp as spears and fists probably big enough to separate her head from her shoulders. She stands her ground, armed with nothing but the indifference of an almost-eight-year-old to her own physical shortcomings. Which goes a long way.

The wurse stops itself midleap and lands softly beside her. The Monster takes a few steps back. Slowly, muscles relax and lungs release air. Neither of them meets her gaze.

"The idea here is that you're supposed to protect *me*," Elsa says in a quieter voice, trying not to cry, which doesn't go so terrifically well. "I've never had any friends and now you two try to kill the only two I've ever had, just after I've found you!"

The wurse lowers its nose. The Monster rubs his hands, disappears into his hood, and makes a rocking motion towards the wurse.

"Started it," The Monster manages to say.

The wurse growls back.

"Stop it!" She tries to sound angry but realizes she mainly just sounds as if she's crying.

The Monster, concerned, moves the palm of his hand up and down along her side, as close as possible without actually touching her.

"Sor . . . ry," he mumbles. The wurse buffets her shoulder. She rests her forehead against its nose.

"We have an important mission here, so you can't keep messing about. We have to deliver this letter because I think Granny wants to say sorry to someone else. And there are more letters. This is our fairy tale: to deliver every single one of Granny's sorries."

With her face in the wurse's fur, she inhales deeply and closes her eyes.

"We have to do it for my mum's sake. Because I'm hoping that the last sorry will be to her."

16

DUST

It turns into an epic adventure. A monstrous fairy tale.

Elsa decides they should begin by taking the bus, like normal knights on normal quests in more or less normal fairy tales when there aren't any horses or cloud animals available. But when all the other people at the bus stop start eyeing The Monster and the wurse and nervously shuffling as far away from them as it's possible to be without ending up at the next bus stop, she realizes it's not going to be quite so straightforward.

On boarding the bus it becomes immediately clear that wurses are not all that partial to traveling by public transport. After it has snuffled about and stepped on people's toes and overturned bags with its tail and accidentally dribbled a bit on a seat a little too close to The Monster for The Monster to feel entirely comfortable, Elsa decides to forget the whole thing, and then all three of them get off. Exactly one stop later.

Elsa pulls the Gryffindor scarf tighter around her face, pushes her hands into her pockets, and leads them through the snow. The wurse is so delighted about escaping the bus that it skips in circles around Elsa and The Monster like an overexcited puppy. The Monster looks disgusted. He doesn't seem used to being outdoors by daylight, Elsa notices. Maybe it's because Wolfheart is used to living in the dark forests outside Miamas where the daylight doesn't dare penetrate. At least, that is where he lives in Granny's fairy tales, so if there is any sort of order to this story, this must surely be the logical explanation.

People who see them on the pavement react as people generally do when they catch sight of a girl, a wurse, and a monster strolling along side by side: they cross the street. Some of them try to pretend that it has nothing to do with the fact that they are scared of monsters and wurses and girls, by demonstratively pretending to be having loud telephone conversations with someone who suddenly gives them different directions and tells them to go the opposite way. That is also what Elsa's dad does sometimes when he's gone the wrong way and he doesn't want strangers to realize he's one of those types who go the wrong way. Elsa's mum never has that problem, because if she goes the wrong way she just keeps going until whoever she was supposed to be meeting has to follow her. Granny used to solve the problem by shouting at the road signs. It varies, how people deal with it.

But others who run into the adventuring trio are not as discreet, and they watch Elsa from the other side of the road as if she's being abducted. Elsa feels that The Monster would probably be good at many things, but a kidnapper who can be put out of action by sneezing at him would probably not be a particularly effective kidnapper. It's a curious sort of Achilles' heel for a superhero, she feels. Snot.

The walk takes more than two hours. Elsa wishes it were Halloween, because then they could take the bus without scaring normal people, everyone would just assume they were dressed up. That's why Elsa likes Halloween: on Halloween it's normal to be different.

It's almost lunchtime by the time they find the right address. Elsa's feet hurt and she's hungry and in a bad mood. She knows that a knight of Miamas would never whine or be afraid of a grand adventure when sent out on a treasure hunt, but whoever said a knight can't be hungry or ill-tempered?

There's a high-rise at the address, but also a hamburger restaurant across the street. Elsa tells the wurse and The Monster to wait, and she goes across even though she has firm moral objections to hamburger chains, as every almost-eight-year-old should. But even almost-eight-year-olds can't eat their principles, so she grudgingly buys ice cream for the wurse, a hamburger for The Monster, and a veggie burger for herself. And as she leaves she sneaks out her red felt-tip pen and crosses out the dash between "Lunch" and "menu" on the sign outside.

Despite the below-freezing temperature clawing at their faces, they sit on a bench opposite the high-rise building. Or rather, Elsa and the wurse sit, because The Monster looks at the bench as if it's also about to lick him. He refuses to even touch the greaseproof paper around his hamburger, so the wurse eats that as well. At one point the wurse drops a bit of ice cream on the bench and licks it up without concern, and The Monster looks close to asphyxiation. After the wurse takes a bite of Elsa's burger and she carries on eating it regardless, she has to help him breathe from a paper bag.

When they're finally done, Elsa leans her head back and looks up the façade of the building. It must be fifteen floors high. She takes the envelope from her pocket, slides off the bench, and marches inside. The Monster and the wurse follow her in silence, surrounded by a strong smell of alcogel. Elsa quickly scans the board of residents on the wall and finds the name as written on the envelope, though preceded by the words "Reg. Psychotherapist." Elsa doesn't know what that means, but she's heard a good deal about terropists setting off bombs and causing all sorts of trouble, so a psychoterropist must be even worse.

She heads over to the lift at the other end of the corridor. The wurse stops when they get there, and refuses to take another step. Elsa shrugs and goes in. The Monster follows her, after a certain amount of hesitation, though he is careful not to touch any of the walls.

Elsa evaluates The Monster as they're going up. His beard sticks out of the hood like a large, curious squirrel, which makes him seem less and less dangerous the longer she knows him. The Monster clearly takes note of her examination of him, and he twists his hands uncomfortably. To her own surprise, Elsa realizes that his attitude hurts her feelings.

"If it bothers you so much, you could just stay on guard downstairs with the wurse, you know. It's not like something's going to happen to me while I'm handing over a letter to the terropist."

She talks in normal language, because she refuses to speak in the secret language with him. Her jealousy about Granny's language not even being Granny's from the very beginning hasn't gone away.

"Anyway, you don't have to be right beside me the whole time to be able to guard me," she says, sounding more resentful than she means to. She'd started thinking of The Monster as a friend, but remembers now that he's only here because Granny told him. The Monster just stands there in silence.

When the elevator doors glide open Elsa marches out ahead of him. They pass rows of doors until they find the terropist's door. Elsa knocks so hard she actually hurts her knuckles. The Monster backs off towards the wall on the other side of the narrow corridor, as if he realizes that the person on the other side of the door may peer through the spyhole. He seems to be trying to make himself as small and unfrightening as possible. It's hard not to find this endearing, thinks Elsa—even if "unfrightening" is not a proper word.

Elsa knocks on the door again. Puts her ear against the lock. Another knock. Another silence.

"Empty," says The Monster slowly.

"No shit, Sherlock."

She really doesn't mean to be angry with him, because it's Granny she's angry with. She's just tired. So very, very tired. She looks around and catches sight of two wooden chairs.

"They must be out for lunch, we'll have to wait," she says glumly, and drops despondently into one of the chairs.

As far as Elsa is concerned, the silence goes from pleasant to hard work to unbearable in about one and a half eternities. And when she has occupied herself with everything she has been able to come up with—drumming her fingers against the tabletop, poking out all the stuffing from the chair cushion through a little hole in the fabric, and carving her name into the soft wood of the armrest with the nail of her index finger—she shatters the silence with one of those questions that sound much more accusing than she means it to be.

"Why do you wear soldier's trousers if you're not a soldier?"

The Monster breathes slowly under his hood.

"Old trousers."

"Have you been a soldier?"

The hood moves up and down.

"War is wrong and soldiers are wrong. Soldiers kill people!"

"Not that sort of soldier," The Monster intones.

"There's only one sort of soldier!"

The Monster doesn't answer. Elsa carves a swearword into the wood of the armrest, using her nail. In actual fact she doesn't want to ask the question that's burning inside of her, because she doesn't want The Monster to know how wounded she is. But she can't stop herself. It's one of Elsa's big problems, they say at school. That she can never control herself.

"Was it you who showed my granny Miamas, or was it Granny who showed you?"

She spits out the words. The hood doesn't move, but she can see him breathing. She's just about to repeat the question when she hears, from the inside of it:

"Your granny. Showed. As a child."

He says it the way he says everything in the normal language. As if the words come bickering out of his mouth.

"You were about my age," Elsa says, thinking of the photos of the Werewolf Boy.

The hood moves up and down.

"Did she tell you fairy tales?" she asks quietly, and wishes he'd say no, even though she knows better.

The hood moves up and down.

"Did you meet during a war? Is that why she called you Wolf-heart?" She really doesn't want to ask anymore, because she can feel her jealousy growing. But the hood continues to nod.

"Camp. Camp for the one who flees."

"A refugee camp. Did Granny bring you here with her? Was she the one who arranged it so you could live in the flat?"

There's a long exhalation from the hood.

"Lived in many places. Many homes."

"Foster homes?" He nods. "Why didn't you stay there?"

The hood moves from side to side, very slowly.

"Bad homes. Dangerous. Your granny came to get me."

"Why did you become a soldier when you grew up? Was it so you could go to the same places as Granny?" He nods. "Did you also want to help people? Like she does?" Slowly, the hood moves up and down. "Why didn't you become a doctor like Granny, then?" The Monster rubs his hands together.

"Blood. Don't like . . . blood."

"Smart idea to become a soldier. Are you an orphan?"

The hood is still. The Monster is silent. But she notices that the beard withdraws even deeper into the darkness. Suddenly Elsa nods exuberantly to herself.

"Like the X-Men!" she exclaims with more enthusiasm than she's really willing to give away. Then she clears her throat, composes herself. "X-Men are . . . mutants. And many X-Men are sort of orphans. It's quite cool."

The hood doesn't move. Elsa pulls out some more stuffing from the chair cushion and feels stupid. She was about to add that Harry Potter was also an orphan, and to be like Harry Potter in any way at all is actually the coolest thing there is, but she's starting to realize that The Monster probably doesn't read as much quality literature as one might hope.

"Is Miamas a word in the secret language?" she asks instead. "I mean, is it a word in your language? It doesn't sound like other words in the secret language—I mean, your language."

The hood doesn't move. But the words come more softly now. Not like all the other words from The Monster, which all seem to be on their guard. These sound almost dreamy.

"Mama's language. 'Miamas.' My . . . mama's language."

Elsa looks up and gazes intently into the darkness inside the hood.

"Did you not have the same language?"

The hood moves from side to side.

"Where did your mother come from?" asks Elsa.

"Other place. Other war."

"What does Miamas mean, then?"

The words come out like a sigh.

"'I love.'"

"So it was your kingdom. That was why it was called Miamas. It wasn't at all because I called pajamas 'mjamas.'"

Elsa pulls out the last bit of stuffing and rolls it into a ball to distract herself from her churning jealousy. Typical bloody Granny thing, making up Miamas for you so you'd know your mother loved you, she thinks, abruptly silencing herself when she realizes she is mumbling it aloud.

The Monster shifts his weight from foot to foot. Breathing more slowly. Rubbing his hands.

"Miamas. Not made up. Not pretend. Not for . . . a little one. Miamas. For real for . . . children."

And then, while Elsa closes her eyes to avoid showing her agreement, he goes on tentatively:

"In letter. Grandmother's apology. Was apology to mother," he whispers from under his hood.

Elsa's eyes open and she frowns.

"What?"

The Monster's chest heaves up and down.

"You asked. About Granny's letter. What Granny wrote. Wrote apology to mother. We never found . . . mother."

Their eyes meet halfway, on different terms. A tiny but mutual respect is created between them, there and then, as Miamasians. Elsa realizes that he is telling her what was in the letter because he understands what it's like when people have secrets from you just because you're a child. So she sounds considerably less angry when she asks:

"Did you look for your mother?"

The hood moves up and down.

"For how long?"

"Always. Since . . . the camp."

Elsa's chin drops slightly.

"So that's why Granny was always going off on all these trips? Because you were looking for your mother?"

The speed of The Monster's hand-rubbing increases. His chest heaves. His hood moves down a fraction, then up again, infinitely slowly. And then everything is silent.

Elsa nods and looks down at her lap and, once again, her anger wells up unreasonably inside her.

"My granny was also someone's mother! Did you ever think about that?"

The Monster doesn't answer.

"You don't have to guard me!" Elsa snaps and starts scratching more swearwords into the wooden armrest.

"Not guard," The Monster finally growls. His black eyes emerge from under the hood. "Not guard. Friend."

He disappears back in under the hood. Elsa burrows her gaze into the floor and scrapes her heels against the wall-to-wall carpet, stirring up more dust.

"Thanks," she whispers grumpily. But she says it in the secret language now. The Monster doesn't say anything, but when he rubs his hands together it's no longer as hard and frenetic.

"You don't like talking so much, do you?"

"No . . . but you do. All the time."

And that's the first time Elsa believes he's smiling. Or almost, anyway.

"Touché." Elsa grins.

Elsa doesn't know how long they wait, but they keep waiting long after Elsa has really decided to give up. They wait until the lift door opens with a little *pling* and the woman in the black skirt walks into the corridor. She approaches the office with big strides but freezes midair as she sees the enormous, bearded man and the small girl who looks as if she'd fit into the palm of one of his hands. The girl stares at her. The woman in the black skirt is holding a small plastic box of salad. It's trembling. She looks as if she's considering turning and running away, or maybe, like a child, believes that if she closes her eyes, she'll no longer be visible. Instead, she stands frozen to the spot a few yards away from them, her hands grasping the edge of the box as if it were the edge of a cliff.

Elsa rises from her chair. Wolfheart backs away from them both. If Elsa had been looking at him, she would have noticed, as he moved away, an expression on his face that she had never seen in him before. A sort of fear that no one in the Land-of-Almost-Awake would have believed Wolfheart capable of. But Elsa doesn't look at him as she rises from the chair; she is only looking at the woman in the black skirt.

"I think I have a letter for you," Elsa eventually manages to say.

The woman stands still with her knuckles whitening around the plastic box. Elsa insistently reaches towards her with the envelope.

"It's from my granny. I think she's saying sorry about something."

The woman takes it. Elsa puts her hands in her pockets, because she doesn't quite know what to do with them. It's unclear what the woman in the black skirt is doing here, but Elsa is certain that Granny had some reason for making her bring the letter. Because there's no coincidence in Miamas, or in fairy tales. Everything that's there is meant to be there.

"It's not your name on the envelope, I know that, but it has to be for you."

The woman smells of mint today, not wine. Carefully she opens the letter. Her lips tighten; the letter trembles in her hands.

"I . . . used to have this name, a long time ago. I changed back to my maiden name when I moved into your house, but this was my name when . . . when I met your grandmother."

"After the wave," ventures Elsa.

The woman's lips pinch inwards until they disappear.

"I . . . I planned to change the name on the office door as well. But . . . well, I don't know. It never . . . never happened."

The letter starts trembling even more violently.

"What does it say?" asks Elsa, regretting that she didn't have a quick peek before handing it over. The woman in the black skirt makes all the right movements to start crying, but seems to be out of tears.

"Your grandmother writes 'sorry,'" she says slowly.

"For what?" Elsa asks at once.

"Because she sent you here."

Elsa is just about to correct her and point at Wolfheart and say, "Sent *us* here!" But when she looks up he's already gone. She didn't hear the elevator or the ground-floor door closing. He's just disappeared. "Like a fart through an open window," as Granny used to say when things weren't where they were supposed to be.

The woman with the black skirt moves towards the door, emblazoned with the words "Reg. Psychotherapist," followed by the name she once had. She puts the key in the lock and gestures quickly for Elsa to come in, although it's quite obviously not what she wants at all.

When she notices that Elsa's eyes are still searching for her large-hewn friend, the woman with the black skirt whispers morosely: "I had another office when your granny last came to see me with him. That's why he didn't know you were coming to me. He would never have come if he had known you were coming here. He is . . . is frightened of me."

17

CINNAMON BUN

In one fairy tale from the Land-of-Almost-Awake, a girl from Miamas broke the curse and released the sea-angel. But Granny never explained how it happened.

Elsa sits by the desk of the woman with the black skirt in a chair that Elsa assumes must be for visitors. Judging by the cloud of dust that enveloped Elsa when she sat down, as if she'd accidentally stumbled into a smoke machine at a magic show, she decides the woman can't have very many visitors. Ill at ease, the woman sits on the other side of the desk, reading and rereading the letter from Granny, though Elsa is quite sure by now that she's only pretending to read it so she doesn't have to start talking to Elsa. The woman looked as if she regretted it as soon as she invited Elsa in. A bit like when people in TV series invite vampires in and then, as soon as they've crossed the threshold, think Oh shit! to themselves just before they get bitten. At least this is what Elsa imagines one would be thinking in that type of situation. And that's also how the woman looks. The walls of the office are covered in bookshelves. Elsa has never seen so many books outside a library. She wonders if the woman in the black skirt has ever heard of an iPad.

And then, once again, her thoughts drift off to Granny and the

Land-of-Almost-Awake. For if this woman is the sea-angel, basically she's the third creature from that world, along with Wolfheart and the wurse, that lives in Elsa's building. Elsa doesn't know if this means that Granny took all her stories from the real world and placed them in Miamas, or if the stories from Miamas became so real that the creatures came across to the real world. But the Land-of-Almost-Awake and her house are obviously merging.

Elsa remembers how Granny said that "the best stories are never completely realistic and never entirely made-up." That was what Granny meant when she called certain things "reality-challenged." To Granny, there was nothing that was entirely one thing or another. Stories were completely for real and at the same time not.

Elsa just wishes Granny had said more about the curse of the sea-angel, and how to break it. Because she supposes this is why she sent Elsa here, and if Elsa doesn't figure out what to do she'll probably never find the next letter. And then she'll never find the apology for Mum.

She looks up at the woman on the other side of the desk and clears her throat demonstratively. The woman's eyelids flicker, but she keeps staring down at the letter.

"Did you ever hear about the woman who read herself to death?" asks Elsa.

The woman's gaze glides up from the paper, brushes against her, and then flees back into the letter.

"I don't know what . . . it means," says the woman almost fearfully.

Elsa sighs.

"I've never seen so many books, it's almost insane. Haven't you heard of an iPad?"

The woman's gaze suddenly moves up again. Lingers for a longer time on Elsa.

"I like books."

"You think I don't like books? You can keep your books on the iPad. You don't need a million books in your office."

The woman's pupils dither back and forth over the desk. She gets out a mint tab from a little box and puts it on her tongue, with awkward movements as if her hand and tongue belonged to two different people.

"I like physical books."

"You can have all sorts of books on an iPad."

The woman's fingers tremble slightly. She peers at Elsa, a little as one peers at a person one meets outside a bathroom, where one has spent just a tad too long.

"That's not what I mean by 'a book.' I mean a 'book' in the sense of the dust jacket, the cover, the pages. . . ."

"A book is the text. And you can read the text on an iPad!"

The woman's eyes close and open like large fans.

"I like holding the book when I'm reading."

"You can hold an iPad."

"I mean I like being able to turn the pages," the woman tries to explain.

"You can turn the pages on an iPad."

The woman nods, with the slowest nod Elsa has seen in all her life. Elsa throws her arms out.

"But, you know, do what you like! Have a million books! I was only, like, asking. It's still a book if you're reading it on an iPad. Soup is soup whatever bowl it's in."

The woman's mouth moves spasmodically at the corners, spreading cracks in the surrounding skin.

"I've never heard that proverb."

"It's from Miamas," says Elsa.

The woman looks down at her lap. Doesn't answer.

She really doesn't look like an angel, thinks Elsa. But on the other hand she doesn't look like a drunk either. So maybe it evens itself out. Maybe this is how halfway creatures look.

"Why did Granny bring Wolfheart here?" asks Elsa.

"Sorry—who?"

"You said Granny brought him here. And that's why he's afraid of you."

"I didn't know you called him Wolfheart."

"That's his name. Why is he afraid of you if you don't even know who he is?"

The woman puts her hands in her lap and studies them as if she just caught sight of them for the first time and wonders what in the name of God they're doing there.

"Your grandmother brought him here to talk about the war. She thought I'd be able to help him, but he got scared of me. He got scared of all my questions and scared of . . . of his memories, I think," she says at last. "He has seen many, many wars. He has lived almost his whole life at war, in one way or another. It does . . . does unbearable things to a human."

"Why does he carry on like that with his hands?"

"Sorry?"

"He washes his hands all the time. Like he's trying to wash off a smell of poo, sort of thing."

"Sometimes the brain does strange things to one after a tragedy. I think maybe he's trying to wash away . . ."

She becomes silent. Looks down.

"What?" Elsa demands to know.

" . . . the blood," the woman concludes, emptily.

"Has he killed someone?"

"I don't know."

"Is he sick in the head?"

"Excuse me?"

"You're a terropist, aren't you?"

"Yes."

"Can't they be fixed, people who are sick in the head? Maybe it's sort of rude to call them sick. Is it? Is he all broken up in the head?"

"All people who have seen war are broken."

Elsa shrugs. "He shouldn't have become a soldier, then. It's because of soldiers that we have wars."

"I don't think he was that sort of soldier. He was a peace soldier."

"There's only one sort of soldier," Elsa snorts.

And she knows she's a hypocrite for saying it. Because she hates soldiers and she hates war, but she knows that if Wolfheart had not fought the shadows in the War-Without-End, the entire Land-of-Almost-Awake would have been swallowed up by gray death. And she thinks a lot about that. Times you're allowed to fight, and times when you're not. Elsa thinks about how Granny used to say, "You have standards and I have double standards, and so I win." But having double standards doesn't make Elsa feel like a winner.

"Maybe so," says the woman in a low voice that skims over Elsa's thoughts.

"You don't have very many patients here, do you?" says Elsa with a pointed nod across the room.

The woman doesn't answer. Her hands fidget with Granny's letter. Elsa sighs impatiently.

"What else does Granny write? Does she say sorry for not being able to save your family?"

The woman's eyes waver.

"Yes. Among . . . among other things."

Elsa nods.

"And for sending me here?"

"Yes."

"Why?"

"Because she knew you'd ask a lot of questions. As a psychologist, I suppose I'm used to being the one who asks the questions."

"What does 'Reg. Psychoterropist' mean?"

"Registered psychotherapist."

"Oh, I thought it had something to do with bombs."

The woman doesn't quite know how to respond to that one. Elsa throws out her arm defensively, and snorts, "Well, maybe it sounds stupid now, but it seemed more logical at the time! Everything seems obvious in hindsight!"

The woman does something with the corner of her mouth that Elsa thinks might be a smile of some kind. But it's more like a stiff twitching, as if the muscles around her mouth are new to this game. Elsa looks around the office again. There are no photos here, as there were in the woman's flat. Only books.

"You got any good ones, then?" she asks, scanning the shelves.

"I don't know what you think is good," the woman answers carefully.

"Do you have any Harry Potters?"

"No."

"Not even one?" Elsa asks, incredulous.

"No."

"You have *all these books* and not a *single* Harry Potter? And they let you fix people whose heads are broken?"

The woman doesn't answer. Elsa leans back and tips the chair in that exact way her mum really hates. The woman takes another mint from the tin on the desk. She makes a movement towards Elsa to offer her one, but Elsa shakes her head.

"Do you smoke?" asks Elsa.

The woman looks surprised. Elsa shrugs.

"Granny also used to have a lot of sweets when she couldn't smoke, and she usually wasn't allowed to indoors."

"I've stopped," says the woman.

"Stopped or taking a break? It's not the same thing," Elsa informs her.

The woman nods, setting a new record for slowness.

"That would be more of a philosophical question. So it's difficult to answer."

Elsa shrugs again.

"Where did you meet Granny? Was it after the wave? Or is that also difficult to answer?"

"It's a long story."

"I like long stories."

The woman's hands take cover in her lap.

"I was on holiday. Or . . . we . . . me and my family. We were on holiday. And it happened . . . an accident happened."

"The tsunami," says Elsa gently.

The woman's gaze flies around the room and then she says, in passing, as if it only just occurred to her:

"Your grandmother found . . . found me . . ."

The woman sucks so hard on the mint in her mouth that her cheeks look like Granny's that time she was going to "borrow" petrol from Elsa's dad's Audi by sucking it out of a plastic tube.

"After my husband and my . . . my boys . . ." the woman begins to say. The last words stumble and fall into the chasm between the others as they pass. As if the woman had suddenly forgotten that she was in the middle of a sentence.

"Drowned?" Elsa fills in, and then feels ashamed of herself when she realizes that it's probably very unpleasant to speak that word to someone whose family did.

But the woman just nods, without looking angry. And then Elsa switches to the secret language and asks briskly:

"Do you also know our secret language?"

"Excuse me?"

"Ah, nothing," Elsa mumbles in the usual language and looks down at her shoes.

It was a test. And Elsa is surprised that the sea-angel doesn't know the secret language, because everyone in the Land-of-Almost-Awake knows the secret language. But maybe that's a part of the curse, she thinks.

The woman looks at her watch.

"Shouldn't you be at school?"

Elsa shrugs.

"It's Christmas holidays."

The woman nods. Probably more or less at a normal speed now.

"Have you been to Miamas?" asks Elsa.

"Is this some kind of joke?"

"If I'd been joking I would have said, a blind guy walks into a bar. And a table. And a couple of chairs."

The woman doesn't answer. Elsa throws out her arms.

"You get it? That a *bliiind* guy walks into a bar and a tab—"

The woman looks into her eyes. Smiles faintly.

"I got it. Thanks."

Elsa shrugs sourly.

"If you get it, laugh."

The woman takes such a deep breath that if you threw a coin into it you'd never hear it hit the bottom.

"Did you think of that one yourself?" she asks after that.

"Which one?" Elsa counters.

"About the blind guy."

"No. Granny told me."

"My boys used to . . . they used to tell jokes like that. Asking something strange and then you had to answer and then they said something and laughed." As she says the world "laughed" she stands up, her legs as fragile as the wings of paper planes.

And then everything changes quickly. Her whole manner. Her way of talking. Even her way of breathing.

"I think you should leave now," she says, standing by the window with her back towards Elsa. Her voice is weak, but almost hostile.

"Why?"

"I want you to leave," the woman repeats in a hard voice.

"But why? I've walked halfway across the city to give you Granny's letter and you've hardly had time to tell me anything and now you want me to leave? Do you get how cold it is out there?"

"You . . . shouldn't have come here."

"I came here because you were Granny's friend."

"I don't need charity! I can manage on my own," says the woman grimly.

"Sure, you're really managing bloody well. Really. But I'm not here out of charity," Elsa manages to reply.

"Well, get out then, you little brat! Get the hell out!" hisses the woman, still without turning around.

Elsa starts breathing hard, frightened by the sudden aggression, and insulted by the woman not even looking at her. She hops off the chair with clenched fists.

"Right, then! So my mum was wrong when she said you were just tired! And Granny was right! You're just a bloody—"

And then it goes as with all anger attacks. They don't just consist of one anger, but of many. A long series of angers, flung into a volcano in one's breast until it erupts. Elsa is angry at the woman in the black skirt because she doesn't say anything to make anything more understandable in this idiotic fairy tale. And she's angry at

Wolfheart for abandoning her because he's afraid of this idiotic psychoterropist. And most of all she's angry at Granny. And this idiotic fairy tale. And all those angers together are too much for her. She knows long before the word leaves her lips how wrong it is to yell it out:

"DRUNK! YOU'RE NOTHING BUT A DRUNK!!!"

She regrets it terribly in the same instant. But it's too late. The woman in the black skirt turns around. Her face is contorted into a thousand broken pieces of a mirror.

"Out!"

"I didn't m—" Elsa begins to say, reeling backwards across the office floor, holding out her hands, wanting to apologize. "Sorr—"

"OOOUUUT!" screams the woman, hysterically clawing at the air as if looking for something to throw at her.

And Elsa runs.

She hurtles along the corridor and down the stairs and through a door to the vestibule, sobbing so violently that she loses her footing, tumbles blindly, and falls headlong. She feels her backpack whack against the back of her head and waits for the pain when her cheekbone meets the floor. But instead she feels soft, black fur. And then everything bursts for her. She hugs the enormous animal so hard that she can feel it gasping for air.

"Elsa." Alf's voice can be heard from the front door. Absolutely cut-and-dried. Not like a question. "Come on, for Christ's sake," he grunts. "Let's go home. You can't lie there bloody sobbing your heart out."

Elsa wants to yell out the whole story to Alf. Everything about the sea-angel and how Granny sends her out on idiotic adventures and she doesn't even know what she's expected to do, and how Wolfheart abandoned her when she needed him most and everything about Mum and the "sorry" Elsa had hoped to find here, and everything about Halfie who will come and change everything. How Elsa is drowning in loneliness. She wants to shout it all out to Alf. But she knows he wouldn't understand anyway. Because no one does when you're almost eight.

"What are you doing here?" she sobs.

"You gave me the damned address," he mutters. "Someone had to bloody pick you up. I've been driving a taxicab for thirty years, so I know you just don't leave little girls anywhere, any-old-how." He's quiet for a few breaths before adding, into the floor: "And your grandmother would have bloody beaten the life out of me if I hadn't picked you up."

Elsa nods and wipes her face on the wurse's pelt.

"Is that thing coming as well?" Alf asks grouchily. The wurse looks back at him even more grumpily. Elsa nods and tries not to start crying again.

"It'll have to go in the trunk, then," says Alf firmly.

But obviously that is not how things end up. Elsa keeps her face buried in its fur all the way home. It's one of the very, very best things about wurses: they're waterproof.

There's opera coming from the car stereo. At least Elsa thinks it must be opera. She hasn't really heard very much opera, but she's heard it mentioned and she supposes this is what it sounds like. When they're about halfway home, Alf peers with concern at her in the rearview mirror.

"Is there anything you want?"

"Like what?"

"I don't know. Coffee?"

Elsa raises her head and glares at him.

"I'm seven!"

"What the hell's that got to do with it?"

"Do you know any seven-year-olds who drink coffee?"

"I don't know very many seven-year-olds."

"I can tell."

"Well, bloody forget it, then," he grunts.

Elsa lowers her face into the wurse's pelt. Alf swears a bit in the front, and then after a while he passes her a paper bag. It has the same writing on it as the bakery where Granny always went.

"There's a cinnamon bun in there," he says, adding, "But don't bloody cry all over it or it won't taste good."

Elsa cries on it. It's good anyway.

When they get to the house she runs from the garage up to the flat without even thanking Alf or saying good-bye to the wurse, and without thinking about how Alf has seen the wurse now and might even call the police. Without saying a word to him, she walks right past the dinner that George has put on the kitchen table. When Mum comes home she pretends to be asleep.

And when the drunk starts yelling on the stairs that night, and the singing starts again, Elsa, for the first time, does what all the others in the house do.

She pretends she doesn't hear.

18

SMOKE

Every fairy tale has a dragon. Thanks to Granny, that is. . . .

Elsa is having terrible nightmares tonight. She's always dreaded closing her eyes and no longer being able to get to the Land-of-Almost-Awake. The worst thing would be a dreamless sleep. But this is the night she learns of something even worse. Because she can't get to the Land-of-Almost-Awake, and yet she dreams about it. She can see it clearly from above, as if she's lying on her stomach on top of a huge glass dome, peering down at it. Without being able to smell any smells or hear any laughter or feel the rush of wind over her face when the cloud animals take off. It's the most terrifying dream of all the eternities.

Miamas is burning.

She sees all the princes and princesses and the wurses and the dream hunters and the sea-angel and the innocent people of the Land-of-Almost-Awake running for their lives. Behind them the shadows are closing in, banishing imagination and leaving nothing but death as they pass. Elsa tries to find Wolfheart in the inferno, but he's gone. Cloud animals, mercilessly butchered, lie in the ashes. All of Granny's tales are burning.

One figure wanders among the shadows. A slim man enveloped

in a cloud of cigarette smoke. That's the only scent Elsa can smell up there on top of the dome, the smell of Granny's tobacco. Suddenly the figure looks up and two clear blue eyes penetrate the haze. A shroud of mist seeps between his thin lips. Then he points directly at Elsa, his forefinger deformed into a gray claw, and he shouts something, and in the next moment hundreds of shadows launch themselves from the ground and engulf her.

Elsa wakes up when she throws herself out of the bed and lands facedown against the floor. She cowers there, her chest heaving, her hands covering her throat. It feels as if millions of eternities have passed before she can trust that she's back in the real world. She's not had a single nightmare since Granny and the cloud animals first brought her to the Land-of-Almost-Awake. She had forgotten how nightmares feel. She stands up, sweaty and exhausted, checks to see that she's not been bitten by one of the shadows, and tries to get her thoughts into order.

She hears someone talking in the hall and has to muster all her powers of concentration to scatter the mists of sleep and be able to hear what's happening.

"I see! But surely you understand, Ulrika, that it's a bit odd for them to be calling you. Why don't they call Kent? Kent is actually the chairman of this residents' association and I am in charge of information, and it's common practice for the accountant to call the chairman with these types of errands. Not just any old person!"

Elsa understands that "any old person" is an insult. Mum's sigh as she answers is so deep that it feels as if Elsa's sheets are ruffled by the draft:

"I don't know why they called me, Britt-Marie. But the accountant said he would come here today to explain everything."

Elsa opens the bedroom door and stands in her pajamas in the doorway. Not only Britt-Marie is standing there in the hall; Lennart and Maud and Alf are also there. Samantha is sleeping on the landing. Mum is wearing only her dressing gown, hurriedly tied across her belly. Maud catches sight of Elsa and smiles mildly, with a cookie tin in her arms. Lennart gulps from a coffee thermos.

For once Alf doesn't look entirely in a bad mood, which means he only looks irritated in an everyday way. He nods curtly at Elsa, as if she has forced him into a secret. Only then does Elsa remember that she left him and the wurse in the garage yesterday when she ran up to the flat. Panic wells up inside of her, but Alf glares at her and makes a quick "stay calm" gesture, so that's what she tries to do. She looks at Britt-Marie and tries to figure out if she's worked up today because she has found the wurse, or if it's a quite normal fuss about the usual Britt-Marie stuff. It seems to be the latter, thank God, but directed at Mum.

"So the landlords have suddenly had the notion that they might be willing to sell the flats to us? After all the years that Kent has been writing them letters! Now they have *suddenly* decided! Just like that, easy-peasy? And then they contact you instead of Kent? That's curious, don't you find that curious, Ulrika?"

Mum tightens her dressing gown sash. "Maybe they couldn't get hold of Kent. And maybe since I've lived here so long they thought—"

"We've actually lived here the longest, Ulrika. Kent and I have lived here longer than anyone else!"

"Alf has lived in the house the longest," Mum corrects her.

"Granny has lived here the longest," Elsa mumbles, but no one seems to hear her. Especially not Britt-Marie.

"Isn't Kent away on a business trip?" asks Mum.

Britt-Marie pauses at this and nods imperceptibly.

"Maybe that's why they didn't get hold of him. That's why I called you as soon as I hung up after speaking to the acc—"

"But surely it's *common practice* to contact the chairperson of the leaseholders' association!" says Britt-Marie with consternation.

"It isn't a leaseholders' association yet," Mum sighs.

"But it will be!"

"And that is what the landlords' accountant wants to come and talk about today—he says they're finally willing to convert our rental contracts into leaseholds. That's what I've been trying to tell you. As soon as I'd hung up the phone after talking to him, I contacted you. And then you woke up the whole house and now here we are. What more do you want me to do, Britt-Marie?"

"What sort of nonsense is that, coming here on a Saturday? Surely one doesn't have meetings like this on a Saturday, surely one doesn't, Ulrika? Do you think one does? Probably you do, Ulrika!"

Mum massages her temples. Britt-Marie inhales and exhales fairly demonstratively and turns to Lennart and Maud and Alf for support. Maud tries to smile encouragingly. Lennart offers Britt-Marie a shot of coffee while they are waiting. Alf looks as if he's now approaching his usual level of ill-humor.

"Well we can't have the meeting without Kent," Britt-Marie splutters.

"No, of course, only if Kent can make it back," Mum agrees exhaustedly. "Why don't you try calling him again?"

"His plane hasn't landed yet! He's actually on a *business trip*, Ulrika!"

Alf grunts something behind them. Britt-Marie spins around. Alf pushes his hands into his jacket pockets and grunts something again.

"Sorry?" say Mum and Britt-Marie at the same time, but in diametrically opposed tones of voice.

"I'm just bloody saying that I sent Kent a text twenty minutes ago when you started making a bloody racket about this, and he got back to tell me he's on his bloody way," says Alf, and then adds, "The idiot wouldn't miss this for all the tea in China."

Britt-Marie seems not to hear the last bit. She brushes invisible dust from her skirt and folds her hands and gives Alf a superior glance, because she knows quite clearly that it's impossible for Kent to be on his way here, because, in fact, his plane hasn't landed yet and, in fact, he's on a business trip. But then there comes the sound of the door slamming on the ground floor and Kent's footsteps. You can tell they're Kent's because someone is screaming German into a telephone, the way Nazis speak in American films.

"Ja, Klaus! JA! We will dizcuzz thiz in Frankfurt!"

Britt-Marie immediately sets off down the stairs to meet him and tell him about the impudence that's been impudent enough to take place here in his absence.

George comes out of the kitchen behind Mum, wearing jogging shorts, a very green sweater, and an even greener apron. He gives them an amused look, while holding a smoking frying pan.

"Anyone want some breakfast? I've made eggs." He looks as if he's going to add that there are also some newly bought protein bars on offer, but seems to change his mind when he realizes they may run out.

"I've brought some cookies," says Maud expansively, giving Elsa the whole tin and patting her tenderly on the cheek. "You have that, I can get some more," she whispers and walks into their flat.

"Is there coffee?" asks Lennart nervously, having another shot of standby coffee as he follows her.

Kent strides up the stairs and appears in the doorway. He is wearing jeans and an expensive jacket. Elsa knows that because Kent usually tells her how much his clothes cost, as if he's awarding points in the final of the Eurovision Song Contest. Britt-Marie hurries along behind him, mumbling repeatedly, "The rudeness, the sheer *rudeness* of not calling you, of just calling any old person. Isn't that just so rude? Things can't be allowed to go on like this, Kent."

Kent doesn't really acknowledge his wife's raving, but points dramatically at Elsa's mum.

"I want to know *exactly* what the accountant said when he called."

But before Mum has time to say anything, Britt-Marie brushes off some invisible dust from Kent's arm, and whispers to him in a radically changed tone of voice.

"Maybe you should go down first and change your shirt, Kent?"

"Please, Britt-Marie, we're doing business here," Kent says dismissively, more or less like Elsa when Mum wants her to wear something green.

She looks crestfallen.

"I can throw it in the machine, come along, Kent. There are freshly ironed shirts in your wardrobe. You really can't be wearing a wrinkly shirt when the accountant comes, Kent, what will the accountant think of us then? Will he think we can't iron our shirts?" She laughs nervously.

Mum opens her mouth to try to say something again, but Kent catches sight of George.

"Ah! You've got eggs?" Kent bursts out enthusiastically.

George nods with satisfaction. Kent immediately darts past Mum into the flat. Britt-Marie hurries after him with a frown. When she passes Mum, Britt-Marie looks bothered as she lets slip, "Oh well, when one is busy with a career like you are, Ulrika, there's no time to clean, of course not." Even though every inch of the flat is in perfect order.

Mum ties the sash of her dressing gown round her a little tighter, and says, with a deeply controlled sigh, "Just come on in, all of you. Make yourselves at home."

Elsa dives into her room and changes out of her pajamas into jeans as quick as she can, so she can run down and check on the wurse in the cellar while everyone is busy up here. Kent interrogates Mum in the kitchen about the accountant, and Britt-Marie echoes him with an "mmm" after every other word.

The only one who stays in the front hall is Alf. Elsa sticks her thumbs in her jeans pockets and pokes her toes against the edge of the threshold, trying to avoid looking him in the eye.

"Thanks for not saying anything about the . . ." she starts to say, but she stops herself before she has to say "wurse."

Alf shakes his head grumpily.

"You shouldn't have rushed off like that. If you've taken that animal on, you have to bloody shoulder your responsibility for it, even if you're a kid."

"I'm not a bloody kid!" snaps Elsa.

"So quit behaving like one, then."

"Touché," Elsa whispers at the threshold.

"The animal is in the storage unit. I've put up some sheets of plywood so people can't see inside. Told it to keep its mouth shut. I think it got the point. But you have to find a better hiding place. People will find it sooner or later," says Alf.

Elsa understands that when he says "people" he means Britt-Marie. And she knows he's right. She has a terribly bad conscience about abandoning the wurse yesterday. Alf could have called the police and they would have shot it. Elsa abandoned it like Granny abandoned Mum, and this scares her more than any nightmares.

"What are they talking about?" she asks Alf, with a nod towards the kitchen, to shake off the thought.

Alf snorts.

"The bloody leaseholds."

"What does it mean?"

"Jesus, I can't stand here explaining everything," he groans. "The difference between a rental contract and a leasehold in a bloo—"

"I know what a bloody leasehold is, I'm not bloody thick," says Elsa.

"Why are you asking, then?" says Alf defensively.

"I'm asking what it *means*; why are they all talking about it!" Elsa clarifies, in the way one clarifies things without being very clear at all.

"Kent has been going on about these sodding leaseholds ever since he moved back in, he won't be satisfied until he can wipe his ass with the money he's shat out first," explains Alf, in the manner of one who doesn't know very many seven-year-olds. At first Elsa is going to ask what Alf meant when he said that Kent "moved back in," but she decides to take one thing at a time.

"Won't we all make money? You and Mum and George and all of us?"

"If we sell the flats and move, yeah," grunts Alf.

Elsa ponders. Alf creaks his leather jacket.

"And that's what Kent wants, the bastard. He's always wanted to move out of here."

That is why she's having all these nightmares, she realizes. Because if the creatures from the Land-of-Almost-Awake turn up in the house now, then maybe the house will start to become a part of the Land-of-Almost-Awake, and if they all want to sell their flats, then . . .

"Then we won't be escaping Miamas. We'll be leaving of our own free will," says Elsa out loud to herself.

"What?"

"Nothing," mumbles Elsa.

The door slamming at the bottom of the house echoes through the stairwell. Then discreet footsteps, heading up. It's the accountant.

Britt-Marie drowns out Kent's voice in the kitchen. She doesn't get any response from Kent insofar as the shirt change goes, so she compensates with a lot of indignation about other things. There is a rich supply of such topics. It's difficult for her to decide which is most upsetting, of course, but she has time to run through several matters, including her threat to call the police if Elsa's mum doesn't *immediately* move Granny's car from Britt-Marie's space in the garage, and also that Britt-Marie will make the police break the lock of the stroller that's still chained up by the entrance, and that she won't hesitate to put pressure on the landlord to put up cameras on the stairs, so they can stop the vile malpractice of people coming and going as they please and putting up notices without first informing the head of information. She's interrupted by the very short man with the very friendly face now standing in the doorway, knocking tentatively against the doorframe.

"I'm the accountant," he says amicably.

And when he catches sight of Elsa, he winks at her. As if they share a secret. Or at least Elsa thinks that's what he means.

Kent steps authoritatively out of the kitchen with his hands on his hips over his overcoat and looks the accountant up and down.

"Well, well? What about these leaseholds, then?" he demands at once. "What price per square foot are you offering?"

Britt-Marie storms out of the kitchen from behind and points at the accountant accusingly.

"How did you get in?"

"The door was open," says the accountant amicably.

Kent breaks in impatiently. "So about the leaseholds: What's your price?"

The accountant points amicably at his briefcase and makes an amicable gesture towards the kitchen.

"Should we sit down, perhaps?"

"There's coffee," Lennart says expansively.

"And cookies," Maud says with a nod.

"And eggs!" George hollers from the kitchen.

"Please excuse the mess, they're all so preoccupied with their careers in this family," says Britt-Marie well-meaningly. Mum does her absolute best to pretend she didn't hear that. As they all head into the kitchen, Britt-Marie stops, turns to Elsa, and clasps her hands together.

"You do understand, dear, I would obviously never ever think you and your grandmother's friends had anything to do with junkies. Obviously I'm not to know if the gentleman who was looking for you yesterday took drugs or not. That's not at all what I mean to say."

Elsa gawks at her, puzzled.

"What? What friends? Who was asking for me yesterday?"

She almost asks, "Was it Wolfheart?" and then stops herself, because she can't imagine how Britt-Marie could possibly know that Wolfheart is her friend.

"Your friend who was here looking for you yesterday. The one I jettisoned from the premises. There's a smoking ban on the stairs, you can tell him that. That is not how we behave in this leaseholders' association. I understand that you and your granny have very curious acquaintances, but rules apply to everyone, they really do!" She straightens an invisible wrinkle in her skirt and clasps her hands on her stomach before continuing: "You know who I mean. He was very slim and stood here smoking on the stairs. He was looking for a child, a family friend, he said, and then he described you. He looked exceedingly unpleasant, actually, so I told him that in this leaseholders' association we do not allow smoking indoors."

Elsa's heart shrinks. Consumes all the oxygen in her body. She has to hold on to the doorframe to stop herself collapsing. No one sees her, not even Alf. But she understands what's about to happen in this adventure now.

Because every fairy tale has a dragon.

19

SPONGE CAKE MIX

Fairy tales from Miamas tell of an infinite number of ways to defeat a dragon. But if this dragon is a shadow, the most evil kind of being one can possibly imagine, and yet it looks like a human, then what? Elsa doubts that even Wolfheart could defeat something like that, even when he was the most renowned warrior in the Land-of-Almost-Awake. And now? When he's afraid of snot and can't wash away the thought of blood from his own fingers?

Elsa doesn't know anything about the shadow. Only that she has seen it twice, the first time at the undertaker's and then from the bus that day on her way to school. And that she's dreamed of it, and now it's come to the house looking for her. And there's no coincidence in Miamas. In fairy tales everything is always exactly as it's meant to be.

So this must have been what Granny meant by "protect your castle, protect your friends." Elsa only wishes that Granny had given her an army to do it with.

She waits until late at night, when it's dark enough for a child and a wurse to pass unseen under Britt-Marie's balcony, before she goes down to the cellar. George is out jogging; Mum is still out preparing everything for tomorrow. Since the meeting with the accountant this morning she's been talking endlessly on the telephone with the whale-woman from the undertaker's and the florist and the vicar and then with the hospital and the vicar again. Elsa has been sitting in her room reading *Spider-Man*, doing her best not to think of tomorrow. It hasn't gone very well.

She brings the wurse some cookies she got from Maud and, once the contents have been mopped up, she has to snatch back the tin so quickly that she almost gets an incisor manicure. Granny always said that wurse saliva was bloody hard to get off in the washing-up, and Elsa is planning to give the tin back to Maud. But the wurse, who in all ways is a typical wurse, rummages quite ravenously in her backpack, apparently having considerable difficulty understanding how she could have come down with just one paltry tin for it.

"I'll try to get you some more cookies, but for now you're going to have to eat this." She opens a thermos. "This is sponge cake mix. I don't know how to mix it properly though," she mumbles apologetically. "I found it in the cupboard in the kitchen and it said 'ready sponge cake mix' on the packet, but it was only powder. So I added water. It's more like gunk than proper mix."

The wurse looks skeptical, but its towel-sized tongue immediately licks all the gunk out of the thermos anyway. Just to be on the safe side. An insanely flexible tongue is one of the most prominent superpowers of wurses.

"There's been a man here looking for me," whispers Elsa into its ear, trying to sound brave. "I think he's one of the shadows. We have to be on our guard."

The wurse buffets its nose against her throat. She throws her arms around it, and feels the taut muscles under its fur. It tries to seem playful, but she understands that it's doing what wurses do best: preparing for battle. She loves it for that.

"I don't know where it comes from, Granny never told me about those kinds of dragons."

The wurse buffets her throat again and looks at her with large, empathic eyes. It seems to be wishing it could tell her everything. Elsa wishes Wolfheart were here. She rang his bell just now but there was no answer. She didn't want to call out, in case Britt-Marie smelled a rat, but she made a loud sniffing sound through the mail slot to clearly signal she was about to sneeze the kind of sticky sneeze that instantly covers everything in camouflage paint. It had no effect.

"Wolfheart has disappeared," she finally admits to the wurse.

Elsa tries to be brave. It goes quite well while they are walking through the cellar. And it's quite okay while they go up the cellar stairs. But when they're standing in the vestibule inside the main door, she senses the smell of tobacco smoke, the same kind of tobacco that Granny used to smoke, and a lingering fear from her nightmare paralyzes her. Her shoes weigh a thousand tons. Her head thumps as if something has worked itself loose and is rattling around in there.

It's strange how quickly the significance of a certain smell can change, depending on what path it decides to take through the brain. It's strange how close love and fear live to each other.

She tells herself she's just imagining it, but it doesn't help. The wurse stands patiently next to her, but her shoes won't budge.

A newspaper blows past outside the window. It's the kind of newspaper you get through the mail slot even if you have a "No junk mail, please!" sticker on the door. It reminds Elsa of Granny. She stands there, still frozen, and the newspaper makes her angry, because it's Granny who put her in this situation. It's all Granny's fault.

Elsa remembers the time Granny called the newspaper office and gave them a roasting for putting the paper in her mail slot even though she had a "No junk mail, ever. Thanks!" message in surprisingly clear letters on the door. Elsa had thought a lot about why it said "Thanks!" because Elsa's mum always said that if one can't say thanks as if one means it, one may as well not bother. And it didn't sound like the note on Granny's door meant it at all.

But the people answering the telephone at the office of the newspaper told Granny their newspaper wasn't in the business of advertising but in fact "social information," which can be put in people's mailboxes irrespective of whether people thank them not to do so. Granny had demanded to know who owned the company that produced the newspaper, and after that she demanded a word with him. The people at the other end of the telephone line said that surely Granny could understand that the owner did not have time for this sort of nonsense.

Of course, they shouldn't have said that, because there were actually an awful lot of things that Granny didn't "surely understand" at all. Also, unlike the man who owned the company that produced the free newspaper, she had a lot of spare time. "Never mess with someone who has more spare time than you do," Granny used to say. Elsa used to translate that as, "Never mess with someone who's perky for her age."

In the following days Granny had picked up Elsa as usual from school, and then they'd patrolled the block with yellow IKEA carrier bags, ringing all the doorbells. People seemed to find it a bit weird, especially since everyone knows you're actually not allowed to take those yellow IKEA bags from the store. If anyone started asking too many questions, Granny just said they were from an environmental organization collecting recyclable paper. And then people didn't dare make any more fuss. "People are afraid of environmental organizations, they think we'll storm the flat and accuse them of not handling their waste properly. They watch too many films," Granny had explained as she and Elsa loaded the stuffed carrier bags into Renault. Elsa never quite understood what kinds of films Granny had seen, and where that sort of thing would ever happen. She did know that Granny hated environmental organizations, which she called "panda fascists."

Whatever the case, you're actually not supposed to take those yellow carrier bags out of the store. Of course, Granny had just shrugged it off. "I never stole the bags, I just haven't given them back yet," she muttered, and gave Elsa a thick felt-tip pen to write with. And then Elsa said she wanted at least four tubs of Ben & Jerry's New York Super Fudge Chunk for this. And then Granny said, "One!" and then Elsa said, "Three!" and then Granny said, "Two!" and then Elsa said, "Three, or I'm telling Mum!" and then Granny yelled, "I'm not negotiating with terrorists!" And then Elsa pointed out that if one looked up "terrorist" on Wikipedia there were quite a lot of things in the definition of the word that applied to Granny but not a single one that applied to Elsa. "The goal of terrorists is to create chaos, and Mum says that's exactly what you're busy doing all day long," said Elsa. And then Granny had agreed to give Elsa four tubs if she just took the felt-tip pen and promised to keep her mouth shut. And so that's what Elsa did. Late into the night she'd sat in the dark in Renault on the other side of town, on guard duty, while Granny ran in and out of houses' entrances with her yellow IKEA carrier bags. The next morning the man who owned the company that produced the free newspaper was woken by the neighbors ringing his doorbell, very upset because someone had apparently filled the lift with hundreds of copies of the free newspaper. Every mailbox was stuffed full of them, and every square inch of the large glass entrance door had been covered in taped-up copies, and outside every flat great tottering piles had been left that collapsed and fell down the stairs when the doors were opened. On every copy of the newspaper, the man's name had been written in large, neat felt-tip letters, and just below, "Complimentry social information, for yor reading plesure!!!"

On the way back home, Granny and Elsa had stopped at a gas station to buy ice cream. A few days later Granny called the newspaper once again, and after that she never received a single free copy.

"Coming in or going?"

Alf's voice cuts through the gloom of the stairwell like laughter. Elsa turns around and instinctively wants to throw herself into his arms, but she stops herself because she realizes he would probably dislike that almost as much as Wolfheart would. He shoves his hands in his pockets with a creak of his leather jacket and nods sharply at the door.

"In or out? There are others apart from you who fancy a bloody walk, you know."

Elsa and the wurse give him blank looks. He mutters something and goes past them and opens the door. Immediately they fall into step just behind him, though he never asked for their company. When they've gone around the corner of the house, out of sight from Britt-Marie's balcony, the wurse backs into a bush and growls at them as politely as can be expected of a wurse in need of a bit of concentration. They turn away. Alf looks unamused in every possible way by his uninvited company. Elsa clears her throat and tries to think of something to make small talk about, to keep him there.

"The car's going well, is it?" she bursts out, because that's what she's heard her dad say when he's at a loss.

Alf nods. Nothing more. Elsa breathes loudly.

"What did the accountant say at the meeting?" she asks instead, in the hope that this might make Alf as upset and talkative as he gets at the residents' meetings. It's easier to get people talking about things they dislike than things they like, Elsa has noticed. And it's easier not to get frightened of shadows in the dark when someone is talking, whatever they're talking about.

"That accountant bastard said the owners had decided to sell the bloody flats to the residents' association bastards, if everyone in the house agrees."

Elsa observes the corners of his mouth. He almost seems to be smiling.

"Is that funny?"

"Are you living in the same house as me? They'll solve the Israel-Palestine conflict before people in this house agree about anything."

"Will anyone want to sell their flat if the house is converted to leaseholds?" she asks.

The corners of Alf's mouth flatten into a more Alf-like shape.

"I don't know about wanting, most will bloody well have to."

"Why?"

"Good area. Expensive bloody flats. Most people in the house won't be able to afford that kind of bastard bank loan."

"Will you have to move?"

"Probably."

"Mum and George and me, then?"

"I don't bloody know, do I?"

Elsa thinks.

"What about Maud and Lennart?"

"You've got a bloody lot of questions."

"Well, what are you doing out here if you don't want to talk?"

Alf's jacket creaks towards the wurse in the bush.

"I was only going for a bloody walk. No one bloody invited you and that thing."

"It's just insane how much you swear, did anyone ever tell you that? My dad says it's a sign of a bad vocabulary."

Alf glares at her and shoves his hands in his pockets.

"Maud and Lennart will have to move. And the girl and her kid on the first bloody floor as well, most likely. The psychologist wench you went to yesterday, I don't know, she probably has a hell of a lot of money—"

He stops himself. Summons some kind of self-restraint.

"That . . . lady. She probably has a . . . heck of a lot of money, that . . . woman," he self-corrects.

"What did my granny think about the leasehold?"

There's another brief twitch at the corners of Alf's mouth.

"Usually the diametric opposite of what Britt-Marie thought."

Elsa draws miniature snow-angels with her shoe.

"Maybe it'll be good? If there are leaseholds, then maybe everyone can move somewhere . . . good?" she says tentatively.

"It's good here. We're doing fine here. This is our bloody home."

Elsa doesn't protest. This is her home too.

Another free newspaper tumbles past in the wind. It gets caught on her foot for a moment, before it tears itself free and keeps rolling like an angry little starfish. It makes Elsa furious again. Gets her thinking about how much Granny was willing to fight to get them to stop putting newspapers in her letter box. It makes Elsa furious because it was a typical Granny thing to do, because Granny was only doing it for Elsa's sake. Granny things were always like that. For Elsa's sake.

Because Granny actually liked those newspapers, she used to stuff them into her shoes when it had been raining. But one day when Elsa read on the Internet how many trees it took to make just one edition of a newspaper, she put up "No junk mail ever, thanks!" notices on both Mum's and Granny's doors, because Elsa is a big fan of the environment. The newspapers kept coming, and when Elsa called the company they just laughed at her. And they shouldn't have done that. Because no one laughs at Granny's grandchild.

Granny hated the environment, but she was the kind of person you brought along when you were going to war. So she became a terrorist for Elsa's sake. Elsa is furious at Granny for that, in fact, because Elsa wants to be furious at Granny. For everything else. For the lies and for abandoning Mum and for dying. But it's impossible to stay angry at someone who's prepared to turn terrorist for the sake of her grandchild. And it makes Elsa furious that she can't be furious.

She can't even be angry at Granny in a normal way. Not even that is normal about Granny.

She stands in silence next to Alf and blinks until her head hurts. Alf tries to look unconcerned, but Elsa notices that he's scanning the darkness, as if looking for someone. He watches their surroundings much like Wolfheart and the wurse. As if he's also on guard duty. She squints and tries to fit him into Granny's life, like a piece of a puzzle. She can't recall Granny ever talking very much about him, except that he never knew how to lift his feet, which was why the soles of his shoes were always so worn down.

"How well did you know Granny?" she asks.

The leather jacket creaks.

"What do you mean, 'knew'? We were bloody neighbors, that's all," Alf answers evasively.

"So what did you mean when you picked me up in the taxi, when you said Granny would never have forgiven you if you'd left me there?"

More creaking.

"I didn't mean anything, not a blo—nothing. I just happened to be in the area. Bloody . . ."

He sounds frustrated. Elsa nods, pretending to understand in a way that Alf clearly doesn't appreciate at all.

"Why are you here, then?" she asks teasingly.

"What?"

"Why did you follow me outside? Shouldn't you be driving your taxi now or something?"

"You don't have a blo— you don't have exclusive rights to taking walks, you know."

"Sure, sure."

"I can't let you and the mutt run loose here at night on your own. Your granny would have blo—"

He interrupts himself. Grunts. Sighs.

"Your granny would never have forgiven me if something happened to you."

He looks as if he already regrets saying that.

"Did you and Granny have an affair?" Elsa asks, after waiting for what seems a more than adequate length of time. Alf looks like she just threw a yellow snowball in his face.

"Aren't you a bit young to know what that means?"

"There are loads of things I'm too young to know about, but I know about them anyway." She clears her throat and carries on: "Once when I was small, Mum was going to explain what her work was, because I'd asked Dad and he didn't really seem to know. And then Mum said she worked as an economist. And then I said, 'What?' and then she said, 'I work out how much money the hospital has, so we know what we can buy.' And then I said, 'What, like in a shop?' And then she said that, yeah, sort of like in a shop, and it wasn't hard to get it at all and so really Dad was being a bit thick about it."

Alf checks his watch.

"But then, anyway, I saw a TV series where two people had a shop. And *they* had an affair, or at least I think they did. So now I get what it means, sort of thing. And I thought that was kind of how you and Granny knew each other! So . . . did you or didn't you?"

"Is that mutt done now or what? Some of us have jobs to go to,"

Alf mutters, which isn't much of an answer. He turns towards the bushes.

Elsa scrutinizes him thoughtfully.

"I just thought you could be Granny's type. Because you're a bit younger than she is. And she always flirted with policemen who were about your age. They were sort of too old to be policemen but they were still policemen. Not that you're a policeman, I mean. But you're also old without being . . . really old. Get what I mean?"

Alf doesn't look like he really gets it. And he looks like he's got a bit of a migraine.

The wurse finishes, and the three of them head back inside, Elsa in the middle. It's not a big army, but it's an army, thinks Elsa and feels a little less afraid of the dark. When they part ways in the cellar between the door to the garage and the door to the storage units, Elsa scrapes her shoe against the floor and asks Alf, "What was that music you were listening to in the car when you came to pick me up? Was it opera?"

"Holy Christ, enough questions!"

"I was only asking!"

"Blo— yeah. It was a bastard opera."

"What language was it in?"

"Italian."

"Can you talk Italian?"

"Yeah."

"For real?"

"What other bloody way is there to know Italian?"

"But, like, fluently?"

"You have to find another hiding place for that thing, I told you," he says, gesturing at the wurse, clearly trying to change the subject. "People will find it sooner or later."

"Do you know Italian or not?"

"I know enough to understand an opera. You got any other bast— questions?"

"What was that opera about in the car, then?" she persists.

Alf pulls open the garage door.

"Love. They're all about love, the whole lot."

He pronounces the world "love" a little as one would say words like "refrigerator" or "two-inch screw."

"WERE YOU IN LOVE WITH MY GRANNY, THEN?" Elsa yells after him, but he's already slammed the door.

She stays there, grinning. The wurse does too, she's almost sure about that. And it's much more difficult being afraid of shadows and the dark while grinning.

"I think Alf is our friend now," she whispers.

The wurse looks like it agrees.

"We're going to need all the friends we can get. Because Granny didn't tell me what happens in this fairy tale."

The wurse snuggles up against her.

"I miss Wolfheart," Elsa whispers into its fur.

Reluctantly, the wurse seems to agree with that too.

20

CLOTHES SHOP

Today's the day. And it starts with the most terrible night.

Elsa wakes with her mouth wide open but her scream fills her head rather than the room. She roars silently and reaches out with her hand to toss aside the bedclothes, but they're already on the floor. She walks into the flat—it smells of eggs. George smiles carefully at her from the kitchen. She doesn't smile back. He looks upset. She doesn't care.

She has a shower so hot her skin feels as if it's about to come away from her flesh like clementine peel. Walks out into the flat. Mum left home hours ago. She's gone to fix everything, because that is what Mum does.

George calls out something behind Elsa, but she neither listens nor answers. She puts on the clothes that Mum has put out for her and crosses the landing, locking the front door behind her. Granny's flat smells wrong. It smells clean. The towers of packing boxes throw shadows across the entry hall, like monuments to everything that is now absent.

She stands inside the door, incapable of going any farther. She was here last night, but it's more difficult by daylight. It's harder work remembering things when the sun is forcing its way in through the blinds. Cloud animals soar past in the sky. It's a beautiful morning but a terrible day.

Elsa's skin is still burning after her shower. It makes her think of Granny, because Granny's shower hasn't worked in over a year, and instead of calling the landlord and asking him to fix the problem, she just used Mum and George's shower. And sometimes she forgot to do up her dressing gown when she went back through the flat. And sometimes she forgot her dressing gown altogether. Once, Mum shouted at her for what must have been fifteen minutes because she didn't show any respect about George also living in Mum and Elsa's flat. But that was soon after Elsa had starting reading the collected works of Charles Dickens. Granny was not much use at reading books, so Elsa used to read them to her while they were driving Renault, because Elsa wanted to have someone she could discuss them with afterwards. Especially *A Christmas Carol*, which Elsa had read several times, because Granny liked Christmas stories.

So when Mum said that thing about how Granny shouldn't run about naked in the flat, out of respect for George, then Granny, still naked, turned to George and said, "What's all this respect rubbish? You're cohabiting with my daughter, for goodness sake." And then Granny bowed very deeply and very nakedly and added ceremoniously: "I am the spirit of future Christmases, George!"

Mum was very angry at Granny about that, but she tried not to show it, for Elsa's sake. So, for Mum's sake, Elsa tried not to show how proud she was of Granny for being able to quote Charles Dickens.

Elsa goes into the flat without taking off her shoes. She's wearing the kind of shoes that scratch the parquet flooring, so Mum has told her she can't wear them inside, but it doesn't matter in Granny's place, because the floor already looks as if someone went skating on it. Partly because it's old, and partly because Granny actually once went skating on it.

Elsa opens the door of the big wardrobe. The wurse licks her face. It smells of protein bars and sponge cake mix. Elsa had just gone to bed last night when she realized that Mum would most likely send George down to the cellar storage unit today to get the spare chairs, because everyone is coming here afterwards for coffee. Because today is the day, and everyone drinks coffee somewhere after days like this.

Mum and George's cellar unit is next to Granny's unit, and it's the only storage unit you can see the wurse from now that Alf has put up the plywood sheets. So Elsa sneaked down in the night, unable to decide whether she was more afraid of shadows or ghosts or Britt-Marie, and brought the wurse upstairs.

"There would be more space to hide you in here if Granny wasn't dead," says Elsa apologetically, because then the wardrobe wouldn't have stopped growing. "Then again, if Granny hadn't died, you wouldn't need to hide in the first place."

The wurse licks her face again and squeezes its head through the opening and looks for her backpack. Elsa runs to fetch it from the hall and pulls out three tins of dreams and a quart of milk.

"Maud left them with Mum last night," Elsa explains, but when the wurse immediately starts snuffling her hands as if about to eat the cookies with the tin still around them, she raises an admonishing forefinger.

"You can only have two tins! One is for ammunition!"

The wurse barks at her a bit about that, but in the end recognizes its poor bargaining position and only polishes off two of the tins and half of the third. It is a wurse, after all. And these are cookies.

Elsa takes the milk and goes looking for her moo-gun. She's a bit slow on the uptake today. Because she hasn't had any nightmares in years, she's only realizing now that she may need it. The first time the shadow came to her in the nightmare, she tried to shake it all off the next morning. As you do. Tried to persuade herself that "it was only a nightmare." But she should have known better. Because everyone who has ever been in the Land-Of-Almost-Awake knows better.

So last night when she had the same dream, she realized where she had to go to fight the nightmares. To reclaim her nights from them.

"Mirevas!" she calls out firmly to the wurse, when it comes out of one of Granny's smaller wardrobes followed by an unnameable jumble of things that Mum has not yet had time to put into boxes.

"We have to go to Mirevas!" announces Elsa to the wurse, waving her moo-gun.

Mirevas, one of the kingdoms adjoining Miamas, is the smallest principality in the Land-of-Almost-Awake and for that reason almost forgotten. When children in the Land-of-Almost-Awake are learning geography and have to reel off the names of the six kingdoms, Mirevas is the one they always forget. Even those who live there. Because the Mirevasians are incredibly humble, kindly, and cautious creatures who go to great lengths to avoid taking up unnecessary space or causing the slightest inconvenience. Yet they have a very important task, actually one of the most important tasks in a kingdom where imagination is the most important thing you can have: for it is in Mirevas that the nightmare hunters are trained.

Only smart-asses in the real world who don't know any better would say something as idiotic as "it was only a nightmare." There are no "only" nightmares—they're living creatures, dark little clouds of insecurity and anguish that come sneaking between the houses when everyone is asleep, trying all the doors and windows to find some place to slip inside and start causing a commotion. And that is why there are nightmare hunters. And anyone who knows anything about anything knows one has to have a moo-gun to chase a nightmare. Someone who doesn't know better might mistake a moo-gun for a quite ordinary paintball gun customised by someone's granny with a milk carton at the side and a catapult glued to the top. Elsa, though, knows what she's got in her hands. She loads the carton with milk and puts a cookie in the firing chamber in front of the rubber band on the cookie gun.

You can't kill a nightmare, but you can scare it. And there's nothing so feared by nightmares as milk and cookies.

Just as she's starting to feel more confident, though, she's startled by the doorbell, and to the infinite chagrin of the wurse she accidentally fires loads of milk at it but no cookie, and it scurries off in a huff. For a moment she wonders how a nightmare can be ringing the doorbell, but it's only George. He looks upset. She doesn't care.

"I'm going down to pick up the spare chairs in the cellar storage," he says and tries to smile at her like stepdads do on days when they have an extra-strong sense of being sidelined.

Elsa shrugs and slams the door in his face. The wurse has reappeared, so she climbs onto its back and peers out of the spyhole to see George lingering there for what must be a minute, looking upset. Elsa hates him for that. Mum always tells Elsa that George just wants her to like him because he cares. As if Elsa doesn't get that. She knows he cares, and that's why she can't like him. Not because she wouldn't like him if she tried, but rather because she knows she definitely would. Because everyone likes George. It's his superpower.

And she knows that in this case she'll only be disappointed when Halfie is born and George forgets she exists. It's better not to like him from the start.

If you don't like people, they can't hurt you. Almost-eight-year-olds who are often described as "different" learn that very quickly.

She jumps down from the wurse's back. The wurse closes its jaws around the moo-gun and gently but firmly takes it away from her, then shambles off and puts it on a stool out of reach of her trigger finger. But it avoids eating the cookie, which, as anyone who understands just how much wurses love cookies knows, is a significant sign of respect for Elsa.

There's another ring at the door. Elsa throws it open and is just about to snap impatiently at George when she realizes just in time that it's not George.

There's a silence lasting for probably half a dozen eternities.

"Hello, Elsa," says the woman in the black skirt, sounding a bit lost. She's wearing jeans, not a black skirt, today, admittedly. And she smells of mint and looks scared. She breathes so slowly that Elsa fears she's about to expire from a shortage of oxygen.

"I'm . . . I'm very sorry I shouted at you in my office," she begins.

They scrutinize each other's shoes.

"It's cool," Elsa manages to say at last.

The corners of the woman's mouth vibrate gently.

"I was a bit caught off guard when you came to the office. I don't get many people visiting me there. I'm . . . I'm not so good at visits."

Elsa nods guiltily without looking up from the woman's shoes.

"It doesn't matter. Sorry for saying that about . . ." she whispers, unable to get out the last few words.

The woman waves her hand dismissively.

"It was my fault. It's difficult for me to talk about my family. Your grandmother tried to make me do it, but it only made me . . . well . . . angry."

Elsa pokes at the floor with the tip of her toe.

"People drink wine to forget things that are hard, right?"

"Or to have the strength to remember. I think."

Elsa snuffles.

"You're also broken, right? Like Wolfheart?"

"Broken in . . . in another way. Maybe."

"Couldn't you mend yourself, then?"

"You mean because I'm a psychologist?"

Elsa nods. "Doesn't that work?"

"I don't think surgeons can operate on themselves. It's probably more or less the same thing."

Elsa nods again. For an instant the woman in the jeans looks as if she's about to reach out towards her, but she stops herself and absentmindedly scratches the palm of her hand instead.

"Your granny wrote in the letter that she wanted me to look after you," she whispers.

Elsa nods.

"That's what she writes in all the letters, apparently."

"You sound angry."

"She didn't write any letters to me."

The woman reaches into a bag on the floor and gets something out.

"I . . . I bought these Harry Potter books yesterday. I haven't had time to get very far yet, but, you know."

"What made you change your mind?"

"I . . . I understand Harry Potter is important to you."

"Harry Potter is important for everyone!"

The skin around the woman's mouth cracks again. She takes another long, deep breath, looks into Elsa's eyes and says:

"I like him a lot too, that's what I wanted to say. It's been a long time since I had such an amazing reading experience. You almost never do, once you grow up, things are at their peak when you're a child and then it's all downhill from there . . . well . . . because of the cynicism, I suppose. I just wanted to thank you for reminding me of how things used to be."

Those are more words than Elsa has ever heard the woman say

without stuttering. The woman offers her what's in the bag. Elsa takes it. It's also a book. A fairy tale. *The Brothers Lionheart*, by Astrid Lindgren. Elsa knows that, because it's one of her favorite stories that doesn't come from the Land-of-Almost-Awake. She read it aloud to Granny many times while they were driving around in Renault. It's about Karl and Jonatan, who die and come to Nangijala, where they have to fight the tyrant Tengil and the dragon Katla.

The woman's gaze loses its footing again.

"I used to read it to my boys when their granny died. I don't know if you've read it. You probably have."

Elsa shakes her head and holds the book tightly.

"No," she lies. Because she's polite enough to know that if someone gives you a book, you owe that person the pretense that you haven't read it.

The woman in jeans looks relieved. Then she takes such a deep breath that Elsa fears her wishbone is about to snap.

"You know . . . you asked if we met at the hospital. Your granny and I. After the tsunami I . . . they . . . they had laid out all the dead bodies in a little square. So families and friends could look for their . . . after . . . I . . . I mean, she found me there. In the square. I had been sitting there for . . . I don't know. Several weeks. I think. She flew me home and she said I could live here until I knew where I was . . . was going."

Her lips open and close, in turn, as if they're electric.

"I just stayed here. I just . . . stayed."

Elsa looks down at her own shoes this time.

"Are you coming today?" she asks.

In the corner of her eye she can see the woman shaking her head. As if she wants to run away again.

"I don't think I . . . I think your grandmother was very disappointed in me."

"Maybe she was disappointed in you because you're so disappointed in yourself."

There's a choking sound in the woman's throat. It takes a while before Elsa understands it's probably laughter. As if that part of her throat has been in disuse and has just found the key to itself and flicked some old electrical switch.

"You're really a very different little child," says the woman.

"I'm not a little child. I'm almost eight!"

"Yes, sorry. You were a newborn. When I moved in here. Newborn."

"There's nothing wrong with being different. Granny said that only different people change the world."

"Yes. Sorry. I . . . I have to go. I just wanted to say . . . sorry."

"It's okay. Thanks for the book."

The woman's eyes hesitate, but she looks straight at Elsa again.

"Has your friend come back? Wolf— what was it you called him?"

Elsa shakes her head. There's something in the woman's eyes that actually looks like genuine concern.

"He does that sometimes. Disappears. You shouldn't worry. He . . . gets scared of people. Disappears for a while. But he always comes back. He just needs time."

"I think he needs help."

"It's hard to help those who don't want to help themselves."

"Someone who wants to help himself is possibly not the one who most needs help from others," Elsa objects.

The woman nods without answering.

"I have to go," she repeats.

Elsa wants to stop her but she's already halfway down the stairs. She has almost disappeared on the floor below when Elsa leans over the railing, gathers her strength, and calls out:

"Did you find them? Did you find your boys in the square?"

The woman stops. Holds the banister very hard.

"Yes."

Elsa bites her lip.

"Do you believe in life after death?"

The woman looks up at her.

"That's a difficult question."

"I mean, you know, do you believe in God?" asks Elsa.

"Sometimes it's hard to believe in God," answers the woman.

"Because you wonder why God didn't stop the tsunami?"

"Because I wonder why there are tsunamis at all."

Elsa nods.

"I saw someone in a film once say, 'Faith can move mountains,'" Elsa goes on, without knowing why, maybe mainly because she doesn't want to lose sight of the woman before she has time to ask the question she really wants to ask.

"So I hear," says the woman.

Elsa shakes her head.

"But you know that's actually true! Because it comes from Miamas, from a giant called Faith. She was so strong it was insane. And she could literally move mountains!"

The woman looks as if she's trying to find a reason to disappear down the stairs. Elsa takes a quick breath.

"Everyone says I may miss Granny now but it'll pass. I'm not so sure."

The woman looks up at her again. With her empathic eyes.

"Why not?"

"It hasn't passed for you."

The woman half-closes her eyes.

"Maybe it's different."

"How?"

"Your granny was old."

"Not to me. I only knew her for seven years. Almost eight."

The woman doesn't answer. Elsa rubs her hands together like Wolfheart does.

"You should come today!" Elsa calls out after her, but the woman has already disappeared.

Elsa hears the door of her flat closing and then everything is silent until she hears Dad's voice from the door at the bottom.

She collects herself and wipes her tears and forces the wurse to hide in the wardrobe again with half of the moo-gun ammunition as a bribe. Then she closes the door of Granny's flat without locking it and runs down the stairs, and a few moments later she's lying in Audi with the seat reclined as far as it'll go, staring out of the glass ceiling.

The cloud animals are soaring lower now. Dad is wearing a suit and is also silent. It feels strange, because Dad hardly ever wears a suit. But today is the day.

"Do you believe in God, Dad?" asks Elsa, in the way that always catches him unaware like water balloons thrown from a balcony. Elsa knows that because Granny loved water balloons and Dad learned never to walk right beneath her balcony.

"I don't know," he answers.

Elsa hates him for not having an answer but she loves him a bit for not lying. Audi stops outside a black steel gate. They sit for a while, waiting.

"Am I like Granny?" says Elsa without taking her eyes off the sky.

"You mean in physical appearance?" asks Dad hesitantly.

"No, like, as a *person*," sighs Elsa.

Dad looks as if he's fighting his hesitation for a moment, like you do when you have daughters aged about eight. It's almost as if Elsa has just asked him to explain where babies come from. Again.

"You must stop saying 'like' and 'sort of' all the time. Only people with a bad vocabulary—" he begins to say instead, because he can't stop himself. Because that's the way he is. One of those who find it very important to say "one of those" and not "one of them."

"So bloody leave it then!" Elsa snaps, much more vehemently than she means to, because she's not in the mood for his corrections today.

Usually it's their thing, correcting one another. Their only thing. Dad has a word jar, where Elsa puts difficult words she has learned, like "concise" and "pretentious," or complex phrases like "My fridge is a taco sauce graveyard." And every time the jar is full she gets a gift voucher for a book to download on the iPad. The word jar has financed the entire Harry Potter series for her, although she knows Dad is ridiculously dubious about Harry Potter because Dad can't get his head around a story unless it's based on reality.

"Sorry," mumbles Elsa.

Dad sinks into his seat. They compete at seeing who can feel most ashamed. Then he says, slightly less tentatively:

"Yes. You're very much like her. You got all your best qualities from her and your mother."

Elsa doesn't answer, because she doesn't know if that was the answer she wanted. Dad doesn't say anything either, because he's unsure whether that was what he should have said. Elsa wants to tell him she wants to stay with him more. Every other weekend is not enough. She wants to yell at him that once Halfie comes along and is quite normal, George and Mum won't want to have Elsa at home anymore, because parents want normal children, not different children. And Halfie will stand next to Elsa and remind them of all the differences between them. She wants to yell that Granny was wrong, that different is not always good, because different is a mutation and almost no one in *X-Men* has a family.

She wants to yell out the whole thing. But she doesn't. Because she knows he'd never understand. And she knows he wouldn't want her to live with him and Lisette because Lisette has her own children. Undifferent children.

Dad sits in silence like you do when you don't feel like wearing a suit. But just as Elsa opens Audi's door to jump out, he turns to her hesitantly and says in a low voice:

". . . but there are moments when I sincerely hope that not ALL your best traits come from Granny and Mum, Elsa."

And then Elsa squeezes her eyes together tightly and puts her forehead against his shoulder and her fingers into her jacket pocket and spins the lid of the red felt-tip pen that he gave her when she was small, so she could add her own punctuation marks, and which is still the best present he's ever given her. Or anyone.

"You gave me your words," she whispers.

He tries to blink his pride out of his eyes. She sees that. And she wants to tell him that she lied to him last Friday. That she was the one who sent the text from Mum's phone about how he didn't have to pick her up from school. But she doesn't want to disappoint him, so she stays quiet. Because you hardly ever disappoint anybody if you just stay quiet. All almost-eight-year-olds know that.

Dad kisses her hair. She raises her head and says as if in passing, "Will you and Lisette have children?"

"I don't think so," Dad replies sadly, as if it's quite self-evident.

"Why not?"

"We have all the children we need."

And it sounds as if he stops himself from saying "more than we need." Or at least that's how it feels.

"Is it because of me you don't want more children?" she asks, and hopes he'll say no.

"Yes," he says.

"Because I turned out different?" she whispers.

He doesn't answer. And she doesn't wait. But just as she's about to slam the door of Audi from the outside, Dad reaches across the seat and catches her fingertips, and when she meets his eyes he looks back tentatively, like he always does. But then he whispers:

"Because you turned out to be perfect."

She's never heard him so nontentative. And if she'd said that aloud, he would have told her that there's no such word. And she loves him for that.

George stands by the gate looking sad. He's also wearing a suit. Elsa runs past him and Mum catches hold of her, her mascara running, and Elsa presses her face against Halfie. Mum's dress smells of boutique. The cloud animals are flying low.

And that's the day they bury Elsa's granny.

21

CANDLE GREASE

There are storytellers in the Land-of-Almost-Awake who say we all have an inner voice, whispering to us what we must do, and all we must do is listen. Elsa has never really believed it, because she doesn't like the thought of someone else having a voice inside her, and Granny always said that only psychologists and murderers have "inner voices." Granny never liked proper psychology. Though she really did try with the woman in the black skirt.

But, in spite of all, in a moment Elsa will hear a voice in her head as clear as a bell. It won't be whispering, it will be yelling. It will be yelling, "Run!" And Elsa will run for her life. With the shadow behind her.

Of course, she doesn't know that when she goes into the church. The quiet murmuring of hundreds of strangers rises towards the ceiling, like the hissing of a broken car stereo. The legions of smart-asss point at her and whisper. Their eyes are oppressive.

She doesn't know who they are and it makes her feel tricked. She doesn't want to share Granny with others. She doesn't want to be reminded of how Granny was her only friend, while Granny herself had hundreds of others.

She concentrates hard on walking straight-backed through the crush, doesn't want them to see that she feels as if she's going to collapse any moment and doesn't even have the strength to be upset anymore. The church floor sucks at her feet, the coffin up there stings her eyes.

The mightiest power of death is not that it can make people die, but that it can make the people left behind want to stop living, she thinks, without remembering where she heard that. On second thought, she decides it probably comes from the Land-of-Almost-Awake, although this seems unlikely when one considers what Granny thought about death. Death was Granny's nemesis. That's why she never wanted to talk about it. And that was also why she became a surgeon, to cause death as much trouble as she could.

But it might also come from Miploris, realizes Elsa. Granny never wanted to ride to Miploris when they were in the Land-of-Almost-Awake, but sometimes she did it anyway because of Elsa's nagging. And sometimes Elsa rode there on her own when Granny was at some inn in Miamas playing poker with a troll or arguing about wine with a snow-angel.

Miploris is the most beautiful of all the kingdoms of the Land-of-Almost-Awake. The trees sing there, the grass massages the soles of your feet, and there's always a smell of fresh-baked bread. The houses are so beautiful that, to be on the safe side, you have to be sitting down when you look at them. But no one lives there, they are only used for storage. For Miploris is where all fairy creatures bring their sorrow, and where all leftover sorrow is stored. For an eternity of all fairy tales.

People in the real world always say, when something terrible happens, that the sadness and loss and aching pain of the heart will "lessen as time passes," but it isn't true. Sorrow and loss are constant, but if we all had to go through our whole lives carrying them the whole time, we wouldn't be able to stand it. The sadness would paralyze us. So in the end we just pack it into bags and find somewhere to leave it.

That is what Miploris is: a kingdom where lone storytelling travelers come slowly wandering from all directions, dragging unwieldy luggage full of sorrow. A place where they can put it down and go back to life. And when the travelers turn back, they do so with lighter steps, because Miploris is constructed in such a way that irrespective of what direction you leave it, you always have the sun up ahead and the wind at your back.

The Miplorisians gather up all the suitcases and sacks and bags of sorrow and carefully make a note of them in little pads. They scrupulously catalogue every kind of sadness and pining. Things are kept in very good order in Miploris; they have an extensive system of rules and impeccably clear areas of responsibility for all kinds of sorrows. "Bureaucratic bastards" was what Granny called the Miplorisians, because of all the forms that have to be filled out nowadays by whoever is dropping off some sorrow or other. But you can't put up with disorder when it comes to sorrow, say the Miplorisians.

Miploris used to be the smallest kingdom in the Land-of-Almost-Awake, but after the War-Without-End it became the biggest. That was why Granny didn't like riding there, because so many of the storehouses had her name on signs outside. And in Miploris people talk of inner voices, Elsa remembers now. Miplorisians believe that the inner voices are those of the dead, coming back to help their loved ones.

Elsa is pulled back into the real world by Dad's gentle hand on her shoulder. She hears his voice whispering, "You've arranged everything very nicely, Ulrika," to Mum. In the corner of her eye she sees how Mum smiles and nods at the programs lying on the church pews and then replies: "Thanks for doing the programs. Lovely font."

Elsa sits at the far end of the wooden pew at the front of the chapel, staring down into the floor until the mumbling dies down. The church is so packed that people are standing all along the walls. Many of them have insanely weird clothes, as if they've been playing outfit roulette with someone who can't read washing instruction tags.

Elsa will put "outfit roulette" in the word jar, she thinks. She tries to focus on that thought. But she hears languages she can't understand, and she hears her name being squeezed into strange pronunciations, and this takes her back to reality. She sees strangers pointing at her, with varying degrees of discretion. She understands that they all know who she is, and it makes her mad, so that when she glimpses a familiar face along one of the walls she has trouble placing him at first. Like when you see a celebrity in a café and instinctively burst out,"Oh, hi there!" before you realize that your brain has had time to tell you, "Hey, that's probably someone you know, say hi!" but not, "No, wait, it's just that guy from the TV!" Because your brain likes to make you look like an idiot.

His face disappears behind a shoulder for a few moments, but when he reappears he's looking right at Elsa. It's the accountant who came to speak about the leasehold conversion yesterday. But he's dressed as a priest now. He winks at her.

Another priest starts talking about Granny, then about God, but Elsa doesn't listen. She wonders if this is what Granny would have wanted. She's not sure that Granny liked church so very much. Granny and Elsa hardly ever talked about God, because Granny associated God with death.

And this is all fake. Plastic and makeup. As if everything's going to be fine just because they're having a funeral. Everything is not going to be fine for Elsa, she knows that. She breaks into a cold sweat. A couple of the strangers in the weird clothes come up to the microphone and talk. Some of them do so in other languages and have a little lady who translates into another microphone. But no one says "dead." Everyone just says that Granny has "passed away" or that they've "lost her." As if she's a sock that's been lost in the tumble-dryer. A few of them are crying, but she doesn't think they have the right. Because she wasn't their granny, and they have no right to make Elsa feel as if Granny had other countries and kingdoms to which she never brought Elsa.

So when a fat lady who looks like she's combed her hair with a toaster starts reading poems, Elsa thinks it's just about enough and she pushes her way out between the pews. She hears Mum whispering something behind her, but she just shuffles along the shiny stone floor and squeezes out of the church doors before anyone has time to come after her.

The winter air bites at Elsa; it feels like she's being yanked out of a boiling hot bath by her hair. The cloud animals are hovering low and ominous. Elsa walks slowly and takes such deep breaths of the December air that her eyes start to black out. She thinks about Storm. Storm has always been one of Elsa's favorite superheroes, because Storm's superpower is that she can change the weather. Even Granny used to admit that as superpowers went, that one was pretty cool.

Elsa hopes that Storm will come and blow away this whole bloody church. The whole bloody churchyard. Bloody everything.

The faces from inside spiral around inside her head. Did she really see the accountant? Was Alf standing in there? She thinks so. She saw another face she recognized, the policewoman with the green eyes. She walks faster, away from the church because she doesn't want any of them to come after her and ask if she's okay. Because she's not okay. None of this will ever be okay. She doesn't want to listen to their mumbling or have to admit that they are talking about her. Over her. Around her. Granny never talked around her.

She's gone about fifty yards between the headstones when she picks up a smell of smoke. At first there's something familiar about it, something almost liberating. Something that Elsa wants to turn and embrace and bury her nose in, like a freshly laundered pillowcase on a Sunday morning. But then there's something else.

And her inner voice comes to her.

She knows where the man between the headstones is before she has even turned around. He's only a few yards away from her. Casually holding his cigarette between his fingertips. It's too far from the church for anyone to hear Elsa scream, and with calm, cold movements he blocks her way back.

Elsa glances over her shoulder towards the gate at the road. Twenty yards away. When she looks back he's taken a long stride towards her.

And the inner voice comes to Elsa. And it's Granny's voice. But it isn't whispering. It's yelling.

Run.

Elsa feels his rough hand grasping her arm, but she slips out of his grip. She runs until the wind scrapes her eyes like nails against a frosty windshield. She doesn't know for how long. Eternities. And when the memory of his eyes and his cigarette crystallizes in her brain, when every breath punches into her lungs, she realizes that he was limping; that's why she got away. Another second of hesitation and he would have grabbed her by her dress, but Elsa is too used to running. Too good at it. She runs until she's no longer sure whether it's the wind or her grief that is making her eyes run. Runs until she realizes she's almost at her school.

She slows down. Looks round. Hesitates. Then she charges right into the black park on the other side of the street, with her dress tossing around her. Even the trees look like enemies in there. The sun seems too exhausted to go down. She hears scattered voices, the wind screaming through the branches, the rumbling of traffic farther and farther away. Out of breath and furious, she stumbles towards the interior of the park. Hears voices. Hears that some of them are calling out after her. "Hey! Little girl!" they call out.

She stops, exhausted. Collapses on a bench. Hears the "little-girl" voice coming closer. She understands that it means her harm. The park seems to be creeping under a blanket. She hears another voice beside the first, slurring and stumbling over its words as if it's put on its shoes the wrong way round. Both of the voices seem to be picking up speed as they come towards her. Realizing the danger, she's on her feet and running in a fluid movement. They follow. It dawns on her with sudden despair that the winter gloom is making everything look the same in the park, and she doesn't know the way out. Good God, she's a seven-year-old girl who watches television a hell of a lot, how could she be so stupid? This is how people end up on the sides of milk cartons, or however they advertise missing children these days.

But it's too late. She runs between two dense black hedges that form a narrow corridor, and she feels her beating heart in her throat. She doesn't know why she charged into the park—the junkies will get her, just as everyone at school said they would. Maybe that's just it, she thinks. Maybe she wants someone to catch her and kill her.

Death's greatest power is not that it can make people die, but that it can make people want to stop living.

She never hears the snapping of branches in the bush. Never hears the ice being crushed under his feet. But in an instant the slurring voices behind her are gone. Her eardrums grate until she wants to scream. And then everything goes back to silence. Slowly she's lifted off the ground. Closes her eyes. Doesn't open them until she's been carried out of the park.

Wolfheart stares down at her. She stares back, lying in his arms. Her consciousness seems to float off. If it wasn't for the realization, in some part of her inner self, that there aren't enough paper bags in the whole world to breathe into if she dribbles on Wolfheart in her sleep, she would probably have gone to sleep there and then. So she struggles to stay awake and, after all, it would be a bit impolite to go to sleep now that he's saved her. Again.

"Not run alone. Never run alone," growls Wolfheart.

She's still not quite sure if she wanted to be saved, although she's happy to see him. Happier than she expected to be, actually. She thought she'd be angrier at him.

"Dangerous place," growls Wolfheart towards the park, and starts putting her back down on the ground.

"I know," she mumbles.

"Never again!" he orders, and she can hear that he's afraid.

She puts her arms around his neck and whispers "Thanks" in the secret language before he can straighten up his enormous body. Then she sees how uncomfortable it makes him and she lets go at once.

"I washed my hands really carefully, I had a mega-long shower this morning!" she whispers.

Wolfheart doesn't answer, but she can see in his eyes that he'll be, like, bathing in alcogel when he gets home.

Elsa looks around. Wolfheart rubs his hands together and shakes his head when he notices.

"Gone now," he says gently.

Elsa nods.

"How did you know I was here?"

Wolfheart's gaze drops into the asphalt.

"Guard you. Your granny said . . . guard you."

Elsa nods.

"Even if I don't always know you're close by?"

Wolfheart's hood moves up and down. She feels that her legs are about to give way beneath her.

"Why did you disappear?" she whispers accusingly. "Why did you leave me with that terropist?" Wolfheart's face disappears under his hood.

"Psychologists want to talk. Always talk. About war. Always. I . . . don't want to."

"Maybe you'd feel better if you talked?"

Wolfheart rubs his hands together in silence. He watches the street as if waiting to catch sight of something.

Elsa wraps her arms around her body and realizes that she left both her jacket and her Gryffindor scarf in the church. It's the only time she's ever forgotten her Gryffindor scarf.

Who the hell could do that to a Gryffindor scarf?

She also looks up and down the street, searching for she doesn't know what. Then she feels something being swept over her shoulders, and when she turns she realizes that Wolfheart has put his coat around her. It drags along the ground by her feet. Smells of detergent. It's the first time she's seen Wolfheart without the upturned hood. Oddly enough, he looks even bigger without it. His long hair and black beard billow in the wind.

"You said 'Miamas' means 'I love' in your mother's language, right?" asks Elsa, and tries not to look directly at his scar, because she can see he rubs his hands even harder when she does.

He nods. Scans the street.

"What does 'Miploris' mean?" asks Elsa.

When he doesn't answer, she assumes it's because he doesn't understand the question, so she clarifies:

"One of the six kingdoms in the Land-of-Almost-Awake is called Miploris. That's where all the sorrow is stored. Granny never wanted t—"

Wolfheart interrupts her, but gently.

"I mourn."

Elsa nods.

"And Mirevas?"

"I dream."

"And Miaudacas?"

"I dare."

"And Mimovas?"

"Dance. I dance."

Elsa lets the words touch down inside her before she asks about the last kingdom. She thinks about what Granny always said about Wolfheart, that he was the invincible warrior who defeated the shadows and that only he could have done it, because he had the heart of a warrior and the soul of a storyteller. Because he was born in Miamas, but he grew up in Mibatalos.

"What does Mibatalos mean?" she asks.

He looks right at her when she asks that. With those big dark eyes wide open with everything that is kept in Miploris.

"Mibatalos—I fight. Mibatalos . . . gone now. No Mibatalos anymore."

"I know! The shadows destroyed it in the War-Without-End and all the Mibatalosians died except you, for you are the last of your people and—" Elsa starts saying, but Wolfheart rubs his hands together so hard that she stops herself.

Wolfheart's hair falls into his face. He backs away a step.

"Mibatalos not exist. I don't fight. Never more fight."

And Elsa understands, the way you always understand such things when you see them in the eyes of those saying them, that he did not hide in the forests at the far reaches of the Land-of-Almost-Awake because he was afraid of the shadows, but because he was afraid of himself. Afraid of what they made him into in Mibatalos.

His eyes flit past her and she hears Alf's voice. When she spins around, Taxi is parked with its engine running by the edge of the pavement. Alf's shoes shuffle through the snow. The policewoman stays by Taxi, her eyes making rapid hawklike sweeps over the park. When Alf picks up Elsa, still rolled up in Wolfheart's sleeping bag–size coat, he says calmly: "Let's get you home now, shall we, you can't bloody stay here getting frozen!" But Elsa hears in his voice that he's afraid, afraid as one can only be if one knows what was chasing Elsa in the churchyard, and she can tell by the watchful gaze in the policewoman's green eyes that she also knows. They all know more than they are letting on.

Elsa doesn't look around as Alf carries her towards Taxi. She knows that Wolfheart has already gone. And when she throws herself into Mum's arms back at the church, she also knows that Mum knows more than she's letting on. And she's always known more than she lets on.

Elsa thinks about the story of the Lionheart brothers. About the dragon, Katla, who could not be defeated by any human. And about the terrible constrictor snake, Karm, the only one that could destroy Katla in the end. Because sometimes in the tales, the only thing that can destroy a terrible dragon is something even more terrible than the dragon.

A monster.

22

O'BOY

Elsa has been chased hundreds of times before, but never like in that churchyard. And the fear she feels now is something else. Because she had time to see his eyes just before she ran, and they looked so determined, so cold, like he was ready to kill her. That's a lot for an almost-eight-year-old to handle.

Elsa tried never to be afraid while Granny was alive. Or at least she tried never to show it. Because Granny hated fears. Fears are small, fiery creatures from the Land-of-Almost-Awake, with rough pelts that coincidentally look quite a lot like blue tumble-dryer fluff, and if you give them the slightest opportunity, they jump up and nibble your skin and try to scratch your eyes. Fears are like cigarettes, said Granny: the hard thing isn't stopping, it's not starting.

It was the Noween who brought the fears to the Land-of-Almost-Awake, in another of Granny's tales, more eternities ago than anyone could really count. So long ago that at the time there were only five kingdoms, not six.

The Noween is a prehistoric monster that wants everything to happen immediately. Every time a child says "in a minute" or "later" or "I'm just going to . . ." the Noween bellows with furious force: "Nooo! IT HAS TO BE DONE NOOOW!" The Noween hates children, because children refuse to accept the Noween's lie that time is linear. Children know that time is just an emotion, so "now" is a meaningless word to them, just as it was for Granny. George used to say that Granny wasn't a time-optimist, she was a time-atheist, and the only religion she believed in was Do-It-Later-Buddhism.

The Noween brought the fears to the Land-of-Almost-Awake to catch children, because when a Noween gets hold of a child it engulfs the child's future, leaving the victim helpless where it is, facing an entire life of eating now and sleeping now and tidying up right away. Never again can the child postpone something boring till later and do something fun in the meantime. All that's left is now. A fate far worse than death, Granny always said, so the tale of the Noween started by clarifying that it hated fairy tales. Because nothing is better at making a child postpone something than a fairy tale. So one night the Noween slithered up Telling Mountain, the highest mountain peak in the Land-of-Almost-Awake, where it caused a massive landslide, which demolished the entire peak. Then it lay in wait in a dark cave. For Telling Mountain is the mountain the enphants have to climb in order to release the tales so they can glide over into the real world, and if the tales can't leave Telling Mountain the whole kingdom of Miamas will suffocate, and then the whole Land-of-Almost-Awake will suffocate. For no stories can live without children listening to them.

When dawn came, all the bravest fighters from Mibatalos tried to climb the mountain and defeat the Noween, but no one managed it. Because the Noween was breeding fears in the caves. Fears need to be handled carefully, because threats just make them grow bigger. So every time a parent somewhere threatened a child, it worked as fertilizer. "Soon," a child said somewhere, and then a parent yelled, "No, nooow! Or I'll—" And, *bang*, another fear was hatched in one of the Noween's caves.

When the warriors from Mibatalos came up the mountain, the Noween released the fears, and they immediately transformed themselves into each individual soldier's worst nightmare. For all beings have a mortal fear, even the warriors from Mibatalos, and the air in the Land-of-Almost-Awake slowly grew thinner. Storytellers found it increasingly difficult to breathe.

(Elsa obviously interrupted Granny at this point because her whole thing about fears transforming themselves into what you are most afraid of was actually nicked from Harry Potter, because that's how a boggart works. And then Granny had snorted and answered, "Maybe it's that Harry muppet who nicked it from me?" And then Elsa had sneered, "Harry Potter doesn't steal!" And then they had argued for quite a long time about that, and in the end Granny gave up and mumbled, "Fine, then! Forget the whole bloody thing! Fears don't transform themselves, they just bite and try to scratch your eyes, are you SATISFIED now or what?" And then Elsa had left it there and they went on with the story.)

That's when the two golden knights showed up. Everyone tried to warn them about riding up the mountain, but they didn't listen, of course. Knights can be so damned obstinate. But when they came up the mountain and all the fears welled out of the caves, the golden knights didn't fight. They didn't yell and swear as other warriors would have done. Instead the knights did the only thing you can do with fears: they laughed at them. Loud, defiant laughter. And then all the fears were turned to stone, one by one.

Granny was fond of rounding off fairy tales with things being turned to stone because she wasn't very good at endings. Elsa never complained, though. The Noween was obviously put in prison for an indeterminate length of time, which made it insanely angry. And the ruling council of the Land-of-Almost-Awake decided to appoint a small group of inhabitants from each of the kingdoms, warriors from Mibatalos and dream hunters from Mirevas and sorrow-keepers from Miploris and musicians from Mimovas and storytellers from Miamas, to keep guard over Telling Mountain. The stones of the fears were used to rebuild the peak higher than ever, and at the foot of the mountain the sixth kingdom was built: Miaudacas. And in the fields of Miaudacas, courage was cultivated, so that no one would ever again have to be afraid of the fears.

Or, well. That is what they did until, as Granny once told Elsa, after the harvest they took all the courage plants and made a special drink of them, and if you had some of it you became incredibly brave. And then Elsa did a bit of Googling and then she pointed out to Granny that it wasn't a very responsible analogy to divulge to a child. And then Granny groaned, "Oh, right, okay, let's say they don't drink it, it's just THERE, okay?!" So that's the whole story of the two golden knights who defeated the fears. Granny told it every time Elsa was afraid of anything, and even though Elsa was often quite right in her criticism of Granny's storytelling technique, it actually worked every time. She wasn't at all as afraid afterwards.

The only thing the story never worked on was Granny's fear of death. And now it wasn't working on Elsa either. Because not even fairy tales defeat shadows.

"Are you scared?" asks Mum.

"Yes," admits Elsa.

Mum doesn't tell Elsa not to be afraid, and she doesn't try to trick her into believing that she shouldn't be. Elsa loves her for that.

They are in the garage and have pushed the backrest down in

Renault. The wurse floats out over everything between them, and Mum unconcernedly scratches its pelt. She wasn't even angry when Elsa confessed that she'd been keeping it hidden in the storage unit. And she wasn't scared when Elsa introduced her. She just started stroking it behind its ear as if it were a kitten.

Elsa reaches out and feels Mum's belly and Halfie contentedly kicking in there. Halfie is not afraid either. Because she/he is completely Mum and George, whereas Elsa is half her dad and Elsa's dad is afraid of everything. So Elsa gets afraid of about half of everything.

Shadows more than anything.

"Do you know who he is? The man who was chasing me?" she asks.

The wurse buffets its head against hers. Mum gently caresses her cheek.

"Yes. We know who he is."

"Who's we?"

Mum takes a deep breath.

"Lennart and Maud. And Alf. And me." It sounds as if she's going to reel off more names, but she stops herself.

"Lennart and Maud?" Elsa bursts out.

Mum nods. "I'm afraid they know him best of all."

"So why did you never tell me about him, then?" Elsa demands.

"I didn't want to scare you."

"That hardly worked, did it?"

Mum sighs. Scratches the wurse's pelt. The wurse, in turn, licks Elsa's face. It still smells of sponge cake mix. Unfortunately, it's quite difficult to be angry when someone smelling of sponge cake mix is licking your face.

"It's a shadow," whispers Elsa.

"I know," whispers Mum.

"Do you?"

"Your grandmother tried to tell me the stories, darling. About the Land-of-Almost-Awake and the shadows."

"And Miamas?" asks Elsa.

Mum shakes her head.

"No. I know you had things there that she never showed me. And it was long ago. I was about as old as you are now. The Land-of-Almost-Awake was very small then. The kingdoms didn't have names yet."

Elsa interrupts impatiently:

"I know! They got their names when Granny met Wolfheart, she named them after things in his mother's language. And she took his own language and made it into the secret language so he'd teach her and she could talk to him. But why didn't she bring you with her, in that case? Why didn't Granny show you the Land-of-Almost-Awake?"

Gently, Mum bites her lip.

"She wanted to bring me, darling. Many times. But I didn't want to go."

"Why not?"

"I was getting older. I was an angry teenager, and I didn't want my mother telling me fairy tales on the phone anymore, I wanted to have her here. I wanted her in reality."

Elsa hardly ever hears her say "my mother." She almost always says, "your grandmother."

"I wasn't an easy child, darling. I argued a lot. I said no to everything. Your grandmother always called me 'the girl who said no.'"

Elsa's eyes open wide. Mum sighs and smiles at the same time, as if one emotional expression is trying to swallow the other.

"Well, I was probably many things in your grandmother's stories. Both the girl and the queen, I think. In the end I didn't know where the fantasy ended and reality began. Sometimes I don't even think your grandmother knew herself."

Elsa lies in silence staring up at the ceiling, with the wurse breathing softly in her ear. She thinks about Wolfheart and the sea-angel, living next door for so many years without anyone knowing the first thing about them. If holes were drilled in the walls and floors of the house, all the neighbors could reach out and touch one another, that was how close their lives were, and yet in the end they knew almost nothing about the others. And so the years just went by.

"Have you found the keys?" asks Elsa, pointing at Renault's dashboard.

Mum shakes her head.

"I think your grandmother hid them. Presumably just to tease Britt-Marie. That must be why it's parked in Britt-Marie's space. . . ."

"Does Britt-Marie even have her own car?" asks Elsa, because from where she's lying she can clearly see BMW, Kent's ridiculously oversize car.

"No. But she had a car many years ago. A white one. And it's still her parking spot. I think it's about the principle. It's usually about the principle with Britt-Marie," says Mum with a smirk.

Elsa doesn't quite know what that means. She doesn't know if it makes any difference either.

"How did Renault get here, then? If no one has the key for it?" she thinks aloud, although she knows Mum won't be able to answer because she doesn't know either. So she asks Mum to tell her about the shadow. Mum brushes her hand over her cheek again and levers herself up laboriously from the seat, with one hand over Halfie.

"I think Maud and Lennart will have to tell you about him, darling."

Elsa wants to protest, but Mum has already climbed out of Renault, so Elsa doesn't have much choice but to follow her. That is

Mum's superpower, after all. Mum brings Wolfheart's coat. She says she's going to wash it so he can have it when he comes home. Elsa likes thinking about that. How he's coming home.

They put blankets over the wurse in the backseat and Mum calmly cautions it to stay still if it hears anyone coming. And it agrees. Elsa promises it several times that she'll find a better hiding place, although it can't seem to see the point of this. On the other hand, it looks very pleased about her going off to find more cookies.

Alf is standing guard at the bottom of the cellar stairs.

"I made coffee," he mutters.

Mum gratefully accepts a cup. Alf hands Elsa the other cup.

"I told you I don't drink coffee," says Elsa tiredly.

"It's not bloody coffee, it's one of those O'boy drinking-chocolate bastards," Alf answers indignantly.

Elsa peers into the cup, surprised.

"Where'd you get this from?" she asks. Mum never lets her have O'boy at home because there's too much sugar in it.

"From home," mutters Alf.

"You have O'boy at home?" Elsa asks skeptically.

"I can bloody go to the shop, can't I?" says Alf sourly.

Elsa grins at him. She's thinking of calling Alf the Knight of Invective because she's read about invective on Wikipedia and she feels all in all there are too few knights of it. Then she takes a deep gulp and comes close to spitting it out all over Alf's leather jacket.

"How many spoonfuls of O'boy did you put in this?"

"I don't know. Fourteen or fifteen, maybe?" Alf mutters defensively.

"You're supposed to put in, like, three!"

Alf looks indignant. Or at least Elsa thinks so. She put "indignant" in Dad's word jar one time, and she imagines that's what it looks like.

"It should bloody taste of something, shouldn't it?"

Elsa eats the rest with a spoon.

"So you also know who was chasing me in the churchyard, don't you?" she asks Alf, with half of the cup's contents in the corners of her mouth and on the tip of her nose.

"It's not you he's after."

"Err, hello? He was *chasing* me."

Alf just slowly shakes his head.

"Yes. But you're not the one he's hunting."

23

DISHCLOTH

Elsa has a thousand questions about what Alf just said, but doesn't ask any of them because Mum is so tired once they've gone up into the flat that she and Halfie have to go straight to bed. Mum gets like that these days, tired as if someone pulled the plug. It's Halfie's fault, apparently. George says that to compensate for Halfie keeping them awake for the next eighteen years, Halfie is making Mum fall asleep all the time for the first nine months. Elsa sits on the edge of the bed stroking her hair; Mum kisses her hands, whispering, "It will get better, darling. It will be fine." Like Granny used to say. And Elsa wants so, so much to believe that. Mum smiles sleepily.

"Is Britt-Marie still here?" she says, with a nod towards the door.

Britt-Marie's nagging voice emanates from the kitchen, so the question immediately becomes rhetorical. She's demanding "a decision" from George on Renault, which is still parked in Britt-Marie's slot in the garage. ("We can't live without rules, George! Even Ulrika has to understand that!") George answers cheerfully that he can understand that well enough, because George can understand everyone's point of view. It's one of the annoying things about him, and, sure enough, seems to be getting Britt-Marie into a huff. And then George offers her some eggs, which she ignores, insisting instead that all tenants "submit to a full investigation" regarding the stroller, which is still locked up at the bottom of the stairs.

"Don't worry, darling, we'll find a better hiding place for your friend tomorrow," Mum mumbles half-asleep, and then adds with a smile: "Maybe we can hide it in the stroller?"

Elsa laughs. But only a little. And she thinks that the mystery of the locked stroller is like the opening of an insanely awful Agatha Christie novel. Elsa knows that because almost all of Agatha Christie's novels can be read on the iPad, and Agatha Christie has never had such a stereotypical villain as Britt-Marie. More likely she'd be a victim, becausc Elsa can imagine a murder mystery in which someone has bludgeoned Britt-Marie to death with a candlestick in the library, and then everyone who knew her would be a suspect because everyone would have a motive: "The hag was a nightmare!" And then Elsa feels a bit ashamed for thinking along these lines. But only a little.

"Britt-Marie doesn't mean any harm, she just needs to feel important," Mum tries to explain.

"She's still just a nagging old busybody," Elsa mutters.

Mum smiles.

And then she gets comfortable on the pillows and Elsa helps her push one of them under her back, and Mum strokes her cheek and whispers:

"I want to hear the stories now, if that's all right. I want to hear the fairy tales from Miamas."

And then Elsa whispers calmly that Mum has to close her eyes but only halfway, and then Mum does as she says, and Elsa has a thousand questions but does not ask any of them. Instead she talks about the cloud animals and the enphants and the regretters and lions and trolls and knights and the Noween and Wolfheart and the snow-angels and the sea-angel and the dream hunters, and she starts talking about the Princess of Miploris and the two princelings who fought for her love, and the witch who stole the princess's treasure, but by then Mum and Halfie are asleep.

And Elsa still has a thousand questions but does not ask any of them. She just covers Mum and Halfie with the blanket and kisses Mum on the cheek and forces herself to be brave. Because she has to do what Granny made her promise to do: protect the castle, protect her family, protect her friends.

Mum's hand fumbles for her as she's standing up, and just as Elsa is about to go, Mum whispers in a half-asleep state:

"All the photos on the ceiling in your grandmother's bedroom, darling. All the children in the photos. They were the ones who came to the funeral today. They're grown-up now. They were allowed to grow up because your granny saved their lives. . . ."

And then Mum is asleep again. Elsa is not entirely sure that she even woke up.

"No shit, Sherlock," whispers Elsa as she switches off the lamp. Because it wasn't so hard working out who the strangers were. It was forgiving them that was hard.

Mum sleeps with a smile on her lips. Elsa carefully shuts the door.

The flat smells of dishcloth, and George is collecting used coffee cups. The strangers were all here today drinking coffee after the funeral. They smiled sympathetically at Elsa and Elsa hates them for it. Hates that they knew Granny before she did. She goes into Granny's flat and lies on Granny's bed. The streetlight outside plays against the photos on the ceiling, and, as she watches, Elsa still doesn't know if she can forgive Granny for leaving Mum on her own so she could save other children. She doesn't know if Mum can forgive it either. Even if she seems to be trying.

She goes out the door, into the stairwell, thinking to herself that she'll go back to the wurse in the garage. But instead, she sinks listlessly onto the floor. Sits there forever. Tries to think but only finds emptiness and silence where usually there are thoughts.

She can hear the footsteps coming from a couple of floors down—soft, padding gently, as if they're lost. Not at all the self-assured, energetic pacing the woman in the black skirt used to have when she was still smelling of mint and talking into a white cable. She wears jeans now. And no white cable. She stops about ten steps below Elsa.

"Hi," says the woman.

She looks small. Sounds tired, but it's a different kind of tiredness than usual. A better tiredness, this time. And she smells of neither mint nor wine. Just shampoo.

"Hello," says Elsa.

"I went to the churchyard today," says the woman slowly.

"You were at the funeral?"

The woman shakes her head apologetically. "I wasn't there. Sorry. I . . . I couldn't. But I . . ." She swallows the words. Looks down at her hands. "I went to my . . . my boys' graves. I haven't been there in a very long time."

"Did it help?" asks Elsa.

The woman's lips disappear.

"I don't know."

Elsa nods. The lights in the stairwell go out. She waits for her eyes to grow accustomed to the darkness. Finally the woman seems to gather all her strength into a smile, and the skin around her mouth doesn't crack quite as much anymore.

"How was the funeral?" she asks.

Elsa shrugs.

"Like a normal funeral. Far too many people."

"Sometimes it's hard to share one's sorrow with people one doesn't know. But I think . . . there were many people who were very fond of your grandmother."

Elsa lets her hair fall over her face. The woman scratches her neck.

"It's . . . I understand it's hard. To know that your granny left home to help strangers somewhere else. . . . Me, for instance."

Elsa looks slightly suspicious. It's as if the woman read her thoughts.

"It's known as 'the trolley problem.' In ethics. I mean, for students. At university. It's . . . it's the discussion of whether it's morally right to sacrifice one person in order to save many others. You can probably read about it on Wikipedia."

Elsa doesn't respond. The woman seems to become ill at ease.

"You look angry."

Elsa shrugs and tries to decide what she's most angry about. There's a fairly long list.

"I'm not angry at you. I'm just angry at stupid Britt-Marie," she decides to say in the end.

The woman looks slightly confused and glances down at what she's holding in her hands. Her fingers drum against it.

"Don't fight with monsters, for you can become one. If you look into the abyss for long enough, the abyss looks into you."

"What are you talking about?" Elsa bursts out, secretly pleased that the woman speaks to her as if Elsa is not a child.

"Sorry, that's . . . that was Nietzsche. He was a German philosopher. It's . . . ah, I'm probably misquoting him. But I think it could mean that if you hate the one who hates, you could risk becoming like the one you hate."

Elsa's shoulders shoot up to her ears.

"Granny always said: 'Don't kick the shit, it'll go all over the place!'"

And that's the first time Elsa hears the woman in the black skirt, who now wears jeans, really burst out laughing.

"Yes, yes, that's probably a better way of putting it."

She's beautiful when she laughs. It suits her. And then she takes two steps towards Elsa and reaches out as far as she can to give her the envelope that she's holding, without having to move too close.

"This was on my boys' . . . on their . . . it was on their headstone. I don't . . . don't know who put it there. But your granny—maybe she figured out that I'd come. . . ."

Elsa takes the envelope. The woman in jeans has disappeared down the stairs before she has time to look up from the envelope. On it, it says, "To Elsa! Give this to Lennart and Maud!"

And that is how Elsa finds Granny's third letter.

Lennart is holding a coffee cup in his hand when he opens the door. Maud and Samantha are behind him, both looking very sweet. They smell of cookies.

"I have a letter for you," Elsa declares.

Lennart takes it and is just about to say something, but Elsa goes on:

"It's from my granny! She's probably sending her regards and saying sorry, because that's what she's doing in all the letters."

Lennart nods meekly. Maud nods even more meekly.

"We're so terribly sad about this whole thing with your grandmother, dear Elsa. But it was such a wonderfully beautiful funeral, we thought. We're so glad that we were invited. Come in and have a dream—and Alf brought over some of that chocolate drink as well." Maud beams.

Samantha barks. Even her bark sounds friendly. Elsa takes a

dream from the proffered tin, filled to the top. She smiles cooperatively at Maud.

"I have a friend who likes dreams very much. And he's been on his own all day. Do you think it would be all right to bring him up?"

Maud and Lennart nod as if it goes without saying.

24

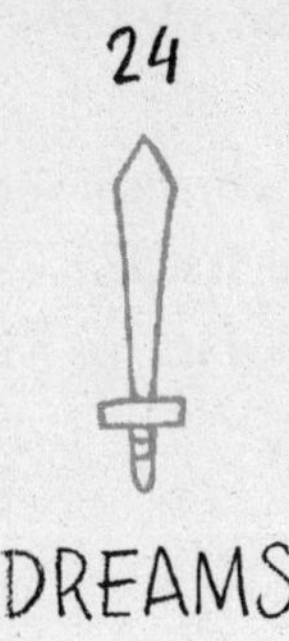

DREAMS

Maud doesn't look quite as convinced once the wurse is sitting on her kitchen rug a few moments later. Especially as it's literally sitting on the entire kitchen rug.

"I told you it likes dreams, didn't I?" says Elsa cheerfully.

Maud nods mutely. Lennart sits on the other side of the table, with an immeasurably terrified-looking Samantha on his lap. The wurse eats dreams, a dozen at a time.

"What breed is that?" says Lennart very quietly to Elsa, as if he's afraid the wurse may take offense.

"A wurse!" says Elsa with satisfaction.

Lennart nods like you do when you don't have a clue what something means. Maud opens a new tin of dreams and carefully pushes it across the floor with the tips of her toes. The wurse empties it in three slavering bites, then lifts its head and peers at Maud with eyes as big as hubcaps. Maud takes down another two tins and tries not to look flattered. It doesn't go so very well.

Elsa looks at the letter from Granny. It's lying unfolded and open on the table. Lennart and Maud must have read it while she was in the cellar getting the wurse. Lennart notices her looking, and he puts his hand on her shoulder.

"You're right, Elsa. Your grandmother says sorry."

"For what?"

Maud gives the wurse some cinnamon buns and half a length of sweet cake.

"Well, it was quite a list. Your grandmother was certainly—"

"Different," Elsa interjects.

Maud laughs warmly and pats the wurse on the head.

Lennart nods at the letter.

"First of all she apologizes for telling us off so often. And for being angry so often. And for arguing and causing problems. It's really nothing to apologize about, all people do that from time to time!" he says, as if apologizing for Granny apologizing.

"You don't," says Elsa and likes them for it. Maud starts giggling. "And then she apologized about that time she happened to shoot Lennart from her balcony with one of those, what are they called, paint-bomb guns!"

Suddenly she looks embarrassed.

"Is that what it's called? Paint-bomb?"

Elsa nods. Even though it isn't. Maud looks proud.

"Once your grandmother even got Britt-Marie—there was a big pink stain on her floral-print jacket, and that's Britt-Marie's favorite jacket and the stain wouldn't even go away with Vanish! Can you imagine?"

Maud titters. And then she looks very guilty.

"What else does Granny apologize about?" Elsa asks, hoping for more stories about someone shooting that paintball gun at Britt-Marie. But Lennart's chin drops towards his chest. He looks at Maud and she nods, and Lennart turns to Elsa and says:

"Your granny wrote that she was sorry for asking us to tell you the whole story. Everything you have to know."

"What story?" Elsa's about to ask, but she suddenly becomes

aware of someone standing behind her. She twists round in her chair, and the boy with a syndrome is standing in the bedroom doorway with a cuddly lion in his arms.

He looks at Elsa, but when she looks back at him he lets his hair fall over his brow, like Elsa sometimes does. He's about a year younger, but almost exactly as tall, and they have the same hairstyle and almost the same color too. The only thing that sets them apart is that Elsa is different and the boy has a syndrome, which is a very special kind of difference.

The boy doesn't say anything, because he never does. Maud kisses his forehead and whispers, "Nightmare?" and the boy nods. Maud gets a big glass of milk and a whole tin of dreams, takes his hand, and leads him back into the bedroom, while robustly saying: "Come on, let's chase it away at once!"

Lennart turns to Elsa.

"I think your grandmother wanted me to start at the beginning."

And that was the day Elsa heard the story of the boy with a syndrome. A fairy tale she'd never heard before. A tale so terrible it makes you want to hug yourself as hard as you can. Lennart tells her about the boy's father, who has more hatred in him than anyone could think would be possible to fit into one person. The father used narcotics. Lennart stops himself, and seems worried about frightening Elsa, but she straightens her back and buries her hands in the wurse's fur and says it doesn't matter. Lennart asks if she knows what narcotics are, and she says she's read about them on Wikipedia.

Lennart describes how the father became a different creature when he used drugs. How he became dark in his soul. How he hit the boy's mother while she was pregnant, because he didn't want to become anyone's father. Lennart's eyes start blinking more and more slowly, and he says that maybe it was because the father feared the child would be as he was. Filled with hatred and violence. So when the boy was born, and the doctors said he had a syndrome, the father was beside himself with rage. He couldn't tolerate that the child was different. Maybe it was because he hated everything that was different. Maybe because, when he looked at the boy, he saw everything that was different in himself.

So he drank alcohol, took more of that stuff on Wikipedia, and disappeared for entire nights and sometimes for weeks on end, without anyone knowing where he was. Sometimes he came home utterly calm and withdrawn. Sometimes he cried, explaining that he'd had to keep out of the way until he'd wrung his own anger out of himself. As if there were something dark living in him that was trying to transform him, and he was struggling against it. He could remain calm for weeks after that. Or months.

Then one night the dark took possession of him. He hit and hit and hit them until neither of them was moving anymore. And then he ran.

Maud's voice moves gently through the silence that Lennart leaves behind him in the kitchen. In the bedroom the boy with a syndrome snores, which is one of the first sounds Elsa has ever heard him make. Maud's fingertips scramble about among the empty cookie tins on the kitchen counter.

"We found them. We'd been trying, for such a long time, to make her take the boy and leave, but she was so afraid. We were all so afraid. He was a terribly dangerous man," she whispers.

Elsa grips the wurse tighter.

"Then what did you do?"

Maud crumples up by the kitchen table. She has an envelope in her hand, just like the one Elsa arrived with.

"We knew your grandmother. From the hospital. We ran a café back then, you see, for the doctors, and your grandmother came there every day. A dozen dreams and a dozen cinnamon buns, every single day! I don't know how it started, really. But your grandmother was the sort of person one told things to, if you see what I mean? I didn't know what to do about Sam. I didn't know who to turn to. We were so terribly frightened, all of us, but I called her. She arrived in her rusty old car in the middle of the night—"

"Renault!" Elsa exclaims, because for some reason she has a sense that he deserves his name in the fairy tale if he's the one who came to their rescue. Lennart clears his throat with a sad smile.

"Her Renault, yes. We took the boy and his mother with us and your grandmother drove here. Gave us the keys to the flats. I can't think how she got her hands on them, but she said she'd clear it with the owners of the building. We've been living here ever since."

"And the father? What happened when he realized everyone was gone?" Elsa wants to know, although she actually doesn't want to know.

Lennart's hand seeks Maud's fingers.

"We don't know. But your grandmother came here with Alf, and said this is Alf and he's going to fetch all the boy's things. And she went back there with Alf and the boy's father turned up and he was . . . nothing but darkness then. Darkness from deep inside. He hit Alf something terrible—"

Lennart stops himself the way one does when suddenly reminding oneself that one is talking to a child. Fast-forwards through the story.

"Well, of course, he was already gone by the time the police came. And Alf, gosh, I don't know. He was patched up at the hospital and drove home by himself and never said a word about it again. And two days later he was driving his cab again. He's made of steel, that man."

"And the father?" Elsa persists.

"He disappeared. Disappeared for years. We thought he'd

never give up trying to find us, but he was gone for so long that we hoped—" says Lennart, interrupting himself as if the words are too heavy for his tongue.

"But now he's found us," Maud fills in.

"How?" asks Elsa.

Lennart's eyes creep along the tabletop.

"Alf thinks he found your grandmother's death notice, you see. And using that he found the undertaker's. And there he found—" he starts to say, then looks as if he's reminding himself of something once again.

"Me?" Elsa gulps.

Lennart nods and Maud lets go of his hand and runs around the table and embraces Elsa.

"Dear, dear Elsa! You have to understand, he hasn't seen the boy in many years. And you're about the same size and you have the same hair. He thinks you're our grandchild."

Elsa closes her eyes. Her temples are burning, and for the first time in her life she uses pure and furious willpower to go to the Land-of-Almost-Awake without even being close to sleeping. With all the most powerful force of imagination she can muster she calls up the cloud animals and flies to Miaudacas. Gathers up all the courage she can carry. Then she pries her eyes open and looks at Lennart and Maud and says:

"So you're his mother's parents?"

Lennart's tears fall onto the tablecloth like rain against a windowsill.

"No. We're his father's parents."

Elsa squints.

"You're the father's parents?"

Maud's chest rises and sinks and she pats the wurse on the head and goes to fetch a chocolate cake. Samantha looks cautiously at the wurse. Lennart goes to get more coffee. His cup trembles so much that it spills onto the countertop.

"I know it sounds terrible, Elsa, taking a child from his father. To do that to your own son. But when you become grandparents, then you are grandparents first and foremost. . . ." he whispers sadly.

"You're a grandmother and grandfather above all things! Always! *Always!*" Maud adds with unshakable defiance, and her eyes burn in a way that Elsa wouldn't have believed was possible in Maud.

Then she gives Elsa the envelope she got from the bedroom.

It has Granny's handwriting on it. Elsa doesn't recognize the name, but she understands it's for the boy's mother.

"She changed her name when we moved here," Maud explains and, in the softest voice possible, adds: "Your grandmother left this letter with us months ago. She said you had to come for it. She knew you'd come."

Lennart inhales unhappily. His and Maud's eyes meet again, then he explains:

"But I'm afraid that first of all we have to tell you about our son, Elsa. We have to tell you about Sam. And that's one of the things your grandmother apologizes for in her letter. She writes that she's sorry she saved Sam's life. . . ."

Maud's voice cracks until her words are like little whistles:

"And then she wrote that she was sorry for writing to say she was sorry about it, sorry for regretting that she had saved our son's life. Sorry because she no longer knew if he deserved to live. Even though she was a doctor . . ."

Night comes to the streets outside the window. The kitchen smells of coffee and chocolate cake. And Elsa listens to the story of Sam.

The son of the world's kindest couple, who became more evil than anyone could understand. Who became the father of the boy with a syndrome, who, in turn, had less evil in him than anyone could have believed, as if his father took it all on his shoulders and passed none of it on. She heard the story of how Sam was once a little boy himself, and how Maud and Lennart, who had waited for a child for so long, had loved him, as parents love their children. As all parents, even the very, very worst possible, must at some point have loved their children. That is how Maud puts it. "Because otherwise one can't be a human being, I just can't imagine one could be a human otherwise," she whispers. And she insists that it has to be her fault, because she can't imagine that any child is born evil. It has to be the mother's fault if a boy who was once so small and helpless grows up into something so terrible, she's quite sure of that. In spite of Elsa saying that Granny always said some people are actually just shits and that it's no one else's fault other than the shit's.

"But Sam was always so angry, I don't know where all that anger came from. There must have been a darkness in me that I passed over to him, and I don't know where it came from," Maud whispers, quite crushed.

And then she talks about a boy who grew up and always fought, always tormented other children at school, always chased those who were different. And about how when he was an adult he became a soldier and went to far-off lands because he thirsted for war, and how he met a friend there. His first real friend. About how everyone who saw it said that it had changed him, brought out something good in him. His friend was also a soldier, but another sort of soldier, without that thirst. They became inseparable. Sam said his friend was the bravest warrior he had ever seen.

They went home together and his friend introduced Sam to a girl he knew, and she saw something in Sam and for a brief moment Lennart and Maud also got to see a glimpse of someone else. A Sam beyond the darkness.

"We thought she'd save him, we all hoped so much that she'd

save him, because it would have been like a fairy tale, and when one has lived in the dark for so long it's so very difficult not to believe in fairy tales," Maud admits, while Lennart clasps her hand.

"But then those little circumstances of life came up," Lennart sighs, "like in so many fairy tales. And maybe it wasn't Sam's fault. Or maybe it was entirely Sam's fault. Maybe it's for people much wiser than I to decide whether every person is completely responsible for their actions or not. But Sam went back to the wars. And he came home even darker."

"He used to be an idealist," Maud interjects gloomily. "Despite all that hatred and anger, he was an idealist. That's why he wanted to be a soldier."

And then Elsa asks if she can borrow Maud and Lennart's computer.

"If you have a computer, I mean!" she adds apologetically, because she thinks about the palaver she had with Wolfheart when she asked him the same thing.

"Of course we have a computer," says Lennart, puzzled. "Who doesn't these days?"

Quite right, thinks Elsa, and decides to bring it up with Wolfheart next time he turns up. If there is another time.

Lennart leads her past the bedroom. In the little study at the far end of the flat, he explains that their computer is very old, of course, so she has to have a bit of patience. And on a table in there is the most unwieldy computer Elsa has ever seen, and at the back of the actual computer is a gigantic box, and on the floor is another box.

"What's that?" says Elsa, pointing at the box on the floor.

"That's the actual computer," says Lennart.

"And what about that?" asks Elsa and points at the other box.

"That's the monitor," says Lennart and presses a big button on the box on the floor, then adds: "It'll take a minute or so before it starts, so we'll have to wait a bit."

"A MINUTE!" Elsa bursts out, then mumbles: "Wow. It really is old."

But when the old computer has eventually started and Lennart after many ifs and buts has gotten her onto the Internet and she has found what she is looking for, she goes back into the kitchen and sits opposite Maud.

"So it means a dreamer. An idealist, I mean. It means a dreamer."

"Yes, yes, you could probably say that," says Maud with a friendly smile.

"It's not that you could say it. It's what it actually means," Elsa corrects.

And then Maud nods, even friendlier. And then she tells the story of the idealist who turned into a cynic, and Elsa knows what that means because a teacher at Elsa's preschool once called Elsa that. There was an uproar when Elsa's mum found out about it, but the teacher stood his ground. Elsa can't remember the exact details, but she thinks it was that time she told the other preschool pupils how sausages were made.

She wonders if she's thinking about these things as a kind of defense mechanism. For this tale really has too much reality in it. It often happens, when you're almost eight, that there's just too much reality.

Maud describes how Sam went off to a new war. He had his friend with him, and for several weeks they had been protecting a village from attack by people who, for some reason unknown to Maud, wanted to kill all who lived there. In the end they received an order to abandon the place, but Sam's friend refused. He convinced Sam and the rest of the soldiers to stay until the village was safe, and took as many injured children as they could fit into their cars to the nearest hospital, many miles away, because Sam's friend knew a woman who worked as a doctor there, and everyone said she was the most skillful surgeon in the whole world.

They were on their way through the desert when they hit the mine. The explosion was merciless. There was a rain of fire and blood.

"Did anyone die?" asks Elsa, without really wanting to know the answer.

"All of them," says Lennart, without wanting to speak the words out loud. Except Sam's friend and Sam himself. Sam was unconscious, but his friend dragged him out of the fire, Sam was the only one he had time to save. The friend had shrapnel in his face and terrible burns, but when he heard the shots and realized they'd been ambushed, he grabbed his rifle and ran into the desert and didn't stop firing until only he and Sam lay there in the desert, panting and bleeding.

The people who had been shooting at him were boys. Children, just like the children the soldiers had just tried to save. Sam's friend could see that, as he stood over their dead bodies, with their blood on his hands. And he was never the same again.

Somehow he managed to carry Sam through the desert and didn't stop until he came to the hospital and Elsa's grandmother came running towards them. She saved Sam's life. He would always have a slight limp in one leg, but he would survive, and it was at that hospital that Sam started smoking Granny's brand of cigarettes. Granny also apologizes about that in the letter.

Maud carefully places the photo album in front of Elsa, as if it were a small creature with feelings. Points at a photo of the boy with a syndrome's mother. She's standing between Lennart and Maud and wearing a bridal gown and they are laughing, all three of them.

"I think Sam's friend was in love with her. But he introduced her to Sam and they fell in love instead. I don't think Sam's friend ever said anything. They were like brothers, those two, can you imagine? I think his friend was just too kind to mention his own feelings, do you understand?"

Elsa understands. Maud smiles.

"He was always such a soft boy, Sam's friend. I always thought he had the soul of a poet. They were so different, him and Sam. It's so terribly difficult to imagine he would do all that he did to save Sam's life. That the place they were in could have made him such a fearsome . . ."

She is silent for a long time, overcome with sorrow.

"Warrior," she whispers, turning the page of the photo album.

Elsa doesn't need to see the photo to know who it's of.

It's Sam. He is standing somewhere in a desert, wearing a uniform and supporting himself on crutches. Next to him stands Elsa's granny with a stethoscope around her neck. And between them stands Sam's best friend. Wolfheart.

25

SPRUCE

It was the cloud animals that saved the Chosen One when the shadows came in secret to the kingdom of Mimovas to kidnap him. For while Miamas is made of fantasy, Mimovas is made of love. Without love there is no music, and without music there is no Mimovas, and the Chosen One was the most beloved in the whole kingdom. So if the shadows had taken him, it would eventually have led to the downfall of the Land-of-Almost-Awake. If Mimovas falls then Mirevas falls, and if Mirevas falls then Miamas falls, and if Miamas falls then Miaudacas falls, and if Miaudacas falls then Miploris falls. Because without music there can't be any dreams, and without dreams there can't be any fairy tales, and without fairy tales there can't be any courage, and without courage no one would be able to bear any sorrows, and without music and dreams and fairy tales and courage and sorrow there would only be one kingdom left in the Land-of-Almost-Awake: Mibatalos. But Mibatalos can't live alone, because the warriors there would be worthless without the other kingdoms, because they'd no longer have anything to fight for.

Granny also stole that from Harry Potter, that bit about having something to fight for. But Elsa forgave her because it was quite good. You're allowed to nick stuff if it's good.

And it was the cloud animals that saw the shadows stealing along between the houses in Mimovas, and they did what cloud animals do: they swept down like arrows and up again like mighty ships, they transformed themselves into dromedaries and apples and old fishermen with cigars, and the shadows threw themselves into the trap. Because soon they didn't know who or what they were chasing. Then all at once the cloud animals disappeared, and one of them bore away the Chosen One. All the way to Miamas.

And that was how the War-Without-End began. And if it hadn't been for the cloud animals it would have ended there, that day, and the shadows would have won.

Elsa is in the Land-of-Almost-Awake all night. She can get there whenever she wants now, as if it had never been a problem. She doesn't know why, but assumes it's because she has nothing to lose anymore. The shadow is in the real world now, Elsa knows who he is, and she knows who Granny was and who Wolfheart is and how it all hangs together. She's not frightened anymore. She knows that the war will come, that it's inevitable, and the mere fact of knowing it makes her strangely calm.

The Land-of-Almost-Awake is not burning as it was in the dream. Wherever she rides, it's as beautiful and tranquil as ever. Only when she wakes up does she realize that she has avoided venturing into Miamas. She rides to all five other kingdoms, even the ruins where Mibatalos used to be before the War-Without-End. But never to Miamas. Because she doesn't want to know if Granny is there. Doesn't want to know if Granny *isn't* there.

Dad is standing in the doorway of her bedroom. At once she's wide awake, as if someone had just squirted menthol up her nose. (Which, just as an aside, works insanely well if you want to wake someone up. You'd know that if you have the kind of granny Elsa had.)

"What's the matter? Is Mum ill? Is it Halfie?"

Dad looks dubious. And slightly nonplussed. Elsa blinks away her sleep and remembers that Mum is at a meeting at the hospital, because she tried to wake Elsa up before she left, but she pretended to be asleep. And George is in the kitchen, because he came in a bit earlier to ask if she wanted any eggs, but she pretended to be asleep. So she looks at her father with confusion.

"It's not your day for you to be with me, is it?"

Dad clears his throat. Looks like dads do when it suddenly dawns on them that something they used to do because it was important to their daughters has now become one of those things their daughters do because it's important to their dads. It's a very thin line to cross. Neither dads nor their daughters ever forget when they do cross it.

Elsa counts the days in her head, instantly remembers, and instantly apologizes. She was right, it isn't Dad's day. But she was wrong, because today's the day before Christmas Eve, which is a terrible thing to forget. Because the day before Christmas Eve is her and Dad's day. Christmas-tree day.

As the name subtly suggests, this is the day that Elsa and Dad buy their Christmas tree. A plastic one, obviously, because Elsa refuses to buy a real tree. But because Dad enjoys the annual tradition so much, Elsa insists on buying a new plastic tree every year. Some people find it a bit of an odd tradition, but Granny used to say that "every child of divorce has the right to get a bit bloody eccentric now and then."

Mum, of course, was very angry at Granny about the whole plastic tree thing, because she likes the smell of a real spruce tree and always said that the plastic tree was something Granny had duped Elsa about. Because it was Granny who had told Elsa about the

Christmas tree dance in Miamas, and no one who's heard that story wants to have a spruce tree that someone has amputated and sold into slavery. In Miamas, spruce trees are living, thinking creatures with—considering that they're coniferous trees—an unaccountably strong interest in home design.

They don't live in the forest but in the southern districts of Miamas, which have become quite trendy in recent years, and they often work in the advertising industry and wear scarves indoors. And once every year, soon after the first snow has fallen, all the spruce trees gather in the big square below the castle and compete for the right to stay in someone's house over Christmas. The spruce trees choose the houses, not the other way around, and the choice is decided by a dance competition. In the olden days they used to have duels about it, but spruce trees are generally such bad shots that it used to take forever. So now they do spruce dancing, which looks a bit unusual, because spruce trees don't have feet. And if a non–spruce tree wants to imitate a dancing spruce tree, they just jump up and down. It's quite handy, particularly on a crowded dance floor.

Elsa knows that because when Dad drinks a glass and a half of champagne on New Year's Eve, he sometimes does the spruce dance in the kitchen with Lisette. But for Dad it's just known as "dancing."

"Sorry, Dad, I do know what day it is!" Elsa yells, hopping into her jeans, getting into her sweater and jacket, and running into the hall. "I just have to do one thing first!"

Elsa hid the wurse in Renault last night. She brought it down a bucket of cinnamon buns from Maud and told it to hide under the blankets in the backseat if anyone came down into the garage. "You have to pretend you're a pile of clothes or a TV or something!" suggested Elsa, though the wurse didn't look entirely convinced. So Elsa had to go and get a sack of dreams from Maud, after which the wurse gave in and crept under the blankets. It didn't look much like a TV, though.

Elsa said good night, sneaked back up the stairs, and stood in the dark outside the flat where the mother and the boy with a syndrome live. She was going to ring at the door, but she couldn't quite make herself do it. Didn't want to hear any more stories. Didn't want to know about shadows and darkness. So she just put the letter in the slot in the door and ran away.

Their door is locked and shut today. All the other doors too. Anyone who's awake has left the house; everyone else is still asleep. So Elsa hears Kent's voice several floors up, even though he's whispering, because that's how the acoustics of stairwells work. Elsa knows that because "acoustics" is a word for the word jar. She hears Kent whispering, "Yes, I promise I'll be back tonight." But when he comes down the last flight of stairs, past the wurse's and Wolfheart's flats and the boy and the mother's flat, Kent suddenly starts talking in a loud voice and calling out, "Yes, Klaus! In Frankfurt! Yez, yez, yez!" And then he turns around and pretends that he's only just noticed Elsa standing behind him.

"What are you doing?" asks Elsa suspiciously.

Kent asks Klaus to hold the line, as you do when there is actually no Klaus at all on the line. He is wearing a rugby shirt with numbers and a little man on a horse on his chest. Kent has told Elsa that this sort of shirt costs more than a thousand kronor, and Granny always used to say that those sorts of shirts were a good thing, because the horse functioned as a sort of manufacturer's warning that the shirt was highly likely to be transporting a muppet.

"What do you want?" Kent sneers.

Elsa stares at him. Then at the small red bowls of meat that he's distributing down the stairwell.

"What are those?"

Kent throws out his hands so quickly that he almost throws Klaus into the wall.

"That hound is still running around here, it reduces the value of the leasehold conversion!"

Elsa backs away watchfully, without taking her eyes off the bowls of meat. Kent seems to realize that he has expressed himself a little clumsily, so he makes another attempt, in the sort of voice that men of Kent's age think one must put on when talking to girls of Elsa's age, so they'll understand:

"Britt-Marie found dog hairs on the stairs, you understand, darling? We can't have wild animals roving around the building—it reduces the value of the leasehold conversion, you see?" He smiles condescendingly; she can see that he's glancing insecurely at his telephone. "It's not like we're going to kill it! It'll just go to sleep for a bit, okay? Now, why don't you be a good girl and go home to your mummy?"

Elsa doesn't feel so very good. And she doesn't like the way Kent makes quotation marks in the air when he says "go to sleep." "Who are you talking to on the phone?"

"Klaus, a business contact from Germany," answers Kent as one does when doing no such thing.

"Sure," says Elsa.

Kent's eyebrows sink.

"Are you giving me attitude?"

Elsa shrugs.

"I think you should run home to your mummy now," Kent repeats, a touch more menacingly.

Elsa points at the bowls. "Is there poison in them?"

"Listen, girlie, stray dogs are *vermin*. We can't have vermin running about here, and rust-heaps down in the garage, and all kinds of crap. It'll lower the value, don't you understand? It's better for everyone this way."

But Elsa hears something ominous in his voice when he says "rust-heaps," so she pushes past him and charges down the cellar stairs. Throws open the door to the garage and stands there with her hands shaking and her heartbeat thumping through her body. She knocks her knees against every step on the way back up.

"WHERE'S RENAULT! WHAT THE HELL HAVE YOU DONE WITH RENAULT!?" she yells at Kent. She waves her fists at him, but only manages to grab hold of Klaus, so she throws Klaus down the cellar stairs so the glass display and plastic cover are smashed and tumble down in a miniature electronic avalanche towards the storage units.

"Are you out of your fu— bloody . . . out of your bloody *mind*, you stupid kid? You know what that telephone *cost*?" yells Kent, and then he tells her it bloody cost eight thousand kronor.

Elsa informs him that she couldn't give a damn what it cost. And then Kent informs her with a sadistic gleam in his eye exactly what he did with Renault.

She runs up the stairs to fetch Dad, but stops abruptly on the penultimate floor. Britt-Marie is standing in her doorway. She's clasping her hands over her stomach, and Elsa can see that she's sweating. The kitchen behind her smells of Christmas food, and she's wearing her flower-print jacket with her large brooch. The pink paintball stain is hardly visible at all.

"You mustn't let Kent kill it," pleads Elsa, wide-eyed. "Please, Britt-Marie, it's my friend. . . ."

Britt-Marie meets her eyes, and for a single fleeting second there's some humanity in them. Elsa can see that. But then Kent's voice can be heard, calling to Britt-Marie from the stairwell that she has to bring more poison, and then the normal Britt-Marie is back.

"Kent's children are coming here tomorrow. They're afraid of dogs," she explains firmly.

She straightens out a wrinkle that isn't there on her skirt, and brushes something invisible off her floral-print jacket.

"We're having a traditional Christmas dinner here tomorrow. With some normal Christmas food. Like a civilized family. We're not barbarians, you know."

Then she slams the door. Elsa stays where she is and realizes that Dad is not going to be able to solve this, because tentativeness is not a very useful superpower in this type of emergency situation. She needs reinforcements.

She has been banging on the door for more than a minute before she hears Alf's dragging footsteps. He opens it with a cup of coffee in his hand that smells so strong that she's sure a spoon would get stuck in it.

"I'm sleeping," he grunts.

"He's killing Renault!" sobs Elsa.

"Killing? Nothing's going to be killed around here. It's only a bloody car," says Alf, swallows a mouthful of coffee and yawns.

"It's not just a car! It's RENAULT!"

"Who the hell has told you he's going to kill Renault?"

"Kent!"

Elsa hasn't even had time to explain what's in Renault's backseat before Alf has put down the coffee cup, stepped into his shoes, and set off down the stairs. She hears Alf and Kent roaring at each other so terribly that she has to cover her ears. She can't hear what they're saying, except that it's a lot of swearwords, and Kent shouts something about leaseholds and how one can't have "rust-heaps" parked in the garage because then people will think the house is full of "socialists." Which is Kent's way of saying "bloody idiots," Elsa understands. And then Alf shouts, "Bloody idiot," which is his way of saying exactly that, because Alf is not big on complicating things.

And then Alf comes stamping up the stairs again, wild-eyed, muttering:

"The bastard got someone to tow the car away. Is your dad here?"

Elsa nods. Alf storms up the stairs without a word, and a few moments later Elsa and Dad are sitting in Taxi, even though Dad doesn't want to at all.

"I'm not sure I want to do this," says Dad.

"Someone has to bloody drive the damned Renault home," grunts Alf.

"How do we find out where Kent sent it, then?" asks Elsa, at the same time that Dad does his best not to look completely tentative.

"I've been driving a damned taxi for thirty years," says Alf.

"And?" hisses Elsa.

"And so I bloody know how to find a Renault that's been towed away!"

Twenty minutes later they're standing in a scrapyard outside the city, and Elsa is hugging the hood of Renault in the exact same way you hug a cloud animal: with your whole body. She can see that the TV in the backseat is shuffling about, fairly displeased about not being the first to be hugged, but if you're almost eight and forget to hug a wurse in a Renault, it's because you're less worried about the wurse than the poor scrapyard worker who happens to find it.

Alf and the fairly fat foreman argue for a short while about what it's going to cost to take Renault away. And then Alf and Elsa argue for a fairly long time about why she never mentioned that she didn't have a key to Renault. And then the fat man walks around mumbling that he was sure he left his moped here earlier and where the hell was it now? And then Alf and the fat man negotiate about what it'll cost to tow Renault back to the house. And then Dad has to pay for it all.

It's the best present he's ever given Elsa. Even better than the red felt-tip pen.

Alf ensures that Renault is parked in Granny's slot in the garage, not in Britt-Marie's. When Elsa introduces them to each other, Dad stares at the wurse with the expression of someone preparing for a root canal. The wurse glares back, a bit cocky. Too cocky, thinks Elsa, so she hauls it over the coals about whether it ate the scrapyard foreman's moped. Whereupon the wurse stops looking cocky and goes to lie down under the blankets and looks a bit as if it's thinking that if people don't want it to eat mopeds, then people should be more generous with the cinnamon buns.

She tells Dad, to his immense relief, that he can go and wait in Audi. Then Elsa and Alf gather all the red food bowls from the stairwell and put them in a big black trash bag. Kent catches them and fumes that the poison bloody cost him six hundred kronor. Britt-Marie just stands there.

And then Elsa goes with Dad to buy a plastic tree. Because Britt-Marie is wrong, Elsa's family are no barbarians. Anyway the proper term is "baa-baa-rians," because in Miamas that is what the spruce trees call those dumb sheep in the real world who chop down living trees, then carry them off and sell them into slavery.

"I'll give you three hundred," says Elsa to the man in the shop.

"My dear, there's no bargaining in this shop," says the man in the shop in exactly the sort of tone one might expect of men in shops. "It costs four hundred and ninety-five."

"I'll give you two fifty."

The man smiles mockingly.

"Now I'll only give you two hundred," Elsa informs him.

The man looks at Elsa's dad. Dad looks at his shoes. Elsa looks at the man and shakes her head seriously.

"My dad is not going to help you. I'll give you two hundred."

The man arranges his face into something that's probably supposed to look like an expression of how you look at children when they're cute but stupid.

"This is not how it works, my dear."

Elsa shrugs. "What time do you close today?"

"In five minutes," sighs the man.

"And do you have a big warehouse space here?"

"What's that got to do with it?"

"I was just wondering."

"No. We don't have any warehouse space at all."

"And are you open on Christmas Eve?"

He pauses. "No."

Elsa pouts her lips with pretend surprise.

"So you have a tree here. And no warehouse. And what day is it tomorrow, again?"

Elsa gets the tree for two hundred. She gets a box of balcony lights and an insanely big Christmas elk thrown in for the same price.

"You MUSTN'T go back in and give him any extra money!" Elsa warns Dad while he's loading it all into Audi. Dad sighs.

"I only did it once, Elsa. On one occasion. And that time you were actually exceptionally unpleasant to the salesman."

"You have to negotiate!"

Granny taught Elsa to do that. Dad also used to hate going to the shops with her.

Audi stops outside the house. As usual, Dad has turned down the volume of the stereo so Elsa doesn't have to listen to his music. Alf comes out to help Dad carry up the box, but Dad insists on carrying it himself. Because it's a tradition that he brings the tree home for his daughter. Before he leaves, Elsa wants to tell him that she'd like to stay with him more after Halfie's been born. But she doesn't want to upset him, so in the end she says nothing. She just whispers, "Thanks for the tree, Dad," and he's happy and then he goes home to Lisette and her children. And Elsa stands there watching as he leaves.

Because no one gets upset if you don't say anything. All almost-eight-year-olds know that.

26

PIZZA

In Miamas you celebrate Christmas the evening before, just like in Sweden, but it's because that's when the Christmas tales are told. All tales are regarded as treasures in Miamas, but the Christmas tales are something truly special. A normal story can either be funny or sad or exciting or scary or dramatic or sentimental, but a Christmas tale has to be all those things. "A Christmas tale has to be written with every pen you own," Granny used to say. And they have to have happy endings, which is something that Elsa has decided completely on her own.

Because Elsa's no fool. She knows if there was a dragon at the beginning of the story, the dragon will turn up again before the story is done. She knows everything has to become darker and more horrible before everything works out just fine at the end. Because that is how all the best stories go.

She knows she's going to have to fight, even though she's tired of fighting. So it has to end happily, this fairy tale.

It has to.

She misses the smell of pizza when she goes down the stairs. Granny said there was a law in Miamas about having to eat pizza at Christmas Eve. Granny was full of nonsense, of course, but Elsa went along with it, because she likes pizza and Christmas food kind of sucks if you're a vegetarian.

The pizza also had the added bonus of making a cooking smell in the stairwell that drove Britt-Marie into a fury. Because Britt-Marie hangs Christmas decorations on her and Ken's front door, because Kent's children always come for Christmas and Britt-Marie wants to "make the stairs look nice for everyone!" And then the Christmas decorations smell of pizza all year, which provokes Britt-Marie and makes her condemn Granny as "uncivilized."

"As if THAT old bat can talk about being uncivilized?! No one is more damned civilized than I am!" Granny would snort every year while she sneaked about, as was the tradition, hanging little pieces of calzone all over Britt-Marie's Christmas decorations. And when Britt-Marie appeared at Mum and George's flat on Christmas Eve morning in such a foul mood, in that way of hers, that she said everything twice, Granny defended herself by saying that they were "pizza Christmas decorations" and that Granny actually just wanted to "make things look nice for everyone!" On one occasion she actually dropped the whole calzone through Britt-Marie and Kent's mail slot, and then Britt-Marie got so angry on Christmas morning that she forgot to put on her floral-print jacket.

No one was ever able to explain how one can drop a whole calzone through someone's letter box.

Elsa takes a couple of deep, controlled breaths on the stairs, because that's what Mum has told her to do when she gets angry. Mum really does everything that Granny never did. Such as asking Elsa to invite Britt-Marie and Kent for Christmas dinner with all the other neighbors, for example. Granny would never have done that. "Over my dead body!" Granny would have roared if Mum had suggested it.

Which she couldn't have done now that her body was actually dead, Elsa realizes, but still. It's about the principle. That's what Granny would have said if she'd been here.

But Elsa can't say no to Mum right now, because Mum, after a lot of nagging, has agreed to let the wurse hide in Granny's flat over Christmas. It's quite difficult saying no to a mum who lets you bring a wurse home, even if Mum still sighs about Elsa "exaggerating" when Elsa says Kent is trying to kill it.

On the other hand, Elsa is happy that the wurse took an instant dislike to George. Not that Elsa feels anyone should hate George, but really no one ever has, so it's nice just for a change.

The boy with a syndrome and his mum are about to move into Granny's flat. Elsa knows that because she played hide-the-key with the boy all afternoon while Mum, George, Alf, Lennart, Maud, and the boy's mother sat in the kitchen talking about secrets. They deny it, of course, but Elsa knows how secretive voices sound. You know that when you're almost eight. She hates that Mum has secrets from her. When you know someone is keeping secrets from you it makes you feel like an idiot, and no one likes feeling like an idiot. Mum of all people should know that.

Elsa knows they're talking about Granny's flat being easier to defend if Sam comes here. She knows that Sam will come sooner or later, and that Mum is going to assemble Granny's army on the top floor. Elsa was in Lennart and Maud's flat with the wurse when Mum told Maud to just "pack the essentials" and tried to sound as if it wasn't at all serious. And then Maud and the wurse packed all the cookie tins they could find into big bags, and when Mum saw that she sighed and said: "Please, Maud, I said just the essentials!" And then Maud looked at Mum in a puzzled way and replied: "Cookies *are* the essentials."

The wurse growled happily at that statement, then looked at Mum as if it was more disappointed than angry and pointedly pushed an extra tin of chocolate and peanut cookies into the bag. Then they carried it all upstairs to Granny's flat and George invited everyone for mulled wine. The wurse drank the most mulled wine of them all. And now all the grown-ups are sitting in Mum and George's kitchen, having secrets together.

Although Britt-Marie and Kent's door is full of Christmas decorations, no one answers when Elsa rings the doorbell. She finds Britt-Marie in the corridor downstairs, just inside the entrance. She stands with her hands clasped together on her stomach, staring disconsolately at the stroller, which is still locked to the banister. She's wearing the floral-print jacket and the brooch. And there's a new notice on the wall.

The first sign was the one that said it was forbidden to leave strollers there. And then someone took that sign down. And now someone has put up a new sign. And the stroller is still there. And it's actually not a sign, Elsa notices when she goes closer. It's a crossword.

Britt-Marie is startled when she catches sight of her.

"I suppose you find this funny," she starts, "you and your family. Making the rest of us look foolish in this house. But I'll get to the bottom of it and find those who are responsible for this, you can be quite sure about that. It's actually a fire risk to have strollers in the stairwell and to keep taping up notices on the walls! The paper can actually start burning!"

She rubs an invisible stain from her brooch.

"I'm actually not an idiot, I'm actually not. I know you talk behind my back in this leaseholders' association, I know you do!"

Elsa doesn't quite know what happens inside her at that point, but it must be the combination of the words "not an idiot" and "behind my back," perhaps. Something very unpleasant and acidic and foul-smelling rises in Elsa's throat, and it takes a long time before, with disgust, she has to admit to herself that it's sympathy.

No one likes feeling like an idiot.

So Elsa says nothing about how maybe Britt-Marie could try to stop being such a bloody busybody all the time, if she wants people to talk to her a bit more. She doesn't even mention that this is not actually a leaseholders' association. She just swallows all the pride she's feasting on and mumbles:

"Mum and George want to invite you and Kent for Christmas dinner tomorrow. Everyone in the house is going to be there."

Britt-Marie's gaze wavers for just an instant. Elsa briefly recalls the look she gave earlier today, the human look, but then she seems to snap out of it.

"Well, well, I can't respond to invitations just like that, because Kent is actually at the office right now, and certain people in this house have *jobs* to take care of. You can give your mother that message. Not all people have *time off* all Christmas. And Kent's children are coming tomorrow and they actually don't like running about, going to other people's parties, they like being home with me and Kent. And we're eating some ordinary Christmas food, like a civilized family. We are. You can give your mother that message!"

Britt-Marie storms off; Elsa stays where she is, shaking her head and mumbling, "Muppet, muppet, muppet." She looks at the crossword above the stroller; she doesn't know who put it there, but now she wishes she'd thought of it herself, because it's obviously driving Britt-Marie barmy.

Elsa goes back up the stairs and knocks on the door of the woman with the black skirt.

"We're having Christmas dinner at our house tomorrow. You're welcome, if you like," says Elsa, and adds: "It could actually be quite nice, because Britt-Marie and Kent aren't coming!"

The woman freezes.

"I . . . I'm not so good at meeting people."

"I know. But you don't seem so good at being on your own either."

The woman looks at her for a long time, drags her hand slowly through her hair. Elsa stares back determinedly.

"I . . . maybe I can come. A . . . short while."

"We can buy pizza! If you don't, you know, like Christmas food," says Elsa hopefully.

The woman smiles. Elsa smiles back.

Alf comes out of Granny's flat just as Elsa's climbing the stairs. The boy with a syndrome is circling him happily, doing a little dance, and Alf has an enormous toolbox in one hand, which he tries to hide when he catches sight of Elsa.

"What are you doing?" asks Elsa.

"Nothing," Alf says evasively.

The boy jumps into Mum and George's flat and heads towards a large bowl of chocolate Santas. Alf tries to get past Elsa on the stairs but Elsa stands in his way.

"What's that?" she asks, pointing at the toolbox.

"Nothing!" Alf repeats and tries to hide it behind his back.

He smells strongly of wood shavings, Elsa notices.

"Sure it's nothing!" she says grumpily.

She tries to stop feeling like an idiot. It doesn't go so very well.

She looks into the flat at the boy. He looks happy in the way that only an almost-seven-year-old can look happy when standing in front of a whole big bowl of chocolate Santas. Elsa wonders if he's waiting for the real Santa, who isn't made of chocolate. Obviously,

Elsa doesn't believe in Santa, but she has a lot of faith in people who do believe in him. She used to write letters to Santa every Christmas, not just wish lists but whole letters. They weren't very much about Christmas, mainly about politics. Because Elsa mostly felt that Santa wasn't involving himself enough in social questions, and believed he needed to be informed about that, in the midst of the floods of greedy letters that she knew he must be receiving from all the other children every year. Someone had to take a bit of responsibility. One year she'd seen the Coca-Cola ad, and that time her letter was quite a lot about how Santa was a "soulless sellout." Another year she'd seen a TV documentary about child labor and, immediately after that, quite a few American Christmas comedies, and because she was unsure whether Santa's definition of "elf" should be classified as the same as the elves that exist in Old Norse mythology or the ones that live in forests in Tolkien's world, or just in the general sense of a short person, sort of thing, she demanded that Santa immediately get back to her with a precise definition.

Santa never did, so Elsa sent another letter that was very long and angry. The year after, Elsa had learned how to use Google, so then she knew the reason for Santa never answering was that he didn't exist. So she didn't write any more letters. She mentioned to Mum and Granny the next day that Santa didn't exist, and Mum got so upset that she choked on her mulled wine, and when Granny saw this she immediately turned dramatically to Elsa and pretended to be even more upset, and burst out: "DON'T you talk like that, Elsa! If you do, you're just reality-challenged!"

Mum didn't laugh at all about that, which didn't bother Granny, but on the other hand Elsa did laugh a good deal, and that pleased Granny immeasurably. And the day before Christmas, Elsa had a letter from Santa in which he gave her a right ticking-off because she'd "got herself an attitude," and then there followed a long haranguing passage that started with "you ungrateful bloody brat" and went on to say that because Elsa had stopped believing in Santa, the elves hadn't been able to reach a proper collective agreement on salaries that year.

"I know you wrote this," Elsa had hissed at Granny.

"How?" Granny asked with exaggerated outrage

"Because not even Santa is so dumb that he spells 'collective' with a double 't'!"

And then Granny had looked a little less outraged and apologized. And then she tried to get Elsa to run to the shop to buy a cigarette lighter, in exchange for Granny "timing her." But Elsa didn't fall for that one.

And then Granny had grumpily got out her newly purchased Santa suit, and they went to the children's hospital where Granny's friend worked. Granny went around all day telling fairy tales to children with terrible diseases and Elsa followed behind her, distributing toys. That was Elsa's best-ever Christmas. They would make a tradition of it, Granny promised, but it was a really crappy tradition because they only had time to do it one year before she went and died.

Elsa looks at the boy, then at Alf, and locks eyes with him. When the boy catches sight of a bowl of chocolate Santas and disappears from view, Elsa slips into the flat's front hall, opens the chest in there, and pulls out the Santa suit. She goes back onto the landing and presses it into Alf's arms.

Alf looks at it as if just tried to tickle him.

"What's that?"

"What does it look like?" asks Elsa.

"Forget it!" says Alf dismissively, pushing the costume back towards Elsa.

"Forget that you can forget about it!" says Elsa, and pushes the costume back even more.

"Your grandmother said you don't even believe in bloody Santa," mutters Alf.

Elsa rolls her eyes.

"No, but not everything in the world is about me, right?"

She points into the flat. The boy is sitting on the floor in front of the TV. Alf looks at him and grunts.

"Why can't Lennart be Santa?"

"Because Lennart couldn't keep a secret from Maud," Elsa answers impatiently.

"What's the bloody relevance of that?"

"The relevance is that Maud can't keep a secret from anyone!"

Alf squints at Elsa. Then he reluctantly mutters that that's true enough. Because Maud really couldn't keep a secret even if it was glued to the insides of her hands. While George was playing hide-the-key with Elsa and the boy with a syndrome earlier, Maud had walked behind them and repeatedly whispered, "Maybe you should look in the flowerpot in the bookshelf," and when Elsa's mum explained to Maud that the whole point of the game was sort of to find out for yourself where the key was hidden, Maud looked disconsolate and said, "The children look so sad while they're searching, I don't want them to be sad."

"So you have to be Santa," Elsa says conclusively.

"What about George?" Alf tries.

"He's too tall. And anyway it'll be too obvious, because he'll wear his jogging shorts on the outside of the Santa suit."

Alf doesn't look as if that would make much of a difference to him. He takes a couple of dissatisfied steps across the landing and into the hall, where he peers over the edge of the chest as if hoping to find a better option. But the only things he sees there are bedsheets and then Elsa's Spider-Man suit.

"What's that?" asks Alf, and pokes at it, as if it might poke him back.

"My Spider-Man suit," grunts Elsa, trying to close the lid.

"When do you get to wear that?" wonders Alf, apparently expecting to know the exact date of the annual Spider-Man day.

"I was supposed to be wearing it when school starts again. We've got a class project." She closes the chest with a slam. Alf stands there with the Santa suit in his hand and doesn't seem interested. At all, actually. Elsa groans.

"If you *haaave* to know, I'm not going to be Spider-Man, because apparently girls aren't allowed to be Spider-Man! But I don't care because I haven't got the energy to fight with everyone all the bloody time!"

Alf has already started walking back to the stairs. Elsa swallows her tears, so he doesn't hear them. Maybe he hears them all the same, though. Because he stops by the corner of the railing. Crumples up the Santa suit in his fist. Sighs. Says something that Elsa doesn't hear.

"What?" Elsa says irritably.

Alf sighs again, harder.

"I said I think your grandmother would have wanted you to dress up as any bloody thing you like," he repeats brusquely, without turning around.

Elsa pushes her hands into her pockets and glares down at the floor.

"The others at school say girls can't be Spider-Man. . . ."

Alf takes two dragging steps down the stairs. Stops. Looks at her.

"Don't you think a lot of bastards said that to your grandmother?"

Elsa peers at him.

"Did she dress up as Spider-Man?"

"No."

"What are you talking about, then?"

"She dressed up as a doctor."

"Did they tell her she couldn't be a doctor? Because she was a girl?"

Alf shifts something in the toolbox and then stuffs in the Santa suit.

"Most likely they told her a whole lot of damned things she wasn't allowed to do, for a range of different reasons. But she damned well did them all the same. A few years after she was born they were still telling girls they couldn't vote in the bleeding elections, but now the girls do it all the same. That's damned well how you stand up to bastards who tell you what you can and can't do. You bloody do those things all the bloody same."

Elsa watches her shoes. Alf watches his toolbox. Then Elsa goes into the hall, takes two chocolate Santas, eats one of them, and throws the other to Alf, who catches it in his free hand. He shrugs slightly.

"I think your grandmother would have wanted you to dress up as any old damned thing you wanted."

With that he shuffles off, his Italian opera music seeping out as he opens his door and closes it behind him. Elsa goes into the hall and fetches the whole bowl of chocolate Santas. Then she takes the boy's hand and calls the wurse. All three of them go across the landing to Granny's flat, where they crawl into the magic wardrobe that stopped growing when Granny died. It smells of wood shavings in there. And, in fact, it has magically grown to the exact dimensions needed to accommodate two children and a wurse.

The boy with a syndrome mainly keeps his eyes shut, and Elsa brings him to the Land-of-Almost-Awake. They fly over all six kingdoms, and when they turn towards Mimovas the boy recognizes where he is. He jumps off the cloud animal and starts running. When he gets to the city gates, where the music of Mimovas comes pouring out, he starts dancing. He dances beautifully. And Elsa dances with him.

27

MULLED WINE

The wurse wakes Elsa up later that night because it needs a pee. She mumbles sleepily that maybe the wurse shouldn't have drunk so much mulled wine and tries to go back to sleep. But unfortunately the wurse begins to look sort of like wurses do when they're planning to pee on a Gryffindor scarf, whereupon Elsa snatches the scarf away and reluctantly agrees to take it out.

When they get out of the wardrobe, Elsa's mum and the boy with a syndrome's mum are still up making up the beds.

"It needs a pee," Elsa explains wearily. Mum nods reluctantly but says she has to take Alf with her.

Elsa nods. The boy with a syndrome's mum smiles at her.

"I understand from Maud that it might have been you that left your grandmother's letter in our mailbox yesterday."

Elsa fixes her gaze on her socks.

"I was going to ring the bell, but I didn't want to, you know. Disturb. Sort of thing."

The boy's mum smiles again.

"She wrote sorry. Your grandmother, I mean. Sorry for not being able to protect us anymore. And she wrote that I should trust you. Always. And then she asked me to try to get you to trust me."

"Can I ask you something that could be sort of impolite?" ventures Elsa, poking at the palm of her hand.

"Absolutely."

"How can you stand being alive and being afraid all the time? I mean, when you know there's someone like Sam out there hunting you?"

"Darling, Elsa . . ." whispers Elsa's mum and smiles apologetically at the boy's mother, who just waves her hand dismissively to show that it doesn't matter at all.

"Your grandmother used to say that sometimes we have to do things that are dangerous, because otherwise we aren't really human."

"She nicked that from *The Brothers Lionheart*," says Elsa.

The boy's mother turns to Elsa's mum and looks as if she'd like to change the subject. Maybe more for Elsa's sake than her own. "Do you know if it's a boy or a girl?"

Mum grins almost guiltily and shakes her head.

"We want to wait until the birth."

"It's going to be a she/he," Elsa informs her. Her mum looks embarrassed.

"I didn't want to know either until he was born," says the boy's mother warmly, "but then I wanted to know everything about him immediately!"

"Yes, exactly, that's how I feel. It doesn't matter what it is, as long as it's healthy!"

Guilt wells up in Mum's face as soon as the last word has escaped her lips. She glances past Elsa towards the wardrobe, where the boy lies sleeping.

"Sorry. I didn't mean to—" she manages to say, but the boy's mum interrupts her at once.

"Oh, don't say sorry. It's fine. I know what people say. But he is healthy. He's just a bit of extra everything, you could say."

"I like extra everything!" Elsa exclaims happily, but then she also looks ashamed and mumbles: "Except veggie burgers. I always get rid of the tomato."

And then both the mothers laugh so hard that the flat echoes. And that's what they both seem to be most in need of. So even though it wasn't her intention, Elsa decides to take the credit for that.

Alf is waiting for her and the wurse on the stairs. She doesn't know how he knew they were coming. The darkness outside the house is so compact that if you threw a snowball, you'd lose sight of it before it left your glove. They sneak under Britt-Marie's balcony so they don't give the wurse away. The wurse backs into a bush and looks as though it would have appreciated having a newspaper or something.

Elsa and Alf turn away respectfully. Elsa clears her throat.

"Thanks for helping me with Renault."

Alf grunts. Elsa shoves her hands in her jacket pockets.

"Kent's an asswipe. Someone should poison *him*!"

Alf's head turns slowly.

"Don't say that."

"What?"

"Don't bloody talk like that."

"What? He is an asswipe, isn't he?"

"Maybe so. But you don't damn well call him that in front of me!"

"You call him a bloody idiot, like, all the time!"

"Yes. I'm allowed to. You're not."

"Why not?"

Alf's leather jacket creaks.

"Because I'm allowed to get shitty about my little brother. You're not."

It takes many different kinds of eternities for Elsa to digest that piece of information.

"I didn't know that," she manages to say at last. "Why are you so horrible to each other if you're brothers?"

"You don't get to choose your siblings," mutters Alf.

Elsa doesn't really know how to answer that. She thinks about Halfie. She'd rather not, so she changes the subject:

"Why don't you have a girlfriend?"

"Never you bloody mind."

"Have you ever been in love?"

"I'm a damned grown-up. It's bloody obvious I've been in love. Everyone's been in bloody love sometime."

"How old were you?"

"The first time?"

"Yes."

"Ten."

"And the second time?"

Alf's leather jacket creaks. He checks his watch and starts heading back to the house.

"There was no second time."

Elsa is about to ask something else. But that's when they hear it. Or rather, it's the wurse that hears it. The scream. The wurse leaps out of the bush and hurtles into the darkness like a black spear. Then Elsa hears its bark for the first time. She thought she'd heard it barking before, but she was wrong. All she's heard before are yelps and whines compared to this. This bark makes the foundations of the house quake. It's a battle cry.

Elsa gets there first. She's better at running than Alf.

Britt-Marie is standing, white-faced, a few yards from the door. There's a carrier bag of food dropped on the snow. Lollipops and comic books have spilled out of it. A stone's throw away stands Sam.

With a knife in his hand.

The wurse stands resolutely between them, its front paws planted like concrete pillars in the snow, its teeth bared. Sam isn't moving, but Elsa can see that he's hesitating. He slowly turns around and sees her, and his gaze pulverizes her spine. Her knees want to give way and let her sink into the snow and disappear. The knife glitters in the glow of the streetlights. Sam's hand hovers in the air, his body rigid with animosity. His eyes eat their way into her, cold and warlike. But the knife isn't directed at her, she can see that.

Elsa can hear Britt-Marie sobbing. She doesn't know where the instinct comes from, or the courage, or maybe it's just pure stupidity—Granny always used to say that she and Elsa were the sort of people who, deep down, were a bit soft in the head, and it would get them in trouble sooner or later—but Elsa runs. Runs right at Sam. She can see him bring the knife down confidently by a few inches, and that the other hand is raised like a claw to catch her as she leaps.

But she doesn't have time to get there. She collides with something dry and black. Feels the smell of dry leather. Hears the creaking of Alf's jacket.

And then Alf is standing in front of Sam, with the same ominous body language. Elsa sees the hammer sliding into his palm from the coat's arm. Alf swings it calmly from side to side. Sam's knife doesn't move. They do not take their eyes off each other.

Elsa doesn't know how long they stand there. For how many eternities of fairy tales. It feels like all of them. It feels as if she has time to die. As if the terror is cracking her heart.

"The police are on their way," Alf finally utters in a low voice. He sounds as if he thinks it's a pity. That they can't just finish this here and now.

Sam's eyes wander calmly from Alf to the wurse. The wurse's hackles are raised. It growls like rolling thunder from its lungs. A faint smile steals across Sam's lips for an unbearable length of time. Then he takes a single step back and the darkness engulfs him.

The police car skids into the street, but Sam is long gone by then. Elsa collapses into the snow as if her clothes have been emptied of whatever was in there. She feels Alf catching her and hears him hissing at the wurse to run up the stairs before the police catch sight of it. She hears Britt-Marie panting and the police crunching through the snow. But her consciousness is already fading, far away. She's ashamed of it, ashamed of being so afraid that she just closes her eyes and escapes into her mind. No knight of Miamas was ever so paralyzed with fear. A real knight would have stayed in position, straight-backed, not taken refuge in sleep. But she can't help it. It's too much reality for an almost-eight-year-old.

She wakes up on the bed in Granny's bedroom. It's warm. She feels the wurse's nose against her shoulder and pats its head.

"You're so brave," she whispers.

The wurse looks as if maybe it deserves a cookie. Elsa slips out of the sweaty sheets, onto the floor. Through the doorway she sees Mum standing in the front hall, her face gray. She's shouting furiously at Alf, so angry she's crying. Alf stands there in silence, taking it. Elsa runs through into Mum's arms.

"It wasn't their fault, they were only trying to protect me!" Elsa sobs.

Britt-Marie's voice interrupts her.

"No, it was obviously my fault! My fault, it was. Everything was obviously my fault, Ulrika."

Elsa turns to Britt-Marie, realizing as she does so that Maud and Lennart and the boy with a syndrome's mum are also in the hall. Everyone looks at Britt-Marie. She clasps her hands together over her stomach.

"He was standing outside the door, hiding, but I caught the smell of those cigarettes, I did. So I told him that in this leaseholders' association we don't smoke! And then he got out that . . ."

Britt-Marie can't bring herself to say "knife" without her voice breaking again. She looks offended, as you do when you're the last to learn a secret.

"You all know who he is, of course! But obviously none of you thought to warn me about it, oh no. Even though I'm the information officer in this residents' association!"

She straightens out a wrinkle in her skirt. A real wrinkle, this time. The bag of lollipops and comics is by her feet. Maud tries to put a tender hand on Britt-Marie's arm, but Britt-Marie removes it. Maud smiles wistfully.

"Where is Kent?" she asks softly.

"He's at a business meeting!" Britt-Marie snaps.

Alf looks at her, then at the bag from the supermarket, and then at her again.

"What were you doing out so late?" Mum says.

"Kent's children get lollipops and comics when they come for Christmas! Always! I was at the shop!"

"Sorry, Britt-Marie. We just didn't know what to say. Look, why don't you just stay here tonight, at least? It may be safer if we're all together?"

Britt-Marie surveys them over the tip of her nose.

"I'm sleeping at home. Kent is coming home tonight. I'm always home when Kent arrives."

The policewoman with the green eyes comes up the stairs

behind her. Britt-Marie spins around. The green eyes stay on her, watchfully.

"It's about time you turned up!" Britt-Marie says. The green-eyed officer doesn't say anything. Another officer is standing behind her, and Elsa can see that he's flummoxed by just having caught sight of Elsa and Mum. He seems to remember escorting them to the hospital only to be given the slip once they got there.

Lennart tries to invite them both in for coffee, and the summer-intern policeman looks like this would be preferable to searching the area with dogs, but after a stern glance from his superior he shakes his head at the floor. The green-eyed policewoman talks with the sort of voice that effortlessly fills a room.

"We're going to find him," she says, her gaze still riveted to Britt-Marie. "Also, the dog that Kent called about yesterday, Britt-Marie? He said you'd found dog hairs on the stairs. Did you see it tonight?"

Elsa stops breathing. So much that she forgets to wonder about why Green-eyes is referring to Kent and Britt-Marie by their first names. Britt-Marie peers around the room, at Elsa and Mum and Maud and Lennart and the boy with a syndrome's mum. Last of all at Alf. His face is devoid of expression. The green eyes sweep over the front hall. There's sweat all over Elsa's palms when she opens and closes her hands to make them stop shaking. She knows that the wurse is sleeping just a few yards behind her, in Granny's bedroom. She knows that everything is lost, and she doesn't know what to do to stop it. She'll never be able to escape with the wurse through all the police she can hear at the bottom of the stairs, not even a wurse could pull that off. They'll shoot it. Kill it. She wonders if that was what the shadow had been planning all along. Because it didn't dare fight the wurse. Without the wurse, and without Wolfheart, the castle is defenseless.

Britt-Marie purses her lips when she sees Elsa staring at her.

Changes her hands around on her stomach and snorts, with a sudden, newly acquired self-confidence, at Green-eyes.

"Maybe we misjudged it, Kent and I. Maybe they weren't dog hairs, it may have been some other nuisance. It wouldn't be so strange, with so many odd people running about on these stairs these days," she says, half-apologetically and half-accusingly, and adjusts the brooch on the floral-print jacket.

The green eyes glance quickly at Elsa. Then the policewoman nods briskly, as if the matter is over and done with, and assures them they'll keep the house under surveillance for the night. Before anyone has time to say anything else, the two officers are already on their way down the stairs. Elsa's mum is breathing heavily. She holds out her hand to Britt-Marie, but Britt-Marie moves away.

"Obviously you find it amusing to have secrets from me. It's amusing to make me look like an idiot, that's what you think!"

"Please, Britt-Marie," Maud tries to say, but Britt-Marie shakes her head, picks up her bag, and stamps out the door. Well-meaningly.

But Elsa sees the way Alf looks at her when she leaves. The wurse is standing in the bedroom doorway with the same expression. And now Elsa knows who Britt-Marie is.

Mum also goes down the stairs, Elsa doesn't know why. Lennart puts on some coffee. George gets out some eggs and makes more mulled wine. Maud distributes cookies. The boy with a syndrome's mother crawls into the wardrobe to find her son, and Elsa hears him laughing. That's one good superpower he's got there.

Alf goes onto the balcony and Elsa goes after him. Stands hesitantly behind him for a long time before joining him and peering over the railing. Green-eyes is standing in the snow, talking to Elsa's mum. She smiles the way she smiled at Granny that time in the police station.

"Do they know each other?" Elsa asks, surprised. Alf nods.

"Knew, at least. They were best friends when they were your age."

Elsa looks at Mum, and she can see that she's still angry. Then she peers at the hammer that Alf has set down in a corner of the balcony floor.

"Were you going to kill Sam?"

Alf's eyes are apologetic but honest.

"No."

"Why was Mum so angry at you, then?"

Alf's leather jacket heaves slightly.

"She was angry because she wasn't there holding the hammer."

Elsa's shoulders sink; she wraps her arms around herself against the cold. Alf hangs his leather jacket over her. Elsa hunches up inside it.

"Sometimes I think I'd like someone to kill Sam."

Alf doesn't answer. Elsa looks at the hammer.

"I mean . . . sort of kill, anyway. I know one shouldn't think people deserve to die. But sometimes I'm not sure people like him deserve to live. . . ."

Alf leans against the balcony railing.

"It's human."

"Is it human to want people to die?"

Alf shakes his head calmly.

"It's human not to be sure."

Elsa hunches up even more inside the jacket. Tries to feel brave.

"I'm scared," she whispers.

"Me too," says Alf.

And they don't say anything else about it.

They sneak out with the wurse when everyone has gone to sleep, but Elsa knows that her mum sees them go. She's certain that Green-eyes also sees them. That she's also keeping watch over them, somewhere in the dark, like Wolfheart would have done, if he were there.

And Elsa tries not to feel reproachful toward Wolfheart, for not being there, for letting her down after he promised to always protect her. It doesn't go very well.

She doesn't talk to Alf. He doesn't say anything either. It's the night before Christmas Eve, but everything just feels odd.

As they're making their way back up the stairs, Alf stops briefly outside Britt-Marie's front door. Elsa sees the way he looks at it. Looks at it, as one does when there was once a first time, but never a second, and never anything more. Elsa looks at the Christmas decorations, which, for the first time ever, don't smell of pizza.

"How old are Kent's children?" she asks.

"They're grown-ups," says Alf bitterly.

"So why did Britt-Marie say they want comics and lollipops, then?"

"Britt-Marie invites them over for dinner every Christmas. They never come. The last time they came they were still children. They liked lollipops and comics then," Alf answers emptily.

When he moves off up the stairs with his dragging footsteps and Elsa follows, the wurse stays where it is. Considering how smart she is, it takes Elsa an unaccountably long time before she realizes why.

The Princess of Miploris was so beloved of the two princes that they fought for her love, until they hated one another. The Princess of Miploris once had a treasure stolen by a witch, and now she lives in the kingdom of sorrow.

And the wurse is guarding the gates of her castle. Because that's what wurses do.

28

POTATOES

Elsa wasn't eavesdropping. She's not the sort of person who eavesdrops. Especially on Christmas Eve morning.

She just happened to be standing there on the stairs early the next morning, and that's when she heard Britt-Marie and Kent talking. It wasn't on purpose—she was looking for the wurse and her Gryffindor scarf. And the door of Kent and Britt-Marie's flat was open. After she'd stood there for a while listening she realized that if she walked past their door now, they'd spot her, and it would look as if maybe she'd been standing on the stairs eavesdropping *deliberately*. So she just stayed put.

"Britt-Marie!" hollered Kent from inside—judging by the echo he was in the bathroom, and judging by the volume of his shouting she was very far away.

"Yes?" answered Britt-Marie, sounding as if she was standing quite close to him.

"Where is my damn electric razor?" yelled Kent without apologizing for yelling. Elsa disliked him a lot for that. Because it's "damned," not "damn."

"Second drawer," answered Britt-Marie.

"Why did you put it there? It's always in the first drawer!"

"It's always been in the second drawer."

A second drawer was opened; then came the sound of an electric razor. But not the slightest little sound of Kent saying "thanks." Britt-Marie went into the flat's foyer and leaned out the front door with Kent's suit in her hand. Gently brushed invisible fluff from one arm. She didn't see Elsa, or at least Elsa didn't think she did. And because Elsa wasn't quite sure, she realized that now she had to stay where she was and look as if she was supposed to be there. As if she was just out inspecting the quality of the railings, or something like that. Not at all as if she was eavesdropping. It got very complicated, the whole thing.

Britt-Marie disappeared back into the flat.

"Did you talk to David and Pernilla?" she asked pleasantly.

"Yes, yes."

"So when are they coming?"

"Damned if I know."

"But I have to plan the cooking, Kent. . . ."

"Let's just eat when they come—six, or seven maybe," Kent said dismissively.

"Well which, Kent?" asked Britt-Marie, sounding worried. "Six or seven?"

"Jesus Christ, Britt-Marie, it doesn't make any damn difference."

"If it doesn't make any difference, then maybe half past six is about right?"

"Fine, whatever."

"Did you tell them we normally eat at six?"

"We *always* eat at six."

"But you did you say that to David and Pernilla?"

"We've been having dinner at six since the beginning of time; they've probably worked that out by now," said Kent with a sigh.

"I see. Is there something wrong with that now, all of a sudden?"

"No, no. Let's say six, then. If they're not here, they're not here," said Kent, as if he was anyway quite sure they wouldn't come. "I have to go now, I have a meeting with Germany," he added, walking out of the bathroom.

"I'm only trying to arrange a nice Christmas for the whole family, Kent," said Britt-Marie despondently.

"Can't we just bloody heat up the food when they come?!"

"If I can just know when they are coming, I can make sure the food is hot when they arrive," said Britt-Marie.

"Let's just eat when everyone is here, if it's so bloody important."

"And when will everyone be here, then?"

"Damn, Britt-Marie! I don't know! You know what they're like—they could come at six or they could come at half past eight!"

Britt-Marie stood in silence for a few grim seconds. Then she took a deep breath and tried to stabilize her voice as you do when not wanting it to be obvious that you're yelling inside.

"We can't have Christmas dinner at half past eight, Kent."

"I know that! So the kids will just have to eat when they damn well get here, won't they!"

"There's no need to get short," said Britt-Marie, sounding a bit short.

"Where are my damn cuff links?" asked Kent, and started tottering around the flat with his half-knotted tie trailing behind him.

"In the second drawer in the chest," Britt-Marie replied.

"Aren't they usually in the first?"

"They've always been in the second. . . ."

Elsa just stands there. Not eavesdropping, obviously. But there's a big mirror hanging in the foyer just inside the front door, and when Elsa stands on the stairs she can see Kent's reflection in it. Britt-Marie is neatly turning down his shirt collar over the tie and gently brushing the lapel of his suit jacket.

"When are you coming home?" she asks in a low voice.

"I don't bloody know, you know how the Germans are, don't wait up for me," Kent answers evasively, extricating himself and heading for the door.

"Put the shirt directly in the washing machine when you come in, please," says Britt-Marie, and comes padding after him to brush something from his trouser leg.

Kent looks at his watch the way men with very expensive watches do when they look at them. Elsa knows that because Kent told Elsa's mum that his watch cost more than Kia.

"In the washing machine, please, Kent! Directly, as soon as you come home!" Britt-Marie calls out.

Kent steps onto the landing without answering. He catches sight of Elsa. He doesn't seem to think she's been eavesdropping at all, but on the other hand he doesn't look very pleased to see her.

"Yo!" he says with a grin, in that way grown men say "yo" to children because they think that's how children talk.

Elsa doesn't answer. Because she doesn't talk like that. Kent's telephone rings. It's a new telephone, Elsa notices. Kent looks as if he'd like to tell her what it cost.

"That's Germany calling!" he says to Elsa, and looks as if he's only just remembering that she was very much implicated in the cellar-stairs-related incident yesterday that resulted in his last phone being put out of action.

He looks as if he remembers the poison as well, and what it cost. Elsa shrugs, as if she's challenging him to a fight. Kent starts yelling "Yez Klaus!" into his new phone as he disappears down the stairs.

Elsa takes a few steps towards the stairs, but stops in the doorway. In the hall mirror she sees the bathroom. Britt-Marie is standing in there, carefully rolling up the cord of Ken's electric shaver before putting it in the third drawer.

She comes out into the hall. Catches sight of Elsa. Folds her hands over her stomach.

"Oh, I see, I see. . . ." she starts.

"I wasn't eavesdropping!" says Elsa at once.

Britt-Marie straightens the coats on the hangers in the hall and carefully brushes the back of her hand over all of Kent's overcoats and jackets. Elsa shoves the tips of her fingers into the pockets of her jeans and mumbles:

"Thanks."

Britt-Marie turns around, surprised.

"Pardon me?"

Elsa groans like you do when you're almost eight and have to say thanks twice.

"I said thanks. For not saying anything to the police about—" she says, stopping herself before she says "the wurse."

Britt-Marie seems to understand.

"You should have informed me about that horrible creature, young lady."

"It's not a horrible creature."

"Not until it bites someone."

"It never will bite anyone! And it saved you from Sam!" growls Elsa.

Britt-Marie looks as if she's about to say something. But she leaves it. Because she knows it's true. And Elsa is going to say something, but she also leaves it. Because she knows that Britt-Marie actually returned the favor.

She looks into the flat through the mirror.

"Why did you put the razor in the wrong drawer?" she asks.

Britt-Marie brushes, brushes, brushes her skirt. Folds her hands.

"I don't know what you're talking about," she says, even though Elsa very well sees that she does.

"Kent said it was always in the first drawer. But you said it was always in the second drawer. And then after he'd gone, you put it in the third drawer," says Elsa.

And then Britt-Marie looks distracted for just a few moments. Then something else. Alone, perhaps. And then she mumbles:

"Yes, yes, maybe I did. Maybe I did."

Elsa tilts her head.

"Why?"

And then there's a silence for an eternity of fairy-tale silences. And then Britt-Marie whispers, as if she's forgotten that Elsa is standing there in front of her:

"Because I like it when he shouts my name."

And then Britt-Marie closes the door.

And Elsa stands outside and tries to dislike her. It doesn't go all that well.

29

SWISS MERINGUES

You have to believe. Granny always said that. You have to believe in something in order to understand the tales. "It's not important what exactly you believe in, but there's got to be something, or you may as well forget the whole damned thing."

And maybe in the end that's what everything, all of this, is about.

Elsa finds her Gryffindor scarf in the snow outside the house, where she dropped it when she charged at Sam the night before. The green-eyed policewoman is standing a few yards away. The sun has hardly risen. The snow sounds like popcorn popping as she walks over it.

"Hello," offers Elsa.

Green-eyes nods, silently.

"You're not much of a talker, are you?"

Green-eyes smiles. Elsa wraps the scarf around herself.

"Did you know my granny?"

The policewoman scans along the house wall and over the little street.

"Everyone knew your grandmother."

"And my mum?" Green-eyes nods again. Elsa squints at her. "Alf says you were best friends." She nods again. Elsa wonders how that would feel. To have a best friend who's your own age. Then she stands in silence beside the policewoman and watches the sun come up. It's going to be a beautiful Christmas Eve, despite everything that's happened. She clears her throat and heads back to the front entrance, stopping with her hand on the door handle.

"Have you been on guard here all night?"

She nods again.

"Will you kill Sam if he comes back?"

"I hope not."

"Why not?"

"Because it's not my job to kill."

"What is your job, then?"

"To protect."

"Him or us?" Elsa asks reproachfully.

"Both."

"He's the one who's dangerous. Not us."

Green-eyes smiles without looking happy.

"When I was small your grandmother used to say that if you become a police officer, you can't choose who to protect. You have to try to protect everyone."

"Did she know you wanted to become a policewoman?" asks Elsa.

"She's the one who made me want to become one."

"Why?"

Green-eyes starts smiling. Genuinely, this time.

"Because I was afraid of everything when I was small. And she told me I should do what I was most afraid of. I should laugh at my fears."

Elsa nods, as if this confirms what she already knew.

"It was you and Mum, wasn't it—the golden knights who saved the Telling Mountain from the Noween and the fears. And built Miaudacas. It was you and Mum."

The policewoman raises her eyebrows imperceptibly.

"We were many things in your grandmother's fairy tales, I think."

Elsa opens the door, puts her foot in the opening, and stops there.

"Did you know my mum first or my granny?"

"Your grandmother."

"You're one of the children on her bedroom ceiling, aren't you?"

Green-eyes looks directly at her. She smiles again in the real way.

"You're smart. She always said you were the smartest girl she ever met."

Elsa nods. The door closes behind her. And it ends up being a beautiful Christmas Eve. Despite everything.

She looks for the wurse in the cellar storage unit and in Renault, but they are both empty. She knows the wardrobe in Granny's flat is also empty, and the wurse is definitely not in Mum and George's flat because no healthy being can stand being there on a Christmas morning. Mum is even more efficient than usual at Christmas.

She normally starts her Christmas shopping in May each year. She says it's because she's "organized," but Granny used to disagree and say it was actually because she was "anal," and then Elsa used to have to wear her headphones for quite a long time. But this year Mum decided to be a bit free-spirited and crazy, so she waited until the first of August before asking what Elsa wanted for Christmas. She was very angry when Elsa refused to tell her, even though Elsa expressly asked if she understood how much someone changes as a person in half a year when they're almost eight. So Mum did what Mum always does: she went and bought a present on her own initiative. And it went as it usually went: to hell. Elsa knew that because she knew where Mum hid her presents. What do you expect when you buy an almost-eight-year-old her present five months early?

So this year, Elsa is getting three books that are about different themes in some way or other touched upon by various characters in the Harry Potter books. They're wrapped in a paper that Elsa likes very much. Elsa knows that because Mum's first present was utterly useless and when Elsa informed her of that in October they argued for about a month and then Elsa's mum gave up and gave Elsa money instead, so she could go and buy "what you want, then!" And then she wrapped them in a paper she liked very much. And put the parcel in Mum's not-so-secret place and praised Mum for again being so considerate and sensitive that she knew exactly what Elsa wanted this year. And then Mum called Elsa a "Grinch."

Elsa has become very attached to this tradition.

She rings Alf's bell half a dozen times before he opens. He's got his dressing gown on, his irritated expression, and his Juventus coffee cup.

"What's the matter?" he barks.

"Merry Christmas!" says Elsa without answering the question.

"I'm sleeping," he grunts.

"It's Christmas Eve morning," Elsa informs him.

"I do know that," he says.

"Why are you sleeping, then?"

"I was up late last night."

"Doing what?"

Alf takes a sip of his coffee.

"What are you doing here?"

"I asked first," Elsa insists.

"I'm not the one standing at your door in the middle of the night!"

"It's not the middle of the night. And it's *Christmas*!"

He drinks some more coffee. She kicks his doormat irritably.

"I can't find the wurse."

"I know that as well." Alf nods casually.

"How?"

"Because it's here."

Elsa's eyebrows shoot up as if they just sat down in wet paint.

"The wurse is here?"

"Yes."

"Why didn't you say so?"

"I just bloody did."

"Why is it here?"

"Because Kent came home at five this morning, and it couldn't sit on the stairs. Kent would have bloody called the police if he'd found out it was still in the house."

Elsa peers into Alf's flat. The wurse is sitting on the floor, lapping at something in a big metal bowl in front of it. It says Juventus on it. The metal bowl, that is.

"How do you know what time Kent came home?"

"Because I was in the garage when he arrived in his bastard BMW," says Alf impatiently.

"What were you doing in the garage?" asks Elsa patiently.

Alf looks as if that is an incredibly stupid question.

"I was waiting for him."

"How long did you wait?"

"Until five o'clock, I bloody said," he grunts.

Elsa thinks about giving him a hug, but leaves it. The wurse peers up from the metal bowl, looking enormously pleased. Something black is dripping from its nose. Elsa turns to Alf.

"Alf, did you give the wurse . . . coffee?"

"Yes," says Alf, and looks as if he can't understand what could reasonably be wrong about that.

"It's an ANIMAL! Why did you give it COFFEE?"

Alf scratches his scalp, which, for him, is the same thing as scratching his hair. Then he adjusts his dressing gown. Elsa notices that he has a thick scar running across his chest. He sees her noticing and looks grumpy about it.

Alf goes into his bedroom and closes the door, and when he comes out again he is wearing his leather jacket with the taxi badge. Even though it's Christmas Eve. They have to let the wurse pee in the garage, because there are even more police outside the building now, and not even a wurse can hold out for very long after drinking a bowl of coffee.

Granny would have loved that one. Peeing in the garage. It will drive Britt-Marie to distraction.

When they come up, Mum and George's flat smells of Swiss meringues and pasta gratin with béarnaise sauce, because Mum has decided that everyone in the house is having Christmas together this year. No one disagreed with her, partly because it was a good idea, and partly because no one ever disagrees with Mum. And then George suggested that everyone should make their own favorite dish for a Christmas buffet. He's good like that, George, which infuriates Elsa.

The boy with a syndrome's favorite food is Swiss meringue, so his mum made it for him. Well, his mum got out all the ingredients and Lennart picked all the meringues up off the floor and Maud made the actual Swiss meringue while the boy and his mother were dancing.

And then Maud and Lennart thought it was important that the woman in the black skirt also felt involved, because they're good like that, so they asked if she wanted to prepare anything in particular. She just sat glued to her chair at the far end of the flat and looked very embarrassed and mumbled that she hadn't cooked any food for several years. "You don't cook very much when you live alone," she explained. And then Maud looked very upset and apologized for being so insensitive. And then the woman in the black skirt felt so sorry for Maud that she made a pasta gratin with béarnaise sauce. Because that was her boys' favorite dish. So they all have Swiss meringue and pasta gratin with béarnaise sauce, because that's the sort of Christmas it is. In spite of it all.

The wurse gets two buckets of cinnamon buns from Maud, and George goes to the cellar to fetch up the bathing tub Elsa had when she was a baby and fills it with mulled wine. With this as an incentive, the wurse agrees to hide for an hour in the wardrobe in Granny's flat, and then Mum goes down and invites the police up from outside the house. Green-eyes sits next to Mum. They laugh. The summer intern is there too; he eats the most Swiss meringue of them all and falls asleep on the sofa.

The woman in the black skirt sits in silence at the table, in the far corner. After they've eaten, while George is washing up and Maud wiping down the tables and Lennart sitting on a stool with a standby cup of coffee, waiting for the percolator and making sure it's not going to get up to any tricks, the boy with a syndrome goes through the flat and crosses the landing and goes into Granny's flat. When he comes back he has cinnamon bun crumbs all around his mouth and so many wurse hairs on his sweater that he looks like someone invited him to a fancy dress party and he decided to dress up as a carpet. He gets a blanket from Elsa's room and walks up to the woman in the black skirt, looks at her for a long time, then reaches up, standing on his tiptoes, and pinches her nose. Startled, she jumps, and the boy's mother makes the sort of scream that mothers make when their children pinch complete strangers' noses and rushes towards him. But Maud gently catches hold of her arm and stops her, and when the boy holds up his thumb, poking out between his index finger and his middle finger, while looking at the woman in the black skirt, Maud explains pleasantly:

"It's a game. He's pretending he stole your nose."

The woman stares at Maud. Stares at the boy. Stares at the nose. And then she steals his nose. And he laughs so loudly that the windows start rattling. He falls asleep in her lap, wrapped up in the blanket. When his mother, with an apologetic smile, tries to lift him off, observing as she does so that "it's actually not at all like him to be so direct," the woman in the black skirt touches her hand tremulously and whispers:

"If . . . if it's all right I . . . could I hold him a little longer . . . ?"

The boy's mother puts both her hands around the woman's hand and nods. The woman puts her forehead against the boy's hair and whispers:

"Thanks."

George makes more mulled wine and everything feels almost normal and not at all frightening. After the police have thanked them for their hospitality and headed back down the stairs, Maud looks unhappily at Elsa and says she can understand it must have been frightening for a child to have police in the house on Christmas Eve. But Elsa takes her by the hand and says:

"Don't worry, Maud. This is a Christmas tale. They always have a happy ending."

And it's clear that Maud believes it.

Because you have to believe.

30

PERFUME

Only one person collapses with a heart attack late on Christmas Eve. But two hearts are broken. And the house is never quite the same again.

It all starts with the boy waking up late in the afternoon and feeling hungry. The wurse and Samantha come flopping out of the wardrobe because the mulled wine is finished. Elsa marches in circles around Alf and intimates that it's time to get the Santa suit. Elsa and the wurse follow Alf down to the garage. He gets into Taxi. When Elsa opens the passenger door and sticks her head in and asks what he's doing, he turns the ignition key and grunts:

"If I have to impersonate Santa for the rest of the day, I'm nipping out for a newspaper first."

"I don't think my mum wants me to go anywhere."

"No one invited you!"

Elsa and the wurse ignore him and jump in. When Alf starts railing at her that you can't just jump into people's cars like that, Elsa says that this is actually Taxi and that is precisely what one does with Taxi. And when Alf grumpily taps the meter and points out that taxi journeys cost money, Elsa says that she'd like to have this taxi journey as her Christmas present. And then Alf looks very grumpy for a long time, and then they go off for Elsa's Christmas present.

Alf knows of a kiosk that's open even on Christmas Eve. He buys a newspaper. Elsa buys two ice creams. The wurse eats all of its own and half of hers. Which, if one knows how much wurses like ice cream, shows how immensely considerate it is being. It spills some of it in the backseat, but Alf only shouts at it for about ten minutes. Which, if one knows how much Alf dislikes wurses spilling ice cream in the backseat of Taxi, shows how immensely considerate he was being.

"Can I ask you something?" asks Elsa, even though she knows full well that this is also a question. "Why didn't Britt-Marie spill the beans about the wurse to the police?"

"She can be a bit of a nagbag sometimes. But she's not bloody evil," Alf clarifies.

"But she hates dogs," Elsa persists.

"Ah, she's just scared of them. Your granny used to bring back loads of strays to the house when she moved in. We were just little brats back then, Britt-Marie and Kent and me. One of the mutts bit Britt-Marie and her mum made a hell of a commotion about it," Alf says, a shockingly lengthy description given that it's coming from Alf.

Taxi pulls into the street. Elsa thinks of Granny's stories about the Princess of Miploris.

"So you've been in love with Britt-Marie since you were ten years old?" she asks.

"Yes," Alf replies as if it's absolutely self-evident. Bowled over by this, Elsa looks at him and waits, because she knows that only by waiting will she get him to tell the whole story. You know things like that when you're almost eight.

She waits for as long as she needs to.

Then after two red lights Alf sighs resignedly, like you do while preparing yourself to tell a story even though you don't like telling stories. And then he recounts the tale of Britt-Marie. And himself. Although the latter part may not be his intention. There are quite a lot of swearwords in it, and Elsa has to exert herself quite a lot not to correct the grammar. But after a lot of "ifs" and "buts" and quite a few "damneds," Alf has explained that he and Kent grew up with their mother in the flat where Alf now lives. When Alf was ten, another family moved into the flat above theirs, with two daughters of the same age as Alf and Kent. The mother was a renowned singer and the father wore a suit and was always at work. The elder sister, Ingrid, apparently had an outstanding singing talent. She was going to be a star, her mother explained to Alf and Kent's mother. She never said anything about the other daughter, Britt-Marie. Alf and Kent caught sight of her anyway. It was impossible not to.

No one remembers exactly when the young female medical student first showed up in the house. One day she was just there in the enormous flat that took up the entire top floor of the house in those days, and when Alf and Kent's mother interrogated her about why she lived by herself in such a big flat, the young female medical student replied that she'd "won it in a game of poker." She wasn't at home a great deal, of course, and whenever she was, she was always accompanied by outlandish friends and, from time to time, stray dogs. One evening she brought home a large black cur that she'd apparently also won in a game of poker, Alf explains. Alf and Kent and the daughters of the neighboring family only wanted to play with it; they didn't understand that it was sleeping. Alf was quite certain it never meant to bite Britt-Marie, it was just caught unawares. She was too.

The dog disappeared after that. But Britt-Marie's mother still hated the young medical student, and nothing anyone said could make her change her mind. And then came the car accident in the street just outside the house. Britt-Marie's mother never saw the truck. The impact shook the whole building. The mother emerged from the front seat of the car with nothing worse than a few grazes, reeling and confused, but no one came out of the backseat. The mother screamed the most terrible of screams when she saw all the blood. The young medical student came running out in her nightie, her whole face full of cinnamon bun crumbs, and she saw the two girls in the backseat. She had no car of her own and she could only carry one girl. She wedged the door open and saw that one of them was breathing and the other wasn't. She picked up the girl who was still breathing and ran. Ran all the way to the hospital.

Alf goes silent. Elsa asks what happened to the sister. Alf is silent for three red lights. Then he says, in a voice heavy with bitterness:

"It's a terrible bloody thing when a parent loses a child. That family was never properly whole again. It wasn't the mother's fault. It was a bastard car accident, it was no one's fault. But she probably never got over it. And she damned well never forgave your grandmother."

"For what?"

"Because she thought your grandmother saved the wrong daughter."

Elsa's silence feels like a hundred red lights.

"Was Kent also in love with Britt-Marie?" she asks at last.

"We're brothers. Brothers compete."

"And Kent won?"

A sound comes from Alf's throat; Elsa can't quite tell if it's a cough or a laugh.

"Like hell. I won."

"What happened then?"

"Kent moved. Got married, too damned young, to a nasty piece of work. Had the twins, David and Pernilla. He loves those kids, but that woman made him bloody unhappy."

"What about you and Britt-Marie?"

One red light. Another.

"We were young. People are bloody idiots when they're young. I went away. She stayed here."

"Where did you go?"

"To a war."

Elsa stares at him.

"Were you also a soldier?"

Alf pulls his hand through his lack of hair.

"I'm old, Elsa. I've been a hell of a lot of things."

"What happened to Britt-Marie, then?"

"I was on my way home. She was going to come and give me a surprise. And she saw me with another woman."

"You had an affair?"

"Yes."

"Why?"

"Because people are bloody idiots when they're young."

Red light.

"Then what did you do?" asks Elsa.

"Went away," he answers.

"For how long?"

"Bloody long."

"And Kent?"

"He got divorced. Moved back in with Mum. Britt-Marie was still there. Yeah, what the hell, he'd always loved her. So when her parents died they moved into their flat. Kent had got wind of the owners maybe selling the whole place as leasehold flats. So they stayed on and waited for the dough. They got married and Britt-Marie probably wanted children but Kent thought the ones he already had were bloody enough. And now things are the way they are."

Elsa opens and closes Taxi's glove compartment.

"Why did you come home from the wars, then?"

"Some wars finish. And Mum got ill. Someone had to take care of her."

"Didn't Kent do that?"

Alf's nails wander around his forehead like nails do when wandering among memories and opening doors that have long been closed.

"Kent took care of Mum while she was still alive. He's an idiot but he was always a good son, you can't take that away from the bastard. Mother never lacked for anything while she was alive. So I took care of her while she was dying."

"And then?"

Alf scratches his head. Doesn't seem to know the exact answer himself.

"Then I just sort of . . . stayed on."

Elsa looks at him with seriousness. Takes a deep, concluding breath and says:

"I like you very much, Alf. But you were a bit of a shit when you went away like that."

Alf coughs or laughs again.

After the next red light he mutters:

"Britt-Marie took care of your mother when her father died. While your grandmother was still traveling a lot, you know. She wasn't always the nagbag she is now."

"I know," says Elsa.

"Did your grandmother tell you that?"

"In a way. She told me a story about a princess in a kingdom of sorrow, and two princes who loved her so much that they began to hate each other. And the wurses were driven into exile by the princess's parents, but then the princess fetched them back when the war came. And about a witch who stole a treasure from the princess."

She goes silent. Crosses her arms. Turns to Alf.

"I was the treasure, right?"

Alf sighs.

"I'm not so big on fairy tales."

"You could make an effort!"

"Britt-Marie has given her whole life to being there for a man who is never home, and trying to make someone else's children love her. When your grandfather died and she could be there for your mother, it was perhaps the first time she felt . . ."

He seems to be looking for the right word. Elsa gives it to him.

"Needed."

"Yes."

"And then Mum grew up?"

"She moved away. Went to university. The house went bloody quiet, for a bloody long time. And then she came back with your father and was pregnant."

"I was going to be all of Britt-Marie's second chances," Elsa says in a low voice, nodding.

"And then your grandmother came home," says Alf, and stops by a stop sign.

They don't say a lot more about that. Like you don't when there's not a great deal more to be said. Alf briefly puts his hand on his chest, as if something is itching under his jacket.

Elsa looks at the zip.

"Did you get that scar in a war?"

Alf's gaze becomes somewhat defensive. She shrugs.

"You've got a massive scar on your chest. I saw it when you were wearing your dressing gown. You really should buy yourself a new dressing gown, by the way."

"I was never in that sort of war. No one ever fired at me."

"So that's why you're not broken?"

"Broken like who?"

"Sam. And Wolfheart."

"Sam was broken before he became a soldier. And not all soldiers are like that. But if you see the shit those boys saw, you need some help when you get back. And this country's so bloody willing to put billions into weapons and fighter jets, but when those boys come home and they've seen the shit they've seen, no one can be bothered to listen to them even for five minutes."

He looks gloomily at Elsa.

"People have to tell their stories, Elsa. Or they suffocate."

"Where did you get the scar, then?"

"It's a pacemaker."

"Oh!"

"You know what it is?" Alf asks skeptically.

Elsa looks slightly offended.

"You really are a different damned kid."

"It's good to be different."

"I know."

They drive up the highway while Elsa tells Alf that Iron Man, who's a kind of superhero, has a type of pacemaker. But really it's more of an electromagnet, because Iron Man has shrapnel in his heart and without the magnet the shrapnel would cut holes in it and then he'd die. Alf doesn't look as though he entirely understands the finer points of the story, but he listens without interrupting.

"But they operate on him and remove the magnet at the end of the third film!" Elsa tells him excitedly, then clears her throat and adds, slightly shamefaced: "Spoiler alert. Sorry."

Alf doesn't look as if this is concerning him very much. To be entirely honest, he doesn't look as if he knows exactly what a "spoiler" is, unless it's a part of a car.

It's snowing again, and Elsa decides that even if people she likes have been shits on earlier occasions, she has to learn to carry on liking them. You'd quickly run out of people if you had to disqualify all those who at some point have been shits. She thinks that this will have to be the moral of this story. Christmas stories are supposed to have morals.

Alf's telephone rings from the compartment between the seats. He checks the display, but doesn't answer. It rings again.

"Aren't you going to answer?" wonders Elsa.

"It's Kent. I suppose he wants to mouth off about some crap to do with the accountant and those leasehold conversion bastards, that's all he ever thinks about. He can bloody go on about it tomorrow," mutters Alf.

The telephone rings again; Alf doesn't answer. It rings a third time. Elsa picks it up, irritated, and answers even though Alf swears at her. There's a woman at the other end. She's crying. Elsa hands the phone to Alf. It trembles against his ear. His face becomes transparent.

It's Christmas Eve. The taxi makes a U-turn. They go to the hospital.

Alf doesn't stop for a single red light.

Elsa sits on a bench in a corridor talking to Mum on the telephone, while Alf is in a room talking to a doctor. The nurses think Elsa is a grandchild, so they tell her that he had a heart attack but he's going to be all right. Kent is going to survive.

There's a young woman standing outside the room. She's crying and she's beautiful. Smells strongly of perfume. She smiles faintly at Elsa and Elsa smiles back. Alf steps out of the room and nods without smiling at the woman; the woman disappears out the door without meeting his eyes.

Alf doesn't say a word, just marches back to the entrance and out into the parking lot, with Elsa behind him. And only then does Elsa see Britt-Marie. She's sitting absolutely still on the bench, wearing her floral-print jacket although it's below freezing. She's forgotten her brooch. The paintball stain is shining. Britt-Marie's cheeks are blue and she's spinning her wedding ring on her finger. She has one of Kent's shirts in her lap; it smells freshly laundered and has been perfectly ironed.

"Britt-Marie?" Alf's voice rasps out in the evening gloom, and he stops a yard from her.

She doesn't answer. Just lets her hand wander over the shirt collar in her lap. Gently brushes away something invisible from a fold. Carefully folds one cuff link under the other. Straightens out a wrinkle that isn't there.

Then she lifts her chin. Looks old. Every word seems to leave a little track on her face.

"I've actually been absolutely brilliant at pretending, Alf," she whispers firmly.

Alf doesn't answer. Britt-Marie looks down into the snow and spins her wedding ring.

"When David and Pernilla were small, they always said I was so bad at coming up with stories. I always wanted to read the ones that were in books. They always said, 'Make one up!' but I don't understand why one should sit there and make things up just like that, when there are books where everything has been written down from the very start. I really don't."

She has raised her voice now. As if someone needed convincing.

"Britt-Marie—" Alf says quietly, but she interrupts him coldly.

"Kent told the children I couldn't make up stories because I didn't have any imagination, but it isn't true. It's not. I have an absolutely excellent imagination. I am very good at pretending." Alf runs his fingers across his head and blinks for a long time. Britt-Marie caresses the shirt in her lap as if it were a baby about to go to sleep. "I always bring a newly washed shirt if I'm meeting him somewhere. Because I don't use perfume."

Her voice grows muted. "David and Pernilla never came for Christmas dinner. They were busy, they said. I can understand they're busy, they've been busy for years. So Kent called and said he was staying at the office for a few hours. Just a few hours, he was having another conference call with Germany. Even though it's actually Christmas in Germany as well. But he never came home. So I tried calling him. He didn't answer. I left a message. Eventually the telephone rang, but it wasn't Kent."

Her lower lip trembles.

"I don't use perfume, but she does. So I always see to it that he has a fresh shirt. That's all I ask, that he should put his shirt directly in the washing machine when he comes home. Is that so much to ask?"

"Please, Britt-Marie . . ."

She swallows spasmodically and spins her wedding ring.

"It was a heart attack. I know that because she called and told me, Alf. She called me. Because she couldn't stand it, she couldn't. She said she couldn't sit there in the hospital and know that maybe Kent would die without my knowing. She simply couldn't stand it. . . ." She puts one hand in the other, closes her eyes and adds in a quivering voice:

"I have an excellent imagination, actually. It is excellently good. Kent always said he was going for dinners with the Germans or that the plane was delayed by snow or that he was just passing by the office for a bit. And then I pretended I believed it. I pretended so brilliantly that I believed it myself."

She rises from the bench, turns around, and hangs the shirt elaborately on the edge of the bench. As if she cannot allow herself even now to take out her feelings on something freshly ironed.

"I'm very good at pretending," she whispers.

"I know that," whispers Alf.

And then they leave the shirt on the bench and go home.

It has stopped snowing. They travel in silence. Mum comes to meet them at the front entrance. She hugs Elsa. Tries to hug Britt-Marie. Britt-Marie keeps her at a distance. Not vehemently, just with determination.

"I don't hate her, Ulrika," she says.

"I know," Mum says with a slow nod.

"I don't hate her and I don't hate the dog and I don't hate her car."

Mum nods and takes her hand. Britt-Marie closes her eyes.

"I don't hate at all, Ulrika. I actually don't. I only wanted you to listen to me. Is that so much to ask? I just didn't want you to leave the car in my place. I actually just didn't want you to come and take my place." She spins her wedding ring.

Mum leads her up the stairs, her hand firmly but lovingly around the floral-print jacket. Alf never shows up in the flat, but Santa does. The boy with a syndrome's eyes light up as children's eyes do when someone tells them about ice cream and fireworks and climbing trees and splashing about in puddles.

Maud sets an extra place at the table and gets out more gratin. Lennart puts on more coffee. George washes up. After the parcels have been handed around, the boy and the woman in the black skirt sit on the floor and watch *Cinderella* on the TV.

Britt-Marie sits slightly ill at ease next to Elsa on the sofa. They peer at one another. They don't say anything, but probably this is their cessation of hostilities. So when Elsa's mum tells her she has to stop eating chocolate Santas now or she'll get a stomachache, and Elsa keeps eating them, Britt-Marie doesn't say anything.

And when the evil stepmother turns up in *Cinderella*, and Britt-Marie discreetly gets up and straightens out a crease in her skirt and goes into the front hall to cry, Elsa follows her.

And they sit on the chest together and eat chocolate Santas.

Because you can be upset while you're eating chocolate Santas. But it's much, much, much more difficult.

31

PEANUT CAKE

The fifth letter drops into Elsa's lap. Literally.

She wakes the next morning in Granny's magic wardrobe. The boy sleeps surrounded by his dreams, with the moo-gun in his arms. The wurse has dribbled a bit on Elsa's sweater and it's set like cement.

She lies in the darkness for a long time. Breathing in the smell of wood shavings. She thinks about the Harry Potter quotation that Granny nicked for one of her stories from the Land-of-Almost-Awake. It's from *Harry Potter and the Order of the Phoenix*, which is obviously ironic, and to understand this one would need to be fairly well informed about the differences between the Harry Potter books and Harry Potter films, as well as fairly well informed about the meaning of "ironic."

Because *Harry Potter and the Order of the Phoenix* is the Harry Potter film Elsa likes the least, in spite of it having one of the Harry Potter quotations Elsa likes best. The one where Harry says that he and his friends have one advantage in the approaching war with Voldemort, because they have one thing that Voldemort doesn't have: "Something worth fighting for."

It's ironic because that quotation isn't in the book, which Elsa likes a lot more than the film, though the book is not one of her favorite Harry Potter books. Now when she thinks of it, possibly it isn't ironic after all. She has to Wikipedia this properly, she thinks, sitting up. And that is when the letter drops into her lap. It's been taped to the wardrobe ceiling. She has no idea how long it's been there.

But this sort of thing is logical in fairy tales.

A minute later, Alf is standing in his doorway. He's drinking coffee and looks like he hasn't slept all night. He looks at the envelope. It just says "ALF" on it, in unnecessarily large letters.

"I found it in the wardrobe. It's from Granny. I think she wants to say sorry about something," Elsa informs him.

Alf makes a *shush* sound and points to the radio behind him, which she really doesn't appreciate. There's the traffic news on the radio. "There's been some damned accident up on the highway. All city-bound traffic has been stuck for hours," he says, as if this is something that will interest Elsa. It doesn't—she's too interested in the letter. Alf only reads it after a lot of nagging.

"What does it say, then?" Elsa demands the second he seems to have finished.

"It says sorry."

"Yes, but sorry for *what*?"

Alf sighs in the way he's generally been sighing at Elsa lately.

"It's my damned letter, isn't it?"

"Does she write sorry for always saying that you didn't lift your feet when you walked and that's why you have such worn-out shoes?"

"What's wrong with my shoes?" says Alf, looking at his shoes. This doesn't seem to have been one of the themes of the letter.

"Nothing. There's nothing at all wrong with your shoes," mumbles Elsa.

"I've had these shoes for more than five years!"

"They're very nice shoes," Elsa lies.

Alf doesn't quite look as if he trusts her. Again, he looks down at the letter skeptically.

"Me and your grandmother had a bloody row before she died, all right? Just before she had to go to the hospital. She'd borrowed my electric screwdriver and never bloody bothered to give it back, but she said she bloody had given it back even though I knew damned well she never bloody did."

Elsa sighs in that way she's started generally sighing at Alf lately.

"Did you ever hear about the bloke who swore himself to death?"

"No," says Alf, as if the question was seriously meant.

Elsa rolls her eyes.

"What does Granny write about the electric screwdriver, then?"

"She just writes sorry for losing it."

He folds up the letter and puts it back in the envelope. Elsa stubbornly stays where she is.

"What else? I saw there was more than that in the letter. I'm not an idiot, you know!"

Alf puts the envelope on the hat shelf.

"It says sorry about loads of things."

"Is it complicated?"

"There wasn't a crap in your grandmother's life that wasn't complicated."

Elsa presses her hands farther into her pockets. Peers down her chin at the Gryffindor emblem on her scarf. At the stitches, where Mum mended it after the girls at school had torn it. Mum still thinks it tore when Granny climbed the fence at the zoo.

"Do you believe in life after death?" she asks Alf, without looking at him.

"Haven't got a bloody clue," says Alf, not unpleasantly and not all pleasantly, just in a very Alf-like way.

"I mean, like, do you believe in . . . paradise . . . sort of thing," mumbles Elsa.

Alf drinks his coffee and thinks about it.

"It would be bloody complicated. Logistically, I mean. Paradise must be where there aren't so many damned people," he mutters at last.

Elsa considers this. Realizes the logic of it. Paradise for Elsa is, after all, a place where Granny is, but paradise for Britt-Marie must probably be a place totally dependent on Granny not being there.

"You're quite deep sometimes," she says to Alf.

He drinks coffee and looks as if he finds that a bit of a bloody mouthful for an almost-eight-year-old.

Elsa is intending to ask him something else about the letter, but she never has time. And when she looks back she will think that if she'd made some different choices, this day would not have worked out as terribly as it did in the end. But by then it's too late for that.

And Dad is standing on the stairs behind her. He's out of breath. Which is not at all like Dad.

Elsa's eyes open wide when she sees him, and then she looks at Alf's flat. At the radio. Because there's no coincidence in fairy tales. And there's a Russian playwright who once said that if there's a pistol hanging on the wall in the first act, it has to be fired before the last act is over. Elsa knows that. And those who can't understand by now how Elsa understands things like that just haven't been paying attention. So Elsa understands that the whole thing with the radio and the accident on the highway must have something to do with the fairy tale they're in.

"Is it . . . Mum?" she manages to say.

Dad nods and throws a nervous glance at Alf. Elsa's face trembles.

"Is she at the hospital?"

"Yes, she was called in this morning to take part in a meeting. There was some kind of cri—" Dad starts, but Elsa interrupts him:

"She was in the car accident, wasn't she? The one on the highway?"

Dad looks spectacularly puzzled.

"What accident?"

"The car accident!" Elsa repeats, quite beside herself.

"No . . . no!" And then he smiles. "You're someone's big sister now. Your mum was at the meeting when her water broke!"

It doesn't quite go into Elsa's head, it really doesn't. It's quite obvious. Although she's very familiar with what happens when the water breaks.

"But the car accident? What's it got to do with the car accident?" she mumbles.

Dad looks breathtakingly tentative.

"Nothing, I think. Or, I mean, what do you mean?"

Elsa looks at Alf. Looks at Dad. Thinks about it so hard that she feels the strain right inside her sinuses.

"Where's George?" she asks.

"At the hospital," answers Dad.

"How did he get there? They said on the radio all traffic on the highway is stuck!"

"He ran," says Dad, with a small twinge of what dads experience when they have to say something positive about the new guy.

And that's when Elsa smiles. "George is good in that way," she whispers.

"Yes," Dad admits.

And she decides that maybe the radio by now has in some way earned its place in this fairy tale, in spite of it all. Then she bursts out anxiously:

"But how are we going to get to the hospital if the highway is blocked?"

"You take the old bloody road," Alf says impatiently. Dad and

Elsa look at him as if he'd just spoken to them in a make-believe language. Alf sighs. "The old road, damn it. Past the old slaughterhouse. Where that factory used to be where they made heat exchangers before the bastards moved everything to Asia. You can take that road to the hospital. Young people today, I tell you—they think the whole bloody world is a highway."

And there's the moment right there when Elsa is thinking that she and the wurse will go in Taxi. But then she changes her mind and decides they'll go in Audi instead, because she doesn't want Dad to be upset. And if she hadn't changed her mind, it's possible that the day wouldn't have ended up as loathsome and terrible as it will soon become. Because when terrible things happen one always thinks, "If I only hadn't . . ." And, afterwards, this will turn out to be one of those moments.

Maud and Lennart also decide to come along to the hospital. Maud has brought cookies and Lennart decides when he gets to the house's entrance to bring the coffee percolator, because he's worried they may not have one at the hospital. And even if they do, Lennart has the feeling it will probably be one of those modern coffeemakers with a lot of buttons. Lennart's percolator only has one button. Lennart is very fond of that button.

The boy with a syndrome and his mother are also coming along. Also the woman in jeans. Because they're sort of a team now, which Elsa is very pleased about. Mum told her yesterday that now, when so many people are living in Granny's flat, the whole house feels like that house Elsa always goes on about where all the X-Men live. She rings at Britt-Marie's door as well. But no one opens it.

In retrospect, Elsa will recall that she paused briefly by the locked stroller in the stairwell. The notice with the crossword was still on the wall above it. And someone had solved it. All the squares were filled. In pencil.

If Elsa had stopped and reflected a little on it, maybe things would have turned out differently. But she didn't. So they didn't. It's possible that the wurse hesitated for a moment outside Britt-Marie's door. Elsa would have understood if it had done that, just like she supposes that wurses hesitate sometimes when they're unsure about who in this fairy tale they've really been sent to protect. Wurses actually guard princesses in normal fairy tales, and even in the Land-of-Almost-Awake, Elsa was never more than a knight. Yet if the wurse had any hesitation, it didn't show it. It went with Elsa. Because that's the sort of friend it is.

If it hadn't gone with Elsa, maybe things would have worked out differently.

Alf convinces the police to make a pass around the block "to make sure everything is safe." Elsa never finds out exactly what he says to them, but Alf can be quite persuasive when he wants to be. Maybe he says that he's seen footprints in the snow. Or heard someone in the house on the other side of the street tell him something. Elsa doesn't know, but she sees the summer-intern policeman get into the car, and sees Green-eyes do the same after lengthy deliberation. Elsa meets her gaze for a second, and if she had only told Green-eyes the truth about the wurse, then maybe everything would have ended up differently. But she didn't. Because she wanted to protect the wurse. Because that's the sort of friend she is.

Alf goes back into the house and down into the garage to fetch Taxi.

When the police car swings around the corner at the end of the street, Elsa and the wurse and the boy with a syndrome scurry out of the front entrance and across the street and into Audi, which is parked there. The children jump in first.

The wurse stops midstep. Its hackles rise.

Probably only a few seconds go by, but it feels like forever. Afterwards Elsa will remember that it felt both as if she had time to think a billion thoughts and as if she didn't have time to think at all.

There's a smell inside Audi that makes her feel surprisingly peaceful. She doesn't quite know why. She looks at the wurse through the open door, and before she has time to realize what is about to happen, she wonders if maybe it doesn't want to jump into the car because it's in pain. She knows it is feeling pain, pain the way Granny had pain everywhere in her body at the end.

Elsa starts getting out a cookie from her pocket. Because no real friend of a wurse would leave home nowadays without at least one cookie for emergencies. But she doesn't have time, of course, because she realizes what is causing that smell in Audi.

Sam comes darting out from behind the backseat, Elsa feels the coldness against her lips when his hand closes over her mouth. His muscles tense around her throat; she feels the hairs on his skin scraping like gravel through the gaps in the Gryffindor scarf. She has time to see the brief confusion in Sam's eyes when he sees the boy. It's the moment when he realizes he's been hunting the wrong child. She has time to understand that the shadows in the fairy tale didn't want to kill the Chosen One. Only steal him. Make him their own. Kill whoever stood in their way.

And then the wurse's jaws close around Sam's other wrist, just as he's making a grab for the boy. Sam roars. Elsa has a split second to react, when he lets go of her. She sees the knife in the rearview mirror.

And everything after that is black.

Elsa can feel herself running, she feels the boy's hand in hers, and she knows that they have to make it to the front entrance. They have to have time to scream so Dad and Alf can hear them.

Elsa sees her feet moving, but she's not guiding them herself. Her body is running by instinct. She thinks that she and the boy have had time to make half a dozen steps when she hears the wurse howling in horrendous pain, and she doesn't know if it's the boy who lets go of her hand or if she lets go of his. Her pulse is beating so hard that she can feel it in her eyes. The boy slips and falls to the ground. Elsa hears the back door of Audi opening and sees the knife in Sam's hand. Sees the blood on it. She does the only thing she can do: picks the boy up as best she can and runs as fast as possible.

She's good at running. But she knows it won't be enough. She can hear Sam straining behind her, feels the tug at her arm as the boy is torn from her grasp; her heart lurches, she closes her eyes, and the next thing she remembers is the pain in her forehead. And Maud's scream. And Dad's hands. The hard floor in the stairwell. The world spins until it lands, swaying upside down in front of her, and she thinks that this must be how it is when you die. Like falling inwards, towards who-knows-what.

She hears banging without understanding where it comes from. Then the echo. Echo, she has time to think, and realizes she is indoors. She feels as if she's got gravel under her eyelids. She hears the light feet of the boy running up the stairs as a boy's feet can run only when they have known for many years that this could happen. She hears the terrified voice of the boy's mother, trying to keep herself calm and methodical as she runs after him, as only a mother can do and only when she has grown accustomed to fear as the natural state of things.

The door of Granny's house closes and locks behind them. Elsa feels that Dad's hands aren't holding her up, they're holding her back. She doesn't know from what. Until she sees the shadow through the glass in the entrance door. Sees Sam on the other side. He's standing still. And something about his face is so deeply uncharacteristic of him that, at first, Elsa can't quite shake off the feeling that she is imagining the whole thing.

Sam is afraid.

In the blink of an eye another shadow descends over him, so enormous that Sam's shadow is engulfed in it. Wolfheart's heavy fists rain down with fury, with a violence and a darkness no fairy tale could describe. He doesn't hit Sam, he hammers him into the snow. Not to make him harmless. Not to protect. To destroy.

Elsa's dad picks her up and runs up the stairs. Presses her against his jacket so she can't see. She hears the door flung open from inside and she hears Maud and Lennart pleading with Wolfheart to stop hitting, stop hitting, stop hitting. But judging by the dull thumping sounds, like when you drop milk cartons on the floor, he isn't stopping. He doesn't even hear them. In the tales Wolfheart fled into the dark forests long before the War-Without-End, because he knew what he was capable of.

Elsa tears herself free of Dad and sprints down the stairs. Maud and Lennart stop screaming before she has reached the bottom. Wolfheart's mallet of a fist is raised so high above Sam that it brushes the stretched-out fingers of the cloud animals before it turns back and hurtles down.

But Wolfheart freezes in the middle of the movement. Between him and the blood-covered man stands a woman who looks so small and frail that the wind should be able to pass right through her. She has an insignificant ball of blue tumble-dryer fluff in her hand, and a thin white line on her finger where her wedding ring used to be. Every ounce of her being seems to be yelling at her to run for her life. But she stays where she is, staring at Wolfheart with the resolute gaze of someone who has nothing left to lose.

She rolls up the tumble-dryer fluff in the palm of one hand and puts that hand against her other hand and clasps them together on her stomach; then she looks with determination at Wolfheart and says, with authority:

"We don't beat people to death in this leaseholders' association."

Wolfheart's fist is still vibrating in the air. His chest heaves up and down. But his arms slowly fall down at his sides.

She is still standing between Wolfheart and Sam, between the monster and the shadow, when the police car comes skidding into their street. The green-eyed policewoman jumps out, her weapon drawn, long before the car has stopped. Wolfheart has dropped on his knees in the snow.

Elsa shoves the door open and charges outside. The police roar at Wolfheart. They try to stop Elsa, but it's like holding water in cupped hands: she slips through their fingers. For reasons she won't understand for many years, Elsa has time to think about what her mother said to George once when she thought Elsa was sleeping. That this is how it is, being the mother of a daughter who is starting to grow up.

The wurse lies immobile on the ground halfway between Audi and the front entrance. The snow is red. It tried to get to her. Crawled out of Audi and crept along until it collapsed. Elsa wriggles out of her jacket and the Gryffindor scarf and spreads them over the animal's body, curling up in the snow next to it and hugging it hard, hard, feeling how its breath smells of peanut cake, and she whispers, "Don't be afraid, don't be afraid" over and over again into its ear. "Don't be afraid, don't be afraid, Wolfheart has defeated the dragon and no fairy tale can end until the dragon has been defeated."

When she feels Dad's soft hands picking her up off the ground, she calls out loudly, so the wurse will hear her even if it's already halfway to the Land-of-Almost-Awake:

"YOU CAN'T DIE! YOU HEAR?! YOU CAN'T DIE BECAUSE ALL CHRISTMAS TALES HAVE HAPPY ENDINGS!"

32

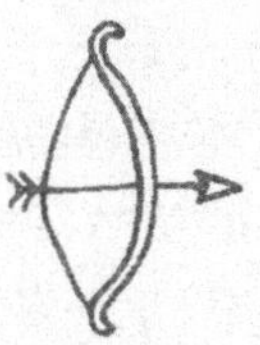

GLASS

It's hard to reason about death. Hard to let go of someone you love.

Granny and Elsa used to watch the evening news together. Now and then Elsa would ask Granny why grown-ups were always doing such idiotic things to each other. Granny usually answered that it was because grown-ups are generally people, and people are generally shits. Elsa countered that grown-ups were also responsible for a lot of good things in between all the idiocy—space exploration, the UN, vaccines, and cheese slicers, for instance. Granny then said the real trick of life was that almost no one is entirely a shit and almost no one is entirely not a shit. The hard part of life is keeping as much on the not-a-shit side as one can.

Once Elsa asked why so many not-shits had to die everywhere, and why so many shits didn't. And why anyone at all had to die, whether a shit or not. Granny tried to distract Elsa with ice cream and change the subject, because Granny preferred ice cream to death. But Elsa was capable of being a bewilderingly obstinate kid, so Granny gave up in the end and admitted that she supposed something always had to give up its own space so that something else could take its place.

"Like when we're on the bus and some old people get on?" asked

Elsa. And then Granny asked Elsa if she'd agree to more ice cream and another topic of conversation if Granny answered "Yes." Elsa said she could go for that.

In the oldest fairy tales from Miamas they say a wurse can die only of a broken heart. Otherwise, they're immortal. This is why it became possible to kill them after they were sent into exile from the Land-of-Almost-Awake for biting the princess: because they were sent away by the very people they had protected and loved. "And that was why they could be killed in the last battle of the War-Without-End," Granny explained—for hundreds of wurses died in that last battle—"because the hearts of all living creatures are broken in war."

Elsa thinks about that while sitting in the waiting room at the veterinary clinic. It smells of birdseed. Britt-Marie sits next to her with her hands clasped together in her lap, watching a cockatoo sitting in its cage on the other side of the room. Britt-Marie doesn't seem so very keen on cockatoos. Elsa isn't wholly conversant with the exact emotional utterances of cockatoos, but she reckons the feeling is mutual.

"You don't have to wait here with me," says Elsa, her voice clogged with sorrow and anger.

Britt-Marie brushes some invisible seeds from her jacket and answers, without taking her eyes off the cockatoo, "It's no trouble, dear Elsa. You shouldn't feel like that. No trouble at all."

Elsa understands that she doesn't mean it unpleasantly. The police are interviewing Dad and Alf about everything that has happened, and Britt-Marie was the first to be questioned, so she offered to sit with Elsa and wait for the veterinary surgeon to come out and say something about the wurse. So Elsa does understand that there's nothing unpleasant about it. It's just difficult for Britt-Marie to say anything at all without it sounding that way.

Elsa wraps her hands in her Gryffindor scarf. Inhales deeply.

"It was very brave of you to step between Wolfheart and Sam," she offers in a low voice.

Britt-Marie brushes some invisible seeds and possibly some invisible crumbs from the table in front of her into the palm of her hand. Sits there with her hand closed around them, as if looking for an invisible wastepaper bin to throw them in.

"As I said, we don't beat people to death in this leaseholders' association," she replies quickly, so Elsa can't hear how her emotion is overwhelming her.

They are silent. As you are when you make peace for the second time in two days, but don't quite want to spell it out to the other person. Britt-Marie fluffs up a cushion at the edge of the waiting-room sofa.

"I didn't hate your grandmother," she says without looking at Elsa.

"She didn't hate you either," says Elsa, without looking back.

"And actually, I've never wanted the flats to be converted to leaseholds. Kent wants it, and I want Kent to be happy, but he wants to sell the flat and make money and move. I don't want to move."

"Why not?"

"It's my home."

It's hard not to like her for that.

"Why were you and Granny always fighting?" Elsa asks, although she already knows the answer.

"She thought I was a . . . a nagging busybody," says Britt-Marie, not revealing the actual reason.

"Why are you like that, then?" asks Elsa, thinking about the princess and the witch and the treasure.

"Because you need to care about *something*, Elsa. As soon as anyone cared about anything in this world, your granny always dismissed it as 'nagging,' but if you don't care about anything, you're actually not alive at all. You're only existing. . . ."

"You're quite deep, you know, Britt-Marie."

"Thanks." She clearly has to resist the impulse to start brushing something invisible from Elsa's coat's-arm. She satisfies herself with fluffing up the sofa cushion again, even though it's been many years since there was last any stuffing in it to fluff up. Elsa threads the scarf around each of her fingers.

"There's this poem about an old man who says he can't be loved, so he doesn't mind, sort of, being disliked instead. As long as someone sees him," says Elsa.

"*Doctor Glas,*" says Britt-Marie with a nod.

"Wikipedia," Elsa corrects.

"No, it's a quote from *Doctor Glas*," insists Britt-Marie.

"Is that a site?"

"It's a play."

"Oh."

"What's Wikipedia?"

"A site."

Britt-Marie puts her hands together in her lap.

"In fact, *Doctor Glas* is a novel, as I understand. I haven't read it. But they put it on in the theater," she says hesitantly.

"Oh," says Elsa.

"I like theater."

"Me too."

They both nod.

"Doctor Glas would have been a good superhero name," Elsa says.

She thinks it would actually have been a better name for a superhero nemesis, but Britt-Marie doesn't look like she reads quality literature on a regular basis, so Elsa doesn't want to make it too complicated for her.

"'We want to be loved,'" quotes Britt-Marie. "'Failing that, admired; failing that, feared; failing that, hated and despised. At all costs we want to stir up some sort of feeling in others. The soul abhors a vacuum. At all costs it longs for contact.'"

Elsa is not quite sure what this means, but she nods all the same. "What do you want to be, then?"

"It's complicated being a grown-up sometimes, Elsa," Britt-Marie says evasively.

"It's not, like, easy-peasy being a kid either," Elsa replies belligerently.

The tips of Britt-Marie's fingers wander carefully over the white circle on the skin of her ring finger.

"I used to stand on the balcony early in the mornings. Before Kent woke up. Your grandmother knew this, that's why she made those snowmen. And that's why I got so angry. Because she knew my secret and it felt as if she and the snowmen were trying to taunt me for it."

"What secret?"

Britt-Marie clasps her hands together firmly.

"I was never like your grandmother. I never traveled. I was just here. But sometimes I liked to stand on the balcony in the mornings, when it was windy. It's silly, of course, everyone obviously thinks it's silly, they do, of course." She purses her mouth. "But I like to feel the wind in my hair."

Elsa thinks about how Britt-Marie may, despite everything, not be a total shit after all.

"You didn't answer the question—what do you want to be?" she says, winding her scarf through her fingers.

Britt-Marie's fingertips move hesitantly over her skirt, like a person moving across a dance floor to ask someone to dance. And then, cautiously, she utters the words:

"I want someone to remember I existed. I want someone to know I was here."

Unfortunately Elsa doesn't hear the last bit, because the veterinary surgeon comes through the door with a look on his face that creates a surging noise inside Elsa's head. She has run past him before he has even had time to open his mouth. Elsa hears them shouting after her as she charges down the corridor and starts throwing doors open, one after the other. A nurse tries to grab her, but she just keeps running, throws more doors open, doesn't stop until she hears the wurse howling. As if it knows she's on her way and is calling for her. When she finally storms into the right room, she finds it lying on a cold table, a bandage round its stomach. There's blood everywhere. She buries her face deep, deep, deep in its coat.

Britt-Marie is still there in the waiting room. Alone. If she left right now, probably no one would remember that she'd been there. She looks as if she's thinking about that for a moment, then brushes something invisible from the edge of the table, straightens a crease in her skirt, stands up, and leaves.

The wurse closes its eyes. It almost looks as if it's smiling. Elsa doesn't know if it can hear her. Doesn't know if it can feel her heavy tears dropping into its pelt. "You can't die. You can't die, because I'm here now. And you're my friend. No real friend would just go and die like that, do you understand? Friends don't die on each other," Elsa whispers, trying to convince herself more than the wurse.

It looks as if it knows. Tries to dry her cheeks with the warm air from its nose. Elsa lies next to it, curled up on the treatment table, as she lay in the hospital bed that night when Granny didn't come back with her from Miamas.

She lies there forever. With her Gryffindor scarf buried in the wurse's pelt.

The policewoman's voice can be heard between the wurse's breaths as they grow slower and the thumping on the other side of the thick black fur gets more and more drawn out. Her green eyes watch the girl and the animal from the doorway.

"We have to take your friend to the police station, Elsa." Elsa knows she's talking about Wolfheart.

"You can't put him in prison! He did it in self-defense!" Elsa roars.

"No, Elsa, he didn't. He wasn't defending himself."

And then she backs away from the door. Checks her watch as if pretending to be disoriented, as if she has just realized there is something extremely important that she has to get on with in an entirely different place, and how crazy it would be if someone she was under very clear orders to bring to the police station would not be watched for a moment so that he could talk to a child who was about to lose a wurse. It would be crazy, really.

And then she's gone. And Wolfheart is standing in the doorway. Elsa flings herself off the table and throws her arms around him and couldn't give a crap about whether or not he has to bathe in alcogel when he gets home.

"The wurse mustn't die! Tell him he mustn't die!" whispers Elsa.

Wolfheart breathes slowly. Stands with his hands held out awkwardly, as if someone has spilled something acidic on his sweater. Elsa realizes she still has his coat at home in the flat.

"You can have your coat back, Mum has washed it really carefully and hung it up in the wardrobe inside a plastic cover," she whispers apologetically and keeps hugging him.

He looks as if he'd really appreciate it if she didn't. Elsa doesn't care.

"But you're not allowed to fight again!" she orders, her face thrust into his sweater, before she lifts her head and wipes her eyes with her wrist. "I'm not saying you can never fight, because I haven't quite decided where I stand on that question. I mean morally, sort of thing. But you can't fight when you're as good at fighting as you are!" she sobs.

And then Wolfheart does something very curious. He hugs her back.

"The wurse. Very old. Very old wurse, Elsa," he growls in the secret language.

"I can't take everyone dying all the time," Elsa weeps.

Wolfheart holds her by both her hands. Gently squeezes her forefingers. He's trembling as if he's holding white-hot iron, but he doesn't let go, as one doesn't when one realizes there are more important things in life than being afraid of children's bacteria.

"Very old wurse. Very tired now, Elsa."

And when Elsa just shakes her head hysterically and yells at him that no one else can die on her now, he lets go of one of her hands and reaches into his trouser pocket, from which he takes a very crumpled piece of paper and puts it in her hand. It's a drawing. It's obvious that it's Granny who drew it, because she drew about as well as she spelled.

"It's a map." Elsa sobs as she unfolds it, the way one sobs when the tears have run out but not the crying.

Wolfheart gently rubs his hands together in circles. Elsa brushes her fingers over the ink.

"It's a map of the seventh kingdom," she says, more to herself than to him.

She lies down again on the table with the wurse. So close that its pelt pricks her through her sweater. Feels its warm breathing from the cold nose. It's sleeping. She hopes it's sleeping. She kisses its nose, so her tears end up in its whiskers. Wolfheart gently clears his throat.

"Was in the letter. Grandmother's letter," he says in the secret language and points at the letter. "Mipardonus." The seventh kingdom. Your grandmother and I . . . we were going to build it."

Elsa studies the map more carefully. It's actually of the whole of the Land-of-Almost-Awake, but with completely the wrong proportions, because proportions were never really Granny's thing.

"This seventh kingdom is exactly where the ruins of Mibatalos lie," she whispers.

Wolfheart rubs his hands together.

"Can only build Mipardonus on Mibatalos. Your grandmother's idea."

"What does Mipardonus mean?" asks Elsa, with her cheek pressed to the wurse's.

"Means 'I forgive.'"

The tears from his cheeks are the size of swallows. His enormous hand descends softly on the wurse's head. The wurse opens its eyes, but only slightly, and looks at him.

"Very old, Elsa. Very, very tired," whispers Wolfheart.

Then he tenderly puts his fingers over the wound that Sam's knife cut through the thick pelt.

It's hard to let go of someone you love. Especially when you are almost eight.

Elsa crawls close to the wurse and holds it hard, hard, hard. It manages to look at her one last time. She smiles and whispers, "You're the best first friend I've ever had," and it slowly licks her on the face and smells of sponge cake mix. And she laughs out loud, with her tears raining down.

When the cloud animals land in the Land-of-Almost-Awake, Elsa hugs it as hard as she can, and whispers: "You've completed your mission, you don't have to protect the castle anymore. Protect Granny now. Protect all the fairy tales!" It licks her face one final time.

And then it runs off.

When Elsa turns to Wolfheart, he squints at the sun as you do when you haven't been to the Land-of-Almost-Awake for an eternity of many fairy tales. Elsa points down at the ruins of Mibatalos.

"We can bring Alf here. He's good at building things. At least he's good at making wardrobes. And we'll also need wardrobes in the seventh kingdom, won't we? And Granny will be sitting on a bench in Miamas when we're ready. Just like the granddad in *The Brothers Lionheart*. There's a fairy tale with that name, I read it to Granny, so I know she'll wait on a bench because it's typical of her to nick something like that from other people's fairy tales. And she knows *The Brothers Lionheart* is one of my favorite fairy tales!"

She is still crying. Wolfheart as well. But they do what they can. They construct words of forgiveness from the ruins of fighting words.

The wurse dies on the same day that Elsa's brother is born. Elsa decides that she will tell her brother all about it when he's older. Tell him about her first best friend. Tell him that sometimes things have to clear a space so something else can take its place. Almost as if the wurse gave up its place on the bus for Halfie.

And she thinks about how she will be very particular about pointing out to Halfie that he mustn't feel sad or have a bad conscience about it.

Because wurses hate traveling by bus.

33

BABY

It's difficult ending a fairy tale. All tales have to end sometime, of course. Some can't finish soon enough. This one, for example, could feasibly have been rounded off and packed away long ago. The problem is this whole issue of heroes at the ends of fairy tales, and how they are supposed to "live happily to the end of their days." This gets tricky, from a narrative perspective, because the people who reach the end of their days must leave others who have to live out their days without them.

It is very, very difficult to be the one who has to stay behind and live without them.

It's dark by the time they leave the vet's. They used to make snow-angels outside the house on the night before Elsa's birthday. That was the only night of the year Granny didn't say crappy things about the angels. It was one of Elsa's favorite traditions. She goes with Alf in Taxi. Not so much because she doesn't want to go with Dad, but because Dad told her Alf was furious with himself for being in the garage with Taxi when the whole thing with Sam happened. Angry because he wasn't there to protect Elsa.

Alf and Elsa don't talk very much in Taxi, of course; this is what happens when you don't have so much to say. And when Elsa at last says she has to do something at home on their way to the hospital, Alf doesn't ask why. He just drives. He's good in that way, Alf.

"Can you make snow-angels?" asks Elsa when Taxi stops outside the house.

"I'm bloody sixty-four years old," grunts Alf.

"That's not an answer."

Alf turns off Taxi's engine. "I may be sixty-four years old, but I wasn't sixty-four when I was born! Course I can make bloody snow-angels!"

And then they make snow-angels. Ninety-nine of them. And they never talk much about it afterwards. Because certain kinds of friends can be friends without talking much.

The woman in jeans sees them from her balcony. She laughs. She's getting good at that.

Dad is waiting for them at the hospital entrance when they get there. A doctor goes past who, for a moment, Elsa thinks she might recognize. And then she sees George, and she runs across the entire waiting room and throws herself into his arms. He is wearing his shorts over his leggings and he has a glass of ice-cold water for Mum in his hand.

"Thanks for running!" says Elsa, with her arms around him.

Dad looks at Elsa and you can see he's jealous but trying not to show it. He's good like that. George looks at her too, overwhelmed.

"I'm quite good at running," he says quietly.

Elsa nods.

"I know. That's because you're different."

And then she goes with Dad to see Mum. And George stays behind for so long with the glass of water that in the end it's back to room temperature.

There's a stern-looking nurse standing outside Mum's room who refuses to let Elsa inside, because apparently Mum has had a complicated delivery. That's how the nurse puts it, sounding very firm and emphatic when she pronounces the "com" in "complicated." Elsa's dad clears his throat.

"Are you new here, by any chance?"

"What's that got to do with anything?" the nurse thunders. "No visitors today!" she snaps with absolute certainty before spinning around and marching back into Mum's room.

Dad and Elsa stay where they are, patiently waiting and nodding, because they suspect this will sort itself out. For Mum may be Mum, but she is also Granny's daughter. Remember the man in the silver car, just before Elsa was born? No one should mess with Mum when she's giving birth.

It takes maybe thirty seconds before the corridor reverberates until the pictures on the wall are practically rattling.

"BRING MY DAUGHTER IN HERE BEFORE I THROTTLE YOU WITH THE STETHOSCOPE AND LEVEL THE HOSPITAL TO THE GROUND, DO YOU UNDERSTAND?"

Thirty seconds was considerably longer than Elsa and Dad thought it would take. But in probably no more than another three or four seconds, Mum adds another roar:

"I COULDN'T GIVE A SHIT! I'LL FIND A STETHOSCOPE SOMEWHERE IN THIS HOSPITAL AND THEN I'LL THROTTLE YOU WITH IT!"

The nurse steps out into the corridor again. She doesn't look quite as self-assured anymore. The doctor that Elsa thought she recognized turns up behind her and says in a friendly voice that they can "probably make an exception this time." He smiles at Elsa. Elsa inhales determinedly and steps over the threshold.

Mum has tubes everywhere, all over her body. They hug as hard as Elsa dares without accidentally pulling one of them out. She imagines that one of them may be an electrical power cable, and that Mum will go out like a light if that happens. Mum repeatedly runs her hand through Elsa's hair.

"I am so very, very sorry about your friend the wurse," she says gently.

Elsa sits in silence for so long on the edge of her bed that her cheeks dry and she has time to think about an entirely new way of measuring time. This whole thing with eternities and the eternities of fairy tales is becoming a bit unmanageable. There must be something less complicated—blinking, for example, or the beating of a hummingbird's wings. Someone must have thought about this. She's going to Wikipedia it when she gets home.

She looks at Mum, who looks happy. Elsa pats her hand. Mum grabs on to it.

"I know I'm not a perfect mum, darling."

Elsa puts her forehead against Mum's forehead.

"Not everything has to be perfect, Mum."

They sit so close that Mum's tears run down the tip of Elsa's nose.

"I work so much, darling. I used to be so angry at your grandmother for never being home, and now I'm just the same myself. . . ."

Elsa wipes both their noses with her Gryffindor scarf.

"No superheroes are perfect, Mum. It's cool."

Mum smiles. Elsa as well.

"Can I ask you something?"

"Of course you can," says Mum.

"How am I like your father?"

Mum looks hesitant. As mums get when they are accustomed to being able to predict their daughters' questions, and then suddenly find they were wrong about that. Elsa shrugs.

"From Granny I have the thing about being different. And I'm a know-it-all like Dad, and I always end up rowing with everyone, which I have from Granny. So what do I have from your dad? Granny never told me any stories about him."

Mum can't quite bring herself to answer. Elsa breathes tensely through her nose. Mum lays her hands on Elsa's cheeks and Elsa dries Mum's cheeks with the Gryffindor scarf.

"I think she talked about your grandfather without your noticing," whispers Mum.

"How am I like him, then?"

"You have his laugh."

Elsa retracts her hands into her sweater. And slowly swings the empty sleeves in front of her.

"Did he laugh a lot?"

"Always. Always, always, always. That was why he loved your grandmother. Because she got him to laugh with every bit of his body. Every bit of his soul."

Elsa climbs up next to Mum in the hospital bed and lies there for probably a billion wingbeats of a hummingbird. "Granny wasn't a complete shit. She just wasn't not a complete shit either," she says.

"Elsa! Language!" And then Mum laughs out loud. Elsa as well. Grandfather's laugh.

And then they lie there talking about superheroes for quite a while. Mum says now that Elsa has become someone's big sister, she has to bear in mind that big sisters are always idols to their younger siblings. And it's a great power to have. A great force.

"And with great power comes great responsibility," whispers Mum.

Elsa sits bolt upright in the bed.

"Have you been reading *Spider-Man*?!"

"I Googled him," Mum says with a proud grin.

And then all the guilty feelings rush over her face. As they do with mothers who have realized that the time has come to reveal a great secret.

"Elsa . . . my darling . . . the first letter from Grandmother. It wasn't you who got it. There was another letter before yours. Grandmother gave it to me. The day before she died. . . ."

Mum looks as if she's standing on the edge of a high diving board with everyone watching and has just decided she can't go through with it.

But Elsa just nods calmly, shrugs, and pats Mum on the cheek, as you do with a small child who has done wrong because it doesn't know any better.

"I know, Mum. I know."

Mum blinks awkwardly at her.

"What? You know? How do you know?"

Elsa sighs patiently.

"I mean, yeah, okay, it took me a bit of time to figure it out. But it wasn't exactly, like, quantum physics. First of all, not even Granny would have been so irresponsible as to send me out on a treasure hunt without telling you first. And secondly, only you and I can drive Renault, because he's a bit different, but I drove him sometimes when Granny was eating kebab and you drove him sometimes when Granny was drunk. So it must have been one of us who parked him in the garage in Britt-Marie's space. And it wasn't me. And I'm sort of not an idiot. I can count."

Mum laughs so loudly and for so long about it that Elsa starts getting seriously worried about the hummingbird.

"You're the sharpest person I know, do you know that?"

And she thinks, Well, that's nice and all that, but Mum really needs to get out there and meet a few more people.

"What did Granny write in your letter?" asks Elsa.

Mum's lips come together.

"She wrote sorry."

"For being a bad mother?"

"Yes."

"Have you forgiven her?"

Mum smiles and Elsa wipes her cheeks again with the Gryffindor scarf.

"I'm trying to forgive us both, I think. I'm like Renault. I have a long braking distance," whispers Mum.

Elsa hugs her until the hummingbird gives up and just goes off to do something else.

"Your grandmother saved children because she was saved herself when she was small, darling. I never knew that, but she wrote it in the letter. She was an orphan," whispers Mum.

"Like the X-Men." Elsa nods.

"You know whereabouts the next letter is hidden, I take it?" says Mum with a smile.

"It's enough to say 'where,'" says Elsa, because she can't stop herself.

But she does know, of course she knows. She's known all along. She's not stupid. And this isn't exactly the most unpredictable of fairy tales.

Mum laughs again. Laughs until the evil nurse comes stamping in and says there's got to be an end to this now, or she'll have problems with the tubes.

Elsa stands up. Mum takes her hand and kisses it.

"We've decided what Halfie's going to be called. It's not going to be Elvir. It'll be another name. George and I decided as soon as we saw him. I think you're going to like it."

She's right about that. Elsa likes it. She likes it a lot.

A few moments later she's standing in a little room, looking at him through a pane of glass. He's lying inside a little plastic box. Or a very big lunchbox. It's hard to tell which. He's got tubes everywhere and his lips are blue and his face looks as if he is running against an insanely strong wind, but all the nurses tell Elsa it's not dangerous. She doesn't like it. This is the most obvious way of figuring out that it actually is dangerous.

She cups her hands against the glass when she whispers, so he'll be able to hear on the other side. "Don't be afraid, Halfie. You've got a sister now. And it's going to get better. Everything's going to be fine."

And then she switches to the secret language:

"I'll try not to be jealous of you. I've been jealous of you for an insane length of time, but I have a pal whose name is Alf and he and his little brother have been at loggerheads for like a hundred years. I don't want us to be at loggerheads for a hundred years. So I think we have to start working at liking each other right from the start, you get what I mean?"

Halfie looks like he gets it. Elsa puts her forehead against the glass.

"You have a granny as well. She's a superhero. I'll tell you all about her when we get home. Unfortunately I gave the moo-gun to the boy downstairs but I'll make you another one. And I'll bring you to the Land-of-Almost-Awake, and we'll eat dreams and dance and laugh and cry and be brave and forgive people, and we'll fly with the cloud animals and Granny will be sitting on a bench in Miamas, smoking and waiting for us. And one day my granddad will come wandering along as well. We'll hear him from far away because he laughs with his whole body. He laughs so much that I think we'll have to build an eighth kingdom for him. I'll ask Wolfheart what 'I laugh' is in his mother's language. And the wurse is also there in the Land-of-Almost-Awake. You're going to like the wurse. There's no better friend than a wurse!"

Halfie looks at her from the plastic box. Elsa wipes the glass with the Gryffindor scarf.

"You've got a good name. The best name. I'll tell you all about the boy you got it from. You'll like him."

She stays by the glass until she realizes that the whole hummingbird thing was probably basically a bad idea, in spite of all. She'll stick to eternities and the eternities of fairy tales for a bit longer. Just for the sake of simplicity. And maybe because it reminds her of Granny.

Before she goes she whispers through cupped hands to Halfie, in the secret language:

"It's going to be the greatest adventure ever having you as a brother, Harry. The greatest, greatest adventure!"

Things are turning out as Granny said. Things are getting better. Everything is going to be fine.

The doctor that Elsa felt she recognized is standing next to Mum's bed when she comes back into the room. He's waiting, without moving, as if he knows that it will take her a moment to remember where she saw him. And when the penny finally drops, he smiles as if there was never any other alternative.

"You're the accountant," Elsa bursts out suspiciously, and then adds, "And the vicar from the church. I saw you at Granny's funeral and you were dressed as a vicar!"

"I am many things," the doctor answers in a blithe tone of voice, with the sort of expression on his face that no one ever had when Granny was around.

"Also a doctor?" asks Elsa.

"A doctor first and foremost," says the doctor, and offers his hand as he introduces himself:

"Marcel. I was a good friend of your grandmother's."

"I'm Elsa."

"So I understand," Marcel says, smiling.

"You were Granny's lawyer," says Elsa, as one does when remembering details of telephone calls from the beginning of a fairy tale, say around the end of chapter two.

"I am many things," Marcel repeats, and gives her a paper.

It's a printout from a computer, and it's correctly spelled, so she knows it's Marcel and not Granny who wrote it. But some of Granny's handwriting can be seen on the bottom of it. Marcel folds his hands together on his stomach, not unlike the way Britt-Marie does it.

"Your grandmother owned the house you live in. Maybe you already worked that out. She says she won it in a game of poker, but I don't know for certain."

Elsa reads the paper. Pouts her lips.

"And what? Now it's mine? The whole house?"

"Your mother will act as your guardian until you're eighteen. But your grandmother has ensured that you'll be able to do what you want with it. If you want to, you can sell the flats as leaseholds. And if you don't want to, you don't have to."

"So why did you tell everyone in the house that it would be turned into leaseholds if everyone agreed?"

"If you don't agree then, technically, you're not all agreed. Your grandmother was convinced you would go with what the neighbors wanted if they were all agreed about it, but she was also certain you wouldn't do anything with the house that might bring anyone who lived in it to harm. That was why she had to make sure you'd got to know all your neighbors by the time you saw the will."

He puts his hand on her shoulder.

"It's a big responsibility, but your grandmother forbade me to give it to anyone but you. She said you were 'smarter than all those other lunatics put together.' And she always said that a kingdom consists of the people who live in it. She said you'd understand that."

Elsa's fingertips caress Granny's signature at the bottom of the paper.

"I understand."

"I can run through the details with you, but it's a very complicated contract," says Marcel helpfully.

Elsa brushes her hair out of her face.

"Granny wasn't exactly an uncomplicated person."

Marcel belly-laughs. You'd have to call it that. A belly-laugh. It's far too noisy to be a laugh. Elsa likes it a great deal. It's quite impossible not to.

"Did you and Granny have an affair?" she asks suddenly.

"ELSA!" Mum interrupts, so distressed that the tubes almost come loose.

Offended, Elsa throws out her arms.

"What's wrong with ASKING?" She turns demandingly to Marcel. "Did you have an affair or not?"

Marcel puts his hands together. Nods with sadness, also happiness. Like when one has eaten a very large ice cream and realizes it is now gone.

"She was the love of my life, Elsa. She was the love of many men's lives. Women as well, actually."

"Were you hers?"

Marcel pauses. He doesn't look angry. Or bitter. Just slightly jealous.

"No," he says, "That was you. It was always you, dear Elsa."

Tenderly he reaches out and pats Elsa's cheek, as you do when you see someone you have loved in the eyes of their grandchild.

Elsa and Mum and the letter share the silence for seconds and eternities and hummingbird wingbeats. Then Mum touches Elsa's hand and tries to make the question sound as if it's not so terribly important, just something she just thought of spontaneously:

"What do you have from me?"

Elsa stands in silence. Mum looks despondent.

"I was just, well, you know. You said you had inherited certain things from your grandmother and from your father, and I was just thinking, you know . . ."

She goes silent. Ashamed of herself as mothers are when they realize they have passed that point in life when they want more from their daughters than their daughters want from them. And Elsa puts her hands over Mum's cheeks and says mildly:

"Just everything else, Mum. I just have everything else from you."

Dad gives Elsa a lift back to the house. He turns off the stereo in Audi so Elsa doesn't have to listen to his music, and he stays the night in Granny's flat. They sleep in the wardrobe. It smells of wood shavings and it's just big enough for Dad to be able to stretch out and touch the walls on both sides with his fingertips and the tips of his toes. It's good in that way, the wardrobe.

When Dad has gone to sleep, Elsa sneaks down the stairs. Stands in front of the stroller, which is still locked up inside the front entrance. She looks at the crossword on the wall. Someone has filled it in with a pencil. In every word is a letter, which, in turn, meshes with four longer words. And in each of the four words is a letter written in a square that's bolder than the others. E-L-S-A.

Elsa checks the padlock with which the stroller is fixed to the stair railing. It's a combination lock, but the four rolls don't have numbers. They have letters.

She spells her name and unlocks it. Pushes the stroller away. And that is where she finds Granny's letter to Britt-Marie.

34

GRANNY

You never say good-bye in the Land-of-Almost-Awake. You just say "See you later." It's important to people in the Land-of-Almost-Awake that it should be this way, because they believe that nothing really ever completely dies. It just turns into a story, undergoes a little shift in grammar, changes tense from "now" to "then."

A funeral can go on for weeks, because few events in life are a better opportunity to tell stories. Admittedly on the first day it's mainly stories about sorrow and loss, but gradually as the days and nights pass, they transform into the sorts of stories that you can't tell without bursting out laughing. Stories about how the deceased once read the instructions "Apply to the face but not around the eyes" on the packaging of some skin cream, and then called the manufacturer with extreme annoyance to point out that this is precisely where the face is positioned. Or how she employed a dragon to caramelize the tops of all the crème brûlées before a big party in the castle, but forgot to check whether the dragon had a cold. Or how she stood on her balcony with her dressing gown hanging open, shooting at people with a paintball gun.

And the Miamasians laugh so loudly that the stories rise up like lanterns around the grave. Until all stories are one and the tenses are one and the same. They laugh until no one can forget that this is what we leave behind when we go: the laughs.

"Halfie turned out to be a boy-half. He's going to be called Harry!" Elsa explains proudly as she scrapes snow from the stone.

"Alf says it's lucky he turned out to be a boy, because the women in our family are 'so bonkers they're a safety hazard.'" She chuckles, making quotation marks in the air and grumpily dragging her feet through the snow, Alf-style. The cold is nipping at her cheeks. She nips it back. Dad digs away the snow and scrapes his spade along the top layer of earth. Elsa tightens her Gryffindor scarf around her neck. Scatters the wurse's ashes over Granny's grave and a thick layer of cinnamon bun crumbs over the ashes.

Then she hugs the gravestone tight, tight, tight, and whispers:

"See you later!"

She's going to tell all their stories. She's already telling him the first few as she wanders back to Audi with Dad. And Dad listens. He turns down the volume of the stereo before Elsa has time to jump in. Elsa scrutinizes him.

"Were you upset yesterday when I hugged George at the hospital?" she asks.

"No."

"I don't want you to be upset."

"I don't get upset."

"Not even a little?" says Elsa, offended.

"Am I allowed to be upset?" wonders Dad.

"You can be a *little* bit upset," mutters Elsa.

"Okay . . . I am a bit upset," Dad tries, and actually does look upset.

"That looks too upset."

"Sorry," says Dad, beginning to sound stressed.

"You shouldn't be so upset that I feel guilty about it. Just upset enough so it doesn't feel like you're not bothered!" explains Elsa.

He tries again.

"Now you're not looking *at all* upset!"

"Maybe I'm upset on the inside?"

Elsa scrutinizes him before conceding:

"Deal." She says it in English.

Dad nods dubiously and manages to stop himself from pointing out that she should avoid using English words when there are perfectly good alternatives in her own language. Elsa opens and shuts the glove compartment as Audi glides up the highway.

"He's quite okay. George, I mean."

"Yes," says Dad.

"I know you don't mean that," Elsa protests.

"George is okay." Dad nods as if he means it.

"So why don't we ever have Christmas together, then?" mutters Elsa with irritation.

"How do you mean?"

"I thought you and Lisette never came to us at Christmas because you don't like George."

"I have nothing at all against George."

"But?"

"But?"

"But there's a 'but' coming here, isn't there? It feels like there's a 'but' coming," mumbles Elsa.

Dad sighs.

"But I suppose George and I are quite different in terms of our . . . personalities, perhaps. He's very . . ."

"Fun?"

Dad looks stressed again.

"I was going to say he seems very outgoing."

"And you're very . . . ingoing?"

Dad fingers the steering wheel nervously.

"Why can't it be your mother's fault? Perhaps we don't visit you at Christmas because Mum doesn't like Lisette."

"Is that it?"

Dad looks uncomfortable. He's a terrible liar. "No. *Everyone* likes Lisette. I'm well aware of it." He says it as people do when considering an extremely irritating character trait in the person they live with.

Elsa looks at him for a long time before she asks:

"Is that why Lisette loves you? Because you are very ingoing?"

Dad smiles.

"I don't know why she loves me, if I'm to be quite honest."

"Do you love her?"

"Incredibly," he says without any hesitation.

But then he immediately looks quite hesitant again.

"Are you going to ask why Mum and I stopped loving each other?"

"I was going to ask why you started."

"Was our marriage so terrible, in your view?"

Elsa shrugs.

"I mean, you're very different, that's all. She doesn't like Apple, that sort of thing. And you kind of don't like *Star Wars*."

"There are plenty of people who don't like *Star Wars*."

"Dad, there's NO ONE who doesn't like *Star Wars* except you!"

Dad seems unwilling to take issue with this.

"Lisette and I are also very different," he points out.

"Does she like *Star Wars*?"

"I have to admit I've never asked."

"How can you NOT have asked her that?!"

"We're different in other ways. I'm almost sure about that."

"So why are you together, then?"

"Because we accept each other as we are, perhaps."

"And you and Mum tried to change each other?"

He leans over and kisses her forehead.

"I worry about how wise you are sometimes, darling."

Elsa blinks intensely. Takes a deep breath. Gathers her energy and whispers:

"Those texts from Mum you got on the last day of school before the Christmas holiday. About not having to pick me up? I wrote them. I lied, so I could deliver one of Granny's letters—"

"I knew," he interrupts.

Elsa squints suspiciously at him. He smiles.

"The grammar was too perfect. I knew right away."

It's still snowing. It's one of those magical winters when it never seems to end. After Audi has stopped outside Mum's house, Elsa turns to Dad very seriously.

"I want to stay with you and Lisette more often than every other weekend. Even if you don't want that."

"You . . . my darling . . . you can stay with us as often as you like!" Dad stammers, quite overwhelmed.

"No. Only every other weekend. And I get that it's because I'm different and it upsets your 'family harmony.' But Mum is having Halfie now. And actually Mum can't do everything all the time because no one's perfect all the time. Not even Mum!"

"Where . . . 'family harmony' . . . where did you get that from?"

"I read things."

"We didn't want to take you away from the house," he whispers.

"Because you didn't want to take me away from Mum?"

"Because none of us wanted to take you away from your granny."

The last words between them dissipate into the air and leave nothing behind. The snowflakes are falling so densely against Audi's windshield that the world in front of them seems to have disappeared. Elsa holds Dad's hand. Dad holds hers even tighter.

"It's hard for a parent to accept that you can't protect your child from everything."

"It's hard for a child to accept it too," says Elsa, and pats him on the cheek. He holds on to her fingers.

"I'm an ambivalent person. I know this makes me a bad father. I've always worried that my life should be in better order before you start living with us for longer periods. I thought it was for your sake. That's what parents often do, I think, we persuade ourselves we're doing everything for the sake of the child. It's too painful to us to admit that our children won't wait to grow up because their parents are busy with other things. . . ."

Elsa's forehead rests in the palm of his hand when she whispers: "You don't need to be a perfect dad, Dad. But you have to be my dad. And you can't let Mum be more of a parent than you just because she happens to be a superhero."

Dad buries his nose in her hair.

"We just didn't want you to become one of those children who have two homes but feel like a visitor in both," he says.

"Where's that from?" Elsa snorts.

"We read things."

"As smart people go, you and Mum are really insanely unsmart sometimes," Elsa says, and then smiles. "But don't worry about how it'll be when you're living with me, Dad. I promise we can make some things really boring!"

Dad nods and tries not to look puzzled when Elsa tells him they're going to celebrate her birthday at his and Lisette's house, because Mum and George and Halfie are still at the hospital. And Dad tries not to look stressed when Elsa says that she has already called Lisette and arranged everything. But he looks much calmer when Elsa tells him he can make the invitation cards. Because Dad immediately starts thinking about suitable fonts, and fonts have a very calming effect on Dad.

"They have to be ready this afternoon, though!" says Elsa, and Dad promises they will be.

They actually end up being ready in March. But that's another story.

Elsa is about to jump out of the car. But since Dad already seems more hesitant and stressed than usual, she turns his stereo on so he can listen to his crappy music for a while. But no music comes out, and it probably takes two or three pages before it really sinks in for Elsa.

"This is the last chapter of *Harry Potter and the Sorceror's Stone*," she finally manages to say.

"It's an audiobook," Dad admits with embarrassment.

Elsa stares at the stereo. Dad keeps his hands on the steering wheel, concentrating. Even Audi has been stationary for a while now.

"When you were small, we always read together. I always knew which chapter you were on in every book. But you read so quickly now, and keep up with all the things you like. Harry Potter seems to mean such a lot to you, and I want to understand the things that mean a lot to you," he says, red-faced, as he looks down at the horn.

Elsa sits in silence. Dad clears his throat.

"It's actually a bit of a pity that you get on so well with Britt-Marie nowadays, because while I was listening to this book it struck me I could have called her She-Who-Must-Not-Be-Named at some suitable opportunity. I had a feeling that would make you laugh. . . ."

And it is actually a bit of a pity, thinks Elsa. Because it's the funniest thing Dad has ever said. It seems to set him off, as he suddenly becomes animated.

"There's a film about Harry Potter, did you know that?" He grins.

Elsa pats him indulgently on the cheek.

"Dad. I love you. I really do. But do you live under a stone or what?"

"You knew that already?" asks Dad, a little surprised.

"Everyone knows that, Dad."

Dad nods. "I don't really watch films. But maybe we could see this Harry Potter one sometime, you and me? Is it very long?"

"There are seven books, Dad. And eight films," says Elsa carefully.

And then Dad looks very, very stressed again.

Elsa hugs him and gets out of Audi. The sun is reflecting off the snow.

Alf is trudging about outside the entrance, trying not to slip in his worn-down shoes, with a snow shovel in his hands. Elsa thinks about the tradition in the Land-of-Almost-Awake of giving away presents on your birthday, and decides that next year she'll give Alf a pair of shoes. But not this year, because this year he's getting an electric screwdriver.

Britt-Marie's door is open. She's wearing her floral-print jacket. Elsa can see in the hall mirror that she's making the bed in the bedroom. There are two suitcases inside the threshold. Britt-Marie straightens a last crease in the bedspread, sighs deeply, turns around, and goes into the hall.

She looks at Elsa and Elsa looks at her and neither of them can quite bring herself to say anything, until they both burst out at the same time:

"I have a letter for you!"

And then Elsa says "What?" and Britt-Marie says "Excuse me?" at the exact same moment. It's all rather disorienting.

"I have a letter for you, from Granny! It was taped to the floor under the stroller by the stairs!"

"I see, I see. I also have a letter for you. It was in the tumble-dryer filter in the laundry room."

Elsa tilts her head. Looks at the suitcases.

"Are you going somewhere?"

Britt-Marie clasps her hands together slightly nervously over her stomach. Looks as if she'd like to brush something off the sleeve of Elsa's jacket.

"Yes."

"Where?"

"I don't know," admits Britt-Marie.

"What were you doing in the laundry?"

Britt-Marie purses her mouth.

"I was hardly going to leave without making the beds and cleaning the dryer filter first, Elsa. Just imagine if something were to happen to me while I was away? I'm not going to let people think I was some sort of barbarian!"

Elsa grins. Britt-Marie doesn't grin, but Elsa has a feeling she may be grinning on the inside.

"It was you who taught the drunk to sing that song when she was on the stairs, yelling, wasn't it? And then the drunk grew completely calm and went to bed. And your mother was a singing teacher. And I don't think drunks can sing songs like that."

Britt-Marie clasps her hands together even harder. Nervously rubs the white streak where her wedding ring used to be.

"David and Pernilla used to like it when I sang them that song, when they were small. Of course they don't remember that now, but they used to like it very much, they really did."

"You're not a complete shit, Britt-Marie, are you?" says Elsa with a smile.

"Thanks," says Britt-Marie hesitantly, as if she's been asked a trick question.

And then they exchange letters. On Elsa's envelope it says "ELSA," and, on Britt-Marie's, "THE BAT." Britt-Marie reads hers out loud without Elsa even having to ask. She's good in that way, Britt-Marie. It's quite long, of course. Granny has quite a lot to apologize about, and most people haven't had anywhere near as many reasons over the years to be apologized to as Britt-Marie. There's an apology about that thing with the snowman. And an apology about the blanket fluff in the tumble-dryer. And an apology about that time Granny happened to shoot at Britt-Marie with the paintball gun when she had just bought it and was "testing it out a bit" from the balcony. Apparently, one time she hit Britt-Marie on the bum when Britt-Marie was wearing her best skirt, and you actually can't even hide stains with brooches if the stains are on your bum. Because it's not civilized to wear brooches on your bum. Granny writes that she can understand that now.

But the biggest apology comes at the end of the letter, and when Britt-Marie is reading it out the words get stuck at the back of her throat, so Elsa has to lean forward and read it herself.

"'Sorry I never told you you desserve much better then Kent. Because you do. Even if you are an old bat!'"

Britt-Marie carefully folds up the letter with the edges exactly together, and then she looks at Elsa and tries to smile like a normal human being.

Elsa pats her on the arm.

"Granny knew you'd solve the crossword on the stairs."

Britt-Marie fidgets with Granny's letter, as if at a loss.

"How did you know it was me?"

"It was done in pencil. Granny always said you were one of those who had to make all the beds before you went on holiday and couldn't even solve a crossword in ink unless you'd had two glasses of wine first. And I've never seen you drink wine."

And then she points at the envelope in Britt-Marie's hand. There's something else inside. Something that's jingling. Britt-Marie opens the seal and leans her head over the opening, peering inside as if she assumes Granny in person will shortly be jumping out and roaring, "WAAAAAAAAAAAAH!"

And then she sticks her hand inside and gets out Granny's car keys.

Elsa and Alf help her with the bags. Renault starts on the first try. Britt-Marie takes the deepest breath Elsa has ever seen any person take. Elsa sticks her head inside on the passenger side and yells over the din of the engine:

"I like lollipops and comics!"

Britt-Marie looks as if she's trying to answer but something is lodged in her throat. So Elsa grins and shrugs and adds:

"I'm just saying. In case you ever have any to spare."

Britt-Marie seems to brush her damp eyes with the sleeve of the floral-print jacket. Elsa closes the door. And then Britt-Marie drives off. She doesn't know where. But she's going to see the world and she's going to feel the wind in her hair. And she's going to solve all her crosswords in ink.

But that, as in all fairy tales, is a completely different story.

Alf stays in the garage and keeps looking long after she's out of sight. He shovels snow the whole evening and most of the next morning.

Elsa sits in Granny's wardrobe. It smells of Granny. The whole house smells of Granny. There's something quite special about a granny's house. Even if ten or twenty or thirty years go by, you never forget how it smells. And the envelope with her last letter smells just like the house. Smells of tobacco and monkey and coffee and beer and lilies and cleaning agents and leather and rubber and soap and alcohol and protein bars and mint and wine and tires and wood shavings and dust and cinnamon buns and smoke and sponge cake mix and clothes shop and candle grease and O'boy and dish-cloth and dreams and spruce tree and pizza and mulled wine and potato and meringues and perfume and peanut cake and glass and baby. It smells of Granny. Smells like the best of someone who was mad in the best possible way.

Elsa's name is written in almost-neat letters on the envelope and it's apparent that Granny really did her utmost to spell everything correctly. It didn't go so very well.

But the first five words are: "Sorry I have to dye."

And that's the day Elsa forgives her granny about that.

EPILOGUE

To my knight Elsa.

Sorry I have to dye. Sorry I dyed. Sorry I got old.

Sorry I left you and sorry for this bloody cancer. Sorry I was a shit moor than a not-shit sometimes.

I luv you more than 10000 eternities of fairytails. Tell Halfie the fairytails! And protect the castel! Protect your frends because they will protect you. The castel is yours now. No one is braver and wyser and stronger than you. You are the best of us all. Grow up and be diffrent and don't let anyone tell you not to be diffrent, because all superheros are diffrent. And if they mess with you then kick them in the fusebox! Live and larf and dream and bring new fairytails to Miamas. I will wait there. Maybe grandad as well—buggered if I know. But it's going to be a grate adventure anyways.

Sorry I was mad.

I luv you.

Damn, how I luv you.

Granny's spelling really was atrocious.

Epilogues in fairy tales are also difficult. Even more difficult than endings. Because although they aren't necessarily supposed to give you all the answers, it can be a bit unsatisfying if they stir up even more questions. Because life, once the story has ended, can be both very simple and very complicated.

Elsa celebrates her eighth birthday with Dad and Lisette. Dad drinks three glasses of mulled wine and dances the "spruce dance." Lisette and Elsa watch *Star Wars*. Lisette knows all the dialogue by heart. The boy with a syndrome and his mum are there, and they laugh a lot, because that is how you overcome fears. Maud bakes cookies and Alf is in a bad mood and Lennart gives Lisette and Dad a new coffee percolator. Lennart noticed that Lisette and Dad's coffee percolator has loads of buttons, and Lennart's is better because it only has one button. Dad seems to appreciate this observation.

And it's getting better. It's going to be fine.

Harry is christened in a little chapel in the churchyard where Granny and the wurse are buried. Mum insists on all the windows being kept open, even though it's snowing outside, so everyone can see.

"And what will the boy's name be?" asks the vicar, who's also an accountant and a doctor and, it's emerged, works a bit on the side as a librarian.

"Harry," says Mum, smiling.

The vicar nods and winks at Elsa.

"And will the child have godparents?"

Elsa snorts loudly.

"He doesn't need any godparents! He has a big sister!"

And she knows that people in the real world don't understand that sort of thing. But in Miamas a newborn doesn't get a godparent, newborns get a Laugher instead. After the child's parents and granny and a few other people that Elsa's granny, when she was telling Elsa the story, didn't seem to think were terribly important, the Laugher is the most important person in a child's life in Miamas. And the Laugher is not chosen by the parents, because Laughers are far too important to be chosen by parents. It's the child who does the choosing. So when a child is born in Miamas, all the family's friends come to the cot and tell stories and pull faces and dance and sing and make jokes, and the first one to make the child laugh becomes the Laugher. The Laugher is personally responsible for making it happen as often and as loudly and in as many situations as possible, particularly those that cause embarrassment to the parents.

Of course, Elsa knows very well that everyone will tell her Harry is too small to understand the whole thing about having a big sister. But when she looks down at him in her arms, the two of them know damned well that it's the first time he's laughing.

They go back to the house, where the people continue to live their lives. Once every other week, Alf gets into Taxi and drives Maud and Lennart to a large building where they get to sit in a little room and wait for a very long time. And when Sam enters through a small door with two large security guards, Lennart gets out some coffee and Maud produces some cookies. Because cookies are the most important thing.

And probably a lot of people think Maud and Lennart shouldn't do that, and that types like Sam shouldn't even be allowed to live, let alone eat cookies. And those people are probably right. And they're probably wrong too. But Maud says she's firstly a grandmother and secondly a mother-in-law and thirdly a mother, and this is what grandmothers and mothers-in-law and mothers do. They fight for the good. And Lennart drinks coffee and agrees. And Maud bakes cookies, because when the darkness is too heavy to bear and too many things have been broken in too many ways to ever be fixed again, Maud doesn't know what weapon to use if one can't use dreams.

So that's what she does. One day at a time. One dream at a time. And one could say it's right and one could say it's wrong. And probably both would be right. Because life is both complicated and simple.

Which is why there are cookies.

Wolfheart comes back to the house on New Year's Eve. The police have decided it was self-defense even though everyone knows it wasn't himself he was protecting. That could also be right or wrong, possibly.

He stays on in his flat. The woman in jeans stays on in hers. And they do what they can. Try to learn to live with themselves, try to live rather than just existing. They go to meetings. They tell their stories. No one knows if this is the way they are going to mend everything that's broken inside them, but at least it's a way towards something. It helps them breathe. They have dinner with Elsa and Harry and Mum and George every Sunday. Everyone in the house does. Sometimes Green-eyes also comes. She's surprisingly good at telling stories. And the boy with a syndrome still doesn't talk, but he teaches them all how to dance beautifully.

Alf wakes up one morning because he's thirsty. He gets up and has some coffee and is just on his way back to bed when there's a knock on the door. He opens it, taking a deep slug of coffee. Looks at his brother for a long time. Kent is supporting himself on a crutch and looking back at him.

"I've been a bloody idiot," mutters Kent.

"Yes," mutters Alf.

Kent's fingers grip the crutch even harder.

"The company went bankrupt six months ago."

They stand there in craggy silence, with a whole life of conflict between them. As brothers do.

"You want some coffee, or what?" grunts Alf.

"If you have some ready," grunts Kent.

And then they drink coffee. As brothers do. Sit in Alf's kitchen and compare postcards from Britt-Marie. Because she writes to them both every week. As women like Britt-Marie do.

They all still have a residents' meeting once every month in the room on the bottom floor. They all argue, as ever. Because it's a normal house. By and large. And neither Granny nor Elsa would have wanted it any other way.

The Christmas holidays come to an end and Elsa goes back to school. She knots her gym shoes tightly and carefully tightens the straps of her backpack as children like Elsa do after the Christmas holidays. But Alex starts in her class that day and she is also different. They become best friends immediately, as you only can when you've just turned eight, and they never have to run away again. When they're called into the headmaster's office the first time that term, Elsa has a black eye and Alex has scratch marks on her face. When the headmaster sighs and tells Alex's mum that she "has to try to fit in," Alex's mum tries to throw the globe at him. But Elsa's mum gets there first.

Elsa will always love her for that.

A few days go by. Maybe a few weeks. But after that, one by one, other different children start tagging along with Alex and Elsa in the playground and corridors. Until there are so many of them that no one dares to chase them anymore. Until they're an army in themselves. Because if a sufficient number of people are different, no one has to be normal.

In the autumn, the boy with a syndrome starts in the first year. When there's a costume party, he comes dressed up as a princess. A group of older boys laugh and make fun of him, until he starts crying. Elsa and Alex notice this and take him outside into the parking area and Elsa calls her dad. He arrives with a bag of new clothes.

When they go back in, Elsa and Alex are also dressed up as princesses. Spider-Man princesses.

And after that, they're the boy's superheroes.

Because all seven-year-olds deserve superheroes.

And whoever disagrees with that needs their head examined.

ACKNOWLEDGMENTS

Neda. Everything is still to make you laugh. Never forget that. (Sorry about the wet towels on the bathroom floor.) Asheghetam.

My maternal grandmother, who is not the least bit crazy, but has always baked some of the best cookies a seven-year-old could ever ask for.

My paternal grandmother. Who has always believed in me most of all.

My sister. Who is stronger than a lion.

My mother. Who taught me to read.

Astrid Lindgren. Who taught me to love it.

All the librarians of my childhood. Who saw that a boy was afraid of heights and lent him wings.

Thanks also to:

My Obi-Wan, Niklas Natt och Dag. My editor, John Häggblom.

My agent, Jonas Axelsson. The language attack force, Vanja Vinter. Fredrik Söderlund (for letting me borrow the Noween).

Johan Zillén (who got it before all others). Kersti Forsberg (for giving a kid a chance once). Nils Olsson (for two amazing covers). All who have been involved in both this book and *A Man Called Ove* at Forum, Månpocket, Bonnier Audio, Bonnier Agency, Tre Vänner, and Partners in Stories. An extra thanks in advance to the linguistic "besserwissers" who will no doubt locate the grammatical failings in the names of the seven kingdoms (tense high five).

Most of all, thanks to you who read. Without whose highly dubious judgment I would very likely have to go out and find myself a proper job.

MY GRANDMOTHER ASKED ME TO TELL YOU SHE'S SORRY

FREDRIK BACKMAN

A Readers' Club Guide

Topics for Discussion

1. *My Grandmother Asked Me to Tell You She's Sorry* begins with the pronouncement, "Every seven-year-old deserves a superhero" (page 1). Do you agree? Why is it so important that children have heroes? Who were your heroes when you were a child?

2. Names play a significant part in Elsa's grandmother's stories. How do the various kingdom and heroine names from the Land-of-Almost-Awake (Miamas, Miploris, Mimovas, Wolfheart, the Chosen One, the sea-angel, etc.) inform your understanding of Granny's stories? Did you agree with how their real world counterparts were portrayed in the stories?

3. Elsa's mother grew up in a nontraditional family environment. Do you think this influenced her parenting style with Elsa? In what ways?

4. Were you surprised by the ways in which each of the apartment tenants were connected to the others? Which relationship surprised you the most? Why?

5. Granny is a polarizing figure in *My Grandmother Asked Me to Tell You She's Sorry*. Describe the way each of the characters reacts to her. Do you think their opinions of her are justified? Why or why not? What did you think of Granny? Do you know anyone like her?

6. Discuss the role that books, especially the Harry Potter novels, play in Elsa's life. Why do you think Elsa relates to the Harry Potter books more than other novels? When you were growing up, were there books you particularly loved? Which ones and why?

7. What did you think of Britt-Marie when you first encountered her? Did she remind you of anyone in your life? Where do you think Britt-Marie goes at the end of the novel?

8. Elsa believes that her "teachers are wrong. [She] has no problems concentrating. She just concentrates on the right things" (page 47). What kinds of things does Elsa concentrate on? How does this create problems for her? Do you think Elsa is a good student? Why or why not?

9. Which of the characters in *My Grandmother Asked Me to Tell You She's Sorry* surprised you the most? Why?

10. Discuss Britt-Marie's marriage to Kent. Did you think they were well suited for each other? Do you think the marriage changed Britt-Marie? How can being in a bad relationship affect someone's personality?

11. Fairy tales can provide a way to teach children some fundamental truths about the world. How do Granny's fairy tales help Elsa understand the world around her? What lessons does Elsa take away from the tales Granny tells her about life in the land of Miamas?

12. When her grandmother dies, Elsa is of course sad, but she also experiences a wide range of other emotions, including anger. Can you name some of the others? Consider how the loss of a loved one can lead us to have feelings that are much more complicated than sadness.

13. In this book, as in his previous novel, *A Man Called Ove*, Fredrik Backman paints a vivid portrait of the relationship between an older person nearing the end of his or her life, and a young child. What can people at the opposite ends of life learn from one another? How are the very old and the very young alike? How are they different? When you were very young, was there an elderly person who played a significant role in your life? What did you learn from him or her?

Enhance Your Book Club

1. *Kirkus Reviews* says *My Grandmother Asked Me to Tell You She's Sorry* puts Backman "firmly in league with Roald Dahl and Neil Gaiman." Read some of Dahl's and Gaiman's works and discuss them with your book club. Do you see any similarities between the works? What are they?

2. Granny's fairy tales provide comfort to Elsa. Why do you think that fairy tales are comforting to her and other children? Share some of your favorite fairy tales with your book club.

3. One of the themes in *My Grandmother Asked Me to Tell You She's Sorry* is the attempt of one generation to reach another via fantastic stories, both successfully in the case of Elsa and Granny, and unsuccessfully in the case of Granny and Elsa's mother. As a group, watch the movie *Big Fish*, which similarly explores this idea, and contrast the ways in which the fairy tales in each story play a part in the intergenerational relationships.

Turn the page for a sneak peek at Fredrik Backman's irresistible novel about finding love and second chances in the most unlikely of places.

Available from Atria Books

1

Forks. Knives. Spoons.

In that order.

Britt-Marie is certainly not the kind of person who judges other people. Far from it.

But surely no civilized person would even think of arranging a cutlery drawer in a different way from how cutlery drawers are supposed to be arranged?

We're not animals, are we?

It's a Monday in January. She's sitting at a desk in the unemployment office. Admittedly there's no cutlery in sight, but it's on her mind because it sums up everything that's gone wrong recently. Cutlery should be arranged as it always has been, because life should go on unchanged. Normal life is presentable. In normal life you clean up the kitchen and keep your balcony tidy and take care of your children. It's hard work—harder than one might think. In normal life you certainly don't find yourself sitting in the unemployment office.

The girl who works here has staggeringly short hair, Britt-Marie thinks, like a man's. Not that there's anything wrong with that, of course—it's modern, no doubt. The girl points at a piece of paper and smiles, evidently in a hurry.

"Just fill in your name, social security number, and address here, please."

Britt-Marie has to be registered. As if she were a criminal. As if she has come to steal a job rather than find one.

"Milk and sugar?" the girl asks, pouring some coffee into a plastic mug.

Britt-Marie doesn't judge anyone. Far from it. But who would behave like that? A plastic mug! Are we at war? She'd like to say just that to the girl, but because Kent is always urging Britt-Marie to "be more socially aware" she just smiles as diplomatically as she can and waits to be offered a coaster.

Kent is Britt-Marie's husband. He's an entrepreneur. Incredibly, incredibly successful. Has business dealings with Germany and is extremely, extremely socially aware.

The girl offers her two tiny disposable cartons of the sort of milk that doesn't have to be kept in the fridge. Then she holds out a plastic mug with plastic teaspoons protruding from it. Britt-Marie could not have looked more startled if she'd been offered roadkill.

She shakes her head and brushes her hand over the table as if it was covered in invisible crumbs. There are papers everywhere, in any old order. The girl clearly doesn't have time to tidy them up, Britt-Marie realizes—she's probably far too busy with her career.

"Okay," says the girl pleasantly, turning back to the form, "just write your address here."

Britt-Marie fixes her gaze on her lap. She misses being at home with her cutlery drawer. She misses Kent, because Kent is the one who fills in all the forms.

When the girl looks like she's about to open her mouth again, Britt-Marie interrupts her.

"You forgot to give me a coaster," says Britt-Marie, smiling, with all the social awareness she can muster. "I don't want to make marks on your table. Could I trouble you to give me something to put my . . . coffee cup on?"

She uses that distinctive tone, which Britt-Marie relies on whenever she has to summon all her inner goodness, to refer to it as a "cup" even though it is a plastic mug.

"Oh, don't worry, just put it anywhere."

As if life was as simple as that. As if using a coaster or organizing the cutlery drawer in the right order didn't matter. The girl—who clearly doesn't appreciate the value of coasters, or proper cups, or even mirrors, judging by her hairstyle—taps her pen against the paper, by the "address" box.

"But surely we can't just put our cups on the table? That leaves marks, surely you see that."

The girl glances at the surface of the desk, which looks as if toddlers have been trying to eat potatoes off it. With pitchforks. In the dark.

"It really doesn't matter; it's so old and scratched up already!" she says with a smile.

Britt-Marie is screaming inside.

"I don't suppose you've considered that it's because you don't use coasters," she mutters, not at all in a "passive-aggressive" way, which is how Kent's children once described her when they thought she wasn't listening. Britt-Marie is not actually passive-aggressive. She's considerate. After she heard Kent's children saying she was passive-aggressive she was extra considerate for several weeks.

The unemployment office girl looks a little strained. "Okay . . . what did you say your name was? Britt, right?"

"Britt-Marie. Only my sister calls me Britt."

"Okay, Britt-Marie, if you could just fill in the form. Please."

Britt-Marie peers at the paper, which requires her to give assurances about where she lives and who she is. An unreasonable amount of paperwork is required these days just to be a human being. A preposterous amount of administration for society to let one take part. In the end she reluctantly fills in her name, social security number, and her cell phone number. The address box is left empty.

"What's your educational background, Britt-Marie?"

Britt-Marie squeezes her handbag.

"I'll have you know that my education is excellent."

"But no formal education?"

"For your information, I solve an enormous number of crosswords. Which is not the sort of thing one can do without an education."

She takes a very small gulp of the coffee. It doesn't taste like Kent's coffee at all. Kent makes very good coffee, everyone says so. Britt-Marie takes care of the coasters and Kent takes care of the coffee.

"Okay . . . what sort of life experience do you have?"

"My latest employment was as a waitress. I had outstanding references."

The girl looks hopeful. "And when was that?"

"Nineteen seventy-eight."

"Ah . . . and you haven't worked since then?"

"I have worked *every day* since then. I've helped my husband with his company."

Again the girl looks hopeful. "And what sorts of tasks did you perform in the company?"

"I took care of the children and saw to it that our home was presentable."

The girl smiles to hide her disappointment, as people do when they don't have the ability to distinguish between "a place to live" and "a home." It's actually thoughtfulness that makes the difference. Because of thoughtfulness there are coasters and proper coffee cups and beds that are made so tightly in the mornings that Kent jokes with his acquaintances about how, if you stumble on the threshold on your way into the bedroom, there's "a smaller risk of breaking your leg if you land on the floor than the bedspread." Britt-Marie loathes it when he talks that way. Surely civilized people lift their feet when they walk across bedroom thresholds?

Whenever Britt-Marie and Kent go away, Britt-Marie sprinkles the mattress with baking soda for twenty minutes before she makes the bed. The baking soda absorbs dirt and humidity, leaving the mattress much fresher. Baking soda helps almost everything, in Britt-Marie's experience. Kent usually complains about being late; Britt-Marie clasps her hands together over her stomach and says: "I absolutely must be allowed to make the bed before we leave, Kent. Just imagine if we die!"

This is the actual reason why Britt-Marie hates traveling. Death. Not even baking soda has any effect on death. Kent says she exaggerates, but people do actually drop dead all the time when they're away, and what would the landlord think if they had to break down the door only to find an unclean mattress? Surely they'd conclude that Kent and Britt-Marie lived in their own dirt?

The girl checks her watch.

"*Okay*," she says.

Britt-Marie feels her tone has a note of criticism in it.

"The children are twins and we have a balcony. It's more work than you think, having a balcony."

The girl nods tentatively.

"How old are your children?"

"Kent's children. They're thirty."

"So they've left home?"

"Obviously."

"And you're sixty-three years old?"

"Yes," says Britt-Marie dismissively, as if this was highly irrelevant.

The girl clears her throat as if, actually, it's very relevant indeed.

"Well, Britt-Marie, quite honestly, because of the financial crisis and all that, I mean, there's a scarcity of jobs for people in your . . . situation."

The girl sounds a bit as if "situation" was not her first choice as a way of concluding the sentence. Britt-Marie smiles patiently.

"Kent says that the financial crisis is over. He's an entrepreneur, you must understand. So he understands these kind of things, which are possibly a little outside your field of competence."

The girl blinks for an unnecessary amount of time. Checks her watch. She seems uncomfortable, which vexes Britt-Marie. She quickly decides to give the girl a compliment, just to show her goodwill. She looks around the room for something to compliment her about, and finally manages to say, with as generous a smile as she can muster:

"You have a very modern hairstyle."

"What? Oh. Thanks," she replies, her fingertips moving self-consciously towards her scalp.

"It's very courageous of you to wear your hair so short when you have such a large forehead."

Why does the girl look offended? Britt-Marie wonders. Clearly that's what happens when you try to be sociable towards young people these days. The girl rises from her chair.

"Thanks for coming, Britt-Marie. You are registered in our database. We'll be in touch!"

She holds out her hand to say good-bye. Britt-Marie stands up and places the plastic mug of coffee in her hand.

"When?"

"Well, it's difficult to say."

"I suppose I'm supposed to just sit and wait," counters Britt-Marie with a diplomatic smile, "as if I didn't have anything better to do?"

The girl swallows.

"Well, my colleague will be in touch with you about a jobseekers' training course, an—"

"I don't want a course. I want a job."

"Absolutely, but it's difficult to say when something will turn up. . . ."

Britt-Marie takes a notebook from her pocket.

"Shall we say tomorrow, then?"

"What?"

"Could something turn up tomorrow?"

The girl clears her throat.

"Well, it could, or I'd rather . . ."

Britt-Marie gets a pencil from her bag, eyes the pencil with some disapproval, and then looks at the girl.

"Might I trouble you for a pencil sharpener?" she asks.

"A pencil sharpener?" asks the girl, as if she had been asked for a thousand-year-old magical artifact.

"I need to put our meeting on the list."

Some people don't understand the value of lists, but Britt-Marie is not one of those people. She has so many lists that she has to keep a separate list to list all the lists. Otherwise anything could happen. She could die. Or forget to buy baking soda.

The girl offers her a pen and says something to the effect of, "Actually I don't have time tomorrow," but Britt-Marie is too busy peering at the pen to hear what she's saying.

"Surely we can't write lists in *ink*?" she bursts out.

"That's all I've got." The girl says this with some finality. "Is there anything else I can help you with today, Britt-Marie?"

"Ha," Britt-Marie responds after a moment.

Britt-Marie often says that. "Ha." Not as in "ha-ha" but as in "aha," spoken in a particularly disappointed tone. Like when you find a wet towel thrown on the bathroom floor.

"Ha." Immediately after saying this, Britt-Marie always firmly closes her mouth, to emphasize this is the last thing she intends to say on the subject. Although it rarely is the last thing.

The girl hesitates. Britt-Marie grasps the pen as if it's sticky. Looks at the list marked "Tuesday" in her notebook, and, at the top, above "Cleaning" and "Shopping," she writes "Unemployment office to contact me."

She hands back the pen.

"It was very nice to meet you," says the girl robotically. "We'll be in touch!"

"Ha," says Britt-Marie with a nod.

Britt-Marie leaves the unemployment office. The girl is obviously under the impression that this is the last time they'll meet, because she's unaware of how scrupulously Britt-Marie sticks to her lists. Clearly the girl has never seen Britt-Marie's balcony.

It's an astonishingly, astonishingly presentable balcony.

It's January outside, a winter chill in the air but no snow on the ground—below freezing without any evidence of it being so. The very worst time of year for balcony plants.

After leaving the unemployment office, Britt-Marie goes to a supermarket that is not her usual supermarket, where she buys everything on her list. She doesn't like shopping on her own, because she doesn't like pushing the shopping cart. Kent always pushes the shopping cart while Britt-Marie walks at his side and holds on to a corner of it. Not because she's trying to steer, only that she likes holding on to things while he is also holding on to them. For the sake of that feeling they are going somewhere at the same time.

She eats her dinner cold at exactly six o'clock. She's used to sitting up all night waiting for Kent, so she tries to put his portion in the fridge. But the only fridge here is full of very small bottles of alcohol. She lowers herself onto a bed that isn't hers, while rubbing her ring finger, a habit she falls into when she's nervous.

A few days ago she was sitting on her own bed, spinning her wedding ring, after cleaning the mattress extra carefully with baking soda. Now she's rubbing the white mark on her skin where the ring used to be.

The building has an address, but it's certainly neither a place to live nor a home. On the floor are two rectangular plastic boxes for balcony flowers, but the hostel room doesn't have a balcony. Britt-Marie has no one to sit up all night waiting for.

But she sits up anyway.

Fredrik Backman's new novel,

BEARTOWN,

will be published in April 2017
by Atria Books.

Praise for

A MAN CALLED OVE

"Even the most serious reader of fiction needs light relief, and for that afternoon when all you want is charm, this is the perfect book."

—*San Francisco Chronicle*

"You will laugh, you will cry, as his heartbreaking story unfolds through the diverse cast of characters that enter his life, all uninvited. You will never look at the grumpy people who come into your life in quite the same way. A very memorable read."

—*The San Diego Union Tribune*, Best Books of 2015

"This quirky debut is a thoughtful and charming exploration of the impact one life has on countless others—and an absolute delight."

—*CBS Local*

"Exquisite. The lyrical language is the confetti thrown liberally throughout this celebration-of-life story, adding sparkle and color to an already spectacular party. Backman's characters feel so authentic that readers will likely find analogues living in their own neighborhoods."

—*Shelf Awareness* (starred review)

"Readers seeking feel-good tales with a message will rave about the rantings of this solitary old man with a singular outlook."

—*Booklist* (starred review)

"Backman writes with winning charm."

—*Publishers Weekly* (starred review)

"A charming debut. . . . Wry descriptions, excellent pacing. . . . In the contest of 'Most Winning Combination,' it would be hard to beat grumpy Ove and his hidden, generous heart."

—*Kirkus Reviews*

"You can't help but be moved."

—*Psychology Today*,
"Thirteen Successful and Risky New Novels"

"An inspiring affirmation of love for life and acceptance of people for their essence and individual quirks. . . . The book is bittersweet, tender, often wickedly humorous and almost certain to elicit tears. I contentedly wept my way through a box of tissues when I first read the novel and again when I savored it for a second time."

—*BookBrowse*

ALSO BY FREDRIK BACKMAN

My Grandmother Asked Me to Tell You She's Sorry

Britt-Marie Was Here

And Every Morning the Way Home Gets Longer and Longer

A MAN CALLED OVE

- A NOVEL -

FREDRIK BACKMAN

WASHINGTON SQUARE PRESS

New York London Toronto Sydney New Delhi

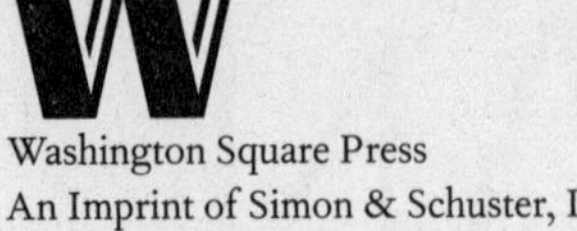

Washington Square Press
An Imprint of Simon & Schuster, Inc.
1230 Avenue of the Americas
New York, NY 10020

This book is a work of fiction. Any references to historical events, real people, or real places are used fictitiously. Other names, characters, places, and events are products of the author's imagination, and any resemblance to actual events or places or persons, living or dead, is entirely coincidental.

Copyright © 2012 by Fredrik Backman
Translation copyright © 2014 by Henning Koch

All rights reserved, including the right to reproduce this book or portions thereof in any form whatsoever. For information, address Washington Square Press Subsidiary Rights Department, 1230 Avenue of the Americas, New York, NY 10020.

First Washington Square Press trade paperback edition May 2015
Originally published in Swedish in 2014 as *En man som heter Ove*
Published by arrangement with Hodder & Stoughton

WASHINGTON SQUARE PRESS and colophon are trademarks of Simon & Schuster, Inc.

For information about special discounts for bulk purchases, please contact Simon & Schuster Special Sales at 1-866-506-1949 or business@simonandschuster.com.

The Simon & Schuster Speakers Bureau can bring authors to your live event. For more information or to book an event contact the Simon & Schuster Speakers Bureau at 1-866-248-3049 or visit our website at www.simonspeakers.com.

Interior design by Paul Dippolito

Manufactured in the United States of America

40 39 38

The Library of Congress has catalogued the hardcover as follows:
Backman, Fredrik, 1981–
[Man som heter Ove. English]
A man called Ove : a novel / by Fredrik Backman.—First Atria Books hardcover edition.
pages cm
I. Title.
PT9877.12.A32M3613 2014
839.73'8—dc23

2014015618

ISBN 978-1-4767-3801-7
ISBN 978-1-4767-3802-4 (trade paperback)
ISBN 978-1-4767-3803-1 (ebook)

A MAN CALLED OVE

1

A MAN CALLED OVE BUYS A COMPUTER THAT IS NOT A COMPUTER

Ove is fifty-nine.

He drives a Saab. He's the kind of man who points at people he doesn't like the look of, as if they were burglars and his forefinger a policeman's flashlight. He stands at the counter of a shop where owners of Japanese cars come to purchase white cables. Ove eyes the sales assistant for a long time before shaking a medium-sized white box at him.

"So this is one of those O-Pads, is it?" he demands.

The assistant, a young man with a single-digit body mass index, looks ill at ease. He visibly struggles to control his urge to snatch the box out of Ove's hands.

"Yes, exactly. An iPad. Do you think you could stop shaking it like that . . . ?"

Ove gives the box a skeptical glance, as if it's a highly dubious sort of box, a box that rides a scooter and wears tracksuit pants and just called Ove "my friend" before offering to sell him a watch.

"I see. So it's a computer, yes?"

The sales assistant nods. Then hesitates and quickly shakes his head.

"Yes . . . or, what I mean is, it's an iPad. Some people call it a 'tablet' and others call it a 'surfing device.' There are different ways of looking at it. . . ."

Ove looks at the sales assistant as if he has just spoken backwards, before shaking the box again.

"But is it good, this thing?"

The assistant nods confusedly. "Yes. Or . . . How do you mean?"

Ove sighs and starts talking slowly, articulating his words as if the only problem here is his adversary's impaired hearing.

"Is. It. Goooood? Is it a good computer?"

The assistant scratches his chin.

"I mean . . . yeah . . . it's really good . . . but it depends what sort of computer you want."

Ove glares at him.

"I want a computer! A normal bloody computer!"

Silence descends over the two men for a short while. The assistant clears his throat.

"Well . . . it isn't really a normal computer. Maybe you'd rather have a . . ."

The assistant stops and seems to be looking for a word that falls within the bounds of comprehension of the man facing him. Then he clears his throat again and says:

". . . a laptop?"

Ove shakes his head wildly and leans menacingly over the counter.

"No, I don't want a 'laptop.' I want a *computer*."

The assistant nods pedagogically.

"A laptop is a computer."

Ove, insulted, glares at him and stabs his forefinger at the counter.

"You think I don't know that!"

Another silence, as if two gunmen have suddenly realized they have forgotten to bring their pistols. Ove looks at the box for a long time, as though he's waiting for it to make a confession.

"Where does the keyboard pull out?" he mutters eventually.

The sales assistant rubs his palms against the edge of the counter and shifts his weight nervously from foot to foot, as young men employed in retail outlets often do when they begin to understand that something is going to take considerably more time than they had initially hoped.

"Well, this one doesn't actually have a keyboard."

Ove does something with his eyebrows. "Ah, of course," he splutters. "Because you have to buy it as an 'extra,' don't you?"

"No, what I mean is that the computer doesn't have a *separate* keyboard. You control everything from the screen."

Ove shakes his head in disbelief, as if he's just witnessed the sales assistant walking around the counter and licking the glass-fronted display cabinet.

"But I have to have a keyboard. You do understand that?"

The young man sighs deeply, as if patiently counting to ten.

"Okay. I understand. In that case I don't think you should go for this computer. I think you should buy something like a MacBook instead."

"A McBook?" Ove says, far from convinced. "Is that one of those blessed 'eReaders' everyone's talking about?"

"No. A MacBook is a . . . it's a . . . laptop, with a keyboard."

"Okay!" Ove hisses. He looks around the shop for a moment. "So are *they* any good, then?"

The sales assistant looks down at the counter in a way that seems to reveal a fiercely yet barely controlled desire to begin clawing his own face. Then he suddenly brightens, flashing an energetic smile.

"You know what? Let me see if my colleague has finished with his customer, so he can come and give you a demonstration."

Ove checks his watch and grudgingly agrees, reminding the assistant that some people have better things to do than stand around all day waiting. The assistant gives him a quick nod, then disappears and comes back after a few moments with a colleague. The colleague looks very happy, as people do when they have not been working for a sufficient stretch of time as sales assistants.

"Hi, how can I help you?"

Ove drills his police-flashlight finger into the counter.

"I want a computer!"

The colleague no longer looks quite as happy. He gives the first sales assistant an insinuating glance as if to say he'll pay him back for this.

In the meantime the first sales assistant mutters, "I can't take anymore, I'm going for lunch."

"Lunch," snorts Ove. "That's the only thing people care about nowadays."

"I'm sorry?" says the colleague and turns around.

"Lunch!" He sneers, then tosses the box onto the counter and swiftly walks out.

2

(THREE WEEKS EARLIER) A MAN CALLED OVE MAKES HIS NEIGHBORHOOD INSPECTION

It was five to six in the morning when Ove and the cat met for the first time. The cat instantly disliked Ove exceedingly. The feeling was very much reciprocated.

Ove had, as usual, gotten up ten minutes earlier. He could not make head nor tail of people who overslept and blamed it on "the alarm clock not ringing." Ove had never owned an alarm clock in his entire life. He woke up at quarter to six and that was when he got up.

Every morning for the almost four decades they had lived in this house, Ove had put on the coffee percolator, using exactly the same amount of coffee as on any other morning, and then drank a cup with his wife. One measure for each cup, and one extra for the pot—no more, no less. People didn't know how to do that anymore, brew some proper coffee. In the same way as nowadays nobody could write with a pen. Because now it was all computers and espresso machines. And where was the world going if people couldn't even write or brew a pot of coffee?

While his proper cup of coffee was brewing, he put on his navy blue trousers and jacket, stepped into his wooden clogs, and shoved his hands in his pockets in that particular way of a middle-aged man who expects the worthless world outside to disappoint him. Then he made his morning inspection of the street. The surrounding row houses lay in silence and darkness as he walked out the door, and there wasn't a soul in sight. Might have known, thought Ove. On this street no one took the trouble to get up any earlier than they had to. Nowadays, it was just self-employed people and other disreputable sorts living here.

The cat sat with a nonchalant expression in the middle of the footpath that ran between the houses. It had half a tail and only one ear. Patches of fur were missing here and there as if someone had pulled it out in handfuls. Not a very impressive feline.

Ove stomped forward. The cat stood up. Ove stopped. They stood there measuring each other up for a few moments, like two potential troublemakers in a small-town bar. Ove considered throwing one of his clogs at it. The cat looked as if it regretted not bringing its own clogs to lob back.

"Scram!" Ove bellowed, so abruptly that the cat jumped back. It briefly scrutinized the fifty-nine-year-old man and his clogs, then turned and lolloped off. Ove could have sworn it rolled its eyes before clearing out.

Pest, he thought, glancing at his watch. Two minutes to six. Time to get going or the bloody cat would have succeeded in delaying the entire inspection. Fine state of affairs that would be.

He began marching along the footpath between the houses. He stopped by the traffic sign informing motorists that they were prohibited from entering the residential area. He gave the metal pole a firm kick. Not that it was wonky or anything, but it's always best to check. Ove is the sort of man who checks the status of all things by giving them a good kick.

He walked across the parking area and strolled back and forth along all the garages to make sure none of them had been burgled in the night or set on fire by gangs of vandals. Such things had never happened around here, but then Ove had never skipped one of his inspections either. He tugged three times at the door handle of his own garage, where his Saab was parked. Just like any other morning.

After this, he detoured through the guest parking area, where cars could only be left for up to twenty-four hours. Carefully he noted down all the license numbers in the little pad he kept in his jacket pocket, and then compared these to the licenses he had noted down the day before. On occasions when the same license numbers turned up in Ove's notepad, Ove would go home and call the Vehicle Licensing Authority to retrieve the vehicle owner's details, after which he'd call up the latter and inform him that he was a useless bloody imbecile who couldn't even read signs. Ove didn't really care who was parked in the guest parking area, of course. But it was a question of principle. If it said twenty-four hours on the sign, that's how long you were allowed to stay. What would it be like if everyone just parked wherever they liked? It would be chaos. There'd be cars bloody everywhere.

Today, thank goodness, there weren't any unauthorized cars in the guest parking, and Ove was able to proceed to the next part of his daily inspection: the trash room. Not that it was really his responsibility, mind. He had steadfastly opposed from the very beginning the nonsense steamrollered through by the recently arrived jeep-brigade that household trash "had to be separated."

Having said that, once the decision was made to sort the trash, someone had to ensure that it was actually being done. Not that anyone had asked Ove to do it, but if men like Ove didn't take the initiative there'd be anarchy. There'd be bags of trash all over the place.

He kicked the bins a bit, swore, and fished out a jar from the glass recycling, mumbled something about "incompetents" as he unscrewed its metal lid. He dropped the jar back into glass recycling, and the metal lid into the metal recycling bin.

Back when Ove was the chairman of the Residents' Association, he'd pushed hard to have surveillance cameras installed so they could monitor the trash room and stop people tossing out unauthorized trash. To Ove's great annoyance, his proposal was voted out. The neighbors felt "slightly uneasy" about it; plus they felt it would be a headache archiving all the videotapes. This, in spite of Ove repeatedly arguing that those with "honest intentions" had nothing to fear from "the truth."

Two years later, after Ove had been deposed as chairman of the Association (a betrayal Ove subsequently referred to as "the coup d'état"), the question came up again. The new steering group explained snappily to the residents that there was a newfangled camera available, activated by movement sensors, which sent the footage directly to the Internet. With the help of such a camera one could monitor not only the trash room but also the parking area, thereby preventing vandalism and burglaries. Even better, the video material erased itself automatically after twenty-four hours, thus avoiding any "breaches of the residents' right to privacy." A unanimous decision was required to go ahead with the installation. Only one member voted against.

And that was because Ove did not trust the Internet. He accentuated the *net* even though his wife nagged that you had to put the emphasis on *Inter*. The steering group realized soon enough that the Internet would watch Ove throwing out his trash over Ove's own dead body. And in the end no cameras were installed. Just as well, Ove reasoned. The daily inspection was more effective anyway. You knew who was doing what and who was keeping things under control. Anyone with half a brain could see the sense of it.

When he'd finished his inspection of the trash room he locked the door, just as he did every morning, and gave it three good tugs to ensure it was closed properly. Then he turned around and noticed a bicycle leaning up against the wall outside the bike shed. Even though there was a huge sign instructing residents not to leave their bicycles there. Right next to it one of the neighbors had taped up an angry, handwritten note: "This is not a bicycle parking area! Learn to read signs!" Ove muttered something about ineffectual idiots, opened the bike shed, picked up the bicycle, put it neatly inside, then locked the shed and tugged the door handle three times.

He tore down the angry notice from the wall. He would have liked to propose to the steering committee that a proper "No Leafleting" sign should be put up on this wall. People nowadays seemed to think they could swan around with angry signs here, there, and anywhere they liked. This was a wall, not a bloody notice board.

Ove walked down the little footpath between the houses. He stopped outside his own house, stooped over the paving stones, and sniffed vehemently along the cracks.

Piss. It smelled of piss.

And with this observation he went into his house, locked his door, and drank his coffee.

When he was done he canceled his telephone line rental and his newspaper subscription. He mended the tap in the small bathroom. Put new screws into the handle of the door from the kitchen to the veranda. Reorganized boxes in the attic. Rearranged his tools in the shed and moved the Saab's winter tires to a new place. And now here he is.

Life was never meant to turn into this.

It's four o'clock on a Tuesday afternoon in November. He's turned off the radiators, the coffee percolator, and all the lights. Oiled the wooden countertop in the kitchen, in spite of those mules at IKEA saying the wood does not need oiling. In this house all wooden worktops get an oiling every six months, whether it's necessary or not. Whatever some girlie in a yellow sweatshirt from the self-service warehouse has to say about it.

He stands in the living room of the two-story row house with the half-size attic at the back and stares out the window. The forty-year-old beard-stubbled poser from the house across the street comes jogging past. Anders is his name, apparently. A recent arrival, probably not lived here for more than four or five years at most. Already he's managed to wheedle his way onto the steering group of the Residents' Association. The snake. He thinks he owns the street. Moved in after his divorce, apparently, paid well over the market value. Typical of these bastards, they come here and push up the property prices for honest people. As if this was some sort of upper-class area. Also drives an Audi, Ove has noticed. He might have known. Self-employed people and other idiots all drive Audis. Ove tucks his hands into his pockets. He directs a slightly imperious kick at the baseboard. This row house is slightly too big for Ove and his wife, really, he can just about admit that. But it's all paid for. There's not a penny left in loans. Which is certainly more than one could say for the clotheshorse.

It's all loans nowadays; everyone knows the way people carry on. Ove has paid his mortgage. Done his duty. Gone to work. Never taken a day of sick leave. Shouldered his share of the burden. Taken a bit of responsibility. No one does that anymore, no one takes responsibility. Now it's just computers and consultants and council bigwigs going to strip clubs and selling apartment leases under the table. Tax havens and share portfolios. No one wants to work. A country full of people who just want to have lunch all day.

"Won't it be nice to slow down a bit?" they said to Ove yesterday at work. While explaining that there was a lack of employment prospects and so they were "retiring the older generation." A third of a century in the same workplace, and that's how they refer to Ove. Suddenly he's a bloody "generation." Because nowadays people are all thirty-one and wear too-tight trousers and no longer drink normal coffee. And don't want to take responsibility. A shed-load of men with elaborate beards, changing jobs and changing wives and changing their car makes. Just like that. Whenever they feel like it.

Ove glares out of the window. The poser is jogging. Not that Ove is provoked by jogging. Not at all. Ove couldn't give a damn about people jogging. What he can't understand is why they have to make such a big thing of it. With those smug smiles on their faces, as if they were out there curing pulmonary emphysema. Either they walk fast or they run slowly, that's what joggers do. It's a forty-year-old man's way of telling the world that he can't do anything right. Is it really necessary to dress up as a fourteen-year-old Romanian gymnast in order to be able to do it? Or the Olympic tobogganing team? Just because one shuffles aimlessly around the block for three quarters of an hour?

And the poser has a girlfriend. Ten years younger. The Blond Weed, Ove calls her. Tottering around the streets like an inebriated panda on heels as long as box wrenches, with clown paint all over her face and sunglasses so big that one can't tell whether they're a pair of glasses or some kind of helmet. She also has one of those handbag animals, running about off the leash and pissing on the paving stones outside Ove's house. She thinks Ove doesn't notice, but Ove always notices.

His life was never supposed to be like this. Full stop. "Won't it be nice taking it a bit easy?" they said to him at work yesterday. And now Ove stands here by his oiled kitchen countertop. It's not supposed to be a job for a Tuesday afternoon.

He looks out the window at the identical house opposite. A family with children has just moved in there. Foreigners, apparently. He doesn't know yet what sort of car they have. Probably something Japanese, God help them. Ove nods to himself, as if he just said something which he very much agrees with. Looks up at the living room ceiling. He's going to put up a hook there today. And he doesn't mean any kind of hook. Every IT consultant trumpeting some data-code diagnosis and wearing one of those non-gender-specific cardigans they all have to wear these days would put up a hook any old way. But Ove's hook is going to be as solid as a rock. He's going to screw it in so hard that when the house is demolished it'll be the last thing standing.

In a few days there'll be some stuck-up real estate agent standing here with a tie knot as big as a baby's head, banging on about "renovation potential" and "spatial efficiency," and he'll have all sorts of opinions about Ove, the bastard. But he won't be able to say a word about Ove's hook.

On the floor in the living room is one of Ove's "useful-stuff" boxes. That's how they divide up the house. All the things Ove's wife has bought are "lovely" or "homey." Everything Ove buys is useful. Stuff with a function. He keeps them in two different boxes, one big and one small. This is the small one. Full of screws and nails and wrench sets and that sort of thing. People don't have useful things anymore. People just have shit. Twenty pairs of shoes but they never know where the shoehorn is; houses filled with microwave ovens and flat-screen televisions, yet they couldn't tell you which anchor bolt to use for a concrete wall if you threatened them with a box cutter.

Ove has a whole drawer in his useful-stuff box just for concrete-wall anchor bolts. He stands there looking at them as if they were chess pieces. He doesn't stress about decisions concerning anchor bolts for concrete. Things have to take their time. Every anchor bolt is a process; every anchor bolt has its own use. People have no respect for decent, honest functionality anymore, they're happy as long as everything looks neat and dandy on the computer. But Ove does things the way they're supposed to be done.

He came into his office on Monday and they said they hadn't wanted to tell him on Friday as it would have "ruined his weekend."

"It'll be good for you to slow down a bit," they'd drawled. Slow down? What did they know about waking up on a Tuesday and no longer having a purpose? With their Internets and their espresso coffees, what did they know about taking a bit of responsibility for things?

Ove looks up at the ceiling. Squints. It's important for the hook to be centered, he decides.

And while he stands there immersed in the importance of it, he's mercilessly interrupted by a long scraping sound. Not at all unlike the type of sound created by a big oaf backing up a Japanese car hooked up to a trailer and scraping it against the exterior wall of Ove's house.

3

A MAN CALLED OVE BACKS UP WITH A TRAILER

Ove whips open the green floral curtains, which for many years Ove's wife has been nagging him to change. He sees a short, black-haired, and obviously foreign woman aged about thirty. She stands there gesticulating furiously at a similarly aged oversize blond lanky man squeezed into the driver's seat of a ludicrously small Japanese car with a trailer, now scraping against the exterior wall of Ove's house.

The Lanky One, by means of subtle gestures and signs, seems to want to convey to the woman that this is not quite as easy as it looks. The woman, with gestures that are comparatively unsubtle, seems to want to convey that it might have something to do with the moronic nature of the Lanky One in question.

"Well, I'll be bloody . . ." Ove thunders through the window as the wheel of the trailer rolls into his flower bed. A few seconds later his front door seems to fly open of its own accord, as if afraid that Ove might otherwise walk straight through it.

"What the hell are you doing?" Ove roars at the woman.

"Yes, that's what I'm asking myself!" she roars back.

Ove is momentarily thrown off-balance. He glares at her. She glares back.

"You can't drive a car here! Can't you read?"

The little foreign woman steps towards him and only then does Ove notice that she's either very pregnant or suffering from what Ove would categorize as selective obesity.

"I'm not driving the car, am I?"

Ove stares silently at her for a few seconds. Then he turns to her husband, who's just managed to extract himself from the Japanese car and is approaching them with two hands thrown expressively into the air and an apologetic smile plastered across his face. He's wearing a knitted cardigan and his posture seems to indicate a very obvious calcium deficiency. He must be close to six and a half feet tall. Ove feels an instinctive skepticism towards all people taller than six feet; the blood can't quite make it all the way up to the brain.

"And who might you be?" Ove inquires.

"I'm the driver," says the Lanky One expansively.

"Oh, really? Doesn't look like it!" rages the pregnant woman, who is probably a foot and a half shorter than him. She tries to slap his arm with both hands.

"And who's this?" Ove asks, staring at her.

"This is my wife." He smiles.

"Don't be so sure it'll stay that way," she snaps, her pregnant belly bouncing up and down.

"It's not as easy as it loo—" the Lanky One tries to say, but he's immediately cut short.

"I said RIGHT! But you went on backing up to the LEFT! You don't listen! You NEVER listen!"

After that, she immerses herself in half a minute's worth of haranguing in what Ove can only assume to be a display of the complex vocabulary of Arabic cursing.

The husband just nods back at her with an indescribably harmonious smile. The very sort of smile that makes decent folk want to slap Buddhist monks in the face, Ove thinks to himself.

"Oh, come on. I'm sorry," he says cheerfully, hauling out a tin of chewing tobacco from his pocket and packing it in a ball the size of a walnut. "It was only a little accident, we'll sort it out!"

Ove looks at the Lanky One as if the Lanky One has just squatted over the hood of Ove's car and left a turd on it.

"Sort it out? You're in my flower bed!"

The Lanky One looks ponderously at the trailer wheels.

"That's hardly a flower bed, is it?" He smiles, undaunted, and adjusts his tobacco with the tip of his tongue. "Naah, come on, that's just soil," he persists, as if Ove is having a joke with him.

Ove's forehead compresses itself into one large, threatening wrinkle.

"It. Is. A. Flower bed."

The Lanky One scratches his head, as if he's got some tobacco caught in his tangled hair.

"But you're not growing anything in it—"

"Never you bloody mind what I do with my own flower bed!"

The Lanky One nods quickly, clearly keen to avoid further provocation of this unknown man. He turns to his wife as if he's expecting her to come to his aid. She doesn't look at all likely to do so. The Lanky One looks at Ove again.

"Pregnant, you know. Hormones and all that . . ." he tries, with a grin.

The Pregnant One does not grin. Nor does Ove. She crosses

her arms. Ove tucks his hands into his belt. The Lanky One clearly doesn't know what to do with his massive hands, so he swings them back and forth across his body, slightly shamefully, as if they're made of cloth, fluttering in the breeze.

"I'll move it and have another go," he finally says and smiles disarmingly at Ove again.

Ove does not reciprocate.

"Motor vehicles are not allowed in the area. There's a sign."

The Lanky One steps back and nods eagerly. Jogs back and once again contorts his body into the under-dimensioned Japanese car. "Christ," Ove and the pregnant woman mutter wearily in unison. Which actually makes Ove dislike her slightly less.

The Lanky One pulls forward a few yards; Ove can see very clearly that he does not straighten up the trailer properly. Then he starts backing up again. Right into Ove's mailbox, buckling the green sheet metal.

Ove storms forward and throws the car door open.

The Lanky One starts flapping his arms again.

"My fault, my fault! Sorry about that, didn't see the mailbox in the rearview mirror, you know. It's difficult, this trailer thing, just can't figure out which way to turn the wheel . . ."

Ove thumps his fist on the roof of the car so hard that the Lanky One jumps and bangs his head on the doorframe. "Out of the car!"

"What?"

"Get out of the car, I said!"

The Lanky One gives Ove a slightly startled glance, but he doesn't quite seem to have the nerve to reply. Instead he gets out of his car and stands beside it like a schoolboy in the dunce's corner. Ove points down the footpath between the row houses, towards the bicycle shed and the parking area.

"Go and stand where you're not in the way."

The Lanky One nods, slightly puzzled.

"Holy Christ. A lower-arm amputee with cataracts could have backed this trailer more accurately than you," Ove mutters as he gets into the car.

How can anyone be incapable of reversing with a trailer? he asks himself. How? How difficult is it to establish the basics of right and left and then do the opposite? How do these people make their way through life at all?

Of course it's an automatic, Ove notes. Might have known. These morons would rather not have to drive their cars at all, let alone reverse into a parking space by themselves. He puts it into drive and inches forward. Should one really have a driver's license if one can't drive a real car rather than some Japanese robot vehicle? he wonders. Ove doubts whether someone who can't park a car properly should even be allowed to vote.

When he's pulled forward and straightened up the trailer—as civilized people do before backing up with a trailer—he puts it into reverse. Immediately it starts making a shrieking noise. Ove looks around angrily.

"What the bloody hell are you . . . why are you making that noise?" he hisses at the instrument panel and gives the steering wheel a whack.

"Stop it, I said!" he roars at a particularly insistent flashing red light.

At the same time the Lanky One appears at the side of the car and carefully taps the window. Ove rolls the window down and gives him an irritated look.

"It's just the reverse radar making that noise," the Lanky One says with a nod.

"Don't you think I know that?" Ove seethes.

"It's a bit unusual, this car. I was thinking I could show you the controls if you like . . ."

"I'm not an idiot, you know!" Ove snorts.

The Lanky One nods eagerly.

"No, no, of course not."

Ove glares at the instrument panel.

"What's it doing now?"

The Lanky One nods enthusiastically.

"It's measuring how much power's left in the battery. You know, before it switches from the electric motor to the gas-driven motor. Because it's a hybrid. . . ."

Ove doesn't answer. He just slowly rolls up the window, leaving the Lanky One outside with his mouth half-open. Ove checks the left wing mirror. Then the right wing mirror. He reverses while the Japanese car shrieks in terror, maneuvers the trailer perfectly between his own house and his incompetent new neighbor's, gets out, and tosses the cretin his keys.

"Reverse radar and parking sensors and cameras and crap like that. A man who needs all that to back up with a trailer shouldn't be bloody doing it in the first place."

The Lanky One nods cheerfully at him.

"Thanks for the help," he calls out, as if Ove hadn't just spent the last ten minutes insulting him.

"You shouldn't even be allowed to rewind a cassette," grumbles Ove. The pregnant woman just stands there with her arms crossed, but she doesn't look quite as angry anymore. She thanks him with a wry smile, as if she's trying not to laugh. She has the biggest brown eyes Ove has ever seen.

"The Residents' Association does not permit any driving in this area, and you have to bloody go along with it," Ove huffs, before stomping back to his house.

He stops halfway up the paved path between the house and his shed. He wrinkles his nose in the way men of his age do, the wrinkle traveling across his entire upper body. Then he sinks down on his knees, puts his face right up close to the paving stones, which he neatly and without exception removes and re-lays every other year, whether necessary or not. He sniffs again. Nods to himself. Stands up.

His new neighbors are still watching him.

"Piss! There's piss all over the place here!" Ove says gruffly.

He gesticulates at the paving stones.

"O . . . kay," says the black-haired woman.

"No! Nowhere is bloody okay around here!"

And with that, he goes into his house and closes the door.

He sinks onto the stool in the hall and stays there for a long time. Bloody woman. Why do she and her family have to come here if they can't even read a sign right in front of their eyes? You're not allowed to drive cars inside the block. Everyone knows that.

Ove goes to hang up his coat on the hook, among a sea of his wife's overcoats. Mutters "idiots" at the closed window just to be on the safe side. Then goes into his living room and stares up at his ceiling.

He doesn't know how long he stands there. He loses himself in his own thoughts. Floats away, as if in a mist. He's never been the sort of man who does that, has never been a daydreamer, but lately it's as if something's twisted up in his head. He's having increasing difficulty concentrating on things. He doesn't like it at all.

When the doorbell goes it's like he's waking up from a warm slumber. He rubs his eyes hard, looks around as if worried that someone may have seen him.

The doorbell rings again. Ove turns around and stares at the bell as if it should be ashamed of itself. He takes a few steps into the hall, noting that his body is as stiff as set plaster. He can't tell if the creaking is coming from the floorboards or himself.

"And what is it now?" he asks the door before he's even opened it, as if it had the answer.

"What is it now?" he repeats as he throws the door open so hard that a three-year-old girl is flung backwards by the draft and ends up very unexpectedly on her bottom.

Beside her stands a seven-year-old girl looking absolutely terrified. Their hair is pitch black. And they have the biggest brown eyes Ove has ever seen.

"Yes?" says Ove.

The older girl looks guarded. She hands him a plastic container. Ove reluctantly accepts it. It's warm.

"Rice!" the three-year-old girl announces happily, briskly getting to her feet.

"With saffron. And chicken," explains the seven-year-old, far more wary of him.

Ove evaluates them suspiciously.

"Are you selling it?"

The seven-year-old looks offended.

"We LIVE HERE, you know!"

Ove is silent for a moment. Then he nods, as if he might possibly be able to accept this premise as an explanation.

"Okay."

The younger one also nods with satisfaction and flaps her slightly-too-long sleeves.

"Mum said you were 'ungry!"

Ove looks in utter perplexity at the little flapping speech defect.

"What?"

"Mum said you *looked* hungry. So we have to give you dinner," the seven-year-old girl clarifies with some irritation. "Come on, Nasanin," she adds, taking her sister by the hand and walking away after directing a resentful stare at Ove.

Ove keeps an eye on them as they skulk off. He sees the pregnant woman standing in her doorway, smiling at him before the girls run into her house. The three-year-old turns and waves cheerfully at him. Her mother also waves. Ove closes the door.

He stands in the hall again. Stares at the warm container of chicken with rice and saffron as one might look at a box of nitroglycerin. Then he goes into the kitchen and puts it in the fridge. Not that he's habitually inclined to go around eating any old food provided by unknown, foreign kids on his doorstep. But in Ove's house one does not throw away food. As a point of principle.

He goes into the living room. Shoves his hands in his pockets. Looks up at the ceiling. Stands there a good while and thinks about what sort of concrete-wall anchor bolt would be most suitable for the job. He stands there squinting until his eyes start hurting. He looks down, slightly confused, at his dented wristwatch. Then he looks out the window again and realizes that dusk has fallen. He shakes his head in resignation.

You can't start drilling after dark, everyone knows that. He'd have to turn on all the lights and no one could say when they'd be turned off again. And he's not giving the electricity company the pleasure, his meter notching up another couple of thousand kronor. They can forget about that.

Ove packs up his useful-stuff box and takes it to the big upstairs hall. Fetches the key to the attic from its place behind the radiator in the little hall. Goes back and reaches up and opens the trapdoor to the attic. Folds down the ladder. Climbs up into the attic and puts the useful-stuff box in its place behind the kitchen chairs that his wife made him put up here because they creaked too much. They didn't creak at all. Ove knows very well it was just an excuse, because his wife wanted to get some new ones. As if that was all life was about. Buying kitchen chairs and eating in restaurants and carrying on.

He goes down the stairs again. Puts back the attic key in its place behind the radiator in the little hall. "Taking it a bit easy," they said to him. A lot of thirty-one-year-old show-offs working with computers and refusing to drink normal coffee. An entire society where no one knows how to back up with a trailer. Then they come telling him *he's* not needed anymore. Is that reasonable?

Ove goes down to the living room and turns on the TV. He doesn't watch the programs, but it's not like he can just spend his evenings sitting there by himself like a moron, staring at the walls. He gets out the foreign food from the fridge and eats it with a fork, straight out of the plastic container.

It's Tuesday night and he's canceled his newspaper subscription, switched off the radiators, and turned out all the lights.

And tomorrow he's putting up that hook.

4

A MAN CALLED OVE DOES NOT PAY A THREE-KRONOR SURCHARGE

Ove gives her the plants. Two of them. Of course, there weren't supposed to be two of them. But somewhere along the line there has to be a limit. It was a question of principle, Ove explains to her. That's why he got two flowers in the end.

"Things don't work when you're not at home," he mutters, and kicks a bit at the frozen ground.

His wife doesn't answer.

"There'll be snow tonight," says Ove.

They said on the news there wouldn't be snow, but, as Ove often points out, whatever they predict is bound not to happen. He tells her this; she doesn't answer. He puts his hands in his pockets and gives her a brief nod.

"It's not natural rattling around the house on my own all day when you're not here. It's no way to live. That's all I have to say."

She doesn't reply to that either.

He nods and kicks the ground again. He can't understand people who long to retire. How can anyone spend their whole life longing for the day when they become superfluous? Wandering about, a burden on society, what sort of man would ever wish for that? Staying at home, waiting to die. Or even worse: waiting for them to come and fetch you and put you in a home. Being dependent on other people to get to the toilet. Ove can't think of anything worse. His wife often teases him, says he's the only man she knows who'd rather be laid out in a coffin than travel in a mobility service van. And she may have a point there.

Ove had risen at quarter to six. Made coffee for his wife and himself, went around checking the radiators to make sure she hadn't sneakily turned them up. They were all unchanged from yesterday, but he turned them down a little more just to be on the safe side. Then he took his jacket from the hook in the hall, the only hook of all six that wasn't burgeoning with her clothes, and set off for his inspection. It had started getting cold, he noticed. Almost time to change his navy autumn jacket for his navy winter jacket.

He always knows when it's about to snow because his wife starts nagging about turning up the heat in the bedroom. Lunacy, Ove reaffirms every year. Why should the power company directors feather their nests because of a bit of seasonality? Turning up the heat five degrees costs thousands of kronor per year. He knows because he's calculated it himself. So every winter he drags down an old diesel generator from the attic that he swapped at a rummage sale for a gramophone. He's connected this to a fan heater he bought at a sale for thirty-nine kronor. Once the generator has charged up the fan heater, it runs for thirty minutes on the little battery Ove has hooked it up to, and his wife keeps it on her side of the bed. She can run it a couple of times before they go to bed, but only a couple—no need to be lavish about it ("Diesel isn't free, you know"). And Ove's wife does what she always does: nods and agrees that Ove is probably right. Then she goes around all winter sneakily turning up the radiators. Every year the same bloody thing.

Ove kicks the ground again. He's considering telling her about the cat. If you can even call that mangy, half-bald creature a cat. It was sitting there again when he came back from his inspection, practically right outside their front door. He pointed at it and shouted so loudly that his voice echoed between the houses. The cat just sat there, looking at Ove. Then it stood up elaborately, as if making a point of demonstrating that it wasn't leaving because of Ove, but rather because there were better things to do, and disappeared around the corner.

Ove decides not to mention the cat to her. He assumes she'll only be disgruntled with him for driving it away. If she was in charge the whole house would be full of tramps, whether of the furred variety or not.

He's wearing his navy suit and has done up the top button of the white shirt. She tells him to leave the top button undone if he's not wearing a tie; he protests that he's not some urchin who's renting out deck chairs, before defiantly buttoning it up. He's got his dented old wristwatch on, the one that his dad inherited from his father when he was nineteen, the one that was passed on to Ove after his sixteenth birthday, a few days after his father died.

Ove's wife likes that suit. She always says he looks so handsome in it. Like any sensible person, Ove is obviously of the opinion that only posers wear their best suits on weekdays. But this morning he decided to make an exception. He even put on his black going-out shoes and polished them with a responsible amount of boot shine.

As he took his autumn jacket from the hook in the hall before he went out, he threw a thoughtful eye on his wife's collection of coats. He wondered how such a small human being could have so many winter coats. "You almost expect if you stepped through this lot you'd find yourself in Narnia," a friend of Ove's wife had once joked. Ove didn't have a clue what she was talking about, but he did agree there were a hell of a lot of coats.

He walked out of the house before anyone on the street had even woken up. Strolled up to the parking area. Opened his garage with a key. He had a remote control for the door, but had never understood the point of it. An honest person could just as well open the door manually. He unlocked the Saab, also with a key: the system had always worked perfectly well, there was no reason to change it. He sat in the driver's seat and twisted the tuning dial half forward and then half back before adjusting each of the mirrors, as he did every time he got into the Saab. As if someone routinely broke into the Saab and mischievously changed Ove's mirrors and radio channels.

As he drove across the parking area he passed that Pregnant Foreign Woman from next door. She was holding her three-year-old by the hand. The big blond Lanky One was walking beside her. All three of them caught sight of Ove and waved cheerfully. Ove didn't wave back. At first he was going to stop and give her a dressing-down about letting children run about in the parking area as if it were some municipal playground. But he decided he didn't have the time.

He drove along, passing row after row of houses identical to his own. When they'd first moved in here there were only six houses; now there were hundreds of them. There used to be a forest here but now there were only houses. Everything paid for with loans, of course. That was how you did it nowadays. Shopping on credit and driving electric cars and hiring tradesmen to change a lightbulb.

Laying click-on floors and fitting electric fireplaces and carrying on. A society that apparently could not see the difference between the correct anchor bolt for a concrete wall and a smack in the face. Clearly this was how it was meant to be.

It took him exactly fourteen minutes to drive to the florist's in the shopping center. Ove kept exactly to every speed limit, even on that 35 mph road where the recently arrived idiots in suits came tanking along at 55. Among their own houses they put up speed bumps and damnable numbers of signs about "Children Playing," but when driving past other people's houses it was apparently less important. Ove had repeated this to his wife every time they drove past over the last ten years.

"And it's getting worse and worse," he liked to add, just in case by some miracle she hadn't heard him the first time.

Today he'd barely gone a mile before a black Mercedes positioned itself a forearm's length behind his Saab. Ove signaled with his brake lights three times. The Mercedes flashed its high beams at him in an agitated manner. Ove snorted at his rearview mirror. As if it was his duty to fling himself out of the way as soon as these morons decided speed restrictions didn't apply to them. Honestly. Ove didn't move. The Mercedes gave him a burst of its high beams again. Ove slowed down. The Mercedes sounded its horn. Ove lowered his speed to 15 mph. When they reached the top of a hill the Mercedes overtook him with a roar. The driver, a man in his forties in a tie and with white cables trailing from his ears, held up his finger through the window at Ove. Ove responded to the gesture in the manner of all men of a certain age who've been properly raised: by slowly tapping the tip of his finger against the side of his head. The man in the Mercedes shouted until his saliva spattered against the inside of his windshield, then put his foot down and disappeared.

Two minutes later Ove came to a red light. The Mercedes was at the back of the line. Ove flashed his lights at it. He saw the driver craning his neck around. The white earpieces dropped out and fell against the dashboard. Ove nodded with satisfaction.

The light turned green. The line didn't move. Ove sounded his horn. Nothing happened. Ove shook his head. Must be a woman driver. Or roadwork. Or an Audi. When thirty seconds had passed without anything happening, Ove put the car into neutral, opened the door, and stepped out of the Saab with the engine still running. Stood in the road and peered ahead with his hands on his hips, filled with a kind of Herculean irritation: the way Superman might have stood if he'd got stuck in a traffic jam.

The man in the Mercedes gave a blast on his horn. Idiot, thought Ove. In the same moment the traffic started moving. The cars in front of Ove moved off. The car behind him, a Volkswagen, beeped at him. The driver waved impatiently at Ove. Ove glared back. He got back into the Saab and leisurely closed the door. "Amazing what a rush we're in," he scoffed into the rearview mirror and drove on.

At the next red light he ended up behind the Mercedes again. Another line. Ove checked his watch and took a left turn down a smaller, quiet road. This entailed a longer route to the shopping center, but there were fewer traffic lights. Not that Ove was mean. But as anyone who knows anything knows, cars use less fuel if they keep moving rather than stopping all the time. And, as Ove's wife often says: "If there's one thing you could write in Ove's obituary, it's 'At least he was economical with gas.'"

As Ove approached the shopping center from his little side road, he could just make out that there were only two parking spaces left. What all these people were doing at the shopping center on a normal weekday was beyond his comprehension. Obviously people no longer had jobs to go to.

Ove's wife usually starts sighing as soon as they even get close to a parking lot like this. Ove wants to park close to the entrance. "As if there's a competition about who can find the best parking spot," she always says as he completes circuit after circuit and swears at all the imbeciles getting in his way in their foreign cars. Sometimes they end up doing six or seven loops before they find a good spot, and if Ove in the end has to concede defeat and content himself with a slot twenty yards farther away, he's in a bad mood for the rest of the day. His wife has never understood it. Then again, she never was very good at grasping questions of principle.

Ove figured he would go around slowly a couple of times just to check the lay of the land, but then suddenly caught sight of the Mercedes thundering along the main road towards the shopping center. So this was where he'd been heading, that suit with the plastic cables in his ears. Ove didn't hesitate for a second. He put his foot down and barged his way out of the intersection into the road. The Mercedes slammed on its brakes, firmly pressing down on the horn and following close behind. The race was on.

The signs at the parking lot entrance led the traffic to the right, but when they got there the Mercedes must also have seen the two empty slots, because he tried to slip past Ove on the left. Ove only just managed to maneuver himself in front of him to block his path. The two men started hunting each other across the tarmac.

In his rearview mirror, Ove saw a little Toyota turn off the road behind them, follow the road signs, and enter the parking area in a wide loop from the right. Ove's eyes followed it while he hurtled forward in the opposite direction, with the Mercedes on his tail. Of course, he could have taken one of the free slots, the one closest to the entrance, and then had the kindness of letting the Mercedes take the other. But what sort of victory would that have been?

Instead Ove made an emergency stop in front of the first slot and stayed where he was. The Mercedes started wildly sounding its horn. Ove didn't flinch. The little Toyota approached from the far right. The Mercedes also caught sight of it and, too late, understood Ove's devilish plan. Its horn wailed furiously as it tried to push past the Saab, but it never stood a chance: Ove had already waved the Toyota into one of the free slots. Only once it was safely in did Ove nonchalantly swing into the other space.

The side window of the Mercedes was so covered in saliva when it drove past that Ove couldn't even see the driver. He stepped out of the Saab triumphantly, like a gladiator who had just slain his opponent. Then he looked at the Toyota.

"Oh, damn," he mumbled, irritated.

The car door was thrown open.

"Hi there!" the Lanky One sang merrily as he untangled himself from the driver's seat. "Hello hello!" said his wife from the other side of the Toyota, lifting out their three-year-old.

Ove watched repentantly as the Mercedes disappeared in the distance.

"Thanks for the parking space! Bloody marvelous!" The Lanky One was beaming.

Ove didn't reply.

"Wass ya name?" the three-year-old burst out.

"Ove," said Ove.

"My name's Nasanin!" she said with delight.

Ove nodded at her.

"And I'm Pat—" the Lanky One started saying.

But Ove had already turned around and left.

"Thanks for the space," the Pregnant Foreign Woman called after him.

Ove could hear laughter in her voice. He didn't like it. He just muttered a quick "Fine, fine," without turning and marched through the revolving doors into the shopping center. He turned left down the first corridor and looked around several times, as if afraid that the family from next door would follow him. But they turned right and disappeared.

Ove stopped suspiciously outside the supermarket and eyed the poster advertising the week's special offers. Not that Ove was intending to buy any ham in this particular shop. But it was always worth keeping an eye on the prices. If there's one thing in this world that Ove dislikes, it's when someone tries to trick him. Ove's wife sometimes jokes that the three worst words Ove knows in this life are "Batteries not included." People usually laugh when she says that. But Ove does not usually laugh.

He moved on from the supermarket and stepped into the florist's. And there it didn't take long for a "rumble" to start up, as Ove's wife would have described it. Or a "discussion," as Ove always insisted on calling it. Ove put down a coupon on the counter on which it said: "2 plants for 50 kronor." Given that Ove only wanted one plant, he explained to the shop assistant, with all rhyme and reason on his side, he should be able to buy it for 25 kronor. Because that was half of 50. However, the assistant, a brain-dead phone-texting nineteen-year-old, would not go along with it. She maintained that a single flower cost 39 kronor and "2 for 50" only applied if one bought two. The manager had to be summoned. It took Ove fifteen minutes to make him see sense and agree that Ove was right.

Or, to be honest about it, the manager mumbled something that sounded a little like "bloody old sod" into his hand and hammered 25 kronor so hard into the cash register that anyone would have thought it was the machine's fault. It made no difference to Ove. He knew these retailers were always trying to screw you out of money, and no one screwed Ove and got away with it. Ove put his debit card on the counter. The manager allowed himself the slightest of smiles, then nodded dismissively and pointed at a sign that read: "Card purchases of less than 50 kronor carry a surcharge of 3 kronor."

Now Ove is standing in front of his wife with two plants. Because it was a question of principle.

"There was no *way* I was going to pay three kronor," rails Ove, his eyes looking down into the gravel.

Ove's wife often quarrels with Ove because he's always arguing about everything.

But Ove isn't bloody arguing. He just thinks right is right. Is that such an unreasonable attitude to life?

He raises his eyes and looks at her.

"I suppose you're annoyed I didn't come yesterday like I promised," he mumbles.

She doesn't say anything.

"The whole street is turning into a madhouse," he says defensively. "Complete chaos. You even have to go out and back up their trailers for them nowadays. And you can't even put up a hook in peace," he continues as if she's disagreeing.

He clears his throat.

"Obviously I couldn't put the hook up when it was dark outside. If you do that there's no telling when the lights go off. More likely they'll stay on and consume electricity. Out of the question."

She doesn't answer. He kicks the frozen ground. Sort of looking for words. Clears his throat briefly once again.

"Nothing works when you're not at home."

She doesn't answer. Ove fingers the plants.

"I'm tired of it, just rattling around the house all day while you're away."

She doesn't answer that either. He nods. Holds up the plants so she can see them.

"They're pink. The ones you like. They said in the shop they're perennials but that's not what they're bloody called. Apparently they die in this kind of cold, they also said that in the shop, but only so they could sell me a load of other shit."

He looks as if he's waiting for her approval.

"The new neighbors put saffron in their rice and things like that; they're foreigners," he says in a low voice.

A new silence.

He stands there, slowly twisting the wedding ring on his finger. As if looking for something else to say. He still finds it painfully difficult being the one to take charge of a conversation. That was always something she took care of. He usually just answered. This is a new situation for them both. Finally Ove squats, digs up the plant he brought last week, and carefully puts it in a plastic bag. He turns the frozen soil carefully before putting in the new plants.

"They've bumped up the electricity prices again," he informs her as he gets to his feet.

He looks at her for a long time. Finally he puts his hand carefully on the big boulder and caresses it tenderly from side to side, as if touching her cheek.

"I miss you," he whispers.

It's been six months since she died. But Ove still inspects the whole house twice a day to feel the radiators and check that she hasn't sneakily turned up the heating.

5

A MAN CALLED OVE

Ove knew very well that her friends couldn't understand why she married him. He couldn't really blame them.

People said he was bitter. Maybe they were right. He'd never reflected much on it. People also called him antisocial. Ove assumed this meant he wasn't overly keen on people. And in this instance he could totally agree with them. More often than not people were out of their minds.

Ove wasn't one to engage in small talk. He had come to realize that, these days at least, this was a serious character flaw. Now one had to be able to blabber on about anything with any old sod who happened to stray within an arm's length of you purely because it was "nice." Ove didn't know how to do it. Perhaps it was the way he'd been raised. Maybe men of his generation had never been sufficiently prepared for a world where everyone spoke about doing things even though it no longer seemed worth doing them. Nowadays people stood outside their newly refurbished houses and boasted as if they'd built them with their own bare hands, even though they hadn't so much as lifted a screwdriver. And they weren't even trying to pretend that it was any other way. They boasted about it! Apparently there was no longer any value in being able to lay your own floorboards or refurbish a room with rising damp or change the winter tires. And if you could just go and buy everything, what was the value of it? What was the value of a man?

Her friends couldn't see why she woke up every morning and voluntarily decided to share the whole day with him. He couldn't either. He built her a bookshelf and she filled it with books by people who wrote page after page about their feelings. Ove understood things he could see and touch. Wood and concrete. Glass and steel. Tools. Things one could figure out. He understood right angles and clear instruction manuals. Assembly models and drawings. Things one could draw on paper.

He was a man of black and white.

And she was color. All the color he had.

The only thing he had ever loved until he saw her was numbers. He had no other particular memory of his youth. He was not bullied and he wasn't a bully, not good at sports and not bad either. He was never at the heart of things and never on the outside. He was the sort of person who was just there. Nor did he remember so very much about his growing up; he had never been the sort of man who went around remembering things unless there was a need for it. He remembered that he was quite happy and that for a few years afterwards he wasn't—that was about it.

And he remembered the sums. The numbers, filling his head. Remembered how he longed for their mathematics lessons at school. Maybe for the others they were a sufferance, but not for him. He didn't know why, and didn't speculate about it either. He'd never understood the need to go around stewing on why things turned out the way they did. You are what you are and you do what you do, and that was good enough for Ove.

He was seven years old when his mum called it a day one early August morning. She worked at a chemicals plant. In those days people didn't know much about air safety, Ove realized later. She smoked as well, all the time. That's Ove's clearest memory of her, how she sat in the kitchen window of the little house where they lived outside town, with that billowing cloud around her, watching the sky every Saturday morning. And how sometimes she sang in her hoarse voice and Ove used to sit under the window with his mathematics book in his lap, and he remembered that he liked listening to her. He remembers that. Of course, her voice was hoarse and the odd note was more discordant than one would have liked, but he remembers that he liked it anyway.

Ove's father worked for the railways. The palms of his hands looked like someone had carved into leather with knives, and the wrinkles in his face were so deep that when he exerted himself the sweat was channeled through them down to his chest. His hair was thin and his body slender, but the muscles on his arms were so sharp that they seemed cut out of rock. Once when Ove was very young he was allowed to go with his parents to a big party with his dad's friends from the rail company. After his father had put away a couple of bottles of pilsner, some of the other guests challenged him to an arm-wrestling competition. Ove had never seen the likes of these giants straddling the bench opposite him. Some of them looked like they weighed about four hundred pounds. His father wore down every one of them. When they went home that night, he put his arm around Ove's shoulders and said: "Ove, only a swine thinks size and strength are the same thing. Remember that." And Ove never forgot it.

His father never raised his fists. Not to Ove or anyone else. Ove had classmates who came to school with black eyes or bruises from a belt buckle after a thrashing. But never Ove. "We don't fight in this family," his father used to state. "Not with each other or anyone else."

He was well liked down at the railway, quiet but kind. There were some who said he was "too kind." Ove remembers how as a child he could never understand how this could be something bad.

Then Mum died. And Dad grew even quieter. As if she took away with her the few words he'd possessed.

So Ove and his father never talked excessively, but they liked each other's company. They sat in silence on either side of the kitchen table, and had ways of keeping busy. Every other day they put out food for a family of birds living in a rotting tree at the back of the house. It was important, Ove understood, that it had to be every other day. He didn't know why, but that didn't matter.

In the evenings they had sausages and potatoes. Then they played cards. They never had much, but they always had enough.

His father's only remaining words were about engines (apparently his mother was content to leave these behind). He could spend any amount of time talking about them. "Engines give you what you deserve," he used to explain. "If you treat them with respect they'll give you freedom; if you behave like an ass they'll take it from you."

For a long time he did not own a car of his own, but in the 1940s and '50s, when the bosses and directors at the railway started buying their own vehicles, a rumor soon spread in the office that the quiet man working on the track was a person well worth knowing. Ove's father had never finished school, and didn't understand much about the sums in Ove's schoolbooks. But he understood engines.

When the daughter of the director was getting married and the wedding car broke down rather than ceremoniously transporting the bride to the church, Ove's father was sent for. He came cycling with a toolbox on his shoulder so heavy that it took two men to lift it when he got off the bicycle. Whatever the problem was when he arrived, it was no longer a problem when he cycled back. The director's wife invited him to the wedding reception, but he told her that it was probably not the done thing to sit with elegant people when one was the sort of man whose forearms were so stained with oil that it seemed a natural part of his pigmentation. But he'd gladly accept a bag of bread and meat for the lad at home, he said. Ove had just turned eight. When his father laid out the supper that evening, Ove felt like he was at a royal banquet.

A few months later the director sent for Ove's father again. In the parking area outside the office stood an extremely old and worse-for-wear Saab 92. It was the first motorcar Saab had ever manufactured, although it had not been in production since the significantly upgraded Saab 93 had come onto the market. Ove's dad recognized it very well. Front-wheel-driven and a side-mounted engine that sounded like a coffee percolator. It had been in an accident, the director explained, sticking his thumbs into his suspenders under his jacket. The bottle-green body was badly dented and the condition of what lay under the hood was certainly not pretty. But Ove's father produced a little screwdriver from the pocket of his dirty overalls and after lengthily inspecting the car, he gave the verdict that with a bit of time and care and the proper tools he'd be able to put it back into working order.

"Whose is it?" he wondered aloud as he straightened up and wiped the oil from his fingers with a rag.

"It belonged to a relative of mine," said the director, digging out a key from his suit trousers and pressing it into his palm. "And now it's yours."

With a pat on his shoulder, the director returned to the office. Ove's father stayed where he was in the courtyard, trying to catch his breath. That evening he had to explain everything over and over again to his goggle-eyed son and show all there was to know about this magical monster now parked in their garden. He sat in the driver's seat half the night, with the boy on his lap, explaining how all the mechanical parts were connected. He could account for every screw, every little tube. Ove had never seen a man as proud as his father was that night. He was eight years old and decided that night he would never drive any car but a Saab.

Whenever he had a Saturday off, Ove's father brought him out into the yard, opened the hood, and taught him all the names of the various parts and what they did. On Sundays they went to church. Not because either of them had any excessive zeal for God, but because Ove's mum had always been insistent about it. They sat at the back, each of them staring at a patch on the floor until it was over. And, in all honesty, they spent more time missing Ove's mum than thinking about God. It was her time, so to speak, even though she was no longer there. Afterwards they'd take a long drive in the countryside with the Saab. It was Ove's favorite part of the week.

That year, to stop him rattling around the house on his own, he also started going with his father to work at the railway yard after school. It was filthy work and badly paid, but, as his father used to mutter, "It's an honest job and that's worth something."

Ove liked all the men at the railway yard except Tom. Tom was a tall, noisy man with fists as big as flatbed carts and eyes that always seemed to be looking for some defenseless animal to kick around.

When Ove was nine years old, his dad sent him to help Tom clean out a broken-down railway car. With sudden jubilation, Tom snatched up a briefcase left by some harassed passenger. It had fallen from the luggage rack and distributed its contents over the floor. Before long Tom was darting about on all fours, scrabbling together everything he could see.

"Finders keepers," he spat at Ove. Something in his eyes made Ove feel as if there were insects crawling under his skin.

As Ove turned to go, he stumbled over a wallet. It was made of such soft leather that it felt like cotton against his rough fingertips. And it didn't have a rubber band around it like Dad's old wallet, to keep it from falling to bits. It had a little silver button that made a click when you opened it. There was more than six thousand kronor inside. A fortune to anyone in those days.

Tom caught sight of it and tried to tear it out of Ove's hands. Overwhelmed by an instinctive defiance, the boy resisted. He saw how shocked Tom was at this, and out of the corner of his eye he had time to see the huge man clenching his fist. Ove knew he'd never be able to get away, so he closed his eyes, held on to the wallet as hard as he could, and waited for the blow.

But the next thing either of them knew, Ove's father was standing between them. Tom's furious, hateful eyes met his for an instant, but Ove's father stood where he stood. And at last Tom lowered his fist and took a watchful step back.

"Finders keepers, it's always been like that," he growled, pointing at the wallet.

"That's up to the person who finds it," said Ove's father without looking away.

Tom's eyes had turned black. But he retreated another step, still clutching the briefcase in his hands. Tom had worked many years at the railway, but Ove had never heard any of his father's colleagues say one good word about Tom. He was dishonest and malicious, that was what they said after a couple of bottles of pilsner at their parties. But he'd never heard it from his dad. "Four children and a sick wife," was all he used to say to his workmates, looking each of them in the eye. "Better men than Tom could have ended up worse for it." And then his workmates usually changed the subject.

His father pointed to the wallet in Ove's hand.

"You decide," he said.

Ove determinedly fixed his gaze on the ground, feeling Tom's eyes burning holes into the top of his head. Then he said in a low but unwavering voice that the lost property office would seem to be the best place to leave it. His father nodded without a word, and then took Ove's hand as they walked back for almost half an hour along the track without a word passing between them. Ove heard Tom shouting behind them, his voice filled with cold fury. Ove never forgot it.

The woman at the desk of the lost property office could hardly believe her eyes when they put the wallet on the counter.

"And it was just lying there on the floor? You didn't find a bag or anything?" she asked. Ove gave his dad a searching look, but he just stood there in silence, so Ove did the same.

The woman behind the counter seemed satisfied enough with the answer.

"Not many people have ever handed in this much money," she said, smiling at Ove.

"Many people don't have any decency either," said his father in a clipped voice, and took Ove's hand. They turned around and went back to work.

A few hundred yards down the track Ove cleared his throat, summoned some courage, and asked why his father had not mentioned the briefcase that Tom had found.

"We're not the sort of people who tell tales about what others do," he answered.

Ove nodded. They walked in silence.

"I thought about keeping the money," Ove whispered at long last, and took his father's hand in a firmer grip, as if he was afraid of letting go.

"I know," said his father, and squeezed his hand a little harder.

"But I knew you would hand it in, and I knew a person like Tom wouldn't," said Ove.

His father nodded. And not another word was said about it.

Had Ove been the sort of man who contemplated how and when one became the sort of man one was, he might have said this was the day he learned that right has to be right. But he wasn't one to dwell on things like that. He contented himself with remembering that on this day he'd decided to be as little unlike his father as possible.

He had only just turned sixteen when his father died. A hurtling carriage on the track. Ove was left with not much more than a Saab, a ramshackle house a few miles out of town, and a dented old wristwatch. He was never able to properly explain what happened to him that day. But he stopped being happy. He wasn't happy for several years after that.

At the funeral, the vicar wanted to talk to him about foster homes, but he found out soon enough that Ove had not been brought up to accept charity. At the same time, Ove made it clear to the vicar that there was no need to reserve a place for him in the pews at Sunday service for the foreseeable future. Not because Ove did not believe in God, he explained to the vicar, but because in his view this God seemed to be a bit of a bloody swine.

The next day he went down to the wages office at the railway and handed back the wages for the rest of the month. The ladies at the office didn't understand, so Ove had to impatiently explain that his father had died on the sixteenth, and obviously wouldn't be able to come in and work for the remaining fourteen days of that month. And because he got his wages in advance, Ove had come to pay back the balance.

Hesitantly the ladies asked him to sit down and wait. After fifteen minutes or so the director came out and looked at the peculiar sixteen-year-old sitting on a wooden chair in the corridor with his dead father's pay packet in his hand. The director knew very well who this boy was. And after he'd convinced himself that there was no way of persuading him to keep the money he felt he had no right to, the director saw no alternative but to propose to Ove that he should work for the rest of the month and earn his right to it. Ove thought this seemed a reasonable offer and notified his school that he'd be absent for the next two weeks. He never went back.

He worked for the railways for five years. Then one morning he boarded a train and saw her for the first time. That was the first time he'd laughed since his father's death.

And life was never again the same.

People said Ove saw the world in black and white. But she was color. All the color he had.

6

A MAN CALLED OVE AND A BICYCLE THAT SHOULD HAVE BEEN LEFT WHERE BICYCLES ARE LEFT

Ove just wants to die in peace. Is that really too much to ask? Ove doesn't think so. Fair enough, he should have arranged it six months ago, straight after her funeral. But you couldn't bloody carry on like that, he decided at the time. He had his job to take care of. How would it look if people stopped coming to work all over the place because they'd killed themselves? Ove's wife died on a Friday, was buried on Sunday, and then Ove went to work on Monday. Because that's how one handles things. And then six months went by and out of the blue the managers came in on Monday and said they hadn't wanted to deal with it on Friday because "they didn't want to ruin his weekend." And on Tuesday he stood there oiling his kitchen worktops.

So he's prepared everything. He's paid the undertakers and arranged his place in the churchyard next to her. He's called the lawyers and written a letter with clear instructions and put it in an envelope with all his important receipts and the deeds of the house and the service history of the Saab. He's put this envelope in the inside pocket of his jacket. He's paid all the bills. He has no loans and no debts, so no one will have to clear up anything after him. He's even washed up his coffee cup and canceled the newspaper subscription. He is ready.

And all he wants is to die in peace, he thinks, as he sits in the Saab and looks out of the open garage door. If he can just avoid his neighbors he may even be able to get away by this afternoon.

He sees the heavily overweight young man from next door slouching past the garage door in the parking area. Not that Ove dislikes fat people. Certainly not. People can look any way they like. He has just never been able to understand them, can't fathom how they do it. How much can one person eat? How does one manage to turn oneself into a twin-size person? It must take a certain determination, he reflects.

The young man notices him and waves cheerfully. Ove gives him a curt nod. The young man stands there waving, setting his fat breasts into motion under his T-shirt. Ove often says that this is the only man he knows who could attack a bowl of chips from all directions at once, but whenever he makes this comment Ove's wife protests and tells him one shouldn't say things like that.

Or rather, she used to.

Used to.

Ove's wife liked the overweight young man. After his mother passed away she would go over once a week with a lunchbox. "So he gets something home-cooked now and then," she used to say. Ove noticed that they never got the containers back, adding that maybe the young man hadn't noticed the difference between the box and the food inside it. At which point Ove's wife would tell him that was enough. And then it was enough.

Ove waits until the lunchbox eater has gone before he gets out of the Saab. He tugs at the handle three times. Closes the garage door behind him. Tugs at the door handle three times. Walks up the little footpath between the houses. Stops outside the bicycle shed. There's a woman's bicycle leaning up against the wall. Again. Right under the sign clearly explaining that cycles should not be left in this precise spot.

Ove picks it up. The front tire is punctured. He unlocks the shed and places the bicycle tidily at the end of the row. He locks the door and has just tugged at it three times when he hears a late-pubescent voice jabbering in his ear.

"Whoa! What the hell're you doin'?!"

Ove turns around and finds himself eye to eye with a whelp standing a few yards away.

"Putting a bike away in the bike shed."

"You can't do that!"

On closer inspection he may be eighteen or so, Ove suspects. More of a stripling than a whelp, in other words, if one wants to be pedantic about it.

"Yes I can."

"But I'm repairing it!" the youth bursts out, his voice rising into falsetto.

"But it's a lady's bike," protests Ove.

"Yeah, so what?"

"It can hardly be yours, then," Ove states condescendingly.

The youth groans, rolling his eyes; Ove puts his hands into his pockets as if this is the end of the matter.

There's a guarded silence. The lad looks at Ove as if he finds

Ove unnecessarily thick. In return, Ove looks at the creature before him as if it were nothing but a waste of oxygen. Behind the youth, Ove notices, there's another youth. Even slimmer than the first one and with black stuff all around his eyes. The second youth tugs carefully at the first's jacket and murmurs something about "not causing trouble." His comrade kicks rebelliously at the snow, as if it were the snow's fault.

"It's my girlfriend's bike," he mumbles at last.

He says it more with resignation than indignation. His sneakers are too big and his jeans too small, Ove notes. His tracksuit jacket is pulled over his chin to protect him against the cold. His emaciated peach-fuzzed face is covered in blackheads and his hair looks as if someone saved him from drowning in a barrel by pulling him up by his locks.

"Where does she live, then?"

With profound exertion, as if he's been shot with a tranquillizer dart, the creature points with his whole arm towards the house at the far end of Ove's street. Where those communists who pushed through the garbage sorting reform live with their daughters. Ove nods cautiously.

"She can pick it up in the bike shed, then," says Ove, tapping melodramatically at the sign prohibiting bicycles from being left in the area, before turning around and heading back towards his house.

"Grumpy old bastard!" the youth yells behind him.

"Shhh!" utters his soot-eyed companion.

Ove doesn't answer.

He walks past the sign clearly prohibiting motor vehicles from entering the residential area. The one which the Pregnant Foreign Woman apparently could not read, even though Ove knows very well that it's quite impossible not to see it. He should know, because he's the one who put it there. Dissatisfied, he walks down the little footpath between the houses, stamping his feet so that anyone who saw him would think he was trying to flatten the tarmac. As if it wasn't bad enough with all the nutters already living on the street, he thinks. As if the whole area was not already being converted into some bloody speed bump in evolutionary progress. The Audi poser and the Blond Weed almost opposite Ove's house, and at the far end of the row that communist family with their teenage daughters and their red hair and their shorts over their trousers, their faces like mirror-image raccoons. Well, most likely they're on holiday in Thailand at this precise moment, but anyway.

In the house next to Ove lives the twenty-five-year-old who's almost a quarter-tonner. With his long feminine hair and strange T-shirts. He lived with his mother until she died of some illness a year or so ago. Apparently his name is Jimmy, Ove's wife has told him. Ove doesn't know what work Jimmy does; most likely something criminal. Unless he tests bacon for a living?

In the house on the other side of Jimmy live Rune and his wife. Ove wouldn't exactly call Rune his "enemy" . . . or rather, he would. Everything that went to pot in the Residents' Association began with Rune. He and his wife, Anita, moved into the area on the same day that Ove and Sonja moved in. At that time Rune drove a Volvo, but later he bought a BMW. You just couldn't reason with a person who behaved like that.

It was Rune who pushed through the coup d'état that saw Ove deposed as chairman of the association. And just look at the state of the place now. Higher electricity bills and bicycles that aren't put away in the bike shed and people backing up with trailers in the residential area in spite of signs *clearly* stating that it's prohibited. Ove has long warned about these awful things, but no one has listened. Since then he has never showed his face in any meeting of the Residents' Association.

His mouth makes a movement as if it's just about to spit every time he mentally enunciates the words "Residents' Association." As if they were a gross indecency.

He's fifteen yards from his broken mailbox when he sees Blond Weed. At first he can't comprehend what she's doing at all. She's swaying about on her heels on the footpath, gesturing hysterically at the façade of Ove's house.

That little barking thing—more of a mutt than a proper dog—which has been pissing on Ove's paving stones is running around her feet.

Weed yells something so violently that her sunglasses slip down over the tip of her nose. Mutt barks even louder. So the old girl has finally lost her faculties, Ove thinks, standing warily a few yards behind her. Only then does he realize that she's actually not gesticulating at the house. She's throwing stones. And it isn't the house she's throwing them at. It's the cat.

It sits squeezed into the far corner behind Ove's shed. It has little flecks of blood in its coat, or what's left of its coat. Mutt bares its teeth; the cat hisses back.

"Don't you hiss at Prince!" wails Weed, picking up another stone from Ove's flower bed and hurling it at the cat. The cat jumps out of the way; the stone hits the windowsill.

She picks up another stone and prepares to throw it. Ove takes two quick steps forward and stands so close behind her that she can most likely feel his breath.

"If you throw that stone into my property, I'll throw you into your garden!"

She spins around. Their eyes meet. Ove has both hands in his pockets; she waves her fists in front of him as if trying to swat two flies the size of microwave ovens. Ove doesn't concede as much as a facial movement.

"That disgusting thing scratched Prince!" she manages to say, her eyes wild with fury. Ove peers down at Mutt. It growls at him. Then he looks at the cat, sitting humiliated and bleeding but with its head defiantly raised, outside his house.

"It's bleeding. So it seems to have ended in a draw," says Ove.

"Like hell. I'll kill that piece of shit!"

"No you won't," says Ove coldly.

His insane neighbor begins to look threatening.

"It's probably full of disgusting diseases and rabies and all sorts of things!"

Ove looks at the cat. Looks at the Weed. Nods.

"And so are you, most likely. But we don't throw stones at you because of it."

Her lower lip starts trembling. She slides her sunglasses up over her eyes.

"You watch yourself!" she hisses.

Ove nods. Points at Mutt. Mutt tries to bite his leg but Ove stamps his foot down so hard that it backs off.

"That thing should be kept on a leash inside the residential area," says Ove steadily.

She tosses her dyed hair and snorts so hard that Ove half-expects a bit of snot to come flying out.

"And what about that thing?!" she rages at the cat.

"Never you bloody mind," Ove answers.

She looks at him in that particular way of people who feel both utterly superior and deeply insulted.

Mutt bares its teeth in a silent growl.

"You think you own this street or what, you bloody lunatic?" she says.

Ove calmly points at Mutt again.

"The next time that thing pisses on my paving," he says coolly, "I'll electrify the stone."

"Prince hasn't bloody pissed on your disgusting paving," she splutters, and takes two steps forward with her fists raised.

Ove doesn't move. She stops. Looks as if she's hyperventilating. Then she seems to summon what highly negligible amount of common sense she has at her disposal.

"Come on, Prince," she says with a wave.

Then raises her index finger at Ove.

"I'm going to tell Anders about this, and then you'll regret it."

"Tell your Anders from me that he should stop stretching his groin outside my window."

"Crazy old muppet," she spits out and heads off towards the parking area.

"And his car's crap, you tell him that!" Ove adds for good measure.

She makes a gesture at him that he hasn't seen before, although he can guess what it means. Then she and her wretched little dog make off towards Anders's house.

Ove turns off by his shed. Sees the wet splashes of piss on the paving by the corner of the flower bed. If he weren't busy with more important things this afternoon he would have gone off to make a doormat of that mutt right away. But he has other things to occupy him. He goes to his toolshed, gets out his hammer-action drill and his box of drill bits.

When he comes out again the cat is sitting there looking at him.

"You can clear off now," says Ove.

It doesn't move. Ove shakes his head resignedly.

"Hey! I'm not your friend."

The cat stays where it is. Ove throws out his arms.

"Christ, you bloody cat, me backing you up when that stupid bag threw stones at you only means I dislike you less than that weedy nutter across the street. And that's not much of an achievement; you should be absolutely clear about that."

The cat seems to give this some careful thought. Ove points at the footpath.

"Clear off!"

Not at all concerned by this, the cat licks its bloodstained fur. It looks at Ove as if this has been a round of negotiation and it's considering a proposal. Then slowly gets up and pads off, disappearing around the corner of the shed. Ove doesn't even look at it. He goes right into his house and slams the door.

Because it's enough now. Now Ove is going to die.

7

A MAN CALLED OVE DRILLS A HOLE FOR A HOOK

Ove has put on his best trousers and his going-out shirt. Carefully he covers the floor with a protective sheet of plastic, as if protecting a valuable work of art. Not that the floor is particularly new (although he did sand it less than two years ago). He's fairly sure that you don't lose much blood when you hang yourself, and it isn't because of worries about the dust or the drilling. Or the marks when he kicks away the stool. In fact he's glued some plastic pads to the bottoms of its legs, so there shouldn't be any marks at all. No, the heavy-duty sheets of plastic which Ove so carefully unfolds, covering the entire hall, living room, and a good part of the kitchen, are not for Ove's own sake at all.

He imagines there'll be a hell of a lot of running about in here, with eager, jumped-up real estate agents trying to get into the house before the ambulance men have so much as got the corpse out. And those bastards are not coming in here, scratching up Ove's floor with their shoes. Whether over Ove's dead body or not. They had better be quite clear about that.

He puts the stool in the middle of the floor. It's coated in at least seven different layers of paint. Ove's wife decided on principle that she'd let Ove repaint one of the rooms in their house every six months. Or, to be more exact, she decided she wanted a different color in one of the rooms once every six months. And when she said as much to Ove he told her that she might as well forget it. And then she called a decorator for an estimate. And then she told Ove how much she was going to pay the decorator. And then Ove went to fetch his painting stool.

You miss the strangest things when you lose someone. Little things. Smiles. The way she turned over in her sleep. Even repainting a room for her.

Ove goes to get his box of drill bits. These are single-handedly the most important things when drilling. Not the drill, but the bits. It's like having proper tires on your car instead of messing about with ceramic brakes and nonsense like that. Anyone who knows anything knows that. Ove positions himself in the middle of the room and sizes it up. Then, like a surgeon gazing down on his instruments, his eyes move searchingly over his drill bits. He selects one, slots it into the drill, and tests the trigger a little so that the drill makes a growling sound. Shakes his head, decides that it doesn't feel at all right, and changes the drill bit. He repeats this four times before he's satisfied, then walks through the living room, swinging the drill from his hand like a big revolver.

He stands in the middle of the floor staring up at the ceiling. He has to measure this before he gets started, he realizes. So that the hole is centered. The worst thing Ove knows is when someone just drills a hole in the ceiling, hit-or-miss.

He goes to fetch a tape measure. He measures from each of the four corners—twice, to be on the safe side—and marks the center of the ceiling with a cross.

Ove steps down from the stool. Walks around to make sure the protective plastic is in position as it should be. Unlocks the door so they won't have to break it down when they come to get him. It's a good door. It'll last many more years.

He puts on his suit jacket and checks that the envelope is in his inside pocket. Finally he turns the photo of his wife in the window, so that it looks out towards the shed. He doesn't want to make her watch what he's about to do, but on the other hand he daren't put the photograph facedown either. Ove's wife was always horribly ill-tempered if they ever ended up in someplace without a view. She needed "something to look at that's alive," she was always saying. So he points her towards the shed while thinking that maybe that Cat Annoyance would come by again. Ove's wife liked Cat Annoyances.

He fetches the drill, takes the hook, stands up on the stool, and starts drilling. The first time the doorbell goes he assumes he's made a mistake and ignores the sound for that very reason. The second time he realizes that there's actually someone ringing the bell, and he ignores it for that very reason.

The third time Ove stops drilling and glares at the door. As if he may be able to convince whoever is standing outside to disappear by his mental powers alone. It doesn't work. The person in question obviously thinks the only rational explanation for his not opening the door the first time around was that he did not hear the doorbell.

Ove steps off the stool, strides across the plastic sheets through the living room and into the hall. Does it really have to be so difficult to kill yourself without constantly being disturbed?

"What?" fumes Ove as he flings the door open.

The Lanky One only manages by a whisker to pull his big head back and avoid an impact with his face.

"Hi!" the Pregnant One exclaims cheerfully beside him, though a foot and a half lower down.

Ove looks down at her, then up at him. The Lanky One is busy touching every part of his face with some reluctance, as if to check that every protuberance is still where it should be.

"This is for you," she says in a friendly sort of voice, and then shoves a blue plastic box into Ove's arms.

Ove looks skeptical.

"Cookies," she explains encouragingly.

Ove nods slowly, as if to confirm this.

"You've really dressed up," she says with a smile.

Ove nods again.

And then they stand there, all three of them, waiting for someone to say something. In the end she looks at the Lanky One and shakes her head with resignation.

"Oh, please, will you stop fidgeting with your face, darling?" she whispers and gives him a push in the side.

The Lanky One raises his eyes, meets her gaze, and nods. Looks at Ove. Ove looks at the Pregnant One. The Lanky One points at the box and his face lights up.

"She's Iranian, you know. They bring food with them wherever they go."

Ove gives him a blank stare. The Lanky One looks even more hesitant.

"You know . . . that's why I go so well with Iranians. They like to cook food and I like to . . ." he begins, with an over-the-top smile.

Then he goes silent. Ove looks spectacularly uninterested.

". . . eat," the Lanky One finishes.

He looks as if he's about to make a drumroll in the air with his fingers. But then he looks at the Pregnant Foreign Woman and decides that it would probably be a bad idea.

"And?" Ove offers, wearily.

She stretches, puts her hands on her stomach.

"We just wanted to introduce ourselves, now that we're going to be neighbors. . . ."

Ove nods tersely and concisely.

"Okay. Bye."

He tries to close the door. She stops him with her arm.

"And then we wanted to thank you for backing up our trailer. That was very kind of you!"

Ove grunts. Reluctantly he keeps the door open.

"That's not something to thank me for."

"Yeah, it was really nice," she protests.

"No, I mean it shouldn't be something to thank me for, because a grown man should be able to back up with a trailer," he replies, casting a somewhat unimpressed gaze on the Lanky One, who looks at him as if unsure whether or not this is an insult. Ove decides not to help him out of his quandary. He backs away and tries to close the door again.

"My name is Parvaneh!" she says, putting her foot across his threshold.

Ove stares at the foot, then at the face it's attached to.

As if he's having difficulties understanding what she just did.

"I'm Patrick!" says the Lanky One.

Neither Ove nor Parvaneh takes the slightest notice of him.

"Are you always this unfriendly?" Parvaneh wonders, with genuine curiosity.

Ove looks insulted.

"I'm not bloody unfriendly."

"You are a bit unfriendly."

"No I'm not!"

"No, no, no, your every word is a cuddle, it really is," she replies in a way that makes Ove feel she doesn't mean it at all.

He releases his grip on the door handle for a moment or two. Inspects the box of cookies in his hand.

"Right. Arabian cookies. Worth having, are they?" he mutters.

"Persian," she corrects.

"What?"

"Persian, not Arabian. I'm from Iran—you know, where they speak Farsi?" she explains.

"Farcical? That's the least you could say," Ove agrees.

Her laughter catches him off guard. As if it's carbonated and someone has poured it too fast and it's bubbling over in all directions. It doesn't fit at all with the gray cement and right-angled garden paving stones. It's an untidy, mischievous laugh that refuses to go along with rules and prescriptions.

Ove takes a step backwards. His foot sticks to some tape by the threshold. As he tries to shake it off, with some irritation, he tears up the corner of the plastic. When he tries to shake off both the tape and the plastic sheeting, he stumbles backwards and pulls up even more of it. Angrily, he regains his balance. Remains there on the threshold, trying to summon some calm. Grabs hold of the door handle again, looks at the Lanky One, and tries to quickly change the subject.

"And what are you, then?"

He shrugs his shoulder a little and smiles, slightly overwhelmed.

"I'm an IT consultant."

Ove and Parvaneh shake their heads with such coordination they could be synchronized swimmers. For a moment it makes Ove dislike her a little less, although he's very reluctant to admit it to himself.

The Lanky One seems unaware of all this. Instead he looks with curiosity at the hammer-action drill, which Ove is holding in a firm grip, like a guerrilla fighter with an AK-47 in his hand.

Once the Lanky One has finished perusing it, he leans forward and peers into Ove's house.

"What are you doing?"

Ove looks at him, as one does at a person who has just said "What are you doing?" to a man standing with a hammer-action drill in his hand.

"I'm drilling," he replies scathingly.

Parvaneh looks at the Lanky One and rolls her eyes, and if it hadn't been for her belly, which testified to a willingness on her part to contribute to the survival of the Lanky One's genetic makeup, Ove might have found her almost sympathetic at this point.

"Oh," says the Lanky One, with a nod.

Then he leans forward and peers in at the living room floor, neatly covered in the protective sheet of plastic.

He lights up and looks at Ove with a grin.

"Almost looks like you're about to murder someone!"

Ove peruses him in silence. The Lanky One clears his throat, a little more reluctant. "I mean, it's like an episode of *Dexter*," he says with a much less confident grin. "It's a TV series . . . about a guy who murders people." He trails off, then starts poking the toe of his shoe into the gaps between the paving stones outside Ove's front door.

Ove shakes his head. It's unclear to whom the Lanky One was primarily aiming what he just said.

"I have some things to get on with," he says curtly to Parvaneh and takes a firm grip on the door handle.

Parvaneh gives the Lanky One a purposeful jab in the side with her elbow. The Lanky One looks as if he's trying to drum up some courage; he glances at Parvaneh, and looks at Ove with the expression of someone expecting the whole world to start firing rubber bands at him.

"Well, the thing is, we actually came because I could do with borrowing a few things . . ."

Ove raises his eyebrows.

"What 'things'?"

The Lanky One clears his throat.

"A ladder. And an Eileen key."

"You mean an Allen key?"

Parvaneh nods. The Lanky One looks puzzled.

"It's an Eileen key, isn't it?"

"Allen key," Parvaneh and Ove correct at the same time.

Parvaneh nods eagerly at him and points triumphantly at Ove. "He said that's what it's called!"

The Lanky One mumbles something inaudible.

"And you're just like 'Whoa, it's an Eileen key!'" Parvaneh jeers.

He looks slightly crestfallen.

"I never sounded like that."

"You did so!"

"Did not!"

"Yes you DID!"

"I DIDN'T!"

Ove's gaze travels from one to the other, like a large dog watching two mice interfering with its sleep.

"You did," says one of them.

"That's what you think," the other one says.

"Everyone says it!"

"The majority is not always right!"

"Shall we Google it or what?"

"Sure! Google it! Wikipedia it!

"Give me your phone."

"Use your own!"

"Duh! I haven't got it with me, dipshit!"

"Sorry to hear that!"

Ove looks at them as their pathetic argument drones on. They remind him of two malfunctioning radiators, making high-pitched whines at each other.

"Good God," he mutters.

Parvaneh starts imitating what Ove assumes must be some kind of flying insect. She makes tiny whirring sounds with her lips to irritate her husband. It works quite effectively. Both on the Lanky One and on Ove. Ove gives up.

He goes into the hall, hangs up his suit jacket, puts down the hammer-action drill, puts on his clogs, and walks past them both towards the shed. He's pretty sure neither of them even notices him. He hears them still bickering as he starts backing out with the ladder.

"Go on, help him then, Patrick," Parvaneh bursts out when she catches sight of him.

The Lanky One takes a few steps towards him, with fumbling movements. Ove keeps his eyes on him, as if watching a blind man at the wheel of a crowded city bus. And only after that does Ove realize that, in his absence, his property has been invaded by yet another person.

Rune's wife, Anita, from farther down the street, is standing next to Parvaneh, blithely watching the spectacle. Ove decides the only rational response must be to pretend that she's doing no such thing. He feels anything else would only encourage her. He hands the Lanky One a cylindrical case with a set of neatly sorted Allen keys.

"Oh, look how many there are," says the imbecile thoughtfully, gazing into the case.

"What size are you after?" asks Ove.

The Lanky One looks at him as people do when they lack the self-possession to say what they are thinking.

"The . . . usual size?"

Ove looks at him for a long, long time.

"What are you using these things for?" he says at last.

"To fix an IKEA wardrobe we took apart when we moved. And then I forgot where I put the Eileen key," he explains, apparently without a trace of shame.

Ove looks at the ladder.

"And this wardrobe's on the roof, is it?"

The Lanky One sniggers and shakes his head. "Oh, right, see what you mean! No, I need the ladder because the upstairs window is jammed. Won't open." He adds the last part as if Ove would not otherwise be able to understand the implications of that word, "jammed."

"So now you're going to try to open it from the outside?" Ove wonders.

The Lanky One nods and clumsily takes the ladder from him. Ove looks as if he's about to say something else, but he seems to change his mind. He turns to Parvaneh.

"And why exactly are you here?"

"Moral support," she twitters.

Ove doesn't look entirely convinced. Nor does the Lanky One.

Ove's gaze wanders reluctantly back to Rune's wife. She's still there. It seems like years since he last saw her. Or at least since he really looked at her. She's gone ancient. People all seem to get ancient behind Ove's back these days.

"Yes?" says Ove.

Rune's wife smiles mildly and clasps her hands across her hips.

"Ove, you know I don't want to disturb you, but it's about the radiators in our house. We can't get any heat into them," she says carefully and smiles in turn at Ove, the Lanky One, and Parvaneh. Parvaneh and the Lanky One smile back. Ove looks at his dented wristwatch.

"Does no one on this street have a job to go to anymore?" he wonders.

"I'm retired," says Rune's wife, almost apologetically.

"I'm on maternity leave," says Parvaneh, patting her stomach proudly.

"I'm an IT consultant!" says the Lanky One, also proudly.

Ove and Parvaneh again indulge in a bit of synchronized head-shaking.

Rune's wife makes another attempt.

"I think it could be the radiators."

"Have you bled them?" says Ove.

She shakes her head and looks curious.

"You think it could be because of that?"

Ove rolls his eyes.

"Ove!" Parvaneh roars at him at once, as if she's a reprimanding schoolmistress. Ove glares at her. She glares back. "Stop being rude," she orders.

"I told you, I'm not rude!"

Her eyes are unwavering. He makes a little grunt, then goes back to standing in the doorway. He thinks it could sort of be enough now. All he wants is to die. Why can't these lunatics respect that?

Parvaneh puts her hand encouragingly on Rune's wife's arm.

"I'm sure Ove can help you with the radiators."

"That would be amazingly kind of you, Ove," Rune's wife says at once, brightening.

Ove sticks his hands in his pockets. Kicks at the loose plastic by the threshold.

"Can't your man sort out that kind of thing in his own house?"

Rune's wife shakes her head mournfully.

"No, Rune has been really ill lately, you see. They say it's Alzheimer's. He's in a wheelchair as well. It's been a bit uphill. . . ."

Ove nods with faint recognition. As if he has been reminded of something his wife told him a thousand times, although he still managed to forget it all the time.

"Yeah, yeah," he says impatiently.

"You can go and breathe their radiators, can't you, Ove!" says Parvaneh.

Ove glances at her as if considering a firm retort, but instead he just looks down at the ground.

"Or is that too much to ask?" she continues, drilling him with her gaze and crossing her arms firmly across her stomach.

Ove shakes his head.

"You don't breathe radiators, you *bleed* them . . . Jesus."

He looks up and gives them the once-over.

"Have you never bled a radiator before, or what?"

"No," says Parvaneh, unmoved.

Rune's wife looks at the Lanky One a little anxiously.

"I haven't got a clue what they're talking about," he says calmly to her.

Rune's wife nods resignedly. Looks at Ove again.

"It would be really nice of you, Ove, if it isn't too much of a bother. . . ."

Ove just stands there staring down at the threshold.

"Maybe this could have been thought about before you organized a coup d'état in the Residents' Association," he says quietly, his words punctuated by a series of discreet coughs.

"Before she what?" says Parvaneh.

Rune's wife clears her throat.

"But, dear Ove, there was never a coup d'état. . . ."

"Was so," says Ove grumpily.

Rune's wife looks at Parvaneh with an embarrassed little smile. "Well, you see, Rune and Ove here haven't always gotten along so very well. Before Rune got ill he was the head of the Residents' Association. And before that Ove was the head. And when Rune was voted in there was something of a wrangle between Ove and Rune, you could say."

Ove looks up and points a corrective index finger at her.

"A coup d'état! That's what it was!"

Rune's wife nods at Parvaneh.

"Well, yes, well, before the meeting Rune counted votes about his suggestion that we should change the heating system for the houses and Ove thou—"

"And what the hell does Rune know about heating systems? Eh?" Ove exclaims heatedly, but immediately gets a look from Parvaneh which makes him reconsider and come to the conclusion that there's no need to complete his line of thought.

Rune's wife nods.

"Maybe you're right, Ove. But anyway, he's very sick now . . . so it doesn't really matter anymore." Her bottom lip trembles slightly.

Then she regains her composure, straightens her neck with dignity, and clears her throat.

"The authorities have said they'll take him from me and put him in a home," she manages to say.

Ove puts his hands in his pockets again and determinedly backs away, across his threshold. He's heard enough of this.

In the meantime the Lanky One seems to have decided it's time to change the subject and lighten up the atmosphere. He points at the floor in Ove's hall.

"What's that?"

Ove turns to look at the bit of floor exposed by the loose plastic sheet.

"It looks as if you've got, sort of . . . tire marks on the floor. Do you cycle indoors, or what?" says the Lanky One.

Parvaneh keeps her observant eyes on Ove as he backs away another step so he can impede the Lanky One's view.

"It's nothing."

"But I can see it's—" the Lanky One begins confusedly.

"It was Ove's wife, Sonja, she was—" Rune's wife interrupts him in a friendly manner, but she only has time to get to the name "Sonja" when Ove, in turn, interrupts her and spins around with unbridled fury in his eyes.

"That'll do! Now you SHUT UP!"

All four of them fall silent, equally shocked. Ove's hands tremble as he steps back into his hall and slams the door.

He hears Parvaneh's soft voice out there asking Rune's wife what all that was about. Then he hears Rune's wife fumbling nervously for words, and then exclaiming: "Oh, you know, I'd better go home. That thing about Ove's wife . . . oh, forget it. Old bats like me, we talk too much, you know. . . ."

Ove hears her strained laugh and then her little dragging footsteps disappearing as quickly as they can around the corner of his shed. A moment later the Pregnant One and the Lanky One also leave.

And all that's left is the silence of Ove's hall.

He sinks down on the stool, breathing heavily. His hands are still shaking as if he were standing waist-deep in ice-cold water. His chest thumps. It happens more and more these days. He has to sort of struggle for a mouthful of air, like a fish in an overturned bowl. His company doctor said it was chronic, and that he mustn't work himself up. Easy for him to say.

"Good to go home and have a rest now," said his bosses at work. "Now your heart is playing up and all." They called it "early retirement" but they might as well have said what it was: "liquidation." A third of a century in the same job and that's what they reduced him to.

Ove is not sure how long he stays there on the stool, sitting with the drill in his hand and his heart beating so hard that he feels the pulse inside his head. There's a photo on the wall beside the front door, of Ove and Sonja. It's almost forty years old. That time they were in Spain on a bus tour. She's suntanned, wearing a red dress, and looking so happy. Ove is standing next to her, holding her hand. He sits there for what must be an hour, just staring at that photo. Of all the imaginable things he most misses about her, the thing he really wishes he could do again is hold her hand in his. She had a way of folding her index finger into his palm, hiding it inside. And he always felt that nothing in the world was impossible when she did that. Of all the things he could miss, that's what he misses most.

Slowly he stands up. Goes into the living room. Up the steps of the stool. And then once and for all he drills the hole and puts in the hook.

Then gets off the stool and studies his work.

He goes into the hall and puts on his suit jacket. Feels in his pocket for the envelope. He's turned out all the lights. Washed his coffee mug. Put up a hook in his living room. He's done.

He takes down the rope from the clothes-dryer in the hall. Gently, with the back of his hand, he caresses her coats one last time. Then he goes into the living room, ties a noose in the rope, threads it through the hook, climbs up on the stool, and puts his head in the noose.

Kicks the stool away.

Closes his eyes and feels the noose closing around his throat like the jaws of a large wild animal.

8

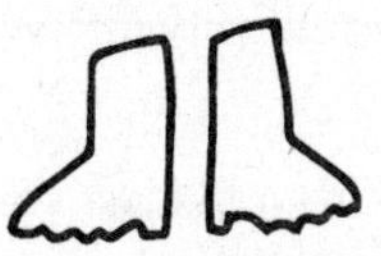

A MAN WHO WAS OVE AND A PAIR OF HIS FATHER'S OLD FOOTPRINTS

She believed in destiny. That all the roads you walk in life, in one way or another, "lead to what has been predetermined for you." Ove, of course, just started muttering under his breath and got very busy fiddling about with a screw or something whenever she started going on like this. But he never disagreed with her. Maybe to her destiny was "something"; that was none of his business. But to him, destiny was "someone."

It's a strange thing, becoming an orphan at sixteen. To lose your family long before you've had time to create your own to replace it. It's a very specific sort of loneliness.

Ove, conscientious and dutiful, completed his two-week stint on the railways. And to his own surprise he found that he liked it. There was a certain liberation in doing a job. Grabbing hold of things with his own two hands and seeing the fruit of his efforts. Ove hadn't ever disliked school, but he hadn't quite seen the point of it either. He liked mathematics, and was two academic years ahead of his classmates. As for the other subjects, quite honestly he was not so concerned about them.

But this was something entirely different. Something that suited him much better.

When he clocked off from his last shift on the last day he was downcast. Not only because he had to go back to school, but because it had only occurred to him now that he didn't know how to earn a living. Dad had been good in many ways, of course, but Ove had to admit he hadn't left much of an estate except a run-down house, an old Saab, and a dented wristwatch. Alms from the church were out of the question, God should be bloody clear about that. Ove said as much to himself while he stood there in the changing rooms, maybe as much for his own benefit as God's.

"If you really had to take both Mum and Dad, keep your bloody money!" he yelled up at the ceiling.

Then he packed up his stuff and left. Whether God or anyone else was listening he never found out. But when Ove came out of the changing rooms, a man from the managing director's office was standing there waiting for him.

"Ove?" he asked.

Ove nodded.

"The director would like to express his thanks for doing such a good job over the past fortnight," the man said, short and to the point.

"Thanks," said Ove as he started walking away.

The man put his hand on Ove's arm. Ove stopped.

"The director was wondering whether you might have an interest in staying and carrying on doing a good job?"

Ove stood in silence, looking at the man. Maybe mostly to check if this was some kind of joke. Then he slowly nodded.

When he'd taken a few more steps the man called out behind him:

"The director says you are just like your father!"

Ove didn't turn around. But his back was straighter as he walked off.

And that's how he ended up in his father's old boots. He worked hard, never complained, and was never ill. The old boys on his shift found him a little on the quiet side and a little odd on top of that. He never wanted to join them for a beer after work and he seemed uninterested in women as well, which was more than weird in its own right. But he was a chip off the old block and had never given them anything to complain about. If anyone asked Ove for a hand, he got on with it; if anyone asked him to cover a shift for them, he did it without any fuss. As time went by, more or less all of them owed him a favor or two. So they accepted him.

When the old truck, the one they used to drive up and down the railway track, broke down one night more than ten miles outside of town, in one of the worst downpours of the whole year, Ove managed to repair it with nothing but a screwdriver and half a roll of gauze tape. After that, as far as the old boys on the tracks were concerned, Ove was okay.

In the evenings he'd boil his sausages and potatoes, staring out the kitchen window as he ate. And the next morning he'd go to work again. He liked the routine, liked always knowing what to expect. Since his father's death he had begun more and more to differentiate between people who did what they should, and those who didn't. People who did and people who just talked. Ove talked less and less and did more and more.

He had no friends. But on the other hand he hardly had any enemies either, apart from Tom, who since his promotion to foreman took every opportunity to make Ove's life as difficult as possible. He gave him the dirtiest and heaviest jobs, shouted at him, tripped him up at breakfast, sent him under railway carriages for inspections and set them in motion while Ove lay unprotected on the cross ties. When Ove, startled, threw himself out of the way just in time, Tom laughed contemptuously and roared: "Look out or you'll end up like your old man!"

Ove kept his head down, though, and his mouth shut. He saw no purpose in challenging a man who was twice his own size. He went to work every day and did justice to himself—that had been good enough for his father and so it would also have to do for Ove. His colleagues learned to appreciate him for it. "When people don't talk so much they don't dish out the crap either," one of his older workmates said to him one afternoon down on the track. And Ove nodded. Some got it and some didn't.

There were also some who got what Ove ended up doing one day in the director's office, while others didn't.

It was almost two years after his father's funeral. Ove had just turned eighteen. Tom had been caught out stealing money from the cash box in one of the carriages. Admittedly no one but Ove saw him take it, but Tom and Ove had been the only two people in the carriage when the money went missing. And, as a serious man from the director's office explained when Tom and Ove were ordered to present themselves, no one could believe Ove was the guilty party. And he wasn't, of course.

Ove was left on a wooden chair in the corridor outside the director's office. He sat there looking at the floor for fifteen minutes before the door opened. Tom stepped outside, his fists so clenched with determination that his skin was bloodless and white on his lower arms.

He kept trying to make eye contact with Ove; Ove just kept staring down at the floor until he was brought into the director's office.

More serious men in suits were spread around the room. The director himself was pacing back and forth behind his desk, his face highly colored, and there was an insinuation that he was too angry to stand still.

"You want to sit down, Ove?" said one of the men in suits at last.

Ove met his gaze, and knew who he was. His dad had mended his car once. A blue Opel Manta. With the big engine. He smiled amicably at Ove and gestured cursorily at a chair in the middle of the floor. As if to let him know that he was among friends now and could relax.

Ove shook his head. The Opel Manta man nodded with understanding.

"Well then. This is just a formality, Ove. No one in here believes you took the money. All you need to do is tell us who did it."

Ove looked down at the floor. Half a minute passed.

"Ove?"

Ove didn't answer. The harsh voice of the director broke the silence at long last. "Answer the question, Ove!"

Ove stood in silence. Looking down at the floor. The facial expressions of the men in suits shifted from conviction to slight confusion.

"Ove . . . you do understand that you have to answer the question. Did you take the money?"

"No," said Ove with a steady voice.

"So who was it?"

Ove stood in silence.

"Answer the question!" ordered the director.

Ove looked up. Stood there with a straight back.

"I'm not the sort that tells tales about what other people do," he said.

The room was steeped in silence for what must have been several minutes.

"You do understand, Ove . . . that if you don't tell us who it was, and if we have one or more witnesses who say it was you . . . then we'll have to draw the conclusion that it was you?" said the director, not as amicable now.

Ove nodded, but didn't say another word. The director scrutinized him, as if he were a bluffer in a game of cards. Ove's face was unmoved. The director nodded grimly.

"So you can go, then."

And Ove left.

Tom had put the blame on Ove when he was in the director's office some fifteen minutes earlier. During the afternoon, two of the younger men from Tom's shift, eager as young men are to earn the approval of older men, came forward and claimed that they had seen Ove take the money with their own eyes. If Ove had pointed out Tom, it would have been one word against another. But now it was Tom's words against Ove's silence. The next morning he was told by the foreman to empty his locker and present himself outside the director's office.

Tom stood inside the door of the changing rooms and jeered at him as he was leaving.

"Thief," hissed Tom.

Ove passed him without raising his eyes.

"Thief! Thief! Thief!" one of their younger colleagues, who had testified against Ove, chanted happily across the changing room, until one of the older men on their shift gave him a slap across the ear that silenced him.

"THIEF!" Tom shouted demonstratively, so loudly that the word was still ringing in Ove's head several days after.

Ove walked out into the morning air without turning around. He took a deep breath. He was furious, but not because they had called him a thief. He would never be the sort of man who cared what other men called him. But the shame of losing a job to which his father had devoted his whole life burned like a red-hot poker in his breast.

He had plenty of time to think his life over as he walked one last time to the office, a bundle of work clothes clutched in his arms. He had liked working here. Proper tasks, proper tools, a real job. He decided that once the police had gone through the motions of whatever they did with thieves in this situation, he'd try to go somewhere where he could get himself another job like this one. He might have to travel far, he imagined. Most likely a criminal record needed a reasonable geographical distance before it started to pale and become uninteresting. He had nothing to keep him here, he realized. But at least he had not become the sort of man who told tales. He hoped this would make his father more forgiving about Ove losing his job, once they were reunited.

He had to sit on the wooden chair in the corridor for almost forty minutes before a middle-aged woman in a tight-fitting black skirt and pointy glasses came and told him he could come into the office. She closed the door behind him. He stood there, still with his work clothes in his arms. The director sat behind his desk with his hands clasped together in front of him. The two men submitted one another to such a long examination that either of them could have been an unusually interesting painting in a museum.

"It was Tom who took that money," said the director.

He did not say it as a question, just a short confirming statement. Ove didn't answer. The director nodded.

"But the men in your family are not the kind who tell."

That was not a question either. And Ove didn't reply.

The director noticed that he straightened a little at the words "the men in your family."

The director nodded again. Put on a pair of glasses, looked through a pile of papers, and started writing something. As if in that very moment Ove had disappeared from the room. Ove stood in front of him for so long that he quite seriously began to doubt whether the director was aware of his presence. The director looked up.

"Yes?"

"Men are what they are because of what they do. Not what they say," said Ove.

The director looked at him with surprise. It was the longest sequence of words anyone at the railway depot had heard the boy say since he started working there two years ago. In all honesty, Ove did not know where they came from. He just felt they had to be said.

The director looked down at his pile of papers again. Wrote something there. Pushed a piece of paper across the desk. Pointed to where Ove should sign his name.

"This is a declaration that you have voluntarily given up your job," he said. Ove signed his name. Straightened up, with something unyielding in his face.

"You can tell them to come in now. I'm ready."

"Who?" asked the director.

"The police," said Ove, clenching his fists at his sides.

The director shook his head briskly and went back to digging in his pile of papers.

"I actually think the witness testimonies have been lost in this mess."

Ove moved his weight from one foot to the other, without really knowing how to respond to this. The director waved his hand without looking at him.

"You're free to go now."

Ove turned around. Went into the corridor. Closed the door behind him. Felt light-headed. Just as he reached the front door the woman who had first let him in caught up with energetic steps, and before he had time to protest she pressed a paper into his hands.

"The director wants you to know that you're hired as a night cleaner on the long-distance train; report to the foreman there tomorrow morning," she said sternly.

Ove stared at her, then at the paper. She leaned in closer.

"The director asked me to pass on another message: You did not take that wallet when you were nine years old. And he'll be deuced if you took anything now. And it would be a damned pity for him to be responsible for kicking a decent man's son into the street just because the son has some principles."

And so it turned out that Ove became a night cleaner instead. And if this hadn't happened, he would never have come off his shift that morning and caught sight of her. With those red shoes and the gold brooch and all her burnished brown hair. And that laughter of hers, which, for the rest of his life, would make him feel as if someone was running around barefoot on the inside of his breast.

She often said that "all roads lead to something you were always predestined to do." And for her, perhaps, it was something.

But for Ove it was someone.

9

A MAN CALLED OVE BLEEDS A RADIATOR

They say the brain functions quicker while it's falling. As if the sudden explosion of kinetic energy forces the mental faculties to accelerate until the perception of the exterior world goes into slow motion.

So Ove had time to think of many different things.

Mainly radiators.

—

Because there are right and wrong ways of doing things, as we all know. And even though it was many years ago and Ove could no longer remember exactly what solution he'd considered to be the right one in the argument about which central heating system should be adopted by the Residents' Association, he did remember very clearly that Rune's approach to it had been wrong.

But it wasn't just the central heating system. Rune and Ove had known one another for almost forty years, and they had been at loggerheads for at least thirty-seven of them.

Ove could not in all honesty remember how it all started. It wasn't the sort of dispute where you did remember. It was more an argument where the little disagreements had ended up so entangled that every new word was treacherously booby-trapped, and in the end it wasn't possible to open one's mouth at all without setting off at least four unexploded mines from earlier conflicts. It was the sort of argument that had just run, and run, and run. Until one day it just ran out.

It wasn't really about cars, properly speaking. But Ove drove a Saab, after all. And Rune drove a Volvo. Anyone could have seen it wouldn't work out in the long run. In the beginning, though, they had been friends. Or, at least, friends to the extent that men like Ove and Rune were capable of being friends. Mostly for the sake of their wives, obviously. All four of them had moved into the area at the same time, and Sonja and Anita became instant best friends as only women married to men like Ove and Rune can be.

Ove recalled that he had at least not disliked Rune in those early years, as far as he could remember. They were the ones who set up the Residents' Association, Ove as chairman and Rune as assistant chairman. They had stuck together when the council wanted to cut down the forest behind Ove's and Rune's houses in order to build even more houses. Of course, the council claimed that those construction plans had been there for years before Rune and Ove moved into their houses, but one did not get far with Rune and Ove using that sort of argumentation. "It's war, you bastards!" Rune had roared at them down the telephone line. And it truly was: endless appeals and writs and petitions and letters to newspapers. A year and a half later the council gave up and started building somewhere else instead.

That evening Rune and Ove had drunk a glass of whiskey each

on Rune's patio. They didn't seem overly happy about winning, their wives pointed out. Both men were rather disappointed that the council had given up so quickly. These eighteen months had been some of the most enjoyable of their lives.

"Is no one prepared to fight for their principles anymore?" Rune had wondered.

"Not a damn one," Ove had answered.

And then they said a toast to unworthy enemies.

That was long before the coup d'état in the Residents' Association, of course. And before Rune bought a BMW.

Idiot, thought Ove on that day, and also today, all these years after. And every day in between, actually. "How the heck are you supposed to have a reasonable conversation with someone who buys a BMW?" Ove used to ask Sonja when she wondered why the two men could not have a reasonable conversation anymore. And at that point Sonja used to find no other course but to roll her eyes while muttering, "You're hopeless."

Ove wasn't hopeless, in his own view. He just had a sense of there needing to be a bit of order in the greater scheme of things. He felt one should not go through life as if everything was exchangeable. As if loyalty was worthless. Nowadays people changed their stuff so often that any expertise in how to make things last was becoming superfluous. Quality: no one cared about that anymore. Not Rune or the other neighbors and not those managers in the place where Ove worked. Now everything had to be computerized, as if one couldn't build a house until some consultant in a too-small shirt figured out how to open a laptop. As if that was how they built the Colosseum and the pyramids of Giza. Christ, they'd managed to build the Eiffel Tower in 1889, but nowadays one couldn't come up with the bloody drawings for a one-story house without taking a break for someone to run off and recharge their cell phone.

This was a world where one became outdated before one's time was up. An entire country standing up and applauding the fact that no one was capable of doing anything properly anymore. The unreserved celebration of mediocrity.

No one could change tires. Install a dimmer switch. Lay some tiles. Plaster a wall. File their own taxes. These were all forms of knowledge that had lost their relevance, and the sorts of things Ove had once spoken of with Rune. And then Rune went and bought a BMW.

Was a person hopeless because he believed there should be some limits? Ove didn't think so.

And yes, he didn't exactly remember how that argument with Rune had started. But it had continued. It had been about radiators and central heating systems and parking slots and trees that had to be felled and snow clearance and lawn mowers and rat poison in Rune's pond. For more than thirty-five years they had paced about on their identical patios behind their identical houses, while throwing meaningful glares over the fence. And then one day about a year ago it all came to an end. Rune became ill. Never came out of the house anymore. Ove didn't even know if he still had the BMW.

And there was a part of him that missed that bloody old sod.

So, as they say, the brain functions quicker when it's falling. Like thinking thousands of thoughts in a fraction of a second. In other words, Ove has a good deal of time to think after he's kicked the stool over and fallen and landed on the floor with a lot of angry thrashing. He lies there, on his back, looking up for what seems like half an eternity at the hook still up on the ceiling. Then, in shock, he stares at the rope, which has snapped into two long stumps.

This society, thinks Ove. Can't they even manufacture rope anymore? He swears profusely while he furiously tries to untangle his legs. How can one fail to manufacture rope, for Christ's sake? How can you get *rope* wrong?

No, there's no quality anymore, Ove decides. He stands up, brushes himself down, peers around the room and ground floor of his row house. Feels his cheeks burning; he's not quite sure if it's because of anger or shame.

He looks at the window and the drawn curtains, as if concerned that someone may have seen him.

Isn't that bloody typical, he thinks. You can't even kill yourself in a sensible way anymore. He picks up the snapped rope and throws it in the kitchen wastebasket. Folds up the plastic sheeting and puts it in the IKEA bags. Puts back the hammer-action drill and the drill bits in their cases, then goes out and puts everything back in the shed.

He stands out there for a few minutes and thinks about how Sonja always used to nag at him to tidy the place up. He always refused, knowing that any new space would immediately be an excuse to go out and buy more useless stuff with which to fill it. And now it's too late for tidying, he confirms. Now there's no longer anyone who wants to go out and buy useless stuff. Now the tidying would just result in a lot of empty gaps. And Ove hates empty gaps.

He goes to the workbench, picks up an adjustable wrench and a little plastic watering can. He walks out, locks the shed, and tugs at the door handle three times. Then goes down the little pathway between the houses, turns off by the last mailbox, and rings a doorbell. Anita opens the door. Ove looks at her without a word. Sees Rune sitting there in his wheelchair, vacantly staring out of the window. It seems that's all he's done these last few years.

"Where have you got the radiators, then?" mutters Ove.

Anita smiles a surprised little smile and nods with equally mixed eagerness and confusion.

"Oh, Ove, that's dreadfully kind of you, if it's not too much trou—"

Ove steps into the hall without letting her finish what she's saying, or removing his shoes.

"Yeah, yeah, this crappy day is already ruined anyway."

10

A MAN WHO WAS OVE AND A HOUSE THAT OVE BUILT

A week after his eighteenth birthday, Ove passed his driving test, responded to an advertisement, and walked fifteen miles to buy his first own car: a blue Saab 93. He sold his dad's old Saab 92 to pay for it. It was only marginally newer, admittedly, and quite a run-down Saab 93 at that, but a man was not a proper man until he had bought his own car, felt Ove. And so it was.

It was a time of change in the country. People moved and found new jobs and bought televisions, and the newspapers started talking about a "middle class." Ove didn't quite know what this was, but he was well aware that he was not a part of it. The middle classes moved into new housing developments with straight walls and carefully trimmed lawns, and it soon grew clear to Ove that his parental home stood in the way of progress. And if there was anything this middle class was not enamored of, it was whatever stood in the way of progress.

Ove received several letters from the council about what was called "the redrawing of municipal boundaries." He didn't quite understand the content of these letters, but he understood that his parental home did not fit among the new-built houses on the street. The council notified him of their intention to force him to sell the land to them so the house could be demolished and another built in its place.

Ove wasn't sure what it was that made him refuse. Maybe because he didn't like the tone of that letter from the council. Or because the house was all he had left of his family.

Whatever the case, he parked his first very own car in the garden that evening and sat in the driver's seat for several hours, gazing at the house. It was, to be blunt, decrepit. His father's specialty had been machines, not building, and Ove was not much better himself. These days he used only the kitchen and the little room leading off it, while the entire second floor was slowly being turned into a recreational stamping ground for mice. He watched the house from the car, as if hoping that it might start repairing itself if he waited patiently enough. It lay exactly on the boundary between two municipal authorities, on a line on the map that would now be moved one way or the other. It was the remnant of an extinguished little village at the edge of the forest, next to the shining residential development into which people wearing suits had now moved with their families.

The suits didn't like the lonely youth in the house due for demolition at the end of the street. The children were not allowed to play around Ove's house. Suits preferred to live in the vicinity of other suits, Ove had come to understand. He had nothing against that, of course—but they were the ones who had moved into his neighborhood, not the other way around.

And so, filled with a kind of strange defiance that made Ove's heart beat a little faster for the first time in years, he decided not to sell his house to the council. He decided to do the opposite. Repair it.

Of course, he had no idea of how to do it. He didn't know a dovetail joint from a pot of potatoes. Realizing that his new working hours left him entirely free in the daytime, he went to a nearby construction site and applied for a job. He imagined this must be the best possible place to learn about building and he didn't need much sleep anyway. The only thing they could offer him was a laboring job, said the foreman. Ove took it.

So he spent his nights picking up litter on the line heading south out of town; then, after three hours of sleep, he used what time remained to dart up and down the scaffolding, listening to the men in hard hats talking about construction techniques. One day a week he was free, and then he dragged sacks of cement and wooden beams back and forth for eighteen hours at a stretch, perspiring and lonely, demolishing and rebuilding the only thing his parents had left him apart from the Saab and his father's wristwatch. Ove's muscles grew and he was a fast learner.

The foreman at the building site took a liking to the hardworking youth, and one Friday afternoon took Ove to the pile of discarded planks, made-to-measure timber that had cracked and was due for burning.

"If I happen to look the other way and something you need goes walking, I'll assume you've burned it," said the foreman and walked off.

Once the rumors of his house-building had spread among his older colleagues, one or other of them occasionally asked Ove about it. When he damaged the wall in the living room, a wiry colleague with wonky front teeth, after spending twenty minutes telling Ove what an idiot he was for not knowing better from the start, taught him how to calculate the load-bearing parameters. When he laid the floor in the kitchen, a more heavy-built colleague with a missing little finger on one hand, after calling him a bonehead three dozen times, showed him how to take proper measurements.

One afternoon, as he was about to head home at the end of his shift, Ove found a little toolbox full of used tools by his clothes. It came with a note that simply read: "To the puppy."

Slowly, the house took shape. Screw by screw and floorboard by floorboard. No one saw it, of course, but there was no need for anyone to see it. A job well done is a reward in its own right, as his father always used to say.

He kept out of the way of his neighbors as much as he could. He knew they didn't like him and he saw no reason to give them further ammunition. The only exception was an elderly man and his wife who lived next door to Ove. This man was the only one on their whole street who did not wear a tie.

Ove had religiously fed the birds every other day since his father died. He only forgot to do it one morning. When the following morning he came out to compensate for his omission, he almost collided headfirst into the older man by the fence under the bird-table. His neighbor gave him an insulted glance; he had bird-seed in his hands. They did not say anything to one another. Ove merely nodded and the older man gave him a little nod back. Ove went back into his house and from that time on made sure he kept to his own days.

They never spoke to one another. But one morning when the older man stepped onto his front step, Ove was painting his fence. And when he was done with that, he also painted the other side of the fence. The older man didn't say anything about it, but when Ove went past his kitchen window in the evening they nodded at one another. And the next day there was a home-baked apple pie on Ove's front step. Ove had not eaten homemade apple pie since his mother died.

Ove received more letters from the council. They became increasingly threatening in their tone and displeased that he still hadn't contacted them about the sale of his property. In the end he started throwing the letters away without even opening them. If they wanted his father's house they could come here and try to take it, the same way Tom had tried to take that wallet from him all those years ago.

A few mornings later Ove walked past the neighbor's house and saw the elderly man feeding the birds in the company of a little boy. A grandchild of his, Ove realized. He watched them surreptitiously through the bedroom window. The way the older man and the boy spoke in low voices with each other, as if they were sharing some great secret. It reminded him of something.

That night he had his supper in the Saab.

A few weeks later, Ove drove home the last nail in his house, and when the sun rose over the horizon he stood in the garden with his hands shoved into the pockets of his navy trousers, proudly surveying his work.

He'd discovered that he liked houses. Maybe mostly because they were understandable. They could be calculated and drawn on paper. They did not leak if they were made watertight; they did not collapse if they were properly supported. Houses were fair, they gave you what you deserved. Which, unfortunately, was more than one could say about people.

And so the days went by. Ove went to work and came home and had sausages and spuds. He never felt alone despite his lack of company. Then one Sunday, as Ove was moving some planks, a jovial man with a round face and an ill-fitting suit turned up at his gate. The sweat ran from his forehead and he asked Ove if there might be a glass of water of the cold variety going spare. Ove saw no reason to deny him this, and while the man drank it by his gate, some small talk passed between them. Or rather, it was mostly the man with the round face who did the talking. It turned out that he was very interested in houses. Apparently he was in the midst of doing up his own house in another part of town. And somehow the man with the round face managed to invite himself into Ove's kitchen for a cup of coffee. Obviously, Ove was not used to this kind of pushy behavior, but after an hour-long conversation about house-building, he was prepared to admit to himself that it wasn't so unpleasant having a bit of company in the kitchen for a change.

Just before the man left he asked in passing about Ove's house insurance. Ove answered candidly that he'd never given it much thought. His father had not been very interested in insurance policies.

The jovial man with the round face was filled with consternation, and he explained to Ove that it would be a veritable catastrophe for him if something happened to the house. After listening carefully to his many admonishments, Ove felt bound to agree with him. He had never given much thought to it until then. Which made him feel rather stupid now.

The man then asked if he might use the telephone; Ove said that would be fine. It turned out that his guest, grateful for a stranger's hospitality on a hot summer's day, had found a way of repaying his kindness. For it transpired that he actually worked for an insurance company, and was able to pull some strings to arrange an excellent quotation for Ove.

Ove was skeptical at first. He asked again about the man's credentials, which he was happy to reiterate. He then spent a considerable amount of time negotiating a better price.

"You're a tough businessman," said the man with the round face with a laugh. Ove felt surprisingly proud when he heard this—"a tough businessman." The man then glanced at his watch, thanked Ove, and said he'd best be on his way. As he left he gave Ove a piece of paper with his telephone number and said that he'd very much like to come by another day and have some more coffee and talk some more about house renovation. This was the first time anyone had ever expressed a wish to be Ove's friend.

Ove paid the man with the round face the full year's premium in cash. They shook hands.

The man with the round face never contacted him again. Ove tried to call him on one occasion but no one answered. He felt a quick stab of disappointment but decided not to think about it again. At least when salesmen called from other insurance companies he was able to say without any bad conscience that he was already insured. And that was something.

Ove continued avoiding his neighbors. He didn't want any problems with them. But unfortunately the problems seemed to have decided to seek out Ove instead. A few weeks after his house repairs were finished, one of his suited neighbors was burgled. It was the second burglary in the area in a relatively short period. The suits got together early next morning to deliberate on that young rascal in the condemned house, who must have had something to do with it. They knew very well "where he'd got the money for all that renovation." In the evening someone stuck a note under Ove's door, on which was written: "Clear off if you know what's good for you!" The night after that a stone was thrown through his window. Ove picked up the stone and changed the glass in the window. He never confronted the suits. Saw no purpose in it. But he wasn't going to move either.

Early the next morning he was woken by the smell of smoke.

He was out of his bed in an instant; the first thing that came into his head was that whoever had thrown that stone had apparently not finished yet. On his way down the stairs he instinctively grabbed a hammer. Not that Ove had ever been a violent man. But you could never be sure, he decided.

He was wearing only his underpants when he stepped onto the front veranda. All that lugging of construction materials in the last months had turned Ove into an impressively muscular young man without him even noticing. His bare upper body and the hammer swinging in his clenched right fist made the group gathered in the street momentarily take their eyes off the fire, and instinctively take a step back.

And that was when Ove realized that it was not his house that was burning, but his neighbor's.

The suits stood in the street, staring like deer into headlights. The elderly man emerged out of the smoke, his wife leaning on his arm. She was coughing terribly. When the elderly man handed her over to one of the suits' wives, and then turned back towards the fire, several of the suits cried out to him, telling him to leave it. "It's too late! Wait for the fire brigade!" they roared. The elderly man didn't listen. Burning material fell over the threshold as he tried to step inside into a sea of fire.

Ove stood in the face of the wind by his gate and saw how scattered glowing balls had already set the dry grass alight between his house and the neighbor's. For a few long-drawn-out seconds he evaluated the situation as best he could: the fire would be all over his house in a few minutes if he didn't charge off to get the water hose at once. He saw the elderly man trying to push his way past an overturned bookcase on his way into the house. The suits shouted his name and tried to make him stop, but the elderly man's wife was screaming out another name.

Their grandchild.

Ove rocked on his heels as he watched the embers stealing their way through the grass. In all honesty he was probably not thinking so much about what he wanted to do, but about what his father would have done. And as soon as that thought had taken root there was not much choice about it.

He muttered, irritated, looking at his house a last time, instinctively calculating to himself how many hours it had taken to build it. And then he ran towards the fire.

The house was so filled with thick, sticky smoke that it was like being struck in the face with a shovel. The elderly man struggled to move the fallen bookcase, which was blocking a door. Ove threw it aside as if it were made of paper and cleared a way up the stairs. By the time they emerged into the light of dawn, the elderly man was carrying the boy in his soot-covered arms. Ove had long, bleeding grazes across his chest and arms.

The bystanders just ran around panicking, screaming. The air was pierced by sirens. Uniformed firemen surrounded them.

Still wearing only his underpants and with aching lungs, Ove saw the first flames climbing his own house. He charged across the lawn but was immediately stopped by a group of firemen. They were everywhere, all of a sudden.

Refused to let him through.

A man in a white shirt, some sort of chief fireman as Ove understood it, stood before him with his legs wide apart and explained that they couldn't let him try to extinguish the fire in his own house. It was much too dangerous. Unfortunately, the white shirt explained after that, the fire brigade could not put it out either until they had the appropriate permissions from the authorities.

It turned out that because Ove's house now lay exactly on the municipal boundary, clearance from the command center was required on the shortwave radio before they could get to work. Permission had to be sought, papers had to be stamped.

"Rules are rules," the man in the white shirt explained in a monotone voice when Ove protested.

Ove tore himself free and ran in fury towards the water hose. But it was futile—by the time the firemen got the all-clear signal, the house was already engulfed by fire.

Ove stood in his garden and watched, helpless and in sorrow, as it burned.

When a few hours later he stood in a telephone booth calling the insurance company, he learned that they had never heard of the jovial man with the round face. There was no valid insurance policy on the house. The woman from the insurance company sighed, impatiently explaining that swindlers often went from door to door claiming to be from their company, and that she hoped at least Ove hadn't given him any cash.

Ove hung up, and clenched his fist in his pocket.

11

A MAN CALLED OVE AND A LANKY ONE WHO CAN'T OPEN A WINDOW WITHOUT FALLING OFF A LADDER

It's quarter to six and the first proper snowfall of the year has laid itself like a cold blanket over the slumbering community of row houses. Ove unhooks his jacket and goes outside for his daily inspection. With equal surprise and dissatisfaction, he sees the cat sitting in the snow outside his door. It seems to have been sitting there all night.

Ove slams the front door extra hard to scare it away. Apparently it doesn't have the common sense to take fright. Instead it just sits there in the snow, licking its stomach. Utterly unconcerned. Ove doesn't like that sort of behavior in a cat. He shakes his head and plants his feet firmly on the ground. The cat gives him the briefest of glances, clearly uninterested, then goes back to licking itself. Ove waves his arms at it. The cat doesn't budge an inch.

"This is private land!" says Ove.

When the cat still fails to give him any sort of acknowledgment,

Ove loses his patience and, in a sweeping movement, kicks one of his clogs towards it. Looking back, he couldn't swear that it wasn't intentional. His wife would have been furious if she'd seen it, of course.

It doesn't make much difference anyway. The clog flies in a smooth arc and passes a good yard and a half to the left of its intended target, before bouncing softly against the side of the shed and landing in the snow. The cat looks nonchalantly first at the clog, and then at Ove.

In the end it stands up, strolls around the corner of Ove's shed, and disappears.

Ove walks through the snow in his socks to fetch the clog. He glares at it, as if he feels it should be ashamed of itself for not having a better sense of aim. Then he pulls himself together and goes on his inspection tour.

Just because he's dying today doesn't mean that the vandals should be given free rein.

When he comes back to his house, he pushes his way through the snow and opens the door to the shed. It smells of mineral spirits and mold in there, exactly as it should in a shed. He steps over the Saab's summer tires and moves the jars of unsorted screws out of the way. Squeezes past the workbench, careful not to knock over the jars of mineral spirits with brushes in them. Lifts aside the garden chairs and the globe barbecue. Puts away the rim wrench and snatches up the snow shovel. Weighs it a bit in his hand, the way one might do with a two-handed sword. Stands there in silence, scrutinizing it.

When he comes out of the shed with the shovel, the cat is sitting in the snow again, right outside his house. Ove glares in amazement at its audacity. Its fur is thawing out, dripping. Or what remains of its fur. There are more bald patches than fur on that creature. It also has a long scar running along one eye, down across its nose. If cats have nine lives, this one is quite clearly working its way through at least the seventh or eighth of them.

"Clear off," says Ove.

The cat gives him a judgmental stare, as if it's sitting on the decision-making side of the desk at a job interview.

Ove grips the shovel, scoops up some snow, and throws it at the cat, which jumps out of the way and glares indignantly at him. Spits out a bit of snow. Snorts. Then turns around and pads off again, around the corner of Ove's shed.

Ove puts his snow shovel to work. It takes him fifteen minutes to free up the paving between the house and the shed. He works with care. Straight lines, even edges. People don't shovel snow that way anymore. Nowadays they just clear a way, they use snowblowers and all sorts of things. Any old method will do, scattering snow all over the place. As if that was the only thing that mattered in life: pushing one's way forward.

When he's done, he leans for a moment against the shovel in a snowdrift on the little pathway. Balances his body weight on it and watches the sun rising over the sleeping houses. He's been awake for most of the night, thinking of ways to die. He has even drawn some diagrams and charts to clarify the various methods. After carefully weighing up the pros and cons, he's accepted that what he's doing today has to be the best of bad alternatives. Admittedly he doesn't like the fact that the Saab will be left in neutral and use up a lot of expensive gas for no good reason afterwards, but it's simply a factor that he'll have to accept in order to get it done.

He puts the snow shovel back in the shed and goes into the

house. Puts on his good navy suit again. It will get stained and foul-smelling by the end of all this, but Ove has decided that his wife just has to go along with it, at least when he gets there.

He has his breakfast and listens to the radio. Washes up and wipes down the counter. Then goes around the house checking the radiators. Turns off all lights. Checks that the coffee percolator is unplugged. Puts on the blue jacket over his suit, then the clogs, and goes back into the shed; he returns with a long, rolled-up plastic tube. Locks the shed and the front door, tugs three times at each door handle. Then goes down the little pathway between the houses.

The white Škoda comes from the left and takes him by such surprise that he almost collapses in a snowdrift by the shed. Ove runs down the pathway in pursuit, shaking his fist.

"Can't you read, you bloody idiot!" he roars.

The driver, a slim man with a cigarette in his hand, seems to have heard him. When the Škoda turns off by the bike shed, their eyes meet through the side window. The man looks directly at Ove and rolls down his window. Lifts his eyebrows, disinterested.

"Motor vehicles prohibited!" Ove repeats, pointing at the sign where the very same message is written. He walks towards the Škoda with clenched fists.

The man hangs his left arm out of the window and unhurriedly taps the ash off his cigarette. His blue eyes are completely unmoved. He looks at Ove as one looks at an animal behind a fence. Devoid of aggression, totally indifferent. As if Ove were something the man might wipe off with a damp cloth.

"Read the si—" says Ove harshly as he gets closer, but the man has already rolled up his window.

Ove yells at the Škoda but the man ignores him. He doesn't even pull away with a wheel spin and screaming tires; he simply rolls off towards the garages and then onward to the main road, as if Ove's gesticulation was of no more consequence than a broken streetlight.

Ove stands rooted to the spot, so worked up that his fists are trembling. When the Škoda has disappeared he turns around and walks back between the houses, so hurried that he almost stumbles over his own legs. Outside Rune and Anita's house, where the white Škoda has quite clearly been parked, are two cigarette butts on the ground. Ove picks them up as if they were clues in a high-level criminal case.

"Hello, Ove," he hears Anita say, cautiously, behind him.

Ove turns towards her. She is standing on the step, wrapped in a gray cardigan. It looks as if it's trying to grab hold of her body, like two hands clutching a wet bar of soap.

"Yeah, yeah. Hello," answers Ove.

"He was from the council," she says, with a nod in the direction in which the Škoda drove off.

"Vehicles are prohibited in this area," says Ove.

She nods cautiously, again.

"He said he has special permission from the council to drive to the house."

"He doesn't have ANY bloody—" Ove begins, then stops himself and clamps his jaws around the words.

Anita's lips are trembling.

"They want to take Rune away from me," she says.

Ove nods without answering. He is still holding the plastic tube in his hand. He pushes his other clenched fist into his pocket. For a moment he thinks about saying something, but then he looks down, turns around, and leaves. He's already gone several yards when he realizes that he has the cigarette butts in his pocket, but by then it's too late to do anything about it.

Blond Weed is standing in the street. Mutt starts barking hysterically as soon as it catches sight of Ove. The door to the house behind them is open and Ove assumes they are standing there waiting for that thing known as Anders. Mutt has something like fur in its mouth; its owner grins with satisfaction. Ove stares at her as he goes past; she doesn't avert her eyes. Her grin gets even broader, as if she's grinning at Ove's expense.

When he passes between his house and that of the Lanky One and Pregnant Woman, he sees the Lanky One standing in the doorway.

"Hi there, Ove!" he calls out inanely.

Ove sees his ladder leaning up against the Lanky One's house. The Lanky One waves cheerfully. Apparently he's got up early today, or at least early by the standard of IT consultants. Ove can see that he's holding a blunt silver dinner knife in one hand. And he realizes he's most likely intending to use it to lever the jammed upstairs window. Ove's ladder, which the Lanky One is clearly about to scale, has been shoved at an angle into a deep snowdrift.

"Have a good day!"

"Yeah, yeah," answers Ove without turning around as he trudges past.

Mutt is outside that Anders thing's house, barking furiously. Out of the corner of his eye, Ove sees the Weed still standing there with a scorching smile in his direction. It disturbs Ove. He doesn't quite know the reason for it, but he feels a disturbance in his bones.

As he walks up between the houses, past the bicycle shed, and into the parking area, he reluctantly admits to himself that he's walking around looking for the cat, but he can't seem to find it anywhere.

He opens his garage door, unlocks the Saab, and then stands there, his hands in his pockets, for what must be in excess of a half hour. He doesn't quite know why he's doing it, he just feels that something like this requires some kind of sanctified silence before one heads off.

He considers whether the paintwork of the Saab will become terribly dirty as a result of this. He supposes so. It's a pity and a shame, he realizes, but not much can be done about it. He gives the tires a couple of evaluating kicks. They're in fine order, they really are. Good for at least another three winters, he estimates, judging by his last kick. Which quickly reminds him about the letter in the inside pocket of his jacket, so he fishes it out to check whether he has remembered to leave instructions about the summer tires. Yes, he has. It's written here under "Saab + Accessories." "Summer tires in the shed," and then clear instructions that even a genuine moron could understand about where the rim bolts can be found in the trunk. Ove slides the letter back into the envelope and puts it in the inside pocket of his jacket.

He glances over his shoulder into the parking area. Not because he's bothered about that damned cat, obviously. He just hopes nothing's happened to it, because then there'll be hell to pay from Ove's wife, he's quite sure about that. He just doesn't want a ticking-off because of the damned cat. That's all.

The sirens of an approaching ambulance can be heard in the distance, but he barely takes any notice. Just gets into the driver's seat and starts the engine. Opens the back electric window a couple of inches. Gets out of the car. Closes the garage door. Fixes the plastic tube tightly over the exhaust pipe. Watches the exhaust fumes slowly bubbling out of the other end of the tube. Then feeds the tube through the open back window. Gets into the car. Closes the door. Adjusts the wing mirrors. Fine-tunes the radio one step forward and one step back. Leans back in the seat. Closes his eyes. Feels the thick exhaust smoke, cubic inch by cubic inch, filling the garage and his lungs.

It wasn't supposed to be like this. You work and pay off the mortgage and pay taxes and do what you should. You marry. For better or for worse until death do us part, wasn't that what they agreed? Ove remembers quite clearly that it was. And she wasn't supposed to be the first one to die. Wasn't it bloody well understood that it was *his* death they were talking about? Well, wasn't it?

Ove hears a banging at the garage door. Ignores it. Straightens the creases of his trousers. Looks at himself in the rearview mirror. Wonders whether perhaps he should have put on a tie. She always liked it when he wore a tie. She looked at him then as the most handsome man in the world. He wonders if she will look at him now. If she'll be ashamed of him turning up in the afterlife unemployed and wearing a dirty suit. Will she think he's an idiot who can't even hold down an honest job without being phased out, just because his knowledge has been found wanting on account of some computer? Will she still look at him the way she used to, like a man who can be relied on? A man who can take responsibility for things and fix a water heater if necessary. Will she like him as much now that he's just an old person with no purpose in the world?

There's more frenetic banging at the garage door. Ove stares sourly at it. More banging. Ove thinks to himself that it's enough now.

"That will do!" he roars and opens the door of the Saab so abruptly that the plastic tube is dislodged from between the window and the molding and falls onto the concrete floor. Clouds of exhaust fumes pour out in all directions.

The Pregnant Foreign Woman should probably have learned by now not to stand so close to doors when Ove is on the other side. But this time she can't avoid getting the garage door right in her face when Ove throws it open violently.

Ove sees her and freezes. She's holding her nose. Looking at him with that distinct expression of someone who just had a garage door slammed into her nose. The exhaust fumes come pouring out of the garage in a dense cloud, covering half of the parking area in a thick, noxious mist.

"I . . . you have to bloo— you have to watch out when the door's being opened. . . ." Ove manages to say.

"What are you doing?" the Pregnant One manages to bite back at him, while watching the Saab with its engine idling and the exhaust spewing out of the mouth of the plastic tube on the floor.

"Me? . . . nothing," says Ove indignantly, looking as if he'd prefer to shut the garage door again.

Thick red drops are forming in her nostrils. She covers her face with one hand and waves at him with the other.

"I need a lift to the hospital," she says, tilting her head back.

Ove looks skeptical. "What the hell? Pull yourself together. It's just a nosebleed."

She swears in something Ove assumes is Farsi and clamps the bridge of her nose hard between her thumb and index finger. Then she shakes her head impatiently, dripping blood all over her jacket.

"Not because of the nosebleed!"

Ove's a bit puzzled by that. Puts his hands in his pockets.

"No, no. Well then."

She groans.

"Patrick fell off the ladder."

She leans her head back, so that Ove stands there talking to the underside of her chin.

"Who's Patrick?" Ove asks the chin.

"My husband," the chin answers.

"The Lanky One?" asks Ove.

"That's him, yeah," says the chin.

"And he fell off the ladder?" Ove clarifies.

"Yes. When he was opening the window."

"Right. What a bloody surprise; you could see that one coming from a mile away. . . ."

The chin disappears and the large brown eyes reappear.

They don't look entirely pleased.

"Are we going to have a debate about this or what?"

Ove scratches his head, slightly bothered.

"No, no . . . but can't you drive yourself? In that little Japanese sewing machine you arrived in the other day?" he tries to protest.

"I don't have a driver's license," she replies, mopping blood from her lip.

"What do you mean you don't have a driver's license?" asks Ove, as if her words are utterly inexplicable to him.

Again she sighs impatiently.

"Look, I don't have a driver's license and that's all, what's the problem?"

"How old are you?" Ove asks, almost fascinated now.

"Thirty," she says impatiently.

"*Thirty?!* And no driver's license? Is there something wrong with you?"

She groans, holding one hand over her nose and snapping her fingers with irritation in front of Ove's face.

"Focus a bit, Ove! The hospital! You have to drive us to the hospital!"

Ove looks almost offended.

"What do you mean, 'us'? You'll have to call an ambulance if the person you're married to can't open a window without falling off a ladder—"

"I already did! They've taken him to the hospital. But there was no space for me in the ambulance. And now because of the snow, every taxi in town is occupied and the buses are getting bogged down everywhere!"

Scattered streams of blood are running down one of her cheeks. Ove clamps his jaws so hard that he starts gnashing his teeth.

"You can't trust bloody buses. The drivers are always drunks," he says quietly, his chin at an angle that might make someone believe he was trying to hide his words on the inside of his shirt collar.

Maybe she notices the way his mood shifts as soon as she mentions the word "bus." Maybe not. Anyway, she nods, as if this in some way clinches it.

"Right, then. So you have to drive us."

Ove makes a courageous attempt to point threateningly at her. But to his own dismay he feels it's not as convincing as he might have hoped.

"There are no have-tos around here. I'm not some bloody mobility service!" he manages to say at last.

But she just squeezes her index finger and thumb even harder around the bridge of her nose. And nods, as if she has not in any way listened to what he just said. She waves, with irritation, towards the garage and the plastic tube on the floor spewing out exhaust fumes thicker and thicker against the ceiling.

"I don't have time to fuss about this anymore. Get things ready so we can leave. I'll go and get the children."

"The CHILDREN???" Ove shouts after her, without getting any kind of answer.

She's already swanned off on those tiny feet that look wholly undersized for that large pregnant bump, disappearing around the corner of the bicycle shed and down towards the houses.

Ove stays where he is, as if waiting for someone to catch up with her and tell her that actually Ove had not finished talking. But no one does. He tucks his fists into his belt and throws a glance at the tube on the floor. It's actually not his responsibility if people can't manage to stay on the ladders they borrow from him—that's his own view.

But of course he can't avoid thinking about what his wife would have told him to do under the circumstances, if she'd been here. And of course it's not so difficult to work it out, Ove realizes. Sadly enough.

At long last he walks up to the car and pokes off the tube from the exhaust pipe with his shoe. Gets into the Saab. Checks his mirrors. Puts it into first and pulls out into the parking area. Not that he cares particularly about how the Pregnant Foreign Woman gets to the hospital. But Ove knows very well that there'll be no end of nagging from his wife if the last thing Ove does in this life is to give a pregnant woman a nosebleed and then abandon her to take the bus.

And if the gas is going to be used up anyway, he may as well give her a lift there and back. Maybe then that woman will leave me in peace, thinks Ove.

But of course she doesn't.

12

A MAN WHO WAS OVE AND ONE DAY HE HAD ENOUGH

People always said Ove and Ove's wife were like night and day. Ove realized full well, of course, that he was the night. It didn't matter to him. On the other hand it always amused his wife when someone said it, because she could then point out while giggling that people only thought Ove was the night because he was too mean to turn on the sun.

He never understood why she chose him. She loved only abstract things like music and books and strange words. Ove was a man entirely filled with tangible things. He liked screwdrivers and oil filters. He went through life with his hands firmly shoved into his pockets. She danced.

"You only need one ray of light to chase all the shadows away," she said to him once, when he asked her why she had to be so upbeat the whole time.

Apparently some monk called Francis had written as much in one of her books.

"You don't fool me, darling," she said with a playful little smile and crept into his big arms. "You're dancing on the inside,

Ove, when no one's watching. And I'll always love you for that. Whether you like it or not."

Ove never quite fathomed what she meant by that. He'd never been one for dancing. It seemed far too haphazard and giddy. He liked straight lines and clear decisions. That was why he had always liked mathematics. There were right or wrong answers there. Not like the other hippie subjects they tried to trick you into doing at school, where you could "argue your case." As if that was a way of concluding a discussion: checking who knew more long words. Ove wanted what was right to be right, and what was wrong to be wrong.

He knew very well that some people thought he was nothing but a grumpy old sod without any faith in people. But, to put it bluntly, that was because people had never given him reason to see it another way.

Because a time comes in every man's life when he decides what sort of man he's going to be: the kind who lets other people walk all over him, or not.

Ove slept in the Saab the nights after the fire. The first morning he tried to clear up among the ashes and destruction. The second morning he had to accept that this would never sort itself out. The house was lost, and all the work he had put into it.

On the third morning two men, wearing the same kind of white shirt as that chief fireman, turned up. They stood by his gate, apparently quite unmoved by the ruin in front of them. They didn't present themselves by name, only mentioned the name of the authority they came from. As if they were robots sent out by the mother ship.

"We've been sending you letters," said one of the white shirts, holding out a pile of documents for Ove.

"Many letters," said the other white shirt and made a note in a pad.

"You never answered," said the first, as if he were reprimanding a dog.

Ove just stood there, defiant.

"Very unfortunate, this," said the other, with a curt nod at what used to be Ove's house.

Ove nodded.

"The fire brigade says it was caused by a harmless electrical fault," continued the first white shirt robotically, pointing at a paper in his hand.

Ove felt a spontaneous objection to his use of the word "harmless."

"We've sent you letters," the second man repeated, waving his pad. "The municipal boundaries are being redrawn."

"The land where your house stands will be developed for a number of new constructions."

"The land where your house *stood*," corrected his partner.

"The council is willing to purchase your land at the market price," said the first man.

"Well . . . a market price now that there's no longer a house on the land," clarified the other.

Ove took the papers. Started reading.

"You don't have much of a choice," said the first.

"This is not so much your choice as the council's," said the other.

The first man tapped his pen impatiently against the papers, pointing at a line at the bottom where it said "signature."

Ove stood at his gate and read their document in silence. He became aware of an ache in his breast; it took a long, long time before he understood what it was.

Hate.

He hated those men in white shirts. He couldn't remember having hated anyone before, but now it was like a ball of fire inside. Ove's parents had bought this house. Ove had grown up here. Learned to walk. His father had taught him everything there was to know about a Saab engine here. And after all that, someone at a municipal authority decided something else should be built here. And a man with a round face sold insurance that was not insurance. A man in a white shirt prevented Ove from putting out a fire and now two other white shirts stood here talking about a "market price."

But Ove really did not have a choice. He could have stood there until the sun had completely risen, but he could not change the situation.

So he signed their document. While keeping his fist clenched in his pocket.

He left the plot where once his parental home had stood, and he never looked back. Rented a little room from an old lady in town. Sat and stared desolately at the wall all day. In the evening he went to work. Cleaned the train compartments. In the morning, he and the other workers were told not to go to their usual changing rooms; they had to go back to the head office to pick up new sets of work clothes.

As Ove was walking down the corridor he met Tom. It was the first time they had seen each other since Ove got blamed for the theft from the carriage. A more sensible man than Tom would probably have avoided eye contact. Or tried to pretend that the incident had never happened. But Tom was not a more sensible sort of man.

"Well, if it isn't the little thief!" he exclaimed with a combative smile.

Ove didn't answer. Tried to get past but got a hard elbow from one of the younger colleagues Tom surrounded himself with. Ove looked up. The younger colleague was smiling disdainfully at him.

"Hold on to your wallets, the thief's here!" Tom called out so loudly that his voice echoed through the corridors.

With one hand, Ove took a firmer grip on the pile of clothes in his arm. But he clenched his fist in his pocket. Went into an empty changing room. Took off his dirty old work clothes, unclipped his father's dented wristwatch and put it on the bench. When he turned around to go into the shower, Tom was standing in the doorway.

"We heard about the fire," he said. Ove could see that Tom was hoping he'd answer.

"That father of yours would have been proud of you! Not even he was useless enough to burn down his own bloody house!" Tom called out to him as he was stepping into the shower.

Ove heard his younger colleagues all laughing together. He closed his eyes, leaned his forehead against the wall, and let the hot water flow over him. Stood there for more than twenty minutes. The longest shower he'd ever had.

When he came out, his father's watch was gone. Ove rooted among the clothes on the bench, searched the floor, fine-combed all the lockers.

A time comes in every man's life when he decides what sort of man he is going to be. Whether he is the kind who lets other people tread on him, or not.

Maybe it was because Tom had put the blame on him for the theft in the carriage. Maybe it was the fire. Maybe it was the bogus insurance agent. Or the white shirts. Or maybe it was just enough now. There and then, it was as if someone had removed a fuse in Ove's mind. Everything in his eyes grew a shade darker. He walked out of the changing room, still naked and with water dripping from his flexing muscles. Walked to the end of the corridor to the foremen's changing room, kicked the door open, and cleared a way through the astonished press of men inside. Tom was standing in front of a mirror at the far end, trimming his bushy beard. Ove gripped him by the shoulder and roared so loudly that the sheet-metal-covered walls echoed.

"Give me back my watch!"

Tom, with a superior expression, looked down at his face. His dark figure towered over Ove like a shadow.

"I don't have your bloo—"

"GIVE IT HERE!" Ove bellowed before Tom had reached the end of the sentence, so fiercely that the other men in the room saw fit to move a little closer to their lockers.

A second later Tom's jacket had been ripped away from him with such power that he didn't even think of protesting. He just stood there like a punished child as Ove hauled out his wristwatch from the inside pocket.

And then Ove hit him. Just once. It was enough. Tom collapsed like a sack of wet flour. By the time the heavy body hit the floor, Ove had already turned and walked away.

A time like that comes for every man, when he chooses what

sort of man he wants to be. And if you don't know the story, you don't know the man.

Tom was taken to the hospital. Again and again he was asked what had happened, but Tom's eyes just flickered and he mumbled something about having slipped. And strangely enough, none of the other men who'd been in the changing rooms at the time had any recollection of what had happened.

That was the last time Ove saw Tom. And, he decided, the last time he'd let anyone trick him.

He kept his job as a night cleaner, but he gave up his job at the construction site. He no longer had a house to build, and anyway he'd learned so much about construction by this point that the men in their hard hats no longer had anything to teach him.

They gave him a toolbox as a farewell present. This time with new-bought tools. "To the puppy. To help you build something that lasts," they'd written on a piece of paper.

Ove had no immediate use for it, so he carried it about aimlessly for a few days. Finally the old lady renting him a room took pity on him and started looking for things around the house for him to mend. It was more peaceful that way for both of them.

Later that year he enlisted for military service. He scored the highest possible mark for every physical test. The recruitment officer liked this taciturn young man who seemed as strong as a bear, and he pressed him to consider a career as a professional soldier. Ove thought it sounded good. Military personnel wore uniforms and followed orders. All knew what they were doing. All had a function. Things had a place. Ove felt he could actually be good as a soldier. In fact, as he went down the stairs to have his obligatory medical examination, he felt lighter in his heart than he had for many years. As if he had been given a sudden purpose. A goal. Something to be.

His joy lasted no more than ten minutes.

The recruitment officer had said that the medical examination was a "mere formality." But when the stethoscope was held against Ove's chest, something was heard that should not have been heard. He was sent to a doctor in the city. A week later he was informed that he had a rare congenital heart condition. He was exempted from any further military service. Ove called and protested. He wrote letters. He went to three other doctors in the hope that a mistake had been made. It was no use.

"Rules are rules," said a white-shirted man in the army's administrative offices the last time Ove went there to try to overturn the decision. Ove was so disappointed that he did not even wait for the bus; instead he walked all the way back to the train station. He sat on the platform, more despondent than at any time since his father's death.

A few months later he would walk down that platform with the woman he was destined to marry. But at that precise moment, of course, he had no idea of this.

He went back to his work as a night cleaner on the railways. Grew quieter than ever. The old lady whose room he rented eventually grew so tired of his gloomy face that she arranged for him to borrow a nearby garage. After all, the boy had that car he was always fiddling with, she said. Maybe he could keep himself entertained with all that?

Ove took his entire Saab to pieces in the garage the next morning. He cleaned all the parts, and then put them together again. To see if he could do it. And to have something to do.

When he was done with it, he sold the Saab at a profit and bought a newer but otherwise identical Saab 93. The first thing he did was to take it to pieces. To see if he could manage it. And he could.

His days passed like this, slow and methodical. And then one morning he saw her. She had brown hair and blue eyes and red shoes and a big yellow clasp in her hair.

And then there was no more peace and quiet for Ove.

13

A MAN CALLED OVE AND A CLOWN CALLED BEPPO

"Ove's funny," titters the three-year-old with delight.

"Yeah," the seven-year-old mumbles, not at all as impressed. She takes her little sister by the hand and walks with grown-up steps towards the hospital entrance.

Their mother looks as if she's going to have a go at Ove, but seems to decide that there's no time for that. She waddles off towards the entrance, one hand on her pouting belly, as if concerned that the child may try to escape.

Ove walks behind, dragging his steps. He doesn't care that she thinks "it's easier just to pay up and stop arguing." Because it's actually about the principle. Why is that parking attendant entitled to give Ove a ticket for questioning why one has to pay for hospital parking? Ove is not the sort of man who'll stop himself from roaring: "You're just a fake policeman!" at a parking attendant. That's all there is to say about it.

You go to the hospital to die, Ove knows that. It's enough that the state wants to be paid for everything you do while you're alive. When it also wants to be paid for the parking when you go to die,

Ove thinks that's about far enough. He explained this in so many words to the parking attendant. And that's when the parking attendant started waving his book at him. And that's when Parvaneh started raging about how she'd be quite happy to pay up. As if *that* was the important part of the discussion.

Women don't seem to get principles.

He hears the seven-year-old complaining in front of him that her clothes are smelling of exhaust. Even though they kept the Saab's windows rolled down all the way, it wasn't possible to get rid of the stench. Their mother had asked Ove what he'd really been doing in the garage, but Ove had just answered with a sound more or less like when you try to move a bathtub by dragging it across some tiles. Of course, for the three-year-old it was the greatest adventure of her life to be able to drive along in a car with all its windows down although it was below freezing outside. The seven-year-old, on the other hand, had burrowed her face into her scarf and vented a good deal more skepticism. She'd been irritated about slipping around with her bottom on the sheets of newspaper Ove had spread across the seat to stop them "filthifying things." Ove had also spread newspaper on the front seat, but her mother snatched it away before she sat down. Ove had looked more than advisably displeased about this, but managed not to say anything. Instead he constantly glanced at her stomach all the way to the hospital, as if anxious that she might suddenly start leaking on the upholstery.

"Stand still here now," she says to the girls when they are in the hospital reception.

They're surrounded by glass walls and benches smelling of disinfectant. There are nurses in white clothes and colorful plastic slippers and old people dragging themselves back and forth in the corridors, leaning on rickety walkers. On the floor is a sign announcing that Elevator 2 in Entrance A is out of order, and that visitors to Ward 114 are therefore asked to go to Elevator 1 in Entrance C. Beneath that is another message, announcing that Elevator 1 in Entrance C is out of order and visitors to Ward 114 are asked to go to Elevator 2 in Entrance A. Under that message is a third message, announcing that Ward 114 is closed this month because of repairs. Under that message is a picture of a clown, informing people that Beppo the hospital clown is visiting sick children today.

"Where did Ove get to now?" Parvaneh bursts out.

"He went to the bathroom, I think," mumbles the seven-year-old.

"Clauwn!" says the three-year-old, pointing happily at the sign.

"Do you know you have to *pay* them here to go to the bathroom?" Ove exclaims incredulously.

Parvaneh spins around and gives Ove a harassed look.

"Do you need change?"

Ove looks offended.

"Why would I need change?"

"For the bathroom?"

"I don't need to go to the bathroom."

"But you said—" she begins, then stops herself and shakes her head. "Forget it, just forget it. . . . When does the parking meter run out?" she asks instead.

"Ten minutes."

She groans.

"Don't you understand it'll take longer than ten minutes?"

"In that case I'll go out and feed the meter in ten minutes," says Ove, as if this was quite obvious.

"Why don't you just pay for longer and save yourself the

bother?" she asks and looks like she wishes she hadn't as soon as the question crosses her lips.

"Because that's exactly what they want! They're not getting a load of money for time we might not even *use*!"

"Oh, I don't have the strength for this. . . ." sighs Parvaneh and holds her forehead.

She looks at her daughters.

"Will you sit here nicely with Uncle Ove while Mum goes to see how Dad is? Please?"

"Yeah, yeah," agrees the seven-year-old grumpily.

"Yeeeees!" the three-year-old shrieks with excitement.

"What?" whispers Ove.

Parvaneh stands up.

"What do you mean, 'with Ove'? Where do you think you're going?" To his great consternation, the Pregnant One seems not to register the level of upset in his voice.

"You have to sit here and keep an eye on them," she states curtly and disappears down the corridor before Ove can raise further objections.

Ove stands there staring after her. As if he is expecting her to come rushing back and cry out that she was only joking. But she doesn't. So Ove turns to the girls. And in the next second he looks as if he's just about to shine a desk lamp into their eyes and interrogate them on their whereabouts at the time of the murder.

"BOOK!" screams the three-year-old at once and rushes off towards the corner of the waiting room, where there's a veritable chaos of toys, games, and picture books.

Ove nods and, having confirmed to himself that this three-year-old seems to be reasonably self-motivating, he turns his attention to the seven-year-old.

"Right, and what about you?"

"What do you mean, me?" she counters with indignation.

"Do you need food or do you have to go for a wee or anything like that?"

The child looks at him as if he just offered her a beer and a cigarette.

"I'm almost EIGHT! I can go to the bathroom MYSELF!"

Ove throws out his arms abruptly.

"Sure, sure. So bloody sorry for asking."

"Mmm," she snorts.

"You swored!" yells the three-year-old as she turns up again, running to and fro between Ove's trouser legs.

He skeptically peruses this grammatically challenged little natural disaster. She looks up and her whole face smiles at him.

"Read!" she orders him in an excitable manner, holding up a book with her arms stretched out so far that she almost loses her balance.

Ove looks at the book more or less as if it just sent him a chain letter insisting that the book was really a Nigerian prince who had a "very lucrative investment opportunity" for Ove and now only needed Ove's account number "to sort something out."

"Read!" she demands again, climbing the bench in the waiting room with surprising agility.

Ove reluctantly sits about a yard away on the bench. The three-year-old sighs impatiently and disappears from sight, her head reappearing seconds later under his arm with her hands leaning against his knee for support and her nose pressed against the colorful pictures in the book.

"Once upon a time there was a little train," reads Ove, with all the enthusiasm of someone reciting a tax statement.

Then he turns the page. The three-year-old stops him and goes back. The seven-year-old shakes her head tiredly.

"You have to say what happens on that page as well. And do voices," she says.

Ove stares at her.

"What bloo—"

He clears his throat midsentence.

"What voices?" he corrects himself.

"Fairy-tale voices," replies the seven-year-old.

"You swored," the three-year-old announces with glee.

"Did not," says Ove.

"Yes," says the three-year-old.

"We're not doing any bloo—we're not doing any voices!"

"Maybe you're no good at reading stories," notes the seven-year-old.

"Maybe you're no good at listening to them!" Ove counters.

"Maybe you're no good at TELLING THEM!"

Ove looks at the book, very unimpressed.

"What kind of sh—nonsense is this anyway? Some talking train? Is there nothing about cars?"

"Maybe there's something about nutty old men instead," mutters the seven-year-old.

"I'm not an 'old man,'" Ove hisses.

"Clauwn!" the three-year-old cries out jubilantly.

"And I'm not a CLOWN either!" he roars.

The older one rolls her eyes at Ove, not unlike the way her mother often rolls her eyes at Ove.

"She doesn't mean you. She means the clown."

Ove looks up and catches sight of a full-grown man who's quite seriously got himself dressed up as a clown, standing in the doorway of the waiting room.

He's got a big stupid grin on his face as well.

"CLAAUUWN," the toddler howls, jumping up and down on the bench in a way that finally convinces Ove that the kid is on drugs.

He's heard about that sort of thing. They have that attention-deficit hyperactivity disorder and get to take amphetamines on prescription.

"And who's this little girl here, then? Does she want to see a magic trick, perhaps?" the clown exclaims helpfully and squelches over to them like a drunken moose in a pair of large red shoes which, Ove confirms to himself, only an utterly meaningless person would prefer to wear rather than getting himself a proper job.

The clown looks gaily at Ove.

"Has Uncle got a five-kronor piece, perhaps?"

"No, Uncle doesn't, perhaps," Ove replies.

The clown looks surprised. Which isn't an entirely successful look for a clown.

"But . . . listen, it's a magic trick, you do have a coin on you, don't you?" mumbles the clown in his more normal voice, which contrasts quite strongly with his character and reveals that behind this idiotic clown a quite ordinary idiot is hiding, probably all of twenty-five years old.

"Come on, I'm a hospital clown. It's for the children's sake. I'll give it back."

"Just give him a five-kronor coin," says the seven-year-old.

"CLAAUUWN!" screams the three-year-old.

Ove peers down with exasperation at the tiny speech defect and wrinkles his nose.

"Right," he says, taking out a five-kronor piece from his wallet.

Then he points at the clown.

"But I want it back. Immediately. I'm paying for the parking with that."

The clown nods eagerly and snatches the coin out of his hand.

Minutes later, Parvaneh comes back down the corridor to the waiting room. She stops, confusedly scanning the room from side to side.

"Are you looking for your girls?" a nurse asks sharply behind her.

"Yes," Parvaneh answers, perplexed.

"There," says the nurse in a not entirely appreciative way and points at a bench by the large glass doors leading onto the parking area.

Ove is sitting there with his arms crossed, looking very angry.

On one side of him sits the seven-year-old, staring up at the ceiling with an utterly bored expression, and on the other side sits the three-year-old, looking as if she just found out she's going to have an ice cream breakfast every day for a whole month. On either side of the bench stand two particularly large representatives of the hospital's security guards, both with very grim facial expressions.

"Are these your children?" one of them asks. He doesn't look at all as if he's having an ice cream breakfast.

"Yes, what did they do?" Parvaneh wonders, almost terrified.

"*They* didn't do anything," the other security guard replies, with a hostile stare at Ove.

"Me neither," Ove mutters sulkily.

"Ove hit the clauwn!" the three-year-old shrieks delightedly.

"Sneak," says Ove.

Parvaneh stares at him, agape, and can't even think of anything to say.

"He was no good at magic anyway," the seven-year-old groans. "Can we go home now?" she asks, standing up.

"Why . . . hold on . . . what . . . what clown?"

"The clauwn Beppo," the toddler explains, nodding wisely.

"He was going to do magic," says her sister.

"Stupid magic," says Ove.

"Like, he was going to make Ove's five-kronor coin go away," the seven-year-old elaborates.

"And then he tried to give back *another* five-kronor coin!" Ove interjects, with an insulted stare at the nearby security guards, as if this should be enough of an explanation.

"Ove HIT the clauwn, Mum," the three-year-old titters as if this was the best thing that ever happened in her whole life.

Parvaneh stares for a long time at Ove, the three-year-old, seven-year-old, and the two security guards.

"We're here to visit my husband. He's had an accident. I'm bringing in the children now to say hello to him," she explains to the guards.

"Daddy fall!" says the three-year-old.

"That's fine." One of the security guards nods.

"But this one stays here," confirms the other security guard and points at Ove.

"I hardly hit him. I just gave him a little poke," Ove mumbles, adding, "Bloody fake policemen," just to be on the safe side.

"Honestly, he was no good at magic anyway," says the

seven-year-old grumpily in Ove's defense as they leave to visit their father.

An hour later they are back at Ove's garage. The Lanky One has one arm and one leg in casts and has to stay at the hospital for several days, Ove has been informed by Parvaneh. When she told him, Ove had to bite his lip very hard to stop himself laughing. He actually got the feeling Parvaneh was doing the same thing. The Saab still smells of exhaust when he collects the sheets of newspaper from the seats.

"Please, Ove, are you sure you won't let me pay the parking fine?" says Parvaneh.

"Is it your car?" Ove grunts.

"No."

"Well then," he replies.

"But it feels a bit like it was my fault," she says, concerned.

"You don't hand out parking fines. The council does. So it's the bloody council's fault," says Ove and closes the door of the Saab. "And those fake policemen at the hospital," he adds, clearly still very upset that they forced him to sit without moving on that bench until Parvaneh came back to pick him up and they went home. As if he couldn't be trusted to wander about freely among the other hospital visitors.

Parvaneh looks at him for a long time in thoughtful silence. The seven-year-old gets tired of waiting and starts walking across the parking area towards the house. The three-year-old looks at Ove with a radiant smile.

"You're funny!" she declares.

Ove looks at her and puts his hands in his trouser pockets.

"Uh-huh, uh-huh. You shouldn't turn out too bad yourself."

The three-year-old nods excitedly. Parvaneh looks at Ove, looks at the plastic tube on the floor of his garage. Looks at Ove again, a touch worried.

"I could do with a bit of help taking the ladder away. . . ." she says, as if she was in the middle of a much longer thought.

Ove kicks distractedly at the asphalt.

"And I think we have a radiator, as well, that doesn't work," she adds—a passing thought. "Would be nice of you if you could have a look at it. Patrick doesn't know how to do things like that, you know," she says and takes the three-year-old by the hand.

Ove nods slowly.

"No. Might have known."

Parvaneh nods. Then she suddenly gives off a satisfied smile. "And you can't let the girls freeze to death tonight, Ove, right? It's quite enough that they had to watch you assault a clown, no?"

Ove gives her a dour glance. Silently, to himself, as if negotiating, he concedes that he can hardly let the children perish just because their no-good father can't open a window without falling off a ladder. There'd be a hellish amount of nagging from Ove's wife if he went and arrived in the next world as a newly qualified child murderer.

Then he picks up the plastic tube from the floor and hangs it up on a hook on the wall. Locks the Saab with the key. Closes the garage. Tugs at it three times to make sure it's closed. Then goes to fetch his tools from the shed.

Tomorrow's as good a day as any to kill oneself.

14

A MAN WHO WAS OVE AND A WOMAN ON A TRAIN

She had a golden brooch pinned to her dress, in which the sunlight reflected hypnotically through the train window. It was half past six in the morning, Ove had just clocked off his shift and was actually supposed to be taking the train home the other way. But then he saw her on the platform with all her rich auburn hair and her blue eyes and all her effervescent laughter. And he got back on the outbound train. Of course, he didn't quite know himself why he was doing it. He had never been spontaneous before in his life. But when he saw her it was as if something malfunctioned.

He convinced one of the conductors to lend him his spare pair of trousers and shirt, so he didn't have to look like a train cleaner, and then Ove went to sit by Sonja. It was the single best decision he would ever make.

He didn't know what he was going to say. But he had hardly had time to sink into the seat before she turned to him cheerfully, smiled warmly, and said hello. And he found he was able to say hello back to her without any significant complications. And when she saw that he was looking at the pile of books she had in her lap, she tilted them slightly so he could read their titles. Ove understood only about half the words.

"You like reading?" she asked him brightly.

Ove shook his head with some insecurity, but it didn't seem to concern her very much. She just smiled, said that she loved books more than anything, and started telling him excitedly what each of the ones in her lap was about. And Ove realized that he wanted to hear her talking about the things she loved for the rest of his life.

He had never heard anything quite as amazing as that voice. She talked as if she were continuously on the verge of breaking into giggles. And when she giggled she sounded the way Ove imagined champagne bubbles would have sounded if they were capable of laughter. He didn't quite know what he should say to avoid seeming uneducated and stupid, but it proved to be less of a problem than he had thought.

She liked talking and Ove liked keeping quiet. Retrospectively, Ove assumed that was what people meant when they said that people were compatible.

Many years later she told him that she had found him quite puzzling when he came to sit with her in that compartment. Abrupt and blunt in his whole being. But his shoulders were broad and his arms so muscular that they stretched the fabric of his shirt. And he had kind eyes. He listened when she talked, and she liked making him smile. Anyway, the journey to school was so boring that it was pleasant just to have some company.

She was studying to be a teacher. Came on the train every day; after a couple miles she changed to another train, then a bus. All in all, it was a one-and-a-half-hour journey in the wrong direction for Ove. Only when they crossed the platform that first time, side by side, and stood by her bus stop, did she ask what he was doing there. And when Ove realized that he was only five or so kilometers from the military barracks where he would have been had it not been for that problem with his heart, the words slipped out of him before he understood why.

"I'm doing my military service over there," he said, waving vaguely.

"So maybe we'll see each other on the train going back as well. I go home at five. . . ."

Ove couldn't think of anything to say. He knew, of course, that one does not go home from military installations at five o'clock, but she clearly did not. So he just shrugged. And then she got on her bus and was gone.

Ove decided that this was undoubtedly very impractical in many ways. But there was not a lot to be done about it. So he turned around, found a signpost pointing the way to the little center of the tiny student town where he now found himself, at least a two-hour journey from his home. And then he started walking. After forty-five minutes he asked his way to the only tailor in the area, and, after eventually finding the shop, ponderously stepped inside to ask whether it would be possible to have a shirt ironed and a pair of trousers pressed and, if so, how long it would take. "Ten minutes, if you wait," came his answer.

"Then I'll be back at four," said Ove and left. He wandered back down to the train station and lay down on a bench in the waiting hall. At quarter past three he went all the way back to the tailor's, had his shirt and trousers pressed while he sat waiting in his underwear in the staff restroom, then walked back to the station and took the train with her for an hour and a half back to her station. And then traveled for another half hour to his own station.

He repeated the whole thing the day after. And the day after that. On the following day the man from the ticket desk at the train station intervened and made it clear to Ove that he couldn't sleep here like some loafer, surely he could understand that? Ove saw the point he was making, but explained that there was a woman at stake here. When he heard this, the man from the ticket desk gave him a little nod and from then on let him sleep in the left-luggage room. Even men at train station ticket desks have been in love.

Ove did the same thing every day for three months. In the end she grew tired of his never inviting her out for dinner. So she invited herself instead.

"I'll be waiting here tomorrow evening at eight o'clock. I want you to be wearing a suit and I'd like you to invite me out for dinner," she said succinctly as she stepped off the train one Friday evening.

And so it was.

Ove had never been asked how he lived before he met her. But if anyone had asked him, he would have answered that he didn't.

On Saturday evening he put on his father's old brown suit. It was tight around his shoulders. Then he ate two sausages and seven potatoes, which he prepared in the little kitchenette in his room, before doing his rounds of the house to put in a couple of screws, which the old lady had asked him to do.

"Are you meeting someone?" she asked, pleased to see him coming down the stairs. She had never seen him wearing a suit. Ove nodded gruffly.

"Yeah," he said in a way that could be described as either a word or an inhalation. The older woman nodded and probably tried to hide a little smile.

"It must be someone very special if you've dressed yourself up like that," she said.

Ove inhaled again and nodded curtly. When he was at the door, she called out from the kitchen.

"Flowers, Ove!"

Perplexed, Ove stuck his head around the partition wall and stared at her.

"She'd probably like some flowers," the old woman declared with some emphasis.

Ove cleared his throat and closed the front door.

For more than fifteen minutes he stood waiting for her at the station in his tight-fitting suit and his new-polished shoes. He was skeptical about people who came late. "If you can't depend on someone being on time, you shouldn't trust 'em with anything more important either," he used to mutter when people came dribbling along with their time cards three or four minutes late, as if this didn't matter. As if the railway line would just lie there waiting for them in the morning and not have something better to do.

So for each of those fifteen minutes that Ove stood waiting at the station he was slightly irritated. And then the irritation turned into a certain anxiety, and after that he decided that Sonja had only been ribbing him when she'd suggested they should meet. He had never felt so silly in his entire life. Of course she didn't want to go out with him, how could he have got that into his head? His humiliation, when the insight dawned on him, welled up like a stream of lava, and he was tempted to toss the flowers in the nearest trash can and march off without turning around.

Looking back, he couldn't quite explain why he stayed. Maybe because he felt, in spite of it all, that an agreement to meet was an agreement. And maybe there was some other reason. Something a little harder to put his finger on. He didn't know it at that moment, of course, but he was destined to spend so many quarter hours of his life waiting for her that his old father would have gone cross-eyed if he'd found out. And when she did finally turn up, in a long floral-print skirt and a cardigan so red that it made Ove shift his weight from his right foot to his left, he decided that maybe her inability to be on time was not the most important thing.

The woman at the florist's had asked him what he wanted. He informed her gruffly that this was a bit of a bloody question to ask. After all, she was the one who sold the greens and he the one who bought them, not the other way around. The woman had looked a bit bothered about that, but then she asked if the recipient of the flowers had some favorite color, perhaps? "Pink," Ove had said with great certainty, although he did not know.

And now she stood outside the station with his flowers pressed happily to her breast, in that red cardigan of hers, making the rest of the world look as if it were made in grayscale.

"They're absolutely beautiful," she said, smiling in that candid way that made Ove stare down at the ground and kick at the gravel.

Ove wasn't much for restaurants. He had never understood why one would ever eat out for a lot of money when one could eat at home. He wasn't so taken with show-off furniture and elaborate cooking, and he was very much aware of his conversational shortcomings as well. Whatever the case, he had eaten in advance so he could afford to let her order whatever she wanted from the menu, while opting for the cheapest dish for himself. And at least if she asked him something he wouldn't have his mouth full of food. To him it seemed like a good plan.

While she was ordering, the waiter smiled ingratiatingly. Ove knew all too well what both he and the other diners in the restaurant had thought when they came in. She was too good for Ove, that's what they'd thought. And Ove felt very silly about that. Mostly because he entirely agreed with their opinion.

She told him with great animation about her studies, about books she'd read or films she'd seen. And when she looked at Ove she made him feel, for the first time, that he was the only man in the world. And Ove had enough integrity to realize that this wasn't right, that he couldn't sit here lying any longer. So he cleared his throat, collected his faculties, and told her the whole truth. That he wasn't doing his military service at all, that in fact he was just a simple cleaner on the trains who had a defective heart and who had lied for no other reason than that he enjoyed riding with her on the train so very much. He assumed this would be the only dinner he ever had with her, and he did not think she deserved having it with a fraudster. When he had finished his story he put his napkin on the table and got out his wallet to pay.

"I'm sorry," he mumbled, shamefaced, and kicked his chair leg a little, before adding in such a low voice that it could hardly even be heard: "I just wanted to know what it felt like to be someone you look at." As he was getting up she reached across the table and put her hand on his.

"I've never heard you say so many words before." She smiled.

He mumbled something about how this didn't change the facts. He was a liar. When she asked him to sit down again, he obliged her and sank back into his chair. She wasn't angry, the way he thought she'd be. She started laughing. In the end she said it hadn't actually been so difficult working out that he wasn't doing his military service, because he never wore a uniform.

"Anyway, everyone knows soldiers don't go home at five o'clock on weekdays."

Ove had hardly been as discreet as a Russian spy, she added. She'd come to the conclusion that he had his reasons for it. And she'd liked the way he listened to her. And made her laugh. And that, she said, had been more than enough for her.

And then she asked him what he really wanted to do with his life, if he could choose anything he wanted. And he answered, without even thinking about it, that he wanted to build houses. Construct them. Draw the plans. Calculate the best way to make them stand where they stood. And then she didn't start laughing as he thought she would. She got angry.

"But why don't you *do* it, then?" she demanded.

Ove did not have a particularly good answer to that one.

On the following Monday she came to his house with brochures for a correspondence course leading to an engineering qualification. The old landlady was quite overwhelmed when she looked at the beautiful young woman walking up the stairs with self-confident steps. Later she tapped Ove's back and whispered that those flowers were probably a very good investment. Ove couldn't help but agree.

When he came up to his room she was sitting on his bed. Ove stood sulkily in the doorway, with his hands in his pockets. She looked at him and laughed.

"Are we an item now?" she asked.

"Well, yes," he replied hesitantly, "I suppose it could be that way."

And then it was that way.

She handed him the brochures. It was a two-year course, and it proved that all the time Ove had spent learning about house building had not, after all, been wasted as he'd once believed. Maybe he did not have much of a head for studying in a conventional sense, but he understood numbers and he understood houses. That got him far. He took the examination after six months. Then another. And another. Then he got a job at the housing office and stayed there for more than a third of a century. Worked hard, was never ill, paid his mortgage, paid taxes, did his duty. Bought a little two-story row house in a recently constructed development in the forest. She wanted to get married, so Ove proposed. She wanted children, which was fine with him, said Ove. And their understanding was that children should live in row housing developments among other children.

And less than forty years later there was no forest around the house anymore. Just other houses. And one day she was lying there in a hospital and holding his hand and telling him not to worry. Everything was going to be all right. Easy for her to say, thought Ove, his breast pulsating with anger and sorrow. But she just whispered, "Everything will be fine, darling Ove," and leaned her arm against his arm. And then gently pushed her index finger into the palm of his hand. And then closed her eyes and died.

Ove stayed there with her hand in his for several hours. Until the hospital staff entered the room with warm voices and careful movements, explaining that they had to take her body away. Ove rose from his chair, nodded, and went to the undertakers to take care of the paperwork. On Sunday she was buried. On Monday he went to work.

But if anyone had asked, he would have told them that he never lived before he met her. And not after either.

15

A MAN CALLED OVE AND A DELAYED TRAIN

The slightly porky man on the other side of the Plexiglas has back-combed hair and arms covered in tattoos. As if it isn't enough to look like someone has slapped a pack of margarine over his head, he has to cover himself in doodles as well. There's not even a proper motif, as far as Ove can see, just a lot of patterns. Is that something an adult person in a healthy state of mind would consent to? Going about with his arms looking like a pair of pajamas?

"Your ticket machine doesn't work," Ove informs him.

"No?" says the man behind the Plexiglas.

"What do you mean, 'no'?"

"I mean . . . I'm asking, doesn't it work?"

"I just told you, it's broken!"

The man behind the Plexiglas looks dubious. "Maybe there's something wrong with your card? Some dirt on the magnetic strip?" he suggests.

Ove looks as if the man behind the Plexiglas had just raised the possibility of Ove having erectile dysfunction. The man behind the Plexiglas goes silent.

"There's no dirt on my magnetic strip, you can be sure of that," Ove splutters.

The man behind the Plexiglas nods. Then changes his mind and shakes his head. Tries to explain to Ove that the machine "actually worked earlier in the day." Ove dismisses this as utterly irrelevant, of course, because it is clearly broken now. The man behind the Plexiglas wonders if Ove has cash instead. Ove replies that this is none of his bloody business. A tense silence settles.

At long last the man behind the Plexiglas asks if he can "check out the card." Ove looks at him as if they just met in a dark alley and he's asked to "check out" Ove's private parts.

"Don't try anything," Ove warns as he hesitantly pushes it under the window.

The man behind the Plexiglas grabs the card and rubs it against his leg in a vigorous manner. As if Ove had never read in the newspaper about that thing they call "skimming." As if Ove was an idiot.

"What are you DOING?" Ove cries and bangs the palm of his hand against the Plexiglas window.

The man pushes the card back under the window.

"Try it now," he says.

Ove thinks that any old fool could figure out that if the card wasn't working half a minute ago it isn't going to work now either. Ove points this out to the man behind the Plexiglas.

"Please?" says the man.

Ove sighs demonstratively. Takes his card again, without taking his eyes off the Plexiglas. The card works.

"You see!" jeers the man behind the Plexiglas.

Ove glares at the card as if he feels it has double-crossed him, before he puts it back in his wallet.

"Have a good day," the man behind the Plexiglas calls out behind him.

"We'll see," mutters Ove.

For the last twenty years practically every human being he's met has done nothing but drone on at Ove about how he should be paying for everything by card. But cash has always been good enough for Ove; cash has in fact served humanity perfectly well for thousands of years. And Ove doesn't trust the banks and all their electronics.

But his wife insisted on getting hold of one of those prepaid cards in spite of it all, even though Ove warned her against it. And when she died the bank simply sent Ove a new card in his name, connected to her account. And now, after he's been buying flowers for her grave for the past six months, there's a sum of 136 kronor and 54 öre left on it. And Ove knows very well that this money will disappear into the pocket of some bank director if Ove dies without spending it first.

But now when Ove actually wants to use that damned plastic card, it doesn't work, of course. Or there are a lot of extra fees when he uses it in the shops. Which only goes to prove that Ove was right all along. And he's going to say as much to his wife as soon as he sees her, she had better be quite clear about that.

He had gone out this morning long before the sun had drummed up the energy to rise over the horizon, much less any of his neighbors. He had carefully studied the train timetable in the hall. Then he'd turned out the lights, switched off the radiators, locked his front door, and left the envelope with all the instructions on the hall mat inside the door. He assumed that someone would find it when they came to take the house.

He fetched the snow shovel, cleared the snow away from the

front of the house, put the shovel back in the shed. Locked the shed. Had Ove been a bit more attentive he would have noticed the fairly large cat-shaped cavity in the quite large snowdrift just outside his shed as he started heading off towards the parking area. But because he had more important things on his mind he did not.

Chastened by recent experiences, he did not take the Saab, but walked instead to the station. Because this time neither Pregnant Foreign Woman, Blond Weed, Rune's wife, nor low-quality rope would be given any opportunity of ruining Ove's morning. He'd bled these people's radiators, loaned them his things, given them lifts to the hospital. But now he was finally on his way.

He checked the train timetable once more. He hated being late. It ruined the planning. Made everything out of step. His wife had been utterly useless at it, keeping to plans. But it was always like that with women. They couldn't stick to a plan even if you glued them to it, Ove had learned. When he was driving somewhere he drew up schedules and plans and decided where they'd fill up and when they'd stop for coffee, all in the interest of making the trip as time-efficient as possible. He studied maps and estimated exactly how long each leg of the journey would take and how they should avoid rush-hour traffic and the shortcuts to take that people with GPS systems wouldn't be able to make head nor tail of. Ove always had a clear travel strategy. His wife, on the other hand, always came up with insanities like "going by a sense of feel" and "taking it easy." As if that was a way for an adult person to get anywhere in life. And then she always remembered that she had to make a call or had forgotten some scarf or other. Or she didn't know which coat to pack at the last moment. Or something else. She always forgot the thermos of coffee on the draining board, which was actually the *only* important thing. There were four coats in those damned bags but no coffee. As if one could just turn off into a gas station every hour and buy the burned fox piss they were selling in there. And get even more delayed. And when Ove got disgruntled she always had to challenge the importance of having a time plan when driving somewhere. "We're not in a hurry anyway," she'd say. As if *that* had anything to do with it.

Now, standing at the station platform, he presses his hands into his pockets. He isn't wearing his suit jacket. It's much too stained and smells too strongly of car exhaust, so he feels she'd probably have a crack at him if he were to turn up in that. She doesn't like the shirt and sweater he's wearing now, but at least they're clean and in decent condition. It's about ten degrees outside. He hasn't yet changed the blue autumn jacket for the blue winter coat, and the cold is blowing straight through it. He's been a bit distracted of late, he has to admit. He hasn't given any real thought to how one is supposed to present oneself when arriving upstairs. Initially he thought one should be all spruced up and formal. Most likely there'll be some kind of uniform up there, to avoid confusion. He supposes there will be all sorts of people—foreigners, for instance, each one wearing a stranger outfit than the next. Presumably it will be possible to organize your clothes once you get there—surely there will even be some sort of wardrobe department?

The platform is almost empty. On the other side of the track are some sleepy-looking youths with oversize backpacks which, Ove decides, are most likely filled with drugs. Alongside them is a man in his forties in a gray suit and a black overcoat. He's reading the newspaper. A little farther off are some small-talking women in their best years with county council logos on their chests and purple tresses of hair. They're chain-smoking long menthol cigarettes.

On Ove's side of the track it's empty but for three overdimensioned municipal employees in their midthirties in workmen's trousers and hard hats, standing in a ring and staring down into a hole. Around them is a carelessly erected loop of cordon tape. One of them has a mug of coffee from 7-Eleven; another is eating a banana; the third is trying to poke his cell phone without removing his gloves. It's not going so well. And the hole stays where it is. And still we're surprised when the whole world comes crashing down in a financial crisis, Ove thinks. When people do little more than standing around eating bananas and looking into holes in the ground all day.

He checks his watch. One minute left. He stands at the edge of the platform. Balancing the soles of his shoes over the edge. It's a fall of no more than five feet, he estimates. Five and a half, possibly. There's a certain symbolism in a train taking his life and he doesn't like this much. He doesn't think the train driver should have to see the awfulness of it. For this reason he has decided to jump when the train is very close, so it's rather the side of the first carriage that throws him onto the rails than the big windshield at the front. He looks in the direction the train is coming from and slowly starts counting. It's important that the timing is absolutely right, he determines. The sun is just up; it shines obstinately into his eyes like a child who has just been given a flashlight.

And that's when he hears the first scream.

Ove looks up just in time to see the suit-wearing man in his black overcoat starting to sway back and forth, like a panda that's been given a Valium overdose. It continues for a second or so, then the suit-wearing man looks up blindly and his whole body is struck with some form of nervous twitching. His arms shake convulsively. And then, as if the moment is a long sequence of still photographs, the newspaper falls out of his hands and he passes out, falling off the edge onto the track with a thump, as if he were a sack of cement mixture.

The chain-smoking old girls with the county council logos on their breasts start shrieking in panic. The drug-taking youths stare at the track, their hands enmeshed in their backpack straps as if fearing that they might otherwise fall over. Ove stands on the edge of the platform on the other side and looks with irritation from one to the other.

"For Christ's sake," fumes Ove to himself at long last as he jumps down onto the track. "GRAB HOLD HERE WILL YOU!" he calls out to one of the backpackers on the platform. The stultified youth drags himself slowly to the edge. Ove hoists up the suit-wearing man in a way that men who have never put their foot in a gym yet have spent their entire lives carrying a concrete plinth under each arm tend to be able to do. He heaves up the body into the backpacker's arms in a way that Audi-driving men wearing neon-bright jogging pants are often incapable of doing.

"He can't stay here in the path of the train, you get that, don't you?!"

The backpackers nod in confusion, and finally by their collective efforts manage to drag the suit-wearing body onto the platform. The county council women are still screaming, as if they sincerely believe this is a constructive approach under the circumstances. The man appears to be breathing, but Ove stays down there on the track. He hears the train coming. It's not quite the way he planned it, but it'll have to do.

Then he calmly goes into the middle of the track, puts his hands in his pockets, and stares into the headlights. He hears the warning whistle like a foghorn. Feels the track shaking powerfully under his feet, as if a testosterone-fueled bull were trying to charge him. He breathes out. In the midst of that inferno of shaking and yelling and the chilling scream of the train's brakes he feels a deep relief.

At last.

To Ove, the moments that follow are elongated as if time itself has applied its brakes and made everything around him travel in slow motion. The explosion of sounds is muted into a low hiss in his ears, the train approaching so slowly that it's as if it's being pulled along by two decrepit oxen. The headlights flash despairingly at him. And in the interval between two of the flashes, while he isn't blinded, he finds himself establishing eye contact with the train driver. He can't be more than twenty years old. One of those who still gets called "the puppy" by his older colleagues.

Ove stares into the puppy's face. Clenches his fists in his pockets as if he's cursing himself for what he's about to do. But it can't be helped, he thinks. There's a right way of doing things. And a wrong way.

So the train is perhaps fifteen yards away when Ove swears with irritation and, as calmly as if he were getting up to fetch himself a cup of coffee, steps out of the way and jumps up on the platform again.

The train has drawn level with him by the time the driver has managed to stop it. The puppy's terror has sucked all the blood out of his face. He is clearly holding back his tears. The two men look at each other through the locomotive window as if they had just emerged from some apocalyptic desert and now realized that neither of them was the last human being on earth. One is relieved by this insight. And the other disappointed.

The boy in the locomotive nods carefully. Ove nods back with resignation.

Fair enough that Ove no longer wants his life. But the sort of man who ruins someone else's by making eye contact with him seconds before his body is turned into blood paste against said person's windshield; damn it, Ove is not that sort of man. Neither his dad nor Sonja would ever have forgiven him for that.

"Are you all right?" one of the hard hats calls out behind Ove.

"Another minute and you'd have been a goner!" yells one of the others.

They stand there staring at him, not at all unlike the way they were standing just now and staring into that hole. It seems to be their prime area of competence, in fact: to stare at things. Ove stares back.

"Another second, I mean," clarifies the man who still has a banana in his hand.

"It could have gone quite badly, that," sniggers the first hard hat.

"Really badly," the other one agrees.

"Could have died, actually," clarifies the third.

"You're a real hero!"

"Saved their life!"

"His. Saved *his* life," Ove corrects and hears Sonja's voice in his own.

"Would have died otherwise," the third one reiterates, taking a forthright bite of his banana.

On the track is the train with all its red emergency lights turned on, puffing and screeching like a very fat person who's just run into a wall. A great number of examples of what Ove assumes must be IT consultants and other disreputable folk come streaming out and stand about dizzily on the platform. Ove puts his hands in his trouser pockets.

"I suppose now you'll have a lot of bloody delayed trains as well," he says and looks with particular displeasure at the chaotic press of people on the platform.

"Yeah," says the first hard hat.

"Reckon so," says the second.

"Lots and lots of delays," the third one agrees.

Ove makes a sound like a heavy bureau that's got a rusted-up hinge. He goes past all three of them without a word.

"Where you off to? You're a hero!" the first hard hat yells at him, surprised.

"Yeah," yells the second.

"A hero!" yells the third.

Ove doesn't answer. He walks past the man behind the Plexiglas, back out into the snow-covered streets, and starts walking home.

The town slowly wakes up around him with its foreign-made cars and its statistics and credit-card debt and all its other crap.

And so this day was also ruined, he confirms with bitterness.

As he is walking alongside the bicycle shed by the parking area, he sees the white Škoda coming past from the direction of Anita and Rune's house. A determined woman with glasses is sitting in the passenger seat, her arms filled with files and papers. Behind the wheel sits the man in the white shirt. Ove has to jump out of the way to avoid being run over as the car races round the corner.

The man lifts a smoldering cigarette towards Ove through the windshield, and offers a superior half smile. As if it's Ove's fault that he's in the way, but he's generous enough to let it go.

"Idiot!" Ove yells after the Škoda, but the man in the white shirt doesn't seem to react at all.

Ove memorizes the license number before the car disappears round the corner.

"Soon it'll be your turn, you old fart," hisses a malevolent voice behind him.

Ove spins around with his fist instinctively raised, and finds himself staring at his own reflection in Blond Weed's sunglasses. She's holding that damned mutt in her arms. It growls at him.

"They were from Social Services," she jeers, with a nod towards the road.

In the parking area, Ove sees that imbecile Anders backing his Audi out of his garage. It has those new, wave-shaped headlights, Ove notes, presumably designed so that no one at night will be able to avoid the insight that here comes a car driven by an utter shit.

"What business is it of yours?" Ove says to the Weed.

Her lips are pulled into the sort of grimace that comes as close to a real smile as a woman whose lips have been injected with environmental waste and nerve toxins is ever likely to achieve.

"It's my business because this time it's that bloody old man at the end of the road they're putting in a home. And after that it'll be you!"

She spits at the ground beside him and walks towards the Audi. Ove watches her, his chest puffing in and out under his shirt. As the Audi swings around she shows him the middle finger on the other side of the window. Ove's first instinct is to run after them and tear that German sheet-metal monster, inclusive of imbeciles, weeds, growling mutts, and wave-shaped headlights, to smithereens. But then suddenly he feels out of breath, as if he's been running full-tilt through the snow. He leans forward, puts his hands on his knees, and notices to his own fury that he's panting for air, his heart racing.

He straightens up after a minute or so. There's a slight flickering effect in his right eye. The Audi has gone. Ove turns and slowly heads back to his house, one hand pressed to his chest.

When he gets to his house he stops by the shed. Stares down into the cat-shaped hole in the snowdrift.

There's a cat at the bottom of it.

Might have bloody known.

16

A MAN WHO WAS OVE AND A TRUCK IN THE FOREST

Before that day when the dour and slightly fumbling boy with the muscular body and the sad blue eyes sat down beside Sonja on the train, there were really only three things she loved unconditionally in her life: books, her father, and cats.

She'd obviously had quite a lot of attention, it wasn't that. The suitors had come in all shapes and sizes. Tall and dark or short and blond and fun-loving and dull and elegant and boastful and handsome and greedy, and if they hadn't been slightly dissuaded by the stories in the village of Sonja's father keeping one or two firearms in the isolated wooden house out there in the woods, they would most likely have been a bit pushier. But none of them had looked at her the way that boy looked at her when he sat down beside her on the train. As if she were the only girl in the world.

Sometimes, especially in the first few years, some of her girlfriends questioned the choice she had made. Sonja was very beautiful, as the people around her seemed to find it so important to keep telling her. Furthermore she loved to laugh and, whatever life threw at her, she was the sort of person who took a positive view of it. But Ove was, well, Ove was Ove. Something the people around her also kept telling Sonja.

He'd been a grumpy old man since he started elementary school, they insisted. And she could have someone so much better.

But to Sonja, Ove was never dour and awkward and sharp-edged. To her, he was the slightly disheveled pink flowers at their first dinner. He was his father's slightly too tight-fitting brown suit across his broad, sad shoulders. He believed so strongly in things: justice and fair play and hard work and a world where right just had to be right. Not so one could get a medal or a diploma or a slap on the back for it, but just because that was how it was supposed to be. Not many men of his kind were made anymore, Sonja had understood. So she was holding on to this one. Maybe he didn't write her poems or serenade her with songs or come home with expensive gifts. But no other boy had gone the wrong way on the train for hours every day just because he liked sitting next to her while she spoke.

And when she took hold of his lower arm, thick as her thigh, and tickled him until that sulky boy's face opened up in a smile, it was like a plaster cast cracking around a piece of jewelry, and when this happened it was as if something started singing inside Sonja. And they belonged only to her, those moments.

She didn't get angry with him that first night they had dinner, when he told her he'd lied about his military service. Of course, she got angry with him on an immeasurable number of occasions after that, but not that night.

"They say the best men are born out of their faults and that they often improve later on, more than if they'd never done anything wrong," she'd said gently.

"Who said that?" asked Ove and looked at the triple set of cutlery in front of him on the table, the way one might look at a box that had just been opened while someone said, "Choose your weapon."

"Shakespeare," said Sonja.

"Is that any good?" Ove wondered.

"It's fantastic." Sonja nodded, smiling.

"I've never read anything with him," mumbled Ove into the tablecloth.

"*By* him," Sonja corrected, and lovingly put her hand on his.

In their almost four decades together Sonja taught hundreds of pupils with learning difficulties to read and write, and she got them to read Shakespeare's collected works. In the same period she never managed to make Ove read a single Shakespeare play. But as soon as they moved into their row house he spent every evening for weeks on end in the toolshed. And when he was done, the most beautiful bookcases she had ever seen were in their living room.

"You have to keep them somewhere," he muttered, and poked a little cut on his thumb with the tip of a screwdriver.

And she crept into his arms and said that she loved him.

And he nodded.

She only asked once about the burns on his arms.

And she had to piece together the exact circumstances of how he lost his parental home, from the succinct fragments on offer when Ove reluctantly revealed what had happened. In the end she found out how he got the scars. And when one of her girlfriends asked why she loved him she answered that most men ran away from an inferno. But men like Ove ran into it.

Ove did not meet Sonja's father more times than he could count on his fingers. The old man lived a long way north, a good way into the forest, almost as if he had consulted a map of all the population centers in the country before concluding that this was as far from other people as one could live.

Sonja's mother had died in the maternity bed. Her father never remarried.

"I have a woman. She is just not home at the moment," he spat out the few times anyone dared bring up the question.

Sonja moved to the local town when she started studying for her upper secondary examinations—all in humanities subjects—at a sixth-form college. Her father looked at her with boundless indignation when she suggested that he might like to come with her. "What can I do there? Meet folk?" he growled. He always spoke the word "folk" as if it were a swear word. So Sonja let him be. Apart from her weekend visits and his monthly trip in the truck to the grocery store in the nearest village, he only had Ernest for company.

Ernest was the biggest farm cat in the world. When Sonja was small she actually thought he was a pony. He came and went in her father's house as he pleased, but he didn't live there. Where he lived, in fact, was not known to anyone. Sonja named him Ernest after Ernest Hemingway. Her father had never bothered with books, but when his daughter sat reading the newspaper at the age of five he wasn't so stupid that he tried to avoid doing something about it. "A girl can't read shit like that: she'll lose her head," he stated as he pushed her towards the library counter in the village. The old librarian didn't quite know what he meant by that, but there was no doubt about the girl's quite outstanding intellect.

The monthly trip to the grocery store simply had to be extended to a monthly trip to the library, the librarian and father decided together, without any particular need to discuss it further. By the time Sonja passed her twelfth birthday she had read all the books at least twice. The ones she liked, such as *The Old Man and the Sea*, she'd read so many times that she'd lost count.

So Ernest ended up being called Ernest. And no one owned him. He didn't talk, but he liked to go fishing with her father, who appreciated his qualities. They would share the catch equally once they got home.

The first time Sonja brought Ove out to the old wooden house in the forest, Ove and her father sat in buttoned-up silence opposite each other, staring down at their food for almost an hour, while she tried to encourage some form of civilized conversation. Neither of the men could quite understand what they were doing there, apart from the fact that it was important to the only woman either of them cared about. They had both protested about the whole arrangement, insistently and vociferously, but without success.

Sonja's father was negatively disposed from the very beginning. All he knew about this boy was that he came from town and that Sonja had mentioned that he did not like cats very much. These were two characteristics, as far as he was concerned, that gave him reason enough to view Ove as unreliable.

As for Ove, he felt he was at a job interview, and he had never been very good at that sort of thing. So when Sonja wasn't talking, which admittedly she did almost all of the time, there was a sort of silence in the room that can only arise between a man who does not want to lose his daughter and a man who has not yet completely understood that he has been chosen to take her away from there. Finally Sonja kicked Ove's shinbone to make him say something. Ove looked up from his plate and noted the angry twitches around the edges of her eyes. He cleared his throat and looked around with a certain desperation to find something to ask this old man about. Because this was what Ove had learned: if one didn't have anything to say, one had to find something to ask. If there was one thing that made people forget to dislike one, it was when they were given the opportunity to talk about themselves.

At long last Ove's gaze fell on the truck, visible through the old man's kitchen window.

"That's an L10, isn't it?" he said, pointing with his fork.

"Yup," said the old man, looking down at his plate.

"Saab is making them now," Ove stated with a short nod.

"Scania!" the old man roared, glaring at Ove.

And the room was once again overwhelmed by that silence which can only arise between a woman's beloved and her father.

Ove looked down grimly at his plate. Sonja kicked her father on his shin. Her father looked back at her grumpily. Until he saw those twitches around her eyes. He was not so stupid a man that he had not learned to avoid what tended to happen after them. So he cleared his throat irately and picked at his food.

"Just because some suit at Saab waved his wallet around and bought the factory it don't stop being a Scania," he grunted in a low voice, which was slightly less accusing, and then moved his shinbones a little farther from his daughter's shoe.

Sonja's father had always driven Scania trucks. He couldn't understand why anyone would have anything else. Then, after years of consumer loyalty, they merged with Saab. It was a treachery he never quite forgave them for.

Ove, who, in turn, had become very interested in Scania when they merged with Saab, looked thoughtfully out of the window while chewing his potato.

"Does it run well?" he asked.

"No," muttered the old man irascibly and went back to his plate. "None of their models run well. None of 'em are built right. Mechanics want half a fortune to fix anything on it," he added, as if he were actually explaining it to someone sitting under the table.

"I can have a look at it if you'll let me," said Ove and looked enthusiastic all of a sudden.

It was the first time Sonja could ever remember him actually sounding enthusiastic about anything.

The two men looked at each other for a moment. Then Sonja's father nodded. And Ove nodded curtly back. And then they rose to their feet, objective and determined, in the way two men might behave if they had just agreed to go and kill a third man. A few minutes later Sonja's father came back into the kitchen, leaning on his stick, and sank into his chair with his chronically dissatisfied mumbling. He sat there for a good while stuffing his pipe with care, then at last nodded at the saucepans and managed to say:

"Nice."

"Thanks, Dad." She smiled.

"You cooked it. Not me," he said.

"The thanks was not for the food," she answered and took away the plates, kissing her father tenderly on his forehead at the same time that she saw Ove diving in under the hood of the truck in the yard.

Her father said nothing, just stood up with a quiet snort and took the newspaper from the kitchen counter. Halfway to his armchair in the living room he stopped himself, however, and stood there slightly unresolved, leaning on his stick.

"Does he fish?" he finally grunted without looking at her.

"I don't think so," Sonja answered.

Her father nodded gruffly. Stood silent for a long while.

"I see. He'll have to learn, then," he grumbled at long last, before putting his pipe in his mouth and disappearing into the living room.

Sonja had never heard him give anyone a higher compliment.

17

A MAN CALLED OVE AND A CAT ANNOYANCE IN A SNOWDRIFT

"Is it dead?" Parvaneh asks in terror as she rushes forward as quickly as her pregnant belly will allow and stands there staring down into the hole.

"I'm not a vet," Ove replies—not in an unfriendly way. Just as a point of information.

He doesn't understand where this woman keeps appearing from all the time. Can't a man calmly and quietly stand over a cat-shaped hole in a snowdrift in his own garden anymore?

"You have to get him out!" she cries, hitting him on the shoulder with her glove.

Ove looks displeased and pushes his hands deeper into his jacket pockets. He is still having a bit of trouble breathing.

"Don't have to at all," he says.

"Jesus, what's wrong with you?"

"I don't get along with cats very well," Ove informs her and plants his heels in the snow.

But her gaze when she turns around makes him move a little farther away.

"Maybe he's sleeping," he offers, peering into the hole. Before adding: "Otherwise he'll come out when it thaws."

When the glove comes flying towards him again he confirms to himself that keeping a safe distance was a very sound idea.

But the next thing he knows Parvaneh has dived into the snowdrift; she emerges seconds later with the little deep-frozen creature in her thin arms. It looks like four ice pops clumsily wrapped in a shredded scarf.

"Open the door!" she yells, really losing her composure now.

Ove presses the soles of his shoes into the snow. He had certainly not begun this day with the intention of letting either women or cats into his house, he'd like to make that very clear to her. But she comes right at him with the animal in her arms and determination in her steps. It's really only a question of the speed of his reactions whether she walks through him or past him. Ove has never experienced a worse woman when it comes to listening to what decent people tell her. He feels out of breath again. He fights the impulse to clutch his breast.

She keeps going. He gives way. She strides past.

The small icicle-decorated package in her arms obstinately brings up a flow of memories in Ove's head before he can put a stop to them: memories of Ernest, fat, stupid old Ernest, so beloved of Sonja that you could have bounced five-kronor coins on her heart whenever she saw him.

"OPEN THE DOOR THEN!" Parvaneh roars and looks round at Ove so abruptly that there's a danger of whiplash.

Ove hauls out the keys from his pocket. As if someone else

has taken control of his arm. He's having a hard time accepting what he's actually doing. One part of him in his head is yelling "NO" while the rest of his body is busy with some sort of teenage rebellion.

"Get me some blankets!" Parvaneh orders and runs across the threshold with her shoes still on.

Ove stands there for a few moments, catching his breath; he furtively scoops up the envelope with his final instructions from the mat before he ambles off after her.

"It's bloody freezing in here. Turn up the radiators!" Parvaneh tosses out the words as if this is something quite obvious, gesturing impatiently at Ove as she puts the cat down on his sofa.

"There'll be no turning up of radiators here," Ove announces firmly. He parks himself in the living room doorway and wonders whether she might try to swat him again with the glove if he tells her at least to put some newspapers under the cat. When she turns to him again he decides to give it a miss. Ove doesn't know if he's ever seen such an angry woman.

"I've got a blanket upstairs," he says at long last, avoiding her gaze by suddenly feeling incredibly interested in the hall lamp.

"Get it then!"

Ove looks as if he's repeating her words to himself, though silently, in an affected, disdainful voice; but he takes off his shoes and crosses the living room at a cautious distance from her glove-striking range.

All the way up and down the stairs he mumbles to himself about why it has to be so damned difficult to get any peace and quiet on this street. Upstairs he stops and takes a few deep breaths. The pain in his chest has gone. His heart is beating normally again. It happens now and then, and he no longer gets stressed about it. It always passes. And he won't be needing that heart for very much longer, so it doesn't matter either way.

He hears voices from the living room. He can hardly believe his ears. Considering how they are constantly preventing him from dying, these neighbors of his are certainly not shy when it comes to driving a man to the brink of madness and suicide. That's for sure.

When Ove comes back down the stairs with the blanket in his hand, the overweight young man from next door is standing in the middle of his living room, looking with curiosity at the cat and Parvaneh.

"Hey, man!" he says cheerfully and waves at Ove.

He's only wearing a T-shirt, even though there's snow outside.

"Okay," says Ove, silently appalled that you can pop upstairs for a moment only to find when you come back down that you've apparently started a bed-and-breakfast operation.

"I heard someone shouting, just wanted to check that everything was cool here," says the young man jovially, shrugging his shoulders so that his back blubber folds the T-shirt into deep wrinkles.

Parvaneh snatches the blanket out of the Ove's hand and starts wrapping the cat in it.

"You'll never get him warm like that," says the young man pleasantly.

"Don't interfere," says Ove, who, while perhaps not an expert at defrosting cats, does not appreciate at all having people marching into his house and issuing orders about how things should be done.

"Be quiet, Ove!" says Parvaneh and looks entreatingly at the young man. "What shall we do, then? He's ice-cold!"

"Don't tell me to be quiet," mumbles Ove.

"He'll die," says Parvaneh.

"Die my ass, he's just a bit chilly—" Ove interjects, in a new attempt to regain control over the situation.

The Pregnant One puts her index finger over his lips and hushes him. Ove looks so absurdly irritated at this it's as if he's going to break into some sort of rage-fueled pirouette.

When Parvaneh holds up the cat, it has started shifting in color from purple to white. Ove looks a little less sure of himself when he notices this. He glances at Parvaneh. Then reluctantly steps back and gives way.

The young, overweight man takes off his T-shirt.

"But what the . . . this has got to be . . . what are you DOING?" stutters Ove.

His eyes flicker from Parvaneh by the sofa, with the defrosting cat in her arms and water dripping onto the floor, to the young man standing there with his torso bare in the middle of Ove's living room, the fat trembling over his chest down towards his knees, as if he were a big mound of ice cream that had first melted and then been refrozen.

"Here, give him to me," says the young man unconcernedly and reaches over with two arms thick as tree trunks towards Parvaneh.

When she hands over the cat he encloses it in his enormous embrace, pressing it against his chest as if trying to make a gigantic cat spring roll.

"By the way, my name's Jimmy," he says to Parvaneh and smiles.

"I'm Parvaneh," says Parvaneh.

"Nice name," says Jimmy.

"Thanks! It means 'butterfly.'" Parvaneh smiles.

"Nice!" says Jimmy.

"You'll smother that cat," says Ove.

"Oh, give it a rest, will you, Ove," says Jimmy.

"I reckon it would rather freeze to death in a dignified manner than be strangled," he says to Jimmy, nodding at the dripping ball of fluff pressed into his arms.

Jimmy pulls his good-tempered face into a big grin.

"Chill a bit, Ove. You can say what you like about us fatties, but we're awesome when it comes to pumping out a bit of heat!"

Parvaneh peers nervously over his blubbery upper arm and gently puts the palm of her hand against the cat's nose. Then she brightens.

"He's getting warmer," she exclaims, turning to Ove in triumph.

Ove nods. He was about to say something sarcastic to her. Now he finds, uneasily, that he's relieved at the news. He distracts himself from this emotion by assiduously inspecting the TV remote control.

Not that he's concerned about the cat. It's just that Sonja would have been happy. Nothing more than that.

"I'll heat some water," says Parvaneh, and in a single snappy movement she slips past Ove and is suddenly standing in his kitchen, tugging at his kitchen cabinets.

"What the hell," mumbles Ove as he lets go of the remote control and tears off in pursuit.

When he gets there, she's standing motionless and slightly confused in the middle of the floor with his electric kettle in her hand. She looks a bit overwhelmed, as if the realization of what's happened has only just hit her.

It's the first time Ove has seen this woman run out of something to say. The kitchen has been cleared and tidied, but it's dusty.

It smells of brewed coffee, there's dirt in the crannies, and everywhere are Ove's wife's things. Her little decorative objects in the window, her hair clips left on the kitchen table, her handwriting on the Post-it notes on the fridge.

The kitchen is filled with those soft wheel marks. As if someone has been going back and forth with a bicycle, thousands of times.

The stove and kitchen counter are noticeably lower than is usual.

As if the kitchen had been built for a child. Parvaneh stares at them the way people always do when they see it for the first time. Ove has got used to it. He rebuilt the kitchen himself after the accident. The council refused to help, of course.

Parvaneh looks as if she's somehow got stuck.

Ove takes the electric kettle out of her outstretched hands without looking into her eyes. Slowly he fills it with water and plugs it in.

"I didn't know, Ove," she whispers, contrite.

Ove leans over the low sink with his back to her. She comes forward and puts her fingertips gently on his shoulder.

"I'm sorry, Ove. Really. I shouldn't have barged into your kitchen without asking first."

Ove clears his throat and nods without turning around. He doesn't know how long they stand there. She lets her enervated hand rest on his shoulder. He decides not to push it away.

Jimmy's voice breaks the silence.

"You got anything to eat?" he calls out from the living room.

Ove's shoulder slips away from Parvaneh's hand. He shakes his head, wipes his face with the back of his hand, and heads off to the fridge still without looking at her.

Jimmy clucks gratefully when Ove comes out of the kitchen

and hands him a sausage sandwich. Ove parks himself a few yards away and looks a bit grim.

"So how is he, then?" he says with a curt nod at the cat in Jimmy's arms.

Water is dripping liberally onto the floor now, but the animal is slowly but surely regaining both its shape and color.

"Seems better, no?" Jimmy grins as he wolfs down the sandwich in a single bite.

Ove gives him a skeptical look. Jimmy is perspiring like a bit of pork left on a sauna stove. There's something mournful in his eyes when he looks back at Ove.

"You know it was . . . pretty bad with your wife, Ove. I always liked her. She made, like, the best chow in town."

Ove looks at him, and for the first time all morning he doesn't look a bit angry.

"Yes. She . . . cooked very well," he agrees.

He goes over to the window and, with his back to the room, tugs at the latch as if to check it. Pokes the rubber seal.

Parvaneh stands in the kitchen doorway, wrapping her arms around herself and her belly.

"He can stay here until he's completely defrosted, then you have to take him," says Ove, shrugging towards the cat.

He can see in the corner of his eye how she's peering at him. As if she's trying to figure out what sort of hand he has from the other side of a casino table. It makes him uneasy.

"I'm afraid I can't," she says after that. "The girls are . . . allergic," she adds.

Ove hears a little pause before she says "allergic." He scrutinizes her suspiciously in the reflection in the window, but does not answer. Instead he turns to the overweight young man.

"So you'll have to take care of it," he says.

Jimmy, who's not only sweating buckets now but also turning blotchy and red in his face, looks down benevolently at the cat. It's slowly started moving its stump of a tail and burrowing its dripping nose deeper into Jimmy's generous folds of upper-arm fat.

"Don't think it's such a cool idea me taking care of the puss, sorry, man," says Jimmy and shrugs tremulously, so that the cat makes a circus tumble and ends up upside down. He holds out his arms. His skin is red, as if he's on fire.

"I'm a bit allergic as well. . . ."

Parvaneh gives off a little scream, runs up to him, and takes the cat away from him, quickly enfolding it in the blanket again.

"We have to get Jimmy to a hospital!" she yells.

"I'm barred from the hospital," Ove replies, without thinking.

When he peers in her direction and she looks ready to throw the cat at him, he looks down again and groans disconsolately. All I want is to die, he thinks and presses his toes into one of the floorboards.

It flexes slightly. Ove looks up at Jimmy. Looks at the cat.

Surveys the wet floor. Shakes his head at Parvaneh.

"We'll have to take my car then," he mutters.

He takes his jacket from the hook and opens the front door. After a few seconds he sticks his head back into the hall. Glares at Parvaneh.

"But I'm not bringing the car to the house because it's prohibit—"

She interrupts him with some words in Farsi which Ove can't understand. Nonetheless he finds them unnecessarily dramatic. She wraps the cat more tightly in the blanket and walks past him into the snow.

"Rules are rules, you know," says Ove truculently as she heads off to the parking area, but she doesn't answer.

Ove turns around and points at Jimmy.

"And you put on a sweater. Or you're not going anywhere in the Saab, let's be clear about that."

Parvaneh pays for the parking at the hospital. Ove doesn't make a fuss about it.

18

A MAN WHO WAS OVE AND A CAT CALLED ERNEST

Ove didn't dislike this cat in particular. It's just that he didn't much like cats in general. He'd always perceived them as untrustworthy. Especially when, as in the case of Ernest, they were as big as mopeds. It was actually quite difficult to determine whether he was just an unusually large cat or an outstandingly small lion. And you should never befriend something if there's a possibility it may take a fancy to eating you in your sleep.

But Sonja loved Ernest so unconditionally that Ove managed to keep this kind of perfectly sensible observation to himself. He knew better than to speak ill of what she loved; after all he understood very keenly how it was to receive her love when no one else could understand why he was worthy of it. So he and Ernest learned to get along reasonably well when they visited the cottage in the forest, apart from the fact that Ernest bit Ove once when he sat on his tail on one of the kitchen chairs. Or at least they learned to keep their distance. Just like Ove and Sonja's father.

Even if Ove's view was that this Cat Annoyance was not

entitled to sit on one chair and spread his tail over another, he let it go. For Sonja's sake.

Ove learned to fish. In the two autumns that followed their first visit, the roof of the house for the first time ever did not leak. And the truck started every time the key was turned without as much as a splutter. Of course Sonja's father was not openly grateful about this. But on the other hand he never again brought up his reservations about Ove "being from town." And this, from Sonja's father, was as good a proof of affection as any.

Two springs passed and two summers. And in the third year, one cool June night, Sonja's father died. And Ove had never seen anyone cry like Sonja cried then. The first few days she hardly got out of bed. Ove, for someone who had run into death as much as he had in his life, had a very paltry relationship to his feelings about it, and he pushed it all away in some confusion in the kitchen of the forest cottage. The pastor from the village church came by and ran through the details of the burial.

"A good man," stated the pastor succinctly and pointed at one of the photos of Sonja and her father on the living room wall. Ove nodded. Didn't know what he was expected to say to that one. Then he went outside to see if anything on the truck needed fiddling with.

On the fourth day Sonja got out of bed and started cleaning the cottage with such frenetic energy that Ove kept out of her way, in the way that insightful folk avoid an oncoming tornado. He meandered about the farm, looking for things to do. He rebuilt the woodshed, which had collapsed in one of the winter storms. In the coming days he filled it with newly cut wood. Mowed the grass. Lopped overhanging branches from the surrounding forest. Late on the evening of the sixth day they called from the grocery store.

Everyone called it an accident, of course. But no one who had met Ernest could believe that he had run out in front of a car by accident. Sorrow does strange things to living creatures. Ove drove faster than he had ever driven on the roads that night. Sonja held Ernest's big head in her hands all the way. He was still breathing when they made it to the vet, but his injuries were far too serious, the loss of blood too great.

After two hours crouching at his side in the operating room, Sonja kissed the cat's wide brow and whispered, "Good-bye, darling Ernest." And then, as if the words were coming out of her mouth wrapped in whisks of cloud: "And good-bye to you, my darling father."

And then the cat closed his eyes and died.

When Sonja came out of the waiting room she rested her forehead heavily against Ove's broad chest.

"I feel so much loss, Ove. Loss, as if my heart was beating outside my body."

They stood in silence for a long time, with their arms around each other. And at long last she lifted her face towards his, and looked into his eyes with great seriousness.

"You have to love me twice as much now," she said.

And then Ove lied to her for the second—and last—time: he said that he would. Even though he knew it wasn't possible for him to love her any more than he already did.

They buried Ernest beside the lake where he used to go fishing with Sonja's father. The pastor was there to read the blessing. After that, Ove loaded up the Saab and they drove back on the small roads, with Sonja's head leaning against his shoulder. On the way he stopped in the first little town they passed through. Sonja had arranged to meet someone there. Ove did not know who. It was one of the traits she appreciated most about him, she often said long after the event. She knew no one else who could sit in a car for an hour, waiting, without demanding to know what he was waiting for or how long it would take. Which was not to say that Ove did not moan, because moaning was one thing he excelled at. Especially if he had to pay for the parking. But he never asked what she was doing. And he always waited for her.

Then when Sonja came out at last and got back inside, closing the Saab's door with a soft squeeze, which she knew was required to avoid a wounded glance from him as if she had kicked a living creature, she gently took his hand.

"I think we need to buy a house of our own," she said softly.

"What's the point of that?" Ove wondered.

"I think our child has to grow up in a house," she said and carefully moved his hand down to her belly.

Ove was quiet for a long time; a long time even by Ove's standards. He looked thoughtfully at her stomach, as if expecting it to raise some sort of flag. Then he straightened up, twisted the tuning button half a turn forward and half a turn back. Adjusted his wing mirrors. And nodded sensibly.

"We'll have to get a Saab station wagon, then."

19

A MAN CALLED OVE AND A CAT THAT WAS BROKEN WHEN HE CAME

Ove spent most of yesterday shouting at Parvaneh that this damned cat would live in Ove's house over his dead body.

And now here he stands, looking at the cat. And the cat looks back.

And Ove remains strikingly nondead.

It's all incredibly irritating.

A half-dozen times Ove woke up in the night when the cat, with more than a little disrespect, crawled up and stretched out next to him in the bed. And just as many times the cat woke up when Ove, with more than a bit of brusqueness, booted it down to the floor again.

Now, when it's gone quarter to six and Ove has got up, the cat is sitting in the middle of the kitchen floor. It sports a disgruntled expression, as if Ove owes it money. Ove stares back at it with a suspicion normally reserved for a cat that has rung his doorbell with a Bible in its paws, like a Jehovah's Witness.

"I suppose you're expecting food," mutters Ove at last.

The cat doesn't answer. It just nibbles its remaining patches of fur and nonchalantly licks one of its paw pads.

"But in this house you don't just lounge about like some kind of consultant and expect fried sparrows to fly into your mouth."

Ove goes to the sink. Turns on the coffeemaker. Checks his watch. Looks at the cat. After leaving Jimmy at the hospital, Parvaneh had managed to get hold of a friend who was apparently a veterinarian. The veterinarian had come to have a look at the cat and concluded that there was "serious frostbite and advanced malnutrition." And then he'd given Ove a long list of instructions about what the cat needed to eat and its general care.

"I'm not running a cat repair company," Ove clarifies to the cat. "You're only here because I couldn't talk any sense into that pregnant woman." He nods across the living room towards the window facing onto Parvaneh's house.

The cat, busying itself trying to lick one of its eyes, does not reply.

Ove holds up four little socks towards it. He was given them by the veterinarian. Apparently the Cat Annoyance needs exercise more than anything, and this is something Ove feels he may be able to help it achieve. The farther from his wallpaper those claws are, the better. That's Ove's reasoning.

"Hop into these things and then we can go. I'm running late!"

The cat gets up elaborately and walks with long, self-conscious steps towards the door. As if walking on a red carpet. It gives the socks an initial skeptical look, but doesn't cause too much of a fuss when Ove quite roughly puts them on. When he's done, Ove stands up and scrutinizes the cat from top to bottom. Shakes his head. A cat wearing socks—it can't be natural. The cat, now standing there checking out its new outfit, suddenly looks immeasurably pleased with itself.

Ove makes an extra loop to the end of the pathway. Outside Anita and Rune's house he picks up a cigarette butt. He rolls it between his fingers. That Škoda-driving man from the council seems to drive about in these parts as if he owned them. Ove swears and puts the butt in his pocket.

When they get back to the house, Ove reluctantly feeds the wretched animal, and once it's finished, announces that they've got errands to run. He may have been temporarily press-ganged into cohabiting with this little creature, but he'll be damned if he's going to leave a wild animal on its own in his house. So the cat has to come with him. Immediately there's a disagreement between Ove and the cat about whether or not the cat should sit on a sheet of newspaper in the Saab's passenger seat. At first Ove sets the cat on two supplements of entertainment news, which the cat, much insulted, kicks onto the floor with its back feet. It makes itself comfortable on the soft upholstery. At this Ove firmly picks up the cat by the scruff of its neck, so that the cat hisses at him in a not-so-passive-aggressive manner, while Ove shoves three cultural supplements and book reviews under him. The cat gives him a furious look. Ove puts it down, but oddly enough it stays on the newspaper and only looks out of the window with a wounded, dismal expression. Ove concludes that he's won the battle, nods with satisfaction, puts the Saab into gear, and drives onto the main road. Only then does the cat slowly and deliberately drag its claws in a long tear across the newsprint, and then put both its front paws through the rip. While at the same time giving Ove a highly challenging look, as if to ask: "And what are you going to do about it?"

Ove slams on the brakes of the Saab so that the cat, shocked, is thrown forward and bangs its nose against the dashboard. "THAT's what I have to say about it!" Ove's triumphant expression seems to say. After that, the cat refuses to look at Ove for the rest of the journey and just sits hunched up in a corner of the seat, rubbing its nose with one of its paws in a very offended way. But while Ove is inside the florist's, it licks long wet streaks across Ove's steering wheel, safety belt, and the inside of Ove's car door.

When Ove comes back with the flowers and discovers that his whole car is full of cat saliva, he waves his forefinger in a threatening manner, as if it were a scimitar. And then the cat bites his scimitar. Ove refuses to speak to him for the rest of the journey.

When they get to the churchyard, Ove plays it safe and scrunches up the remains of the newspaper into a ball, with which he roughly pushes the cat out of the car. Then he gets the flowers out of the trunk, locks the Saab with his key, makes a circuit around it, and checks each of the doors. Together they climb the frozen graveled slope leading up to the church turn-off and force their way through the snow, before they stop by Sonja. Ove brushes some snow off the gravestone with the back of his hand and gives the flowers a little shake.

"I've brought some flowers with me," he mumbles. "Pink. Which you like. They say they die in the frost but they only tell you that to trick you into buying the more expensive ones."

The cat sinks down on its behind in the snow. Ove gives it a sullen look, then refocuses on the gravestone.

"Right, right. . . . This is the Cat Annoyance. It's living with us now. Almost froze to death outside our house."

The cat gives Ove an offended look. Ove clears his throat.

"He looked like that when he came," he clarifies, a sudden defensive note in his voice. Then, with a nod at the cat and the gravestone:

"So it wasn't me who broke him. He was already broken," he adds to Sonja.

Both the gravestone and the cat wait in silence beside him. Ove stares at his shoes for a moment. Grunts. Sinks onto his knees in the snow and brushes a bit more snow off the stone. Carefully lays his hand on it.

"I miss you," he whispers.

There's a quick gleam in the corner of Ove's eye. He feels something soft against his arm. It takes a few seconds before he realizes that the cat is gently resting its head in the palm of his hand.

20

A MAN CALLED OVE AND AN INTRUDER

For almost twenty minutes, Ove sits in the driver's seat of the Saab with the garage door open. For the first five minutes the cat stares at him impatiently from the passenger seat. During the next five it begins to look properly worried. In the end it tries to open the door itself; when this fails, it promptly lies down on the seat and goes to sleep.

Ove glances at it as it rolls onto its side and starts snoring. He has to concede that the Cat Annoyance has a very direct approach to problem-solving.

He looks out over the parking area again at the garage opposite. He must have stood out there with Rune a hundred times. They were friends once. Ove can't think of very many people in his life he could describe as such. Ove and Ove's wife were the first people to move into this street of row houses all those years ago, when it had only recently been built and was still surrounded by trees. That same day, Rune and Rune's wife moved in. Anita was also pregnant and, of course, immediately became best friends with Ove's wife in that way only women knew how. And just like all women who become best friends they both had the idea that Rune and Ove had to become best friends. Because they had so many "interests in common." Ove couldn't really understand what they meant by that. After all, Rune drove a Volvo.

Not that Ove exactly had anything against Rune apart from that. He had a proper job and he didn't talk more than he had to. Admittedly he did drive that Volvo but, as Ove's wife kept insisting, this did not necessarily make a person immoral. So Ove put up with him. After a period he even lent him tools. And one afternoon, standing in the parking area, thumbs tucked into their belts, they got caught up in a conversation about lawn mower prices. When they parted they shook hands. As if the mutual decision to become friends was a business agreement.

When the two men later found out that all sorts of people were moving into the area, they sat down in Ove and Sonja's kitchen for consultations. By the time they emerged from these, they had established a shared framework of rules, signs clarifying what was permitted or not, and a newly setup steering group for the Residents' Association. Ove was the chairman; Rune, the vice chairman.

In the months that followed they went to the dump together. Grumbled at people who had parked their cars incorrectly. Bargained for better deals on paint and drainpipes at the hardware store, stood on either side of the man from the telephone company when he came to install telephones and jacks, brusquely pointing out where and how he should best go about it. Not that either of them knew exactly how telephone cables should be installed, but they were both well versed in keeping an eye on whippersnappers like this one, to stop them pulling a fast one. That was all there was to it.

Sometimes the two couples had dinner together. Insofar as one could have dinner when Ove and Rune mostly just stood about in the parking area the whole evening, kicking the tires of their cars and comparing their load capacity, turning radius, and other significant matters. And that was all there was to it.

Sonja's and Anita's bellies kept growing steadily, which, according to Rune, made Anita "doolally in the brain." Apparently he had to look for the coffeepot in the fridge more or less daily once she was in her third month. Sonja, not to be outdone, developed a temper that could flare up quicker than a pair of saloon doors in a John Wayne film, which made Ove reluctant to open his mouth at all. This, of course, gave further cause for irritation. When she wasn't breaking out in a sweat she was freezing. And as soon as Ove tired of arguing with her and agreed to turn up the radiators by a half step she started sweating again, and he had to run around and turn them back down again. She also ate bananas in such quantities that the people at the supermarket must have thought Ove had started a zoo.

"The hormones are on the warpath," Rune said with an insightful nod during one of the nights when he and Ove sat in the outside space behind his house, while the women kept to Sonja and Ove's kitchen, talking about whatever it is women talk about.

Rune told him that he had found Anita crying her eyes out by the radio the day before, for no other reason than that it "was a nice song."

"A . . . nice song?" said Ove, perplexed.

"A nice song," Rune answered.

The two men shook their heads in mutual disbelief and stared out into the darkness. Sat in silence.

"The grass needs cutting," said Rune at last.

"I bought new blades for the mower." Ove nodded.

"How much did you pay for them?"

And so their friendship went on.

In the evenings, Sonja played music for her belly, because she said it made the child move. Ove mostly just sat in his armchair on the other side of the room and pretended to be watching television while she was doing it. In his innermost thoughts he was worried about what it would be like once the child finally decided to come out. What if, for example, the kid disliked Ove because Ove *wasn't* so fond of music?

It wasn't that Ove was afraid. He just didn't know how to prepare himself for fatherhood. He had asked for some sort of manual but Sonja had just laughed at him. Ove didn't understand why. There were manuals for everything else.

He was doubtful about whether he'd be any good at being someone's dad. He didn't like children an awful lot. He hadn't even been very good at *being* a child. Sonja thought he should talk to Rune about it because they were "in the same situation." Ove couldn't quite understand what she meant by that. Rune was not in fact going to be the father of Ove's child, but of an altogether different one. At least Rune agreed with Ove about the point of not having much to discuss, and that was something. So when Anita came over in the evenings and sat in the kitchen with Sonja, talking about the aches and pains and all those things, Ove and Rune made the excuse of having "things" to talk about and went out to Ove's shed and just stood there in silence, picking at various bits on Ove's workbench.

Standing there next to each other behind a closed door for the third night running without knowing what they were supposed to do with themselves, they agreed that they needed to get busy with something before, as Rune put it, "the new neighbors start thinking there's some sort of monkey business going on in here."

Ove agreed that it might be best to do as he said. And so it was. They didn't talk much while they were doing it, but they helped each other with the drawings and measuring the angles and ensuring that the corners were straight and properly done. And late one evening when Anita and Sonja were in the fourth month, two light blue cribs were installed in the prepared nurseries of their row houses.

"We can sand it down and repaint it pink if we get a girl," mumbled Ove when he showed it to Sonja. Sonja put her arms around him, and he felt his neck getting all wet with her tears. Completely irrational hormones.

"I want you to ask me to be your wife," she whispered.

And so it was. They married in the Town Hall, very simply. Neither of them had any family, so only Rune and Anita came. Sonja and Ove put on their rings and then all four of them went to a restaurant. Ove paid but Rune helped check the bill to make sure it "had been done properly." Of course it hadn't. So after conferring with the waiter for about an hour, the two men managed to convince him it would be easier for him if he halved the bill or they'd "report him." Obviously it was a bit hazy exactly who would report whom for what, but eventually, with a certain amount of swearing and arm-waving, the waiter gave up and went into the kitchen and wrote them a new bill. In the meantime Rune and Ove nodded grimly at one another without noticing that their wives, as usual, had taken a taxi home twenty minutes earlier.

Ove nods to himself as he sits there in the Saab looking at Rune's garage door. He can't remember when he last saw it open. He turns off the headlights of the Saab, gives the cat a poke to wake it up, and gets out.

"Ove?" says a curious, unfamiliar voice.

Suddenly an unknown woman, clearly the owner of the unfamiliar voice, has stuck her head into the garage. She's about forty-five, wearing tatty jeans and a green windbreaker that looks too large for her. She doesn't have any makeup on and her hair is in a ponytail. The woman blunders into his garage and looks around with interest. The cat steps forward and gives her a threatening hiss. She stops. Ove puts his hands in his pockets.

"Ove?" she bursts out again, in that exaggerated chummy way of people who want to sell you something, while pretending it's the very last thing on their mind.

"I don't want anything," says Ove, nodding at the garage door—a clear gesture that she needn't bother about finding another door, it'll be just fine if she walks out the same way that she came.

She looks utterly unchastened by that.

"My name is Lena. I'm a journalist at the local newspaper and, well . . ." she begins, and then offers her hand.

Ove looks at her hand. And looks at her.

"I don't want anything," he says again.

"What?"

"I suppose you're selling subscriptions. But I don't want one."

She looks puzzled.

"Right. . . . Well, actually . . . I'm not selling the paper. I write for it. I'm a *journalist*," she repeats slowly, as if there were something wrong with him.

"I still don't want anything," Ove reiterates as he starts shooing her out the garage door.

"But I want to talk to *you*, Ove!" she protests and starts trying to force herself back inside.

Ove waves his hands at her as if trying to scare her away by shaking an invisible rug in front of her.

"You saved a man's life at the train station yesterday! I want to interview you about it," she calls out excitedly.

Clearly she's about to say something else when she notices that she's lost Ove's attention. His gaze falls on something behind her. His eyes turn to slits.

"I'll be damned," he mumbles.

"Yes. . . . I'd like to ask y—" she begins sincerely, but Ove has already squeezed past her and started running towards the white Škoda that's turned in by the parking area and started driving down towards the houses.

The bespectacled woman is caught off guard when Ove charges forward and bangs on the window and she throws the file of documents into her own face. The man in the white shirt, on the other hand, is quite unmoved. He rolls down the window.

"Yes?" he asks.

"Vehicle traffic is prohibited in the residential area," Ove hisses and points at each of the houses, at the Škoda, at the man in the white shirt, and at the parking area.

"In this Residents' Association we park in the *parking* area!"

The man in the white shirt looks at the houses. Then at the parking area. Then at Ove.

"I have permission from the council to drive up to the houses. So I have to ask you to get out of the way."

Ove is so agitated by his answer that it takes him many seconds just to formulate some swear words by way of an answer. Meanwhile, the man in the white shirt has picked up a pack of cigarettes from the dashboard, which he taps against his trouser leg.

"Would you be kind enough to get out of the way?" he asks Ove.

"What are you doing here?" Ove blurts out.

"That's nothing for you to worry yourself about," says the man in the white shirt in a monotone voice, as if he's a computer-generated voice mail message letting Ove know that he's been placed in a telephone line.

He puts the cigarette he's shaken out in his mouth and lights it. Ove breathes so heavily that his chest is pumping up and down under his jacket. The woman gathers up her papers and files and adjusts her glasses. The man just sighs, as if Ove is a cheeky child refusing to stop riding his skateboard on the sidewalk.

"You know what I'm doing here. We're taking Rune, in the house at the end of the road, into care."

He hangs his arm out the window and flicks the ash against the wing mirror of the Škoda.

"Taking him into care?"

"Yes," says the man, nodding indifferently.

"And if Anita doesn't want that?" Ove hisses, tapping his index finger against the roof of the car.

The man in the white shirt looks at the woman in the passenger seat and smiles resignedly. Then he turns to Ove again and speaks very slowly. As if otherwise Ove might not understand his words.

"It's not up to Anita to make that decision. It's up to the investigation team."

Ove's breathing becomes even more strained. He can feel his pulse in his throat.

"You're not bringing this car into this area," he says through gritted teeth.

His fists are clenched. His tone is pointed and threatening. But his opponent looks quite calm. He puts out the cigarette against the paintwork of the door and drops it on the ground.

As if everything Ove had said was nothing more than the inarticulate raving of a senile old man.

"And what exactly are you going to do to stop me, Ove?" says the man at long last.

The way he flings out his name makes Ove look as if someone just shoved a mallet in his gut. He stares at the man in the white shirt, his mouth slightly agape and his eyes scanning to and fro over the car.

"How do you know my name?"

"I know a lot about you."

Ove only manages by a whisker to pull his foot out of the way of the wheel as the Škoda moves off again and drives down towards the houses. Ove stands there, in shock, staring after them.

"Who was that?" says the woman in the windbreaker behind him.

Ove spins around.

"How do you know my name?" he demands.

She takes a step back. Pushes a few evasive wisps of hair out of her face without taking her eyes off Ove's clenched fists.

"I work for the local newspaper—we interviewed people on the platform about how you saved that man. . . ."

"How do you know my name?" says Ove again, his voice shaking with anger.

"You swiped your card when you paid for your train ticket. I went through the receipts in the register," she says and takes a few more steps back.

"And him!!! How does HE know my name?" Ove roars and

waves in the direction in which the Škoda went, the veins on his forehead bulging.

"I . . . don't know," she says.

Ove breathes violently through his nose and nails her with his eyes. As if trying to see whether she's lying.

"I have no idea. I've never seen that man before," she promises.

Ove rivets his eyes into her even harder. Finally he nods grimly to himself. Then he turns around and walks towards his house. She calls out to him but he doesn't react. The cat follows him into the hall. Ove closes the door. Farther down the road, the man in the white shirt and the woman with glasses ring the doorbell of Anita and Rune's house.

Ove sinks onto the stool in his hall. Shaking with humiliation.

He had almost forgotten that feeling. The humiliation of it. The powerlessness. The realization that one cannot fight men in white shirts.

And now they're back. They haven't been here since he and Sonja came home from Spain. After the accident.

21

A MAN WHO WAS OVE AND COUNTRIES WHERE THEY PLAY FOREIGN MUSIC IN RESTAURANTS

Of course, the bus tour was her idea. Ove couldn't see the use of it. If they had to go anywhere, why not just take the Saab? But Sonja insisted that buses were "romantic," and that sort of thing was incredibly important, Ove had learned. So that's how it ended up. Even though everyone in Spain seemed to think they were somehow exceptional because they went around yawning and drinking and playing foreign music in restaurants and going to bed in the middle of the day.

Ove did his best not to like any of it. But Sonja got so worked up about it all that in the end it inevitably affected him too. She laughed so loudly when he held her that he felt it through his whole body. Not even Ove could avoid liking it.

They stayed in a little hotel, with a little pool, and a little restaurant run by a man whose name, as Ove understood it, was Schosse.

It was spelled "José" but it seemed people weren't too particular about pronunciation in Spain. Schosse couldn't speak any Swedish but he was very interested in speaking anyway. Sonja had a little book in which she looked things up, so she could say things like "sunset" and "ham" in Spanish. Ove felt it didn't stop being the butt end of a pig just because you said it another way, but he never mentioned this.

On the other hand he tried to point out to her that she shouldn't give money to the beggars in the street, as they'd only buy schnapps with it. But she kept doing it.

"They can do what they like with the money," she said.

When Ove protested she just smiled and took his big hands in hers and kissed them, explaining that when a person gives to another person it's not just the receiver who's blessed. It's the giver.

On the third day she went to bed in the middle of the day. Because that was what people did in Spain, she said, and one should adopt the "local customs of a place." Ove suspected it was not so much about customs as her own preferences, and this suited her very well as an excuse. She already slept sixteen hours out of twenty-four since she got pregnant.

Ove occupied himself by going for walks. He took the road leading past the hotel into the village. All the houses were made of stone, he noted. Many of them didn't appear to have thresholds under their front doors, and there were no decent window seals to be seen. Ove thought it slightly barbaric. One couldn't bloody build houses like this.

He was on his way back to the hotel when he saw Schosse leaning over a smoking brown car at the side of the road. Inside sat two children and a very old woman with a shawl around her head. She didn't seem to be feeling very well.

Schosse caught sight of Ove and waved at him in an agitated manner with something almost like panic in his eyes. "Sennjaur," he called out to Ove, the way he'd done every time he'd spoken to him since their arrival. Ove assumed it meant "Ove" in Spanish, but he hadn't checked Sonja's phrase book so carefully. Schosse pointed at the car and gesticulated wildly at Ove again. Ove stuck his hands into his trouser pockets and stopped at a safe distance, with a watchful look on his face.

"Hospital!" Schosse shouted again and pointed at the old woman in the car. In fact, she didn't look in very good shape, Ove reaffirmed to himself. Schosse pointed to the woman and pointed under the hood at the smoking engine, repeating despairingly, "Hospital! Hospital!" Ove cast his evaluating eye on the spectacle and finally drew the conclusion that this smoking, Spanish-manufactured car must be known as a "hospital."

He leaned over the engine and peered down. It didn't look so complicated, he thought.

"Hospital," Schosse said again and nodded several times and looked quite worried.

Ove didn't know what he was expected to say to that; clearly the whole matter of car makes was considered quite important in Spain, and certainly Ove could empathize with that.

"Saaaab," he said, therefore, pointing demonstratively at his chest.

Schosse stared in puzzlement at him for a moment. Then he pointed at himself.

"Schosse!"

"I wasn't bloody asking for your name, I was only sayi—" Ove started saying, but he stopped himself when he was met on the other side of the hood by a stare as glazed as an inland lake.

Obviously this Schosse's grasp of Swedish was even worse than Ove's Spanish. Ove sighed and looked with some concern at the children in the backseat. They were holding the old woman's hands and looked quite terrified. Ove looked down at the engine again.

Then he rolled up his shirtsleeves and motioned for Schosse to move out of the way. Within ten minutes they were back on the road, and Ove had never seen anyone so relieved to have his car fixed.

However much she flicked through her little phrase book, Sonja never found out the exact reason why they weren't charged for any of the food they ate in José's restaurant that week. But she laughed until she was positively simmering every time the little Spanish man who owned the restaurant lit up like a sun when he saw Ove, held out his arms, and exclaimed: "Señor Saab!!!"

Her daily naps and Ove's walks became a ritual. On the second day, Ove walked past a man putting up a fence, and stopped to explain that this was absolutely the wrong way to do it. The man couldn't understand a word of what he was saying, so Ove decided in the end that it would be quicker to show him how. On the third day he built a new exterior wall on a church building, with the assistance of the village priest. On the fourth day he went with Schosse to a field outside the village, where he helped one of Schosse's friends pull out a horse that had got stuck in a muddy ditch.

Many years later it occurred to Sonja to ask him about all that. When Ove at last told her, she shook her head both long and hard. "So while I was sleeping you sneaked out and helped people in need . . . and mended their fences? People can say whatever they like about you, Ove. But you're the strangest superhero I ever heard about."

On the bus on the way home from Spain she put Ove's hand on her belly and he felt the child kicking—faintly, as if someone had prodded the palm of his hand through a very thick oven mitt. They sat there for several hours feeling the little bumps. Ove didn't say anything but Sonja saw the way he wiped his eyes with the back of his hand when he rose from his seat and mumbled something about needing the bathroom.

It was the happiest week of Ove's life.

It was destined to be followed by the very unhappiest.

22

A MAN CALLED OVE AND SOMEONE IN A GARAGE

Ove and the cat sit in silence in the Saab outside the hospital.

"Stop looking at me as if this is my fault," says Ove to the cat.

The cat looks back at him as if it isn't angry but disappointed.

It wasn't really the plan that he would be sitting outside this hospital again. He hates hospitals, after all, and now he's bloody been here three times in less than a week. It's not right and proper. But no other choice was available to him.

Because today went to pot from the very beginning.

It started with Ove and the cat, during their daily inspection, when they discovered that the sign forbidding vehicular traffic within the residential area had been run over. This inspired such colorful profanities from Ove that the cat looked quite embarrassed. Ove marched off in fury and emerged moments later with his snow shovel. Then he stopped, looking towards Anita and Rune's house, his jaws clamped so hard that they made a creaking sound.

The cat looked at him accusingly.

"It's not my fault the old sod went and got old," he said more firmly.

When the cat didn't seem to find this to be in any way an acceptable explanation, Ove pointed at it with the snow shovel.

"You think this is the first time I've had a run-in with the council? That decision about Rune, do you think they've actually come to a real conclusion about it? They NEVER will! It'll go to appeal and then they'll drag it out and put it through their shitty bureaucratic grind! You understand? You think it'll happen quickly, but it takes months! Years! You think I'm going to stick around here just because that old sod went all helpless?"

The cat didn't answer.

"You don't understand! Understand?" Ove hissed and turned around.

He felt the cat's eyes on his back as he marched inside.

That is not the reason why Ove and the cat are sitting in the Saab in the parking area outside the hospital. But it does have a fairly direct connection with Ove standing there shoveling snow when that journalist woman in her slightly too large green jacket turned up outside his house.

"Ove?" she asked behind him, as if she was concerned that he might have changed his identity since she last came here to disturb him.

Ove continued shoveling without in any way acknowledging her presence.

"I only want to ask you a few questions. . . ." she tried.

"Ask them somewhere else. I don't want them here," Ove answered, scattering snow about him in a way that made it difficult to tell whether he was shoveling or digging.

"But I only want t—" she said, but she was interrupted by Ove and the cat going into the house and slamming the door in her face.

Ove and the cat squatted in the hall and waited for her to leave. But she didn't leave. She started banging on the door and calling out: "But you're a hero!!!"

"She's absolutely psychotic, that woman," said Ove to the cat.

The cat didn't disagree.

When she carried on banging and shouting even louder, Ove didn't know what to do, so he threw the door open and put his finger over his mouth, hushing her, as if in the next moment he was going to point out that this was actually a library.

She attempted to grin up at his face, waving something that Ove instinctively perceived as a camera of some sort. Or something else. It wasn't so easy knowing what cameras looked like anymore in this bloody society.

Then she tried to step into his hall. Maybe she shouldn't have done that.

Ove raised his big hand and pushed her back over the threshold as a reflex, so that she almost fell headfirst into the snow.

"I don't want anything," said Ove.

She regained her balance and waved the camera at him, while yelling something. Ove wasn't listening. He looked at the camera as if it were a weapon, and then decided to flee. This person was clearly not a reasonable person.

So the cat and Ove stepped out the door, locked it, and headed off as quick as they could towards the parking area. The journalist woman jogged along behind them.

To be absolutely clear about it, though, no part of this bears any relation to why Ove is now sitting outside the hospital. But when Parvaneh stood knocking on the door of Ove's house, fifteen minutes or so later, holding her three-year-old by the hand, and when no one opened and then she heard voices from the parking area, this, so to speak, has a good deal to do with Ove sitting outside the hospital.

Parvaneh and the child came around the corner of the parking area and saw Ove standing outside his closed garage door with his hands sullenly shoved into his pockets. The cat was sitting at his feet looking guilty.

"What are you doing?" said Parvaneh.

"Nothing," said Ove defensively.

Some knocking sounds were coming from the inside of the garage door.

"What was that?" said Parvaneh, staring at it with surprise.

Ove suddenly seemed extremely interested in a particular section of the asphalt under one of his shoes. The cat looked a bit as if it were about to start whistling and trying to walk away.

Another knock came from the inside of the garage door.

"Hello?" said Parvaneh.

"Hello?" answered the garage door.

Parvaneh's eyes widened.

"Christ . . . have you locked someone in the *garage*, Ove?!" Ove didn't answer. Parvaneh shook him as if trying to dislodge some coconuts.

"OVE!"

"Yes, yes. But I didn't do it on purpose, for God's sake," he muttered and wriggled out of her grip.

Parvaneh shook her head.

"Not on purpose?"

"No, not on purpose," said Ove, as if this should wrap up the discussion.

When he noticed that Parvaneh was obviously expecting some sort of clarification, he scratched his head and sighed.

"Her. Well. She's one of those journalist people. It wasn't bloody me who locked her in. I was going to lock myself and the cat in there. But then she followed us. And, you know. Things took their course."

Parvaneh started massaging her temples.

"I can't deal with this. . . ."

"Naughty," said the three-year-old and shook her finger at Ove.

"Hello?" said the garage door.

"There's no one here!" Ove hissed back.

"But I can hear you!" said the garage door.

Ove sighed and looked despondently at Parvaneh. As if he was about to exclaim: "You hear that, even garage doors are talking to me these days?"

Parvaneh waved him aside, walked up to the door, leaned her face up close, and knocked tentatively. The door knocked back. As if it expected to communicate by Morse code from now on. Parvaneh cleared her throat.

"Why do you want to talk to Ove?" she said, relying on the conventional alphabet.

"He's a hero!"

"A . . . what?"

"Okay, sorry. So: my name is Lena; I work at the local newspaper, and I want to intervie—"

Parvaneh looked at Ove in shock.

"What does she mean, a hero?"

"She's just prattling on!" Ove protested.

"He saved a man's life; he'd fallen on the track!" yelled the garage door.

"Are you sure you've got the right Ove?" said Parvaneh.

Ove looked insulted.

"I see. So now it's out of the question that I could be a hero, is it?" he muttered.

Parvaneh peered at him suspiciously. The three-year-old tried to grab hold of what was left of the cat's tail, with an excitable "Kitty!" "Kitty" did not look particularly impressed by this and tried to hide behind Ove's legs.

"What have you done, Ove?" said Parvaneh in a low, confidential voice, taking two steps away from the garage door.

The three-year-old chased the cat around his feet. Ove tried to figure out what he should do with his hands.

"Ah, so I hauled a suit off the rails, it's nothing to make a bloody fuss about," he mumbled.

Parvaneh tried to keep a straight face.

"Or to have a giggle about, actually," said Ove sourly.

"Sorry," said Parvaneh.

The garage door called out something that sounded like: "Hello? Are you still there?"

"No!" Ove bellowed.

"Why are you so terrifically angry?" the garage door wondered.

Ove was starting to look hesitant. He leaned towards Parvaneh.

"I . . . don't know how to get rid of her," he said, and if Parvaneh had not known better she might have concluded that there was something pleading in his eyes. "I don't want her in there on her own with the Saab!" he whispered gravely.

Parvaneh nodded, in confirmation of the unfortunate aspects of the situation. Ove lowered a tired, mediating hand between the three-year-old and the cat before that situation went out of control around his shoes. The three-year-old looked as if she was ready to try to hug the cat. The cat looked as if it was ready to pick out the three-year-old from a lineup at a police station. Ove managed to catch the three-year-old, who burst into peals of laughter.

"Why are you here in the first place?" Ove demanded of Parvaneh as he handed over the little bundle like a sack of potatoes.

"We're taking the bus to the hospital to pick up Patrick and Jimmy," she answered.

She saw the way Ove's face twitched above his cheekbones when she said "bus."

"We . . ." Parvaneh began, as if articulating the beginnings of a thought.

She looked at the garage door, then looked at Ove.

"I can't hear what you're saying! Talk louder!" yelled the garage door.

Ove immediately took two steps away from it. At once, Parvaneh smiled confidently at him. As if she had just worked out the solution to a crossword.

"Hey, Ove! How about this: if you give us a lift to the hospital, I'll help you get rid of this journalist! Okay?"

Ove looked up. He didn't look a bit convinced. Parvaneh threw out her arms.

"Or I'll tell the journalist that I can tell a story or two about you, Ove," she said, raising her eyebrows.

"Story? What story?" the garage door called out and started banging in an excitable manner.

Ove looked dejectedly at the garage door.

"This is blackmail," he said desperately to Parvaneh.

Parvaneh nodded cheerfully.

"Ove ackatted de clauwn!" said the three-year-old and nodded in an initiated way at the cat, clearly because she felt that Ove's aversion to the hospital needed further explanation to whoever was not there the last time they went.

The cat seemed not to know what this meant. But if the clown had been anywhere near as tiresome as this three-year-old, the cat didn't take an entirely negative view of Ove hitting someone.

And so this is the reason why Ove is sitting here now. The cat looks personally let down by Ove for making it travel all the way in the backseat with the three-year-old. Ove adjusts the newspapers on the seats. He feels he's been tricked. When Parvaneh said she'd "get rid of" the journalist, he didn't have a very clear idea of exactly how she'd manage it. Obviously he didn't have expectations of the woman being conjured away in a puff of smoke or knocked out with a spade or buried in the desert or anything of that kind.

In fact the only thing Parvaneh had done was to open the garage door, give that journalist her card, and say, "Call me and we'll talk about Ove." Was that really a way of getting rid of anyone? Ove doesn't think, properly speaking, that it's a way of getting rid of anyone at all.

But now it's too late, of course. Now, damn it, he's sitting here waiting outside the hospital for the third time in less than a week. Blackmail, that's what it is.

Added to this, Ove has the cat's resentful stares to contend with.

Something in its eyes reminds him of the way Sonja used to look at him.

"They won't be coming to take Rune away. They say they're going to do it, but they'll be busy with the process for many years," says Ove to the cat.

Maybe he's also saying it to Sonja. And maybe to himself. He doesn't know.

"At least stop feeling so sorry for yourself. If it wasn't for me you'd be living with the kid, and then you wouldn't have much left of what you have now for a tail. Think about that!" He snorts at the cat, in an attempt to change the subject.

The cat rolls onto its side, away from Ove, and goes to sleep in protest. Ove looks out the window again. He knows very well that the three-year-old isn't allergic at all. He knows very well that Parvaneh just lied to him so she wouldn't have to take care of the Cat Annoyance.

He's not some bloody senile old man.

23

A MAN WHO WAS OVE AND A BUS THAT NEVER GOT THERE

"Every man needs to know what he's fighting for." That was apparently what people said. Or at least it was what Sonja had once read out aloud to Ove from one of her books. Ove couldn't remember which one; there were always so many books around that woman. In Spain she had bought a whole bag of them, despite not even speaking Spanish. "I'll learn while I'm reading," she said. As if that was the way you did it. Ove told her he was a bit more about thinking for himself rather than reading what a lot of other clots had on their minds. Sonja just smiled and caressed his cheek.

Then he carried her absurdly oversize bags to the bus. Felt the driver smelling of wine as he went by, but concluded that maybe this was the way they did things in Spain and left it at that. Sat there in the seat as Sonja moved his hand to her belly and that was when he felt his child kicking, for the first and last time. He stood up and went to the bathroom and when he was halfway down the aisle the bus lurched, scraped against the central barrier, and then there was a moment of silence. As if time was taking a deep breath.

Then: an explosion of splintering glass. The merciless screeching of twisting metal. Violent crunches as the cars behind the bus slammed into it.

And all the screams. He'd never forget them.

Ove was thrown about and only remembered falling on his stomach. He looked around for her, terrified, among the tumult of human bodies, but she was gone. He threw himself forward, cutting himself under a rain of glass from the ceiling, but it was as if a furious wild animal were holding him back and forcing him down on the floor in unreflecting humiliation. It would pursue him every night for the rest of his life: his utter impotence in the situation.

He sat by her bed every moment of the first week. Until the nurses insisted that he shower and change his clothes. Everywhere they looked at him with sympathetic stares and expressed their "condolences." A doctor came in and spoke to Ove in an indifferent, clinical voice about the need to "prepare himself for the likelihood of her not waking up again." Ove threw that doctor through a door. A door that was locked and shut. "She isn't dead," he raved down the corridor. "Stop behaving as if she was dead!" No one at the hospital dared make that mistake again.

On the tenth day, as the rain smattered against the windows and the radio spoke of the worst storm in several decades, Sonja opened her eyes in torturous little slits, caught sight of Ove, and stole her hand into his. Enfolded her finger in the palm of his hand.

Then she fell asleep and slept through the night. When she woke up again the nurses offered to tell her, but Ove grimly insisted that he was the one who would do it. Then he told her everything in a composed voice, while caressing her hands in his, as if they were very, very cold. He told her about the driver smelling of wine and the bus veering into the crash barrier and the collision. The smell of burned rubber. The earsplitting crashing sound.

And about a child that would never come now.

And she wept. An ancient, inconsolable despair that screamed and tore and shredded them both as countless hours passed. Time and sorrow and fury flowed together in stark, long-drawn darkness. Ove knew there and then that he would never forgive himself for having got up from his seat at that exact moment, for not being there to protect them. And knew that this pain was forever.

But Sonja would not have been Sonja if she had let the darkness win. So, one morning, Ove did not know how many days had passed since the accident, expressing herself quite succinctly, she declared that she wanted to start having physiotherapy. And when Ove looked at her as if it were his own spine screaming like a tortured animal every time she moved, she gently leaned her head against his chest and whispered: "We can busy ourselves with living or with dying, Ove. We have to move on."

And that's how it was.

In the following months, back in Sweden, Ove met innumerable men in white shirts. They sat behind desks made of light-colored wood in various municipal offices and they apparently had endless amounts of time to instruct Ove in what documents had to be filled in for various purposes, but no time at all to discuss the measures that were needed for Sonja to get better.

A woman was dispatched to the hospital from one of the municipal authorities, where she bullishly explained that Sonja could be placed in "a service home for other people in her situation." Something about how "the strain of everyday life" quite understandably could be "excessive" for Ove. She didn't say it right out, but it was clear as crystal what she was driving at. She did not believe that Ove could see himself staying with his wife now. "Under present conditions," she kept repeating, nodding discreetly at the bedside. She spoke to Ove as if Sonja were not even in the room.

Admittedly Ove opened the door this time, but she was ejected all the same.

"The only home we're going to is our own! Where we LIVE!" Ove roared at her, and in pure frustration and anger he threw one of Sonja's shoes out of the room.

Afterwards he had to go and ask the nurses, who'd almost been hit by it, if they knew where it had gone. Which of course made him even angrier. It was the first time since the accident that he heard Sonja laughing. As if it was pouring out of her, without the slightest possibility of stopping it, like she was being wrestled to the ground by her own giggling. She laughed and laughed and laughed until the vowels were rolling across the walls and floors, as if they meant to do away with the laws of time and space. It made Ove feel as if his chest was slowly rising out of the ruins of a collapsed house after an earthquake. It gave his heart space to beat again.

He went home and rebuilt the whole house, ripped out the old countertop and put in a new, lower one. Even managed to find a specially made stove. Reconstructed the doorframes and fitted ramps over all the thresholds. The day after Sonja was allowed to leave the hospital, she went back to her teacher training. In the spring she sat her examination. There was an advertisement in the newspaper for a teaching position in a school with the worst reputation in town, with the sort of class that no qualified teacher with all the parts of her brain correctly screwed together would voluntarily face. It was attention-deficit hyperactivity disorder before attention-deficit hyperactivity disorder had been invented.

"There's no hope for these boys and girls," the headmaster soberly explained in the interview. "This is not education, this is storage." Maybe Sonja understood how it felt to be described as such. The vacant position attracted only one applicant, and she got those boys and girls to read Shakespeare.

In the meantime Ove was so weighed down with anger that Sonja sometimes had to ask him to go outside so he didn't demolish the furniture. It pained her infinitely to see his shoulders so loaded down with the will to destroy. Destroy that bus driver. The travel agency. The crash barrier of that highway. The wine producer. Everything and everyone. Punch and keep punching until every bastard had been obliterated. That was all he wanted to do. He put that anger in his shed. He put it in the garage. He spread it over the ground during his inspection rounds. But that wasn't all. In the end he also started putting it in letters. He wrote to the Spanish government. To the Swedish authorities. To the police. To the court. But no one took responsibility. No one cared. They answered by reference to legal texts or other authorities. Made excuses. When the council refused to build a ramp at the stairs of the school where Sonja worked, Ove wrote letters and complaints for months. He wrote letters to newspapers. He tried to sue the council. He literally inundated them with the unfathomable vengefulness of a father who has been robbed.

But everywhere, sooner or later, he was stopped by men in white shirts with strict, smug expressions on their faces. And one couldn't fight them. Not only did they have the state on their side, they *were* the state. The last complaint was rejected. The fighting was over because the white shirts had decided so. And Ove never forgave them that.

Sonja saw everything. She understood where he was hurting.

So she let him be angry, let all that anger find its outlet somewhere, in some way. But on one of those early summer evenings in May that always come along bearing gentle promises about the summer ahead, she rolled up to him, the wheels leaving soft marks on the parquet floor. He was sitting at the kitchen table writing one of his letters, and she took his pen away from him, slipped her hand into his, and pressed her finger into his rough palm. Leaned her forehead tenderly against his chest.

"That's enough now, Ove. No more letters. There's no space for life with all these letters of yours."

And she looked up, softly caressed his cheek, and smiled.

"It's enough now, my darling Ove."

And then it was enough.

The next morning Ove got up at dawn, drove the Saab to her school, and with his own bare hands built the disabled ramp the council was refusing to put up. And after that she came home every evening for as long as Ove could remember and told him, with fire in her eyes, about her boys and girls. The ones who arrived in the classroom with police escorts yet when they left could recite four-hundred-year-old poetry. The ones who could make her cry and laugh and sing until her voice was bouncing off the ceilings of their little house. Ove could never make head nor tail of those impossible kids, but he was not beyond liking them for what they did to Sonja.

Every human being needs to know what she's fighting for. That was what they said. And she fought for what was good. For the children she never had. And Ove fought for her.

Because that was the only thing in this world he really knew.

24

A MAN CALLED OVE AND A BRAT WHO DRAWS IN COLOR

The Saab is so full of people when Ove drives away from the hospital that he keeps checking the fuel gauge, as if he's afraid that it's going to break into a scornful dance. In his rearview mirror he sees Parvaneh unconcernedly giving the three-year-old paper and color crayons.

"Does she have to do that in the car?" barks Ove.

"Would you rather have her restless, so she starts wondering how to pull the upholstery off of the seats?" Parvaneh says calmly.

Ove doesn't answer. Just looks at the three-year-old in his mirror. She's shaking a big purple crayon at the cat in Parvaneh's lap and yelling: "DROORING!" The cat observes the child with great caution, clearly reluctant to make itself available as a decorative surface.

Patrick sits between them, turning and twisting his body to try to find a comfortable position for his leg cast, which he's wedged up on the armrest between the front seats.

It's not easy, because he's doing his best not to dislodge the newspapers that Ove has placed both on his seat and under the cast.

The three-year-old drops a color crayon, which rolls forward under the front passenger seat, where Jimmy is sitting. In what must surely be a move worthy of an Olympian acrobat for a man of his physique, Jimmy manages to bend forward and scoop up the crayon from the mat in front of him. He checks it out for a moment, grins, then turns to Patrick's propped-up leg and draws a large, smiling man on the cast. The toddler shrieks with joy when she notices.

"So you're going to start making a mess as well?" says Ove.

"Pretty neat, isn't it?" Jimmy crows and looks as if he's about to make a high-five at Ove.

Ove rolls his eyes.

"Sorry, man, couldn't stop myself," says Jimmy and, somewhat shamefaced, gives back the crayon to Parvaneh.

There's a plinging sound in Jimmy's pocket. He hauls out a cell phone as large as a full-grown man's hand and occupies himself with frenetically tapping the display.

"Whose is the cat?" Patrick asks from the back.

"Ove's kitty!" the three-year-old answers with rock-solid certainty.

"It is *not*," Ove corrects her at once.

He sees Parvaneh smiling teasingly at him in the rearview mirror.

"Is so!" she says.

"No it ISN'T!" says Ove.

She laughs. Patrick looks very puzzled. She pats him encouragingly on the knee.

"Don't worry about what Ove is saying. It's absolutely his cat."

"He's a bloody vagrant, that's what he is!" Ove corrects.

The cat lifts its head to find out what all the commotion is about, then concludes that all this is sensationally uninteresting and snuggles back into Parvaneh's lap. Or rather, her belly.

"So it's not being handed in somewhere?" Patrick wonders, scrutinizing the feline.

The cat lifts its head a little, hissing briefly at him by way of an answer.

"What do you mean, 'handed in'?" Ove says, cutting him short.

"Well . . . to a cat home or someth—" Patrick begins, but gets no further before Ove bawls:

"No one's being handed in to any bloody home!"

And with this, the subject is exhausted. Patrick tries not to look startled. Parvaneh tries not to burst out laughing. Neither really manages.

"Can't we stop off somewhere for something to eat?" Jimmy interjects and adjusts his seat position; the Saab starts swaying.

Ove looks at the group assembled around him, as if he's been kidnapped and taken to a parallel universe. For a moment he thinks about swerving off the road, until he realizes that the worst-case scenario would be that they all accompanied him into the afterlife. After this insight, he reduces his speed and increases the gap significantly between his own car and the one in front.

"Wee!" yells the three-year-old.

"Can we stop, Ove? Nasanin needs to pee," Parvaneh calls out, in that manner peculiar to people who believe that the backseat of a Saab is two hundred yards behind the driver.

"Yeah! Then we can have something to eat at the same time." Jimmy nods with anticipation.

"Yeah, let's do that, I need a wee as well," says Parvaneh.

"McDonald's has toilets," Jimmy informs them helpfully.

"McDonald's will be fine, stop there," Parvaneh nods.

"There'll be no stopping here," says Ove firmly.

Parvaneh eyes him in the rearview mirror. Ove glares back. Ten minutes later he's sitting in the Saab, waiting for them all outside McDonald's. Even the cat has gone inside with them. The traitor. Parvaneh comes out and taps on Ove's window.

"Are you sure you don't want anything?" she says softly to him.

Ove nods. She looks a little dejected. He rolls up the window again. She walks around the car and hops in on the passenger side.

"Thanks for stopping." She smiles.

"Yeah, yeah," says Ove.

She's eating french fries. Ove reaches forward and puts more newspaper on the floor in front of her. She starts laughing. He can't understand at what.

"I need your help, Ove," she says suddenly.

Ove doesn't seem spontaneously or enormously enthusiastic.

"I thought you could help me pass my driving test," she continues.

"What did you say?" asks Ove, as if he must have heard her wrong.

She shrugs. "Patrick will be in casts for months. I have to get a driver's license so I can give the girls lifts. I thought you could give me some driving lessons."

Ove looks so confused that he even forgets to get upset.

"So in other words you don't have a driver's license?"

"No."

"So it wasn't a joke?"

"No."

"Did you lose your license?"

"No. I never had one."

Ove's brain seems to need a good few moments to process this information, which, to him, is utterly beyond belief.

"What's your job?" he asks.

"What's that got to do with it?" she replies.

"Surely it's got everything to do with it?"

"I'm a real estate agent."

Ove nods.

"And no driver's license?"

"No."

Ove shakes his head grimly, as if this is the very pinnacle of being a human being who doesn't take responsibility for anything. Parvaneh smiles that little teasing smile of hers again, scrunches up the empty french fries bag, and opens the door.

"Look at it this way, Ove: Do you really want *anyone* else to teach me to drive in the residential area?"

She gets out of the car and goes to the trash can. Ove doesn't answer. He just snorts.

Jimmy shows up in the doorway.

"Can I eat in the car?" he asks, a piece of chicken sticking out of his mouth.

At first Ove thinks of saying no, but then realizes they'll never get out of here at this rate. Instead, he spreads so many newspapers over the passenger seat and floor that it's as if he's preparing to give the car a respray.

"Just hop in, will you, so we can get home," he groans and gestures at Jimmy.

Jimmy nods, upbeat. His cell phone plings.

"And stop that noise—this isn't a bloody pinball arcade."

"Sorry, man, work keeps e-mailing me all the time," says Jimmy, balancing his food in one hand and fiddling with the phone in his pocket with the other.

"So you have a job, then?" says Ove.

Jimmy nods enthusiastically.

"I program iPhone apps."

Ove has no further questions.

At least it's relatively quiet in the car for ten minutes until they roll into the parking area outside Ove's garage. Ove stops alongside the bicycle shed, puts the Saab into neutral without turning off the engine, and gives his passengers a meaningful look.

"It's fine, Ove. Patrick can manage on his crutches from here," says Parvaneh with unmistakable irony.

"Cars aren't allowed in the residential area," says Ove.

Undeterred, Patrick extricates himself and his cast from the backseat of the car, while Jimmy squeezes out of the passenger seat, chicken grease all over his T-shirt.

Parvaneh lifts out the three-year-old in her car seat and puts it on the ground. The girl waves something in the air, while yelling out some garbled words.

Parvaneh nods, goes back to the car, leans in through the front door, and gives Ove a sheet of paper.

"What's that?" Ove asks, making not the slightest movement to accept it.

"It's Nasanin's drawing."

"What am I supposed to do with that?"

"She's drawn you," Parvaneh replies, and shoves it into his hands.

Ove gives the paper a reluctant look. It's filled with lines and swirls.

"That's Jimmy, and that's the cat, and that's Patrick and me. And that's you," explains Parvaneh.

When she says that last bit she points at a figure in the middle of the drawing. Everything else on the paper is drawn in black, but the figure in the middle is a veritable explosion of color. A riot of yellow and red and blue and green and orange and purple.

"You're the funniest thing she knows. That's why she always draws you in color," says Parvaneh.

Then she closes the passenger door and walks off.

It takes several seconds before Ove collects himself enough to call out after her: "What do you mean, 'always'?"

But by then they have all started walking back to the houses.

Slightly offended, Ove adjusts the newspaper on the passenger seat. The cat climbs over from the back and makes itself comfortable on it. Ove backs the Saab into the garage. Closes the door. Puts it into neutral without turning off the engine. Feels the exhaust fumes slowly filling the garage and gazes at the plastic tube hanging on the wall. For a few minutes all that can be heard is the cat's breathing and the engine's rhythmic stuttering. It would be easy, just sitting there and waiting for the inevitable. It's the only logical thing, Ove knows. He's been longing for it for a long time now. The end. He misses her so much that sometimes he can't bear existing in his own body. It would be the only rational thing, just sitting here until the fumes lull both him and the cat to sleep and bring this to an end.

But then he looks at the cat. And he turns off the engine.

The next morning they get up at quarter to six. Drink coffee and eat tuna fish respectively. When they've finished their inspection round, Ove carefully shovels snow outside his house. When he's done with that he stands outside his shed, leaning on his snow shovel, looking at the line of row houses.

Then he crosses the road and starts clearing snow in front of the other houses.

25

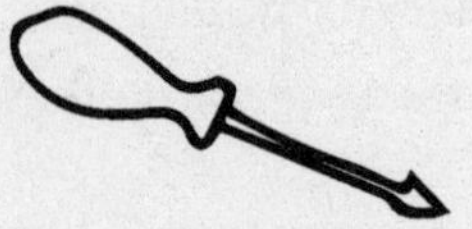

A MAN CALLED OVE AND A PIECE OF CORRUGATED IRON

Ove waits till after breakfast, once he's let the cat out. Only then does he take down a plastic bottle from the top shelf in the bathroom. He weighs it in his hand as if he's about to throw it somewhere, rattles it lightly to see if many pills are left.

Towards the end the doctors prescribed so many painkillers for Sonja. Their bathroom still looks like a storage facility for the Colombian mafia. Ove obviously doesn't trust medicine, has always been convinced its only real effects are psychological and, as a result, it only works on people with feeble brains.

But it's only just struck him that chemicals are not at all an unusual way of taking one's life.

He hears something outside the front door—the cat is back surprisingly quickly, scraping its paws by the threshold and sounding like it's been caught in a steel trap. As if it knows what's going through Ove's mind. Ove can understand that it's disappointed in him. He can't possibly expect it to understand his actions.

He thinks about how it would feel, doing it this way. He has never taken any narcotics. Has hardly even been affected by alcohol. Has never liked the feeling of losing control. He's come to realize over the years that it's this very feeling that normal folk like and strive for, but as far as Ove is concerned only a complete bloody airhead could find loss of control a state worth aiming for. He wonders if he'll feel nauseated, if he'll feel pain when his body's organs give up and stop functioning. Or will he just go to sleep when his body becomes unfit for use?

By now, the cat is howling out there in the snow. Ove closes his eyes and thinks of Sonja. It's not that he's the sort of man who gives up and dies; he doesn't want her to think that. But it's actually *wrong*, all this. She married him. And now he doesn't quite know how to carry on without the tip of her nose in the pit between his throat and his shoulder. That's all.

He unscrews the lid and distributes the pills along the edge of the washbasin. Watches them as if expecting them to transform into little murderous robots. Of course they don't. Ove is unimpressed. He finds it quite inexplicable how those little white dots could do him any harm, regardless of how many of them he takes. The cat sounds as if it's spitting snow all over Ove's front door. But then it's interrupted by another, quite different sound.

A dog barking.

Ove looks up. It's quiet for a few seconds, and then he hears the cat yowling with pain. Then more barking. And Blond Weed roaring something.

Ove stands there gripping the washbasin. Closes his eyes as if he could blink the sound out. It doesn't work. Then at last he sighs and straightens up. Unscrews the lid of the bottle, pushes the pills back into it. Goes down the stairs. As he crosses the living room he puts the jar on the windowsill. And through the window he sees Blond Weed in the road, taking aim and then rushing towards the cat.

Ove opens the door exactly as she's about to kick the animal in the head with all her strength. The cat quickly dodges her needle-sharp heel and backs away towards Ove's toolshed. Mutt growls hysterically, saliva flying around its head as if it were a rabies-infected beast. There's fur in its jaws. This is the first time Ove can remember having seen Weed without her sunglasses. Malevolence glitters in her green eyes. She pulls back, preparing for another kick, then catches sight of Ove and stops herself midflow. Her lower lip is trembling with anger.

"I'll have that thing shot!" she hisses and points at the cat.

Very slowly Ove shakes his head without taking his eyes off her. She swallows. Something about his expression, as if sculpted from a seam of rock, makes her murderous assurance falter.

"It's a f-f-fucking street cat and . . . and it's going to die! It scratched Prince!" she stammers.

Ove doesn't say anything but his eyes turn black. And in the end even the dog backs away from him.

"Come on, Prince," she says, disappearing around the corner as if Ove had physically shoved her from behind.

Ove stays where he is, breathing heavily. He presses his fist to his chest, feels the uncontrolled beating of his heart. He groans a little. Then he looks at the cat. The cat looks back at him. There's a new wound down its flank. Blood in its fur again.

"Nine lives won't last you very long, will they?" says Ove.

The cat licks its paw and looks as if it's not the sort of cat that likes to keep count. Ove nods and steps aside.

"Get inside, then."

The cat traipses in over the threshold. Ove closes the door.

He stands in the middle of the living room. Everywhere, Sonja looks back at him. Only now does it strike him that he's positioned the photographs so they follow him through the house wherever he goes. She's on the table in the kitchen, hangs on the wall in the hall and halfway up the stairs. She's on the window shelf in the living room, where the cat has now jumped up and sits right beside her. It sends Ove a disgruntled look as it sweeps the pills onto the floor, with a crash. When Ove picks up the bottle, the cat looks at him in horror, as if about to shout, "J'accuse!"

Ove kicks a little at a baseboard, then turns around and goes into the kitchen to put the pill bottle in a cupboard. Then he makes coffee and pours water in a bowl for the cat.

They drink in silence.

Ove picks up the empty bowl and puts it next to his coffee cup in the sink. He stands with his hands on his hips for a good while. Then turns around and goes into the hall.

"Tag along, then," he urges the cat without looking at it. "Let's give that village cur something to think about."

Ove puts on the navy winter jacket, steps into his clogs, and lets the cat walk out the door first. He looks at the photo of Sonja on the wall. She laughs back at him. Maybe it's not so enormously important to die that it can't wait another hour, thinks Ove, and follows the cat into the street.

He goes to Rune's house, where it takes several minutes before the door opens. There's a slow, dragging sound inside before anything happens with the lock, as if a ghost is approaching with heavy chains rattling behind it. Then, finally, it opens and Rune stands there looking at Ove and the cat with an empty stare.

"You got any corrugated iron?" wonders Ove, without allowing any time for small talk.

Rune gives him a concentrated stare for a second or two, as if his brain is fighting desperately to produce a memory.

"Corrugated iron?" he says to himself, as if tasting the word, like someone who's just woken up and is intensely trying to remember what he's been dreaming.

"Corrugated iron; that's it," says Ove with a nod.

Rune looks at him, or rather he looks straight through him. His eyes have the gleam of a newly waxed car hood. He's emaciated and hunchbacked; his beard is gray, bordering on white. This used to be a solid bloke commanding a bit of respect, but now his clothes hang on his body in rags. He's grown old: very, very old, Ove realizes, and it hits him with a force he hadn't quite counted on. Rune's gaze flickers for a moment. Then his mouth starts twitching.

"Ove?" he exclaims.

"Yeah, well . . . one thing's for sure, I'm not the pope," Ove replies.

The baggy skin on Rune's face cracks into a sleepy smile. Both men, once as close as men of that sort could be, stare at each other. One of them a man who refuses to forget the past, and one who can't remember it at all.

"You look old," says Ove.

Rune grins.

Then Anita's anxious voice makes itself heard and in the next moment her small, drumming feet are bearing her at speed towards the door.

"Is there someone at the door, Rune? What are you doing there?" she calls out, terrified, as she appears in the doorway. Then she sees Ove.

"Oh . . . hello, Ove," she says and stops abruptly.

Ove stands there with his hands in his pockets. The cat beside him looks as if it would do the same, if it had pockets. Or hands. Anita is small and colorless in her gray trousers, gray knitted cardigan, gray hair, and gray skin. But Ove notices that her face is slightly red-eyed and swollen. Quickly she wipes her eyes and blinks away the pain. As women of that generation do. As if they stood in the doorway every morning, determinedly driving sorrow out of the house with a broom. Tenderly she takes Rune by the shoulders and leads him to his wheelchair by the window in the living room.

"Hello, Ove," she repeats in a friendly, also surprised, voice when she comes back to the door. "What can I do for you?"

"Do you have any corrugated iron?" he asks back.

She looks puzzled.

"Corrected iron?" she mumbles, as if the iron has somehow been wrong and now someone has to put it right.

Ove sighs deeply.

"Good God, corrugated iron."

Anita doesn't look the slightest bit less puzzled.

"Am I supposed to have some?"

"Rune will have some in his shed, definitely," says Ove and holds out his hand.

Anita nods. Takes down the shed key from the wall and puts it in Ove's hand.

"Corrugated. Iron?" she says again.

"Yes," says Ove.

"But we don't have a metal roof."

"What's that got to do with it?"

Anita shakes her head.

"No . . . no, maybe it doesn't, of course."

"One always has a bit of sheet metal," says Ove, as if this was absolutely beyond dispute.

Anita nods. As one does when faced with the undeniable fact

that a bit of corrugated iron is the sort of thing that all normal, right-thinking people keep lying about in their sheds, just in case there's call for it.

"But don't you have any of that metal yourself, then?" she tries, mainly to have something to talk about.

"I've used mine up," says Ove.

Anita nods understandingly. As one does when facing the indisputable fact that there's nothing odd about a normal man without a metal roof getting through his corrugated iron at such a rate that it runs out.

A minute later, Ove turns up triumphantly in the doorway, dragging a gigantic piece of corrugated iron, as big as a living room rug. Anita honestly has no idea how such a large piece of metal has even fitted in there without her knowing about it.

"Told you," Ove says with a nod, giving her back the key.

"Yes . . . yes, you did, didn't you," Anita feels obliged to admit.

Ove turns to the window. Rune looks back. And just as Anita turns around to go back into the house, Rune grins again, and lifts his hand in a brief wave. As if right there, just for a second, he knew exactly who Ove was and what he was doing there.

Anita stops hesitantly. Turns around.

"They've been here from Social Services again, they want to take Rune away from me," she says without looking up.

Her voice cracks like dry newspaper when she speaks her husband's name. Ove fingers the corrugated iron.

"They say I'm not capable of taking care of him. With his illness and everything. They say he has to go into a home," she says.

Ove continues fingering the corrugated iron.

"He'll die if I put him in a home, Ove. You know that. . . ." she whispers.

Ove nods and looks at the remains of a cigarette butt, frozen into the crack between two paving stones. Out of the corner of his eye he notices how Anita is sort of leaning slightly to one side. Sonja explained about a year ago that it was the hip replacement operation, he remembers. Her hands shake as well, these days. "The first stage of multiple sclerosis," Sonja had also explained. And a few years ago Rune got Alzheimer's as well.

"Your lad can come and give you a hand, then," he mumbles in a low voice.

Anita looks up. Looks into his eyes and smiles indulgently.

"Johan? Ah . . . he lives in America, you know. He's got enough on his own plate. You know how young people are!"

Ove doesn't answer. Anita says "America" as if it were the kingdom of heaven where her egotistical son has moved. Not once has Ove seen that brat here on the street since Rune sickened. Grown man now, but no time for his parents.

Anita jumps to attention, as if she's caught herself doing something disreputable. She smiles apologetically at Ove.

"Sorry, Ove, I shouldn't stand here taking up your time with my nattering."

She goes back into the house. Ove stays where he is with the sheet of corrugated iron in his hand and the cat at his side. He mutters something to himself just before the door is closed. Anita turns around in surprise, peers out of the crack, and looks at him.

"Pardon me?"

Ove twists without meeting her eyes. Then he turns and starts to leave, while his words slip out of him involuntarily.

"I said if you have any more problems with those bloody radiators, you can come and ring my doorbell. The cat and me are at home."

Anita's furrowed face pulls itself into a surprised smile. She takes half a step out the door, as if she wants to say something more. Maybe something about Sonja, how deeply she misses her best friend. How she misses what they had, all four of them, when they first moved onto this street almost forty years ago. How she even misses the way Rune and Ove used to argue. But Ove has already disappeared around the corner.

Back in his toolshed, Ove fetches the spare battery for the Saab and two large metal clips. He lays out the sheet of corrugated iron across the paving stones between the shed and the house and carefully covers it with snow.

He stands next to the cat, evaluating his creation for a long time. A perfect dog trap, hidden under snow, bursting with electricity, ready to bite. It seems a wholly proportionate revenge. The next time Blond Weed passes by with that bloody mutt of hers and the latter gets the idea of peeing on Ove's paving, it'll do so onto an electrified, conductive metal plate. And then let's see how amusing they find it, Ove thinks to himself.

The cat tilts its head and looks at the metal sheet.

"Like a bolt of lightning up your urethra," says Ove.

The cat looks at him for a long time. As if to say: "You're not serious, are you?" Eventually Ove sticks his hands in his pockets and shakes his head.

"No . . . no, I suppose not." He sighs glumly.

And then he packs up the battery and clamps and corrugated iron and puts everything in the garage. Not because he doesn't think those morons deserve a proper electric shock. Because they do. But because he knows it's been awhile since someone reminded him of the difference between being wicked because one has to be or because one can.

"It was a bloody good idea, though," he concludes to the cat as they go back into the house.

The cat goes into the living room with the dismissive body language of someone mumbling: "Sure, sure it was. . . ."

And then they have lunch.

26

A MAN CALLED OVE AND A SOCIETY WHERE NO ONE CAN REPAIR A BICYCLE ANYMORE

Many people find it difficult living with someone who likes to be alone. It grates on those who can't handle it themselves. But Sonja didn't whine more than she had to. "I took you as you were," she used to say.

But Sonja was not so silly that she didn't understand that even men like Ove like to have someone to talk to now and then. It had been quite awhile since he'd had that.

"I won," Ove says curtly when he hears the slamming of the mailbox.

The cat jumps off the windowsill in the living room and goes into the kitchen. Bad loser, thinks Ove and goes to the front door. It's been years since he last made a bet with someone about what time the mail would come. He used to make bets with Rune when they were on vacation in the summers, which grew so intensive that they developed complex systems of marginal extensions and half minutes to determine who was most accurate. That was how it was back in those days. The mail arrived at twelve o'clock on the dot, so one needed precise demarcations to be able to say who had guessed right. Nowadays it isn't like that. Nowadays the mail can be delivered halfway through the afternoon any old way it pleases. The post office takes care of it when it feels like it and you just have to be grateful and that's it. Ove tried to make bets with Sonja after he and Rune stopped talking. But she didn't understand the rules. So he gave up.

The youth barely manages to avoid being knocked off the steps when Ove throws the door open. Ove looks at him in surprise. He's wearing a postman's uniform.

"Yes?" demands Ove.

The youth looks like he can't come up with an answer. He fiddles with a newspaper and a letter. And that's when Ove notices that it's the same youth who argued with him about that bicycle a few days ago, by the storage shed. The bicycle the youth said he was going to "fix." Of course Ove knows what that means. "Fix" means "steal and sell on the Internet" to these rascals, that's the long and short of it.

The youth looks, if possible, even less thrilled about recognizing Ove than vice versa. He looks a little like a waiter sometimes does, when he's undecided about whether to serve you your food or take it into the kitchen and spit on it. The lad looks coolly at Ove before reluctantly handing the mail over with a grumpy "There y'go." Ove accepts it without taking his eyes off him.

"Your mailbox is mashed, so I was gonna give you these," says the youth.

He nods at the folded-double pile of junk that used to be Ove's mailbox until the Lanky One who can't back up with a trailer backed his trailer into it—then nods at the letter and newspaper in Ove's hand. Ove looks down at them. The newspaper is one of those local rags they hand out for nothing even when one puts up a sign quite expressly telling them to do no such bloody thing. And the letter is most likely advertising, Ove imagines. Admittedly his name and address have been written in longhand on the front, but that's a typical advertising trick. To make one think it's a letter from a real person, and then one opens it and in a flash one has been subjected to marketing. That trick won't work on Ove.

The youth stands there rocking on his heels and looking down at the ground. As if he's struggling with something inside that wants to come out.

"Was there something else?" Ove wonders.

The youth pulls his hand through his greasy, late-pubescent shock of hair.

"Ah, what the hell. . . . I was just wondering if you have a wife called Sonja," he manages to say.

Ove looks suspicious. The lad points at the envelope.

"I saw the surname. I had a teacher with that name. Was just wondering. . . ."

He seems to be cursing himself for having said anything. He spins around on the spot and starts walking away. Ove clears his throat and kicks the threshold.

"Wait . . . that could be right. What about Sonja?"

The lad stops a yard farther away.

"Ah, shit. . . . I just liked her, that's all I wanted to say. I'm . . . you know . . . I'm not so good at reading and writing and all that."

Ove almost says, "I'd never have guessed," but he leaves it. The youth twists awkwardly. Runs his hand through his hair, somewhat disoriented, as if he's hoping to find the appropriate words up there somewhere.

"She's the only teacher I ever had who didn't think I was thick as a plank," he mumbles, almost choking on his emotion. "She got me reading that . . . Shakespeare, you know. I didn't know I could even read, sort of thing. She got me reading the most hard-core thick book an' all. It felt really shit when I heard she died, you know."

Ove doesn't answer. The youth looks down at the ground. Shrugs.

"That's it. . . ."

He's silent. And then they both stand there, the fifty-nine-year-old and the teenager, a few yards apart, kicking at the snow. As if they were kicking a memory back and forth, a memory of a woman who insisted on seeing more potential in certain men than they saw in themselves. Neither of them knows what to do with their shared experience.

"What are you doing with that bike?" says Ove at last.

"I promised to fix it up for my girlfriend. She lives there," the youth answers, nodding at the house at the far end of their row, opposite Anita and Rune's place. The one where those recycling types live when they're not in Thailand or wherever they go.

"Or, you know. She's not my girlfriend yet. But I'm thinking I'm wanting her to be. Sort of thing."

Ove scrutinizes the youth as middle-aged men often scrutinize younger men who seem to invent their own grammar as they go along.

"So have you got any tools, then?" he asks.

The youth shakes his head.

"How are you going to repair a bike without tools?" Ove marvels, more with genuine surprise than agitation.

The youth shrugs.

"Dunno."

"Why did you promise to repair it, then?"

The youth kicks the snow. Scratches his face with his entire hand, embarrassed.

"Because I love her."

Ove can't quite decide what to say to that one. So he rolls up the local newspaper and envelope and slaps it into his palm, like a baton.

"I have to get going," the youth mumbles almost inaudibly and makes a movement to turn around again.

"Come over after work, then, and I'll get the bike out for you."

Ove's words seem to pop up out of nowhere. "But you have to bring your own tools," he adds.

The youth brightens up.

"You serious, man?"

Ove continues slapping the paper baton into his hand. The youth swallows.

"Awesome! Wait . . . ah, shit . . . I can't pick it up today! I have to go to my other job! But tomorrow, man, I can come tomorrow. Is it cool if I pick it up tomorrow, like, instead?"

Ove tilts his head and looks as if everything that's just been said came from the mouth of a character in an animated film. The youth takes a deep breath and pulls himself together.

"What other job?" asks Ove, as if he's had an incomplete answer in the final of *Jeopardy!*

"I sort of work in a café in the evenings and at the weekends," says the youth, with that new-won hope in his eyes about perhaps being able to rescue his fantasy relationship with a girlfriend who doesn't even know that she's his girlfriend—the sort of relationship that only a boy in late puberty with greasy hair can have. "I need both jobs because I'm saving money," he explains.

"For what?"

"A car."

Ove can't avoid noticing how he straightens up slightly when he says "car." Ove looks dubious for a moment. Then he slowly but watchfully slaps the baton into his palm again.

"What sort of car?"

"I had a look at a Renault," the youth says brightly, stretching a little more.

The air around the two men stops for a hundredth of a breath or so. An eerie silence suddenly envelops them. If this were a scene from a film, the camera would very likely have time to pan 360 degrees around them before Ove finally loses his composure.

"Renault? *Renault?* That's bloody FRENCH! You can't bloody well go and buy a FRENCH car!!!"

The youth seems just about to say something but he doesn't get the chance before Ove shakes his whole upper body as if trying to get rid of a persistent wasp.

"Christ, you puppy! Don't you know anything about cars?"

The youth shakes his head. Ove sighs deeply and puts his hand on his forehead as if he's been struck by a sudden migraine.

"And how are you going to get the bicycle to the café if you don't have a car?" he says at long last, visibly struggling to regain his composure.

"I hadn't . . . thought about that," says the youth.

Ove shakes his head.

"Renault? Christ almighty. . . ."

The youth nods. Ove rubs his eyes in frustration.

"Where's this sodding café you work at, then?" he mutters.

Twenty minutes later, Parvaneh opens her front door in surprise. Ove is standing outside, thoughtfully striking his hand with a paper baton.

"Have you got one of those green signs?"

"What?"

"You have to have one of those green signs when you're a student driver. Do you have one or not?"

She nods.

"Yeah . . . yes, I have, but wh—"

"I'll come and pick you up in two hours. We'll take my car."

Ove turns around and tramps back across the little road without waiting for an answer.

27

A MAN CALLED OVE AND A DRIVING LESSON

It happened now and then in the almost forty years they lived in the row of row houses that some thoughtless and recently moved-in neighbor was bold enough to ask Sonja what the real cause was for the deep animosity between Ove and Rune. Why had two men who had once been friends suddenly started hating one another with such overpowering intensity?

Sonja usually answered that it was quite straightforward. It was simply about how when the two men and their wives moved into their houses, Ove drove a Saab 96 and Rune a Volvo 244. A year or so later Ove bought a Saab 95 and Rune bought a Volvo 245. Three years later Ove bought a Saab 900 and Rune bought a Volvo 265. In the decades that followed, Ove bought another two Saab 900s and then a Saab 9000. Rune bought another Volvo 265 and then a Volvo 745, but a few years later he went back to a sedan model and acquired a Volvo 740. Whereupon Ove bought yet one more Saab 9000 and Rune eventually went over to a Volvo 760, after which Ove got himself a Saab 9000i and Rune part-exchanged to a Volvo 760 Turbo.

And then the day came when Ove went to the car dealer to look at the recently launched Saab 9-3, and when he came home in the evening, Rune had bought a BMW.

"A *BMW*!" Ove had roared at Sonja. "How can you *reason* with a human being like that? *How?*"

And possibly it was not the entire explanation for why these two men loathed one another, Sonja used to explain. Either you understood it or you didn't. And if you didn't understand, there was no point even trying to clarify the rest.

Most people never did understand, Ove often commented. But then people had no idea of loyalty these days. The car was just "a means of transport" and the road just a complication arising between two points. Ove is convinced this is why the roads are as bad as they are. If people were a little more careful with their cars they wouldn't drive like idiots, he thinks, watching with concern as Parvaneh pushes away the newspaper he has spread across her seat. She has to retract the driver's seat as far as it'll go, so she can maneuver her pregnant belly into the car, then bring it forward all the way so she can reach the wheel.

The driving lesson doesn't start so well. Or, to be precise, it begins with Parvaneh trying to get into the Saab with a bottle of carbonated juice in her hand. She shouldn't have done that. Then she tries to fiddle with Ove's radio to find "a more entertaining station." She shouldn't have done that either.

Ove picks up the newspaper from the floor, rolls it up, and starts nervously striking it against his hand, like a more aggressive version of a stress ball. She grabs the wheel and looks at the instruments like a curious child.

"Where do we start?" she yells eagerly, after at long last agreeing to hand over the juice.

Ove sighs. The cat sits in the backseat and looks as if it wished, with intensity, that cats knew how to strap on safety belts.

"Press the clutch pedal," says Ove, slightly grim.

Parvaneh looks around her seat as if searching for something. Then she looks at Ove and smiles ingratiatingly.

"Which one's the clutch?"

Ove's face fills with disbelief.

She looks around the seat again, turns toward the seat belt fixture in the back rest, as if she may find the clutch there. Ove holds his forehead. Parvaneh's facial expression immediately sours.

"I told you I want a driver's license for an automatic! Why did you make me use your car?"

"Because you're getting a proper license!" Ove cuts her short, emphasizing "proper" in a way that makes it plain that a license for an automatic is as much a "proper driver's license" as a car with an automatic gearbox is a "proper car."

"Stop shouting at me!" shouts Parvaneh.

"I'm not shouting!" Ove shouts back.

The cat curls up in the backseat, clearly anxious not to end up in the middle of this, whatever it is. Parvaneh crosses her arms and glares out of the side window. Ove strikes his paper baton rhythmically into the palm of his hand.

"The pedal on the far left is the clutch," he grunts in the end.

After taking a breath so deep that he has to stop halfway for a rest before he inhales again, he continues:

"The one in the middle is the brake. On the far right is the accelerator. You release the clutch slowly until you find the point where it engages, then give it a bit of gas, release the clutch, and move off."

Parvaneh seems to accept this as an apology. She nods and calms down. Takes hold of the steering wheel, starts the car, and follows his instructions. The Saab lurches forward with a little jump, then pauses before catapulting itself with a loud roar towards the guest parking and very nearly crashing into another car. Ove tugs at the hand brake. Parvaneh lets go of the steering wheel and yells in panic, covering her eyes with her hands until the Saab finally comes to an abrupt stop. Ove is puffing as if he'd had to make his way to the hand brake by forcing himself through a military obstacle course. His facial muscles twitch like a man whose eyes are being sprayed with lemon juice.

"What do I do now?!" roars Parvaneh when she realizes that the Saab is an inch from the taillights of the car in front.

"Reverse. You put it in reverse," Ove manages to say through his teeth.

"I almost smashed into that car!" pants Parvaneh.

Ove peers over the edge of the hood. And then, suddenly, a sort of calm comes over his face. He turns and nods at her, very matter-of-fact.

"Doesn't matter. It's a Volvo."

It takes them fifteen minutes to get out of the parking area and onto the main road. Once they're there, Parvaneh revs the first gear until the Saab vibrates like it's about to explode. Ove tells her to change gear and she replies that she doesn't know how. Meanwhile the cat seems to be trying to open the back door.

When they get to the first red light, a big black SUV with two shaven-headed young men in the front pulls up so close to their rear bumper that Ove is pretty sure he'll have their license number etched into his paintwork when they get home. Parvaneh glances nervously in the mirror. The SUV revs its engine, as if giving vent to some sort of opinion. Ove turns and looks out the back window. The two men have tattoos all over their throats, he notes. As if the SUV is not a clear enough advertisement for their stupidity.

The light turns green. Parvaneh brings up the clutch, the Saab splutters, and the instrument panel goes black. Stressed, Parvaneh turns the key in the ignition, which only makes it grind in a heart-rending manner. The engine makes a roar, coughs, and dies anew. The men with the shaved heads and tattooed throats sound the horn. One of them gestures.

"Press down the clutch and give it more gas," says Ove.

"That's what I'm doing!" she answers.

"That's not what you're doing."

"Yes I am!"

"Now you're shouting."

"I'M NOT BLOODY SHOUTING!" she shouts.

The SUV blares its horn. Parvaneh presses down the clutch. The Saab rolls backwards a few inches and bumps into the front of the SUV. The Throat Tattoos are now hanging on the horn as if it's an air raid alarm.

Parvaneh tugs despairingly at the key, only to be rewarded by yet another stall. Then suddenly she lets go of everything and hides her face in her hands.

"Good Go— Are you crying now?" Ove asks in amazement.

"I'M NOT BLOODY CRYING!" she howls, her tears spattering over the dashboard.

Ove leans back and looks down at his knee. Fingers the end of the paper baton.

"It's just such a strain, this, do you understand?" she sobs and leans her forehead against the wheel as if hoping it might be soft and fluffy. "I'm sort of PREGNANT! I'm just a bit STRESSED, can no one show a bit of understanding for a pregnant bloody woman who's a bit STRESSED?!"

Ove twists uncomfortably in the passenger seat. She punches the steering wheel several times, mumbles something about how all she wants is to "drink some bloody lemonade," flops her arms over the top of the steering wheel, buries her face in her sleeves, and starts crying again.

The SUV behind them honks until it sounds as if the Finland ferry is about to run them down. And then something in Ove snaps. He throws the door open, gets out of the car, walks slowly around the SUV, and rips the driver's door open.

"Have you never been a student driver or what?"

The driver doesn't have time to answer.

"You stupid little bastard!" Ove roars in the face of the shaven-headed young man with throat tattoos, his spittle cascading over their seats.

The Throat Tattoo doesn't have time to answer and Ove doesn't wait for him either. Instead he grabs the young man by his collar and pulls him up so hard that his body tumbles clumsily out of the car. He's a muscular sort, easily weighing in at two hundred pounds, but Ove holds his collar in an immovable steel grip. Evidently, Throat Tattoo is so surprised by the strength in the old man's grip that it doesn't occur to him to put up any resistance. Fury burns in Ove's eyes as he presses the probably thirty-five-years-younger man so hard against the side of the SUV that the bodywork creaks. He places the tip of his index finger in the middle of the shaved head and positions his eyes so close to Throat Tattoo's face that they feel each other's breath.

"If you sound that horn one more time, it'll be the LAST thing you do on this earth. Got it?"

Throat Tattoo allows his eyes to divert quickly towards his equally muscular friend inside the car, and then at the growing line of other cars behind the SUV. No one is making the slightest move to come to his assistance. No one beeps. No one moves. Everyone seems to be thinking the same thing: If a non-throat-tattooed man of Ove's age without any hesitation steps up to a throat-tattooed man of the age of this Throat Tattoo and presses him up against a car in this manner, then it's very likely not the throat-tattooed man one should be most worried about annoying.

Ove's eyes are black with anger. After a short moment of reflection, Throat Tattoo seems convinced by the argument that the old man unmistakably means business. The tip of his nose, almost unnoticeably, moves up and down.

Ove nods by way of confirmation and lets him back down on the ground. Then turns around, walks around the SUV, and gets back into the Saab. Parvaneh stares at him, with her mouth hanging open.

"Now, you listen to me," says Ove calmly while he carefully closes the door. "You've given birth to two children and quite soon you'll be squeezing out a third. You've come here from a land far away and most likely you fled war and persecution and all sorts of other nonsense. You've learned a new language and got yourself an education and you're holding together a family of obvious incompetents. And I'll be damned if I've seen you afraid of a single bloody thing in this world before now."

Ove rivets his eyes into her. Parvaneh is still agape. Ove points imperiously at the pedals under her feet.

"I'm not asking for brain surgery. I'm asking you to drive a car. It's got an accelerator, a brake, and a clutch. Some of the greatest twits in world history have sorted out how it works. And you will as well."

And then he utters seven words, which Parvaneh will always remember as the loveliest compliment he'll ever give her.

"Because you are not a complete twit."

Parvaneh pushes a ringlet of hair out of her face, sticky with tears. Clumsily she once again grabs hold of the steering wheel with both hands. Ove nods, puts on his safety belt, and makes himself comfortable.

"Now, push the clutch down and do what I say."

And that afternoon Parvaneh learns to drive.

28

A MAN WHO WAS OVE AND A MAN WHO WAS RUNE

Sonja used to say that Ove was "unforgiving." For instance, he refused to go back to the local bakery eight years after they gave him the wrong change when he bought pastries once at the end of the 1990s. Ove called it "having firm principles." They were never quite in agreement when it came to words and their meanings.

He knows that she is disappointed that he and Rune could not keep the peace. He knows that the animosity between him and Rune to some extent ruined the possibility of Sonja and Anita becoming the great friends they could have been. But when a conflict has been going on for long enough it can be impossible to sort out, for the simple reason that no one can remember how it first started. And Ove didn't know how it first started.

He only knew how it ended.

A BMW. There must have been some people who understood it and some who didn't. There were probably people who thought there was no connection between cars and emotions. But there would never be a clearer explanation as to why these two men had become enemies for life.

Of course, it had started innocently enough, not long after Ove and Sonja came back from Spain and the accident. Ove laid new paving stones in their little garden that summer, whereupon Rune put up a new fence around his. Whereupon Ove put up an even higher fence around his garden, whereupon Rune went off to the building supply store and a few days later started boasting all over the street that he had "built a swimming pool." That was no bloody swimming pool, Ove raged to Sonja. It was a little splash pool for Rune and Anita's newborn urchin, that was all it was. For a while Ove had plans to report it to the Planning Department as an illegal construction, but at that point Sonja put her foot down and sent him out to "mow the lawn" and calm himself down. And so Ove did just that, although it certainly did not calm him down very much at all.

The lawn was oblong, about five yards wide, and ran along the backs of Ove's and Rune's houses and the house in between, which Sonja and Anita had quickly named "the neutral zone." No one quite knew what that lawn was for or what function it was expected to fill, but when row housing was put up in those days, some city architect must have got the idea that there had to be lawns here and there, for no other reason than that they looked so very nice in the drawings. When Ove and Rune formed the Residents' Association and were still friends, the two men decided that Ove should be the "grounds man" and responsible for keeping the grass mowed. It had always been Ove before. On one occasion the other neighbors had proposed that the association should put out tables and benches on the lawn to create a sort of "common space for all the neighbors," but obviously Ove and Rune put a stop to that at once. It would only turn into a bloody mess and lots of noise.

And as far as that went, it was all peace and joy. At least insofar as anything could be "peace and joy" when men like Ove and Rune were involved.

Soon after Rune had built his "pool," a rat ran across Ove's newly mown lawn and into the trees on the other side. Ove immediately called a "crisis meeting" of the association and demanded that all local residents put out rat poison around their houses. The neighbors protested, of course, because they had seen hedgehogs by the edge of the woods and were concerned that they might eat the poison. Rune also protested, because he was afraid that some of it would end up in his pool. Ove suggested to Rune that he button up his shirt and go see a psychologist about his delusions of living on the French Riviera. Rune made a malicious joke at Ove's expense, to the effect that Ove had probably only imagined seeing that rat. All the others laughed. Ove never forgave Rune for that. The next morning someone had thrown birdseed all over Rune's outside space, and Rune had to use a spade to chase away a dozen rats as big as vacuum cleaners in the next few weeks. After that Ove got permission to put out poison, even though Rune mumbled that he'd pay him back for this.

Two years later Rune won the Great Tree Conflict, when he gained permission at the annual meeting to saw down a tree blocking his and Anita's evening sun on one side. The same tree on the other side screened off Ove and Sonja's bedroom from blinding morning sunlight. Further, he managed to block Ove's furious motion that the association would then have to pay for Ove's new awning.

However, Ove got his revenge during the Snow Clearance

Skirmish of the following winter, in which Rune wanted to anoint himself "Chief of Snow Shoveling" and at the same time lumber the Residents' Association with the purchase of a gigantic snowblower. Ove had no intention of letting Rune walk around with some bloody contraption at the expense of the association and spray snow over Ove's windows, which he made crystal clear at the steering group meeting.

Rune was still chosen to be responsible for snow clearance, but to his great annoyance he had to spend all winter shoveling the snow by hand between the houses. The outcome of this, of course, was that he consistently shoveled outside all the houses in their row except Ove and Sonja's. Just to annoy Rune, in mid-January Ove hired a gigantic snowblower to clear the ten square yards outside his door. Rune was incandescent about it, Ove remembers with delight to this day.

Of course, Rune found a way of paying him back the following summer, by buying one of those monstrous lawn tractors. Then, by a combination of treachery, lies, and conspiracies, he managed to get approval at the annual meeting to take over Ove's lawn-mowing responsibilities on the grounds that he had "slightly more adequate equipment than the one who was in charge of it before."

As a partial restitution, Ove managed some four years later to stop Rune's plans of putting in new windows in his house, because after thirty-three letters and a dozen angry telephone calls the Planning Department gave up and accepted Ove's argument that this would "ruin the harmonious architectural character of the area."

In the following three years, Rune refused to speak of Ove as anything but "that bloody red-tapist." Ove took it as a compliment. And the next year he changed his own windows.

When the next winter set in, the steering group decided that the area needed a new collective heating system. Quite coincidentally, of course, Rune and Ove happened to have diametrically different views on what sort of heating system was required, which was jokingly referred to by the other neighbors as "the battle of the water pump." It grew into an eternal struggle between the two men.

And so it continued.

But, as Sonja used to say, there were also some other moments. There weren't many of them, but women like Sonja and Anita knew how to make the most of them. Because there hadn't always been burning conflict. One summer in the 1980s, for instance, Ove had bought a Saab 9000 and Rune a Volvo 760. And they were so pleased with this that they kept the peace for several weeks. Sonja and Anita even managed to get all four of them together for dinner on a few occasions. Rune and Anita's son, who'd had time to turn into a teenager by this stage, with all the divinely sanctioned charmlessness and impoliteness this entailed, sat at one end of the table like an irritable accessory. "That boy was born angry," Sonja used to say with sadness in her voice, but Ove and Rune managed to get along so well that they even had a little whiskey together at the end of the evening.

Unfortunately, at their last dinner that summer Ove and Rune had the idea of having a barbecue. And obviously they started feuding at once about the most effective way of lighting Ove's globe grill. Within fifteen minutes the argument had escalated so much in volume that Sonja and Anita agreed it might be best to eat their dinner separately after all. The two men had time to buy and sell a Volvo 760 (Turbo) and a Saab 9000i before they spoke to one another again.

Meanwhile, the neighbors came and went in the row of houses. In the end there had been so many new faces in the doorways of the other row houses that they all merged in a sea of gray. Where before there had been forest, there were only construction cranes. Ove and Rune stood outside their houses, hands obstinately shoved into their trouser pockets, like ancient relics in a new age, while a parade of uppity real estate agents barely able to see over their grapefruit-size tie knots patrolled the little road between the houses and kept their eyes on them—like vultures watching aging water buffaloes. They could hardly wait to move some bloody consultants' families into their houses, both Ove and Rune knew that very well.

Rune and Anita's son moved away from home when he was twenty, in the early 1990s. Apparently he went to America, Ove found out from Sonja. They hardly saw him again. From time to time Anita had a telephone call around the time of Christmas, but "he was so busy with his own things now," as Anita said when she tried to keep her spirits up, even though Sonja could see that she had to hold back her tears. Some boys leave everything behind and never look back. That was all there was to it.

Rune never said anything about it. But to anyone who had known him a long time, it was as if he shrank a couple of inches in the years that followed. As if he sort of crumpled with a deep sigh and never really breathed properly again.

A few years later Rune and Ove fell out for the hundredth time about that collective heating system. Ove stormed out of a Residents' Association meeting, in a fury, and never returned. The last battle the two men fought was a bit into the noughties when Rune bought one of those automated robotic lawn mowers, which he'd ordered from Asia, and left it to whiz about on the lawn behind the houses. Rune could even remotely program it to cut "special patterns," Sonja said in an impressed tone of voice one evening when she came home from visiting Anita. Ove soon caught on that this "special pattern" was the habit of that robotic little shit to consistently rumble back and forth all night outside Ove and Sonja's bedroom window. One evening Sonja saw Ove fetch a screwdriver and walk out the veranda door. Next morning the little robot, quite inexplicably, had driven right into Rune's pool.

The month after, Rune went into the hospital for the first time. He never bought another lawn mower. Ove did not know himself how their animosity had begun, though he knew very well that it ended there and then. Afterwards it was only memories for Ove, and a lack of them for Rune.

And there were very likely people who thought one could not interpret men's feelings by the cars they drove.

But when they moved onto the street, Ove drove a Saab 96 and Rune a Volvo 244. After the accident Ove bought a Saab 95 so he'd have space for Sonja's wheelchair. That same year Rune bought a Volvo 245 to have space for a stroller. Three years later Sonja got a more modern wheelchair and Ove bought a hatchback, a Saab 900. Rune bought a Volvo 265 because Anita had started talking about having another child.

Then Ove bought two more Saab 900s and after that his first Saab 9000. Rune bought a Volvo 265 and eventually a Volvo 745 station wagon. But no more children came. One evening Sonja came home and told Ove that Anita had been to the doctor.

And a week later a Volvo 740 stood parked in Rune's garage. The sedan model.

Ove saw it when he washed his Saab. In the evening Rune found a half bottle of whiskey outside his door. They never spoke about it.

Maybe their sorrow over children that never came should have brought the two men closer. But sorrow is unreliable in that way. When people don't share it there's a good chance that it will drive them apart instead.

Maybe Ove never forgave Rune for having a son who he could not even get along with. Maybe Rune never forgave Ove for not being able to forgive him for it. Maybe neither of them forgave themselves for not being able to give the women they loved more than anything what they wanted more than anything. Rune and Anita's lad grew up and cleared out of home as soon as he got the chance. And Rune went and bought a sporty BMW, one of those cars that only has space for two people and a handbag. Because now it was only him and Anita, as he told Sonja when they met in the parking area. "And one can't drive a Volvo all of one's life," he said with an attempt at a halfhearted smile. She could hear that he was trying to swallow his tears. And that was the moment when Ove realized that a part of Rune had given up forever. And for that maybe neither Ove nor Rune forgave him.

So there were certainly people who thought that feelings could not be judged by looking at cars. But they were wrong.

29

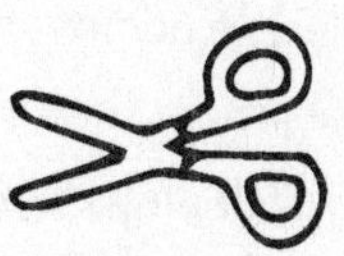

A MAN CALLED OVE AND A BENDER

"Seriously, where are we going?!" Parvaneh wonders, out of breath.

"To fix something," Ove answers curtly, three steps ahead of her, with the cat half jogging at his side.

"What thing?"

"A thing!"

Parvaneh stops and catches her breath.

"Here!" Ove calls out and stops abruptly in front of a little café.

A scent of fresh-baked croissants comes through the glass door. Parvaneh looks at the parking area on the other side of the street where they left the Saab. In the end they could not have parked closer to the café. At first Ove had been absolutely convinced that the café was at the other end of the block. That was when Parvaneh had suggested they could possibly park on that side, but the notion was abandoned once they found that parking cost one kronor more per hour.

Instead they had parked here and walked all around the block looking for the café. Because Ove, as Parvaneh had soon realized, was the sort of man who, when he was not quite certain where he was going, just carried on walking straight ahead, convinced that the road would eventually fall into line. And now when they find that the café is directly opposite the spot where they parked, Ove looks as if this was his plan all along. Parvaneh mops some sweat off her cheek.

A man with a ragged, dirty beard is leaning against a wall halfway down the street. He has a paper cup in front of him. Outside the café Ove, Parvaneh, and the cat meet a slim boy aged about twenty who has what looks very much like black soot around his eyes. It takes Ove a moment to realize it's the boy who was standing behind the lad with the bicycle when Ove met him the first time. He looks a little cautious; although he smiles at Ove, Ove can't think of anything to do but nod back. As if wanting to clarify that while he has no intention of returning the smile, he is prepared to acknowledge receipt of it.

"Why didn't you let me park next to the red car?" Parvaneh wants to know as they open the glass door and step inside.

Ove doesn't answer.

"I would have managed it!" she says self-confidently.

Ove shakes his head wearily. Two hours ago she didn't know where the clutch was; now she's irritated because he won't let her squeeze into a narrow parking space.

Once they're inside the café, Ove sees from the corner of his eye how the slim soot-eyed boy offers the sandwiches he's hiding to the vagrant.

"Hi there, Ove!" a voice calls out so eagerly that it cracks into falsetto in the high notes.

Ove turns around and sees the lad from the bike shed. He's standing behind a long, polished counter at the front of the premises, wearing a baseball cap, Ove notes. Indoors.

The cat and Parvaneh make themselves at home, the latter mopping sweat from her forehead although it's ice-cold in there. Colder than outside in the street, actually. She pours herself some water from a pitcher on the counter. The cat unconcernedly laps up some of it from her glass when she isn't looking.

"Do you know each other?" Parvaneh asks with surprise, looking at the youth.

"Me and Ove are sort of friends." The youth nods.

"Are you? Me and Ove are sort of friends too!" Parvaneh grins, tenderly imitating his enthusiasm.

Ove stops at a safe distance from the counter. As if someone might give him a hug if he gets too close.

"My name's Adrian," says the youth.

"Parvaneh," says Parvaneh.

"You want something to drink?" he asks them.

"A latte for me, please," says Parvaneh, in a tone of voice as if she's suddenly having her shoulders massaged. She dabs her forehead with a napkin. "Preferably an iced latte if you have it!"

Ove shifts his weight from his left foot to his right and peers around the premises. He's never liked cafés. Sonja, of course, loved them. Could sit in them for an entire Sunday "just looking at people," as she put it. Ove used to sit there with her, reading a newspaper. Every Sunday they did it. He hasn't put his foot in a café since she died. He looks up and realizes that Adrian, Parvaneh, and the cat are waiting for his answer.

"Coffee, then. Black."

Adrian scratches his hair under the cap.

"So . . . espresso?"

"No. Coffee."

Adrian transfers his scratching from hair to chin.

"What . . . like black coffee?"

"Yes."

"With milk?"

"If it's with milk it's not black coffee."

Adrian moves a couple of sugar bowls on the counter. Mainly to have something to do, so he doesn't look too silly. A bit late for that, thinks Ove.

"Normal filter coffee. Normal bloody filter coffee," Ove repeats.

Adrian nods.

"Oh, that. . . . Well. I don't know how to make it."

Ove points aggressively at the percolator in the corner, only barely visible behind a gigantic silver spaceship of a machine, which, Ove understands, is what they use for making espresso.

"Oh, that one, yeah," says Adrian, as if the penny has just dropped. "Ah . . . I don't really know how that thing works."

"Should have bloody known. . . ." mutters Ove as he walks around the counter and takes matters into his own hands.

"Can someone tell me what we're doing here?" calls Parvaneh.

"This kid here has a bicycle that needs repairing," explains Ove as he pours water into the carafe.

"The bicycle hanging off the back of the car?"

"You brought it here? Thanks, Ove!"

"You don't have a car, do you?" he replies, while rummaging around a cupboard for coffee filters.

"Thanks, Ove!" says Adrian and takes a step towards him, then comes to his senses and stops before he does something silly.

"So that's your bicycle?" Parvaneh smiles.

"Kind of—it's my girlfriend's. Or the one I want to be my girlfriend . . . sort of thing."

Parvaneh grins.

"So me and Ove drove all this way just to give you a bike so you can mend it? For a girl?"

Adrian nods. Parvaneh leans over the counter and pats Ove on the arm.

"You know, Ove, sometimes one almost suspects you have a heart. . . ."

"Do you have tools here or not?" Ove says to Adrian, snatching his arm away.

Adrian nods.

"Go and get them, then. The bike's on the Saab in the parking lot."

Adrian nods quickly and disappears into the kitchen. After a minute or so he comes back with a big toolbox, which he quickly takes to the exit.

"And you be quiet," Ove says to Parvaneh.

She smirks in a way that suggests she has no intention of keeping quiet.

"I only brought the bicycle here so he wouldn't mess about in the sheds back home. . . ." Ove adds.

"Sure, sure," says Parvaneh with a laugh.

"Oh, hey," says Adrian as the soot-eyed boy appears again a moment later. "This is my boss."

"Hi there—ah, what . . . sorry, what are you doing?" asks the "boss," looking with some interest at the spry stranger who has barricaded himself behind the counter of his café.

"The kid's going to fix a bicycle," answers Ove as if this were something plain and obvious. "Where do you keep the filters for real coffee?"

The soot-eyed boy points at one of the shelves. Ove squints at him.

"Is that makeup?"

Parvaneh hushes him. Ove looks insulted.

"What? What's wrong with asking?"

The boy smiles a little nervously.

"Yes, it's makeup." He nods, rubbing himself around his eyes. "I went dancing last night," he says, smiling gratefully as Parvaneh with the deftness of a fellow conspirator hauls out a wet-wipe from her handbag and offers it to him.

Ove nods and goes back to his coffee-making.

"And do you also have problems with bicycles and love and girls?" he asks absentmindedly.

"No, no, not with bicycles anyway. And not with love either, I suppose. Well, not with girls, anyway." He chuckles.

Ove turns on the percolator and, once it begins to splutter, turns around and leans against the inside of the counter as if this is the most natural thing in the world in a café where one doesn't work.

"Bent, are you?"

"OVE!" says Parvaneh and slaps him on the arm.

Ove snatches back his arm and looks very offended.

"What?!"

"You don't say . . . you don't call it that," Parvaneh says, clearly unwilling to pronounce the word again.

"Queer?" Ove offers.

Parvaneh tries to hit his arm again but Ove is too quick.

"Don't talk like that!" she orders him.

Ove turns to the sooty boy, genuinely puzzled.

"Can't one say 'bent'? What are you supposed to say nowadays?"

"You say homosexual. Or an LGBT person," Parvaneh interrupts before she can stop herself.

"Ah, you can say what you want, it's cool." The boy smiles as he walks around the counter and puts on an apron.

"Right, good. Good to be clear. One of those gays, then," mumbles Ove. Parvaneh shakes her head apologetically; the boy just laughs. "Well then," says Ove with a nod, and starts pouring himself a coffee while it's still going through.

Then he takes the cup and without another word goes outside and across the street to the parking area. The sooty boy doesn't comment on his taking the cup outside. It would seem a little unnecessary, under the circumstances, when this man within five minutes of his arrival at the boy's café has already appointed himself as barista and interrogated him about his sexual preferences.

Adrian is standing by the Saab, looking as if he just got lost in a forest.

"Is it going well?" asks Ove rhetorically, taking a sip of coffee and looking at the bicycle, which Adrian hasn't even unhooked yet from the back of the car.

"Nah . . . you know. Sort of. Well," Adrian begins, compulsively scratching his chest.

Ove observes him for half a minute or so. Takes another mouthful of his coffee. Nods irritably, like someone squeezing an avocado and finding it overly ripe. He forcefully presses his cup of coffee into the hands of the boy, and then steps forward to unhitch the bicycle. Turns it upside down and opens the toolbox the youth has brought from the café.

"Didn't your dad ever teach you how to fix a bike?" he says without looking at Adrian, while he hunches over the punctured tire.

"My dad's in the slammer," Adrian replies almost inaudibly and scratches his shoulder, looking around as if he'd like to find a big black hole to sink into. Ove stops himself, looks up, and gives him an evaluating stare. The boy stares at the ground. Ove clears his throat.

"It's not so bloody difficult," he mutters at long last and gestures at Adrian to sit on the ground.

It takes them ten minutes to repair the puncture. Ove barks monosyllabic instructions; Adrian remains silent throughout. But he's attentive and dextrous and in a certain sense does not make a complete fool of himself, Ove has to admit. Maybe he's not quite as fumbling with his hands as he is with words. They wipe off the dirt with a rag from the trunk of the Saab, avoiding eye contact with each other.

"I hope the lady's worth it," says Ove and closes the trunk.

Now it's Adrian's turn to look nonplussed.

When they go back into the café, there's a short cube-shaped man in a stained shirt standing on a stepladder, tinkering with something that Ove suspects is a fan heater. The sooty boy stands below the stepladder with a selection of screwdrivers held aloft. He keeps mopping the remnants of makeup around his eyes, peering at the fat man on the ladder and looking a little on the nervous side. As if worried that he may be caught out. Parvaneh turns excitedly to Ove.

"This is Amel! He owns the café!" she says in a suitably gushing manner. She points to the cubic man on the ladder.

Amel doesn't turn around, but he emits a long sequence of hard consonants that, even though Ove does not understand them, he suspects to be various combinations of four-letter words and body parts.

"What's he saying?" asks Adrian.

The sooty boy twists uncomfortably.

"Ah . . . he . . . something about the fan heater being a bit of a fairy . . ."

He looks over at Adrian, then quickly turns his face down.

"What's that?" asks Ove, wandering over to him.

"He means it's worthless, like a homo," he says in such a low voice that only Ove catches his words.

Parvaneh, on the other hand, is busy pointing at Amel with delight.

"You can't hear what he's saying but you sort of know that almost all of it is swear words! He's like a dubbed version of you, Ove!"

Ove doesn't look particularly delighted. Nor does Amel.

He stops tinkering with the fan heater and points at Ove with the screwdriver.

"The cat? Is that your cat?"

"No," says Ove.

Not so much because he wants to point out that it isn't his cat, but because he wants to clarify that it's no one's cat.

"Cat out! No animals in café!" Amel slashes at the consonants so that they hop about like naughty children caught inside the sentence.

Ove looks with interest at the fan heater above Amel's head. Then at the cat on the bar stool. Then at the toolbox, which Adrian is still holding in his hand. Then at the fan heater again. And at Amel.

"If I repair that for you, the cat stays."

He offers this more as a statement than a question. Amel seems to lose his self-possession for a few moments. By the time he regains it, in a way he could probably not explain afterwards, he has become the man holding the stepladder rather than the man standing on the stepladder. Ove digs about up there for a few minutes, climbs down, brushes the palm of his hand against his trouser leg, and hands the screwdriver and a little adjustable wrench to the sooty boy.

"You fixed!" cries Amel suddenly as the fan heater splutters back to life.

In an effusive manner, he grabs Ove's shoulders.

"Whiskey? You want? In my kitchen I have the whiskey!"

Ove checks his watch. It's quarter past two in the afternoon. He shakes his head while looking a little uncomfortable, partly about the whiskey and partly because of Amel, who is still holding on to him. The sooty boy disappears through the kitchen door behind the counter, still frenetically rubbing his eyes.

Adrian catches up with Ove and the cat on their way back to the Saab.

"Ove, mate, you won't say anything about Mirsad being . . ."

"Who?"

"My boss," says Adrian. "The one with the makeup."

"The bent person?" says Ove.

Adrian nods.

"I mean his dad . . . I mean Amel . . . he doesn't know Mirsad is . . ."

Adrian fumbles for the right word.

"A bender?" Ove adds.

Adrian nods. Ove shrugs. Parvaneh comes wagging along behind them, out of breath.

"Where did you get to?" Ove asks her.

"I gave my change to him," says Parvaneh, with a nod at the man with the dirty beard by the house wall.

"You know he'll only spend it on schnapps," Ove states.

Parvaneh opens her eyes wide with something Ove strongly suspects to be sarcasm. "Really? Will he? And I was *sooo* hoping he would use it to pay off his student loans from his university education in particle physics!"

Ove snorts and opens the Saab. Adrian stays where he is on the other side of the car.

"Yes?" Ove wonders.

"You won't say anything about Mirsad, will you? Seriously?"

"Why the hell would I say anything?" Ove points at him with exasperation. "You! You want to buy a French car. Don't worry so much about others, you have enough problems of your own."

30

A MAN CALLED OVE AND A SOCIETY WITHOUT HIM

Ove brushes the snow off the gravestone. Digs determinedly into the frozen ground and carefully replenishes the flowers. He stands up, dusts himself off, and looks helplessly at her name, feeling ashamed of himself. He who always used to nag at her about being late. Now he stands here himself, apparently quite incapable of following her as he'd planned.

"It's just been bloody mayhem," he mumbles to the stone.

And then he's silent again.

He doesn't know what happened to him after her funeral. The days and weeks floated together in such a way, and in such utter silence, that he could hardly describe what exactly he was doing. Before Parvaneh and that Patrick backed into his mailbox he could barely remember saying a word to another human being since Sonja died.

Some evenings he forgets to eat. That's never happened before, as far as he can remember. Not since he sat down with her on that train almost forty years ago. As long as Sonja was there they had their routines. Ove got up at quarter to six, made coffee, went off for his inspection. By half past six Sonja had showered and then they had breakfast and drank coffee. Sonja had eggs; Ove had bread. At five past seven, Ove carried her to the passenger seat of the Saab, stowed her wheelchair in the trunk, and gave her a lift to school. Then he drove to work. At quarter to ten they took coffee breaks separately. Sonja took milk in her coffee; Ove had it black. At twelve they had lunch. At quarter to three another coffee break. At quarter past five Ove picked up Sonja in the school courtyard, hoisted her into the passenger seat and the wheelchair into the trunk. By six o'clock they were at the kitchen table having their dinner, usually meat and potatoes and gravy. Ove's favorite meal. Then she solved crosswords with her legs drawn up beneath her on the sofa while Ove pottered about in the toolshed and watched the news. At half past nine Ove carried her upstairs to the bedroom. She nagged him for years about moving into the empty downstairs guest room, but Ove refused. After a decade or so she realized that this was his way of showing her that he had no intention of giving up. That God and the universe and all the other things would not be allowed to win. That the swine could go to hell. So she stopped nagging.

On Friday nights they sat up until half past ten watching television. On Saturdays they had a late breakfast, sometimes as late as eight. Then they went out to do their errands. The building supply store, furniture shop, and garden center. Sonja would buy potting soil and Ove liked to look at tools. They only had a small row house with a tiny outside space, yet there always seemed to be something to plant and something to build. On the way home they'd stop for ice cream. Sonja would have one with chocolate and Ove one with nuts. Once a year the shop raised the price by one krona per ice cream and then, as Sonja put it, Ove would "have a tantrum." When they got back to the house she'd roll out the little terrace door onto the patio and Ove would help her out of the chair and gently put her on the ground so she could do some gardening in her beloved flower beds. In the meantime Ove would fetch a screwdriver and disappear into the house. That was the best thing about the house. It was never finished. There was always a screw somewhere for Ove to tighten.

On Sundays they went to a café and drank coffee. Ove read the newspaper and Sonja talked. And then it was Monday.

And one Monday she was no longer there.

And Ove didn't know exactly when he became so quiet. He'd always been taciturn, but this was something quite different. Maybe he had started talking more inside his own head. Maybe he was going insane (he did wonder sometimes). It was as if he didn't want other people to talk to him, he was afraid that their chattering voices would drown out the memory of her voice.

He lets his fingers run gently across the gravestone, as if running them through the long tassels of a very thick rug. He's never understood young people who natter on about "finding themselves." He used to hear that nonstop from all those thirty-year-olds at work. All they ever talked about was how they wanted more "leisure time," as if that was the only point of working: to get to the point when one didn't have to do it. Sonja used to laugh at Ove and call him "the most inflexible man in the world." Ove refused to take that as an insult. He thought there should be some order in things. There should be routines and one should be able to feel secure about them. He could not see how it could be a bad attribute.

Sonja used to tell people about the time that Ove, in a moment of temporary mental dislocation in the middle of the 1980s, had been persuaded by her to get himself a red Saab, even though in all the years she'd known him he'd always driven a blue one. "They were the worst three years of Ove's life," Sonja tittered. Since then, Ove had never driven anything but a blue Saab. "Other wives get annoyed because their husbands don't notice when they have their hair cut. When I have a haircut my husband is annoyed with me for days because I don't look the same," Sonja used to say.

That's what Ove misses most of all. Having things the same as usual.

People need a function, he believes. And he has always been functional, no one can take that away from him.

It's thirteen years since Ove bought his blue Saab 9-5 station wagon. Not long after, the Yanks at General Motors bought up the last Swedish-held shares in the company. Ove closed the newspaper that morning with a long string of swear words that continued into a good part of the afternoon. He never bought a car again. He had no intention of placing his foot in an American car, unless his foot and the rest of his body had first been placed in a coffin, they should be bloody clear about that. Sonja had of course also read the article and she had certain objections to Ove's exact version of events regarding the company's nationality, but it made no difference. Ove had made up his mind and now he was fixed on it. He was going to drive his car until either he, or it, broke down. Either way, proper cars were not being made anymore, he'd decided. There was only a lot of electronics and crap inside them now. Like driving a computer. You couldn't even take them apart without the manufacturers whining about "invalid warranties." So it was just as well. Sonja said once that the car would break down with sorrow the day Ove was buried. And maybe that was true.

But there was a time for everything, she also said. Often. For example, when the doctors gave her the diagnosis four years ago. She found it easier to forgive than Ove did. Forgive God and the universe and everything. Ove got angry instead. Maybe because he felt someone had to be angry on her behalf, when everything that was evil seemed to assail the only person he'd ever met who didn't deserve it.

So he fought the whole world. He fought with hospital personnel and he fought with specialists and chief physicians. He fought with men in white shirts and the council representatives who in the end grew so numerous that he could barely remember their names. There was an insurance policy for this, another insurance policy for that; there was one contact person because Sonja was ill and another because she was in a wheelchair. Then a third contact person so she did not have to go to work and a fourth contact person to try to persuade the bloody authorities that this was precisely what she wanted: to go to work.

And it was impossible to fight the men in white shirts. And one could not fight a diagnosis.

Sonja had cancer.

"We have to take it as it comes," said Sonja. And that was what they did. She carried on working with her darling troublemakers for as long as she could, until Ove had to push her into the classroom every morning because she no longer had the strength to do it herself. After a year she was down to 75 percent of her full working week. After two years she was on 50 percent. After three years she was on 25 percent. When she finally had to go home she wrote a long personal letter to each of her students and exhorted them to call her if they ever needed anyone to talk to.

Almost everyone did call. They came to visit in long lines. One weekend there were so many of them in the row house that Ove had to go outside and sit in his toolshed for six hours. When the last of them had left that evening he went around the house carefully assuring himself that nothing had been stolen. As usual. Until Sonja called out to him not to forget to count the eggs in the fridge. Then he gave up. Carried her up the stairs while she laughed at him. He put her in the bed, and then, just before they went to sleep, she turned to him. Hid her finger in the palm of his hand. Burrowed her nose under his collarbone.

"God took a child from me, darling Ove. But he gave me a thousand others."

In the fourth year she died.

Now he stands there running his hand over her gravestone. Again and again. As if he's trying to rub her back to life.

"I'm really going to do it this time. I know you don't like it. I don't like it either," he says in a low voice.

He takes a deep breath. As if he has to steel himself against her trying to convince him not to do it.

"See you tomorrow," he says firmly and stamps the snow off his shoes, as if not wanting to give her a chance to protest.

Then he takes the little path down to the parking area, with the cat padding along beside him. Out through the black gates, around the Saab, which still has the learner plate stuck to the back door. He opens the passenger door. Parvaneh looks at him, her big brown eyes filled with empathy.

"I've been thinking about something," she says carefully, as she puts the Saab into gear and pulls off.

"Don't."

But she can't be stopped.

"I was just thinking that maybe I could help you clean out the house. Maybe put Sonja's things in boxes and—"

She hardly has time to speak Sonja's name before Ove's face darkens, anger stiffening it into a mask.

"Not another word," he roars, with a booming sound inside the car.

"But I was only thi—"

"Not another bloody WORD. Have you got it?!"

Parvaneh nods and goes silent. Shaking with anger, Ove stares out the window all the way home.

31

A MAN CALLED OVE BACKS UP A TRAILER. AGAIN.

The next morning, after letting the cat out, he fetched Sonja's father's old rifle from the attic. He'd decided that his dislike of weapons could never be greater than his dislike of all the empty places she has left behind in their silent little house. It was time now.

But it seems that someone, somewhere, knows the only way of stopping him is to put something in his way that makes him angry enough not to do it.

For this reason, he stands now in the little road between the houses, his arms defiantly crossed, looking at the man in the white shirt and saying:

"I am here because there was nothing good on the TV."

The man in the white shirt has been observing him without the slightest hint of emotion through the entire conversation. In fact, whenever Ove has met him, he has been more like a machine than a person. Just like all the other white shirts Ove has run into in his life. The ones who said Sonja was going to die after the coach accident, the ones who refused to take responsibility afterwards and the ones who refused to hold others responsible. The ones who would not build an access ramp at the school. The ones who did not want to let her work. The ones who went through paragraphs of small print to root out some clause meaning they wouldn't have to pay out any insurance money. The ones who wanted to put her in a home.

They had all had the same empty eyes. As if they were nothing but shiny shells walking around, grinding away at normal people and pulling their lives to pieces.

But when Ove says that thing about there being nothing good on TV, he sees a little twitch at the temple of the white shirt. A flash of frustration, perhaps. Amazed anger, possibly. Pure disdain, very likely. It's the first time Ove has noticed that he's managed to get under the skin of the white shirt. Of any white shirt at all.

The man snaps his jaws shut, turns around, and starts to walk away. Not with the measured, objective steps of a council employee in full control, but something else. With anger. Impatience. Vengefully.

Ove can't remember anything having made him feel so good in a long, long time.

Of course, he was supposed to have died today. He had been planning to calmly and peacefully shoot himself in the head just after breakfast. He'd tidied the kitchen and let the cat out and made himself comfortable in his favorite armchair. He'd planned it this way because the cat routinely asked to be let out at this time. One of the few traits of the cat that Ove was highly appreciative of was its reluctance to crap in other people's homes. Ove was a man of the same ilk.

But then of course Parvaneh came banging on his door as if it were the last functioning toilet in the civilized world. As if that woman had nowhere to wee at home. Ove put the rifle away behind the radiator so she wouldn't see it and start interfering. He opened the door and she more or less had to press her telephone into his hand by violent means before he accepted it.

"What is this?" Ove wanted to know, the telephone held between his index finger and his thumb, as if it smelled bad.

"It's for you," groaned Parvaneh, holding her stomach and mopping sweat from her forehead even though it was below freezing outside. "That journalist."

"What do I want with her telephone?"

"God. It's not her telephone, it's my telephone. She's on the line!" Parvaneh said impatiently.

Then, before he could protest, she squeezed past him and headed for his bathroom.

"Yes," said Ove, lifting the telephone to within a couple of inches of his ear, slightly unclear about whether he was still talking to Parvaneh or the person at the other end.

"Hi!" yelled the journalist woman, Lena. Ove felt it might be wise to move the phone farther away from his ear. "So, are you ready to give me an interview now?" she went on in a gung-ho tone.

"No," said Ove, holding the telephone in front of him to work out how to hang up.

"Did you read the letter I sent you? Or the newspaper? Have you read the newspaper? I thought I'd let you see it, so you can form an impression of our journalistic style!"

Ove went into the kitchen. Picked up the newspaper and letter that Adrian fellow had brought over a few days earlier.

"Have you got it?" roared the journalist woman.

"Calm yourself down. I'm reading it, aren't I!" Ove said out loud to the telephone and leaned over the kitchen table.

"I was just wondering if—" she continued valiantly.

"Can you CALM DOWN, woman!" Ove raged.

Suddenly, out the window, Ove noticed a man in a white shirt in a Škoda, driving past his house.

"Hello?" the journalist woman called just before Ove flew out the front door.

"Oh, dear, dear," Parvaneh mumbled anxiously when she came out of the bathroom and caught sight of him careering along between the houses.

The man in the white shirt got out of the Škoda on the driver's side outside Rune and Anita's house.

"It's enough now! You hear? You're NOT driving your car inside the residential area! Not another bloody YARD! You got it?" shouted Ove in the distance, long before he'd even reached him.

The little man in the white shirt, in a most superior manner, adjusted the cigarette packet in his breast pocket while calmly meeting Ove's gaze.

"I have permission."

"Like hell you do!"

The man in the white shirt shrugged. As if to chase away an irritating insect more than anything.

"And what exactly are you going to do about it, Ove?"

The question actually caught Ove off-balance. Again. He stopped, his hands trembling with anger, at least a dozen pieces of invective at his disposal. But to his own surprise he could not bring himself to use any of them.

"I know who you are, Ove. I know everything about all the

letters you've written about your wife's accident and your wife's illness. You're something of a legend in our offices, you should know," said the man in the white shirt, his voice quite unwavering.

Ove's mouth opened into a crack. The man in the white shirt nodded at him.

"I know who you are. And I'm only doing my job. A decision is a decision. You can't do anything about it, you should have learned that by now."

Ove took a step towards him but the man put up a hand against his chest and pressed him back. Not violently. Not aggressively. Just softly and firmly, as if the hand did not belong to him but was directly controlled by some robot at the computer center of a municipal authority.

"Go and watch some TV instead. Before you have more problems with that heart of yours."

On the passenger side of the Škoda the determined woman, wearing an identical white shirt, stepped out with a pile of paper in her arms. The man locked the car with a loud bleep. Then he turned his back on Ove as if Ove had never stood there talking to him.

Ove stayed where he was, his fists clenched at his sides and his chin jutting out as if he were an outraged bull elk. The white shirts disappeared into Anita and Rune's house. It took a minute before he recovered himself enough to even turn around. But then he did so with determined fury and started walking towards Parvaneh's house. Parvaneh was standing halfway up the little road.

"Is that useless husband of yours at home?" Ove growled, walking past her without waiting for an answer.

Parvaneh didn't have time to do more than nod before Ove, in four long strides, reached their front door. Patrick opened it, standing there on crutches, casts apparently covering half of his body.

"Hi, Ove!" he called out cheerfully, trying to wave with a crutch, with the immediate effect that he lost his balance and stumbled into the wall.

"That trailer you had when you moved in. Where did you get it?" Ove demanded.

Patrick leaned with his functioning arm against the wall. Almost as if he wanted it to look as if he'd meant to stumble into it.

"What? Oh . . . *that* trailer. I borrowed it off a guy at work—"

"Call him. You need to borrow it again."

And this was the reason why Ove did not die today. Because he was detained by something that made him sufficiently angry to hold his attention.

When the man and woman in the white shirts come out of Anita and Rune's house almost an hour later, they find that their little white car with the council logo has been boxed into the little cul-de-sac by a large trailer. A trailer that someone, while they were inside the house, must have parked exactly so it blocks the entire road behind them. One could almost think it had been done on purpose.

The woman looks genuinely puzzled. But the man in the white shirt immediately walks up to Ove.

"Have you done this?"

Ove crosses his arms and looks at him coldly.

"No."

The man in the white shirt smiles in a superior manner. The way men in white shirts, who are used to always having things their own way, smile when someone tries to disagree with them.

"Move it at once."

"I don't think so," says Ove.

The man in the white shirt sighs, as if the threatening statement he makes after that were directed at a child.

"Move the trailer, Ove. Or I'll call the police."

Ove shakes his head nonchalantly, pointing at the sign farther down the road.

"Motor vehicles prohibited inside the residential area. It says so clearly on the sign."

"Don't you have anything better to do than standing out here pretending to be the foreman?" groans the man in the white shirt.

"There was nothing good on TV," says Ove.

And that's when there's a little twitch at the temple of the man in the white shirt. As if his mask has slipped a little, just a fraction. He looks at the trailer, his boxed-in Škoda, the sign, Ove standing in front of him with his arms crossed. The man seems to consider for an instant whether he might try to force Ove by violence, but he realizes in another instant that this would very likely be an extremely bad idea.

"This was very silly of you, Ove. This was very, very silly," he hisses finally.

And his blue eyes, for the first time, are filled with genuine fury. Ove's face does not betray the slightest emotion. The man in the white shirt walks away, up towards the garages and the main road, with the sort of steps that make it clear that this will not be the end of this story.

The woman with the papers hurries off after him.

One might have expected Ove to watch them with a look of triumph in his eyes. He would probably have expected this himself, in fact. But instead he just looks sad and tired. As if he hasn't slept in months. As if he hardly has the strength to keep his arms up any longer. He lets his hands glide into his pockets and goes back home. But no sooner has he closed the door than someone starts banging on it again.

"They're going to take Rune away from Anita," says Parvaneh urgently, snatching the front door open before Ove has even reached the handle.

"Pah," Ove snorts tiredly.

The resignation in his voice clearly takes both Parvaneh and Anita, who's standing behind her, by surprise. Maybe it also surprises Ove. He inhales quickly through his nose. Looks at Anita. She's grayer and more sunken than ever; her eyes are red, swollen.

"They say they'll come and pick him up this week, and that I can't manage to take care of him myself," she says, in a voice so fragile that it hardly manages to get past her lips.

"We have to do something!" cries Parvaneh, grabbing him.

Ove snatches his arm back and avoids her eyes.

"Pah! They won't come to get him for years and years. This'll go to appeal and then it'll go through all the bureaucratic shit," says Ove.

He tries to sound more convinced and sure of himself than he actually feels. But he doesn't have the strength to care about how he's coming across. He just wants them to leave.

"You don't know what you're talking about!" roars Parvaneh.

"You're the one who doesn't know what you're talking about—you've never had anything to do with the county council, you don't know what it's like fighting them," he answers in a monotone voice, his shoulders slumped.

"But you have to talk . . ." she begins to say in a faltering voice.

It's as if all the energy in Ove's body is draining out of him even as he stands there.

Maybe it's the sight of Anita's worn-out face. Maybe it's the insight that a simple battle won is nothing in the greater scheme of things. A boxed-in Škoda makes no difference. They always come back. Just like they did with Sonja. Like they always do. With their clauses and documents. Men in white shirts always win. And men like Ove always lose people like Sonja. And nothing can bring her back to him.

In the end, there is nothing left but a long series of weekdays with nothing more meaningful than oiling the kitchen counters. And Ove can't cope with it anymore. He feels it in that moment more clearly than ever. He can't fight anymore. Doesn't want to fight anymore. Just wants it all to stop.

Parvaneh keeps trying to argue with him, but he just closes the door. She hammers at it but he doesn't listen. He sinks down on the stool in the hall and feels his hands trembling. His heart thumps so hard that it feels like his ears are about to explode. The pressure on his chest, as if an enormous darkness has put its boot over his throat, doesn't begin to release till more than twenty minutes later.

And then Ove starts to cry.

32

A MAN CALLED OVE ISN'T RUNNING A DAMNED HOTEL

Sonja said once that to understand men like Ove and Rune, one had to understand from the very beginning that they were men caught in the wrong time. Men who only required a few simple things from life, she said. A roof over their heads, a quiet street, the right make of car, and a woman to be faithful to. A job where you had a proper function. A house where things broke at regular intervals, so you always had something to tinker with.

"All people want to live dignified lives; dignity just means something different to different people," Sonja had said. To men like Ove and Rune dignity was simply that they'd had to manage on their own when they grew up, and therefore saw it as their right not to become reliant on others when they were adults. There was a sense of pride in having control. In being right. In knowing what road to take and how to screw in a screw, or not. Men like Ove and Rune were from a generation in which one was what one did, not what one talked about.

She knew, of course, that Ove didn't know how to bear his

nameless anger. He needed labels to put on it. Ways of categorizing. So when men in white shirts at the council, whose names no normal person could keep track of, tried to do everything Sonja did not want—make her stop working, move her out of her house, imply that she was worth less than a healthy person who was able to walk, and assert that she was dying—Ove fought them. With documents and letters to newspapers and appeals, right down to something as unremarkable as an access ramp at a school. He fought so doggedly for her against men in white shirts that in the end he began to hold them personally responsible for all that happened to her—and to the child.

And then she left him alone in a world where he no longer understood the language.

Later that night, once Ove and the cat have had their dinner and watched the TV for a while, he turns out the lamp in the living room and goes upstairs. The cat follows watchfully at his heels, as if sensing that he's going to do something it hasn't been informed about. It sits on the bedroom floor while Ove gets undressed and looks as if it's trying to figure out a magic trick.

Ove goes to bed and lies still while the bloody cat, on Sonja's side of the bed, takes more than an hour to go to sleep. Obviously, he does not go to such lengths because of some lingering sense of obligation to the cat; he just doesn't have the energy for an argument. He can't be expected to explain the concept of life and death to an animal that can't even take care of its own fur.

When the cat finally rolls onto its back on Sonja's pillow and starts snoring with an open mouth, Ove sneaks out of bed as lightfootedly as he can. Goes down into the living room, gets out the rifle from the hiding place behind the radiator. He gets out four heavy-duty tarpaulins he's fetched in from the toolshed and hidden in the broom cupboard so the cat doesn't notice them. Starts taping them up on the walls in the hall. Ove, after some consideration, has decided that this will probably be the best room for the deed, because it has the smallest surface area. He's assuming that there's a good deal of splattering when one shoots oneself in the head, and he's loath to leave more of a mess behind than he has to. Sonja always hated it when he made a mess.

He's wearing his going-out shoes and suit again. It's dirty and still smells of car exhaust, but it'll have to do. He weighs the rifle in his hands, as if checking its center of gravity. As if this will play a decisive role in the future of the venture. He turns and twists it, tries to angle the barrel almost as if intending to fold the weapon double. Not that Ove knows very much about weapons, but one wants to know if it's a decent piece of equipment one's got, more or less. And because Ove supposes one can't test the quality of a rifle by kicking it, he decides it can be done by bending and pulling at it, to see what happens.

While he's doing this, it strikes him that it was probably a fairly bad idea to put on his best gear. Will be an awful lot of blood on the suit, Ove imagines. Seems silly. So he puts down the rifle, goes into the living room, gets undressed, carefully folds up the suit, and puts it neatly beside his going-out shoes. Then he gets out the letter with all the instructions for Parvaneh and writes "Bury me in my suit" under the heading "Funeral Arrangements" and puts the letter on top of the pile of clothes. He has already stated clearly and unmistakably that there should not be any fuss in other respects. No exaggerated ceremony and rubbish like that. Shove him in the ground next to Sonja, that's all. The spot has already been prepared and paid for, and Ove has put cash in the envelope for the hearse.

So, wearing nothing but his socks and underwear, Ove goes back into the hall and picks up his rifle. He catches sight of his own body in the hall mirror. He hasn't seen himself in this way for probably thirty-five years. He's still quite muscular and robust. Certainly in better shape than most men of his age. But something's happened to his skin that makes him look like he's melting, he notes. It looks terrible.

It's very quiet in the house. In the whole neighborhood, actually. Everyone's sleeping. And only then does Ove realize that the cat will probably wake at the sound of the shot. Will probably scare the living daylights out of the poor critter, Ove admits. He thinks about this for a good while before he determinedly sets down the rifle and goes into the kitchen to turn on the radio. Not that he needs music to take his own life, and not that he likes the idea of the radio clicking its way through units of electricity when he's gone. But because if the cat wakes up from the bang, it may end up thinking that it's just a part of one of those modern pop songs the radio plays all the time these days. And then go back to sleep. That is Ove's train of thought.

There's no modern pop song on the radio, Ove hears, when he comes back into the hall and picks up the rifle again. It's the local news bulletin. So he stays where he is for a moment and listens. Not that it's so important to listen to the local news when you're about to shoot yourself in the head, but Ove thinks there's no harm in keeping yourself updated. They talk about the weather. And the economy. And the traffic. And the importance of local property owners staying vigilant over the weekend because of a large number of burglary rings on the rampage all over town. "Bloody hooligans," Ove mutters, and grips the rifle a little more firmly when he hears that.

From a purely objective point of view, the fact that Ove was wielding a gun was something two other hooligans, Adrian and Mirsad, would ideally have been aware of before they unconcernedly trotted up to Ove's front door a few seconds later. They would then quite likely have understood that when Ove heard their creaking steps in the snow he would not immediately think to himself, Guests, how nice! but rather, Well, I'll be damned! And they'd probably also know that Ove, wearing nothing but socks and underpants, with a three-quarter-century-old hunting rifle in his hands, would kick the door open like an aging, half-naked, suburban Rambo. And maybe then Adrian would not have screamed in a high-pitched voice that went right through every window on the street, nor would he have turned in panic and run into the toolshed, almost knocking himself unconscious.

It takes a few confused cries and a good deal of tumult before Mirsad has time to clarify his identity as that of a normal hooligan, not a burglar hooligan, and for Ove to come to grips with what is happening. Before then he has had time to wave his rifle at them, making Adrian scream like an air raid warning.

"Shush! You'll wake the bloody cat!" Ove hisses angrily while Adrian reels backwards, a swelling as large as a medium-size pack of ravioli on his forehead.

"What in the name of God are you doing here?" he raves, the gun still firmly fixed on them. "It's the middle of the bloody night!"

Mirsad is holding a big bag in his hand, which he gently drops into the snow. Adrian impulsively holds his hands up as if he's about to be robbed, and almost loses his balance and falls into the snow again.

"It was Adrian's idea," Mirsad begins, looking down into the snow.

"Mirsad came out today, you know!" Adrian blurts out.

"What?"

"He . . . came out, you know. Told everyone he was . . ." says Adrian, but he seems slightly distracted, partly by the fact that a fuming old man in his underpants is pointing a gun at him, and partly because he is increasingly convinced that he's sustained some sort of concussion.

Mirsad straightens up and nods at Ove with more determination.

"I told my dad I'm gay."

Ove's eyes grow slightly less threatening. But he doesn't lower his rifle.

"My dad hates gays. He always said he'd kill himself if he found out that any of his children were gay," Mirsad goes on.

After a moment's silence he adds:

"He didn't take it so well. You might say."

"He throwed him out!" Adrian interjects.

"Threw," Ove corrects.

Mirsad picks up his bag from the ground and nods anew at Ove.

"This was a stupid idea. We shouldn't have disturbed—"

"Disturbed me with what?" Ove cuts him short.

Now that he's standing here in his underpants in below-freezing temperatures, he might as well at least find out the reason why, it seems to him.

Mirsad takes a deep breath. As if he's physically shoving his pride down his throat.

"Dad said I was sick and not welcome under his roof with

my . . . 'unnatural ways,'" he says, swallowing hard before he manages to spit out the word "unnatural."

"Because you're a bender?" Ove clarifies.

Mirsad nods.

"I don't have any relatives here in town. I was going to stay the night at Adrian's, but his mum's new boyfriend is staying. . . ."

He goes quiet. Looks like he's feeling very silly.

"It was an idiotic idea," he says in a low voice and makes a move to turn around and leave.

Adrian, on the other hand, seems to be rediscovering a desire for discussion, and he stumbles eagerly through the snow towards Ove.

"What the hell, Ove! You've got a load of space in there! So we thought maybe he could crash here tonight?"

"Here? This is not a damned hotel!" says Ove, raising the rifle so that Adrian's chest collides right into the barrel.

Adrian freezes. Mirsad takes two quick steps forward through the snow and puts his hand on the rifle.

"We had nowhere else to go, sorry," he says in a low voice while gently turning the barrel away from Adrian.

Ove looks like he's coming to his senses slightly. He lowers his weapon to the ground. When he almost imperceptibly takes a half step backwards into the hall, as if he's only now become aware of the cold which envelops his not-so-well-dressed body, he notices, from the corner of his eye, the photo of Sonja on the wall. The red dress. The bus trip to Spain when she was pregnant. He asked her so many times to take that bloody photo down, but she refused. Said it was "a memory worth as much as any other."

Obstinate woman.

So this should have been the day Ove *finally* died. Instead it became the evening before the morning when he woke with not only a cat but also a bent person living in his row house. Sonja would have liked it, most likely. She liked hotels.

33

A MAN CALLED OVE AND AN INSPECTION TOUR THAT IS NOT THE USUAL

Sometimes it is difficult to explain why some men suddenly do the things they do. Sometimes, of course, it's because they know they'll do them sooner or later anyway, and so they may as well just do them now. And sometimes it's the pure opposite—because they realize they should have done them long ago. Ove has probably known all along what he has to do, but all people at root are time optimists. We always think there's enough time to do things with other people. Time to say things to them. And then something happens and then we stand there holding on to words like "if."

As he marches down the stairs the next morning, he stops in the hallway. It hasn't smelled like this in the house since Sonja died. Watchfully he takes the last few steps down, lands on the parquet floor, and stands in the doorway of the kitchen, his body language that of a man who has just caught a thief red-handed.

"Is that you who's been toasting bread?"

Mirsad nods anxiously.

"Yes . . . I hope that's okay. Sorry. I mean, is it?"

Ove notices that he's made coffee too. The cat is on the floor eating tuna. Ove nods, but doesn't answer the question.

"Me and the cat have to go for a little walk around our road," he clarifies instead.

"Can I come?" asks Mirsad quickly.

Ove looks at him a little as if Mirsad has stopped him in a pedestrian arcade, dressed up as a pirate, and asked him to guess under which of the three teacups he's hidden the silver coin.

"Maybe I can help?" Mirsad continues eagerly.

Ove goes into the hall and shoves his feet into his clogs.

"It's a free country," he mutters as he opens the door and lets out the cat.

Mirsad interprets this as "Of course you can!" and quickly puts on his jacket and shoes and goes after Ove.

"Hey, guys!" Jimmy hollers as they reach the pavement. He turns up, puffing energetically, behind Ove in a fiercely green tracksuit that's so tight around his body that Ove wonders at first if it's in fact a garment or a body painting.

"Jimmy!" says Jimmy, panting, and offering Mirsad his hand.

The cat looks as if it would like to rub itself lovingly against Jimmy's legs, but seems to change its mind, bearing in mind that the last time it did something similar Jimmy ended up in the hospital. Instead it opts for the next best available thing and rolls about in the snow. Jimmy turns to Ove.

"I usually see you walking around about this time, so I was gonna check with you if you're cool with me tagging along. I've decided to start exercising, you know!"

He nods with such satisfaction that the fat under his chin sways between his shoulders like a mainsail in stormy conditions. Ove looks highly dubious.

"Do you usually get up at this time?"

"Shit, no, man. I haven't even gone to bed yet!" He laughs.

And this is why a cat, an overweight allergy sufferer, a bent person, and a man called Ove make the inspection round that morning.

Mirsad explains in brief that he and his father are not getting along and that he's temporarily staying with Ove; Jimmy expresses disbelief that Ove is up at this time every single morning.

"Why did you have a fight with the old man, then?" asks Jimmy.

"That's none of your business!" Ove barks.

Mirsad gives Ove a grateful glance.

"But seriously, man. You do this *every* morning?" Jimmy asks cheerfully.

"Yes, to check if there have been any burglaries."

"For real? Are there a lot of burglaries around here?"

"There are never lots of burglaries before the first burglary," Ove mutters and heads off towards the guest parking.

The cat looks at Jimmy as if unimpressed by his fitness drive. Jimmy pouts and touches his stomach, in the apparent belief that he has already lost some weight.

"Did you hear about Rune, then?" he calls out, hastening his steps into a half jog behind Ove.

Ove doesn't answer.

"Social Services is coming to pick him up, you know," Jimmy explains once he's caught up.

Ove opens his pad and starts noting down the license plates of the cars. Jimmy evidently takes his silence as an invitation to keep talking.

"You know, the long and short of it is Anita applied for more home help. Rune is just past it and she couldn't deal with it anymore. So then the Social did some investigation and some guy called and said they'd decided she couldn't handle it. And they were going to put Rune in one of those institutions, you know. And then Anita said they could forget about it, she didn't even want home help anymore. But then that guy got really aggro and started getting totally uncool with her. Going on about how she couldn't take the investigation back now and she was the one who had asked them to look into it. And now the investigation had made a decision and that was all there was to it, you know. Doesn't matter what she says 'cos the Social guy is just running his own race, know what I mean?"

Jimmy goes silent and nods at Mirsad, in the hope of getting some kind of reaction.

"Uncool . . ." Mirsad declares hesitantly.

"BLOODY uncool!" Jimmy nods until his upper body shakes.

Ove puts his pen and pad in the inside pocket of his jacket and steers his steps towards the trash room.

"Ah, it'll take them forever to make those kinds of decisions. They say they're taking him now, but they won't pull their finger out for another year or two," he snorts.

Ove knows how that damned bureaucracy works.

"But . . . the decision is made, man," says Jimmy and scratches his hair.

"Just sodding appeal it! It'll take years!" says Ove grumpily as he strides past him.

Jimmy looks at him as if trying to evaluate whether it's worth the exertion of following him.

"But she has done! She's been writing letters and things for two years!"

Ove doesn't stop when he hears that. But he slows down. He hears Jimmy's heavy steps bearing down on him in the snow.

"Two years?" he asks without turning around.

"More or less," says Jimmy.

Ove looks like he's counting the months in his head.

"That's a lie. Then Sonja would have known about it," he says dismissively.

"I wasn't allowed to say anything to Sonja. Anita didn't want me to. You know . . ."

Jimmy goes silent. Looks down at the snow. Ove turns around. Raises his eyebrows.

"I know what?"

Jimmy takes a deep breath.

"She . . . thought you had enough troubles of your own," he says in a low voice.

The silence that follows is so thick you could split it with an ax. Jimmy does not look up. And Ove doesn't say anything. He goes inside the trash room. Comes out. Goes into the bicycle shed. Comes out. The penny seems to have dropped. Jimmy's last words hang like a veil over his movements and an unfathomable anger builds up inside Ove, picking up speed like a tornado inside his chest. He tugs at doors with increasing violence. Kicks the thresholds. And when Jimmy in the end mumbles something about, "Now it's all screwed, man, now they'll put Rune in a home, you know," Ove slams a door so hard that the entire trash room shakes. He stands in silence with his back to them, panting more and more heavily.

"Are you . . . okay?" asks Mirsad.

Ove turns and points with anything but controlled fury at Jimmy.

"Was that how she put it? She didn't want to ask for Sonja's help because we had 'enough troubles of our own'?"

Jimmy nods anxiously. Ove stares down at the snow, his chest heaving under his jacket. He thinks about how Sonja would have taken it if she'd found out. If she'd known that her best friend had not asked for her help because Sonja had "enough problems." She would have been heartbroken.

Sometimes it's hard to explain why some men suddenly do the things they do. And Ove had probably known all along what he had to do, whom he had to help before he could die. But we are always optimists when it comes to time; we think there will be time to do things with other people. And time to say things to them.

Time to appeal.

Again Ove turns to Jimmy with a grim expression.

"Two years?"

Jimmy nods. Ove clears his throat. For the first time he looks unsure.

"I thought she'd just started. I thought I . . . had more time," he mumbles.

Jimmy looks as if he's trying to figure out who Ove is talking to. Ove looks up.

"And they're coming to get Rune now? Seriously? No bureaucratic rot and appeals and all that shit. You're SURE about this?"

Jimmy nods again. He opens his mouth to say something, but Ove has already started moving off. He makes off between the houses with the movements of a man about to take his revenge for a deadly injustice in a Western. Turns off at the house at the end of the road, where the trailer and the white Škoda are still parked, banging at the door with such force that it's difficult to tell whether it will open before he reduces it to wood chips. Anita opens, in shock. Ove steps right into her hall.

"Have you got the papers from the authorities here?"

"Yes, but I tho—"

"Give them to me!"

In retrospect, Anita will tell the other neighbors that she had not seen Ove so angry since 1977, when there was talk of a merger between Saab and Volvo.

34

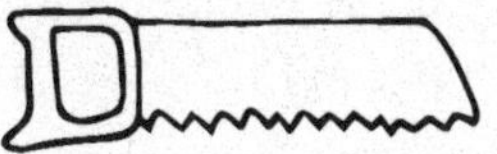

A MAN CALLED OVE AND A BOY IN THE HOUSE NEXT DOOR

Ove has brought along a blue plastic deck chair to push into the snow and sit on. This could take awhile, he knows. It always does when he has to tell Sonja something she doesn't like. He carefully brushes away all the snow from the gravestone, so they can see each other properly.

In just short of forty years a lot of different kinds of people have had time to pass through their block of row houses. The house between Ove's and Rune's has been lived in by quiet, loud, peculiar, unbearable, and hardly noticeable kinds of people. Families have lived there whose teenage children pissed on the fence when they were drunk, or families who tried to plant non-approved bushes in the garden, and families who got the idea that they wanted to paint their house pink. And if there was one single thing Ove and Rune agreed on, irrespective of how much they were feuding at the time, it was that whoever currently populated the neighbor's house tended to be utter imbeciles.

At the end of the 1980s the house was bought by a man who was apparently some sort of bank manager—as "an investment," Ove heard him boast to the real estate agent. He, in turn, rented the house to a series of tenants in the coming years. One summer, to three young men who made an audacious attempt to redefine it as a free zone for a veritable parade of drug addicts, prostitutes, and criminal elements. The parties went on around the clock, broken glass from beer bottles covered the little walkway between the houses like confetti, and the music boomed out so loud that the pictures fell off the wall in Sonja and Ove's living room.

Ove went over to put a stop to the nuisance, and the young men jeered at him. When he refused to go, one of them threatened him with a knife. When Sonja tried to make them see sense the following day, they called her a "paralyzed old bag." The evening after they played louder than ever, and when Anita in pure desperation stood outside and shouted at them, they threw a bottle that went right through her and Rune's living room window.

And that was obviously quite a bad idea.

Ove immediately began working on his plans for revenge by examining the financial doings of their landlord. He called lawyers and the tax authorities to put a stop to the renting of the house, and he intended to persist with it even if he had to take the case "all the bloody way to the Supreme Court," as he put it to Sonja. But he never had time to get that idea off the ground.

Late one night he saw Rune walking towards the parking area with his car keys in his hand. When he came back he had a plastic bag, the contents of which Ove could not determine, in his hand. And the following day the police came and took away the three young men in handcuffs and charged them with possession of a large amount of drugs, which, after an anonymous tip-off, had been found in their shed.

Ove and Rune were both standing in the street when it happened. Their eyes met. Ove scratched his chin.

"Me, I wouldn't even know where to buy narcotics in this town," said Ove thoughtfully.

"On the street behind the train station," said Rune with his hands in his pockets. "At least, that's what I've heard," he added with a grin.

Ove nodded. They stood smiling there in the silence for a long time.

"Car running well?" asked Ove eventually.

"Like a Swiss watch." Rune smiled.

They were on good terms for two months after that. Then, of course, they fell out again over the heating system. But it was nice while it lasted, as Anita said.

The tenants came and went in the following years, most with a surprising amount of forbearance and acceptance from Ove and Rune. Perspective can make a great deal of difference to people's reputations.

One summer halfway through the 1990s, a woman moved in with a chubby boy of about nine, whom Sonja and Anita immediately took to their hearts. The boy's father had left them when the boy was newborn, Sonja and Anita were told. A bull-necked man of about forty who lived with them now, and whose breath the two women tried to ignore for as long as possible, was her new love. He was rarely at home, and Anita and Sonja avoided asking too many questions. They supposed that the girl saw qualities in him that they, perhaps, did not understand. "He has taken care of us, and you know how it is, it's not easy being a single mother," she said with a brave smile at some point, and the women from the neighboring houses left it at that.

The first time they heard the bull-necked man shouting through the walls they decided that each and every one must be allowed to mind their own business in their home. The second time they thought that all families fight sometimes, and maybe this was nothing more serious than that.

When the bull-necked man was away the next time, Sonja invited in the woman and the boy for coffee. The woman explained with a strained laugh that the bruises were because she had thrown open a kitchen cabinet too quickly. In the evening Rune met the bull-necked man in the parking area. He got out of his car in a clear state of intoxication.

In the two nights that followed, the neighboring houses on either side overheard how the man was shouting in there and things were being thrown on the floor. They heard the woman giving a short cry of pain, and when the sound of the weeping nine-year-old boy pleading with the man to stop came through the wall, Ove went outside and stood in front of his house. Rune was already waiting.

They were in the midst of one of their worst-ever power struggles in the steering group of the Residents' Association. Had not even spoken to each other for almost a year. Now they just briefly glanced at one another, and then went back into their houses without a word. Two minutes later they met fully dressed at the front. They rang the bell; the thug lashed out at them as soon as he opened the door, but Ove's fist struck the bridge of his nose. The man lost his footing, got up, grabbed a kitchen knife, and ran at Ove. He never got there. Rune's massive fist slugged him like a mallet. In his heyday he was quite a piece, that Rune. Highly unwise to get involved in fisticuffs with him.

The next day the man left the house and never came back. The young woman slept with Anita and Rune for two weeks before she dared go home again with her boy. Then Rune and Ove went into town and went to the bank, and in the evening Sonja and Anita explained to the young woman that she could see it as a gift or a loan, whichever she preferred. But it wasn't open for discussion. And so it was that the young woman stayed on in the house with her son, a chubby, computer-loving little boy whose name was Jimmy.

Now Ove leans forward and looks with great seriousness at the gravestone.

"I just thought I'd have more time, somehow. To do . . . everything."

She doesn't answer.

"I know how you feel about causing trouble, Sonja. But this time you have to understand. One can't reason with these people."

He pokes his thumbnail into the palm of his hand. The gravestone stays where it is without saying anything, but Ove doesn't need words to know what she would have thought. The silent approach has always been her preferred trick when there are disputes with him. Whether she's alive or dead.

In the morning, Ove had called that Social Services Authority or whatever the hell it was called. He'd called from Parvaneh's house because he no longer had a telephone line. Parvaneh had advised him to be "friendly and approachable." It hadn't started so well, because before long Ove had been connected to the "responsible officer." Which was the smoking man in the white shirt. He directly demonstrated a significant level of agitation about the little white Škoda, which was still parked at the end of the road outside Rune and Anita's house. And, yes, Ove could have established a better negotiating position if he'd immediately apologized about it and maybe even agreed that it was regrettable that he'd intentionally put the man in the white shirt in this nonvehicular predicament. It would certainly have been better than the alternative, which was to hiss: "So maybe you've learned to read signs now! Illiterate bastard!"

Ove's next move involved trying to convince the man that Rune should not be put in a home. The man informed Ove that "Illiterate bastard!" was a very bad choice of words for bringing up that subject. After this, there was a long series of impolite phrases on both ends of the telephone line, before Ove declared in clear terms that things could not be allowed to work like this. One couldn't just come along and remove people from their homes and transport them to institutions any old way one liked, just because their memory was getting a bit defective. The man at the other end answered coldly that it didn't matter very much where they put Rune now "in the state he was in" because for him it "would probably make a very marginal difference where he was." Ove roared a series of invectives back. And then the man in the white shirt said something very stupid.

"The decision has been made. The investigation has been going on for two years. There's nothing you can do, Ove. Nothing. At all."

And then he hung up.

Ove looked at Parvaneh. Looked at Patrick. Slammed Parvaneh's cell phone into their kitchen table and boomed that they needed a "New plan! Immediately!" Parvaneh looked deeply unhappy but Patrick nodded at once, grabbed his crutches, and hobbled quickly out the door. As if he'd just been waiting for Ove to say that. Five minutes later, to Ove's deep dissatisfaction, he came back with that silly fop Anders from the neighboring house. With Jimmy cheerfully tagging along.

"What's he doing here?" said Ove, pointing at the fop.

"I thought you needed a plan?" said Patrick, nodding at the fop and looking very pleased with himself.

"Anders is our plan!" Jimmy threw in.

Anders looked around the hall a little awkwardly, apparently slightly dissuaded by Ove's expression. But Patrick and Jimmy insistently pushed him into the living room.

"Go on, tell him," Patrick prompted.

"Tell me what?"

"Okay, so I heard you had some problems with the owner of that Škoda, yeah?" began Anders, giving Patrick a nervous glance. Ove nodded impatiently for him to continue.

"Well, I don't think I've ever told you what sort of company I have, have I?" Anders went on tentatively.

Ove put his hands in his pockets. Adopted a slightly more relaxed position. And then Anders told him. And even Ove had to admit that it sounded almost more than decently opportune.

"Where are you keeping that blond bimbo—" he started saying once Anders had finished, but he stopped himself when Parvaneh kicked his leg. "Your girlfriend," he corrected himself.

"Oh. We split up. She moved out," said Anders and looked at his shoes.

Whereupon he had to explain that apparently she'd become a bit upset about Ove feuding so much with her and the dog. But her annoyance had been small beer compared to her agitation when Anders found out that Ove called her dog "Mutt" and had not quite been able to stop himself smiling about it.

And so it came to pass that when the chain-smoking man in the white shirt turned up on their road that afternoon accompanied by a police officer to demand that Ove release the white Škoda from its captivity, both the trailer and the white Škoda were already gone. Ove stood outside his house with his hands calmly tucked into his pockets, while his adversary finally lost his composure altogether and started roaring expletives at him. Ove maintained that he had no idea how this had happened, but pointed out in a friendly manner that none of this would have happened in the first place if he'd just respected the sign that made it clear that cars were prohibited in the area. He obviously left out the detail that Anders owned a car towing company, and that one of his tow trucks had picked up the Škoda at lunchtime and then placed it in a large gravel pit twenty-five miles outside town. And when the police officer tactfully asked if he had really not seen anything, Ove looked right into the eyes of the man in the white shirt and answered:

"I don't know. I may have forgotten. You start losing your memory at my age."

When the policeman looked around and then wondered why Ove was standing about here in the street if he had nothing to do with the disappearance of the Škoda, Ove just innocently shrugged his shoulders and peered at the man in the white shirt.

"There's still nothing good on TV."

Anger drained the man's face of color until, if possible, his face was even whiter than his shirt. He stormed off, raging that this was "far from over." And of course it wasn't. Only an hour or so later, Anita opened the door to a courier, who gave her a certified letter from the council. Signed, confirmed, with the time and date of the "transfer into care."

And now Ove stands by Sonja's gravestone and manages to say something about how sorry he is.

"You get so damned worked up when I fight with people, I know that. But the reality of it is this. You'll just have to wait a bit longer for me up there. I don't have time to die right now."

Then he digs up the old, frozen pink flowers out of the ground, plants the new ones, straightens up, folds up his deck chair, and walks towards the parking area while muttering something that sounds suspiciously like "because there's a bloody war on."

35

A MAN CALLED OVE AND SOCIAL INCOMPETENCE

When Parvaneh, with panic in her eyes, runs right into Ove's hall and continues into the bathroom without even bothering to say "Good morning," Ove immediately disputes how one can become so acutely in need of a pee in the space of the twenty seconds it takes her to walk from her own house to his. But "hell has no fury like a pregnant woman in need," Sonja once informed him. So he keeps his mouth shut.

The neighbors are saying he's been "like a different person" these last days, that they've never seen him so "engaged" before. But as Ove irritably explains to them, that's only because Ove has never bloody engaged himself in their particular business before. He's always been a bloody "engaged" person.

Patrick says the way he walks between the houses and slams the doors the whole time is like "a really angry avenging robot from the future." Ove doesn't know what he means by that. But, anyway, he's spent hours at a time in the evenings sitting with Parvaneh and Patrick and the girls, while Patrick to the best of his abilities has tried to get Ove not to put angry fingerprints all over Patrick's computer monitor whenever he wants to show them something. Jimmy, Mirsad, Adrian, and Anders have also been there. Jimmy has repeatedly tried to get everyone to call Parvaneh and Patrick's kitchen "The Death Star" and Ove "Darth Ove." They've considered countless plans over the last few days—including planting marijuana in the white-shirted man's shed, as Rune might have suggested—but after a few nights Ove seems to give up. He nods grimly, demands to use the telephone, and shuffles off into the next room to make a call.

He didn't like doing it. But when there's a war on, there's a war.

Parvaneh comes out of the bathroom.

"Are you done?" Ove wonders, as if he's suspecting this to be some sort of halftime interval.

She nods, but just as they're on their way out the door she notices something in his living room and stops. Ove is standing in the doorway but he knows very well what she's staring at.

"It's . . . Pah! What the hell, it's nothing special," he mumbles and tries to wave her out the door.

When she fails to move he gives the edge of the doorframe a hard kick.

"It was only gathering dust. I sanded it down and repainted it and applied another layer of lacquer, that's all. It's no big bloody deal," he grumbles, irritated.

"Oh, Ove," whispers Parvaneh.

Ove occupies himself checking the threshold with a couple of kicks.

"We can sand it down and repaint it pink. If it's a girl, I mean," he mutters.

Clears his throat.

"Or if it's a boy. Boys can have pink nowadays, can't they?"

Parvaneh looks at the light blue crib, her hand across her mouth.

"If you start crying now you're not having it," warns Ove.

And when she starts crying anyway, Ove sighs—"Bloody women"—and turns around and starts walking down the road.

The man in the white shirt extinguishes his cigarette under his shoe and bangs on Anita and Rune's door about half an hour later. He's brought along three young men in nurse uniforms, as if he's expecting violent resistance. When frail little Anita opens the door, the three young men look a touch ashamed of themselves more than anything, but the man in the white shirt takes a step towards her and waves his document in the air as if holding an axe in his hands.

"It's time," he informs her with a certain impatience and tries to step into the hall.

But she places herself in his way. As much as a person of her size can place herself in anyone's way.

"No!" she says without budging an inch.

The man in the white shirt stops and looks at her. Shakes his head tiredly at her and tightens the skin around his nose until it almost seems to be swallowed up in his cheek-flesh.

"You've had two years to do this the easy way, Anita. And now the decision has been made. And that's all there is to it."

He tries to get past her again but Anita stays where she is on her threshold, immovable as an ancient standing stone.

She takes a deep breath without breaking their eye contact.

"What sort of love is it if you hand someone over when it gets difficult?" she cries, her voice shaking with sorrow. "Abandon someone when there's resistance? Tell me what sort of love that is!"

The man pinches his lips. There's a nervous twitch around his cheekbones.

"Rune doesn't even know where he is half the time, the investigation has showed th—"

"But I KNOW!" Anita interrupts and points at the three nurses. "I KNOW!" she cries at them.

"And who's going to take care of him, Anita?" he asks rhetorically, shaking his head. Then he takes a step forward and gestures for the three nurses to follow him into the house.

"I'm going to take care of him!" answers Anita, her gaze as dark as a burial at sea.

The man in the white shirt just continues shaking his head as he pushes past her. And only then does he see the shadow rising up behind her.

"And so will I," says Ove.

"And I will," says Parvaneh.

"And me!" say Patrick, Jimmy, Anders, Adrian, and Mirsad with a single voice as they push their way into the doorway until they're falling over each other.

The man in the white shirt stops. His eyes narrow into slits.

Suddenly a woman wearing beat-up jeans and a slightly too big green windbreaker turns up at his side with a voice recorder in her hand.

"I'm from the local newspaper," Lena announces, "and I'd like to ask you a few questions."

The man in the white shirt looks at her for a long time. Then he turns his gaze on Ove. The two men stare at one another in silence.

Lena, the journalist, produces a pile of papers from her bag. She presses this into the man's arms.

"These are all the patients you and your section have been in charge of in recent years. All the people like Rune who have been taken into care and put in homes against their own and their families' wishes. All the irregularities that have taken place at geriatric residential care where you have been in charge of the placements. All the points where rules have not been followed and correct procedures have not been observed," she states.

She does so in a tone as if she were handing over the keys of a car he'd just won in the lottery. Then she adds, with a smile:

"The great thing about scrutinizing bureaucracy when you're a journalist, you see, is that the first people to break the laws of bureaucracy are always the bureaucrats themselves."

The man in the white shirt does not spare a single look at her. He keeps staring at Ove. Not a word comes from either of them. Slowly, the man in the white shirt clamps his jaws together.

Patrick clears his throat behind Ove and jumps out of the house on his crutches, nodding at the pile of papers in the man's arms.

"We've also got your bank statements from the last seven years. And all the train and air tickets you've bought with your card and all the hotels you've stayed in. And all the Web history from your work computer. And all your e-mail correspondence, both work and personal . . ."

The eyes of the man in the white shirt wander from one to the other. His jaws so tightly clamped together that the skin on his face is turning pale.

"Not that there *would* be anything you want to keep secret," says Lena with a smirk.

"Not at all," Patrick agrees.

"But you know . . ."

". . . once you start really digging into someone's past . . ."

". . . you usually find something they'd rather keep to themselves," says Lena.

"Something they'd rather . . . forget," Patrick clarifies, with a nod towards the living room, where Rune's head sticks out of one of the armchairs.

The TV is on in there. A smell of fresh-brewed coffee comes through the door. Patrick points one of his crutches, giving a little poke at the pile of paper in the man's arms, so that a sprinkling of snow settles over the man's white shirt.

"I'd especially take a look at that Internet history, if I were you," he explains.

And then they all stand there. Anita and Parvaneh and that journalist woman and Patrick and Ove and Jimmy and Anders and Adrian and Mirsad and the man in the white shirt and the three nurses, in the sort of silence that only exists in the seconds before all the players in a poker game who have bet everything they've got put their cards on the table.

Finally, after an interval that, for all involved, feels like being held underwater with no possibility of breathing, the man in the white shirt starts slowly leafing through the papers in his arms.

"Where did you get all this shit?" he hisses, his shoulders hoisted up around his neck.

"On the InterNET!" rages Ove, abrupt and furious as he steps out of Anita and Rune's row house with his fists clenched by his hips.

The man in the white shirt looks up again. Lena clears her throat and pokes helpfully at the pile of paper.

"Maybe there's nothing illegal in all these old records, but my editor is pretty certain that with the right kind of media scrutiny it would take months for your section to go through all the legal processes. Years, maybe . . ." Gently she puts her hand on the man's shoulder. "So I think it might be easiest for everyone concerned if you just leave now," she whispers.

And then, to Ove's sincere surprise, the little man does just that. He turns around and leaves, followed by the three nurses. He goes around the corner and disappears the way shadows do when the sun reaches its apex in the sky. Or like villains at the ends of stories.

Lena nods, self-satisfied, at Ove. "I told you no one has the stomach for a fight with journalists!"

Ove shoves his hands into his pockets.

"Don't forget what you promised me." She grins.

Ove groans.

"Did you read the letter I sent you, by the way?" she asks.

He shakes his head.

"Do it!" she insists.

Ove answers with something that might either be a "yeah, yeah" or a fierce exhalation of air through the nostrils. Difficult to judge.

When Ove leaves the house an hour later he's been sitting in the living room, talking quietly and one-to-one with Rune for a long time. Because he and Rune needed to "talk without disruption," Ove explained irritably before he drove Parvaneh, Anita, and Patrick into the kitchen.

And if Anita hadn't known better, she could have sworn that in the minutes that followed she heard Rune laughing out loud several times.

36

A MAN CALLED OVE AND A WHISKEY

It is difficult to admit that one is wrong. Particularly when one has been wrong for a very long time.

Sonja used to say that Ove had only admitted he was wrong on one occasion in all the years they had been married, and that was in the early 1980s after he'd agreed with her about something that later turned out to be incorrect. Ove himself maintained that this was a lie, a damned lie. By definition he had only admitted that she was wrong, not that he was.

"Loving someone is like moving into a house," Sonja used to say. "At first you fall in love with all the new things, amazed every morning that all this belongs to you, as if fearing that someone would suddenly come rushing in through the door to explain that a terrible mistake had been made, you weren't actually supposed to live in a wonderful place like this. Then over the years the walls become weathered, the wood splinters here and there, and you start to love that house not so much because of all its perfection, but rather for its imperfections. You get to know all the nooks and crannies. How to avoid getting the key caught in the lock when it's cold outside. Which of the floorboards flex slightly when one steps on them or exactly how to open the wardrobe doors without them creaking. These are the little secrets that make it your home."

Ove, of course, suspected that he represented the wardrobe door in the example. And from time to time he heard Sonja muttering that "sometimes I wonder if there's anything to be done, when the whole foundations are wonky from the very start" when she was angry with him. He knew very well what she was driving at.

"I'm just saying surely it depends on the cost of the diesel engine? And what its consumption is per mile?" says Parvaneh unconcernedly, slowing the Saab down at a red light and trying, with some grunts, to settle herself more comfortably in her seat.

Ove looks at her with boundless disappointment, as if she really hasn't listened to anything he's said. He's made an effort to educate this pregnant woman in the fundamentals of owning a car. He's explained that one has to change one's car every three years to avoid losing money. He has painstakingly run through what all people who know anything are well aware of, namely that one has to drive at least twelve thousand miles per year to save any money by opting for a diesel rather than a gas engine. And what does she do? She starts blabbering, disagreeing as usual, debating things like "surely you don't save money by buying a car new" and it must depend on "how much the car costs." And then she says, "Why?"

"Because!" says Ove.

"Right," says Parvaneh, rolling her eyes in a way that makes Ove suspect she is not accepting his authority on the topic as one might reasonably expect her to.

A few minutes later she's stopped in the parking area on the other side of the street.

"I'll wait here," she says.

"Don't touch my radio settings," orders Ove.

"As if I would," she brays, with a sort of smile that Ove has begun to dislike in the last few weeks.

"It was nice that you came over yesterday," she adds.

Ove replies with one of his sounds that isn't words as such, more a sort of clearing of his air passages. She pats him on the knee.

"The girls are happy when you come over. They like you!"

Ove gets out of the car without answering. There wasn't much wrong with the meal last night, he can stretch to admitting that. Although Ove doesn't feel there's a need to make such a palaver about cooking, as Parvaneh does. Meat and potatoes and gravy are perfectly adequate. But if one has to complicate things like she does, Ove could possibly agree that her rice with saffron is reasonably edible. It is. So he had two portions of it. And the cat had one and a half.

After dinner, while Patrick washed up, the three-year-old had demanded that Ove read her a bedtime story. Ove found it very difficult to reason with the little troll, because she didn't seem to understand normal argumentation, so he followed her with dissatisfaction through the front hall towards her room and sat on her bedside, reading to her with his usual "Ove-excitement," as Parvaneh once described it, although Ove didn't know what the hell she meant by that. When the three-year-old fell asleep with her head partly on his arm and partly on the open book, Ove had put both her and the cat in the bed and turned out the light.

On the way back along the hall he'd gone past the seven-year-old's room. She was sitting in front of her computer, of course, tapping away. This seemed to be all kids did these days, as Ove understood it. Patrick had explained that he'd "tried to give her newer games but she only wanted to play that one," which made

Ove more favorably disposed both to the seven-year-old and to her computer game. Ove liked people who didn't do what Patrick told them to do.

There were drawings everywhere on the walls in her room. Black-and-white pencil sketches, mostly. Not at all bad, considering they had been created by the absence of deductive faculties and highly undeveloped motor function of a seven-year-old, Ove was willing to admit. None of them were of people. Only houses. Ove found this extremely engaging.

He stepped into the room and stood beside her. She looked up from the computer with the dour expression this kid always seemed to lug about with her, and in fact she didn't seem too pleased about his presence. But when Ove stayed where he was, she pointed at last to an upside-down storage crate, made of plastic, on the floor. Ove sat down on it. And she started quietly explaining to him that the game was about building houses and then making cities out of the houses.

"I like houses," she muttered quietly.

Ove looked at her. She looked at him. Ove put his index finger on the screen, leaving a large fingerprint, pointing at an empty space of the town and asking her what happened if she clicked that spot. She moved her cursor there and clicked, and in a flash the computer had put up a house there. Ove looked fairly suspicious about it. Then he made himself comfortable on the plastic box and pointed at another empty space. Two and a half hours later Parvaneh stomped in angrily and threatened to pull out the plug if they didn't call it a night at once.

As Ove stood in the doorway getting ready to leave, the seven-year-old carefully tugged at his shirtsleeve and pointed at a drawing on the wall right next to him. "That's your house," she whispered, as if it was a secret between her and Ove.

Ove nodded. Maybe they weren't totally worthless after all, those two kids.

He leaves Parvaneh in the parking area, crosses the street, opens the glass door, and steps in. The café is empty. The fan heater overhead coughs as if it's full of cigar smoke. Amel stands behind the counter in a stained shirt, wiping glasses with a white towel.

His stocky body has sunk into itself, as if at the end of a very long breath. His face bears that combination of deep sorrow and inconsolable anger which only men of his generation and from his part of the world seem capable of mastering. Ove stays where he is, in the center of the floor. The two men watch one another for a minute or so. One of them a man who can't bring himself to kick out a homosexual youth from his house, and the other who couldn't stop himself. Eventually Ove nods grimly and sits down on one of the bar stools.

He folds his hands together on the counter and gives Amel a dry look.

"I wouldn't be averse to that whiskey now if it's still on offer."

Amel's chest rises and falls in a couple of jerky breaths under the stained shirt. At first he seems to be considering opening his mouth, but then he thinks again. In silence he finishes wiping his glasses. Folds up the towel and puts it next to the espresso machine. Disappears into the kitchen without a word. Comes back with two glasses and a bottle, the letters on the label illegible to Ove. Puts these down on the counter between them.

It is difficult to admit that one is wrong. Particularly when one has been wrong for a very long time.

37

A MAN CALLED OVE AND A LOT OF BASTARDS STICKING THEIR NOSES IN

I'm sorry about this," Ove creaks. He brushes the snow off the gravestone. "But you know how it is. People have no respect at all for personal boundaries anymore. They charge into your house without knocking and cause a commotion, you can hardly even sit on the crapper in peace anymore," he explains, while he digs the frozen flowers out of the ground and presses down the new ones through the snow.

He looks at her as if he's expecting her to nod her agreement. But she doesn't, of course. The cat sits next to Ove in the snow and looks like it absolutely agrees. Especially with that bit about not being allowed to go to the toilet in peace.

Lena had come by Ove's house in the morning to drop off a copy of the newspaper. He was on the front page, looking like the archetypal grumpy old sod. He'd kept his word and let her interview him. But he wasn't smiling like a donkey for the camera; he told them that in no uncertain terms.

"It's a fantastic interview!" she insisted proudly.

Ove didn't respond, but this did not seem to concern her. She looked impatient and sort of paced on the spot, while glancing at her watch as if in a hurry.

"Don't let me hold you up," muttered Ove.

She managed a teenager's repressed titter by way of an answer.

"Me and Anders are going skating on the lake!"

Ove merely nodded at this point, taking this as confirmation that the conversation was over, and closed the door. He put the newspaper under the doormat; it would come in handy for absorbing the snow and slush brought in by the cat and Mirsad.

Back in the kitchen, he began clearing up all the advertising and free newspapers that Adrian had left with the day's mail (Sonja might have managed to teach the rascal to read Shakespeare, but apparently he could not understand a three-word sign that said "NO JUNK MAIL").

At the bottom of the pile he found the letter from Lena, the one Adrian had delivered that first time he rang Ove's doorbell.

Back then the youth rang the doorbell, at least—nowadays he ran in and out of the door as if he lived here, Ove grumbled as he held the letter up to the kitchen lamp like a bank note being checked. Then he got out a table knife from the kitchen drawer. Even though Sonja got mad every time he used a table knife to open an envelope rather than fetching the letter opener.

Dear Ove,

I hope you'll excuse me contacting you like this. Lena at the newspaper has let me know that you don't want to make a big

> thing out of this but she was kind enough to give me your address. Because for me it was a big thing, and I don't want to be the sort of person who does not say that to you, Ove. I respect that you don't want to let me thank you personally, but at least I want to introduce you to some people who will always be grateful to you for your courage and selflessness. People like you are not made anymore. Thanks is too small a word.

It was signed by the man in the gray suit and black overcoat, the one Ove hoisted off the track after he passed out. Lena had told Ove that the swooning fit had been caused by some sort of complicated brain disease. If they hadn't discovered it and started treating it when they did, it would have claimed his life within a few years. "So in a way you saved his life twice over," she'd exclaimed in that excitable tone of voice that made Ove regret a little not having left her locked up inside the garage while he still had the chance.

He folded up the letter and put it back in the envelope. Held up the photo. Three children, the oldest a teenager and the others more or less the same age as Parvaneh's oldest daughter, looked back at him. Or rather, they weren't really looking, they were sort of lying about in a pile, each with a water pistol and apparently laughing until they were practically screaming. Behind them stood a blond woman of about forty-five, with a wide grin and her arms stretched out like a large bird of prey and an overflowing plastic bucket in each hand. At the bottom of the pile lay the man in the gray suit, but wearing a blue polo shirt, and trying in vain to shield himself from the downpour.

Ove threw away the letter along with the advertising, tied up the bag, put it by the front door, went back into the kitchen, got out a magnet from the bottom drawer, and put up the photo on the fridge. Right next to the riotous color drawing the three-year-old had made of him on the way back from the hospital.

Ove brushes his hand over the gravestone again, even though he's already brushed off all the snow that can be brushed off.

"Well, yes, I told them one might like a bit of peace and quiet like a normal human being. But they don't listen, they don't," he moans, waving his arms tiredly towards the gravestone.

"Hi, Sonja," says Parvaneh behind him, with a cheerful wave so that her big mittens slip off her hands.

"Hajj!" the three-year-old hollers happily.

"'Hi,' you're supposed to say 'hi,'" the seven-year-old corrects.

"Hi, Sonja," say Patrick, Jimmy, Adrian, and Mirsad, all nodding in turn.

Ove stamps the snow off his shoes and nods, with a grunt, at the cat beside him.

"Yeah. And the cat you already know."

Parvaneh's belly is now so big that she looks like a giant tortoise when she heaves herself down into a squatting position, one hand on the gravestone and the other hooked around Patrick's arm. Not that Ove dares bring up the giant tortoise metaphor, of course. There are more pleasant ways of killing oneself, he feels. And that's speaking as someone who's already tried quite a few of them.

"This flower is from Patrick and the children and me," says Parvaneh with a friendly smile at the stone.

Then she holds up another flower and adds:

"And this one's from Anita and Rune. They send loads of love."

The multifarious gathering turns around to go back to the parking area, but Parvaneh stays by the gravestone. When Ove wants to know why, she just says, "Never you bloody mind!" to him with the sort of smile that makes Ove want to throw things at her. Nothing hard, perhaps. But something symbolic.

He replies with a snort in the lower octave range, then finds, after a certain amount of inner deliberation, that a discussion with both of those women at the same time would be redundant from the very start. He starts going back to the Saab.

"Girl talk," says Parvaneh succinctly when at last she comes back to the parking area and gets into the driver's seat. Ove doesn't know what she means by that, but he decides to leave it alone. Nasanin's big sister helps her with her belt, in the backseat. In the meantime Jimmy, Mirsad, and Patrick have managed to squeeze into Adrian's new car in front of them. A Toyota. Hardly an optimal choice of car for any kind of thinking person, Ove had pointed out to him many times while they stood there at the dealership. But at least it wasn't French. And Ove managed to get the price reduced by almost eight thousand kronor and made sure that the kid got winter tires thrown in for the same price. So it seemed acceptable, in spite of it all.

When Ove got to the dealership the bloody kid had been checking out a Hyundai. So it could have been worse.

Once they make it back to their street, they go their separate ways. Ove, Mirsad, and the cat wave at Parvaneh, Patrick, Jimmy, and the children and turn off around the corner by Ove's toolshed.

It's difficult to judge how long the stocky man has been waiting outside Ove's house. Maybe all morning. He has the determined look of a straight-backed sentry posted somewhere in the field, in the wilderness. As if he's been cut from a thick tree trunk and the below-freezing temperature is of no concern to him. But when Mirsad comes walking around the corner and the stocky man catches sight of him, he quickly comes to life.

"Hello," he says, stretching, shifting his body weight back to the first foot.

"Hello, Dad," mumbles Mirsad.

That evening Ove has his dinner with Parvaneh and Patrick, while a father and son talk about disappointments and hopes and masculinity in two languages in Ove's kitchen. Maybe most of all they speak of courage. Sonja would have liked it, Ove knows that much. But he tries not to smile so much that Parvaneh notices.

Before the seven-year-old goes to bed she presses a paper into Ove's hand, on which is written "Birthday Party Invitation." Ove reads through it as if it were a legal transfer of rights for a leasehold agreement.

"I see. And then you'll be wanting presents, I expect?" he huffs at last.

She looks down at the floor and shakes her head.

"You don't have to buy anything. I only want one thing anyway."

Ove folds up the invitation and puts it in the back pocket of his trousers. Then, with a degree of authority, presses the palms of his hands against his sides.

"Right?"

"Mum says it's too expensive anyway so it doesn't matter," she says without looking up, and then shakes her head again.

Ove nods conspiratorially, like a criminal who has just made a sign to another criminal that the telephone they are using is wiretapped. He and the girl look around the hall to check that neither her mother nor her father have their nosy ears around some corner, surreptitiously listening to them. And then Ove leans forward and the girl forms her hands in a funnel round her face and whispers into his ear:

"An iPad."

Ove looks a little as if she just said, "An awyttsczyckdront!"

"It's a sort of computer. There are special drawing programs for it. For children," she whispers a little louder.

And something is shining in her eyes.

Something that Ove recognizes.

38

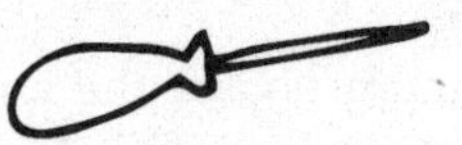

A MAN CALLED OVE AND THE END OF A STORY

Broadly speaking there are two kinds of people. Those who understand how extremely useful white cables can be, and those who don't. Jimmy is the first of these. He loves white cables. And white telephones. And white computer monitors with fruit on the back. That's more or less the sum of what Ove has absorbed during the car journey into town, when Jimmy natters on excitedly about the sorts of things every rational person ought to be so insuperably interested in, until Ove at last sinks into a sort of deeply meditative state of mind, in which the overweight young man's babbling turns to a dull hissing in his ears.

As soon as the young man thundered into the passenger seat of the Saab with a large sandwich in his hand, Ove obviously wished he hadn't asked for Jimmy's help with this. Things are not improved by Jimmy aimlessly shuffling off to "check a few leads" as soon as they enter the shop.

If you want something done you have to do it yourself, as usual, Ove confirms to himself as he steers his steps alone towards the sales assistant. And not until Ove roars, "Have you been frontally lobotomized or what?!" to the young man who's trying to show him the shop's range of portable computers does Jimmy come hurrying to his aid. And then it's not Ove but rather the shop assistant who needs to be aided.

"We're together." Jimmy nods to the assistant with a glance that sort of functions as a secret handshake to communicate the message, "Don't worry, I'm one of you!"

The sales assistant takes a long, frustrated breath and points at Ove.

"I'm trying to help him but—"

"You're just trying to fob me off with a load of CRAP, that's what you're doing!" Ove yells back at him without letting him get to a full stop, and menacing him with something he spontaneously snatches off the nearest shelf.

Ove doesn't quite know what it is, but it looks like a white electrical plug of some sort and it feels like the sort of thing he could throw very hard at the sales assistant if the need arises. The sales assistant looks at Jimmy with a sort of twitching around his eyes that Ove seems adept at generating in people with whom he comes into contact. This is so frequent that one could possibly name a syndrome after him.

"He didn't mean any harm, man," Jimmy tries to say pleasantly.

"I'm trying to show him a MacBook and he's asking me what sort of car I drive," the sales assistant bursts out, looking genuinely hurt.

"It's a relevant question," mutters Ove, with a firm nod at Jimmy.

"I don't have a car! Because I think it's unnecessary and I want to use more environmentally friendly modes of transportation!" says the sales assistant in a tone of voice pitched somewhere between intransigent anger and the fetal position.

Ove looks at Jimmy and throws out his arms, as if this should explain everything.

"You can't reason with a person like that." He nods and evidently expects immediate support. "Where the hell have you been, anyway?"

"I was just checking out the monitors over there, you know," explains Jimmy.

"Are you buying a monitor?" asks Ove.

"No," says Jimmy and looks at Ove as if it was a really strange question, more or less in the way that Sonja used to ask, "What's that got to do with it?" when Ove asked her if she really "needed" another pair of shoes.

The sales assistant tries to turn around and steal away, but Ove quickly puts his leg forward to stop him.

"Where are you going? We're not done here."

The sales assistant looks deeply unhappy now. Jimmy pats him on the back, to encourage him.

"Ove here just wants to check out an iPad—can you sort us out?"

The sales assistant gives Ove a grim look.

"Okay, but as I was trying to ask him earlier, what model do you want? The 16-, 32-, or 64-gigabyte?"

Ove looks at the sales assistant as if he feels the latter should stop regurgitating random combinations of letters.

"There are different versions with different amounts of memory," Jimmy translates for Ove as if he were an interpreter for the Department of Immigration.

"And I suppose they want a hell of a lot of extra money for it," Ove snorts back.

Jimmy nods his understanding of the situation and turns to the sales assistant.

"I think Ove wants to know a little more about the differences between the various models."

The sales assistant groans.

"Well, do you want the normal or the 3G model, then?"

Jimmy turns to Ove.

"Will it be used mainly at home or will she use it outdoors as well?"

Ove pokes his flashlight finger into the air and points it dead straight at the sales assistant.

"Hey! I want her to have the BEST ONE! Understood?"

The sales assistant takes a nervous step back. Jimmy grins and opens his massive arms as if preparing himself for a big hug.

"Let's say 3G, 128-gig, all the bells and whistles you've got. And can you throw in a cable?"

A few minutes later Ove snatches the plastic bag with the iPad box from the counter, mumbling something about "eightthousandtwohundredandninetyfivekronor and they don't even throw in a keyboard!" followed by "thieves," "bandits," and various obscenities.

And so it turns out that the seven-year-old gets an iPad that evening from Ove. And a lead from Jimmy.

She stands in the hall just inside the door, not quite sure what to do with that information, and in the end she just nods and says, "Really nice . . . thanks." Jimmy nods expansively.

"You got any snacks?"

She points to the living room, which is full of people. In the middle of the room is a birthday cake with eight lit candles, towards which the well-built young man immediately navigates. The girl, who is now an eight-year-old, stays in the hall, touching the iPad box with amazement. As if she hardly dares believe that she's actually got it in her hands. Ove leans towards her.

"That's how I always felt every time I bought a new car," he says in a low voice.

She looks around to make sure no one can see; then she smiles and gives him a hug.

"Thanks, Granddad," she whispers and runs into her room.

Ove stands quietly in the hall, poking his house keys against the calluses on one of his palms. Patrick comes limping along on his crutches in pursuit of the eight-year-old. Apparently he's been given the evening's most thankless task: that of convincing his daughter that it's more fun sitting there in a dress, eating cake with a lot of boring grown-ups, than staying in her room listening to pop music and downloading apps onto her new iPad. Ove stays in the hall with his jacket on and stares emptily at the floor for what must be almost ten minutes.

"Are you okay?"

Parvaneh's voice tugs gently at him as if he is coming out of a deep dream. She's standing in the opening to the living room with her hands on her globular stomach, balancing it in front of her as if it were a large laundry basket. Ove looks up, slightly hazy in his eyes.

"Yeah, yeah, of course I am."

"You want to come in and have some cake?"

"No . . . no. I don't like cake. I'll just take a little walk with the cat."

Parvaneh's big brown eyes hold on to him in that piercing way, as they do more and more often these days, which always makes him very unsettled. As if she's filled with dark premonitions.

"Okay," she says at last, without any real conviction in her voice. "Are we having a driving lesson tomorrow? I'll ring your doorbell at eight," she suggests after that.

Ove nods. The cat strolls into the hall with cake in its whiskers.

"Are you done now?" Ove snorts at it, and when the cat looks ready to confirm that it is, Ove glances at Parvaneh, fidgets a little with his keys, and agrees in a low voice:

"Right. Tomorrow morning at eight, then."

The dense winter darkness has descended when Ove and the cat venture out into the little walkway between the houses. The laughter and music of the birthday party well out like a big warm carpet between the walls. Sonja would have liked it, Ove thinks to himself. She would have loved what was happening to the place with the arrival of this crazy, pregnant foreign woman and her utterly ungovernable family. She would have laughed a lot. And God, how much Ove misses that laugh.

He walks up towards the parking area with the cat. Checks all the signposts by giving them a good kick. Tugs at the garage doors. Makes a detour over the guest parking and then comes back. Checks the trash room. As they come back between the houses alongside Ove's toolshed, Ove sees something moving down by the last house on Parvaneh and Patrick's side of the road. At first Ove thinks it's one of the party guests, but soon he sees that the figure is moving by the shed belonging to the dark house of that recycling family. They, as far as Ove knows, are still in Thailand. He squints into the gloom to be sure that the shadows are not deceiving him, and for a few seconds he actually doesn't see anything. But then, just as he's ready to admit that his eyesight is not what it used to be, the figure reappears. And behind him, another two. And then he hears the unmistakable sound of someone tapping with a hammer at a window that's covered in insulation tape. Which is how one minimizes the noise when the glass shatters. Ove knows exactly what it sounds like; he learned how to do it on the railways when they had to knock out broken train windows without cutting their fingers.

"Hey? What are you doing?" he calls through the darkness.

The figures down by the house stop moving. Ove hears voices.

"Hey, you!" he bellows and starts running towards them.

He sees one of them take a couple of steps towards him, and he hears one of them shouting something. Ove increases his pace and charges at them like a human battering ram. He has time to think that he should have brought something from the toolshed to fight with, but now it's too late. From the corner of his eye he notices one of the figures swinging something long and narrow in one fist, so Ove decides he has to hit that bastard first.

When there's a stabbing feeling in his breast he thinks at first that one of them has managed to attack him from behind and thump a fist into his back. But then there's another stab, from inside. Worse than ever, as if someone were skewering him from the scalp down, methodically working a sword all the way through his body until it comes out through the soles of his feet. Ove gasps for air but there's no air to be had. He falls in the middle of a stride, tumbles with his full weight into the snow. Perceives the dulled pain of his cheek scraping against the ice, and feels how something seems to be squeezing the insides of his chest in a big, merciless fist. Like an aluminum can being crushed in the hand.

Ove hears the running steps of the burglars in the snow, and realizes that they are fleeing. He doesn't know how many seconds pass, but the pain in his head, like a long line of fluorescent tubes exploding, is unbearable. He wants to cry out but there's no oxygen in his lungs. All he hears is Parvaneh's remote voice through the deafening sound of pulsating blood in his ears. Perceives the tottering steps when she stumbles and slips through the snow, her disproportionate body on those tiny feet. The last thing Ove has time to think before everything goes dark is that he has to make her promise that she won't let the ambulance drive down between the houses.

Because vehicular traffic is prohibited in the residential area.

39

A MAN CALLED OVE

Death is a strange thing. People live their whole lives as if it does not exist, and yet it's often one of the great motivations for living. Some of us, in time, become so conscious of it that we live harder, more obstinately, with more fury. Some need its constant presence to even be aware of its antithesis. Others become so preoccupied with it that they go into the waiting room long before it has announced its arrival. We fear it, yet most of us fear more than anything that it may take someone other than ourselves. For the greatest fear of death is always that it will pass us by. And leave us there alone.

People had always said that Ove was "bitter." But he wasn't bloody bitter. He just didn't go around grinning the whole time. Did that mean one had to be treated like a criminal? Ove hardly thought so. Something inside a man goes to pieces when he has to bury the only person who ever understood him. There is no time to heal that sort of wound.

And time is a curious thing. Most of us only live for the time that lies right ahead of us. A few days, weeks, years. One of the most painful moments in a person's life probably comes with the insight that an age has been reached when there is more to look back on than ahead. And when time no longer lies ahead of one, other things have to be lived for. Memories, perhaps. Afternoons in the sun with someone's hand clutched in one's own. The fragrance of flower beds in fresh bloom. Sundays in a café. Grandchildren, perhaps. One finds a way of living for the sake of someone else's future. And it wasn't as if Ove also died when Sonja left him. He just stopped living.

Grief is a strange thing.

When the hospital staff refused to let Parvaneh accompany Ove's stretcher into the operating room, it took the combined efforts of Patrick, Jimmy, Anders, Adrian, Mirsad, and four nurses to hold her back, and her flying fists. When a doctor told her to consider the fact that she was pregnant and cautioned her to sit down and "take it easy," Parvaneh overturned one of the wooden benches in the waiting room so that it landed on his foot. And when another doctor came out of a door with a clinically neutral expression and a curt way of expressing himself about "preparing yourselves for the worst," she screamed out loud and collapsed on the floor like a shattered porcelain vase. Her face buried in her hands.

Love is a strange thing. It takes you by surprise.

It's half past three in the morning when a nurse comes to get her. She has refused to leave the waiting room. Her hair is one big mess, her eyes bloodshot and caked with streams of dried tears and mascara. When she steps into the little room at the end of the corridor she looks so weak at first that a nurse rushes forward to stop the pregnant woman crumbling to pieces as she crosses the threshold. Parvaneh supports herself against the doorframe, takes a deep breath, smiles an infinitely faint smile at the nurse, and assures her that she's "okay." She takes a step into the room and remains there for a second, as if for the first time that night she can take in the full enormity of what has happened.

Then she goes up to the bed and stands next to it with fresh tears in her eyes. With both palms she starts thumping Ove's arm.

"You're *not* dying on me, Ove," she weeps. "Don't even think about it." Ove's fingers move weakly; she grabs them with both hands and puts her forehead in the palm of his hand.

"I think you'd better calm yourself down, woman," Ove whispers hoarsely.

And then she hits him on the arm again. And then he sees the wisdom of keeping quiet for a while. But she stays there with his hand in hers and slumps into the chair, with that mix of agitation, empathy, and sheer terror in those big brown eyes of hers. At this point he lifts his other hand and strokes her hair. He has tubes going up his nose and his chest moves strenuously under the covers. As if his every breath is one long impulse of pain. His words come out wheezing.

"You didn't let those sods bring the ambulance into the residential area, did you?"

It takes about forty minutes before any of the nurses finally have the guts to go back into the room. A few moments later a bespectacled young doctor wearing plastic slippers who, in Ove's view, has the distinct appearance of someone with a stick up his ass, comes into the room and stands dozily by the bed. He looks down at a paper.

"Parr . . . nava . . . ?" He broods, and gives Parvaneh a distracted look.

"Parvaneh," she corrects.

The doctor doesn't look particularly concerned.

"You're listed here as the 'next of kin,'" he says, glancing briefly at this emphatically Iranian thirty-year-old woman on the chair, and this emphatically un-Iranian Swede in the bed.

When neither of them makes the slightest effort to explain how this can be, other than Parvaneh giving Ove a little shove and sniggering, "Aaah, next of kin!" and Ove responding, "Shut it, will you!" the doctor sighs and continues.

"Ove has a heart problem. . . ." he begins in an anodyne voice, following this up with a series of terms that no human being with less than ten years of medical training or an entirely unhealthy addiction to certain television series could ever be expected to understand.

When Parvaneh gives him a look studded with a long line of question marks and exclamation marks, the doctor sighs again in that way young doctors with glasses and plastic slippers and a stick up their ass often do when confronted by people who do not even have the common bloody decency to attend medical school before they come to the hospital.

"His heart is too big," the doctor states crassly.

Parvaneh stares blankly at him for a very long time. And then she looks at Ove in the bed, in a very searching way. And then she looks at the doctor again as if she's waiting for him to throw out his arms and start making jazzy movements with his fingers and crying out: "Only joking!"

And when he doesn't do this she starts to laugh. First it's more like a cough, then as if she's holding back a sneeze, and before long it's a long, sustained, raucous bout of giggling. She holds on to the side of the bed, waves her hand in front of her face as if to fan herself into stopping, but it doesn't help. And then at last it turns into one loud, long-drawn belly laugh that bursts out of the room and makes the nurses in the corridor stick their heads through the door and ask in wonder, "What's going on in here?"

"You see what I have to put up with?" Ove hisses wearily at the doctor, rolling his eyes while Parvaneh, overwhelmed with hysterics, buries her face in one of the pillows.

The doctor looks as if there was never a seminar on how to deal with this type of situation, so in the end he clears his throat loudly and sort of brings his foot down with a quick stamping motion, in order to remind them of his authority, so to speak. It doesn't do much good, of course, but after many more attempts, Parvaneh gets herself into order enough to manage to say: "Ove's heart is too big; I think I'm going to die."

"It's me who's bloody dying!" Ove objects.

Parvaneh shakes her head and smiles warmly at the doctor.

"Was that all?"

The doctor closes his file with resignation.

"If he takes his medication we can keep it under control. But it's difficult to be sure about things like this. He could have a few more months or a few years."

Parvaneh gives him a dismissive wave.

"Oh, don't concern yourself about that. Ove is quite clearly UTTERLY LOUSY at dying!"

Ove looks quite offended by that.

Four days later Ove limps through the snow to his house. He's supported on one side by Parvaneh and on the other by Patrick. One is on crutches and the other knocked up; that's the support you get, he thinks. But he doesn't say it; Parvaneh just had a tantrum when Ove wouldn't let her back the Saab down between the houses a few minutes ago. "I KNOW, OVE! Okay! I KNOW! If you say it one more time I swear to God I'll set fire to your bloody sign!" she shouted at him. Which Ove felt was a little overly dramatic, to say the least.

The snow creaks under his shoes. The windows are lit up. The cat sits outside the door, waiting. There are drawings spread across the table in the kitchen.

"The girls drew them for you," says Parvaneh and puts his spare keys in the basket next to the telephone.

When she sees Ove's eyes reading the letters in the bottom corner of one of the drawings, she looks slightly embarrassed.

"They . . . sorry, Ove, don't worry about what they've written! You know how children are. My father died in Iran. They've never had a . . . you know . . ."

Ove takes no notice of her, just takes the drawings in his hand and goes to the kitchen drawers.

"They can call me whatever they like. No need for you to stick your bloody nose in."

And then he puts up the drawings one by one on the fridge. The one that says "To Granddad" gets the top spot. She tries not to smile. Doesn't succeed very convincingly.

"Stop sniggering and put the coffee on instead. I'm fetching down the cardboard boxes from the attic," Ove mumbles and limps off towards the stairs.

So, that evening, Parvaneh and the girls help him clean up his house. They wrap each and every one of Sonja's things in newspaper and carefully pack all her clothes into boxes. One memory at a time. And at half past nine when everything is done and the girls have fallen asleep on Ove's sofa with newsprint on their fingertips and chocolate ice cream around the corners of their mouths, then Parvaneh's hand suddenly grips Ove's upper arm like a voracious metal claw. And when Ove growls, "OUCH!" she growls back, "SHUSH!"

And then they have to go back to the hospital.

It's a boy.

A MAN CALLED OVE AND AN EPILOGUE

Life is a Curious Thing.

Winter turns to spring and Parvaneh passes her driving test. Ove teaches Adrian how to change tires. The kid may have bought a Toyota, but that doesn't mean he's *entirely* beyond help, Ove explains to Sonja when he visits her one Sunday in April. Then he shows her some photographs of Parvaneh's little boy. Four months old and as fat as a seal pup. Patrick has tried to force one of those cell phone camera things on Ove, but he doesn't trust them. So he walks around with a thick wad of paper copies inside his wallet instead, held together by a rubber band. Shows everyone he meets. Even the people who work at the florist's.

Spring turns to summer and by the time autumn sets in, the annoying journalist, Lena, moves in with that Audi-driving fop Anders. Ove drives the moving van; he has no faith in those jackasses being able to back it between the houses without ruining his new mailbox, so it's just as well.

Of course, Lena doesn't believe in "marriage as an institution," Ove tells Sonja with a snort that seems to suggest there have been certain discussions about this along the street, but the following spring he comes to the grave and shows her another wedding invitation.

Mirsad wears a black suit and is literally shaking with nervousness. Parvaneh has to give him a shot of tequila before he goes into the Town Hall. Jimmy is waiting inside. Ove is his best man. Has bought a new suit. They have the party at Amel's café; the stocky man tries to hold a speech three times but he's too overwhelmed by emotion to manage more than a few stuttering words. On the other hand, he names a sandwich after Jimmy, and Jimmy himself says it's the most magnificent present he's ever had. He continues living in his mother's house with Mirsad. The following year they adopt a little girl. Jimmy brings her along to Anita and Rune's every afternoon, without fail, at three o'clock when they have coffee.

Rune doesn't get better. In certain periods, he is virtually uncontactable for days at a time. But every time that little girl runs into his and Anita's house with her arms reaching out for Anita, a euphoric smile fills his entire face. Without exception.

Even more houses are built in the area. In a few years it goes from a quiet backwater to a city district. Which obviously doesn't make Patrick more competent when it comes to opening windows or assembling IKEA wardrobes. One morning he turns up at Ove's door with two men more or less the same age as himself, who apparently are also not so good at it. Both own houses a few streets down, they explain. They're restoring them but they've run into problems with joists over partition walls. They don't know what to do. But Ove knows, of course. He mutters something that sounds a little like "fools" and goes over to show them. The next day another neighbor turns up. And then another. And then another. Within a few months Ove has been everywhere, fixing this and that in almost every house within a radius of four streets. Obviously he always grumbles about people's incompetence. But when he's by himself by Sonja's grave he does mumble on one occasion, "Sometimes it can be quite nice having something to get on with in the daytime."

Parvaneh's daughters celebrate their birthdays and before anyone can explain how it happened, the three-year-old has become a six-year-old, in that disrespectful way often noted in three-year-olds. Ove goes with her to school on her first day. She teaches him to insert smileys into a text message, and he makes her promise never to tell Patrick that he's got himself a cell phone. The eight-year-old, who in a similar disrespectful way has now turned ten, holds her first pajama party. Their little brother disperses his toys all over Ove's kitchen. Ove builds a splash pond for him in his outside space but when someone calls it a splash pond Ove snorts that "Actually it's a bloody pool, isn't it!" Anders is voted in again as the chairman of the Residents' Association. Parvaneh buys a new lawn mower for the lawn behind the houses.

Summers turn to autumns and autumns to winters and one icy-cold Sunday morning in November, almost four years to the day since Parvaneh and Patrick backed that trailer into Ove's mailbox, Parvaneh wakes up as if someone just placed a frozen hand on her brow. She gets up, looks out of her bedroom window, and checks the time. It's quarter past eight. The snow hasn't been cleared outside Ove's house.

She runs across the little road in her dressing gown and slippers, calling out his name. Opens the door with the spare key he's given her, charges into the living room, stumbles up the stairs in her wet slippers, and, with her heart in her mouth, fumbles her way into his bedroom.

Ove looks like he's sleeping very deeply. She has never seen his face looking so peaceful. The cat lies at his side with its little head carefully resting in the palm of his hand. When it sees Parvaneh it slowly, slowly stands up, as if only then fully accepting what has happened, then climbs into her lap. They sit together on the bedside and Parvaneh caresses the thin locks of hair on Ove's head until the ambulance crew gets there and, with tender and gentle words and movements, explains that they have to take the body away. Then she leans forward and whispers, "Give my love to Sonja and thank her for the loan," into his ear. Then she takes the big envelope from the bedside table on which is written, in longhand, "To Parvaneh," and goes back down the stairs.

It's full of documents and certificates, original plans of the house, instruction booklets for the video player, the service booklet for the Saab. Bank account numbers and insurance policy documents. The telephone number of a lawyer to whom Ove has "left all his affairs." A whole life assembled and entered into files. The closing of accounts. At the top is a letter for her. She sits down at the kitchen table to read it. It's not long. As if Ove knew she'll only drench it in tears before she gets to the end.

Adrian gets the Saab. Everything else is for you to take care of. You've got the house keys. The cat eats tuna fish twice per day and doesn't like shitting in other people's houses. Please respect that. There is a lawyer in town who has all the bank papers and so on. There is an account with 11,563,013 kronor and 67 öre. From Sonja's dad. The old man had shares. He was mean as hell. Me and Sonja never knew what to do with it. Your kids should get a million each when they turn eighteen, and Jimmy's girl should get the same. The rest is yours. But please don't let Patrick bloody take care of it. Sonja would have liked you. Don't let the new neighbors drive in the residential area.

Ove

At the bottom of the sheet he's written in capitals "YOU ARE NOT A COMPLETE IDIOT!" And after that, a smiley, as Nasanin has taught him.

There are clear instructions in the letters about the funeral, which mustn't under any circumstances "be made a bloody fuss of." Ove doesn't want any ceremony, he only wants to be thrown in the ground next to Sonja and that's all. "No people. No messing about!" he states firmly and clearly to Parvaneh.

More than three hundred people come to the funeral.

When Patrick, Parvaneh, and the girls come in there are people standing all along the walls and aisles. Everyone holds lit candles with "Sonja's Fund" engraved on them. Because that is what Parvaneh has decided to use most of Ove's money for: a charity fund for orphaned children. Her eyes are swollen with tears; her throat is so dry that she has felt as if she's panting for air for several days now. The sight of the candles eases something in her breathing. And when Patrick sees all the people who have come to say their farewells to Ove, he elbows her gently in her side and grins with satisfaction.

"Shit. Ove would have hated this, wouldn't he?"

And then she laughs. Because he really would have.

In the evening she shows a young, recently married couple around Ove and Sonja's house. The woman is pregnant. Her eyes glitter as she walks through the rooms, the way eyes glitter when a person imagines her child's future memories unfolding there on the floor. Her husband is obviously much less pleased with the place. He's wearing a pair of carpenter's trousers and he mostly goes around kicking the baseboards suspiciously and looking annoyed. Parvaneh obviously knows it doesn't make any difference; she can see in the girl's eyes that the decision has already been made. But when the young man asks in a sullen tone about "that garage place" mentioned in the ad, Parvaneh looks him up and down carefully, nods drily, and asks what car he drives. The young man straightens up for the first time, smiles an almost undetectable smile, and looks her right in the eye with the sort of indomitable pride that only one word can convey.

"Saab."

ACKNOWLEDGMENTS

Jonas Cramby. Brilliant journalist and a real gentleman. Because you discovered Ove and gave him a name that first time, and for so generously allowing me to carry on with his story.

John Häggblom. My editor. Because in a gifted and scrupulous manner you advised me on all my linguistic failings, and because you patiently and humbly accepted all the times I totally ignored your advice.

Rolf Backman. My father. Because I hope I am unlike you in the smallest possible number of ways.

Turn the page for a sneak peek at Fredrik Backman's irresistible novel about finding love and second chances in the most unlikely of places.

Available from Atria Books

1

Forks. Knives. Spoons.

In that order.

Britt-Marie is certainly not the kind of person who judges other people. Far from it.

But surely no civilized person would even think of arranging a cutlery drawer in a different way from how cutlery drawers are supposed to be arranged?

We're not animals, are we?

It's a Monday in January. She's sitting at a desk in the unemployment office. Admittedly there's no cutlery in sight, but it's on her mind because it sums up everything that's gone wrong recently. Cutlery should be arranged as it always has been, because life should go on unchanged. Normal life is presentable. In normal life you clean up the kitchen and keep your balcony tidy and take care of your children. It's hard work—harder than one might think. In normal life you certainly don't find yourself sitting in the unemployment office.

The girl who works here has staggeringly short hair, Britt-Marie thinks, like a man's. Not that there's anything wrong with that, of course—it's modern, no doubt. The girl points at a piece of paper and smiles, evidently in a hurry.

"Just fill in your name, social security number, and address here, please."

Britt-Marie has to be registered. As if she were a criminal. As if she has come to steal a job rather than find one.

"Milk and sugar?" the girl asks, pouring some coffee into a plastic mug.

Britt-Marie doesn't judge anyone. Far from it. But who would behave like that? A plastic mug! Are we at war? She'd like to say just that to the girl, but because Kent is always urging Britt-Marie to "be more socially aware" she just smiles as diplomatically as she can and waits to be offered a coaster.

Kent is Britt-Marie's husband. He's an entrepreneur. Incredibly, incredibly successful. Has business dealings with Germany and is extremely, extremely socially aware.

The girl offers her two tiny disposable cartons of the sort of milk that doesn't have to be kept in the fridge. Then she holds out a plastic mug with plastic teaspoons protruding from it. Britt-Marie could not have looked more startled if she'd been offered roadkill.

She shakes her head and brushes her hand over the table as if it was covered in invisible crumbs. There are papers everywhere, in any old order. The girl clearly doesn't have time to tidy them up, Britt-Marie realizes—she's probably far too busy with her career.

"Okay," says the girl pleasantly, turning back to the form, "just write your address here."

Britt-Marie fixes her gaze on her lap. She misses being at home with her cutlery drawer. She misses Kent, because Kent is the one who fills in all the forms.

When the girl looks like she's about to open her mouth again, Britt-Marie interrupts her.

"You forgot to give me a coaster," says Britt-Marie, smiling, with all the social awareness she can muster. "I don't want to make marks on your table. Could I trouble you to give me something to put my . . . coffee cup on?"

She uses that distinctive tone, which Britt-Marie relies on whenever she has to summon all her inner goodness, to refer to it as a "cup" even though it is a plastic mug.

"Oh, don't worry, just put it anywhere."

As if life was as simple as that. As if using a coaster or organizing the cutlery drawer in the right order didn't matter. The girl—who clearly doesn't appreciate the value of coasters, or proper cups, or even mirrors, judging by her hairstyle—taps her pen against the paper, by the "address" box.

"But surely we can't just put our cups on the table? That leaves marks, surely you see that."

The girl glances at the surface of the desk, which looks as if toddlers have been trying to eat potatoes off it. With pitchforks. In the dark.

"It really doesn't matter; it's so old and scratched up already!" she says with a smile.

Britt-Marie is screaming inside.

"I don't suppose you've considered that it's because you don't use coasters," she mutters, not at all in a "passive-aggressive" way, which is how Kent's children once described her when they thought she wasn't listening. Britt-Marie is not actually passive-aggressive. She's considerate. After she heard Kent's children saying she was passive-aggressive she was extra considerate for several weeks.

The unemployment office girl looks a little strained. "Okay . . . what did you say your name was? Britt, right?"

"Britt-Marie. Only my sister calls me Britt."

"Okay, Britt-Marie, if you could just fill in the form. Please."

Britt-Marie peers at the paper, which requires her to give assurances about where she lives and who she is. An unreasonable amount of paperwork is required these days just to be a human being. A preposterous amount of administration for society to let one take part. In the end she reluctantly fills in her name, social security number, and her cell phone number. The address box is left empty.

"What's your educational background, Britt-Marie?"

Britt-Marie squeezes her handbag.

"I'll have you know that my education is excellent."

"But no formal education?"

"For your information, I solve an enormous number of crosswords. Which is not the sort of thing one can do without an education."

She takes a very small gulp of the coffee. It doesn't taste like Kent's coffee at all. Kent makes very good coffee, everyone says so. Britt-Marie takes care of the coasters and Kent takes care of the coffee.

"Okay . . . what sort of life experience do you have?"

"My latest employment was as a waitress. I had outstanding references."

The girl looks hopeful. "And when was that?"

"Nineteen seventy-eight."

"Ah . . . and you haven't worked since then?"

"I have worked every day since then. I've helped my husband with his company."

Again the girl looks hopeful. "And what sorts of tasks did you perform in the company?"

"I took care of the children and saw to it that our home was presentable."

The girl smiles to hide her disappointment, as people do when they don't have the ability to distinguish between "a place to live" and "a home." It's actually thoughtfulness that makes the difference. Because of thoughtfulness there are coasters and proper coffee cups and beds that are made so tightly in the mornings that Kent jokes with his acquaintances about how, if you stumble on the threshold on your way into the bedroom, there's "a smaller risk of breaking your leg if you land on the floor than the bedspread." Britt-Marie loathes it when he talks that way. Surely civilized people lift their feet when they walk across bedroom thresholds?

Whenever Britt-Marie and Kent go away, Britt-Marie sprinkles the mattress with baking soda for twenty minutes before she makes the bed. The baking soda absorbs dirt and humidity, leaving the mattress much fresher. Baking soda helps almost everything, in Britt-Marie's experience. Kent usually complains about being late; Britt-Marie clasps her hands together over her stomach and says: "I absolutely must be allowed to make the bed before we leave, Kent. Just imagine if we die!"

This is the actual reason why Britt-Marie hates traveling. Death. Not even baking soda has any effect on death. Kent says she exaggerates, but people do actually drop dead all the time when they're away, and what would the landlord think if they had to break down the door only to find an unclean mattress? Surely they'd conclude that Kent and Britt-Marie lived in their own dirt?

The girl checks her watch.

"Okay," she says.

Britt-Marie feels her tone has a note of criticism in it.

"The children are twins and we have a balcony. It's more work than you think, having a balcony."

The girl nods tentatively.

"How old are your children?"

"Kent's children. They're thirty."

"So they've left home?"

"Obviously."

"And you're sixty-three years old?"

"Yes," says Britt-Marie dismissively, as if this was highly irrelevant.

The girl clears her throat as if, actually, it's very relevant indeed.

"Well, Britt-Marie, quite honestly, because of the financial crisis and all that, I mean, there's a scarcity of jobs for people in your . . . situation."

The girl sounds a bit as if "situation" was not her first choice as a way of concluding the sentence. Britt-Marie smiles patiently.

"Kent says that the financial crisis is over. He's an entrepreneur, you must understand. So he understands these kind of things, which are possibly a little outside your field of competence."

The girl blinks for an unnecessary amount of time. Checks her watch. She seems uncomfortable, which vexes Britt-Marie. She quickly decides to give the girl a compliment, just to show her goodwill. She looks around the room for something to compliment her about, and finally manages to say, with as generous a smile as she can muster:

"You have a very modern hairstyle."

"What? Oh. Thanks," she replies, her fingertips moving self-consciously towards her scalp.

"It's very courageous of you to wear your hair so short when you have such a large forehead."

Why does the girl look offended? Britt-Marie wonders. Clearly that's what happens when you try to be sociable towards young people these days. The girl rises from her chair.

"Thanks for coming, Britt-Marie. You are registered in our database. We'll be in touch!"

She holds out her hand to say good-bye. Britt-Marie stands up and places the plastic mug of coffee in her hand.

"When?"

"Well, it's difficult to say."

"I suppose I'm supposed to just sit and wait," counters Britt-Marie with a diplomatic smile, "as if I didn't have anything better to do?"

The girl swallows.

"Well, my colleague will be in touch with you about a jobseekers' training course, an—"

"I don't want a course. I want a job."

"Absolutely, but it's difficult to say when something will turn up. . . ."

Britt-Marie takes a notebook from her pocket.

"Shall we say tomorrow, then?"

"What?"

"Could something turn up tomorrow?"

The girl clears her throat.

"Well, it could, or I'd rather . . ."

Britt-Marie gets a pencil from her bag, eyes the pencil with some disapproval, and then looks at the girl.

"Might I trouble you for a pencil sharpener?" she asks.

"A pencil sharpener?" asks the girl, as if she had been asked for a thousand-year-old magical artifact.

"I need to put our meeting on the list."

Some people don't understand the value of lists, but Britt-Marie is not one of those people. She has so many lists that she has to keep a separate list to list all the lists. Otherwise anything could happen. She could die. Or forget to buy baking soda.

The girl offers her a pen and says something to the effect of, "Actually I don't have time tomorrow," but Britt-Marie is too busy peering at the pen to hear what she's saying.

"Surely we can't write lists in ink?" she bursts out.

"That's all I've got." The girl says this with some finality. "Is there anything else I can help you with today, Britt-Marie?"

"Ha," Britt-Marie responds after a moment.

Britt-Marie often says that. "Ha." Not as in "ha-ha" but as in "aha," spoken in a particularly disappointed tone. Like when you find a wet towel thrown on the bathroom floor.

"Ha." Immediately after saying this, Britt-Marie always firmly closes her mouth, to emphasize this is the last thing she intends to say on the subject. Although it rarely is the last thing.

The girl hesitates. Britt-Marie grasps the pen as if it's sticky. Looks at the list marked "Tuesday" in her notebook, and, at the top, above "Cleaning" and "Shopping," she writes "Unemployment office to contact me."

She hands back the pen.

"It was very nice to meet you," says the girl robotically. "We'll be in touch!"

"Ha," says Britt-Marie with a nod.

Britt-Marie leaves the unemployment office. The girl is obviously under the impression that this is the last time they'll meet, because she's unaware of how scrupulously Britt-Marie sticks to her lists. Clearly the girl has never seen Britt-Marie's balcony.

It's an astonishingly, astonishingly presentable balcony.

It's January outside, a winter chill in the air but no snow on the ground—below freezing without any evidence of it being so. The very worst time of year for balcony plants.

After leaving the unemployment office, Britt-Marie goes to a supermarket that is not her usual supermarket, where she buys everything on her list. She doesn't like shopping on her own, because she doesn't like pushing the shopping cart. Kent always pushes the shopping cart while Britt-Marie walks at his side and holds on to a corner of it. Not because she's trying to steer, only that she likes holding on to things while he is also holding on to them. For the sake of that feeling they are going somewhere at the same time.

She eats her dinner cold at exactly six o'clock. She's used to sitting up all night waiting for Kent, so she tries to put his portion in the fridge. But the only fridge here is full of very small bottles of alcohol. She lowers herself onto a bed that isn't hers, while rubbing her ring finger, a habit she falls into when she's nervous.

A few days ago she was sitting on her own bed, spinning her wedding ring, after cleaning the mattress extra carefully with baking soda. Now she's rubbing the white mark on her skin where the ring used to be.

The building has an address, but it's certainly neither a place to live nor a home. On the floor are two rectangular plastic boxes for balcony flowers, but the hostel room doesn't have a balcony. Britt-Marie has no one to sit up all night waiting for.

But she sits up anyway.

2

The unemployment office opens at 9:00. Britt-Marie waits until 9:02 before going in, because she doesn't want to seem pigheaded.

"You were supposed to contact me today," she announces, not at all pigheadedly, when the girl opens her office door.

"What?" the girl exclaims, her face entirely liberated from any kind of positive emotion. She is surrounded by similarly dressed people clutching plastic mugs. "Erm, look, we're just about to begin a meeting. . . ."

"Oh, right. I suppose it's important?" says Britt-Marie, adjusting a crease in her skirt that only she can see.

"Well, yes . . ."

"And I'm not important, of course."

The girl contorts herself as if her clothes have suddenly changed size.

"You know, I told you yesterday I'd be in touch if something turned up. I never said it would be tod—"

"But I've put it on the list," says Britt-Marie, producing her notebook and pointing at it determinedly. "I wouldn't have put it on the list if you hadn't said it, you must understand that. And you made me write it in ink!"

The girl takes a deep breath. "Look, I'm very sorry if there's been a misunderstanding, but I have to go back to my meeting."

"Maybe you'd have more time to find people jobs if you didn't spend your days in meetings?" observes Britt-Marie as the girl shuts the door.

Britt-Marie is left on her own in the corridor. She notes there are two stickers on the girl's door, just under the handle. At a height where a child would put them. Both have soccer balls on them. This reminds her of Kent, because Kent loves soccer. He loves soccer in a way that nothing else in his life can live up to. He loves soccer even more than he loves telling everyone how much something costs after he's bought it.

During the big soccer championships, the crossword supplements are replaced by special soccer sections, and after that it's hardly possible to get a sensible word out of Kent. If Britt-Marie asks what he wants for dinner, he just mumbles that it doesn't matter, without even taking his eyes off the page.

Britt-Marie has never forgiven soccer for that. For taking Kent away from her, and for depriving her of her crossword supplement.

She rubs the white mark on her ring finger. She remembers the last time the morning newspaper replaced the crossword supplement with a soccer section, because she read the newspaper four times in the hope of finding a small, hidden crossword somewhere. She never found one, but she did find an article about a woman, the same age as Britt-Marie, who had died. Britt-Marie can't get it out of her head. The article described how the woman had lain dead for several weeks before she was found, after the neighbors made a complaint about a bad smell from her flat. Britt-Marie can't stop thinking about that article, can't stop thinking about how vexatious it would be if the neighbors started complaining about bad smells. It said in the article that the cause of death had been "natural." A neighbor said that "the woman's dinner was still on the table when the landlord walked into the flat."

Britt-Marie had asked Kent what he thought the woman had eaten. She thought it must be awful to die in the middle of your dinner, as if the food was terrible. Kent mumbled that it hardly made any difference, and turned up the volume on the TV.

Britt-Marie fetched his shirt from the bedroom floor and put it in the washing machine, as usual. Then she washed it and reorganized his electric shaver in the bathroom. Kent often maintained that she has "hidden" his shaver, when he stood there in the mornings yelling "Briiitt-Mariiie" because he couldn't find it, but she's not hiding it at all. She was reorganizing. There's a difference. Sometimes she reorganized because it was necessary, and sometimes she did it because she loved hearing him call out her name in the mornings.

After half an hour the door to the girl's office opens. People emerge; the girl says good-bye and smiles enthusiastically, until she notices Britt-Marie.

"Oh, you're still here. So, as I said, Britt-Marie, I'm really sorry but I don't have time for . . ."

Britt-Marie stands up and brushes some invisible crumbs from her skirt.

"You like soccer, I see," Britt-Marie offers, nodding at the stickers on the door. "That must be nice for you."

The girl brightens. "Yes. You too?"

"Certainly not."

"Right . . ." The girl peers at her watch and then at another clock on the wall. She's quite clearly bent on trying to get Britt-Marie out of there, so Britt-Marie smiles patiently and decides to say something sociable.

"Your hairstyle is different today."

"What?"

"Different from yesterday. It's modern, I suppose."

"What, the hairstyle?"

"Never having to make up your mind."

Then she adds at once: "Not that there's anything wrong with that, of course. In fact it looks very practical."

In actual fact it mainly looks short and spiky, like when someone has spilled orange juice on a shagpile rug. Kent always used to spill his drink when he was having vodka and orange juice during his soccer matches, until one day Britt-Marie had enough and moved the rug to the guest room. That was thirteen years ago, but she still often thinks about it. Britt-Marie's rugs and Britt-Marie's memories have a lot in common in that sense: they are both very difficult to wash.

The girl clears her throat. "Look, I'd love to talk further, but as I keep trying to tell you I just don't have time at the moment."

"When do you have time?" Britt-Marie asks, getting out her notebook and methodically going through a list. "Three o'clock?"

"I'm fully booked today—"

"I could also manage four or even five o'clock," Britt-Marie offers, conferring with herself.

"We close at five today," says the girl.

"Let's say five o'clock then."

"What? No, we close at five—"

"We certainly can't have a meeting later than five," Britt-Marie protests.

"What?" says the girl.

Britt-Marie smiles with enormous, enormous patience.

"I don't want to cause a scene here. Not at all. But my dear girl, civilized people have their dinner at six, so any later than five is surely a bit on the late side for a meeting, wouldn't you agree? Or are you saying we should have our meeting while we're eating?"

"No . . . I mean . . . What?"

"Ha. Well, in that case you have to make sure you're not late. So the potatoes don't get cold."

Then she writes "6:00. Dinner" on her list.

The girl calls out something behind Britt-Marie but Britt-Marie has already gone, because she actually doesn't have time to stand here going on about this all day.

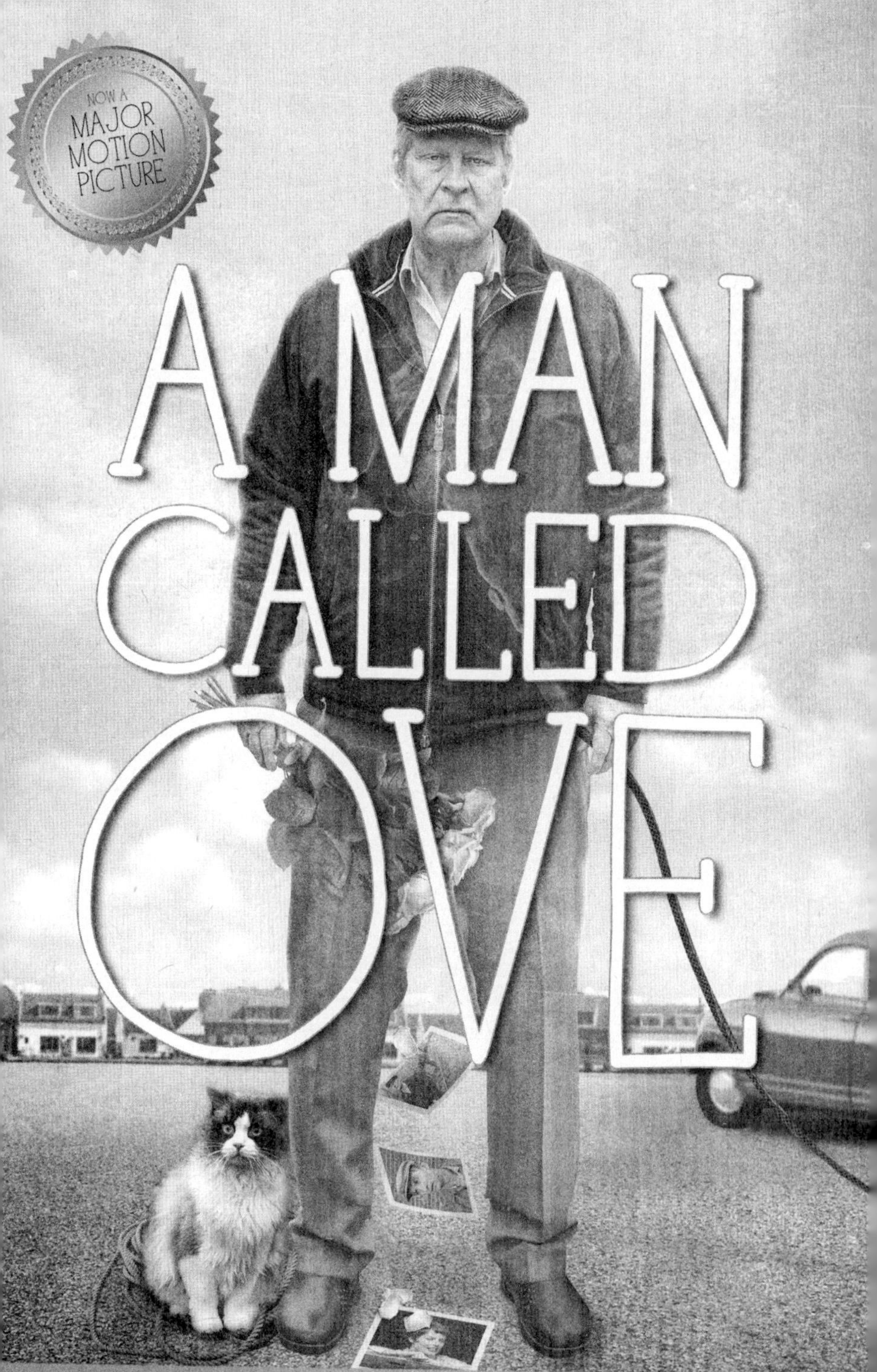

TO LEARN MORE ABOUT THE FILM, VISIT: WWW.MUSICBOXFILMS.COM/OVE

Fredrik Backman's new novel,

BEARTOWN,

will be published in April 2017
by Atria Books.